First thing Jason saw was the tea-chests they'd packed the cats into Tuesday morning, shoved up against a wall. No noise coming from them, not now; but he peered in and saw a single cat crouched in the bottom of one, two in the other. They hissed weakly, their fur matted, their faces scabby from fighting.

Next to them was a treadmill, a length of carpet stretched over rollers in a frame. Jason had never seen one before, but he knew what it was. A strong dog could run for hours on one of those, and just get stronger.

Then there were the pens, made of breeze blocks again, with strong metal mesh for the gates. The first had a nursing bitch in it, with half a dozen pups; the other three each held a solitary dog on a chain. Looked like Staffies, they did, more or less: macho Staffies, maybe, Staffies with a nasty streak.

Only they didn't have any ears. Dead giveaway that was, when you say how their ears had been lopped off right down low, nothing to get your teeth into.

"Pit bulls," Vinny said, but he didn't need to. Jason had figured that out for himself. And what they were for, he'd figured that too.

Also by Chaz Brenchley:

The Samaritan
The Refuge
The Garden
Mall Time

Paradise

Chaz Brenchley

NEW ENGLISH LIBRARY
Hodder and Stoughton

Copyright © 1994 Chaz Brenchley

First published in Great Britain
in 1994 by Hodder and Stoughton

First published in paperback in 1994
by Hodder and Stoughton
A division of Hodder Headline PLC

A NEL paperback

The right of Chaz Brenchley to be identified as the Author of
the Work has been asserted by him in accordance with the
Copyright, Designs and Patents Act 1988.

10 9 8 7 6 5 4 3 2 1

British Library Cataloguing in Publication Data
Brenchley, Chaz
Paradise
I. Title
823.914 [F]

ISBN 0 340 58950 7

Printed and bound in Great Britain by
Cox & Wyman Ltd, Reading, Berkshire

Hodder and Stoughton Ltd
A Division of Hodder Headline PLC
338 Euston Road
London NW1 3BH

For my parents
with my love.

AUTHOR'S NOTE

Like St Paul, I hold myself to be a citizen of no mean city: he of Tarsus, I of Newcastle. And I can't speak for Tarsus, but Newcastle certainly has a district known as Paradise, as do several other cities in Britain. A theory I've not managed to verify suggests that these used to be the red-light areas, where young men got their first taste of Paradise; but that's beside the point. The point is, that the Paradise drawn in these pages is not intended to be a representation of any of them. It's a construct of my own imagination, with no stronger link than that to the real world.

Similarly, the people of Paradise are inventions, pure and simple; any resemblance to real people living or dead is entirely coincidental, and deeply regretted.

Meanwhile, my thanks are due to Nick, who commissioned this; to Bill, who waited for it; to Clare, who read it in a weekend and tore up all the plans on the Monday. And to Helen, who did the messy midwife bit; and of course to Carol, who lets me drink her gin and play with her cat, and is thus the ideal agent.

A world away from London, there is a small host of friends who helped me through this thing and fed me champagne when it was finished. To all of them, my love.

ONE

He is the child of beauty, child of light.

He is the golden boy, blessed and protected; he walks in the way of his Lord, and every single thing he does is right.

Power is with him, glory burns bright in his eyes; words are molten silver on his tongue, all the world listens and believes.

His is the true faith, immutable, uncompromised. Through him all riddles are answered, all doubts dispelled.

He is the lover and the deeply beloved, a man of infinite trust, never betrayed.

Everything that happens, happens because of what he is, of what he does and says.

He is not afraid.

"Okay. So you're standing there, you're inside the hut. All of you?"

"Yes, all of us."

"No," Derry said. "I'm staying outside."

"What for?" That was Mick, otherwise known as Althar the Wizard, leader of their little band: frowning across at him, suspicious of insubordination.

"On guard, right? Dunno what might happen out there. Something might come along."

"Right." Mick nodded, turned back to Stu. "Palidas stays outside, the rest of us go in. What's in there?"

"Hang on. Derry, what's Palidas doing?"

"You know. Watching, listening out for trouble . . . "

"All right." Stu scribbled behind his hand; Derry took the note, and read it slowly.

The sun comes out from behind a cloud. You see rocks and sand and lots of wilderness. That's all.

Derry nodded, keeping the smile off his face. Just another of Stu's red herrings, to keep the rest on edge.

"Okay. Now, Althar, Dael, Simonid: you're standing inside a bare wooden hut. There's a mouldy old mattress in one corner with a wooden chest next to it. On top of the mattress is the mummified body of an old man. Looks like he's been there a long, long time. What are you going to do?"

"Are there any locks on the chest?" Linda, alias Dael Blue-thumb, halfling and thief.

"No. It's just a box."

"I'm going to open it. Carefully, with the blade of my knife."

"Hold it," Mick snapped. "Shouldn't we test it for traps first?"

"Yeah, 'course we should; but Dael wouldn't, would she? She's hoping for jewels or something she can pocket quick, while you two are still looking at the body. I open it," firmly, to Stu. "What happens?"

"Not a lot." He grinned at her. "No jewels, just a big, rusty tin. It's labelled 'Woodworm Powder'," he added helpfully.

"Terrific."

"Might not be woodworm powder inside," pointed out Albie, aka Simonid, rebellious son of a merchant-adventurer.

"Okay, let's see." But this time Dael did ask Althar for a spell to be cast over the tin, "just to check."

"What are you checking for?"

"Booby-traps," Mick said.

Stu made a face. "Bit general. But I guess you're in favour at the moment," confirmed with a roll of the dice, hidden again behind his hand. "All right. You cast your spell, and there are no booby-traps."

"Open it up, Linda. Dael."

Dael prised the lid up with her knife, and:

"It's full of silvery-grey dust, but you can just see a corner of parchment poking out above the surface. Do you want to fish it out?"

"Wait a minute. What's the dust stuff?" Linda asked warily.

"Woodworm powder," Stu said, straight-faced.

"Right. I take the parchment out. Anything else in there?"

"A couple of dead woodworm. It's good stuff, that powder."

The parchment turned out to be a map; and after a break for refreshment – lager and cigarettes shared around, with the windows wide open to the night and the ashtray washed afterwards to keep Stu's parents from guessing – the intrepid adventurers followed the marked route to a wide canyon and a narrow bridge.

8

"It doesn't look good, that bridge," Stu warned them. "Very rickety it looks, very unsafe. There are planks missing, and the handrail's broken away one side. You going over?"

"Althar's casting another spell first," Mick said. "To see if there's any magic on it, or any creatures lurking down in the canyon. You got us with a troll, once."

"Yeah. Didn't you like my troll? I *loved* my troll. But that's two spells, Mick. Takes it out of you. You'll have to rest on the other side."

"So we'll rest. I want to be sure, this time."

"All right." Two rolls of the dice, and, "No magic, and no creatures. Oh, except for woodworm, of course. In the bridge."

"Shut up with your bloody woodworm. We'll go over. One at a time, and lightest first. That's you, Dael."

Dael got across with no alarms; Althar followed, and Simonid. Then it was Derry's turn. Palidas the Paladin, golden-haired warrior-mystic, six foot six of solid muscle: he stepped cautiously onto the creaking, shifting planks, made it halfway over, and —

"Sorry, mate," Stu said, rolling his dice again and shaking his head at the result, trying to hide a triumphant grin. "The whole bridge falls apart under you. Just disintegrates. And it's a long drop. Do you want to scream?"

"Nah. Palidas is a hero, he wouldn't scream."

"Right. Strong, silent type. Okay, you just fall. What about the rest of you?"

"I'll scream," Linda said obligingly. And did.

"Jesus!" Mick scowled at her, then back at Stu. "So what the hell happened, with the bridge?"

"Woodworm." He was openly laughing now. "I did warn you. It was crawling with 'em. Could've gone any time, the rest of you were only lucky with the dice."

"That's not fair." Mick always protested disasters; Derry closed his eyes and let the words roll over him, wondering if he was dead or not, how it would feel to die like that, quick and clean and easy. "You've got to give us a chance. What chance have we got against woodworm? We can't fight that . . . "

"I did give you a chance." Derry heard Stu's voice distantly, as if he really were lying injured or dying at the bottom of a deep canyon. It happened a lot these days, this sudden distancing, this falling away; the only strange thing was to have such a ready excuse tonight. "Remember the powder? Now that *was* magic. If you'd brought that along, it would've killed the woodworm and fixed the bridge up like new."

"Yeah, well, we didn't know, did we?"

9

"Not my fault, if you don't test for the right things. I keep telling you, Mick, if I put something there, it's got a reason. Even woodworm powder."

"Look, never mind that," from Albie. "What about Derry, um, Palidas? Is he dead, or what?"

Yeah, what about me? Derry opened his eyes for this, saw Stu rolling a twenty-sided die.

"No, he's not dead. He's hurt, though."

"How badly? Can he climb out?"

"Not a chance. Um, sorry, Derry," with a flush and an awkward glance, "you've broken your legs. Both of 'em."

Derry just smiled.

"We can fix him, though, can't we?" Mick, urgently. "With a healing spell?"

"Sure. But you've got to rest, I told you that. And then you've got to get to him. I put lots of interesting stuff down in that canyon. I'll have to do you separately for a while, you lot and Derry, now you've been split up. You won't know what's happening to each other."

"In that case," Derry said, glancing at the clock, "how's about if I leave you to it? You can tell me next time, if I get rescued or what."

"Okay, yeah," Stu's worried tone reflecting the concern on all their faces. "Anything wrong?"

"No, I just want to get home. Mam frets if I'm out late."

"Do you want someone to go back with you?" Linda asked.

"Don't be daft. It's only ten minutes, even for me. Just pass us the sticks over, and my bag, and I'll be fine . . . "

So long as he had his crutches, Derry could still get around on his own, if he didn't have far to go; but you couldn't in all fairness say that he walked. Neither did he limp. You need one good leg, for a proper limp. With Derry it was more of a shuffle-drag-scrape, an ugly lurching from stick to stick.

Making his slow and stumbling way down the hill from Stu's house, he heard noises coming from behind a lit and curtained window: a man grunting, a woman moaning softly, then crying out sharp and clear. Derry felt something jerk inside himself, as if in answer. He choked it off in his throat, and tried to hurry on out of earshot. And staggered and almost fell, caught a precarious balance and held himself still for a moment, sweating and shaken; then went on with an inching caution, the sounds of love dogging him all the way to the corner, sharp spurs that hurt more and far more than his legs ever could.

10

"Forget it, boy," mumbling to himself, doing it aloud for a greater authority. "Just something else you ain't never going to get, that's all. Like a trip in Concorde, a million quid in the bank, a medal at the Olympics. Don't matter."

But it did, of course. It mattered in a way that Concorde or money or medals never could, because this at least he could have had and should be getting now. All the way from holding hands to necking in doorways to naked bodies sweating and fumbling and fitting together; and then everything that came after, work and weddings and children. It was all there, free and easy on a plate, just come and help yourselves. But none of it for Derry, no, though he wanted it as much as anyone and maybe more than most. It wasn't just sex he hungered for, it was the whole deal, wife and babies and all. He'd love to have babies.

And wasn't ever going to have babies, or any other part of the dream. He hauled himself around the corner, halfway home now, and had to stop to rest; sagged against the blank brick wall that ended the terrace and saw that the council had been round with their new machine, cleaning off the graffiti.

It wouldn't last, of course. Not round here. Give it a week and the local girls would have their names daubed all over it again, linked with their current fancies, trying to make fragile promises permanent and true.

None of them was going to put Derry's name up there, that was for sure. If he wanted it, he'd have to do it himself; and he had the whole wall to play with after the cleaning, he had spray-paints in his duffel bag and time enough if he sat down to the work, took the weight off his legs . . .

He couldn't resist it, not tonight. Not now, with his lost future riding him so hard. So he lowered himself carefully to the pavement, slipped his arms out of his crutches and started in.

Derry's wall-signature was a work of art, requiring three square metres of brickwork, four different colours and twenty uninterrupted minutes on the job. He worked with an intense concentration, wanting it perfect; and was barely aware of the rising clatter of a heavy engine until a spotlight stabbed down suddenly out of the sky, throwing his shadow thickly black across the wall.

Police helicopter, he thought. *The boys playing with their new toy.* But he didn't move, didn't even glance up into the beam of light. He only sat and waited until it went away, and he could see again; then he picked up his can and got back to work.

Five minutes later, with the job — it was too grand, too

11

ambitious, far too beautiful to be called graffiti – nearly done, there were more lights to disturb him. From a car this time, pulling up at the kerb, too close to be ignored. Derry glanced round and saw a patrol car, a policeman getting out, no one he knew. He sighed, scowled, looked back at the wall. He wouldn't get to finish it now. It'd have to stand as it was, one corner barely sketched in, the colours fading into nothing; but then, that made a savage kind of sense.

"All right, lad. What's your name, then?"

"Derry. Derry Bowen."

"Uh-huh. How old are you, Derry?"

"Sixteen."

"Right. Sixteen, and you haven't got the sense you were born with, have you? Why the hell didn't you scarper when the chopper came over? Never heard of radios, or what?"

For answer, Derry reached for his crutches and began the laborious process of levering himself up off the ground.

"Oh. Um, for Christ's sake, here, let me help . . . "

Derry drove the policeman back with a fierce shake of the head. Made it to his feet alone, unaided; shuffle-dragged a metre or so away from the wet paint and leant sweating against the wall. Looked at the policeman, no words needed.

"What d'you do it for, then, Derry?" With a jerk of his head towards the artwork, Derry's name emblazoned in a technicolour trademark. "What's it all in aid of?"

Derry gave him a sullen shrug; and when that wasn't enough, wasn't accepted, he turned vicious and gave him the truth instead.

"I'll be dead by Christmas," Derry said. Dead at seventeen; and nothing made, nothing done. No girl, no babies. Nothing to be remembered by, but this. And this only till the council came round with their machine again . . .

The policeman looked at him, looked at the wall; said, "All right, son. Pick those paints up, and get in the car."

But he didn't take Derry down to the station, no.

He took him home.

iii

It had been a good day for praying, Arthur thought. Of course praying was a good thing in itself, a duty that uplifted the soul and made the worst times bearable; but still there were days that called to him and caught him, days made for this special purpose,

12

an unbroken dialogue with God.

Like today, when he'd been drawn out early to spend all morning in the spring sunshine, walking the streets or sitting on a bench in the park. When he'd watched the people pass – the men and women hurrying to work; the children running and screaming while their mothers laughed or yelled or ignored them altogether, too busy talking to their friends; the teenagers and students in packs or pairs, cheerful congregations or tender couples – when he'd watched and prayed for them all, discussing each stranger privately with God.

At midday he'd done a little shopping and gone home for a bite to eat. Then it had been out again to the cemetery with fork and trowel in a carrier bag, to tend his wife's grave and make a haven of the afternoon, a time of peace and solitude to set against the busyness of the morning.

This evening was something else again.

This evening, he'd taken his supper at the Corner Café, as he often did: pie, chips and beans and a cup of tea, special price for pensioners and a chocolate biscuit thrown in gratis for regular customers. Then he paid his bill and left, with a word of blessing for Edna behind the counter.

There was the junior school across the road, with open ground surrounding it; on this side, long terraces climbed the hill, the houses and flats Arthur had known all his seventy years. He'd have that climb to face later, going home; but now a walk of fifty yards along the road brought him to a head-high fence of wood and wire netting.

There'd been a hardware shop here once, before the war. Arthur remembered it well: the ladders and brooms stacked outside, the smell of paraffin and beeswax, the dozens of wooden drawers from which screws and nails and hooks were sold by the ounce in blue paper packets. But a stray bomb had accounted for that, one of the few to fall this far upriver. Arthur had come home in his demob suit to find it a rubble playground for the children, half hidden by the tall purple spikes of fireweed.

A couple of years later, with the site still derelict, Arthur had been one of the group that tracked down the owner and bought the land. They'd cleared and levelled it themselves, armed with spades and wheelbarrows and a deep and abiding faith in the work, doing what they were called to do. With the guidance and help of a local builder who believed with them, they erected a wooden hut on the site, confident that soon – in a year, or two

13

years, or five – God's bounty would grant them the money for a more permanent building.

Now, though, four decades later, it was that selfsame hut that Arthur looked at through the fence; or at least its twin, with every timber, every plank replaced piecemeal over the years but nothing changed, nothing added. Even the grilles on the windows had been there since the beginning. There were hooligans and tear-away kids in the fifties too, and religious houses were always vulnerable to stone-throwing and vandalism.

It was a long, low building, this hut, built on raised brick foundations. Its walls were dark with creosote, its roof with pitch. Only the lean-to porch and the doors at front and side were painted, a sombre blue; but the paint at least was fresh, the walls were redone every year and the roof-felt patched or replaced. A humble hut it might be, but still it was God's temple, His house on earth. They were His caretakers, not the owners, and they took their responsibilities seriously.

On the walls of the hut, two posters gave the only touch of colour, fading now but still gaudy against the solemn wood. *CHRIST JESUS CAME INTO THE WORLD TO SAVE SINNERS*, one declared; the other, *HE THAT BELIEVETH ON THE SON HATH EVER-LASTING LIFE*.

Arthur looked at that last, and completed the quotation silently in his head. *He that believeth on the Son hath everlasting life; and he that believeth not the Son shall not see life; but the wrath of God abideth on him.* Time was, when it would have been the second half they put up on a poster – not the promise, but the threat. But that was back in the early days, when old Jim Jones was preacher and guiding light. The Thunderer, they used to call him. One of the old school, Jim was, loved to preach hellfire and damnation. But the world had moved on, since then. The message didn't change, God's truth was eternal; only you had to temper the Word to the mood of the times. People wanted the promise these days, they wanted hope rather than hellfire. It was the good news they'd come for, if they came at all.

Mostly, of course, people didn't come.

Arthur unlocked the front door and walked in with just a glance up at the sign above. *PARADISE PENTECOSTAL GOSPEL HALL*, it read, with *Jesus Saves!* beneath; and you couldn't get more hope-ful than that, you couldn't ask for better news. But still the people didn't come.

Through the porch, its shelves stacked high with hymnals and service sheets; then another door to unlock, and into the main

14

hall. The small windows let only a little murky light in through their grilles and lace curtains, but Arthur didn't need light to find his way. Not in here. He knew every plank, every nail in this building; he could be struck blind and still walk firmly, purposefully from one end to the other without stumbling over a step or banging into a door-jamb.

He passed between the rows of wooden chairs, between the electric organ and the podium with its heavy old Bible; stood for a moment facing the end wall where a cross hung, taller than man-height, constructed from two roof-beams of the old shop and dominating the room as it was meant to; then opened a door under the left arm of the cross and went through.

It was a homely little space they'd made for themselves, the chapel's founding fathers, at this far end of the hut. They'd been all men in those days, it was before the advent of Mrs Dolance; but they'd needed and asked for no woman's touch to guide them when they furnished it with old armchairs, curtained the windows and brought in a kettle and a teapot, a dozen books and a fringed, flowery shade for the light.

Like the structure of the building itself, everything in here had been replaced as it broke or wore out; but like the building, it hadn't really changed. Arthur turned the light on and settled into his favourite chair with a sigh of comfort, a sense of coming home. He closed his eyes and offered up a prayer that was more like a conversation continued, an ongoing talk with a constant companion.

He prayed for a successful evening, for plans to be settled and the necessary commitments made; then he busied himself making a pot of tea, knowing that he wouldn't be long alone.

'The Gang of Six', that's what Arthur had called them, more than once; but watching them arrive one by one tonight, he thought that it wasn't quite right. The Gang of Four Plus Two, that came closer. There were the four originals: himself, Ted Grimes, Arnold Saltley and Jack Dubrowski. They were the ones who'd been here since the beginning, the ones who'd shifted rubble and sweated and made the chapel a labour of love from the very first day. They were all of them old men now, old and slowing down, leaning on walking-sticks or daughters-in-law as much as on faith.

And then there were Alan Parkinson and Jean Dolance. You couldn't call them newcomers, either of them; Alan had been ten years in the congregation, Jean nearly as long, and they'd both won their way onto the Council by sheer effort in the Lord's

15

work. They deserved their places in this room, in this company. And yet . . .

Well, no surprise if it still seemed strange to see them here. After forty years of the same faces, of watching your friends grow old along with you – yes, and watching them die, some of them: Dulcie, Jim, Norman the builder who'd really started it all – it was surely going to take time to adjust.

What was also sure, it was God's will that Alan and Jean should join the Council. There'd been a lot of praying done beforehand, before the decision was made; it hadn't been taken lightly. But they were sorely needed, with the old hands all into their seventies. And never more so than now, Arthur thought, with the arrangements to be made for this year's Mission.

They'd always had a Mission in the summer, two weeks of taking God's word out of the hall and into the streets, organising special events and bearing witness to the local population. It had been a perfunctory affair in recent years, though: a film show and a couple of speakers brought in, leaflets distributed round the houses, little more. It was hard to work up the enthusiasm when your bones ached. This time, though, with the infusion of new blood into the Council, Arthur at least was hoping for something more.

And as he listened to the discussion, he thought that those hopes stood a good chance of being realised. Alan was a great one for testifying in public, soap-box evangelism, preaching on street corners; while Jean promised to take her children canvassing door to door, trying to bring in newcomers.

"Aye, and I'll tell you what," Ted put in, from his corner. "My nephew Richard, Sarah's boy that was raised in London; he's to be staying with us this summer. He's strong in the Lord, he'll do something to help. He's in America just now, he's been working for a mission over there; but I'll write and tell him. He'll put his shoulder to the wheel, I can promise you that."

The meeting broke up at nine, with a good deal accomplished and the promise of more to come. The regular congregation would volunteer their own time and ideas, when they saw how much the Council was proposing to do. That was all that had been lacking recently, positive leadership from the front. This year they'd have it, and who knew how much might be achieved for the Lord this summer?

Arthur saw the others out, locked up the building and turned for home; and was hailed from a passing car, the driver pulling up and leaning over to wind the passenger window down.

16

"Excuse me, I wonder if you can help. I'm looking for Paradise . . . "

Arthur chuckled. "Aren't we all, son?" And added, "But I've found it, and so can you. Come to our service next Sunday, and see if you can find it in your heart to believe."

The young man grimaced distastefully. "No, I mean seriously. It's an address, a district." He produced a sheet of paper. "See, 'Crichton Street, Paradise.' Any idea?"

"Aye. Crichton Street's second left from here. This is Paradise, see," with an all-encompassing wave of his arm. "You've found it." And as the driver nodded his thanks and started to wind the window up: "Don't forget, service is on Sunday, eleven o'clock. And you know where we are now, you can't miss us," with another happy chuckle at the coincidence that had always delighted him, ever since he found his faith as a teenager before the war. "We're right in the heart of Paradise."

TWO

Surprising, almost, that he needs an aeroplane to fly. He should be a wingless angel, floating serenely through the clouds with his own golden nimbus to light his way, only his strong will bringing him back to earth. Only his goodwill keeping him from heaven.

But perhaps that's what he is, in truth: an angel without wings, a spiritual master. Perhaps he doesn't need the plane.

Perhaps he only buys his ticket and takes his seat to help us common mortals, not to show us how far we are from glory by showing us how close he is.

When he does fly, of course, he flies Virgin. What else?

And when they board this day, perhaps it's no coincidence that he's sitting between a businessman sodden with cold and an elderly woman taking her first flight, jittering with nerves.

He shares his smile around, sympathises with the man, helps the woman with her seat-belt and sits talking to her quietly while the plane taxies into position. In a sudden access of terror as the engines race, she grips his hand; and almost gasps at the gold of his touch, fire and honey mixed. And looks up at him and asks,

– What do you do, anyway?

Again that smile, the warm glow of it lighting the whole plane, sinking deep into tired muscles and stressed minds.

– I'm a missionary, he says.

And perhaps he is, perhaps he's no more an angel than you or I. Perhaps we're not seeing him straight; human eyes don't work so well, squinting into his kind of light.

But this much is true, is certain: that the woman leaves the plane at Gatwick feeling infinitely easy in her mind, looking forward to the flight home and already planning other trips.

That the businessman leaves the plane with his packet of tissues still in their cellophane wrapping, with his chest clear and his eyes bright and all his shivering misery left behind.

That everyone who was aboard that plane – captain or cabin staff, bishop or bus-driver or baby – leaves it feeling just a little happier, a little healthier.

And when the stewardess bids our wonder boy goodbye, when she says she hopes to see him flying Virgin again real soon, she means it. Believe me, she really, really means it.

ii

Something had roused Nathan from his dreaming, opening his eyes to the dim light of sunshine through curtains. He frowned, trying to hear it again in his mind as he had heard it in his dream; but a squint at the clock told him *no, don't worry, not your door.* No one was going to knock him up at ten o'clock on a Saturday morning. He rolled over, stretching luxuriantly across the wide mattress, reaching for the concentrated warmth of that other body beside him, relaxed in sleep now but very much his for the waking; and scowled as the knocking came again, firm and insistent this time, unmistakably his door.

He stood up cursing, heedless of the way the duvet fell, back and away from his sleeping bed-mate; blundered through their tangled clothes, snatching up his bathrobe and pulling it on; yawned his way down the passage, and stooped to gather his mail before he opened the door.

It was a girl on the doorstep, a fat and stupid-looking child with lank hair, a year or two short of adolescence. She was wearing a dark and dreary dress, obviously home-made, that fell halfway down her calves. Behind her was a younger boy in a short-trousered suit, his thick curls tugged into a side parting and greased to his scalp; and behind them both was a skeletal woman in another of those dresses. Her greying hair was drawn into a painfully tight bun, which might account for the twisted severity of her gaze, but probably didn't.

The girl's dull eyes were fixed on a pamphlet, that she held screwed up between her clenched fingers. The boy's were on her, his sister, at a guess; their mother's on Nathan, steel-sharp and condemning.

"Good morning, sir," the girl muttered into her chest, in a flat and mechanical voice. "I want . . . "

"Speak up, Lisa."

"I want to talk to you about the love of Jesus Christ," a desperate mumble now, no louder, only faster.

"No, you bloody don't," he said bluntly. Then, turning to the woman, turning savage: "For fuck's sake, where the hell do you get off? What gives you the right to drag people out of bed on a Saturday, just to rant at them?"

"Idleness is an offence in the eyes of the Lord," the woman stabbed back at him, quite undaunted. "And the Bible says it's a Christian's duty to spread the Gospel. No matter what persecution they may suffer for it."

"And you'd love a bit of persecution, wouldn't you, lady? Yeah, I bet you'd really love that. Well, here's something to stiffen your sense of outrage for you. The Bible's full of shit. Read my lips. Full – of – shit. Christ, it wouldn't take in a ten-year-old, that heap of crap you call the word of God. I mean, look at your kids here. Maybe they spout it all when you push the buttons, but you don't think they *believe* it, do you?"

"My children have been washed in the Blood of the Lamb," spat with a sting in it, mother-tiger time. "They know their duty to the Lord, and do it willingly."

"Bullshit. Just look at them," gesturing towards the girl, her downcast eyes, her trembling hands. "They're scared, that's all. What do you do, knock them around if they forget their lines? Or do you keep it strictly psychological, do you just pray over them till they're crazy with it?"

"We're not scared," the boy speaking for the first time, flushed and defiant. "We're counted among the blessed, and, and we're going to be raised up in the last days. With the saints. And you're *not*. You're a sinner, you're a *sinner*."

"Jesus. Brainwashing never loses its charm, does it?"

"An' that's taking the Lord's name in vain. That's a sin, too."

"Damn right, kid." Nathan had lost all taste for the fight, faced with this high treble scorn. "So's fornication, so just let me get back to it, will you?"

He slammed the door in their faces, and turned away; heard muttering voices and the clatter of the letter-box, looked back to see the girl's pamphlet thrust through, falling to the mat.

He left it lying there and went slowly back to the bedroom. Helen was standing just inside the door with the duvet wrapped around her shoulders, clutched loosely across her body and dragging absurdly behind her like a train.

"What was all that about, Nat?"

"Just some God-bothering bitch, with her charming family." He glanced through the post in his hand, dropped it onto a pile of books and walked up to her, grinning. "You look ridiculous."

"I'm cold."

"So let's get warm again."

Worked the duvet free of her grasp, and tossed it aside; stood

20

looking at her naked while he did the same for his bathrobe. Helen was a tall redhead, classy voice with classy bones, big breasts on a slender frame. With all her advantages – the private schooling, the years abroad, the aura of money and privilege – she should have been riding so easily through this life, doing what she wanted, being who she chose. It could have been Helen who undressed him, if only she hadn't been cursed with the over-mastering vulnerability that had brought her so quickly to his bed and made her over to him so completely. He hadn't got a handle on it yet, this emotional weakness that ran so deep within her; he hadn't managed to track it down to its roots. He'd do that, one day. It fascinated him. No hurry, though. For the moment, he was content to exploit it.

As now, taking her by the hand and leading her back to the stripped mattress on the floor, brooking no denial; knowing that she would come as she did come, yielding and complaisant.

Later:

"I'd better go. I'm booked at the squash court."

"Oh. Right. Um, give me, just give me a couple of minutes, I'll get my stuff together . . . "

"There's no need," he murmured, smiling, laying his hands on her hips and pressing the thumbs in deep just above the bone, feeling soft flesh under tight denim. Relishing the sudden spark of joy in her as he said, "You stay, if you want. A couple of hours, that's all. I'll be back."

"You don't, you don't mind?"

"Stupid." He kissed her, hard; then left her standing and crossed to the mantelpiece, fished in a bowl and took out the spare keys to his flat. Tossed them over, saw her drop them and bend, straighten with the ring clutched in her hand like a treasure. "There. Be good."

"Thanks, Nat. I will . . . "

And she would, too. She'd be perfect. She couldn't help herself. He'd come home to the flat cleaned and tidied, a meal ready for when he wanted it and Helen ready for when he wanted her. She'd stay all weekend, bright and glowing in his service, her delight; but he'd have the keys back off her on Monday morning, before college. No one got a permanent right of entry to Nathan's life. She'd hurt, but that was all right, no problems there. Her pain was a gift to him, when the assuagement was so easy and so reward-ing.

He collected his rackets and sports kit, took shampoo and a towel from the bathroom, packed it all into a small rucksack.

21

That on his back, he wheeled his bike out into the street; and Helen came barefoot after him, tousled and blinking in the sunshine.

Freshly laid, Nathan thought, grinning to himself, glancing up and down to see who was around to see her. *Like an egg, still with nest-feathers clinging.*

And to his delight there was a feather from his pillow, tangled in the waves of her hair. He picked it out, gave her one last light kiss and a repeated promise to be home soon, four at the latest (thinking *five*, thinking *half-past, maybe, we'll have a drink or two after the game, probably run into some people*), and powered away up the hill.

And hadn't gone fifty metres, was confident that Helen would still be out there waiting for the chance to wave, when a dog came round the corner just ahead of him. A bull terrier, its owner sauntering behind, both of them heavy with muscle; Nathan swayed over to the centre of the road, watched with a touch of chill. And thought, *Thank Christ they didn't come a minute earlier, while I was stood there. While Helen could see . . .*

And only grateful for that marginal escape, he bent over the handlebars and worked the pedals hard, quickly up to the junction and quickly away.

iii

It was turning into another warm day; but Terry Belderstone was ready for it, following the others out of the restaurant with his jacket slung over one shoulder and his sleeves rolled back. A heavy Rolex gleamed on one wrist, below an old tattoo that he kept for pride's sake, for appearances. He was a working man made good, the son and the grandson of working men, and he was quite happy for the world to know it.

His companions were glancing up at the sky, murmuring about the weather, was it global warming or just the promise of a good summer to come? Terry smiled non-committally. Only one thing he was prepared to state with certainty, and he would brook no denial on this: that it could have rained buckets, it could have thundered and stormed and made no difference at all. The same went for the whole summer, by extension. Let the weather do what it would, let it have a wild time these coming months, Terry didn't care. He'd still count it an excellent year.

The four men lingered a minute longer on the wide pavement,

22

then shook hands and parted. Terry stood still, watching the others move away, savouring the moment. Raymond Adison, Tony Jones, Michael Fournier: respectively – and very respectfully, he was always respectful in the face of power, of patronage – Chairman of the City Council, Head of Planning and Head of Finance. Four men, two hours around a lunch-table, quiet discussion and a handshake, and so much achieved! All the formalities still to come, of course, bids and contracts, all of that; but the real business had been done already, they'd made the agreements and taken the decisions that counted.

Terry set off whistling up the hill, to find the city centre seething. Bound to be, a day this fine, a Saturday. His car was parked in the multi-storey across town, but Terry wasn't in a hurry to get home. He picked his way through the crowds, thinking with every shuffling avoidance, every minor collision and apology, *I've just changed your city for you. Changed your life for you, maybe. Evicted you, maybe, driven a road through your home or your lover's, your grandmother's, your favourite pub. And you don't even know . . .*

He heard a hoarse voice yelling: a few words, a pause, a few more words. Another pause. Looking round, he saw a short bearded man in sports jacket and T-shirt standing on the monument steps and haranguing the passers-by in those odd jerky phrases, glancing constantly at a book held open in his hand.

Bible-thumper, Terry thought dispassionately. And none too good at it, for all his conviction: no one was noticeably listening to him, not even the teenagers and winos who sat or sprawled or fooled around on the warm stone steps. Certainly no one was waiting, eager with questions, ready to give their souls over to God.

Terry's route lay past the monument; and willing to be generous on this most auspicious of days, even to some God-crazed inadequate, he walked more slowly than he might, turning his head to catch the preacher's drift.

" . . . You may have money . . . You may have a fast car . . . You may have a big house in the country . . . But God says, that's nothing! . . . Without Jesus . . . Without Jesus in your heart, you've got nothing! . . . It says, right here in the Bible . . . In God's Word, it says . . . 'Love not the world . . . neither the things that are in the world . . . If any man love the world . . . the love of the Father is not in him.' . . . And without the love of the Father . . . without the love of Jesus . . . you're lost, friends! . . . As I was lost . . . lost and in darkness . . . till I found Jesus . . . till God made His light to shine upon me . . . "

23

And Terry smiled, shook his head, went briskly on his way. Went through the bright sunlight towards his fast car and his big house in the country, thinking about the money he'd arranged to make this day, and the money he'd arranged to spend.

iv

"You want to go through that again, or is everybody happy?"

Rachel looked at her watch, and shook her head. "Sounded good to me, Joe. And it's after ten, we've been at it three hours now. Much more and I won't be singing, I'll just croak."

"What about the rest of you?"

Grunts of agreement, but they were more or less redundant; the boys were already moving to unplug guitars, switch off amplifiers, get their gear together.

Rachel sat down wearily on the edge of the stage, then glanced back with a pang of conscience. "You want a hand with the drum-kit?"

"No, I'll just leave it. We're back here tomorrow afternoon, right?"

"Right." She reached for the giant bottle of Coke and took a swallow against the roughness in her throat, another against the thought of doing it all again tomorrow. And this was still only rehearsals, the concert wasn't till Thursday . . .

A hand tapped lightly on the top of her head. She glanced up to see Robbie grinning down at her.

"It'll be fine, Rache. Don't worry."

"Mind-reader." Another swig from the bottle and she passed it up, watched him empty it in one long chug-a-lug. He'd obviously been practising. On pints, most likely, in any pub that'd take his money.

"You ready, then?" He tossed the empty bottle into the wings, then jumped the three-foot drop to the hall floor, landing with a resounding thud.

"Careful, you'll break it," she advised. "You on guard-duty tonight, are you?"

He smiled, shrugged, didn't answer. She still hadn't worked out how they organised her escort service home, if they had a rota or tossed a coin or what, but it was certainly prearranged every evening. Never any unchivalrous arguments about whose turn it was.

They called goodnight to the others, reminded Joe to turn the

24

lights off and lock up, then pushed the big doors open and came out into the cool night.

They didn't talk much, on the walk to Rachel's house. The route must have been as familiar to Robbie by now as it was to her. Down past the tennis courts and out the school gates, turn left; six hundred metres up the road and left again. Then a quick right-and-left into the cul-de-sac and there you were, home sweet home and thank you very much.

Halfway there, Rachel looked up at the tall figure loping beside her in this awkward silence and asked, "Robbie? Did the Head tell you boys to see me back, when he said we could use the hall this late?"

"Well, yeah. He did, actually. Made it a condition. But we would've done it anyway," in a defensive rush, "we would've thought of it ourselves."

"I'm sure you would."

And she was sure, and wished she could underline that certainty with something physical, her arm linking through his, the reassurance of touch.

But that wasn't on, wouldn't be welcome. Not from her. Rachel grimaced – head down, to hide it – and wished urgently, almost prayed for things to be different. For herself to be a different girl, so that Robbie could be different towards her. She knew why he found it so uncomfortable to be alone with her. Knew, and understood, and resented it: all three at once, a trinity.

Which was appropriate, she supposed, mooching along with hands thrust deep into pockets in imitation of his, nice and safe and virginal.

Sometimes, in the throes of that resentment of him (or which-ever other boy it might be, they were all the same, all carried their hands in their pockets) or of herself, sometimes of God – or else again all three at once, another neat trinity – sometimes Rachel would yearn to lose her faith. Not for long, just a week or two. Just long enough to lose her inhibitions too, and her wretched virginity.

It shouldn't be hard to find a willing boy, there were enough around. Take Robbie, for instance. He was clean, good-looking, friendly; he'd do. She didn't love him, but that surely wouldn't matter. Once she'd lost God – temporarily, of course, must stress that – then love wouldn't come into it, really. It would just be a matter of bodies.

And love wasn't the point, anyway. She wasn't in any hurry for love. Breaking barriers, that was the point, and her hymen the least of them. She wanted to be a normal girl, just for a while, and to be seen to be normal. She wanted to get drunk and get into fights, and sleep around and panic when her period was late and have the boys label her a slag because she'd been out with so many . . .

Except that she didn't want that, if she was honest. She didn't want any of it except the hoped-for reward, to be treated as just another girl, nothing different; and that really didn't seem to be an option. Here she was, sixteen going on seventeen − surely she should at least have struggled with a little temptation by now, battled with the occasional pang of lust? Surely it wasn't natural, to have a soul so obstinately virginal?

It wasn't that she didn't appreciate male beauty in the abstract. She was quite firm, quite positive about that. She had posters on her wall to prove it, pretty pop-stars and rugged macho film heroes both. Though admittedly they had a double purpose, serving to counteract the cross on the wall and the bible by the bed, to dilute the sanctity a little. There was just this yawning, wearisome gulf between aesthetic appreciation and physical desire. The one she had in abundance, but the other − she'd just never managed to achieve it, somehow. And that maddened her sometimes, made her so *angry* . . .

Honestly, Jesus, you don't make it easy for a girl. You could lighten up a little, couldn't you? Slip me a bit of temptation, let me at a little wickedness? Just so's I'll know how it feels . . .

But he didn't, he wouldn't. She was stuck with her rotten virtue, sealed into it like a fly in amber. She'd even tried St Augustine's line, *Lord, give me chastity, but not yet. Please, not already?* Even then she hadn't really meant it, though, couldn't manage that depth of hypocrisy.

And here they were at home; and Robbie was already turning to go, refusing a cup of coffee almost before she could offer it. Suspicious perhaps of her motives, dreading the embarrassment of a sermon with the drink. He wouldn't have got that, but he couldn't know, he'd never let himself close enough to find out.

Rachel sighed, said goodnight and let him go. Went indoors to find her parents out; made a single, a solitary coffee and took it upstairs for her personal rituals, this final half-hour before bed. Her diary first, the blessings and frustrations of the day given equal weight, meticulously recorded. That was followed by formal prayers, formally on her knees, giving over all her problems and pleasures to God. Then a visit to the bathroom and into her pyjamas, under the covers and lights off for the last, the best part of this or any day: a quiet, friendly, serious but teasing talk with

Jesus – strictly private, of course, strictly in her head – until she slipped away into sleep.

v

Grace Bowen was on her knees in the chapel, and her eyes were uplifted to the great empty cross on the wall, symbol of her hope and expectation; but she wasn't praying. Not today.

She was cleaning the paintwork, wiping off the scuffs and heel-marks to have it white and shining for tomorrow's services. Or rather, she wasn't. She had been, and would be again in a minute; but right now, she was eavesdropping.

She was listening to old Ted Grimes as he talked to Arthur Brougham in the little room behind the wall, as his voice rolled out through the door they'd forgotten to close.

" . . . I talked to my nephew," Ted was saying. "On the tele-phone, last night. He's in London now, with his mother. Told him our plans for Easter, how we're making it a dry run, like, for the Mission. He said he'd come up next week, to see how we did things and lend a hand where he could. And when I said about the Sunday, about the long service, he said he'd like to take a part of that. To pray for healing, he said. It's a thing he's done in America, seemingly, and he says the people come. He says it's a great thing, to see the rows packed with people who'd never be in a church ordinarily and to feel the Lord moving among them, healing the sick and the distressed . . . "

Hearing footsteps in the porch behind her, another Council member coming to the meeting, Grace turned to her work again, scrubbing industriously at the wall. She'd been feeling shamed a minute ago, conscience-struck, listening in to a conversation not meant for her to hear; but no longer.

Now she knew that it had all been meant: that it was God's hand and not Arthur's that had left that door ajar, God's will that caused Ted to speak so loudly against his deafness. This was a message for her ears specifically, that was plain as Scripture. *People who'd never be in a church ordinarily* – yes, indeed. She had one of those on her hands. Well, more than one; but one in particular, the special one who stood so much in need.

And he'd be here, on Easter Sunday. She'd see to that.

THREE

Arrivals are crucial, first comings are always symbolic; which is maybe why he times his first coming to the city for the early morning, while it's still asleep. Maybe he wants empty streets and silences because they can more easily be filled with his vision, the city sleeping overpainted with his dream of its waking.

Or maybe not, maybe it's only that the overnight bus from London works out cheaper, and it's not his money that he's spending here.

Whatever, he comes with the sunrise, and he's first off the bus. His aunt and uncle are there to meet him, though it seems more as if he's greeting them, with his kiss of love and his murmured blessing.

He collects his luggage, his single small suitcase from the back of the coach; and he laughs at their surprise, he says,

– I like to travel light.

But they know that already, they're bathed and glowing in the light he travels by.

George Jenner was working on his car, stripped down to T-shirt and tracksuit bottoms in the midday sun. A power cut had forced him to close the gym an hour ago, and he wasn't a man to waste time with idleness.

Anyone looking at George for the first time – as was happening right now, there was someone standing on the waste ground opposite, just standing watching him – any stranger might have thought George a poor advertisement for the Paradise Gym and Health Centre. He was no body-builder, with tanned translucent skin over massive ridges of muscle. Loose flesh hung from his brawny arms and rippled across his broad back, while his heavy belly jutted ponderously over the waistband of his trousers.

But that stranger would have seen his mistake, perhaps, would surely have been impressed – as the watching man was meant to be – when George moved to stand in the road, in front of the open bonnet of his car. When he bent, locked his arms securely around the unbolted engine, stiffened legs and spine – and straightened with no more than a soft grunt, raising the whole engine clear of the chassis.

He took three slow, careful paces back, and lowered it to the tarmac. Stood upright again, and walked over to his toolbox; and glancing casually across to see if the feat had registered, had made its intended mark on the stranger, he saw the man coming across the road towards him.

Tall, but not extravagantly so; well-built and looking fit without the unbalanced, top-heavy appearance of an obsessive iron-pumper; moving with a lithe and easy grace that wasn't assumed, that carried no hint of show. George reached for a rag to wipe the oil and filth from his hands and forearms, sensing a potential customer. Not a fanatic, not a man who'd spend three hours a day sweating to improve his quads, but a regular for sure. Someone who'd work out two or three times a week, just to keep himself in shape . . .

But then there was the scutter of paws and claws on tarmac, a furious barking; and George cursed, seeing the heavy shape of his dog Kyzer come hurtling from the alley beside the gym.

Too late, he remembered letting the dog out and forgetting about it, with the street empty and work to be done. He moved fast now, spurred by a chill certainty; but though he could do that, though he could move faster than anyone would guess, still he wasn't fast enough. The dog still reached the stranger first.

And that should have been trouble; that should have brought blood and pain and terror, with George fighting, needing all his strength to wrestle the dog away.

But it just didn't happen, somehow. Nothing happened the way it ought to. The stranger didn't back off from the menace of a Rottweiler, didn't even look nervous; he only stood there and smiled, brightly blond in the sunshine.

Kyzer's barking died in a moment, in the face of that smile. Its frenzied run finished with a leap at the man's body, but not to attack, no: only to plant two paws firmly on his chest and strain to lick his face.

The stranger laughed, held his chin teasingly out of reach, pulled at cocked ears and dug his fingers deep into thick fur.

And the dog went on playing the untrained puppy, playing the fool. It spared not a glance for George, keeping its gaze fixed on the stranger's face. At a word from him it dropped to the ground again, obedient but whining, softly protesting; and was bouncing and playful again a moment later when the man's left hand cuffed it lightly across the muzzle, announcing a new game. A growl and a retreat, a spring forward and a sudden grab: strong jaws closed over the stranger's fingers, and began to chew.

"Careful," George said through his bewilderment. "It could have your arm off, that one."

"Oh, he won't hurt me. Will you, boy?"

And to prove it the stranger closed his hand tight round the dog's lower jaw and swung the great head from side to side. The dog rumbled threateningly in its chest, scrabbled for purchase on the road, fought back hard; and all the time its stump of a tail was twitching, its whole hindquarters were wagging in a frenzy of delight.

And when the man finally pulled his hand free and wiped the slobber off onto his jeans, there were only a few fading white marks to show where Kyzer's teeth had gripped. Not one had so much as broken the skin.

"I've never seen it behave like that," George said, running a hand over the stubble on his shaven scalp. "Never. Not with anyone."

"He's smart," the stranger smiled, "he knows a friend when he sees one."

"It's meant to be a guard dog. It's not supposed to go soft like that . . . "

"Yes, but a good guard dog knows his enemies, surely? So by definition he should know his friends as well." And the stranger held out his right hand, treating George to one of those dazzling golden smiles that had so bewitched his dog. "So should you, of course. Richard Gould."

"Unh. I'm George Jenner. This is my place," with a jerk of his bullet head back towards the gym, and an unfocused need to save face driving him to one of his bonecrusher handshakes. He'd broken a man's hand before this, for what seemed less cause.

Gould didn't gasp, didn't so much as wince; nor did his own grip tighten, to turn it into a challenge. He only nodded, "Pleased to meet you, Mr Jenner," and disengaged his hand.

"Well," trying to ignore it all, and particularly the odd behaviour of the dog, which was after all only a reflection of the oddness he could sense in the man, "something I can do for you, lad? Interested in the gym, were you? It's closed right now, the power's off so I can't show you round, but . . . "

"It's the building I'm interested in, to be honest. It looks like a church."

"Aye, that's right. It was a warehouse when I bought it, mind, an upholstery company that went bust; but it still had the old signs up. The Paradise Methodist Church, it said. With the times of services, and everything." George chuckled. "Why, wanting to go in and say a prayer, were you?"

"There's no need," the stranger said gently, peaceably. "I'm trying to learn a little about the area, that's all."

"Just arrived, have you?"

"That's right."

"Staying long?"

"I'm not sure. I'll probably have to go back to London next month, but I'm here again for the summer, that's certain."

"Well, I can do you a six-month membership cheap. You'll find us handy, if you want to keep in trim. All the equipment's new; and there's a sauna, jacuzzi, sun-beds if you want to top up that tan. You never got that from English sunshine."

"No," smiling, "I've been in California for a while."

"Right. Shame to lose it. And the local girls come here for their aerobics, they'll stop you feeling lonely in a strange town . . . "

George's spiel was cut off then, by a delivery-van's arriving. It tried to back in to the kerb ahead of George's car, and was stopped by the engine in the road; and it was the stranger who moved first, to help. Who stepped over to the engine, bent and lifted it with no visible effort. Who carried it to the foot of the gym steps and set it down as though it weighed no more than a box of crisps; and who straightened then with an odd, shamed look on his face, a shrug that was like an apology, though George couldn't be sure what he was apologising for or to whom, only that it wasn't himself.

iii

"*Mind* your backs, please, *mind* your backs there . . . "

Billy's familiar call, in Billy's raucous voice; and people did mind their backs, moving to one side or the other to let him through with his wide trolley.

Only there wasn't a trolley, not this time. There was only Billy, only him and his cackling laugh as he paraded regally through the space he'd created for himself.

The people watched him go, watched him walk out into the sunlit street; and they shrugged, smiled, went on into the crush and clamour of the market. *It's only Billy*, the shrugs said to the smiles, the smiles to the shrugs. *No great matter, nothing to get het up about. Just another Billy story to be told if we remember, but we probably won't. There are others we've been saving, better ones; and more to come, that's certain. Billy's a monument, he's a landmark, he won't let us down . . .*

Outside, Billy stood like a monument, like a landmark among the hurrying crowds. He was wondering which way to go.

He had a half-day, that's why he'd got off work during the lunchtime rush. He was seeing the dentist this afternoon, and he had an appointment card to prove it.

But his appointment wasn't till three o'clock, and it was only just after one now; so he stood still on the pavement while his tongue worried at his aching tooth, while he wondered which way to go.

He could go that way, up to the buses, and be good and early for his appointment; or he could go the other way, down to the pubs. If he went to the pubs, he'd be late.

It was a hot day, and Billy was thirsty. He turned to go down the hill, and stopped. He didn't want to be late; so he turned again, and collided with a little girl running after her impatient mother.

The girl fell over, cracked her head on the pavement and started screaming.

Billy stooped to pick her up, smiling and crooning to her, touching silk-soft hair with his gentle fingers. She gaped up at him, forgetting to cry; and suddenly her mother was there, snatching her arm and dragging her off, "You come away from him, what have I told you about strangers? He's soft in the head, that one, you don't have nothing to do with him . . . "

Billy stayed where he was until the two of them were out of sight, the little girl's renewed screams lost in the general noise; then he started moving, his mind made up at last.

He went down the hill, towards the pubs.

In the first, he was turned out before he reached the bar. There were motorbikes outside the second and long-hairs within, leather jackets and loud music on the juke; Billy went straight past.

He had better luck with the third, finding a new boy behind the bar and no sign of snotty Leila. So he got his pint, looked around and saw a couple of students sitting under the window, the boy smoking as he talked quietly to his girl.

Billy took a gulp at his pint then wedged himself beside them, smiling amiably.

"Sell us a tab, lad," he said, fishing for coins. "Only I got no money for a pack, see, and I'm desperate . . . "

"Sure, take one," the boy said. And as Billy sorted coppers in his palm, "No, don't worry about that, just take one."

"Thanks, mate. You're a mate, you are," fumbling a cigarette out of the offered packet and dropping coins as he did so, lighting up blissfully and drawing smoke deep into his lungs. "I'll buy you a drink, next time I'm in. Only I'm short today, don't get paid till Friday, see. I've got a job, me, but they let me go early today, I've got an appointment at the dentist. Three o'clock, that is, time for a pint first . . . "

But Billy's time had run out already, his last seconds counted down by the sound of heels solid on the wooden floor. He glanced up to see Leila approaching, snatched up his glass and buried his face in it, swallowing urgently as she started in.

"What the hell are you doing here? You're barred, Billy, you know that. Out with you, now."

Billy spluttered nervously and started to cough, spraying his drink over the table. "You can't, you can't bar me. I live here . . . "

"Not in here, you don't. And you don't drink here, neither. I won't have you annoying my customers. Come on, move yourself."

No good the boy saying that he wasn't annoying anyone, no good Billy protesting that he hadn't finished his pint, or that his money was all over the floor. Leila had her hands on him already, pulling him up and propelling him towards the door, calling back over her shoulder as she hustled him out.

"Don't you serve this one again, Gareth, you hear me? He's nothing but trouble, and you don't let him through the door from now on. He gives you any lip, call me. I'll deal with him . . . "

With the last of his change left on the pub floor, Billy couldn't manage a bus fare; so he set out to walk to his dentist.

He mooched along the main road, hands in pockets and mumbling, feeling sorry for himself. Loud voices ahead gave him early warning, two teenage lads and a girl coming towards him; Billy stepped warily into the gutter to let them pass. He remembered too many similar encounters, too much trouble. Worse trouble than Leila, kids could be.

He licked his lips, thinking of his abandoned pint, mourning the loss of it; and seeing the open gate of the cemetery just ahead of him, he wandered inside. This wasn't a short cut, exactly, just a nicer way to go, but he had plenty of time. Time enough to sit on his favourite bench in the sunshine, to look at the graves and be alone for a while . . .

33

Only he was hardly through the gate before he heard running footsteps behind him, voices yelling. Billy shivered in the warm breeze, but kept walking, didn't even look round till the lads caught up.

"Hey, you! Did you give my girl the tongue, did you?"

Billy blinked, shook his head, heard the whine in his own voice, "What, no, I never . . . "

"She says you did." And they were pushing him already, shoving him back and forth so that he staggered between them, teetering on the edge of balance, the very edge of terror.

"Calling her a liar, are you?"

"You're the liar."

"And a pervert, you're a fucking pervert . . . "

And this was trouble, sure enough; and could only get worse here in the empty cemetery, a long way from the road, from any chance of help.

"No filthy fucking pervert gives my girl the tongue."

"You keep your tongue in your head, right? Right?"

And they weren't pushing any more, they were hitting him now, hard fists beating in through his flailing arms, catching his stomach, his ribs, the side of his head as he doubled over. Then there were hands in his hair and a knee driving up into his face, mashing lips and tongue between his jolted teeth.

Billy toppled and fell. The lads yelled their scorn, their victory; then the footsteps were blessedly running the other way, and it was over until the next time.

And Billy lay sobbing on the tarmac path, spitting out blood and fragments from a broken tooth, spitting words blindly through the fog of his pain and fear.

"Oh, God, oh God. Oh, Jesus God . . . "

iv

"Well, I don't like it."

Thus Alan Parkinson, in the back room at a Council meeting, holding one of the posters that advertised their Easter services.

Ted Grimes shifted uncomfortably in his chair; Arthur lifted a hand to still him, said, "We pray for healing, Alan. At every service, near enough."

"Aye, but not like this." Alan ran his eye down the poster, and read aloud. "' . . . *A special hour of prayer, for the healing of the sick . . . For those who seek it, the laying on of hands . . . Only ask in faith and you will be healed; that is God's promise to us . . . All welcome . . .* ' You never wrote this, Arthur."

"No," he agreed quietly. "It was Richard wrote it. I asked him to."

"You should have consulted us," from Jean Dolance, who was no more happy than Alan.

Arthur sighed. "We talked about this. We agreed to give him a free hand, to run his hour the way he felt was right. I couldn't pull back once I'd told him that. And if he feels called to lead a service of healing, who are we to forbid it?"

"It's our hall," Alan said, with a degree of spite.

"No." Jack Dubrowski, declaring a position at last. "It's God's hall. We're only the caretakers."

"Aye, then, but we've a responsibility to see that He's not mocked in His own hall, don't we? And this," waving the poster like a flag, "this'll bring the Press and everything. You know what happens then, we've seen it before. Pieces in the paper mocking us, mocking God through us. We've a responsibility," again.

"It's a commandment," Ted said anxiously, obviously feeling responsible himself. "Luke 9, verse 2: 'And he sent them to preach the kingdom of God, and to heal the sick.'"

"Aye, but God heals where He chooses, not where we choose. We can't promise miracles. If you ask me, that boy, he's spent too much time in America. I've seen them, those telly evangelists. Telling people to press themselves against the TV screen and be healed. That's not Scripture, it's mockery. It's corruption of the Gospel, they do it for the money."

"I think we have to trust Richard," Arthur said hastily. "And I'm sure we can, Ted, he's a fine lad. I'll have a word with him tomorrow, but I'm sure he'll not do anything outlandish. Now let's pray, shall we, let's take it to God and put all our troubles into His hands, where they belong . . . "

v

Sam Bowen came home from work to find contention in the family, the whole flat heavy with tension unresolved.

Nothing new there. What was new, what startled him as he hung his jacket up on the landing and went into the lounge, what killed the teasing smile on his lips was the obvious cause of the trouble, Grace glaring at their eldest where he lay on the sofa.

The little ones, Trevor and Sammy were watching wide-eyed,

35

uninvolved for once and fascinated by the sight of their big brother in a row. It was rare enough, that was for sure. Derry had always had a knack for avoiding trouble, slippery as a fish he'd been when he needed it; and then he'd fallen sick. *He'll not be with us long,* Grace had said quietly one night, when she'd finally accepted the truth of what the doctors told them. *Let's give him a good time while he's here. As good as we can. We'll only regret it, else. After he's gone . . .*

Her notion of a good time meant spoiling him rotten, in Sam's eyes, but he never objected. It did Grace good, at least, it made her burden lighter; which made life less of a strain for the whole family. And his practical soul fed him no visions of the boy's growing up into a self-centred monster. No visions of the boy's growing up at all, no delusions for Sam.

Grace's other comfort came from her religion, its only value to Sam. She'd meet her son again, no doubt of that in her mind. Only once had Sam lost patience with her; driven by his own distress, his futile raging, he'd asked her savagely if she could really see Derry sporting wings and a halo, with a harp tucked under his arm. *He's no Christian, that boy,* he'd said. *If you're right about God and that, then he's bound for Hell, same as me. That's the God you believe in, Grace, one that'll kill a fifteen-year-old boy and then send him down into the pit.*

She'd cried and said no, her God was a god of love, He wouldn't separate a boy and his mother, not for eternity He wouldn't. Sam had fallen silent then, too late; and they hadn't mentioned it again, either of them.

As for Sam himself, he'd made his own accommodations with a cruel world. For him Derry was dead already, dead from the time the doctors pronounced sentence. All his grieving had been done then, in advance; which made these final months a gift, a bonus, a generous postponement of the day when they came to take the boy away. Sam saw his son as Lazarus, visiting for a while before going back to the tomb; and he loved him for it.

But now he stood in the doorway, looked from his wife's set face to his son's, and said, "What's to do, then?"

"Ask her," Derry said shortly, one scornful flick of his head to indicate his mother before he dropped back onto the sofa cushions, staring fixedly at the ceiling, giving no ground and offering no help.

"Grace?"

"Oh, you talk to him. I'm sick to here with his stubbornness. All I'm asking is an hour of his precious time," and she choked for a moment, perhaps remembering too late that every hour really was precious to Derry, was something to be seized and cherished from a calendar cut brutally short, "just one hour and the hope of life after; but he'll not listen to me. You're his father, you talk to him."

And she stalked through into the kitchen, slamming the door behind her.

Sam stood still for a moment, his mind whirling giddily, hurting for both of them and no space left to hurt for himself. Then he chased the two younger boys out, and drew a chair up beside the sofa.

"What's this all about, then, Derry son?"

"She wants me to go to chapel with her, Sunday," the words spat out through thin lips. "Some guy's doing a special service, there's a poster about it on the table there. She thinks he's going to heal me." There was almost a hatred in his voice as he said it; and Sam could understand that, could see how easy it would be to hate anyone who held out another hope to someone who'd had three years already to see hope fail and fail.

"Well," Sam said, thinking how needless this was, how stupid of Grace to be so blinded by her own desperate faith, "look, son . . . "

"I'm not going." And there was that special determination on Derry's face as he said it, the same determination that had brought him home two months ago, after he'd refused any more of the chemotherapy that was only making him sicker. Sam hadn't found a way to break it then, and couldn't imagine doing so now.

He tried, briefly; he offered the old and the obvious arguments, that it would do no harm if it did no good, that it would make things easier on his mother and thereby on all of them. And he got nowhere, as he'd expected.

He pushed himself to his feet, meaning to talk to Grace instead; but to delay the moment, he stopped and glanced over the poster on the table. No doubt that would be up in their bedroom window tonight, shouting its message into the street.

He read it through, and paused; read it again, and came back to Derry with a sudden, small hope brightly in his mind. Not for a miracle, nothing so grandiose; only for a way to make peace in his family, to cast a little oil on troubled waters.

"Derry, listen to me. I know you don't want to do this for your mother, and I can understand that. But have you thought what she'll do, what's going to happen if you don't?"

"How d'you mean? She'll be mad, I know that. But . . . " An adolescent shrug, *she'll get over it.*

Sam smiled. "She won't get mad, son. She'll get even. I've been with her twenty years come June, I should know. If you don't go to hear this preacher, she'll bring him to you. Trust me, she'll do that. She'll bring him here, and you'll have him praying over you right in this room. Is that really better than chapel on Sunday?"

Derry licked pale lips with a pale tongue – *like he's had all the blood squeezed out of him*, Sam thought, *that's how he looks these days, my rowdy son* – and said nothing for a minute. Then, "She would, wouldn't she?"

"No question. No warning, either, so you couldn't dodge him." *No slippery fish, you. Not any more. Pale on a slab and ready for gutting, aren't you, my smart boy, my sharp young customer?*

"Christ. Dad . . . "

"I'm sorry, son. It'll be bloody awful, but I can't help you," chuckling quietly inside. "You know your mother, when she's set on something. I can't shift her. She's as stubborn as you are. Where you get it from, I expect."

"Oh, *fuck* it." He ran thin fingers through his patchy tufts of hair, graphic evidence of the failed chemotherapy, and said, "Tell her I'll go, then." And as Sam headed triumphant for the kitchen, his son's querulous voice came after him, seeking urgently for some small victory to set against this vast defeat. "And bring us a lager from the fridge, will you?"

Sam was in no mood to deny him that. In fact, he'd join him. A father should drink with his son, sometimes; and this father decided suddenly, he'd take any chance he got.

FOUR

i

− I need to be alone, he says, I have to pray before the service.

But surely all his life is prayer, he himself is surely prayer made flesh; so now, in the privacy of that small room behind the Cross, he can no longer simply be praying. It's his modesty that speaks there, not his truth.

Rather say that prayer must have encompassed him, must have unbound him to the glory. We don't need to see him, to imagine this. Lost in his Father's greater light, he will no longer be able to sense the limits of his body, of his bones. Kneeling, he will know nothing of the worn carpet he kneels on, the hard boards beneath; nothing of the small noises and motions in the room, his own soft breathing and the creaks of expanding wood, the constant dance of dust in sunlight.

Remote from flesh, no doubt he dreams awake, his spirit cradled in a hand wider than the world and more real. No question of it, he is all song behind that door, all praise and all wonder.

And when he emerges, he will be as ever what he seeks to be, what is needed of him.

ii

Derry came to chapel that Easter Day in style, riding high; or else he came trumped and defeated and brought low, where he hadn't meant to come at all.

"I can't," he'd said as his mother bustled about getting the two younger boys ready, checking that their hair was combed and their laces were tied. "I'm sorry, Mam," lying in his teeth, "I just can't walk that far. It's really bad today."

That was meant to be his own trump, his unassailable excuse; but his father had simply grunted, and said, "You managed to walk up to Stu's, yesterday. And home again."

"Yeah, well, maybe I shouldn't have. Maybe that's why."

"Maybe it is. Just as well you don't have to walk today, then, isn't it?"

39

"How d'you mean?"

"I've borrowed Dave's estate for the day," jingling the keys in his hand, chimes of doom to Derry's hopes. "The kids can squash in behind, so you get the whole back seat to yourself. Can you manage the stairs okay, or do you want me to carry you down?"

Derry had given his father a look, a glare of bitter betrayal, and had received nothing but a smile in response. Had levered himself furiously up on his crutches and made his slow way down the stairs alone, with all the family backed up behind him.

And now he inched himself along the seat to let his legs hang out of the open door; now his mother handed his crutches over from the front; now he pushed himself up and out, rage twisting his body as he shrugged off any help from his traitor father.

He shuffle-drag-scraped his slow way around the car, to see a small crowd gathered on the pavement outside the wooden chapel. Local people, most of them, he knew their faces if not their names. They were smoking, stretching, talking quietly; and he thought, *Great timing, Dad.* It was his father's work, no question, bringing them here just as there was a break in the three-hour service. His mother relied on God to arrange these things; Dad just stepped in occasionally to do the Almighty's job for him, to make sure she wasn't disappointed.

Above the chapel door, the sign: *PARADISE PENTECOSTAL GOSPEL HALL. Jesus Saves!* Derry eyed it cynically, thinking that Jesus showed no signs of saving him. That was what they were all here for, of course, to give the guy another chance; but how many chances did he need? Derry had been here often enough before, too bloody often, dragged along by his mother every Sunday till he was old enough to rebel effectively. Nothing had ever happened then, it had just been people singing too loud and talking too long, no sign of any God around. And it'd be the same today, only worse: people eyeing him covertly, sick with pity and loving themselves for it . . .

And they were eyeing him already, murmuring between themselves, just too low for him to catch it. Not that he needed to. *That's Grace Bowen's lad, is it? Must be. Her eldest, the one with the odd name. Looks terrible, doesn't he? Hasn't got long, by what I hear. But you can see that, it's written all over him . . .*

It was written inside him, too, written deep into every cell in his body. He *hadn't* got long, and he certainly didn't have time for all this crap. But he was here now, and too proud to make a scene; so Derry lifted his resentful head, stared down the murmurers and started forward again, shuffle-drag-scrape through the crowd and

40

into the porch ahead of them all, not waiting for anyone, certainly not waiting for his father.

Almost tripped on the step going in, and caught himself just in time, just ahead of the half-dozen eager hands reaching out to help. Took a second to steady himself, to be sure of balance; and went more cautiously on into the chapel proper.

The room he knew of old. He knew the boredom of the bleak white walls and their mean windows, nothing to see but walls and sky through wire netting; he knew the discomfort of the wooden chairs, the raucous sound of the cheap electric organ and the heavy threat of the great cross at the end. Knew it all and hated it, and hated it more today.

The people, too, he knew them, or some of them. There were the four old men who'd run the place forever, gathered in a huddled group at the front. And there was Alan Parkinson with his new beard, Derry had seen him last Saturday making a fool of himself in town, bellowing God at the crowds; and creepy Mrs Dolance with her two weird kids in tow. They sat on one side, the grown-ups muttering with their heads together while the kids had their hands folded neatly round bibles and hymn-books, eyes front and don't whisper, don't fidget in chapel.

There were others scattered around, shoulders hunched in prayer or heads turning to check out the new arrivals; and more coming in behind. Derry knew many and ignored them all, slumping into a seat at the back and dropping his crutches into the aisle with a deliberate clatter.

His mother squeezed past him, high-stepping awkwardly over his legs and taking the next seat, where she could prod him forward when the time came. Then Trevor and Sammy, and the little one stumbling inevitably over Derry's feet, which really did hurt, too late to be useful. Derry just hissed softly and watched his father swoop the kid up and carry him on along the row.

His mother prodded him in the ribs. "Move down to the front, son. It'll be easier, for when the preacher wants you."

"No fucking way."

That brought a sharp pinch on his arm, and, "Watch your language, Derry Bowen! You're in God's house now."

"Leave it out, Mam. He ain't listening."

"That's what you think ... "

And damn right that was what Derry thought, though he was too wise to say so. It stood to reason. If God existed – big if, but if He did – then He had to be smarter than Derry was, didn't he? And if Derry was bored rigid by what went on here, if he turned

41

off as soon as he was through the door, then why the hell would God bother to listen?

Derry smirked to himself, pleased with that; and forgot to change the smirk to a scowl when a woman appeared beside him with a pile of books, so that she thought he was smiling at her.

"Welcome to the Gospel Hall," she said, clashing horsy yellow teeth as she smiled back. "Here's a hymn-book, and a service sheet. Hullo, Mrs Bowen," talking over his head now, passing more books along the row. "It's good to see the family here. I know the two boys and Mr Bowen, of course, but is this your eldest . . . ?"

As if she didn't know, as if the crutches didn't mark him out for who and what he was, what he was doing here. Derry glowered, and started reading the service sheet to lose the sound of her voice, his mother's reply.

The beginning and the end of this long service had every minute accounted for, between hymns and Bible readings and talks: *"The Truth of the Resurrection"*, Mr A. Saltley; *"The Path to Glory"*, Mr A. Parkinson. And so on, two solid hours of it. If God had any sense, he'd keep a million miles away from this.

The middle stretch, though – what they were here for, what was going to start any minute now – there were no hymns marked down for that, no readings, nothing. Just, "1pm – 2pm: Mr R. Gould will lead a service of prayers for healing."

Derry was glad about the no singing, he'd always hated that and would hate it worse today, having to scrabble for his crutches every time they stood up. But that was a small mercy, in the face of what his mother was demanding . . .

He shifted in his chair, stared sullenly around as the old cow with the books went on yattering to Mam across him, as everyone came back in from outside and found their seats again; and saw a door open under the arm of the cross.

Saw a man walk out, easy and confident and smiling.

Saw him go over to the organ, heard him pick a few notes out one-fingered; felt the sudden silence in the congregation, and thought, *Shit, there's going to be hymns after all.*

Was already bending over to retrieve his crutches when a voice reached out and stilled him, stole all his movement away.

"Hullo, everyone. My name's Richard, for those of you who haven't met me yet. I'm Ted's nephew, and I've been asked to lead the service for the next hour or so . . . "

The words were nothing. It was the voice that gripped Derry: a voice like softened gold, filling the room, filling Derry's head like summer. Like old summer, like summer used to be before he was

42

ill, all fire and light and freedom.

"I know there are some of you who aren't regular members of the congregation here, who've come along hoping for healing. Perhaps some of you aren't even believers," and his smile seemed to find Derry out at the back of the hall, seemed to know him all too well, "but you've turned up anyway, just in case. Well, I can't promise you a miracle this afternoon, I'm not allowed to do that," and now the smile shared itself around, flashed across the old men in the front row, made Alan Parkinson stir in his place by the wall. "One thing I can promise you, though. No, two things. The first is that you're very welcome here, whatever your reasons for coming; and the second is that God truly does have the power to heal. I don't. I'm the world's worst doctor, I can't put a plaster on a cut. I'm just a tool here. A hammer doesn't hit a nail of its own will, it takes a carpenter's hand to do the work; and the carpenter chooses his own tools. He does the work his own way, in his own time. Whether God will choose to work here today, I can't say. What I *can* say is that He has the power, and I've seen it work. I've seen the blind regain their sight, no trickery. I was visiting a retreat in America when there was an accident, a sister there was crushed under a car when the brakes failed. We laid hands on her and prayed, and by the time the ambulance arrived it wasn't needed. Broken bones had been made whole again, deeper injuries had healed completely. The paramedics thought it was some kind of hoax, till we showed them the blood on the road and the car's tyre-marks on her clothes. They took her into hospital for X-rays, but there wasn't so much as a bruise on her body.

"Minds, too, I've seen broken minds made well and madness broken. God can and will work miracles of healing; and I truly believe that if we come to Him in faith this afternoon, if we ask in faith, then those among you who need healing will receive it. Maybe not immediately, because He's not a showman at heart; He chucks down the odd firework to keep us on our toes, but mostly He prefers to work more quietly, behind the scenes. I don't think He likes headlines too much, and I know I don't. So let's just pray, shall we, plant a few mustard seeds of faith . . . "

Derry didn't move, despite everyone else shifting forward in their seats, his mother bowing head into hands and the whispered "Amens" beginning to echo around the room. The guy's voice still held him, though, he couldn't switch off the way he used to. Even the chill of his private visions, even the image of his own funeral service going on in this same room – *sometime this year, most likely; maybe this month, this week, maybe you'd all better hang around for it, don't go home, you could save the petrol money –*

even that couldn't take him away from here today.

So he sat and listened to the prayers, and the talking that came afterwards; and was still listening when nightmare time came round. Still listening and ready for it, not needing his mother's nudging elbow to remind him.

"What I'm going to ask now will be difficult, I know that. You don't have to do it, you can stay right where you are if you want to. God still sees you, He knows your needs.

"But if you've got a special need, if you're here in search of healing, I want you to come up to the front. Don't feel embarrassed, there's no need. You're among friends here. I'll ask you to kneel down, I'll lay hands on you as God instructs His ministers to do; and I'll say a prayer, a personal prayer for each of you. You don't have to tell me what's wrong, I don't need to know that. Nails don't talk to hammers.

"I'll ask the rest of the congregation to bow their heads now and just pray silently, while those of you who are sick or suffering make your way to the front. Don't hold back. Just come. Have faith, put your trust in Jesus, and declare that trust by coming forward. Let Him see your faith . . . "

"Get going, Derry," a soft sibilant whisper.

"He said I didn't have to. He *said* so."

"Never mind him. Go." And another nudge, a warning of trouble otherwise to help him on his way.

And he went, eventually. Slowly, reluctantly, furiously blushing: shuffle-drag-scrape up the aisle he went, behind half a dozen others.

Stood in line before the guy with the golden voice, before his radiant smile; stood in the middle of the line, watched the others kneel on either side of him and stayed aggressively upright, propped awkwardly on his crutches.

Watched the guy – what was his name, Richard something – making his way along the line, laying hands on each bowed head and murmuring softly, keeping it private, something to be grateful for; until at last he reached Derry, smiled down at him, touched his arm and spoke.

"I think you should kneel, really. I think it's better."

"Can't."

"Oh, I think you can. It's not so hard, before God. Pride's so empty, it just flies right out of the window. Come on, now. I'll help."

"It hurts," in a hiss so harsh it made the other supplicants stir on either side.

"I'm sure it does. What's your name?"

44

"Derry."

"Life hurts, Derry; and some people's lives hurt more than others, that's right, isn't it? You'd know. But pain's all right, you've got the strength, you can meet pain face to face and come off best. You'd know that, too."

Then there was a firm hand lifting his, taking his weight, taking his crutch away. The same on the other side, and he just let it happen, he couldn't fight it; and he was left with his fingers panic-tight around two strong wrists as he was lowered slowly to his knees.

And it did hurt, Christ it hurt. He bit his lip frantically against the cry in his throat, not to let it out into the silent chapel; ducked his head against the shaming sting of tears and found himself suddenly empty-handed, the guy's arms gone, nothing to cling to.

Then warm palms and long fingers enclosed his head, pressing down on thin tufts of hair and areas of bare scalp between. He heard that voice again, distantly now, turned elsewhere; and felt the loss of it like a sorrow. And listened anyway, listened blushing, as if eavesdropping on a private conversation.

"Lord, if it be Your will, reach down and touch this boy Derry in his need. You made the world and the stars, You made each of us, You made him; and You made him to be strong in Your service. You have the power to heal him. Don't take him from us now, Lord, before he's had a chance to show his worth, before we've had a chance to love him as You meant him to be loved . . . "

And there was more, but Derry wasn't listening any longer. Fire and light, he'd thought that voice was; but it was all shadow compared to the fire that seized him now, the light that burned behind his closed eyes. He shivered, he gasped, he sobbed in the heart of that fire, cried out against the light; and cried again when it left him, when the fire died.

Opening his eyes again at last, when he didn't dare hide any longer: opening his eyes in fear of what he would find, a world utterly changed, the first thing he saw was a face that mirrored his, streaming tears and a trembling mouth.

The second thing he saw was a pair of hands reaching down to him, an invitation and a plea.

He grabbed at them desperately, and for a minute the two of them clung to each other, needing the comfort of a touch that was nothing more than human.

Then Richard cocked one eyebrow, his mouth twisted itself wryly, and he said, "Come on, then, Derry. Got to try it sometime. Let's have you on your feet again."

Derry shook his head in sudden terror. "I can't. I – I *can't* . . . "

"Yes, you can. If you can't trust God, trust me. I won't let you fall."

But the world hadn't changed that much. This was still the same planet, he still had the same body; and he knew that body too well, despite the memory of flame lingering in his bones.

So he shook his head, didn't or couldn't move any more than that; and was looking, reaching cautiously for the pain again, for something to ground him in a known reality, when he felt the guy slip free and leave him with nothing. He yelled "*No!*" and toppled forward, snatching; and Richard's arms came round him in a bearhug, the smile was wide and glowing once more, Derry could feel his laughter shaking all his ribs as he said,

"On your feet, kid. Right *now*."

And he lifted Derry up, sweet and easy; lifted him right off the ground for a moment, eye to eye and gloriously laughing.

Set him down with a thud that shook the floor, that resounded through the room and should have finished Derry, should have sent a killing pain up through his legs and all the way to his heart to stop it, dead.

Derry felt nothing except the jolt, and searched again for the agony that belonged to him and within him, that defined the world he knew. Couldn't find it, or the last least trace of it; and clung instead to the man who'd done this to him.

"Don't let go," he whispered. "For, for God's sake don't let go . . . "

"For God's sake is exactly why I have to," a soft chuckle in his ear. "He's got His reputation to keep up. Miracles have to be seen, to be believed. But don't worry, I'm not going away. Okay, now, on the count of three. One, two . . . "

Three: and Richard stepped back from Derry's reaching hands and left him standing.

Derry closed his eyes and waited for the pain, waited to fall over.

When neither one happened, he opened his eyes and looked numbly round for his crutches. Saw the guy holding them a few metres away, and held out his hand to ask.

Richard just shook his head, so Derry took a step towards him, two steps, saying, "Please, I can't walk without them . . . "

"Could have fooled me, Derry. You're doing fine."

That stopped him. He looked down at his feet, rock-steady on the floor; and shook his head against the bewilderment that dizzied him, that made the room spin momentarily and could have had him falling after all.

He glanced round to see everyone, the whole congregation staring at him, even the ones still on their knees at the front, no one praying now. Shivered in the intensity of that gaze, that mass fascination, and turned away hurriedly.

"Derry? Would you like to be alone for a bit?"

"Uh, yeah. Yeah . . . "

"Through here." Richard pulled open the door to the back room; and Derry walked all the way over, going slow, shuffling like a man in darkness but getting there in the end.

"Sit down, and rest. You'll need to, if you feel anything like the way I do. Try to get your head around what's happened; and try a prayer, if you can. A quick thank-you, that's all, I just think God might appreciate it. But most of all," wryly, "enjoy the quiet. You won't get much of that for a while after. I'll come through soon, with your family. Okay?"

A hand on his shoulder, and an unexpected kiss on the cheek; then the door closed, and Derry was on his own.

On his feet, and staggering.

He just made it to the nearest chair before the noise hit, coming through the wall, rising and swelling, breaking like a monstrous wave of water.

Derry didn't get long to himself: ten minutes, perhaps, no more than that. What time he had, he spent exploring this strange and sudden gift, his new-made body. He pointed his toes and stretched his heels, twisted his feet one way and then the other, felt nothing but the stretching and twisting, no pain.

His fingers fumbled with the buttons of his jeans, undid them one by one; then a deep breath and almost a prayer, he almost managed a prayer before working the denim over his hips and pushing it down to his ankles.

He sat and looked at his legs, seeing the pale and familiar thinness of them, no extra miracle there; and punched one leg and slapped the other, laughing at the sting of it. Pinched them and pummelled them and still didn't wake up, almost didn't expect to.

Then he sat back, looking; and when even that got too much for him he closed his eyes and simply sat within the shivering wonder of it all. His mind flinched away from both past and future, content to settle simply for what was, the unaccustomed sense of wholeness, of belonging to his body again, no alien presence seeking to thrust him out.

More noises from beyond the wall brought him back: the scrape

47

of chairs, the buzz of conversation, footsteps just the other side of the door and coming closer.

He lost the wonder, in a surge of panic. Scrambled to his feet without even thinking about it, bent to grab his trousers, and was just hauling them above his knees when the door opened.

He froze and reddened, embarrassment hot on his skin and cold in his bones. But it was Richard who came in, only him; and he only laughed, looked back over his shoulder and said, "Hang on a minute, folks." Then he stood guard over the doorway until Derry had straightened, had pulled his trousers up and buttoned the fly, got himself straight for company.

"Okay, Derry?"

A pause, one last moment just for the two of them, before they let others in; and Derry used the time to drink the guy's face with his eyes, to soak it deep into his mind. Gold-blond hair matted now with sweat, tanned skin turned dirty white and glistening, green eyes abruptly sunken into deep shadow. *Takes it out of you, right?* Derry wondered vaguely what he looked like himself. He felt shattered, more than drained, wrung out like a filthy cloth; and he guessed it'd show stark and clear on his fleshless face. But he'd been that way and worse on the chemotherapy, his family was used to seeing him sick; and maybe the change would shine through it all, maybe there'd still be a glow left from the fire to show that he was different now.

Or maybe not, but it didn't matter anyway. He put one hand on the table to steady himself, and nodded.

"Okay. Just, just don't let the kids climb all over me. If I fall over now, I'll fall apart . . . "

Richard smiled a reassurance and beckoned someone in with his eyes, held someone else back with a gesture, *not yet, one by one, that's all he's got the strength for . . .*

Derry's mother: she came first, and she had the right to. No one was going to challenge her taking precedence today. She walked in, hesitant in her large body despite her larger faith, nervous in the face of possibilities turned real.

For a second they only looked at each other, Derry's eyes jittering away from hers, shy of what he could read there. Then she hurried forward, her arms engulfed him, he was pressed deep into her cushions of fat and rocked wordlessly from side to side.

He hugged her for longer than he wanted to, his own emotions burned out, only wanting to be generous to hers. Then he lifted his face from her neck, murmured "Mam . . . " and pushed at her gently, urging her away from him.

48

It took a minute, but at last she let him go, stepped back and pulled a handkerchief from her sleeve. She blew her nose vigorously, gazed at her standing son with an expression that went far beyond joy, far beyond anything Derry had ever seen in her, and let Richard lead her to a chair.

Derry's father came in next, even more awkward and uncertain. His hand reached out for Derry's in a gesture absurdly close to a formal shake; then he gripped his shoulders, embraced him quickly, kissed him and turned away.

The two boys were easier. Richard went outside and brought them in together, holding a hand of each and warning them to go easy with their brother. They wouldn't really need the warning, Derry thought distantly; they'd had to go too easy for too long, it must be second nature by now.

Trevor frowned up at him solemnly, and asked, "Are you going to be better now?"

Derry touched his hair with fingers that were trembling again. "I don't know, Trev. I really don't. I think so, maybe . . . "

"Better enough to play football with me, like you used to?"

Derry looked around for help, looked from his mother's tearful certainty to his father's quiet confusion to Richard by the door, who was saying nothing; and shrugged, shook his head. "Maybe. I just don't know."

Meanwhile little Sammy was clutching uncertainly at Derry's jeans, wary of being warned or swatted away as he had been so often before. Derry tried a grin, and couldn't manage it; so instead he simply sat down, reached out and lifted the chubby boy onto his lap, where he hadn't been allowed for many months.

"Okay, kid?"

Sammy nodded, awed to a rare silence by the company and the occasion; stuck his thumb firmly into his mouth and nestled up against his brother's chest with a contented sigh.

Hugging Sammy was easy and uncomplicated, nothing like hugging the emotional JCB his mother had become. So Derry did that for a while, closing his eyes and his ears to the room, his mind to everything except the warm weight in his arms and the aching fatigue in every muscle. They were talking about things that concerned him, things he ought to listen to: visits to the hospital, visits from the media, what they should say and what they shouldn't. Derry ought to be following this; but oh, he was so *tired*, and it felt so good just to be sitting here without pain, with Sammy squirming softly against him, with his thoughts turning away from all questions, not even touching on tne dangerous promise of tomorrow . . .

49

So that's all he did, he simply sat and let the talk wash over him like a river; and soon after that he did what he most wanted to do, he fell asleep.

Didn't wake till his father shook him roughly by the shoulder, urged him to his feet and out of the room. He shuffled like a sleepwalker through the chapel, past all the staring eyes of the congregation, stopping only to collect his abandoned crutches and carry them loosely under one arm; made it to the car, guided and half-supported by his father's arm, and was asleep again before the five-minute drive was over.

FIVE

i

If he is himself prayer and an answer to prayer – and who could possibly doubt it, who can doubt anything now? – then it should be no surprise that his own prayers are so blatantly, so flagrantly answered.

Nothing he does should surprise us now, nothing he decides to do. His plan is God's plan, that much is transparent. He speaks with more than one voice, a greater authority than his own; and when he speaks, the people listen. What else? When he prays, God listens.

And when God speaks to him, he hears it, as clearly as we see miracles.

He hears, obeys and rejoices; and his joy is beautiful, as he himself is beautiful in joy.

ii

Rachel lay on the living-room carpet in faded pink sweatshirt and black leggings, bare feet kicking aimlessly in the air, the evening paper spread out before her and the television flickering soundlessly in the corner.

Behind her, the door opened and she heard her father's voice.

"Dinner's ready."

She scowled and turned her head, pushing back a heavy fall of hair.

"Can you stick it in the oven or something, Dad? Please?"

"No, I can't. Your mother's made *nasi goren*, and it'll spoil if you don't come now. What are you up to, anyway?"

"Waiting for the local news, it's really important."

"Why," and she felt his hand snag one upraised foot and tweak the toes playfully, "what's happening?"

"Haven't you *heard*? It's all over the paper . . . "

"And you've been monopolising the paper ever since I came in. No, I haven't heard. What is it?"

"Listen, I'll read it to you. '*EASTER MIRACLE IN PARADISE*', it says. '*It is being claimed that a teenage boy was miraculously cured of cancer at a faith healing session in a small chapel yesterday.*

"'*Derry Bowen (16), of Delacorte Road, Paradise, has been suffering from cancer for the last three years. His doctors had given up hope, and he was not expected to live out the year. His mother took him to the service in desperation, and it seems her prayers have been answered . . .*'"

Rachel's father kept his grip on her foot, swinging it idly from side to side as he listened. At last he grunted, drummed his fingers on her instep and said, "All right, young lady. We'll have our dinner in here for once. As you say, it is important. Turn the sound up on that television."

Rachel stabbed a finger at the remote control; her father disappeared, returning a minute later with a plate in each hand. When he passed one down to her, she looked at the heap of fried rice studded with chicken, prawns, ham and peppers under strips of yellow omelette, and groaned.

"What are you trying to do, fatten me up for slaughter?"

"That's right." Her mother, coming in with a tray: her own dinner, a bottle of wine, three glasses. "Why pay butcher's prices, when we can raise our own meat? Now be quiet, and pass that paper up. I want to see."

Rachel picked a prawn out with her fingers and nibbled it while the announcer droned on about programmes later in the evening, while her mother scanned the paper, while her father poured the wine. She took her glass with the proper expression of shocked amazement, "This isn't Christmas, what's going on?"

"Internal marinating. It'll tenderise your tough bits."

"I don't have tough bits, don't be cheeky. Just sweet young flesh. Emphasis on the *young*, you old wrinkly."

But the banter stopped then, before her father could come back at her; it died the death in a moment, as Rachel heard the signature tune for *Northern Eye* and turned all her attention back to the television.

It was a magazine programme, half an hour of local headlines, reports and interviews; and it didn't let Rachel down today. The presenter lifted her head to the camera as the music faded, smiled professionally, and:

"Hullo. The major story this evening: it's being said that a local boy has been miraculously healed of a fatal cancer. But was it God's work or just a normal remission? A full report on that coming up. First, though, over to Michael Dunne for the night's other headlines . . . "

52

Rachel stabbed impatient forkfuls of her meal, scattering rice heedlessly across the carpet until they returned to the only story that interested her. A young reporter interviewed several witnesses outside the chapel and got the same story from each of them, a dying boy suddenly well again, suddenly walking without crutches. The reporter was neutral, nodding, non-committal; then he turned to the camera, and,

"For a medical assessment I spoke earlier to Derry Bowen's consultant at the King George Medical Centre, Mr Simon Yale."

Cut to an untidy shelf-lined office with the blind drawn, the reporter sitting on one side of a cluttered desk and a relaxed man in his fifties on the other.

"Mr Yale, you've spent most of the day examining Derry; can you confirm if he is in fact free of cancer, if he has been cured?"

"That's two questions, young man, and they need two answers. The first," counting it off on a long manicured finger, stock-in-trade of a successful doctor, "yes, as of today Derry appears to be free from his cancer. We've had him through the body scanner inch by inch, and there are no tumours. The second, though – no, I cannot possibly confirm that he's been cured. Cancer is a recurrent disease, it could flare up again at any time. It'll be years yet, before I let that boy think of himself as cured."

"All right, I can understand that. But is there any scientific explanation for this sudden disappearance of the tumours? Or was it a miracle, Mr Yale?"

"Oh, miracle schmiracle, what does that mean? We see spontaneous remissions from cancer all the time, without being able to explain them. And Derry's cancer is very rare, this is only the third case I've seen in twenty years. We know very little about it; we can't begin to lay down rules for its behaviour yet."

"Surely, though, it can hardly be normal for an advanced cancer to reverse itself so suddenly? The way it's been described to me, it all happened in a matter of seconds . . . "

"That's the way it's been described to me, too," Mr Yale agreed, with a wry smile. "That's the way Derry tells it; but he's not necessarily the best witness. Remission could have been going on for weeks, without his being aware of it. On the other hand, he could be entirely right. Maybe some ethereal fire did burn out his cancer for him. There are more things in heaven and earth than are dreamed of in my philosophy, I'll tell you that much. I don't imagine this was a miracle, and I sincerely hope it wasn't; but I've been wrong before. All I'm certain of is this, Mr Singh: that there is no one who can tell you accurately what did go on yesterday in Derry's body or in his mind. Though you're going to meet a lot of people who think they can."

And he slumped a little behind his desk, looked suddenly very weary of the whole affair: the picture of a man who'd given his life to science seeing all his hard-won knowledge, all his confidence swept away by a moment's magic.

And cut, a close-up of Singh outside the chapel again.

"But what about the boy at the heart of this story, what about Derry himself? What does he say? I talked to him too, with his mother, Mrs Grace Bowen . . . "

Cut again: the living-room of a flat that might have been any one of a thousand, of ten thousand flats in this city. A long sofa pushed back against a papered wall, two people on it: a fat middle-aged woman who again might have been any one of a thousand or ten thousand women, and a boy who was totally unique, who even before his healing couldn't have been anyone but himself.

Rachel drank him in with her eyes: the birdbone fragility of him, the face little more than a skull with parchment skin stretched tight, sparse tufts of hair still clinging.

"Derry, this may be a silly question, but how are you feeling today?"

The boy smiled, a death's-head grimace. "Tired," he said; and the word was hopelessly inadequate to explain his deep-sunken eyes, his air of total exhaustion.

"I can understand that, after a long day of tests at the hospital . . . "

Derry shook his head. "Nah, it wasn't that. I've been tired ever since it happened, like. At the chapel. I went to sleep there, and in the car coming home. That's only a couple of minutes, but I still went to sleep. Dad had to carry me up the stairs. Then I went straight to bed, and I didn't wake up till Mam got at me with a cold flannel this morning."

"Well, tell us about what happened at the chapel."

A pause, a squinting of his eyes that looked strange to Rachel till she realised that on anyone else it would have been a frown, only he didn't have skin loose enough to frown with; then he said, "Dunno if I can, really. It was strange, that's all. Scary. Like fire all through me, and this great burning light, only I had my eyes closed . . . "

"Do you think it was a miracle, Derry? Was it the hand of God?"

He just blinked, squinted again, finally shrugged. "I dunno what it was."

It was his mother who stirred impatiently, who said, "Of course it was a miracle, what kind of question is that? It was the Lord answering my prayers, giving my son back to me, restored and whole again."

"His doctor says it's too soon to be sure of that, the cancer could recur at any time . . . "

"Doctors, what do they know? He's my son, and he's been healed by the Lord's good grace, completely healed. I know he has. I *know* it."

"I hope you're right, Mrs Bowen. So, Derry, one final word – what of the future? What's a fit and well Derry Bowen going to do with himself?"

"Sleep," positively. "Sleep a *lot*. And play football with my brothers. And kick cans down the street, stuff like that. I can't remember the last time I really kicked anything. Lots of things I want to kick," meditatively; and surely, Rachel thought, surely he meant more than cans.

And cut back to the chapel again, where Singh was standing with a tall and golden man who drew a soft sigh of appreciation from Rachel, earning a chuckle from her father and a foot nudging her to silence.

"Mr Gould. You're the man who made this happen – "

"Oh, no," a smiling interruption. "No, I'm just a conduit. It's God who makes things happen, not men."

"Well, you're the conduit, then. Give us your perspective. Do you think it was a miracle?"

"Define 'miracle'. Can you? I can't," in a laughing echo, conscious or not, of what the doctor had been saying. "God works many ways. He created the whole of nature, He wrote the laws that men strive to discover; so it doesn't really matter, does it? If what happened to Derry was a purely natural phenomenon, it's still God's work, by definition. He still deserves our thanks for it. And has them."

"But if Derry's cancer recurs . . . ?"

"No. No, that much I'm sure of. God isn't a tease, He wouldn't be that cruel. Call it a miracle, call it spontaneous remission, whatever: it's done now, Derry's nightmare is over. Of course, he could walk under a bus tomorrow, if he forgets to look; but he'll do it on two good legs without a tumour in them."

"I see. I hope you're right," again.

"Don't hope. Pray. God listens, we've proved that. Miracle or nature, Derry's recovery is still a direct answer to prayer. Prayer *works*."

"Well, looking to the future – you've stirred this city to the bones already, and you've only just arrived, I understand you're just visiting at present . . . "

"Oh, I'm staying now. Definitely. I wanted to, in any case; but it wasn't my choice, so I took it to God. He was quite unequivocal about it. God's never content, you see, never will be till the whole world gives itself over to Him. And there's more work for me here, I'm sure of that. It's hardly started yet. God has great plans for this city."

Singh smiled his uncommitted smile, and handed back to the studio. Rachel punched a button, and the picture died.

"I want to go," she said. "Over to Paradise. I want to meet that guy."

"Which one?" her father asked. "Gould, or the boy?"

Rachel made a face at him over her shoulder. "Him, of course. Richard Gould. He's *wonderful* . . . "

"Yes," thoughtfully. "An answer to prayer, I think. There *is* a lot of work to do here."

"There's a lot of work everywhere," from Rachel's mother. "But I'm not happy about you going to Paradise, dear. Not on your own, at any rate. It's a rough area."

"Phooey. I'm nearly seventeen, Mum, I'm a big girl now. I won't go into any dark alleys, I promise; I'm not that thick. Anyway, God'll look after me. Best bodyguard in the world."

"Be that as it may," her father said, "you'll still be careful, please, Rachel. It's as the man said: that Derry boy could walk under a bus, and you could walk into trouble. I think I'll drive you over, if you really want to go; I'm interested myself. Now finish your dinner," his foot nudging her again, "big girls need more fuel. And pick that rice up off the carpet."

iii

Jason Dewey ambled up the hill from the gym, cutting across the waste ground opposite. He slashed his feet through long grass and weeds, and his toe stubbed against something that glinted in the darkness. An empty bottle: he picked it up, weighed it in his hand for a moment and then hurled it high, back towards the cars parked by the far kerb. It fell short of those, but he heard it smash on the road and grinned fleetingly.

His hand went to the back pocket of his jeans, one finger slipping in to check for the stiffness of folded notes. Not much tonight, just fifteen quid; but that was more than he'd expected for a bag of videos and CDs. George must've been in a good mood

— unless he was keeping Jason sweet for something, some job or other coming up. That was more like it.

Waste of money, though. George could dredge up some fucking awful jobs sometimes, but he didn't need to buy Jason's cooperation. It was stupid to say no. Dangerous. Keeping George sweet was number one on Jason's list of priorities, had been ever since he'd seen what happened to a boy who didn't bother.

The rough ground turned to tarmac and wood chippings beneath Jason's feet, a play area for kids; there were people there, a girl sitting on a swing and a boy pushing. Their soft, private laughter followed Jason up to the road and over.

He slouched moodily into a dark alley between two terraces, wondering what to do with the evening. Priority number two was keeping himself amused, but that wasn't so easy tonight.

He made his way slowly past garage doors and back gates, bin-bags leaking rubbish; and stopped, his eyes on one stretch of the high wall. Vertical spikes of glass shone in their bed of cement above the brickwork, but that was no problem, he had a route over. And the lights in the house beyond didn't mean anything. The husband would be out for sure, he'd be up the road at the carry-out, busy in the kitchens; and Jason didn't care if the wife was in or not. He'd do one thing if she was and another if she wasn't, that was all.

He backtracked a short way down the alley, and jumped. Fell back, took a short run at it and jumped again. This time his hand caught the top of the wall; he hung from his fingers for a moment, then jerked himself up and hooked the other arm over, while his feet scrabbled for purchase on the bricks.

A couple of seconds' heaving, and he was up. He sat still for a moment, getting his breath back and checking yards and windows from this high vantage-point. No one in sight, no one watching; Jason stood up confidently on the narrow wall.

From here, the back yards looked like a row of open boxes. He walked casually along, no thought of falling in his head, till he came to that barrier of broken glass. There was a car parked down in the yard, as there always was; Jason grinned to himself as he turned towards the house, picking his way on tiptoe between the shards of glass, arms outstretched now for balance.

Three metres of that cautious progress, and he was standing directly above the car. He glanced up and down the alley one last time, then at the lit and curtained windows of the house; and then he jumped.

A drop of a few feet, and he landed in a crouch on the car roof.

It made a noise, of course, a light thud and a creak from the suspension; but nothing more than that, no electronic wail set off by the jarring shock of his landing.

Stupid bastards, he thought. *Should've got an alarm fitted months back. How the fuck do they think I get in here every time?*

He stepped off the roof onto the bonnet, and from there down to the ground. There was a door on his right, leading into the kitchen extension; but Jason ignored it. Locked and bolted, that would be. He was more interested in the window ahead of him.

It was the old sash type, easily forced. He took a penknife out of his jacket pocket, opened the blade and worked it up into the crack between the window's two frames. Eased the catch aside and put the knife away again, gripped the lower frame and pushed upwards –

– and nothing happened, the frame didn't shift a millimetre. Jason scowled, tried to rattle it loose, tried to force it open; and when he still couldn't move it, accepted grudgingly that they must have learned something, at least. They must have fitted locks, or else simply screwed it shut so it wouldn't open at all.

He was looking round for a stone or a loose brick he could use to smash the glass when the heavy velvet curtain twitched aside, followed by the lacy nylon net covering the inside of the window.

Light speared out and caught him, gripped him tight; for a second he stood in its glare, staring in at a woman's shadow.

Then she drew back, let the curtains fall into place again, left him in the dark.

The frozen feeling slipped away, and Jason shoved a hand angrily through his tangled hair, sneering at himself for that brief spasm of fear. It was just the wife, that's all, nothing to worry about. She wouldn't come out, she'd be too scared. The most she'd do now was phone her husband up at the carry-out, and he'd be too busy to come. She wouldn't even call the police. She'd tried that once during the winter, when they'd all been out the front throwing stones at the chimney, trying to knock the TV aerial down; and she'd learned, had been taught to regret it. They'd come back the following night and done that thing with the cat, as a warning. *No more police*, the cat had said to them, good and loud. It had been Vinny's idea, that cat.

Jason stood in the yard, feeling and relishing the woman's fear even through the wall; and he thought about smashing the window anyway, just to hear her scream.

But then he felt a weight against his hip, a heavy cylinder in his jacket pocket, and went for that instead. He climbed up onto the window-sill, pulled the can of paint out and began to spray the glass.

He was halfway through, finished with the upper frame and jumping down to do the lower when the curtains were pulled aside again, *just checking*. No nerves this time, Jason only smiled widely, aimed the spray-can like a gun and fired it straight at the woman's face. Black paint spread in a circle, began to run in dribbles down the glass; she jerked back, her eyes a momentary flash of white, of sheer terror before the curtains dropped like a veil to hide her.

Jason laughed, and went on with his painting.

When the whole window was black, all six panes thickly coated, he sprayed *PAKI BASTARDS* on the bonnet of the car and a swastika on its roof. Then he calmly unbolted the up-and-over door and raised it, calmly walked out into the empty alley and went back to his dad's for the night.

iv

It wasn't a thing he did often, he liked the comforts of his own fireside and the shelter of known walls around him; but occasionally Arthur Brougham would go for a late walk around the streets of Paradise. It was like a darker reflection of his regular morning walks. He couldn't tell which, God had never granted him that inner sight, but he knew that some of the women he passed were prostitutes, some were battered wives or worse; some of the lads burglars, apprentices to the young men they hung around with, while others perhaps were living rough or living as rent boys, on the run from violence or abuse at home.

He was out tonight on one of these private missions, watching the parade of faces and praying silently for them all; but tonight there was a difference, tonight it wasn't so private.

Tonight he had a companion, a man whom he suspected of seeing directly into the heart of every soul they encountered, knowing the good and the evil in each of them and blessing the good, rebuking the evil as a true disciple should.

So he walked taller than he might otherwise have done, he sensed the power and purity in Richard and felt encouraged, felt proud and hopeful.

As they walked, as he bathed in the effortless warmth of Richard's aura, they talked of plans and promises: of the big prayer meeting organised for Friday, when they would gather with others from across the city to try to discover God's purpose for this summer, the path that should lead on from Derry's miracle.

"There always is a purpose, at times like this," Richard had said. "Derry could have been healed quietly, slowly, and no one been any the wiser. If the Spirit chooses to send a sign like this, there has to be a reason. And I just get the feeling that we're looking at something big . . . "

So they walked, they talked; and then, halfway home, they were interrupted.

"Excuse me . . . "

Scurrying footsteps and a jagged voice ripping at their peaceful progress, leaving it in shreds. They stopped, turned; and Arthur didn't know what Richard might be seeing, what his greater gift was telling him, but for himself he saw a woman whose desperation was masked only by a curious placidity in her face, whose smile was belied by the dreadful rush of her words.

"Excuse me, I'm sorry, I shouldn't have stopped you, I'm sure I'm wrong. I'm only being foolish. But aren't you the man I saw on television the other night, aren't you the man who worked that wonderful miracle on that poor boy?"

She was talking to Richard, of course, solely to Richard. She must have seen Arthur too, seen him and forgotten him in the same instant, blinded to everything but Richard's gift of presence. Arthur didn't resent it. He took a step backward, leaving Richard to admit the fact and deny any responsibility for it; and in moving away he found that he could see the woman more clearly. He saw the oddity of her clothing, the dress that reached almost to her ankles and the headscarf knotted over her hair, neutral colours turned to nothing in the harsh street lighting. He saw how her hands fluttered as she talked, as she listened; he tried to see her age and failed, unable to tell if she were closer to twenty-five or forty.

" . . . It was so good, what you did," she was saying. "I felt so glad you were here, I felt so *uplifted*, even just from seeing it on television. And I'm sure I'm not alone, you're just what we need, you see, what we've needed so long . . . "

Richard waited patiently till the flow of words ran down; then he asked her name.

"Evelyn, Evelyn Somers. But that's not important, heavens, you shouldn't try to remember my name . . . "

"It won't be difficult," he said with a smile. "Can I ask, are you a Christian, Evelyn?"

"Oh, I love God. I mean, I really do, I really love God. But I feel so far from him sometimes, so terribly far . . . "

"That's not true. You know it isn't, you must know that. However lost we are, God's only ever a moment, only a word away."

"I wish I could believe that." And for a moment her voice and her face and her hands all matched, were all equally wistful and yearning. "I really do, it's what I need, what I need to believe. But it's so hard when the world all turns against you, when everyone's so wicked all the time. When they call you mad and take your children away from you, even, when you feel so alone, it's so hard to believe in God or love or anything good . . . "

"No one ever said faith was easy. It isn't, you're right, it's the hardest thing in the world to find and hold to faith; but it's the most rewarding thing, too."

"Yes. Yes, that's so true, even I know that, I've *felt* it, sometimes it's like a great fire in my heart . . . " She hesitated, was suddenly utterly still, voice and face and hands and all; then, "Look, I'm sure you won't want to, you were going somewhere with your friend, you don't want me interrupting; but if there's nothing, nothing important, you wouldn't like to – no. No, I'm sorry, it's too ridiculous."

"What is?"

"You wouldn't like to come and have a cup of coffee with me, would you? At my flat? It's just around the corner here, no distance. We'll have to be quiet going up, my neighbour's peculiar, I'm not being funny but I'm sure there's something *wrong* with him, wrong in his head, he makes up the most fantastic nonsense about me. But we could sit and talk, talk about God, I'd love to do that. You probably won't want to, though, I can quite see that. It's terribly late, and you've got your friend . . . "

"I'd love to come," Richard said. He turned to Arthur, and said, "That's all right, isn't it, Arthur? If I leave you here?"

"Aye, go. I'm fine, I'm just a step from home here. You go, and God bless, the pair of you."

It was God's work he was sending the lad on; Arthur knew the Spirit's hand when he saw it, bringing this woman to Richard in her need. And she was needing, even he could see that. Richard would see more and reach deeper, with the Lord's help could shine his light into the darkest hollows of her trouble and drive the shadows back.

"God bless, Arthur."

Arthur stood for a minute watching after them, before he turned for home; and the last thing he saw, he saw their two hands link.

Back in his flat, he locked and chained the front door carefully behind him, as he'd trained himself to do at his daughter's insistence, though he relied far more on God to be his shield and defender. He made himself a cup of cocoa and drank it while he listened to the radio news; then he undressed, cleaned his teeth, read his Bible and said his prayers.

Between the sheets at last, he sank towards his accustomed easy sleep, and stumbled just once, just briefly on the threshold before slipping over. And the memory, the thought, the question that tripped him, that so fleetingly detained him was the same that had puzzled and concerned him out in the street: had it been Richard he'd seen reaching for Evelyn's hand, or Evelyn reaching for Richard's? And why should it, how could it possibly matter . . . ?

SIX

He's staying with his aunt and uncle still, in the same little box-room they always kept for him as a child, as a teenager; and they love to have him there, they say so often.

– He was never any trouble, they say. Such a good boy, they say; even as a youth, an adolescent, never trouble. Always a pleasure to have him, they say.

– Of course he's changed now, they say wickedly, giving him a laughing glance if he's around. Out till all hours, what was it, four o'clock the other morning? We don't know, they say, we did our best with him, us and his mother both; we got him through the difficult years, they say, and now when he's supposed to be adult and mature he's suddenly debauched, never in his bed and *we* don't know where he is, what he's up to, he doesn't tell us, oh no . . .

– It's the Lord's work, he says, laughing with them.

And of course it is, that much you can be sure of. Whether he's witnessing to the lost and lonely or simply praying alone, out under the great globe of stars, this at least is certain: that everything he does is done to the greater glory of his God. You only have to look at him, to know.

See how he shines?

Two in the afternoon, and Nathan lingered by a notice-board until Helen appeared, coming round the corner with a group of friends.

There was a fractional hesitation in her as she saw him, an uncertain movement of her head, her voice falling silent.

He smiled, walked slowly over to bar her passage and locked his fingers round her wrist.

"Hullo, Nat . . . "

"I've been waiting for you."

He tugged her over to the wall, away from her companions. She shrugged at them vaguely, wordlessly over his shoulder; he heard them moving on, and his smile deepened.

"Well, you've got me." Her eyes were unreadable behind huge sunglasses, but her voice said it all: soft and submissive, not contesting his right to cut her out this way. "What do you want?" Meaning, *anything, just ask, it's already yours*.

"You." And he knew he'd won, just from her reaction: the subtle catch in her breath, the tremor he could feel under her skin. True to what she hadn't quite said aloud, she was already his. But the game still needed to be played out, to appease her conscience; so he slid his fingers slowly up her bare forearm, feeling the shiver in her suddenly intensify. "Come home with me," he murmured, private and persuasive.

"What, now?"

"Now."

"Oh, God." A wild jerk of her head, up the corridor to where her friends were waiting. "Nat, I can't . . . "

"Yes, you can."

"I've got lectures . . . "

"So've I. We can skip them." Gripping her elbow firmly, he reached up with his free hand to lift the sunglasses away and lodge them in the thick red mass of her hair. He watched her pupils contract against the light; then he kissed her, trapped her lower lip between his teeth and bit it gently, watching them dilate again with desire.

Nathan laughed, tipped the shades back onto her nose again with the flick of a teasing finger, slid his arm round her waist and steered her towards the exit, not giving her a chance even to say goodbye to her friends.

They took the bus out to Paradise and walked down to Nathan's flat in the continuing sunshine, Helen's hands tight about his arm now and her feet almost running, trying to draw him on faster.

Nathan grinned, and slowed down.

When they reached his door, he slipped his key into the Yale and tried to turn it.

Felt the lock blocked and immovable; frowned, twisted the key the other way, no result.

"Nat? What's wrong?"

"I think I've got visitors. Or had them."

"Visitors?"

"Burglars. They've put the lock on the snib."

He pushed her roughly out of his way, and took a step back from the door.

"Nat . . . "

"Quiet. And stay outside, till I say."

A moment's concentration, then he lifted one leg high and slammed the flat of his foot sharply against the lock.

The door sprang open, and Nathan went in at a run.

A glance to the left, into the bedroom: a shambles. Mattress overturned, drawers pulled out and contents scattered, wardrobe emptied onto the floor. No one there.

Keep moving.

The spare room: door shut, access still blocked by his bicycle, as he'd left it. Okay, keep moving.

Into the living-room, and here's the action.

A boy standing frozen, middle of the room, his arms wrapped round one massive hi-fi speaker. The other speaker gone already, along with the rest of the stereo, the television and video. Boxes and carrier bags on the floor, stuffed with cameras and records, tapes and CDs, ready to go.

Okay.

A violent shove on the boy's shoulder, to knock him sprawling into the corner and never mind the speaker, insurance'll cover any damage. Just keep moving.

The boy yells as he falls, not a warning, only shock and alarm; but it'll do as a warning too. The briefest glimpse of a face staring in from the yard outside, and then more yelling, a figure sprinting out into the alley.

Down two steps into the kitchen: the small window above the sink broken and open, the back door unbolted and standing wide. A quick look out, just time to see a dirty white van racing away from the gate, someone inside pulling the doors shut. No hope of getting the number.

Okay.

Twist round, jump the steps, back into the living-room. The boy scrambling to his feet, wired for speed: his eyes on the door to the passage, his thoughts on running.

Kick hard and low, hook his ankles out from under him, send him crashing down again . . .

Nathan stood still for a moment, breathing hard. The boy was on the floor, edging away; Nathan grinned down at him, no humour in it, and stepped casually forward. Stepped full onto the boy's stomach, stepped hard. Not hard enough to bruise, just to wind him, to warn, to pin him like a bug to the carpet.

Then – leaving his foot where it was, like a pin, a silent

65

reminder not to move again – he took another look around the room. Saw the empty phone socket, saw the phone's cord trailing from one of the bags, and smiled to himself as he heard Helen calling, "Nat . . . ?" nervously from the front door.

"Yeah, it's okay. Come on in."

She came, she stood in the passage looking in at the tableau – the stripped room, Nathan, the boy on the floor – and she raised a fretful hand, took her shades off, looking for orders.

He savoured the moment briefly – himself totally in control, two people doing nothing but watch him, wait for his decisions – then he smiled broadly at Helen, said, "Got any change, love?"

"What? Yes, I think so . . . Yes. But . . . "

"Go back up the road to the phone-box and call the police, would you? Then wait for them outside. Don't worry, I'll look after this one. He won't be any trouble."

Helen frowned. "What's wrong with . . . " Then her eyes found the empty socket on the wall, and as he'd expected didn't look any further. "Oh. I see. All right. If you're sure . . . "

"I'm sure. Believe me, I'm sure. Off you go, now."

"Right, then," he said, when she was gone. "Just the two of us now, nice and cosy, right?"

"Listen, mister, I never . . . It was my mates, like, I just come along . . . "

A nasal, adolescent whine, the boy blinking up at him, his skin shining with sweat, acne flaring red on his pale face. Nathan's expression didn't change; he lifted his foot from the boy's stomach, gave him a second to hope and then swung it hard, deep into the boy's gut.

The boy doubled up gasping, knees to chin, wrapping himself around the pain; Nathan smiled and kicked again at the curled body, catching him in the kidneys.

"Stand up, you little shit."

When the boy didn't move, when he only whimpered and drew more tightly into himself, Nathan bent down and grabbed a handful of long, lank hair. Pulled him up slowly and laughed at the sobbing yelp of pain, the way the boy unfolded suddenly.

Nathan pushed him against the wall and cuffed his head savagely, once and then again.

"So you didn't do anything, right?" he murmured, soft and incongruous. "You just came along when your mates invited you. You were only helping to carry the stuff – my stuff," digging his nails into the boy's ear, "out to the van, is that it?"

"Yeah, yeah, that's right, mister, I swear . . . "

"Right. Older than you, are they, these mates of yours?"

"Yeah . . . "

"Bigger than you?"

"Yeah, they are. Yeah. So I couldn't say no, see, they'd've laid into me . . . "

"What's your name?"

The boy hesitated just for a second, then flinched away from Nathan's uplifted hand.

"Jason."

"Jason what?"

"Dewey, Jason Dewey." ·

"Well, Jason Dewey, you're a liar, aren't you? You're a filthy lying little shit. If your mates are bigger than you, they couldn't have got in through that window in the kitchen. You did that, didn't you? You broke the window and wriggled your skinny little body in and opened the door for them, you let them in to steal my gear. That's what happened, isn't it? Isn't it?"

The boy stared at him, and muttered something.

"What was that?"

"Fuck off!" in a desperate shriek. "Just fuck off, you . . . "

Nathan's fist sank into the boy's stomach with all his rage behind it, all his contempt. Jason's eyes glazed over, he started to sway, to topple forward; Nathan grabbed his hair again and hauled him up, slamming him back against the wall.

"Listen, you slimy little turd," the words driven low but forceful direct into the boy's ear, above the wheezing gasp of his breathing. "What you're going to do now, you're going to write down the names and addresses of all your big mates, you hear me? No funny stuff, no lies, or I'll beat you senseless. And no cheek, you're not going to give me any more cheek, are you?" A brutal tug at his hair, to bring the boy's rolling eyes up to meet his, just inches away. "Are you?"

"N-no. No, I swear . . . "

"Good boy, Jason. That's what I like to hear," patting the boy's sweat-slick cheek, laughing in his face. "Now just stand there, while I find some paper and a pen in all this mess. Don't do anything silly, you'll only regret it. But you know that, don't you? You're probably regretting you ever got up this morning, isn't that right, Jason . . . ?"

Five minutes later, Nathan stood smiling contentedly in the ruins of his living-room, reading a sheet of paper covered with clumsy childish printing.

Jason Dewey was backed up against the wall where Nathan had

67

required him to be, his narrow face blotched and streaked with tears, bad skin stretched tight over sharp features.

Nathan finished reading, nodded; folded the paper and slid it into his back pocket. "Very good, Jason. I hope it's true, for your sake."

"It's true, it is . . . "

"Well, we'll see, won't we?"

Jason's tongue slid quickly over dry lips. "What now, then?"

"What now? Oh, now we wait for the police, Jason. I don't think they'll be long now."

"Are you, are you going to give them that, like? That paper?"

"Oh, no." Nathan grinned at him, at his obvious relief. "No, this is for me. You tell the police what you like, I've got what I want."

"What's it for, then, what do you want it for?"

"Oh, I thought I might show it to your, um, employer, shall we say? I think that might be useful."

"You wouldn't."

"Oh, I would. I will, Jason. Promise."

"He'll kill me."

"I doubt it. He might beat you up a bit, I guess, when he can get at you; but that's all in a day's work, right, Jason? Oh, and one other little thing," hearing voices suddenly from outside, an abrupt knock on the open door and footsteps in the passage. "I never touched you, Jason. Understand?"

And he smiled, deep into the boy's wide-stretched eyes; and laughed aloud as he caught a sudden smell, saw a dark stain spreading down the leg of Jason's jeans.

iii

Friday evening: and it felt like a rerun to Derry, a repeat. He was lying on the sofa with his feet up, where he'd been watching telly till his mother flicked it off; and now she was looming over him, large and demanding, and he wasn't giving an inch.

"I want you to come, Derry. It's only right."

"No." She blinked at the flatness, the force of that, and didn't come right back at him; left him a hole, to keep talking. "It's a prayer meeting, right? You said that. You're going to sit around praying all night, and I can't do that. I *can't*. And what do you want me for, anyway? I don't believe in God."

"How can you, how can you *say* that? After . . . "

A gesture of her hand encompassed his legs, his miracle and hers; and Derry shook his head wearily, sick of beating his head against the stone wall of her certainty.

"Look, I dunno what happened, Sunday. You say one thing, the doctors say something else, and maybe you're both wrong. All I know is, whatever it was, it hasn't turned me into any bloody Holy Joe, all right?"

"Haven't you got any gratitude?"

"Sure; but it's Richard I'm grateful to, not God."

"Well, come for his sake, then. He'll want to see you there, he'll expect it."

"Yeah, and so's everyone else expecting it. There'll be the newspapers hanging around outside, and all your lot inside, wanting to gawp at me; and I've had enough, Mam. I'm not coming, okay? Couldn't, anyway," finding another excuse and seizing on it gladly. "Someone's got to stay with the kids."

"Your father'll be home in a minute. He'll look after them tonight. I asked him to."

"Well, good. Means I can go out, then, doesn't it?" And he swung himself suddenly to his feet, reminding her and himself that things were different now, that he wasn't pain's prisoner any longer. "But I'm not coming with you."

"Where, then? Where are you going?"

"Up to Stu's."

"Derry . . . "

"Why not? I haven't seen him since it happened, not properly. Only when he came with his dad, and we couldn't talk then, I was too tired. It was like being back in hospital, that was," with a grin that turned to a grimace, remembering the grapes they'd brought and the awkwardness, none of them knowing what to say. "And we've got a game to get on with, if the rest of the gang's around. I'll see you later, okay?"

"Wait, Derry. What do you want me to say to Richard, eh? What am I supposed to tell him, when he asks about you?"

"Tell him I'm just fine," thrown back at her from the door. Then, relenting, "No, straight up, Mam, tell him I said thanks, okay? And, and say I'll go see him soon. Or say he should come here again, tell him I'll be awake this time, honest . . . "

Five days on from his miracle, Derry still found it an unnerving way of getting about, to walk without support. He actually missed his crutches, or at least the security they offered. He could remember a time when it had all been easy, when balance was as natural as breathing; but that was years back, before he got ill.

Now every step needed thinking about, needed to be taken carefully, against the threat of falling.

Making his way up the hill towards Stu's house, he walked like a man on ice, watching his feet. He didn't shuffle, and he didn't stride; he set each foot down in its turn, cat-cautious, feeling for the solidity of ground and desperate to feel nothing else, no sickness in his bones, no sudden return to pain. He walked on danger's edge, between hope and terror, suspicious of any twinge in an underused muscle. And there were twinges and more, there were aches and stabs and moments of real hurting as his unaccustomed legs confronted the reality of even his light weight; but these were fleeting shadows, there and gone, lingering only long enough to make Derry doubt.

And he did doubt, his history didn't grant him the option. Presented with a miracle and lacking the faith to give it credence, he distrusted it profoundly, looking for it to fail as he looked for his feet to stumble and his body to fall.

But he made it to Stu's without his legs letting him down or his miracle slipping away. At the door he looked back the way he'd come, near half a mile and nothing to lean on bar his own determination, and told himself with far more certainty now that he'd been right to go his own way tonight. Mam and the others, even Richard would have taken the glory of his walking away from him, would have seen only the miracle and none of the work. Being alone, at least he knew exactly what he'd done; he could look back and remember every separate step, could almost see them stamped into the pavement, *Derry was here*; and he could claim each of them for himself, his alone and nothing to do with God.

Another ten minutes, and all the glow was gone.

Another ten minutes, and he sat with his friends on the floor of Stu's lounge, searching as hard as any of them for something to say.

The boys had all been there when he rang, Stu and Mick and Albie. Stu's parents were out, as usual; so they'd raided some cans from the fridge, Mick had produced ten Embassy Regal, they'd turned the telly off and sprawled on the floor the way they used to, to leave the sofa free for Derry.

And none of them said a word when he joined them instead on the carpet. They were self-conscious and awkward suddenly; they swigged lager and passed the ashtray around, followed it with their eyes, gazed at the blank TV screen, anything to save looking at him.

All Derry's blazing triumph shrivelled inside him. Like them he played with his can and his cigarette, and waited yearningly for someone else to speak. A comment, a joke about his skinny legs: anything to get them out of this.

It didn't happen, though. His eyes jerked round the circle, and saw them all mute in the face of magic.

"Tell you what," he said, "we could phone Linda, get her round here and go on with the game."

"Can't," from Mick. "I saw her earlier, she's out with some bloke tonight, this guy she met at her Saturday job . . . "

And that should have been the cue for a chorus of teasing; Mick fancied Linda like mad, they all knew that. But everything was so out of kilter tonight, no one bothered even to raise a sympathetic smile. They just nodded, shrugged, fell back on the fidgeting little rituals of alcohol and tobacco.

"Well," Derry, trying again, "we could do something without her, couldn't we? Make it that she's ill or something, she has to stay in camp. You've done that before, Stu."

"Yeah, but . . . " Stu shrugged. "I dunno, Derry, you've got to be in the mood, right? And I'm just not, tonight. I don't think any of us are."

Grunts of agreement, and maybe that was all the problem, or maybe it was more than that: maybe they didn't feel like playing an intense and demanding game with someone they couldn't even talk to. Derry looked around again, saw how they avoided his eyes, and thought that he was more separated from them now than he had been before. That his miracle had cut a crevasse between them wider than his illness ever had.

One last effort, "Get the cards out, Stu. Got to do something, or you dozy lot will be falling asleep on me."

"Cards. Right, yeah, good idea, Derry . . . "

They played a few desultory hands of poker, too uninterested even to gamble with anything more than matchsticks; and as soon as he reasonably could, Derry glanced at the clock, sighed and pushed himself to his feet.

"Deal me out, Albie."

"You going already?" Anyone else, Stu would have reached to pull him down, to keep him in the game; but for Derry he stood up, and the question didn't even pretend to be a protest.

"Yeah. Curfew," Derry lied, wanting to make it easy for them both.

"Oh, right. Makes sense, I guess."

They made their way out into the hall, two gangling boys trying

71

not to touch each other; and it was a last-minute bid to save something at least from the wreckage that made Derry stop and turn in the doorway, just as Stu reached out to grab his shoulder.

"Derry . . . Listen, we are glad, you know, that you're better. It's terrific. It's just, it's a bit hard for us, it's all been so weird. I mean, you on the telly and stuff, and everyone talking about God . . . "

"Yeah, I know. It's a bit hard for me, too."

They met each other eye to eye, just for a moment; then Derry nodded, turned, walked away.

Cursed his doctors silently for not curing him the proper way, for leaving it to God; and cursed God for doing it so flashy, for getting in the way.

Remembered then that he didn't believe in God, but cursed him anyway, just in case; and wandered away down the hill, slow on his feet, time on his hands.

He called in at a corner shop to buy some tabs and a box of matches, and went on all the way down to the river. He skirted the broken lands, the rubble and thin grass of an industrial estate that never got built; found a path to the water and a bench to sit on; and just sat there, smoking and thinking, watching the tide push the water upstream.

It wasn't going to make life any easier, if those lads kept their distance. He didn't have friends to spare. He'd been out of school for the last three years, getting home tuition when he was well enough – and getting away with murder, not bothering at all, seeing no point in education when he wouldn't have the time or the strength to exploit it. His world had shrunk to a tight triangle, home, hospital and Stu's house; he couldn't remember the last time he'd met anyone new. Except for nurses at the hospital, of course, other patients on the ward; and they didn't count, none of them counted.

He flicked his butt-end high, watching it flare red in the dark and disappear as it hit the river. He was going to be dead lonely, he thought, bored out of his skull, without even the interest of watching himself die . . .

Except he wasn't, of course. He shook his head sharply. Things were different now. He was well again; even the doctors had to admit that, for all their awful warnings. He was finished with learning, school and home tuition both. He could apply for jobs, like any normal boy. Okay, he'd got no qualifications, and he wasn't strong – not yet – but he'd find something. He'd land a job, and meet people that way. Make new friends and start right from

72

the beginning again, really start *living* this time . . .

Derry lifted his head, and howled softly at the cloud-blurred image of the moon. Liked the sound of that and did it again, did it louder, teenage werewolf to the core. Then he took out another tab, lit it and inhaled good and deep. He tried to blow smoke-rings like Mick did and made a right mess of it; lay full-length along the concrete bench, propped himself up on one elbow and thought about Richard.

Figured out what it was about Richard that had kept him hiding in bed and pretending to be asleep both times the guy had called round since Sunday; one reason why he was so determined to keep away from chapel, away from Richard tonight.

He was scared, that's what it was.

Not of Richard himself, no way. Not of what Richard had done to him, even; that was scary, sure, but it was a different level of scare. That one he could handle, he could learn to control. But no one was ever going to control Richard; and that was what scared Derry so greatly, never knowing what the man might do. Specifically, what he might do next to Derry Bowen.

Derry remembered the strength and the warmth of him, the sense of closeness those brief moments together in the chapel; and shuddered, jerked his head away from the memory, tried to deny an inescapable bond. It drew him and appalled him, both at the same time; and he dreaded the same thing happening again, Richard's touch reaching still further into his head and heart. The guy had turned his life inside-out once already, Derry barely knew what was real now and what was not. Too much of Richard and he'd be down on his knees and babbling, mad like the maddest of them. Believing like his mam believed, believing anything he was told . . .

Told himself he was being stupid, it was only that they'd both been scorched by that phantom fire, nothing more than that; and to prove it to his stubborn, frightened self, he got to his feet again and set off up to the chapel. Maybe they'd be coming out by now. Maybe he could run into Richard all accidental-like, have a quiet, friendly little chat with him, nothing significant and nothing to be scared of.

When he got there, though, the hum of voices through the thin wooden walls told him that they were a long way from through yet. The chapel was packed out, that much was obvious; there were cars parked nose-to-tail both sides of the street, Volvos and BMWs a lot of them, not what the locals drove around in. Derry guessed that a couple of those might be missing by the time their owners finally came out to claim them.

But what was important was his timing being off, no chance of seeing Richard tonight. He ran a hand over his scalp, fingered his sparse hair, breathed out a long, slow sigh of relief and went on home, his legs aching so much now that it was an effort just to keep going, even with one hand against the nearest wall for balance.

SEVEN

i

It's a wonderful feeling, never to be alone; and he never can be, of course, God must always be with him. But it must surely still be a great reassurance to see that confirmed in his other, his earthly life: to see a full church, to know that he's not, that he's never going to be the only soldier in the fight.

And that's what's happening now, the army is mustering to the flag. Every day there are phone-calls and visitors, believers ready to give time or money or both. At every service there are more worshippers crowding into the small chapel.

And they're all looking to him, that's inevitable. He's the fountainhead, he's the source of all this; they drink deep of his faith and energy, they'd drink him dry if God didn't sustain him.

But he is sustained, and more. He's enriched, he's recharged every moment, he's sparking with life and love and a passionate hunger for his work.

If that work turns to war, as it very well may, he'll have his army marching at his back; and, more potent, he'll have his God by his side. By definition, God gives him the majority. God is the big battalions.

ii

Back at school after the Easter break, Rachel was heading towards the music room when she bumped into Joe in the corridor.

"Rache, good. Don't forget the rehearsal tomorrow night, yeah?"

"Oh. Tomorrow. Um, Joe . . . "

"Me and Robbie have been working on this new number, but we're stuck. What I reckon, we need you to have a listen, tell us where we're going wrong."

"Joe, slow down." Rachel pushed a hand through her long hair, still damp from the shower after an hour's dancing in the gym at lunchtime. "I've been trying to find you all day," *and dreading it*

75

when I did. "I can't, I just can't make it tomorrow. I've got something else . . . "

"Ah, shit." She prayed for him to leave it there, to shrug his long body in a simple acceptance and fix another night; but God wasn't listening, or else – more likely – was wanting her to get this settled now and out of the way, to make her priorities clear. "Well, what, then?" Joe demanded. "What's so important you've got to skip rehearsal?"

Here we go. Rachel knew that she should face him proudly, carry her banner high; but she couldn't manage that, not here, where she felt so much alone. Her cheeks burned, her eyes skittered away from his, not to see the inevitable scorn as she mumbled, "It's a church thing."

"You what?"

"They're . . . " She had a great view of her feet now, she was watching one shoe scuff the other; but she scowled and jerked her head up suddenly, met him eye to eye, riding high on her own self-disgust. "They're starting this new youth group out at Paradise. It's the first meeting tomorrow night, and I really want to be there. It, it *is* important."

"Jesus fucking Christ . . . " And Rachel would have forgiven him the blasphemy, would have forgiven him anything if he'd only left it at that, left her, if he'd only turned on his heel and stormed away. Witnessing to an angry, scornful fifth-former in a busy corridor was the last, the very last thing she wanted to do.

But, "A *youth* group?" he repeated incredulously, his mouth twisting the words into something derisory and contemptible. "You're missing rehearsal with the band just so's you can go to some bloody religious youth group?"

"That's right," she said, trying to be patient, trying to explain. "It's the same chapel where they had that miracle over Easter, you must've heard about that. It's leading to something really big, I was over there last week and they're talking about organising a festival to go on all summer, with lots of outreach into the community." *That's the way, girl, blind him with science.* "There's going to be a whole load of events for young people tied in with it, and I want to be involved, right from the start. So I've got to be there tomorrow."

"Oh, great. Terrific." Joe swung an arm wildly through the air and glowered down at her, six foot plus of furious boy. "So let's get this straight, can we, it's not just tomorrow we're talking about here, is it? It's going to go on for months, is that what you're saying?"

"Probably. I'm sorry, Joe, it's a matter of priorities . . . "

76

"Damn right it is. And the band comes nowhere, right? All that work, we had the chance of some real gigs this summer, and now you throw us in the shit like this."

"I'll do what I can, Joe . . . "

"That's not good enough. It's, what's the fucking word, commitment, that's what it is. If you're not committed to the band, you're no use to us. And you're not the only girl in this school who can sing. So think about that, right, Rachel? If you don't come to rehearsal tomorrow – and come up with a bit of commitment, too, I'll be looking for promises – if you're not there, I start looking for someone who will be."

And with that he did leave her at last, he stalked away, long legs as fluent and expressive as his tongue; and Rachel stood still and watched him go, deaf to the bell clanging out for afternoon lessons. Played with a stray lock of hair, with fingers that trembled slightly in the aftermath of his going, and knew that the story would be all over school by tomorrow. *That Rachel Grant, heard about her? Chucked up the band, she has, just to go God-bothering with a bunch of Jesus freaks . . .*

But there was still no way she'd be at rehearsal tomorrow, no way the band could ever have first claim on her life. She'd been claimed and promised long ago, dedicated to God since childhood – and by her own decision, too, no pressure from parents or anyone else.

She sighed and wandered on towards the music room, reminding herself that no one had ever said it was the easy choice. Trying to find comfort in visions of a glorious summer, herself and a group of other teenagers – unknown as yet, their faces a blank, but surely they were only waiting to meet her, to welcome her to their number – out in the city streets singing and playing, talking and reading from the Bible, drawing people to Jesus . . .

Go on. Please? Make it worthwhile, don't let me throw up everything I've gained here just for a dream. You can do it, big J, you can make it happen – so do it, eh? For me?

And she grinned, almost laughed aloud at the transparent selfishness of that – *sorry, just joking. Do it for you and your Dad, do it for everyone, for the world. Okay?* – and hurried down the suddenly-empty corridor trying to think cello, trying to remember something, anything about that rotten piece she should have learned over the holidays and hadn't.

Terry Belderstone nodded firmly, pushed the sheaf of drawings to one side of his massive desk and stood up smiling.

"Good. Thanks, Michael, those alterations are just what I had in mind."

The man beside him – Michael Grant, just one in his team of consultant architects, but definitely one of the best – took the cue smoothly, rising to his feet and reaching for his case.

"I'm glad. Any idea about dates yet?"

"Nothing certain, my lawyers are still tied up in negotiations over some of the land; but soon, I think. A matter of months, no more than that."

The two men walked slowly towards the door at the far end of the office, and paused by unspoken but mutual consent beside the model that stood there on a low table.

It showed the river spanned by a broad new bridge, with a network of roads looping away on either bank, linking into hotels and housing and major industrial developments. It was Michael's model and Terry's dream, and at this stage little more than that; he only kept it here to impress visitors, to demonstrate just how committed he was to the city's future. The bridge would come, he was sure of that; and when it came it would come to him. But that couldn't be rushed, they needed to prove the need for it, they needed a revived and growing economy urgent for access. So he was starting with a business park on undeveloped land by the river, just the first small part of this model that would begin to turn solid and actual in the summer.

Money in the bank, Terry thought, running a finger lightly between the miniature buildings, the model trees and pathways. That's what it was, come right down to it. The physical reality meant no more than this model; it was only money, pure and simple. Figures in an account, with plenty of zeros attached.

"By the way, Terry, there's something I wanted to ask . . . "

"Sure. Anything," he said expansively.

Michael smiled. "Wait till you've heard it, before you commit yourself. And please, feel free to say no, I'm not trying to put the bite on you . . . "

Terry was interested, suddenly. Could he have been wrong about Michael Grant, would the guy ask for a cut on the side? Terry had always put him down as straight, but he'd been wrong before. Once or twice.

But Michael said, "As you probably know, I'm a Christian,"

and that was surely a strange opener to asking for a slice of some illegal action. Terry frowned, wondering if maybe he'd picked up rumours of the heavy-duty money sliding around under the table, if he would threaten to blow the whole deal . . .

"Yeah," Terry said, "I'd heard that. What about it?"

Another smile, a slightly embarrassed shrug. "I'm involved in a group that's planning a good deal of activity this summer, everything from open-air concerts to providing food and shelter for the homeless. It's all nebulous at the moment, and I'm afraid it'll stay that way unless we can come up with some finance – so I said I'd try to do a little fund-raising among my business contacts. There'll be no publicity," he added quickly, "anything you give will be a purely private affair. You may not be a believer yourself, but please," smiling again, and yes, he was definitely embarrassed by this, "don't let that stop you. Just concentrate on what we'll be doing. It can only be good for the city; and indirectly, that has to be good for you . . . "

Terry was smiling himself now, thinking, *You should never be embarrassed about money, Michael. About asking for it, or about taking it when it's offered. Money's the root of everything, it's the heart's-blood of life; it all comes down to money in the end, so why be embarrassed?*

"Sure I'll give you something," he said. "Why not? I give to every local charity with the sense to ask. Your religion's not going to stop me, why should it?"

He walked back to his desk, and took out a cheque-book. Personal, not business. At bottom this was just another sort of bribe, and it was himself he wanted Michael grateful to, not the company. Gratitude was a useful commodity; Terry dealt in it continually. He bought and sold favours like shares, and hoarded others against an unpredictable need.

He wrote some figures on the blank cheque, thought about them briefly, then added another zero.

"There you go, son. Don't thank me," as Michael started to do just that, "I look on it as an investment, not a gift. Anything improves the image of the city, that's good for business. And come back if you need to, understood? There could be more where that came from, I'm always willing to listen."

iv

Light-footed despite his size, George walked into his gym in

79

tracksuit and trainers. It wasn't busy in there – hell, it never was, and didn't need to be – but there were a few of his regulars in, local blokes helping each other with the free-standing weights, no worries there. A young guy, though, by one of the machines: he was a different matter. Not recognising the lad's face, George headed over. Above his head, tinny music and the regular thump of feet, the occasional burst of women's laughter from an aerobics class.

"New here, aren't you, son?"

"That's right, yeah. First time."

He looked about twenty, student type, wearing a singlet, fraying denim shorts and baseball boots. He was well built, with good muscle tone under a holiday tan; but even so, George gave him the usual warning.

"You shouldn't use these machines unless you're fit. They can be dangerous if you don't know what you're doing."

The lad grinned. "Don't worry, I'm fit enough."

Then he hooked his feet under the bar and proved it, doing thirty lifts nice and smooth and easy, barely breaking sweat.

George nodded approvingly. "Reckon you could go up a bit, on the weights there. Want to try another five kilos?"

"Sure, why not?"

George fitted the weights on, stood back and watched.

"Okay, that's good . . . Take it slow, there's no hurry . . . Just another five, now . . . And four, three, two, one more . . . Right. Good. Take a breather, son. What's your name?"

The boy sat back, panting; wiped his forearm across his face and said, "Nathan Lewis. Nat. Are you Mr Jenner?"

"That's right. Student, are you, Nat?" And, getting a nod, "We've got a good deal on student memberships at the moment, just ask Tracey at the desk . . . "

"I know, I've already joined. Cheaper than town, and it's handy, I live just up the road." He swung his legs off the machine and stood up, saying, "There's something I'd like to see you about, actually, Mr Jenner. Is there somewhere we can talk?"

"Sure, come on through to the office. What's it about?"

Nat glanced at the mirrored wall and said, "Let me shower first. Ten minutes, okay? I'll find you." Then as an afterthought, already turning away, the words tossed casually back over his shoulder: "It's about your friend Jason Dewey."

George had been glad of the warning, and of every minute of respite before this Nat guy reappeared, relaxed in jeans and a hooded sweatshirt. He'd thought hard during those minutes,

80

thought about denying all knowledge of young Jason, and decided against. Decided to stay cool and confident, to see no threat in this.

He looked up from his desk when Nat knocked lightly on the open door, nodded without smiling, gestured him to a chair.

"So. What, about Jason? He was inside, last I heard."

"That's right. I caught him doing a job on my flat, and turned him in. But the point is, Jason talked to me before they took him away. He told me who his mates were, who'd been on the job with him; and he told me who it was sent them to do it, Mr Jenner. Who the paymaster was."

George blinked, and shook his head even against the evidence. "Jason wouldn't do that. He's got more sense."

Nat smiled quietly. "Ordinarily, I'm sure you're right. But – well, it's just a matter of who he's more scared of, really."

And for proof, he slid a sheet of paper across the desk. It was a photocopy, that was so obvious it didn't need saying: and what had been copied was a list, names and addresses misspelt but clear and incontrovertible. There were the two lads George had sent out with Jason; and there at the bottom was George himself, heavily underlined, 'Paradise Jim' below.

He almost smiled, almost cracked a joke, asking who Paradise Jim was supposed to be; but, "I guess young Jason's got himself in trouble," he said instead. "All right if I keep this?"

Nat just shrugged carelessly, unconcerned.

"Thank you." George slipped the sheet into a drawer, for his later attention. Justice would have to wait awhile, until the law was finished with Jason; but justice would be done, and be seen to be done. That was very necessary.

Meantime, he had a more immediate problem. "Well," he said slowly, "what's the deal, then?" There was a deal on offer, that much was apparent. It was just a matter of terms.

"Not much," Nat said immediately, making it clear that he understood there were limits to his advantage, and that it would be foolish or dangerous to trespass beyond them. "I've made a list of what I lost," producing another sheet of paper.

"And I suppose you want them back, right?"

"No. Everything's insured, and I've got a claim in already. It could be embarrassing, if I was discovered later with it all back in my flat again. What I'd like is replacements, Mr Jenner. Of at least as good quality as what was taken. That's all."

And fair enough, the lad was being more reasonable than George had expected; but still, for the sake of show, he snorted dismissively as he ran his eye over the list. "Telly, video, hi-fi –

81

you think I'm running a shop here, or what?"

"More or less, yes," Nat said flatly. "I think you act as a fence for half the burglars in the district, never mind the ones you employ directly. I think you can fill that list, Mr Jenner, no problem."

"Well." A pause, and George capitulated, almost enjoying the sensation for its rarity value. "Well, you could be right. Let's go down and see, shall we?"

George's storerooms were in the basement, at the far end of a dim corridor. His dog Kyzer was kept down there too, first room at the foot of the stairs; as they passed, there was a furious volley of barking, and the sound of a heavy body beating against the locked door. George glanced back, just in time to see Nat go white and press himself against the opposite wall.

George smiled and let Nat see the smile, suddenly enjoying himself a whole lot more.

v

The hills in this town got steeper every year. Jack Dubrowski took a brief rest at a corner, leaning against the wall, hating the ignominy of it even though there was no one around to see. He was still a long way above the river, a long drop from home; and it was the drops that got to him, the downhill stretches. He didn't mind climbing, he'd never been scared of hard work; but downward slopes were dangerous, pulling him constantly forward and off-balance, always on the edge of falling.

He shifted the light box he carried from right hand to left, and his mind slid back across the evening just gone as he started on down the hill again.

After making sure that Anita was comfortable and content, he'd gone up to chapel for the planned campaign meeting. And perhaps he should have stayed till it was over, he thought wearily, and gone straight home after as he'd meant to. He'd have saved himself a lot of walking, a lot of hills.

But they were turning difficult, those meetings, there was an uncomfortable tension in the air. It was an exciting time, no doubt of that, and bless God for it; Richard was an inspiration, and his ideas were stirring people up all over the city. What had been stagnant was suddenly moving again, the spirit of change was abroad and Jack could foresee great works ahead, the power of love sweeping through this forsaken town.

And yet there was no unity in the Council, as there ought to be at a time like this. Ted of course was backing his nephew to the hilt, and seemingly deaf to any dissent. Arthur and Arnold played peacemaker as best they could, as Jack did himself, each of them vaguely trying to recover what they'd lost, the sense of a single purpose. It was the two new members, Alan Parkinson and Jean Dolance, who were joined together in opposition to Richard's plans; though the way Jack saw it, it wasn't the plans they objected to so much as Richard himself.

If he didn't know better, Jack would have said that they were jealous. He would have said that they saw it as their own role, to bring some fresh blood to a group of ageing men; and that they resented having that role usurped by an incomer younger than either and so full of fire, so very much brighter than both.

But Jack did know better, he had to. This was God's work they were embarked on, it was the Lord's will they followed and none of Richard's. Alan and Jean could surely see that as well as any; they must have felt the Lord's spirit blazing in the chapel when young Derry Bowen was healed. Richard was only a tool, as they all were.

So no, not jealousy. It had to be something else that had turned Alan and Jean against him. Undeniable, that there was something; but something simple, surely, something fundamentally human, a clash of personalities and no connection with the work.

But whatever it was, it made Jack uncomfortable. As tonight, when Richard had been outlining an idea he had for the local teenagers, a run up the coast and a party on the beach. Jean had been instantly objecting, saying they could never hope to control a gang of adolescent thugs, it'd only lead to trouble and they'd be responsible, and she didn't see where the good of it was in any case, they'd just be giving a pack of blasphemous vandals the opportunity to indulge in shoplifting and under-age drinking miles away from where they were known and watched out for . . .

Jack hadn't waited for Richard's reply, he'd slipped quietly out of the room with an apologetic grimace to Arthur; and had received a brief wave in reply, *I know why you're going, Jack old lad, and I don't blame you. Take the chance while it's there, and God bless . . .*

Coming out into the twilight, finding the evening still young, Jack had turned left instead of right, up the hill instead of down: had gone to the Polish Club, instead of going home.

He'd spent a couple of hours there, glad to be Jacek again and not Jack, glad of the company of another group he'd grown old with, all exiles like himself. His Protestantism was no barrier between them, their photographs of the Pope no problem to him. They spoke another language here and lived in a different world, one with no interface to his other life. He'd asked after absent children and mourned over their defiant Englishness; had been cheerfully mobbed by half a dozen youngsters, the grandchildren who were still thrilled by an alien culture and the cachet it gave them at school, the mark of otherness that they could wear with pride. They were the ones who'd learn dances and folk-songs, who'd wear the traditional costumes their grandmothers sewed for them; and never mind that they'd lose it all when they hit adolescence, that they'd strive to be indistinguishable where now they strove to be different. For the moment they were the joy of the old ones' hearts, and Jack felt that joy as strongly as any.

He'd fielded questions about Anita's health and welfare, answered them as vaguely as he could. He'd promised to bring her up here as soon as she was strong enough and welcomed promises to visit in the meantime, knowing that most or all of those promises would be broken.

And as he'd been on the point of leaving, as he'd stopped for a final word with Jerzy behind the bar:

"Here," Jerzy had said, pressing a box into his hand. "Give these to Anita, with our love. You've won the raffle tonight."

"Jerzy, there was no raffle tonight."

"You know that, I know that. Does Anita know it? She does not. Give them, Jacek. A love-gift, from all of us."

So he'd accepted them, how not? And carried them now, light in his hand, down the final slope to the river and home.

Home was an isolated terrace, eight small houses that had somehow been missed when the surrounding streets were demolished. If the planned industrial estate had ever been built, no doubt someone would have remembered Cockburn Grove and sent the bulldozers back; but the money hadn't been there in the end, or had gone somewhere else it liked better. They could afford to destroy, but not to build. For ten years Cockburn Grove had stood like a forgotten sentry amid the rubble, guarding nothing, nothing to guard. One by one the other tenants had died or moved out, the unconcerned landlord allowing their properties to stand empty, to fall slowly into decay; and now only Jack and Anita were left to fight a weary battle against the leaking roof and the erratic plumbing. Maybe they should give up now, maybe it was time. But the rent was fixed, a peppercorn rate after so many years of inflation, and he wasn't sure how they would manage anywhere else. And they'd been here so long, Anita was settled, she'd be badly disturbed by a move . . .

Jack shook his head, and picked his way the last few yards over crumbling tarmac to the door. No point hurrying into worry, they could go on as they were for a while yet. There were new plans to redevelop, a business park they called it now, but it was only the same old notion under another name; and there were always plans, and nothing ever came of them.

He let himself in, changed shoes for slippers in the hall and followed the sound of the television into the sitting-room.

His sister was sitting in the dark, only the glow of the TV screen to light his way. Nothing new there. He switched on a table-lamp, not to dazzle her with anything brighter; and saw her face turn to greet him with her vague, charming smile.

"Jacek. You're home."

"Yes, Anita." They spoke in Polish, as ever.

"Did you have a good day at work?"

"Yes, a good day." He never challenged her now, it only confused her further. "I've brought you a present home."

"A present?"

"Here." He pressed the box into her thin, spotted hands, thinking, *Only two years between us, it could be ten, the way she looks, so old. It could be twenty, the way she acts.* "I'm sorry it's not wrapped."

"Oh – chocolate plums! My favourite . . . "

"I know." Then, honesty fighting his trained, his ingrained cautiousness and winning for once, strengthened by his debt of gratitude: "They're not from me, I'm afraid."

"Not . . . ? Oh, did Papa send them, are they from Papa?"

"No, my love," stroking fine white hair back from her forehead, *Papa died fifty years ago and a thousand miles away, my love, my sweet love. We were there, we saw it happen.* "Jerzy sent you these."

"Jerzy?" She frowned, trying to remember. "Oh, I know! Jerzy, he's so sweet, always sending me presents . . . "

"Yes." No point trying to discover which Jerzy she meant, which boy or blend of boys she was remembering or inventing. She was happy with her Jerzy, and that was enough.

She struggled to unwrap the box, ripping at tight cellophane with weak nails. At last it was open; Anita reached inside, then stopped and held the box up to him. "You first, Jacek, you take first."

He smiled, and did what he was told; and bit first too, feeling her eyes on him, her need to see his pleasure in her treat.

Dark bitter chocolate and then dense, juicy fruit inside, heavy with sweetness, a taste from memory: childhood in Kraków, before the Germans came. And almost he could wish to be like Anita, to live all but entirely within that cloudless world, mixing it with this only when necessary . . .

Almost, but not quite. Not after seeing his sister's hurt and distress when her logic occasionally failed her, when she'd been stranded suddenly in a world she could make no sense of.

Those times didn't happen now, bless God. She'd learned to smother them at the first faint signs of danger, or else she was simply further down the road now, out of reason's reach.

She was further from him, that was certain. He lived with a ghost, no true sister; she made a fit pair with his other haunting, his English wife who'd died in pregnancy. Long ago, that was, the day when his world changed irrevocably. The war had had less effect on him than Mary's death. At least he hadn't been responsible for the war . . .

In the darkness afterwards he'd found a new light when he needed one, he'd found God; and had lived by that light ever since, not thinking to look for another. He had his sister to keep house for him, he had his work, religion for comfort and the companionship of fellow exiles: it had always seemed enough.

But now Anita had left him, all but her body. He'd retired long since, and the pension was tight and growing tighter; and even chapel was no longer the solace it should have been, with those hints of strain and dissension biting deep, twisting even at his prayers.

He looked down at Anita and saw that she'd fallen back in her chair, eyes glued on the TV screen as her fingers reached blindly for another chocolate plum.

It was always strange to him, how she could be so absorbed in English television and yet still think she was in Poland in the years before Poland ever saw a television set. She could listen to a storyline in one language and conduct what passed with her for conversation in the other, both at the same time and without a moment's hesitancy or confusion. But then, she could look Jack full in the face and still see the boy he used to be, not the grizzled beard and all the lines of age. Her mind was beyond his fathoming; he only tried to be grateful for what there was of Anita that remained to him, their shared childhood. He did try. Better something than nothing, better Anita's confusion than Mary's grave.

"Come on, my love. Time for bed now."

"Is it? Oh, all right, Jacek. I was just thinking about Jerzy . . . "

"No, you weren't," with a teasing smile, "you were watching television." Switching it off, bending to pull the plug out, you couldn't be too careful in this house. You certainly couldn't trust the wiring.

"No. Jerzy, I was thinking of Jerzy." A soft, dreamy smile on her lips and almost a twirl, almost a skip to her step as she stood up. At least her legs were strong, she was still mobile, that was something to be grateful for. The alternative was something Jack didn't want to think about. *God will provide,* the only thought he would allow that subject. *Though I hope, I pray he doesn't have to.* "Do you think he will call tomorrow, Jacek? Will Jerzy call?"

"I'm certain of it, Anita. If he can fight his way through your other gentleman callers. Now come, take my arm, you'll be dizzy on the stairs with the excitement . . . "

EIGHT

Perfect is how he wants it, he's said so. Not for himself, of course, he's said that too; he's ambitious only for his God, to see His glory reflected here on earth.

Or more specifically, here in Paradise.

And he sees the hope of it, he says, he sees the chance. He can smell the possibilities.

Not that he needs to tell us that, not that it needs to be said. It's there to be seen in him, just exactly what it is he sees when he walks these streets.

He sees the mess and the misery, of course he does; he's never been blind to other people's realities, their sad lives in a sordid world. But at the same time he sees further and deeper, his eyes attuned to a light stronger than the sun's and more truthful, more revealing. He sees gold in the dust beneath his feet, and power in the people; he sees how it can be here, how it should and shall be when every hand is raised to proclaim God's mercy and every voice lifted in His praise.

He sees Paradise as a lighthouse, a great and shining beacon, a testimony to the country and the watching world.

And what he sees now, others will see tomorrow. That's his job and his gift, it's what makes him a missionary. Miracles are a sideshow, the real work lies in the message.

And the city's ready for that message, ready for him. That also is there to be seen. The streets are humming with expectation.

All it wants, all it's going to take is hard work and a little patience; and surely neither of those will be a problem when he can see the goal so clearly, the new Jerusalem so vivid to his eyes that mundane Paradise is only a shadow laid across its broad avenues and perfect squares, between its spires and its glistening domes.

The posters didn't say a word about God. *'PARADISE YOUTH CLUB'*, they said. *'Grand Inaugural Beach Party at Colston Bay. Barbecue, music, dancing. All welcome – everything free.'*

You had to look closely, you had to read the small print at the bottom to find where it said about the youth club being run by the Paradise Pentecostal Gospel Hall.

Derry thought it was a trick, and he didn't like it. Other kids didn't have his advantage, knowing about it from the inside. They'd go along looking for a good time and end up getting religion forced down their necks, ruining their day.

He hadn't planned to go at all. He was quite determined on that, he would have nothing to do with the youth club or any of its sideshows. Worse than the bloody Scouts, it would be: organised fun and games, prayers at the end of the evening and everyone home by ten o'clock. That wasn't for Derry, no way – and it wouldn't be for any of the kids round here. The whole thing was heading for one big disastrous belly-flop, he could see it coming a mile off.

So Derry was holding out against the lure of the posters and the advertisements on local radio; he was holding out against his mother's blandishments too, and finding it easy. No problem, he just kept saying no. He was getting good at that.

Then Richard came to see him.

When it was over, Derry couldn't figure out why he'd been avoiding that meeting so assiduously. There was nothing to be scared of, no threat. They'd talked, that was all. They'd talked for hours. And it seemed like there really was some special link between them still, soul to soul, forged when Richard worked his magic on Derry's bones; because Derry had opened up in a way he never would with anyone else, friends or family or anyone. He remembered talking about loneliness particularly, the loneliness of his illness and the greater loneliness threatened by his miracle.

Richard hadn't exploited that the way anyone else from the chapel would have done, jumping in to offer friendship and company down at the new youth club. Or worse, offering Jesus as a friend for ever. He'd simply counselled patience, giving people time, waiting for them to forget the strangeness.

"It won't take long," he'd said. "You'll see. In six months you'll be just another nuisance teenager. You'll be hanging around on street corners with the lads, talking football and girls; and there will be girls, even if not as many as you boast about. There'll be some girl who lets you walk her home but doesn't ask you in for a coffee, and you'll sweat about her all night, does she fancy you or not; and by then no one's going to remember you were ever ill."

"Ah, leave it out." Derry had pushed an embarrassed hand over his scalp. "I'm half bald, see? No girl's going to fancy me like this . . . "

"You'll be surprised, kid. You will be, I promise."

The conversation had turned to other things, and the constant surprise to Derry was that it never turned to God. And maybe it was gratitude for not getting a sermon, or for the original miracle, or both; or maybe it went deeper than that, or not so deep. It could have been that strong link between them doing its stuff, tugging Derry along in Richard's wake; or it could simply have been the dancing light in Richard's eyes and his irresistible smile, making it impossible to say no.

But it had happened, whatever the reason. Richard had got up to go; he'd given Derry a quick, friendly hug in parting, and then, almost at the door:

"Are you coming on Saturday, by the way?"

Just like that, a straight question, no pressure. No persuasion, even, no promise of new friends and a good time under the stars. He'd simply asked; and Derry had simply answered, gone with the flow, said what he wanted to.

"Yeah, sure. I'll be there. Three o'clock, right?"

"Right. See you then, kid. Take care, and God bless . . . "

And Derry hadn't flinched from the blessing, even internally, the way he usually did. Coming from Richard it only seemed natural and right, something to be cherished even if you didn't believe in God.

So come Saturday, come three o'clock, he was there. Or almost there. In fact he was hanging back on the wrong side of the road, watching and wondering, half inclined to chicken out.

There were two old coaches pulled up by the kerb, and a pack of people milling around on the pavement. Many of the faces surprised him; he knew them from the old days, from before his illness made him outcast, and they were the last people he'd have expected to see on a trip like this.

They must have been conned by the adverts, they were probably expecting a disco on the sand. They couldn't have realised it was a Christian do. Or else they did know, and this was a conspiracy; could be they were all going along to mock, to have a laugh at the God-botherers . . .

That last thought would have been enough to make Derry turn and flee; he'd let Richard down, he'd do anything to avoid the embarrassment of the scene he was imagining. But just then a girl came hurrying, almost running across the road towards him.

Derry stood still, imagining nothing now, only looking. Seeing how the long dark hair flew out behind her, how the baggy sweatshirt flapped around her body, how black leggings clung tight to calf and thigh. How she was so pleased to see him, this stranger, she was actually laughing as she reached to hug him, her body pressing warm and firm against his.

Derry didn't move a muscle, didn't dare. Didn't know what the hell to do with his hands, so just held them stiffly twitching at his sides.

"Oh," she said, "I know *you*."

And then she kissed his cheek.

Derry shook his head in a desperate confusion, said, "Um, no. No, you don't. Sorry, but . . . "

"Yes, I do. You're Derry Bowen, I saw you on the news. And I've been so happy since then, I think it's wonderful . . . "

Oh. Right. She was one of those. He'd had a few of them, mostly little old ladies stopping him in the street and gushing on about how marvellous it all was, and what a lucky boy he must feel. It made him sick. This one was a lot younger than the others and an awful lot prettier, but she must be the same underneath. It wasn't him she was hugging, it was just his miracle, his five minutes of fame on the telly.

He tried to pull away, but she wasn't having any of that. She hung on to his arm and said, "You are coming with us, aren't you? Come on over, you shouldn't be holding back like this. Especially not you."

"Look, I'm nothing special, okay?" His voice tight and fretful, jumping an octave like it always did when he lost his temper, something close to a whine. He winced at the sound of it and watched her bubbling eagerness fade suddenly, saw her turn solemn and serious but still with a smile threatening, still with her fingers lightly linked around his wrist.

"Oh," she said, "I'm sorry. Stupid of me, I should have thought. You've probably had it up to here with total strangers wanting to kiss you, right?"

"Well, yeah," grudgingly, shuffling his feet. "Something like that."

"Okay. No more kisses," and that smile broke through, spread itself into a grin. "I promise. But I *am* glad you're here, Derry; and I still think it's terrific, what happened for you. Now are you coming over, or what?"

"I dunno." He looked over the street again and saw them climbing into the coaches, making a dash for the back. In five minutes they'd have the cans out, and the fags; some of those lads were going to be well pissed before they came home. The return trip would be a nightmare, they'd be necking with their girls and mooning at other traffic through the window ...

"Chicken," she said teasingly. "Don't look so worried. We're going to have a good time, that's all. You can cope with that."

"Are you?" He was doubtful, and doubly so on her behalf. She must be in with the God squad, not just along for the ride. She was going to hate every minute, if it turned into the riot he was half expecting.

"Guaranteed." No doubts on her side. But she was turning serious again, big brown eyes coming at him hard while her hand tightened on his wrist. "Don't walk away from us now, Derry, we really want you along. *I* really want you along."

"Why, what for? I said, you don't know me."

"I know. That's the point, I want to." She shrugged, pushed the hair back from her face with her free hand, said, "Look, don't get paranoid. I just want to talk to you, okay?"

And he might still have said no and walked away, might have let his distrust carry him off up the hill again if she hadn't been so pretty, if his body hadn't been tingling still at the memory of hers. If her fingers loosening on his wrist hadn't gripped him tight as a handcuff, harder to break free.

He stood there helpless, caught between wanting nothing to do with her and wanting more, wanting everything; and then there was a voice, Richard, calling to them from the coaches.

"Rachel, Derry – let's go, we're off now!"

She didn't move, except to cock her head slightly, waiting for his decision. Derry scowled, finally nodded.

"Okay, then. I'll come."

"Good. And try smiling, why don't you? This is supposed to be fun ... "

She let go of him at last, and ran over to one of the coaches. Derry was briefly tempted to get into the other. But she was waiting on the step, watching him; and in the end he followed her up and in, sat beside her on the last free seat at the front.

Derry stretched his legs out into the gangway, giving himself an excuse to sit with his back half-turned to the girl. But the coach lurched hard round a corner and threw him suddenly off balance, sent him toppling sideways into the resilience of her body. He grabbed at the seat to pull himself upright, blushing furiously; and heard her soft chuckle in his ear, heard her say, "Look, it might be easier if you sat straight, don't you think?"

"Uh, yeah. Right . . . "

He twisted around, clenched both hands into the upholstery, stared at the floor.

"That's better. But I wish you'd relax. What are you so uptight about? I told you, I only want to talk."

Derry felt himself turning red again, and shook his head wordlessly. He could see her feet next to his, trendy red baseball boots and those revealing leggings above; but he wasn't going to let his eyes drift up any further, however much they wanted to. He could hear the smile in her voice, he already knew what it looked like on her face, he didn't have to see it again.

"You're dead strange, you are. But look, tell you what. I guess I blew it, slobbering all over you like that; so let's take it from the top, okay? Start all over again." And she thrust her right hand across, dangled it under Derry's nose. "Hullo, Derry. My name's Rachel Grant. Pleased to meet you."

Reluctantly, feeling stupid, Derry lifted his own hand and closed it around hers in a brief shake. Warmth in her palm, an unexpected strength in slender fingers; he pulled abruptly free, against the temptation of letting the grip linger.

Then, finding the courage from somewhere, he lifted his eyes to hers and said, "Just, just do us a favour, right? Just don't ask how it feels, what happened to me."

"Okay. Am I allowed to ask why not, or is that taboo too?"

He wasn't sure whether he was being teased or not, he wasn't sure of anything about this confident, smiling girl. He shrugged, shook his head, said, "I can't tell you, that's all. I don't know how it feels."

"Fair enough. It's only been a couple of weeks, hasn't it? And you'd been living with cancer for years, it's got to take time. But what I don't understand, Derry, what seems really strange to me . . . " She hesitated, as if in acknowledgement that this was dangerous ground again, then went on determinedly. "Well, if it was me, I think I'd be shouting the news from the rooftops. I'm sure I'd be down at the chapel thanking God for it, every chance there was. But you're not, are you? Someone told me you haven't been back since, not once."

"That's right." But seemingly the confirmation wasn't enough for her; she waited patiently for more, and at last he said awkwardly, "It'd be different for you, wouldn't it? I mean, you're religious, right?"

"I'm a Christian, yes." She said it simply, very matter-of-fact. "But even if I wasn't before – well, surely you have to afterwards, don't you? I mean, you can't be touched by God that way and still not believe, that just doesn't make sense . . . "

And there was a minor victory for Derry in seeing her at last a little uncertain, a little doubtful; so he underlined it, good and hard.

"I don't believe," he said. "I don't believe any of it, about God and Jesus and that."

"But . . . " She stopped, shook her head, thought about it; then, "Weird," she said. Smiling, friendly, back on course again. Back on top. "But then, anyone who doesn't believe in God seems a bit weird to me. You're just going for it in a bigger way. Don't worry, though, I'm not going to sit here and preach at you. If I did, you'd clam up on me again, wouldn't you?"

For a wonder, Derry managed to meet her smile with one of his own. It wasn't so hard. "Yeah, reckon I would. I hate that."

"So okay," she said, settling more comfortably into the corner between seat and window, "let's talk ordinary for a bit. Party talk. You tell me about Derry Bowen, and I'll tell you about Rachel Grant, and we'll leave God right out of it."

"Well, maybe. What do you want to know?"

"Everything, of course. I'm very inquisitive . . . "

He didn't tell her everything, of course. Not by a long way. But he talked more than she did, she was a good listener; and would have told her more for sure, might have gone on talking all day if they hadn't been interrupted. If someone hadn't called his name suddenly, as they disembarked at Colston Bay.

He turned, and saw Albie waving at him from the crowd around the other coach.

"Friend of yours?" Rachel asked at his shoulder.

"Yeah. Sort of. We play games together. Used to, before . . . "

"Before you got miracled?"

Derry nodded. "It's been, I dunno, difficult since."

"I can imagine." And when he didn't move, when he only stood there looking at her, waiting for permission and unsure whether he wanted it or not, she laughed and gave him a little shove on the chest. "Well, go on, then. Go and build some bridges. I'll see you later."

"Right . . . "

And he left her with a pang of disappointment to season the relief, torn both ways. She was a girl, and dead pretty, and obviously interested in him; and that was what he wanted, what he ached for. But still he was glad to escape the threat of her, how she left him feeling so clumsy and stupid. And her thing about God, he was well glad to get away from that.

He made his way through to Albie, said, "What the hell are you doing here?"

Albie shrugged. "It's something to do."

"Thought you were Jewish?" And when Albie gave him a stare — *we don't talk about that, what are you on about?* — "Didn't you know this was a Christian do?"

"Christ, is it?" Albie looked around warily, as if he expected to see someone handing out hymn-books. "No one said. What are they going to do, then?"

"God knows. Sermons round the campfire, most likely. But we can always go off if it gets too bad, there's buses back home."

"Yeah, right."

They grinned at each other, each glad to have found safe company; and Derry thought, *She was right, Rachel. That's what I'm doing, building bridges* . . .

Then Albie said, "So who was the skirt, then, eh?" and Derry blushed, shrugged, kicked at a tussock of grass.

"Just a girl, I dunno. I was sitting next to her on the coach, that's all. She's one of the God squad."

"Unh. That's too bad, she looked good from this direction. I was getting jealous for a moment there."

"No point."

"Not if she's religious. Invisible chastity belts, girls get when they get religion. I should know, my sisters are into it in a big way. They only date good Jewish boys, and even those poor buggers don't get past the bedroom door . . . "

They climbed up a steep bank of dunes, ran and slid laughing down the other side and onto the beach, following Richard and a bunch of other young adults. Before they could scatter, Richard backed a little way up the slope again and called for their attention.

"Gather round and listen for a minute. The most important thing is the fire. We're not lighting it yet, but we'll need plenty of fuel when we do. You'll find driftwood up and down this beach, if you look for it; and by sunset I want a pile taller than I am, right here. Anyone who doesn't bring in their share gets raw hamburger and a candle to cook it on, understood?"

Laughter, whistles and cat-calls; but the mood was cheerful, cooperative even, and clearly the wood would be there.

"Good. The second most important thing is for you lot to enjoy yourselves. We've brought towels, so if you want to get wet go right ahead, though I warn you the water's freezing. Otherwise there are footballs, frisbees, things like that. Just ask; if we've got it, you can have it. Oh, and the coaches leave at midnight on the dot. Anyone we can't find gets left behind, and buses don't run that late. That's all. Except, have fun . . . "

And somewhat to Derry's surprise, they did have fun. He and Albie wandered off along the sands, an extended exercise in bridge-building; and when they came back, lugging a driftwood log between them, there was a riotous game of soccer going on. Boys against girls, with Rachel in goal for the girls; and Derry grinned to himself as he saw her surreptitiously kicking her jacket goalposts a couple of feet closer together. She spotted him watching, and winked broadly.

A yell made him glance round, just in time to duck as a frisbee scythed past his head. Albie reached out a hand and caught it neatly, sent it spinning back in a high loop towards the guy who'd thrown it; then he followed after at a run, to join the game. Derry kicked his shoes off, tossed them onto a pile of others and went barefoot down to the water's edge, where Richard was directing the construction of a massive sandcastle.

"Derry! We need a channel to the water, to fill the moat before the tide goes out. Roll your jeans up and get busy . . . "

Derry followed orders, feeling like a fool and a skinny fool at that. But there were boys older than him working on the castle, building ramparts high and carving battlements, shouting and laughing like children. So he shrugged off his embarrassment and joined in with a will, digging a trench down to the surf and scraping it deeper with a length of wood until the sea rushed up into the weed-lined moat.

Then the football flew suddenly past him into the waves. Yells and shrieks, from behind him; Derry plunged to the rescue before it could be dragged further out, soaking his jeans to mid-thigh in the process, and found Rachel running to reclaim it.

Derry tossed it to her feet, and saw her trap it neatly. He tackled her, barefoot; won the ball, dribbled it easily past a couple of giggling, protesting girls and rolled it through their suspiciously-narrow goal to a cheer from the boys' team.

"Not fair!" one of the girls protested, thumping him in the ribs as he punched the air in celebration. "You're not playing."

"I am now."

"Should you?" That was Rachel, appearing beside him.

"Sure, why not? I got miracle legs, remember?"

"Right, then. We're *not* counting that," she said positively, "it was a goal kick to us anyway. But it's still ten-six to you lot."

He grinned. "You let *ten* past you?"

"Yes. But if you're playing, I'm coming out of goal . . . "

Derry managed twenty minutes, mostly either tackling Rachel or being tackled by her. That private battle had to be abandoned with honours even, more or less, when he staggered away to collapse on the soft sand below the dunes, sweating hard, his heart hammering against his labouring ribs.

He closed his eyes, feeling the world swim away; and opened them again to find her kneeling beside him, looking anxious.

"Derry? Are you okay?"

He grunted, pushing himself up on one elbow. "Yeah. Yeah, I'm fine. No problem. Just, I haven't run around like that for three years. I need to get fit again, that's all . . . "

"Oh." She sighed with relief, then scowled and punched him on the shoulder. "Don't scare me like that, all right? I thought it was your legs again."

Derry grinned weakly. "Where's your faith, then? You're supposed to be the one who believes in miracles . . . "

She snorted, giving him a shove that sent him sprawling back onto the sand. He closed his eyes again, listening to the noises around him, the party going with a swing; and didn't open them until he heard something else, soft music and a girl's voice singing.

It was Rachel, sitting on the dune a short way above him, her head bent low over a guitar, her hair fallen forward to veil her face. For a minute he couldn't hear the words and assumed this was some Christian song, the truce was over and she was taking advantage of his weakness to throw her religion at him.

But then her head lifted, tossing the hair back with a practised flick. She sang the next verse bright and clear, out towards the sea; and no, there was nothing Christian in it. It was a love-song, a ballad with an edge of sharpness, a hint of bitterness behind the loss. Derry rolled onto his stomach and propped his head on his hands to listen.

"Hey, that was good," he said as she stilled the strings with a flat hand, killing the resonance of the final chord.

"Thanks."

"Know any more like that?"

"There aren't any more like that."

"Unh?"

Rachel smiled, briefly. "I wrote the words, this bloke I know did the music. A boy at school. It was our first, and we really

97

worked well together. We were going to be Lennon and McCartney, you know? Set the world on fire . . . "

"So what happened?"

A pause, a shrug, another tight smile. "He chucked me out of the band, because I was getting too involved with this," with a gesture around the beach, the party, all that they implied. "So, no more songs. Not with him, anyway, he was really mad."

"Oh. Well, sing something else, then."

"What?"

"Anything. I'm not fussy. Not a hymn," he added sternly.

This time her smile was genuine and easy, with a chuckle behind it. "Okay. No hymns."

Rachel sang 'Blowin' In The Wind', and a couple of boys came over laughing, calling her a hippy; but they still sat down to listen. She sang 'The Night They Drove Old Dixie Down' and a group of girls massed behind Derry, clapping the beat and joining raucously in the chorus.

She sang old songs and new, did some requests and shook her head at others, with a shrug of apology. And Derry sat and listened, barely distracted even by a fight down on the beach. He glanced round briefly at the noise, saw Richard step between the scuffling boys, saw how quickly they quietened; and turned his eyes and all his attention back to Rachel.

There must have been twenty in her audience, might have been more when Richard's voice broke the spell of the music.

"Give the girl a break, you lot! Or aren't you interested in the fire? Or food? I want some help over here . . . "

Someone stood up and drifted over towards the massive pile of firewood. Someone else followed; and then there was a rush, a squabbling clamour of voices eager for a blaze to light the cooling evening. Derry was the last to move, pushing himself slowly to his feet and walking away, walking backwards while Rachel let her head drop again, nursing the guitar close to her chest while her fingers went on picking music out of it.

He was almost out of earshot when he heard her start to sing again, soft and private; but what she was singing took him back, with a mock scowl on his face.

"Oy," he said quietly. "You're cheating again. You promised, no hymns."

She glanced up at him, her dark eyes fierce behind her hair. "I thought you'd gone to play bonfires. Go on, shove off if you don't like it. This one's just for me."

But it wasn't, of course. He stood there listening, no true

complaint in him; and she lifted her head and let her voice ring out across the darkening sand, all the verses of 'Amazing Grace' sung with a passion and a fire, a deep belief that shook Derry all the more because he didn't understand it, couldn't come close to understanding.

Wary of giving her another chance to break through his defences, Derry left her putting her guitar away and joined the milling crowd around the growing fire. He found Albie there, a more predictable companion; and the two of them cooked sausages on twigs above the hissing flames, rolled them in slices of bread and munched contentedly. There were hamburgers as well, smeared with ketchup and mustard and served in buns; and soft drinks for the ill-prepared, the ones who hadn't brought their own lager.

When even teenage appetites were satisfied, they sat or sprawled in little groups on the cool sand. The fire was blazing green on its diet of salted, sun-dried driftwood; Derry pulled aching eyes away from its glare and saw people slipping quietly off into the dunes. Couples looking for somewhere private, bolder spirits going to try their luck in the local pubs. Fine by him. He didn't want a drink, he was quite happy with a full stomach and a can of coke; and tonight he couldn't even feel jealous of the lovers.

Richard stood up, a silhouette against the leaping flames; and Derry thought, *This is it, here comes the sermon.* Maybe he and Albie should have taken the chance to slip off, maybe the pub-goers had the right idea after all.

"Listen up a minute, everyone. Just a couple of things I want to say, before we get on with the party. First off, most of you will probably have realised by now, this whole thing has been put together with the help of the Gospel Hall back in Paradise. And yes, that does mean I'm a Christian. So are Mike and Alice and the rest of us; and so are some of the kids you've been fooling around with. They're my fifth column. However," in defiance of Derry's expectations, "that doesn't mean that we're going to preach at you, now or ever. That's not what the youth club is about.

"Secondly, we'll try to do this again or something like it, as often as we can through the summer; but if you've had a good time today, why not come along to our regular meetings as well? Every Thursday evening they'll be, at the Gospel Hall until we can arrange somewhere bigger. What happens there will more or less depend on who turns up and what they want; it's your club, so come to the early meetings and you can help to shape it.

"And that's enough talking for now. Mike's brought his ghetto-blaster along, with a box of tapes; so if any of you have got any energy left, now's the time to use it up . . . "

Music pulsed heavily into the night, from a rock at the sea's edge. People drifted slowly down to listen, talked and laughed and egged each other on to dance on the hard, wet sand.

Derry stayed where he was, even after Albie had been lured away. He felt comfortably lazy, here in the heat of the roaring fire; and the years of his illness had lost him the habit of discos almost as soon as he'd learned it.

He didn't move until he felt a toe digging hard into his ribs.

No surprise, it was Rachel standing over him, a shadow against the blaze.

"What I reckon," she said, "if you're fit enough to play football, you're fit enough to dance."

"Not me," he said hurriedly, to support his sudden shyness. "You saw what the game did to me, I was knackered . . . "

"You've had time to get your breath back. Come on, up."

Her toe worked its way into his side again, and he squirmed and scrambled to his feet, somehow not resenting the bullying; encouraging it, even, laying himself open to more. "I dunno, I haven't danced for years, I can't remember how . . . "

"It'll come back to you," she said more gently. "Anyone can dance. Just enjoy yourself." And she took his hand, to pull him down the beach; and stopped without warning, met him eye to eye and giggling. "You know what? I'm taller than you are."

He was used to that, too much so to have noticed; but it seemed to matter now. "Well, you're older," he muttered. "We worked it out on the coach."

"Five months, that's all."

"Yeah, well. Cancer stunts your growth, all right? You probably weigh more than I do, too."

"Are you saying I'm fat, Derry Bowen?"

He just looked at her – looked up at her – and after a second her indignant laughter died.

"Well, maybe not. I'll let you off this time. Just do something about it, okay? Grow a bit. You haven't got cancer now, so there's no excuse for it. And get some exercise, put some muscles on. Who wants to dance with a bundle of bones?"

"You don't have to."

"Oh, give me strength! I didn't mean tonight, stupid. Tonight I do. Just get a bit heavier for next time, do some circuit-training. Or go swimming, swimming's good. And so's dancing," added positively, "dancing's great exercise. You should do lots of that. Starting," and her grip tightened as she tugged on his arm, towed him behind her, "starting tonight . . . "

So he danced: self-consciously at first, his body suddenly an awkward and inhibiting shell, a clumsy machine under her eyes and the others'. But slowly the music overrode his mind; and then he only danced, as hard and as fast as he'd played football, with every step and every movement a celebration of itself, of his freedom to step and move this way.

And when he was exhausted – which happened too soon, like the football – when he was weak and sweating and desperate for a break, someone changed the tape. It might have been Rachel, he didn't see. All he knew was that the relentless beat cut off in mid-track, was replaced by something slow and easy. There were cat-calls and complaints, but he was glad; and doubly so when Rachel appeared in front of him, slipping her arms round his waist, her body moving gently against his. He felt a moment of nervousness, unsure of where to put his hands, what was okay to touch and what was not; but he couldn't pull away, didn't want to and didn't dare. So he just held her and hoped, closed his eyes and forgot everything except the moment and the music, the excitement and the threat of her warm body in his arms.

She left him before he was ready, before he'd begun to wonder if she might. Someone murmured something in her ear, and she nodded, smiled at them, said, "Sorry, Derry, got to go. Richard wants me. You keep working on those muscles, there's lots of other girls here to help out . . . "

And then she was gone, running off into the darkness. *Her master's voice,* Derry thought, with a bitter jealousy. *He just has to whistle, doesn't he? Well, sod him. And sod her too. I'm okay . . .*

Except that he wasn't, not really. Everybody must have marked her sudden leaving, his abandonment; or if not everybody, Albie had for one, that was certain. Derry could see him now, standing with his hand on a girl's shoulder, sending indecipherable messages with his eyebrows. Derry scowled, not wanting his sympathy; and not wanting to dance either, without Rachel.

So when the music started again he turned his back, thrust his hands into his pockets – closing his fists tightly around the memory of her, the damp sweatshirt, firm flesh and bone beneath – and walked away. Realised that he was following her, and hesitated. She'd have taken him along if she'd wanted him. And she'd told him to stay put, hadn't she? She might as well have said it straight, *don't come dangling after me.*

So he went over to the fire instead, to throw the last of the wood into the glowing heart of it and send showers of sparks rising high towards the stars. He watched the flames for a while, then scowled, turned, set off down the beach. And yes, he was following her; and no, he didn't care what she thought, what she'd say. Why should he?

He heard her before he saw her. As the strident rhythms of the open-air disco faded behind him, he heard her singing, too soft to make out the words. He slowed, losing his nerve again, shy of simply walking up to her; moved over to the dunes where he'd be harder to see, and made his way more cautiously forward.

Soon he could see a group, six or eight people sitting on the sand. Richard was there, he was easy to make out; the others were just shapes in the darkness, their conversation only a murmur. Rachel was sitting on a rock a little apart from them, half turned away, seemingly playing and singing only for herself or her God. Except that Richard had asked for her . . .

Mood music, Derry realised. *That's what he wants her for, just to lay down a mood . . .*

And he resented that for her sake, as she obviously wasn't resenting it for herself. He didn't like her being used that way; and just to make the point — to her, to Richard, to anyone who could see — he walked openly across the sand towards her.

He sat down a couple of metres away, where she'd be able to see him if she lifted her head, if she looked; and he listened to her as those other kids were listening to Richard.

He listened as she sang hymns and spirituals, more modern songs of faith and praise; and he didn't stop listening until the disco quit and someone came looking for Richard, to put an end to the party.

She acknowledged him then, at last, with a smile and a little gesture that might have meant *thanks*, or might not. He shrugged, held her case while she put the guitar away, then walked wordlessly beside her back to the coaches.

He didn't get to sit with her on the drive home. He lost her somehow in the crush, got into the wrong coach; so he sat by himself, head against the cold glass of the window, welcoming the hard vibration of it as an antidote to thinking.

He didn't get to talk to her after the journey, either. He saw her on the pavement with Richard and an older man; and before he could do anything, before he could even make up his mind what he ought to do, she'd taken the old guy's arm and walked over the road with him, lugging her guitar case and talking hard. Derry was ready to wave, he'd settle for that if he had to; but she didn't even look round, didn't give him the chance.

They got into a car, a big new Volvo estate, and drove away. Derry watched the tail-lights out of sight around the corner, scowling; then he saw Albie heading off hand in hand with the girl he'd been dancing with, and scowled harder.

As he shouldered his way through the dispersing crowd, Richard reached out a hand to grip his shoulder. "Derry. I'm glad you came today. Don't forget, Thursday, eight o'clock."

Derry nodded shortly. He wouldn't forget. Whether he'd be there or not, that was something else.

NINE

i

He knows there are whisperings against him even at the chapel's heart, even among the devout. He knows there are dark looks aimed at his back, knives of distrust sharpened in secret. Of course he does, he must know. How could he not, when he's so much in tune with the souls of his people?

It must be such a grief to him, to feel the small plots and minor conspiracies rise like a web around him; but he won't let it disturb him unduly. It's just another part of his burden, something to be borne with sadness until such time as God turns it all to good, some way that even he can't see as yet. That'll happen, sooner or later. It's inevitable, it's the way life is. His path is all laid out for him, step by step from here to the golden city. All he has to do is walk it, stride boldly through the shadows and trail light behind him like a comet in the night. That's the irony, that's God's little joke, the price He asks of His ambassadors: that they're heralds of glory, but they never get a share of it themselves, they never get to bask in their own reflected light. Their gaze is always forwards, into the dark, where the need is. They don't look back.

ii

Alan Parkinson stood on the monument steps, surveyed the crowd and closed his bible with a satisfied snap. It was Saturday, and he'd had to contend with animal-rights activists and students selling their communist rags, as well as the urgencies of shopping; but still he'd gathered twelve or fifteen onlookers, people who'd actually stopped to listen to his message. Some were sniggering, the ones who wanted only to mock, whose hearts were closed to God. That was inevitable. But others were genuinely interested; he could read it in their faces, in their stillness as they received the Word.

Ted Grimes was moving among those now, handing out leaflets and inviting them to service; and that was another victory right there, that Alan no longer pursued this mission alone.

He glanced at his watch, then stepped down to shake hands, to give his blessing and reiterate the invitation. "Come to Chapel, brother . . . Bless you, sister, will we see you tomorrow?"

As the people dispersed, Ted came up to him. "It's a shame to stop, like, with so much interest."

"Aye. Bit of a change, that. Back at Christmas, no one stopped." *And no one came to help, either. Not you, Ted, not anyone.*

"Right. And you know what's done it, don't you, you know what's got them curious?"

"It's the Lord's work," Alan said flatly. *And mine.* "It's God speaking to them, through me; and praise Him for it."

"But it was Easter planted the seed. This is just the harvest. Young Derry Bowen's miracle, that's what set this off."

Alan scowled, covering it with another check on the time. "I have to go, Ted. Jean Dolance is expecting me."

"Oh, aye. Off you go, then. I'll pack up the stall. See you at service tomorrow, Alan. And," the old man frowning anxiously, sensing that he'd blundered, "well done, for today. You spoke very well."

Alan jerked his head in the necessary denial. "Not me. It was the Lord, Ted. I'm only His mouthpiece. We don't any of us do this ourselves. Not *any* of us."

"No, that's right, of course. But," still fretful, still a little unhappy, "He wouldn't, He couldn't use us if we weren't fit tools for His hand. And that much we have to do ourselves, we have to keep ourselves pure . . . "

Fit, too. They had to keep themselves fit. Alan didn't run a car, and he disdained buses. Sometimes he'd cycle, if he had any distance to cover; but mostly he walked. And as he walked, he'd take pamphlets from his shoulder-bag and push them through doors or leave them under the windscreen wipers of parked cars. His was a constant labour, a duty never to be fulfilled until his death or Christ's second coming.

Today he marched up the steep hill from town, God's soldier, no time to waste in the long war: his stiff-legged gait unfaltering even under the jeering derision of teenagers lounging against a wall on the other side of the road. Time was, when he would have stopped for them; when he would have crossed over and tried to hand out his pamphlets, his mission driving him into the heat, the very heart of ridicule. No longer. He was with Jean Dolance in this, as in so much else: that there were some folk who put themselves deliberately beyond saving, beyond reach of the Word.

It was nothing but folly and pride, the sin of self-aggrandisement, even to attempt to witness to their dark souls. And Pride might walk the streets of Paradise in person these days, in his golden flesh, but Alan wouldn't be seduced into imitation. No man's disciple, he.

So he ignored the laughter, and the hurled beer-can that clattered on the pavement just behind him. It would all be paid for, come the Judgement, all be tallied up and reckoned in the final accounting. Endurance would be rewarded, and mockery punished. Didn't it say in the Bible, that God sent she-bears to punish the children who made fun of Elisha's bald head? That was long ago, but He didn't change. He would still be vengeful, for the wrongs inflicted on His people . . .

To Alan's left, street after street ran sharply down towards the industrial wasteland that bordered the river. Then there were stone walls and high iron railings, the old cemetery; and after that more long terraces, the houses and flats of Paradise.

A few minutes brought him to Jean's door. Her son Luther was out in the tiny patch of front garden, down on his hands and knees, frowning in concentration as he rooted weeds out with his fingers. Odd, to see that; normally it was Lisa who did the work around the house. Luther was more often to be found studying his Bible. Jean meant him for a missionary.

"Helping your mother, Luther? That's good."

The boy looked up from his work. "I'm doing a penance, Mr Parkinson."

"Oh, aye? And what have you done, to be punished for?"

"Not a punishment, a *penance*. Mother said I should. I said a dirty word. A, a *foul* word, Mother said it was. I learned it from Lisa, she said it was all right, but she was being wicked. She was lying to me. Mother's very angry with Lisa."

"Aye, I'm sure." Alan gestured towards the open door. "Your mother in, then, is she?"

"She's upstairs, praying with Lisa."

Alan nodded, touched the bell briefly to announce his arrival and stepped into the hall.

As always, the house smelt of polish and recent hoovering. A reproduction of 'The Light of the World' hung on one wall; opposite it, a plain wooden cross and a Bible verse, framed behind glass. '*He hath shewed thee, O man, what is good; and what doth the Lord require of thee, but to do justly, and to love mercy, and to walk humbly with thy God?*'

Walk humbly, yes, that was the point. There were others in the

106

city, Alan thought, who could do with a sight of that wisdom. Some people would do well to find themselves a little humility, to remember that they were the strangers here and not puff themselves up beyond their deserving . . .

Jean came down the stairs after a minute, thinly smiling.

"Alan."

"Peace be on this house," he said formally, as he always did. They had that as a commandment, from Jesus' own lips. *The gospel of Luke,* his mind supplied, *the tenth chapter.*

"Amen to that. You come at a good time, Alan."

And there was no sarcasm in her voice, she was glad to have him here, glad perhaps of the support he could offer; so he felt no discomfort in saying, "I saw Luther, out at the front there. He said you'd had some trouble . . . "

"Yes. Lisa's at the back of it, of course. The Devil's in that child, Alan; and it's all deliberate, that's clear to see. It's her own sin, she opened herself to him. She must have done."

"There's no one could blame you, Jean. Where is she now?"

"In her room. Locked in, until I see some sign of repentance in her."

"Well. I'll pray for her."

"Do that, I'd be glad of it. And if you'd care to pray with her before you go, I'd be even more glad. She's closed herself off from me, I can't reach her."

"Yes, of course." He didn't relish the prospect; he knew Lisa's dull, doughy sullenness of old. But duty was duty, and couldn't be denied.

"Thank you. Now, a cup of tea. You've been at the monument all day, you'll want it."

And over the kitchen table and the cup of tea came the serious business of the day, the real news:

"You'll not have heard his latest, then, Jean? Ted told me this morning, while we were setting up."

"No, what's this, what is it this time?"

"He wants to bring in a whole troupe from outside. Seems we're not good enough for him. He said at breakfast, apparently, he wants kids here from all over the country. America, too."

"Kids?"

"Aye. Teens and twenties. He's to bring it up at the next Council meeting. A new crusade, he called it."

"Crusade! New disciples for him, more like. A new set of worshippers for Richard Gould."

"Aye."

"Where's he going to put them, has he thought of that?"

"Tents, church halls, anything he can get. A school gym, perhaps. He'd find somewhere."

"He would, you're right." She ran a finger slowly around the rim of her cup, and said, "It's got to be stopped, Alan."

"It has."

"We haven't worked for the chapel all these years, only to have it taken away from us now. This is a test, do you see that? We're being tested. Like Job. God's laying a temptation in our path. It'd be all too easy to sit back and let Richard have his way, let him steal everything to himself. But we'll lose it all in the end, if we let that happen. He's no true guide, that boy. He's too full of himself, he'll lead us all astray if we let him. 'Let not him that is deceived trust in vanity: for vanity shall be his recompence.' That was Job. And others may be deceived, Alan, but not us. We mustn't let ourselves be dazzled."

"There's Jeremiah, too. I was reading Jeremiah last night, the Lord put it into my head to do that. And he says, 'Take ye heed every one of his neighbour, and trust ye not in any brother: for every brother will utterly supplant, and every neighbour will walk with slanders.' There's a message in that for us, Jean. A warning, if you like. We're being supplanted by one as should be a brother."

"And you were led to that passage, to make it clear to you. It's as I said, this is a test."

"So what do we do now?"

Jean smiled, thin lips pulling back from small, uneven teeth. "We fight. For the Lord, Alan, for the chapel, and for ourselves. We fight tooth and claw, and every inch of the way. And we'll win, make no doubt of that. We'll win."

iii

Morning service was over, and Arthur stood in his usual place by the porch door, shaking hands and exchanging blessings as the congregation filed out. There were more hands than ever this morning, more strangers to smile at, to thank for coming and hope to see again. Plenty of youngsters, too, that was the best of it. And this was without Richard; it was widely known, had even been announced in the papers that he was preaching at a Methodist chapel this morning, away on the other side of town.

"Mary, good to see you out and about again . . . Hullo, lad, welcome to Paradise ... God bless ... John, how's the little one getting along ... ?"

Friends and strangers, in a long parade; and then, as the stream died to a trickle, the last lingerers making their slow way out onto the crowded pavement:

"Mr Brougham, isn't it? You don't know me, but ... "

"Yes, I do, son," Arthur replied firmly. "Oh, not your name, not yet; but you've been before, haven't you?" A man in his thirties with a sad, anxious face, hesitancy and determination warring in his eyes, his twitching mouth.

"Aye, that's right. Not regular, like, I'm a Baptist normally; but I've been coming here these last few weeks, my minister said no problem and I thought you wouldn't mind ... "

"Of course not, we're delighted to have you join us for worship. There's no competition between your church and us. I hope you'll come again."

"Aye, I will. But, look, can I have a word? In private, like? It's important ... "

"Yes, of course. If you could just wait a moment ... "

A quick goodbye to the stragglers, and Arthur led the young man back through the chapel to the room at the rear. Arnold Saltley was in there, spooning tea into the pot; but one quick glance and he switched the kettle off and left them alone.

"Sit down, son. Would you like a cuppa? We usually make one, after service."

"No, no thanks. I can't stay long, my wife'll be looking for me. It's just, I've got some news that I think you ought to hear. In confidence," urgently, "it's got to be in confidence. You mustn't let on who you heard it from."

"You can trust me for that, lad."

"Right. Well, thing is, I work for the council, see? In the planning department. And there's something I came across, just by chance, like ... " He lowered himself slowly into a chair and sat uncomfortably on the edge, cracking his knuckles one by one. Then he plunged on, seemingly at a tangent. "Last time I came, it was your Mr Dubrowski ran the service."

"Jack? Aye."

"And he was talking about isolation, he used his own home for an example. Cockburn Grove, he said, and he was the only tenant left in a whole terrace, and nothing but rubble all around. That's right, isn't it, Cockburn Grove?"

"That's right, son. What about it?"

"Just, the story stuck with me, it must be so odd to live like that; so I remembered the name, Cockburn Grove, when I saw it on some papers I was dealing with . . . "

A long pause then, but Arthur didn't prompt him. He could feel bad news coming, and he didn't want to hurry it along.

At last, though, all in a rush:

"You know there are these plans for a business park down there by the river? Well, Cockburn Grove's right in the middle of it, where they want to build. And they've been mucking about for ages, trying to raise the finance, but it's all going ahead now. It's a private developer, but the council's behind him, and there's Government money too, and the EC. Mr Dubrowski's going to lose his home, is what it is. I checked the file, and the woman who owns the property, she's been holding out for a better price, and there's been no hurry before; but if she doesn't sell up soon they'll just do a compulsory purchase, is all. And I thought, I thought you ought to know. So he can be warned. I didn't like to say directly, not to him, it's got to be bad news, hasn't it? But someone should know. A few months, that's all. Could be sooner. And he needs to know, he needs to start looking for somewhere . . . "

"Aye." Arthur breathed out, long and slow. "Thank you, son. You did the right thing, coming to tell me. I'll pass it on to Jack; and don't worry, I'll tell no one where I heard it from. You have my word on that."

"Thanks, Mr Brougham. I, I've got to go now . . . "

Arthur nodded and half-rose in his chair, slumping back again before his visitor was out of the door. He'd have a minute at most before Arnold came in, looking for his tea and the gossip; and a minute wasn't enough, not by a long chalk.

Jack hadn't come to service this morning. Anita must be having a bad day, he wouldn't have missed chapel for any lesser reason. And that only underlined the trouble this news was going to bring him. Anita's health was a worry at the best of times; Arthur couldn't imagine how a forced move would affect her, but he was certain the results couldn't be good.

He closed his eyes and offered up a hurried prayer for strength and comfort, dreading the thought of facing Jack with the news, as he would have to.

Then the door opened, and in came Arnold.

"What was that all about, then, Arthur? Yon boy was running, almost, when he went out . . . "

"Sorry, Arnold, can't tell you yet. It's not good news, I'll say that much; but it's personal, for Jack. He'll have to be told about it first. Don't worry, you'll hear soon enough." Then, suddenly inspired and *thank you, Lord,* seeing a way to make this easier on himself and maybe easier on Jack too: "Are Ted and Ellen expecting Richard back for Sunday lunch, do you know?"

"Aye, I believe so. They went off pretty sharp after service. Likely Ellen wanted to get the joint on."

"Likely she did. Thanks, Arnold. I'll see you tonight."

So Arthur didn't go home when he left the chapel, he headed for Ted's: hoping to find Richard there, hoping to spread the weight of his reluctant mission across those broad shoulders. And never stopping to wonder how it was that he could tell Richard but not Arnold, only glad that it was so; only praying that Richard was free to be enlisted, to set his particular warmth against the chill of that sad house and these sadder tidings.

iv

"So what's the matter with you, then?"

Rachel shrugged one-shouldered, not shifting the other from the doorway she was leaning against.

"Like that, is it?" Her mother snorted, shuffling papers on her desk. "Well, I'm sorry, pet, but I haven't got time for teenage blues tonight. I've got to get this sorted, and I can't concentrate with you haunting the back of my neck. Take yourself off and join your father, you're both as bad as each other, and neither one of you's talking. Go on, I mean it," when Rachel still didn't move. "Vanish. And close the door behind you."

Rachel did that, with a glare at her mother's unheeding back and a sullen toss of her head. What were mothers for, if not to provide comfort and counsel when a daughter needed it?

The accuracy of the diagnosis didn't help, either. Teenage blues was exactly what Rachel was suffering from, and she knew it. And resented it, unfamiliar with the symptoms, taken by surprise and deeply confused.

Ordinarily she lived a life of certainties, grounded on the solid rock of faith. The path ahead had always been clear, even in her greatest troubles; she prayed, she talked things over with her parents, with her friends and with God, and she came through confident at the last, head high and walking tall.

She wasn't used to these clouds of doubt and hesitancy that fogged her mind and her vision now, the nervousness that held her back, fearful of putting a foot wrong in a suddenly treacherous world. Specifically she wasn't used to being plagued, possessed almost by the image of a boy's face, the memory of his voice and a deep concern for his problems.

111

Derry had been much on her mind ever since the beach party last week. She'd been looking forward to seeing him again at Thursday's meeting, perhaps getting to know him better if she could charm or bully or inveigle her way past his prickly defences; and she'd been more than frustrated when he hadn't turned up. She'd been worried, almost worried enough to mention it to Richard and only held back by a stupid shyness, not to be caught asking after a boy.

So okay, she should phone him. Richard would have his number. Or she could go round, see him face to face to bypass the silences and awkwardness of a telephone.

But that's where the doubts crept in, where the hesitancy asserted itself; that's where she found herself backing off, doing nothing for fear of doing something wrong.

She padded barefoot down the stairs and slouched into the living-room. The television was on, but her father wasn't watching it; he was standing at the table by the window, bent over a magazine he wasn't reading, flicking the pages in a restless search for something, anything that might seize his attention.

He looked round at Rachel, seemed briefly lost for a greeting, unable to find even a smile for her; finally said, "Done your school work, have you?"

"Dad, it's Sunday night. Of course I've done my school work."

Done it sketchily, done it badly, her mind a long way from German grammar and Jude the Exceedingly Obscure. Her teachers weren't going to be pleased with her; but that was fair enough. She wasn't pleased with herself, either. Not at all impressed.

She dropped onto the sofa, reached for the TV remote-control and flicked through the channels. Nothing: she gave up in despair, turned the television off and let her head fall back, staring blankly at the ceiling.

After a minute, she felt her father's hands close lightly on her temples.

"Problems?"

"Yeah."

"Want to talk?"

"Dunno. Don't think so, really. It's sort of private." That was another new experience, having things in her head too private to share with her parents. It was enough to make her bitterly resentful of Derry — or his ghost, at least, the tormenting, burdensome image of him — that he could shift all her realities around this way. She knew it was ridiculous, that resentment; he wasn't to blame

112

for her state of mind. For all she knew, he hadn't given her so much as a moment's thought since the party. Lord, he hadn't even travelled back on the same coach as her, nor had she seen him to say goodbye to afterwards.

But still, the resentment was genuine and active; and that only added to her sense of muddle and the muddiness of her thoughts. And no, she couldn't possibly talk about it.

"Fair enough." Her father sounded more relieved than surprised; and it dawned on Rachel that even if she had been ready to talk, he was by no means ready to listen. Which was at least as strange, as out of habit as her own behaviour.

She twisted her head to watch him walk away, and said, "How's about you?"

At least he managed a smile this time, passive and strained though it might be. "Same thing, thanks, pet. Something on my mind, but I can't really discuss it."

"Okay." And she matched his smile with one of her own, albeit just as passive and just as strained; glad at least to have found some common ground, something they could share.

He settled himself in a chair with that magazine in his hands, still as useless to him, only a tool to occupy his fingers. Rachel watched him for a little while, finding just space enough in her own confusion to wonder about his, what could have so perturbed her imperturbable father; then the doorbell sounded like a blessing. She was on her feet in a moment, "I'll get it, don't you move."

It wasn't Derry on the step, of course. She'd hardly dreamed it might be, hardly at all. It was Richard Gould, with one of the old men from the Paradise Chapel; she searched for his name as she let them in, and found it. Arthur Brougham, that's who he was; but her eyes and all her attention were on Richard.

"Hullo, Rachel. Is your father free?"

"Yes, sure. He's in the living-room, come on through . . . "

Richard was grave behind his smile; there was something up, clearly. Something too important to let a teenager in on, no doubt. Rachel brought them to her father, watched him summon up the necessary welcome with a heavy effort to hide his own concerns, and tactfully withdrew before she could be sent away.

She made a pot of coffee, and carried it through on a tray. Her father's voice met her from the open door, "Compulsory purchase orders are pretty final. There's really not much you can do. There is an appeals procedure, but – " and broke off abruptly as he

113

registered her coming. She made like a hostess, dispensed cream and sugar and passed the mugs around; then she gave them a general smile, as big and bright as she could, and said, "I'm off to bed, Dad. Goodnight."

She closed the door firmly on her father's surprise, his quick glance at the clock. So okay, it was early; but at least the point had been made, loud and clear. Conspicuous virtue, this was, not angling to butt in on their discussion. And she surely had nothing else to stay up for ...

Feeling unwontedly dirty she took a quick shower, trying to scrub her mind clean as she scrubbed her body. Then there was a long session with comb and hair-dryer in her bedroom, and the usual determination to have it all cropped short, to save herself the hassle; and at last she could get down to her diary.

Her confession, it had become in recent days. She was still confessing – and enjoying it almost, wallowing in it almost – when there was a light tap at the door.

"Yeah, come in ... " She'd been too engrossed to hear footsteps, but it had to be Dad, this time of night. It was his regular Sunday habit to drop in last thing, for a brief chat about the week gone and a prayer for the week to come. It wouldn't be so easy tonight, with secrets on her side and his, with Rachel feeling so uneasy with herself; but she glanced over her shoulder smiling, not to let their mutual troubles damage a valued ritual.

And felt the smile freeze and crack, felt herself furiously blushing as she saw Richard in the doorway.

"Ohh ... "

A clumsy finger switching the radio to silence, a hasty scramble out of the chair, tugging her skimpy bathrobe tighter; a sudden reach back to flip the diary shut against his accidentally seeing his name, and then another savage tug at the uncooperative robe; and all the time he only stood there grinning at her.

"Relax, Rachel. I just looked in to say goodnight."

"You, uh, you surprised me ... " And she pushed a hand through her wild hair, slid it down over a hot cheek, tried to smile. Managed not to make a dive for the bed, not to hide under the duvet with a pillow across her face. "I thought you were my dad, he usually comes up for a bit, on a Sunday ... "

"I know, he told me. But he's busy with Arthur; there's a lot going on, and we need his advice. So I volunteered instead. Only if you'd like it, I don't want to muscle in on you. Privacy's important too."

"Oh, please. No, do stay. But," with a glance down at the

brevity of her robe, "well, do you mind if I just get into bed?"

He laughed. "Sure, why not? Any way you're comfortable."

So she got to hide after all, at least a little; and that was better, that way she could produce a genuine smile as he glanced curiously around the room. She looked with him, tried to see what he saw: the cross on the wall between the pop posters, the bible balanced on an untidy heap of magazines and schoolbooks.

"*Filia Religiosa*," she murmured; and warmed at his chuckle, felt his quick understanding.

"I know that feeling," he said cheerfully, settling himself at the foot of the bed. "The good news is, it gets better; but I don't suppose you want to hear that, do you? It's not going to help you now."

She tried to imagine him as a muddled teenager; tried, and failed utterly. "Were you, were you always a Christian, Richard?"

"Always and always."

Good, that fitted. He probably came out of the womb glowing. But, "What," she said, "never any doubts?"

"Oh, sure. Everyone has doubts. But what I found, if you look at the doubts hard enough, you'll find there are certainties underneath. Doubt's just cloud cover. It can't touch the bedrock. Can't damage it." Then, turning easily from the general to the particular, to her: "You haven't got doubts, have you, Rachel?"

"No. Not the way you mean, not about God. About me, maybe."

"Want to talk?"

It was the same invitation her father had made; and that reminded her, gave her an alternative. *Yeah, I'll sic Richard on him, that'll teach him to have secrets . . .*

"You haven't talked to Dad at all, have you?" she asked disingenuously.

"What, about you? Of course not."

"No, not about me. I mean generally, you know . . . "

"Ah. No, I haven't; but he's got something on his mind, hasn't he? It struck me, that he did seem worried."

"I know. He hasn't told us what, though. Me or Mum. Maybe you should ask him, maybe that's what he needs, someone else to talk to. I bet he'd talk to you." *I bet anyone would.*

"Well, maybe. A lot of people do."

And then he cocked his head slightly and lifted an eyebrow in invitation, not letting her change the subject after all. Rachel flinched away from the force of his sea-green gaze, fidgeted with her bedclothes, finally made herself ask.

"How, how's Derry, have you seen him?"

"Yes, I have. He's fine."

"Good. I'm glad. I've been, I don't know, sort of fretting about him. When he didn't come on Thursday, I got worried . . . "

"Nothing to worry about. He'll be there next week."

"So what happened, then, why didn't he come?"

"You won't tell anyone?"

"No, of course not. I promise." And a promise to Richard, she found suddenly, was like a promise to God: fixed and firm and irrevocable.

"He chickened out. Got as far as the chapel door, and didn't have the nerve to walk in."

"Oh." And then, thinking about it, "*Ohh!* Isn't he just the giddy *limit*, that boy?" Stealing one of her mother's favourite phrases, as she had to sometimes to keep her mouth out of trouble.

"It's hard for him, Rachel."

"I know. I know it is. But still. I was really anxious, you know? I thought, I don't know what I thought, but anything could've happened to him, I was sure something had. And he just didn't have the guts to come through the door? . . . Oh, I guess I just don't understand him, that's all."

"Give it time," Richard said, smiling. "Just don't hurry him. You've got years, yet."

"Decades is what Mum says, when she says that. But I hope it doesn't take that long," trying to frown sternly and losing it in a giggle, "I'm not giving him decades. A year or two, maybe, but not decades. No way. There's not enough of him, he's too skinny to deserve decades . . . "

Relief made her stupid, her tongue running on, nothing but nonsense; but Richard put an end to that, by reaching for her bible. He opened it almost at random and read a few verses here, a few there; and they all seemed relevant to Rachel's giddy mind.

Then they prayed a little, and that sobered her entirely. Afterwards, when Richard had kissed her and gone, she lay awake for a while and found that nothing much had changed. Okay, she didn't need to worry any longer about Derry being hurt, being sick or dead or treacherous, and that was good, that was blessed relief; but it only made more space for worrying about herself and Derry, why one chance-met boy should have such a grip on her.

He's just new, that's all. He's new to himself, let alone to me. I've never met anyone like him, I don't suppose there is anyone like him, even; so of course I'm interested. Who wouldn't be? And of course I care. Damn it, why am I giving myself a hard time over this?

116

She scowled, rolled over, hugged her pillow hard and thought, *Tomorrow. Now that I know he's okay, I'll go and see him tomorrow. Mustn't leave it till Thursday, in case he chickens out again. I'll go and lean on him a bit, that's what.*

And thought, *No, better not. Leave it till Thursday, girl, you'll only scare him off; and he needs that youth club. He needs something, anyway, and maybe he can find it there.*

And thought, *No, he won't come. If he backed out once, he'll do it again. It's always harder the second time, always easier to quit. I'll go see him. I'll go tomorrow. Or the day after . . .*

TEN

i

Far and wide the news is spreading, to all four corners of this rolling globe; and from far and wide, from those four corners his people come, when he calls to them. How could they not?

Some he calls by name, whose names he knows. He calls to America for them, and from America in love and faith they come. His uncle's phone bill will be very high this quarter, but he says not to worry; money's coming too, he says, and more will come after. God will provide.

Others who will come he does not know. He writes to their churches and their magazines, he spreads the word; and wherever that word is heard, some people will be called and they will come. He has no doubt of that.

Indeed, the first are here already. Almost every day there's a message, almost every day he goes to the airport or the railway station to meet old friends or new faces. They're young people for the most part, travelling alone or in couples, from Melbourne and Rome and Harare: rucksacks and badges, kisses and laughter and eagerness for the task.

He finds temporary beds for them among the congregation, and sends them out to learn the city, to let the city learn them. One thing is certain, bright and joyous as they are: they will not pass unnoticed.

ii

Jason had been crying, but he'd stopped now.

He'd stopped when George put him in the darkness, where terror walked.

Yesterday he'd been bailed to a hostel until his trial came up. He was under a strict curfew, in by ten every night, no exceptions; and there'd be a load of crap from the hostel workers, counselling and offence awareness and all that garbage. But this was familiar territory, he'd been here before; and at least he was back on home

118

ground again, back in Paradise.

He'd been dead glad to get it, yesterday. He'd have said yes to anything to get out of the remand centre, to have a room of his own and at least a daylight freedom.

Yesterday he'd been cocky, sure of himself, king of the heap.

Today he only wanted to be back inside again, to be safe.

He hadn't got more than fifty metres from the hostel this morning, he hadn't reached the bus-stop before he was picked up. A van pulled into the kerb, the driver's door opened, Vinny Armstrong got out; and Jason almost started crying then, that was enough.

Vinny was about forty, maybe, with grey in his crew-cut and gaps in his teeth, fading tattoos on his scrawny neck and the backs of his restless hands. Vinny worked for George sometimes, and he scared Jason shitless.

"In you get, Jase." Vinny smiled his eternal, crooked smile. "George wants a word with you."

There was a dog in the back of the van, squat and dangerous; but Vinny was enough. You didn't argue with Vinny. Jason got in, let Vinny slam the door on him, hunched up against it and closed his eyes to make this only a dream, if only for a moment.

Then, when they were moving, "What's," he worked the words out slowly, one by one through a dry and clumsy mouth, "what's George want, then, Vinny?"

"Wouldn't know, would I, Jase? Maybe he's got a job for you. Maybe he owes you money. Or he just wants to say welcome back, glad you're out, maybe that's it. *I* don't know."

But his smile called him a liar, his tongue moving over stained and broken teeth said that he knew full well. And Jason knew, too. He hadn't been asking a question, really, only looking for a miracle: looking for someone – anyone, even Vinny – to tell him it was okay, he didn't need to worry.

But he did, of course. He did need to worry. George hadn't just sent him a message, he'd sent Vinny; and that meant Jason needed to be very worried indeed . . .

They parked in the alley behind the gym and went in the back way, down a flight of stone steps and through a fire-door left open. Vinny had a hand locked tight around his elbow and was still smiling, still talking shit. Their footsteps in the corridor set George's dog off with its crazy barking, but they didn't go that far; Vinny steered him into a cleared stockroom, white walls and empty shelving. No windows, not down here.

"What, what now, then?" Jason muttered.

119

"Now we wait for George."

Vinny shoved him hard in the back, sent him staggering across the room; then he leant casually in the doorway, scratching at a tooth with his fingernail.

Jason huddled into the corner, trying to make himself smaller, so small he wasn't even here. Wrapped his arms around his chest, shivered and sweated and waited for George.

Finally George came, walking slow and heavy into the room, pulling the door closed behind him.

"You talk too much, Jason." No games for George, no wasted words. "That's stupid. Vinny, show him how stupid it is."

Vinny nodded, detached himself from the wall and drifted over towards Jason, hands in pockets and that terrible smile on his face. Jason cowered back, tried to push himself all the way into the wall; but a heavy boot swung without warning, hooked around his ankles and sent him sprawling.

He got one hand down in time to break his fall. Vinny stamped on it.

Jason screamed, and scrambled uselessly across the floor. Vinny's boot caught him on the knee, then once and twice in the ribs. By now he was almost at George's feet, almost kneeling; he stared up frantically and said, "Please, George . . . Please . . . "

George just looked at him, said, "Learn your lesson, Jason," and kicked him in the face.

That was all from George, but it was enough. Jason didn't plead any more, certainly didn't try to fight. He curled up on the floor, hugged his head in his hands and took tuition from the feet of a master.

Steel toe-caps there were, on Vinny's boots. They found Jason's spine, his kidneys and his shins; and the lesson was still continuing when the dog went wild again, in the next room. Dimly through his own noises, Jason heard frenzied barking and the sound of claws scrabbling on wood.

And, "Hold it, Vin," he heard that too, George's voice above his head.

Then there was no more kicking, no more pain beyond what he had already, as much as his body could hold of pain. The door opened and closed, he was left alone; but he didn't try to move, he didn't dare. He only lay on the cold concrete shaking and sobbing, choking on his tears.

*

Too soon, the door opened again and George came back.

"Get up, Jason."

"Can't, I can't . . . "

He could, though, with George's foot in his ribs for encouragement. "Get up, I said."

George gripped his arm and dragged him stumbling into the corridor, saying, "I haven't finished with you yet, don't think it's over. But I got someone to see now. So I'm going to put you away till I'm ready for you."

He smiled then, as he took a bunch of keys from their clip on his belt.

"I'm going to put you in with Kyzer," he said softly. "It'll teach you to keep quiet, better than Vinny would, even. It doesn't like strangers on its patch, and it doesn't like noise. So you'd better stop that snivelling."

"No . . . No, George. Please, no . . . "

But George unlocked the door, and bellowed an order as he opened it; pushed Jason through and slammed it, locked it again behind him.

Jason stood pressed against the door, feeling how deeply Kyzer's claws had gouged it. No windows, no light; only a rumbling growl in the blackness, sounds of a heavy body restlessly moving.

Jason inched his way into a corner, crouched down slowly, hugged his knees and stared like a crazy man into the dark; and no, he wasn't crying now. He was hardly breathing, just snatching air in soft gasps and fighting not to choke on the stink of it . . .

iii

Coming up the stairs, George found Vinny in the office, laughing. Vinny smiled all the time, but he rarely laughed; George grunted through the high, hysterical cackle, and said, "What's funny?"

"This kid. Wait till you see him, he's a real freak . . . "

That from the cadaverous Vinny with his angular limbs and his dry and flaking skin, his tattoos and his devil's smile. George had seen children, even the tough children of Paradise scream and run from Vinny in the street.

"Well. Send him in, then. And you see that gear gets off okay, when the truck comes. Check the boxes yourself, and let them know you're checking."

Vinny licked his teeth, nodded wisely. "What about young

Jason?"

"He's not going anywhere." George allowed himself a smile of his own. "I'll finish with him later. My own way. You've done enough. Now let's have that kid in."

Vinny disappeared. George settled himself at his desk and started in on some paperwork, the legitimate business of the gym.

A minute later, there was a tap on the open door.

"Yeah, come in."

He didn't look up yet from his reading, despite a strong curiosity. He read on for a minute, for two minutes; scribbled some marginal notes, shuffled the papers into a pile and set it aside. Then at last he lifted his head, and saw.

Saw a boy who was thinner even than Vinny, skeletally thin, like a refugee from Belsen; and half bald with it, more than half, only the odd straggle of fine hair clinging to his scalp. Saw the nerves on the boy's tense face and in his twisting fingers, and nearly laughed as Vinny had laughed, loud and long. Nearly sent the boy away with a gesture of his hand and a shake of his laughing head, no words necessary.

But he saw something else in the boy too, a desperate eagerness to please; and that in itself pleased George, flattered his sense of power. He relished the taste of it enough to drag this charade out a little longer.

"So you want a job, do you, kid?"

"Yeah." The boy's voice was as tight-drawn as his skin, high and rising. "The receptionist said you might have something . . . "

"Sure, sure. There's always work here, for a willing kid. I like a boy who asks. But, see," taking his time, playing with a pencil on his desk, loving it, "the thing is . . . "

The thing is, this is a gym. It's all about health, and strength. That's what the customers are after, that's what they want to see in the staff. And you look sick, sunshine, you look nigh-on dead with your skull face and your white skin and all the bones of you standing out for counting . . .

And he was close to saying all of that out loud, just to cherish the sight of a dream's dying. But the boy must have read something of it in his face already, because he spoke quickly, said, "I'll work hard. I will. I, I'm stronger than I look."

"I'm sure you are," George said, smiling openly now, lying and letting him see the lie. "That's good, a boy your age, you shouldn't be afraid of hard work. That's not what it's about, though, come right down to it. I can get any number of willing boys." *Got one downstairs right now, he doesn't know it yet but he's going to work his guts out for me, little Jason.* "It's image that counts, a

122

place like this," getting to the point at last, laying it on the line.

"And I don't look right, that's what you're saying, isn't it?" The boy was too young to hide his disappointment, the slouch in his body, the slight turn towards the door as if he wanted to be out and away already, without another word.

"That's it, son. Sorry. Build yourself up a bit, and then maybe, yes; but not now. Tell you what, though," rising to his feet, rounding the desk and dropping a big hand onto the boy's sharp-boned shoulder, "that's our business, see? Helping people get fit, put some flesh on. Come on back to reception, and I'll have Tracey give you three months' free membership. You'll only need to pay for the sessions, and it's cheap for juniors. Put in some of that hard work you were talking about, then come and see me again, all right?"

Some of the clouds faded from the boy's face, as he thought about it. "Well – okay, yeah. Thanks."

"My pleasure." George steered the boy down the corridor. "You been ill, then, or what?"

Surprisingly the question was met with a laugh, almost, a quick snort of amusement. "You could say that, yeah. Sort of shows, doesn't it?"

"Ah, you'll be surprised how quickly you get some weight on if you work at it. You're the right age. Still growing. I'll sort out a routine for you, get you started."

In reception, George watched over the boy's shoulder as he filled out a membership form. He wrote slowly, in awkward, clumsy capitals; but they were legible enough. George read the name and thought, *Derry Bowen. I know that, where've I heard that . . . ?*

Gradually he tracked the memory down. The local paper, a headline story for a day or two, that was it. A miracle cure or some such. Cancer, wasn't it? That made sense, the way the boy looked, just turning back from death's door.

George smiled, put his arm round the boy and said, "Wait a minute, though, son. Maybe I was being hasty back there. Maybe I can find work for you after all."

And never mind Tracey's disbelieving stare, or the boy's caution; George's mind was turning over fast, throwing up possibilities. This had to be worth a follow-up story in the paper, *Miracle boy finds job at local gym. Owner to guide him back to health and strength.* Good human-interest stuff, it might even bring the TV cameras in . . .

"Yeah," he said. "I'm sure I can."

The boy's face twisted between hope and suspicion. "Why,

what's changed? I don't look right, you said . . . "

"That's right, you don't. You look bloody awful. But I'll be straight with you, son, you'll be good publicity for me, see?" The boy did see, he saw it all. His eyes narrowed into a squint, thinking no doubt about the papers, but George went blithely, confidently on. "My customers'll see you the way you are, skinny as shit; they'll see you around all the time, they'll see you working out in the gym, and soon they'll notice you're not so skinny any more. They'll see you toning up, getting some good muscle; and they'll reckon if I can do it for you, I can do it for anyone. That's good business, see? It'll bring them back more often, and their friends too, maybe.

"I'm not talking a regular job, mind. There's not enough work to be worth it," *not with Jason all eager to volunteer. No question, that boy's going to be eager.* "And I can't be doing with all the forms, the tax and National Insurance and that. So it'll just be pocket-money, and free use of the gym. Some of my time too, though, to help you train. I'll sweat you hard; but in six months you'll have a body you can be proud of. You'll have the girls bug-eyed over your biceps. That's worth it, isn't it? That's a good deal?"

The boy relaxed, his mind as easy to read as his childish writing. *He reckons I don't know what I've got here,* George thought cheerfully. *He reckons I'm a bloody dildo . . .*

Well, let him reckon. He'd learn. And meantime he was nodding, smiling, "Yeah, that's good. That's terrific, Mr Jenner."

"Right, then. You can start now," checking the time, deciding he could take an hour. The paperwork would keep; and so would Jason, of course. Jason would definitely keep. "Derry Bowen, is it? Welcome aboard, Derry. Tracey, take Derry into the shop and fit him out. T-shirts, shorts. Sweatshirt, tracksuit. Club gear, mind, with the logo on. And some decent trainers. Don't thank me, kid," smilingly, "you can pay it off at a fiver a week. Tracey'll keep a record. Trade prices, though, I don't look for a profit off my staff. And it's good gear. Get kitted up, and I'll see you in the gym in ten minutes. Oh, and give the lad a towel too, Trace. He'll need a shower, after."

iv

" . . . And His banner over me is love,
His banner over me is love . . . "

The chorus ended with a long strumming chord on the guitars, with a dozen voices singing high and clear, with a dozen arms uplifted, a dozen fingers pointing skyward, one way to God.

Ingrid looked around her as she slowly lowered her arm, as she felt the music leave her throat, her tongue, her heart. The music left, but not the joy; and she saw that same joy mirrored all around her on the faces of half a dozen different nationalities, one family.

"Please don't go away, ladies and gentlemen." That was Andreas the Greek boy, talking to the small crowd that had gathered. "We'll sing again in a little while. But now, if you have the time and the interest to listen, we would like to talk to you individually about what Jesus has done for us in our lives, and what he can do for you, the same things."

Bengt touched her hand lightly as the choir began to separate, and one finger linked itself loosely with his, without her even thinking about it.

Bengt had been her travelling companion from Stockholm, a brother member of her church. On the journey he had become a friend, a good friend; and now, perhaps, he was becoming something more than either brother or friend. Her eyes traced the sunlight in his pale hair, and there was a pleasing tingle in her spine, a little shiver on her skin as his grip tightened.

"Come," he said, in Swedish; his English was less happy than hers. "There are people here waiting to hear our witness."

"Yes – but separately, Bengt," and she disengaged herself with a wry, reluctant shrug. "One to one, yes? Two to one is uncomfortable for them, and inefficient for us. Unproductive," with a giggle. "A waste of resources. Yes?"

He nodded and turned away abruptly. Ingrid saw the stiffness in his slim shoulders, and bit her lip fretfully. Witness to strangers was never easy, however deep your commitment; for Bengt it was doubly hard, in a language that could make his tongue stumble, could sometimes abandon him altogether.

She called after him, softly and in Swedish again: "Ben, God will give you the words."

He half-turned his head in acknowledgement, lifted a hand and let it fall again.

She stood where she was, watching while he approached a young man on the fringes of the crowd; she watched until he seemed to be deep in conversation, only an occasional frustrated gesture to show when a word had escaped him.

Satisfied, she turned quickly, apologetically to her own duty, her own witness. Moved among the dispersing crowd handing out

125

leaflets until she found a woman willing to listen, who might be willing to talk.

Ingrid was comfortable in half a dozen languages, fluent in English; it was a gift she was constantly grateful for. Comfortably, fluently she talked about Jesus, about rebirth and the safe promise of salvation; and she broke off only once, and only for a moment. Only for long enough to register that Richard had joined them unexpectedly, that he was just a few metres away speaking to a red-haired girl.

Ingrid closed her eyes briefly, against the soul-shaking warmth of simply being close to Richard. And suppressed it sternly, reminded herself that she had a mission here that neither a budding love nor a gloriously flowering hero-worship could be allowed to distract her from, turned back to the woman and her questions, her doubts, her seeking hunger. Told her about the big meeting on Saturday, in the marquee they'd hired because the chapel wasn't anywhere near big enough; and was sure or almost sure that she would come.

v

"You going to that youth club, then, or not?"

"Oh, Mam, give us a break. I'm shattered . . . "

"Shattered this week, is it? Something else last time, I forget what. If you don't want to go, I wish you'd just say so straight, and stop making promises to Richard."

Okay. I don't want to go. But he didn't say so, he only scowled at the unfairness of it all. Because it was true, he was shattered. He was weary to his very bones, lying stretched out on the sofa the way he had so often before, so many months. His legs were aching cruelly, but not alone now; his arms ached the same way, and all the muscles of his back, almost all the muscles in his body. He'd worked for that aching, he'd sweated for it; and he cherished it for the promises that came with it. *No pain, no gain,* that's what Mr Jenner said; and Derry would put up with any amount of pain, in a good cause. That's what he was best at, after all. He'd had the experience.

But the other was true too, that he had promised Richard he'd go tonight. And it wasn't fair of his mother to fling that at him so scornfully. Things had changed, since he'd made that promise.

"I've got a job now," he reminded her sullenly. "I've been working."

126

She only snorted. She didn't believe the depths of his exhaustion, and never would; and in the face of that disbelief, his pride gave him no alternative.

He pushed himself to his throbbing feet with a grunt, almost a groan; picked up his jacket and said, "All right, I'm going, see me? See me go?"

He walked slowly down towards the chapel – as slow as when he'd first got his legs back, that unbelievable gift to an unbeliever – dwelling on every twinge in his protesting body, not to dwell on other things. He turned a corner and the chapel was in sight now, just a hundred metres down the hill; and that was a bit too near, a bit too close for comfort, so he sat down on a handy wall to think about it.

Lit a cigarette, to help him concentrate; and had just flicked the match in a high flaring arc towards the gutter when he saw a movement, down in the shadows by the chapel porch.

Saw the slender figure of a girl come through the fence, come striding up the hill towards him.

No question who it was, though he couldn't see her face at this distance in the uncertain light. His mouth tightened momentarily; then he shrugged, and took a deep drag on the cigarette. No point running away, she'd only come after him. Catch him, too. She was taller, faster for sure tonight, probably stronger. *Not for long, though,* he thought, cheered by the memory of his sufferings in the gym. That was one reason he'd thrown himself into it so enthusiastically. One of the better reasons, to be stronger than Rachel, to find some ground where he could meet and outmatch her.

But he wasn't there yet, not by a long way. Not even strong enough to meet her eyes as she stood in front of him now, hands on her hips and glaring, snapping at him: "What the *hell* do you think you're doing, Derry Bowen?"

That was a surprise, to hear her swearing; twice so, to have her coming on so mad, right out of the blue. Last time she'd kissed him; now she looked ready to belt him one.

"What? I'm just sitting here, I was coming down in a minute, what's the hurry?"

"Not that. You're *smoking*, you cretin!"

"Yeah, I am." And he smiled his old bitter, certain smile, and said, "Why not? It can't hurt me, I've already . . . "

And stopped with no certainty at all, remembering.

"No, you haven't," she said, quieter now but just as forceful. "You haven't got cancer any more; but that doesn't mean you

127

can't get it. You're not immune. So put that bloody thing out," doing it herself, whisking it from his fingers and crushing it under her heel, grinding it into the pavement, "and don't let me catch you with another one, got it? Not ever."

Sometime, maybe, he'd be able to stand up to her in this mood; sometime he'd tell her that she didn't have the right to make rules for him, it was his life. Sometime when he was stronger, maybe. If he got the muscle on his body, maybe he'd get it in his mind, too.

But tonight he just shrugged, pulled the pack of ten from his pocket and said, "Here, you want to stomp on these too?"

She was actually reaching for them, "You bet," before she checked; before she looked at him, and groaned.

"I'm doing it again, aren't I?"

He nodded, grinning at the dismay on her face.

"Oh, glory. I'm sorry, Derry. Here." And she did take the cigarettes; but only to put them back into his jacket pocket, to button the flap carefully and give it a little pat, *there. Home safe and hands off, Rachel.* "It's your life, they're your fags. Do what you want with them."

What he felt inclined to do was take them out again and hurl them far and wide, to win a smile; but he didn't do that. Tabs cost money, and he might want them later. He might want to light up in front of her, just to assert himself next time she got bossy. So he only nodded, and left them where they were.

"What next, then? Are you coming down, or what?"

Derry pushed himself to his feet. "Yeah, I guess. What's happening?"

"Don't ask me. I haven't been inside since I got here, except for a minute to say hullo."

And she gave him a teasing glance, daring him to ask why not. He didn't, though. He thought he knew. *I've been hanging around,* he thought she'd say, *in case a certain person got this far and lost his nerve again.*

So instead, "I've got a job," he said. "At the gym, just down the hill a bit from here."

And earned his smile and more, earned himself a hug.

"Derry, that's terrific!" with an arm still round his waist, tugging him on down the street. "Wait till Richard hears, he'll be so pleased. What do you do, then, what's the job?"

"Just dogsbody," he said, shrugging. "Sweep the floors, clean the bogs out, fetch and carry for the boss. Hard work, lousy pay. Not a proper job at all, really, just to keep me busy." He didn't mention all the training he'd be doing on the side. He'd rather wait, see how long it took her to notice. Something to surprise her

128

with, he was looking forward to that.

The chapel was more crowded than Derry had expected; and as he had been at the beach party, he was surprised by some of the faces he saw. Albie was there for one thing, and ignorance no excuse this time, he knew what he was getting himself into.

They'd stacked all the chairs up at one end of the hall, and now they were looking with varying degrees of unbelief at a massive pile of folded cardboard.

"Best quality boxes, these would have been," Richard was assuring them, laughing. "And the tape's waterproof — but no, you can't cover the whole boat with tape. One roll per team, and that's your lot. Use as much cardboard as you like, though. And there's string too, if anyone wants string."

"*Boat?*" Rachel murmured in his ear.

"Derry!" Albie was waving violently. "Come on, we need one more. Teams of four . . . "

"Um . . . " He gestured at Rachel, *there's two of us*, or meant to; but when he looked she was gone, claimed by a bunch of giggling girls.

So he joined Albie, and two lads he didn't know; and "What are we supposed to be doing, then, what was that about boats?"

"That's what we're doing. Building a boat."

"Out of *cardboard?*"

"Richard says it works. Well, he says it works sometimes. If you get the design right. We're going to race them on Sunday, across the lake in the park. Bring a towel, he said."

"I bet."

"You'll have to be the jockey," Albie said. "You're the lightest."

"Terrific."

"Tell you what I reckon," from one of the other lads. "I reckon string's the secret. He wouldn't have said string, unless it helped. See, if we make a sort of boat shape," he drew with his finger on the wax-polished floor, "and then run a couple of lengths of string from the front, good and tight, it'll help to keep the nose up . . . "

Then they were off, sketching and scribbling, building and tearing apart and building again; and Richard had to do more than cough politely, had to take Derry's arm and pull him aside simply in order to get noticed.

"Rachel tells me you've found yourself a job."

Typical, that was. She couldn't leave it for him to tell, could she? Derry tried to summon up a little resentment, and failed. It was just Rachel, that was all.

They talked about the job for a minute or two; then Derry looked around the packed hall, all the kids laughing and squabbling and showing off like they did anywhere, any time, and he asked the question that had been building slowly in the back of his mind all evening. "When does the religious bit start, Richard? Straight up?"

"When you lot want it to," Richard said, smiling. "When you're ready."

Derry wasn't satisfied with that. He didn't try to chase Richard any harder; but later he found Rachel quietly alone and asked her the same question.

"It has started, you dimwit. Look," and she nodded over to where people were sharing out cokes and packets of crisps. "It says in the Bible, we're supposed to feed the hungry."

"Seriously, I mean."

"I am being serious. It's not all sermons and singing hymns, Derry. That's what this is for, I reckon; to show you that it's not."

He thought about that for a minute, said, "Does that make me a Christian, then, if I go over and get you some of them crisps?"

Rachel laughed. "No, that just makes you a minor hero. A *major* hero, if you can scrounge a can as well. We'll split it."

"Hey, Rich, man!" One of the girls, shrieking across the room. "Can we have a disco next time? If we bring some tapes?"

"Not here, you can't. The chapel elders won't allow it."

"*Bor*ing!"

"Be patient with them, love. As soon as I fix up somewhere bigger to meet, I promise, you can have your disco. If I can have the first dance. Date?"

Jeers and wolf-whistles; and a man walking into the middle of it, a man who had Rachel up on her feet and waving in a moment. The same man Derry had seen claiming her before.

"Got to go, that's my dad."

"Oh. Okay. 'Bye, then . . . "

Their eyes met; then her toe dug hard into his hip. "Get up, you lazy so-and-so. Come and meet him."

"I dunno, Rachel . . . "

"I do. Up."

That toe again, and an arm reaching down to help, surprising strength in her as she hauled him to his feet.

Derry shuffled after her through the crowded room, hands in pockets, dying of shy; through the porch and out into the evening, where her father stood waiting by his big Volvo.

"Dad, look, this is Derry Bowen . . . "

"Oh. Yes, of course. Hullo."

"Er, hi, Mr . . . " Derry couldn't remember Rachel's surname, and blushed furiously in the dark. Didn't know if the guy would want to shake hands or what, brought his hand halfway out of his pocket in case; but he needn't have bothered, because Rachel's father had already turned his back.

"In you get, Rachel. Quickly, please."

Derry stood motionless, barely noticing Rachel's sudden stiffening, the way she turned to him, the helpless little shrug before she climbed into the car. He watched her father move round to the driver's side without another glance in his direction; watched the car disappear and still didn't move, still couldn't.

When he could, when he did, he reached for his cigarettes first thing. Nothing automatic about it, this was deliberate. He took one out and lit it defiantly, *so much for you, Rachel What's-your-name, and so much for your sodding father.*

It sounded like there was a sudden riot going on in the chapel behind him, but he didn't even turn his head. He was gone from there, utterly gone. Raging silently, he started down the hill towards the gym, towards the river; and knackered or not, there was a long, long walk between here and going home.

ELEVEN

i

His teams are assembling, his people are active, eager as hounds on the scent; they feel the thrill of possibilities, they feel God's hand upon this city.

But they all look to him for guidance, for leadership; and he can't be everywhere at once, even he has limits. He's only human, after all. Or so he says.

What he needs most of all now is a lieutenant, someone to rely on. He needs to delegate; but he has to find the right person, that's crucial. Enthusiasm is not enough.

There's no one among the elders at the chapel, he's quite clear about that; nor among the regular congregation there. Nor, so far, among the newcomers, the strangers who've been drawn to him and his work. Ideally he wants someone local, who knows Paradise and the ways of its people; and he'd prefer someone young. The strength and hope of any city lies in its youth, he says that often. His primary mission is always to the young.

So he prays, and he waits, and watches always for an answer to prayer: for the one boy or girl who can take something of his burden from him. He's a visionary, and his vision is explicit; but he's going to need help to turn that vision into a physical reality, a new Jerusalem, the wonder of the age.

ii

Mrs Patel looked at the two men sitting opposite her, the young lion and the old fretful monkey; and she shook her head in confusion. In the ten years since her husband died she'd learned a lot about the buying and selling of property, but she couldn't recall any offer quite so strange as this.

"Let me see it clearly," she said, addressing herself to the young one who'd done all the talking. "You are wanting to make me an offer for some houses belonging to my company, on Cockburn Grove by the river."

"That's correct."

"But these houses, they are almost worthless. They are not habitable, except for one. Only the land has a value."

"That's probably true, yes."

"And you are aware that I am in discussion with a private developer who wishes to buy the property, who has the approval of the council for a business park on the land, the houses of course to be demolished?"

"Yes, we know that. And we're not trying to cheat you, Mrs Patel. We don't want to buy the property from you and then sell it on at a profit. It's the houses we want, as they stand."

She believed him. She knew dishonesty now, when she met it; and there was no trace of it in him, look though she might, though she did. But still she couldn't understand.

"You do realise that if I sell you these houses and their land, that will not stop it? The council will make out a compulsory purchase order, and take the houses from you. Perhaps for less than you have paid me."

"Yes," he said again, greatly patient. "We know that, too."

"But nevertheless . . . ?"

"Nevertheless," he agreed. "We still want to go ahead with this. It's very important to us."

Mrs Patel frowned, tapping a finger lightly on her desk. "Tell me, then. Why should I sell to you, rather than the other?"

"For profit, for good business. The developer may be making you a fair offer, but he can afford not to be generous; as you say, the property has almost no value, and if you're stubborn he can rely on the council to force a purchase through. We can't do that, so we have to be generous. Get the best offer you can, and we'll give you ten per cent more."

She looked at him appraisingly, and at the other, the unhappy man; and said, "Tell me why. I cannot understand this, and I will not do it unless I understand."

The blond man returned her gaze, her assessment; and nodded. "That's fair enough. Arthur?"

The older man didn't lift his eyes from his twisting fingers. "Aye. You tell her, Richard, if you think it's right. Jack wouldn't mind."

So Mrs Patel heard a story that morning, the history of her last surviving tenants in Cockburn Grove; and at the end she understood only a little better than she had before. It was only sentiment, surely, that was leading them to make this offer. Sentiment had no place in business. It would cost them a good deal of money and to no good purpose, only to buy a few months' delay

133

of the inevitable.

But to refuse them, only for their own good – that too would be sentimental.

"Fifteen," she said. "Fifteen per cent above the best offer."

And the young man stretched his hand across the desk, to shake hers in acceptance.

iii

Domenico Santori might have been born and bred in Paradise, he might have left home at seventeen and have felt nothing but relief at the leaving, he might be a single man with no intention of changing that happy state; but still he was Italian at heart, and still he had all his forefathers' attachment to the idea, the dream of family.

Which was why he'd called this meeting in the school hall tonight; why he'd spent the last week leafleting every house in the district; why he felt a sense of bitter disappointment, looking at the rows of empty seats, the few people who'd bothered to turn up. There was only one face he hadn't seen before, a blond guy sitting over to the side looking alert and interested – and thank God for that, for a bit of interest. The rest of them here were protest junkies or politicos with their own hobby-horses to ride, only looking for a bandwagon to jump on.

Even his friends weren't here this time. Fair enough, they heard him ranting on all the time at work or down the club. But where were the locals? It was this community that was being threatened – didn't the people *care*?

The trouble was, he knew the answer to that, he'd learned it long ago. If they cared, they didn't care enough. Or else they were simply disillusioned. So many battles, so little achieved. Domenico was getting pretty disillusioned himself, come to that.

Still, the fight had to go on. That was the crucial thing: to call meetings and organise marches, to write letters and gather petitions. To keep it all visible and to keep trying, not to let the bastards grind you down . . .

So Domenico pushed himself to his feet, faced the long hall with its pathetic scattering of people and lifted his hands to still the whisper of too few voices.

"Thanks for coming tonight, everyone. Not many of us here, I'm afraid; but still, it's a start. Or a new start, I should say, the campaign's been running for years. It's only circumstances have

134

changed. And Jesus did it all with twelve disciples, so we don't need to give up hope yet, right? Tell you what would help, though, if you could all come closer, up to the front here, so I don't have to shout . . . "

Mutterings, slow stirrings; Domenico stood patiently waiting, making it clear that he wasn't going on with his spiel until the last stragglers had moved at least a few seats forward.

"Okay. Well, I'm Domenico Santori, and I'm the chair" – at present the sole surviving committee member, but no need to mention that yet – "of the Paradise Community Action Group. You all know what this meeting's about; but if you'll bear with me I'll summarise the situation as I see it, and bring you up to date with developments. Things have moved on since our last public meeting, and I'm sorry to tell you it isn't looking good.

"The news is that planning permission for the business park is sure to go through now, and work could start in just a few months' time. Everything's settled, as far as the council's concerned; there's funding from the government and the EC, and they're satisfied with the private finance arrangements. But once they start, they're not going to stop. I've seen the proposals: new roads, a new bridge, they're talking total redevelopment.

"Now, you might think that all this has got to be good for Paradise. It'll bring plenty of money into the area, plenty of jobs during the construction and after.

"It's a fair argument, that; but it's not the whole story. It doesn't take any account of Paradise as a community. That's how I see us, as a community, as a family; and that's how come I'm so concerned about this whole deal. They're not doing it for us, Paradise is only a word on a map to them; and the roads they're talking about will chop Paradise into pieces. Whole streets are going to be demolished, to make way for them. Maybe you'll be one of the lucky ones, maybe you won't lose your own house; but your mother might lose hers, or your uncle or your grandad. Someone you know, that's for sure. And these streets of ours, they're like extended families, people look out for their next-door neighbours and their kin up the road. All that's going to be lost. There are no plans to resettle people together with their friends and relatives. The unlucky ones are going to end up scattered right across the city.

"That's bad enough, but it's not the end of it. There are five schools in this neighbourhood; chances are, there'll suddenly be a dual carriageway between you and the school your kids go to. How are you going to feel about that? Okay, there'll be foot-bridges over; but do you trust your kids to use a footbridge when all their mates are playing chicken with the traffic? There's going to be accidents, there's going to be kids killed on those roads.

"Now you may say there's nothing you or I can do, it's all out of our hands now. They held their public meetings, we protested then, we did everything we could; and the first stage has still got through, and all the rest will follow. Maybe that's right, maybe we can't stop them. But we can still try. Even if we fail, I think it's important. I think we've got to try. We've got to tell them they've got their priorities all wrong. Housing and hope, that's what we need in Paradise, not more traffic and more dead kids . . . "

So Domenico talked, and others. There were contributions as well as questions from the floor; there were nominations to the committee, there were officials elected *ad hoc* and *pro tem*. Domenico smiled, and congratulated, and thanked; but inwardly he only sighed. He'd been down this road so often before, often enough with these self-same people on his committees and action groups – and they just weren't enough, they'd never be enough.

He closed the meeting at last, arranging for the committee to meet at his house in a fortnight; and he was ushering the people out, keys in his hand ready to lock up, when the stranger, the blond guy touched his arm.

"My name's Richard Gould," the stranger said. "I'm not known here, so I didn't put myself forward for your committee; but I agree with the stand you're taking, and I'd like to stay in touch. I'm with the Pentecostal Chapel, just up the road. You can always contact me there."

A religious freak, Domenico thought, from the depths of his private depression. *There's always one.*

But the man smiled, and said, "I think we can help, you see. I'm sure we can."

And somehow that smile made Domenico smile too. It spoke of family, of community; and it was so assured, so confident that he found himself feeling hopeful for the first time that evening, the first time in many long months.

iv

"This money . . . "

Arnold Saltley had always been the chapel's treasurer. In the early days he'd begged donations and materials for its construction; he'd counted and meticulously recorded every penny of the

Sunday collections for forty years and more, sending all they could spare to their preferred missions overseas.

He'd taken his responsibilities seriously, he'd been a precise and careful steward of their meagre funds; but in all that time he'd never worried, he'd never lost a night's sleep over the accounts.

Now, though – now he worried, now he didn't sleep. Now he only had to think about money, he only had to play with the coins in his pocket to be left suddenly cold and shaking and afraid.

"This money," he said, pushing at the account-books with nervous fingers, "what are we going to *do* with all this money?"

They were in the back room of the chapel, the six Council members and Richard; and only Richard smiled now, only Richard spoke.

"Don't worry about it, Arnold," he said.

"How can I help but worry? It's, it's offensive, sums like this coming to us, when so much of the world is in want. There's more comes in every day, cheques from all over, all over the *world*, and we don't need any of it. And I'm responsible, and I don't know what to do with it all . . . "

"Reason not the need," Richard said quietly. "There are people in need and in want here, as much as anywhere in the world. God will show us the need, when he's ready; and when he does, we'll spend the money. That's what it's for, Arnold. It's what you've always done, isn't it, spent what you received on the Lord's work? I know this is more than you're used to dealing with, but so will the expenses be. There's the hire of the marquee, don't forget, that's not cheap; we've only paid the deposit so far, and I can see us using that for six months or more. It's a mobile chapel, effectively; we can take it anywhere. Other towns, out into the villages – the people won't have to come to us any longer, we can go to them."

"One thing at a time," Arthur said, making a quieting gesture with his hands. "Let's get next week over, before we look ahead. That marquee's chancy, Richard. What if no one comes?"

"They'll come. We'll fill it. They'll be standing in the aisles."

Jean stirred in her corner seat. "'Pride goeth before destruction, and an haughty spirit before a fall.'"

"The Lord won't let us fall, Jean, we're on His work. Have faith."

"Oh, I've faith in plenty. It's ambition I'm short of."

"We have to be ambitious for the Lord."

"Aye. Not for ourselves, though. Not to hurry Him along to reap glory for ourselves. Every time I hear you, Richard, you're talking bigger, you're looking for more. How much of it is God's

137

guidance, that's what I want to know; how much of it is His plan and how much of it is yours? He's not spoken to me about travelling with a tent."

This was an old argument, a confrontation that flared up whenever it saw the chance. But Richard always ducked it, consummate politician that he was, never gave fuel to the fire.

"Of course," he said, "you mustn't do anything more than you feel called to, Jean. Each of us has our own role to play. Your mission is to Paradise alone, I think we all understand that."

Jean subsided momentarily, and Arnold seized his chance.

"That marquee?" he said. "That's nothing. We could *buy* that marquee, and not notice. What's it all for, Richard? It's your doing, that we've got all this . . . "

"No. My contacts, perhaps, but not my doing. People have heard, that's all; they hear what's happening, and they want to help. They're led to it, yes, but not by me. Don't be so anxious, Arnold. The purpose will become clear, at the right time."

Arthur grunted, said, "I think this is the right time, Richard. They've got to be told, what we agreed the other day. We can't keep secrets."

"No. Perhaps you're right." Richard seemed to hesitate briefly, his eyes on Jack Dubrowski; then he said, "Well, then. One use we've found, for some of the money. We're going to buy those houses down on Cockburn Grove."

There was silence for a moment, acknowledging the bombshell qualities of the news; then everyone spoke at once.

"What for?"

"How much?"

"What about the council?"

And Jack's voice, rising over the babble, cutting through it, sharp and angry: "*No!*"

They all fell quiet again, granting his anger precedence; and he said no again, said, "No. Thank you, but no. That would not be a proper use, for money given to God. Anita and I, we will find another way, a new home somewhere. We will need help, perhaps, we would be glad of your good help; but not like this."

"You're wrong, Jack." Richard wasn't smiling, for once; he was grave, motionless, magnetic. "For many reasons. I can understand your reaction, but you're not seeing clearly. This isn't a charitable exercise. Helping you is only a happy side-effect. I've been hoping to find some cheap property in the area, and those houses are just about perfect."

"What for? You cannot use them, they are nothing. Empty, useless . . . "

138

"No. They're run-down, they need work; but who better than us, to do that work? We've got builders in the congregation, we can get any number of volunteers to help. You know that, it's how you built this place. Fixing up some derelict houses is small beer, next to that. And think of the value of it, as a symbol. What better way to revitalise a community than to be seen renewing its houses, making them fit to live in?"

"I don't understand. Who is to live in them?"

"Well, I will, for a start. I can't depend on Ted's hospitality forever. And we need somewhere for these kids who are coming over for the mission. They're crashing on people's floors at the moment, but that can't go on all summer; I'd like to give them a base to work from, where they can all be together."

Jack subsided, but only for Alan Parkinson to step in with another argument.

"Aye, but Cockburn Grove's the wrong place for it. It's to be knocked down, so what's the point?"

"That is the point. If we want to help this community, we have to be seen giving a lead; and I think the council's plans are where we start. There won't be a community left, if all that development goes ahead. We can fight it, but we need ground to fight on. Cockburn Grove could be that ground. The people will get behind us, if they see us turning waste and rubble into good houses; it'll be our flagship and our rallying-cry."

Alan shook his head, savagely. "This is a chapel, not a, not a political platform. It's not our business to be fighting the council."

"I think it is, when the council is threatening the people we serve. We can't pick and choose, Alan; we can't preach the king-dom of God on earth, and then sit back and watch it being destroyed around us. I don't think it's any coincidence that God's giving us this opportunity now, when Paradise is so much under threat. His timing is immaculate, always."

Alan looked disposed to argue further; but Richard's own timing was never faulty. He glanced at his watch, and got smoothly to his feet.

"I'm sorry, I have to go. The city ecumenical committee is compiling a report on urban poverty and ways to tackle it, and they've asked me to sit in on a couple of meetings . . . "

After he was gone:

"Ecumenical committees, is it now?" sourly, from Jean Dolance. "And to look into poverty, of all things. That man should read his Bible. Doesn't he know that poverty's a blessing?"

"It's also a blessing to help the poor," Arthur said mildly.

"Not the idle, there's no blessing in that. But that's beside the point. The point is, here's Richard taking yet more on himself; and taking this chapel's name with him without our consent, without consultation, even. We've never had to do with other churches in this town, and for good reasons. They teach a corrupt doctrine. He'll be mixing our name with that corruption, with the idolaters of Rome, even; and what I want to know is, is there no end to this?"

"There's never an end to God's work, Jean."

"Nor any end to Richard's, seemingly. It's where to divide them, that's what worries me . . . "

v

At last, Helen heard what she'd been waiting for: the living-room door, feet in the passage, voices murmuring. Nat's laughter.

She put down the book she hadn't been reading, got to her feet and stood patiently in the bedroom doorway, while people wheeled their stacked bicycles out into the street; smiled at their leaving, wished them a polite goodnight.

Nat had gone outside with someone, not yet tired of talking. Helen sighed, went through to the abandoned living-room and began to collect their empty mugs.

She was in the kitchen, running hot water for the washing-up, when he finally came through to find her.

She glanced at him over her shoulder, trying to gauge his mood; saw the contentment in him and relaxed. It had gone well, then. But still, he'd expect her to ask.

"Good meeting?"

"Excellent. We made a lot of progress, I think."

That meant he'd persuaded the others round to his point of view, whatever it was they were discussing. She smiled and bent over the sink, letting her hair fall down to mask the smile.

"You shouldn't be doing that, it's our mess." His hands made no effort to move her aside, though; they only settled on her waist, fingers sliding under the waistband of her jeans, thumbs working lightly at the muscles of her back.

She shivered, shook her head. "I don't mind."

And she didn't, of course; that was the triumph of it, and the tragedy. His triumph, perhaps, her tragedy; or perhaps nothing so clear-cut, only another bright and clamorous truth. She didn't look for gratitude, not ever, she wasn't that naïve. Simple

140

approval was enough. It brought its rewards, a smile or a nod or — as now — the touch of him, his long body pressed against her while his hands teased and wandered, while he talked.

"We've got a conference coming up in a couple of months. Just a few days. I'm going, of course, but I think you should come with me."

She would, then, if he wanted her to. No question. Never mind that politics bored her, even when she understood it; never mind that she didn't understand one word in three, when Nat got together with his radical comrades. It would be another opportunity to touch his life, to watch what she couldn't share.

"Please," she said. "I'd like to."

And with the mugs washed and draining, she turned round into his hug, her reward.

Soon afterwards, back in the bedroom and nestled into the warmth, the possessive strength of him:

"You'll be here for the weekend, then," he said. An assumption, a prediction; not an invitation.

"If you don't mind . . . "

"I don't mind."

"Oh, good." Pleasure and relief, sighed out gently against his chest; then a swift breath in, remembering, forcing herself to say it now, say it fast. "There's something I want to go to, though, Saturday evening. So don't you, don't you put anything off for my sake . . . "

He chuckled. "I won't," he said; which she'd known in any case. He never did. "But what is it, what's the big attraction?"

What gets priority over me? his hands asked, drumming against her spine, demanding an answer; and thank heaven for his easy mood tonight, or the question would have been put more urgently, might even have come as a statement, a law new-minted against rebellion, *nothing gets priority over me*.

She shifted uncomfortably, and mumbled into his shoulder.

"It's just, I met this bloke in town; and he's, he's not like anyone I've ever *met* before, Nat, and . . . "

"Wait a minute." His hands were still now as his body was still, only his ribs moving under her, breathing slow and quiet and controlled. "What bloke, what are you talking about?"

"Oh, not like that. Though he's very attractive," finding space for a giggle even within these tight walls, this dangerous conversation. "But that's not sex, there's nothing sex about him, really. It's all charisma. He's with those Christians who've been hanging around the town centre, these last weeks."

141

"Uh-huh. So, you met this Christian. What about him, then?"

"Well, I . . . I want to hear what he's got to say, that's all. There's something, I don't know what it is, a light in his eyes or something, a sort of joy that surrounds him . . . I don't believe in God, you know that, but whatever this guy's got, it seems to work. And I'm, I suppose I'm curious."

"So? Where does Saturday evening come into this?"

"They're having a meeting, just down the road from here. On that field opposite the school, they've put up a marquee. And I want to go." She waited, got no response; finally said, "You don't, you don't mind, do you?"

"Mind? Why should I mind? It's your soul, sweetheart. You want to get it scrubbed down or whatever, that's your choice. Nothing to do with me."

Which was nonsense, of course, he could have stopped her with a word. So, "Thanks," she said, meaning it deeply.

He laughed, and stroked the back of her neck. "My pleasure. Tell you what, if this guy's so amazing, maybe I'll come too. I've got my share of curiosity. How's about that, then?"

Truth to tell, Helen wasn't at all sure how she felt about that. She'd set Saturday night aside as a time of private pilgrimage, separated from her regular life, entirely separate from Nat; it wouldn't be the same with him beside her, sharp and cynical and mocking. But then, any changes in her life would have to encompass Nat, or they simply wouldn't happen; and in any case, this wasn't a time for telling the truth.

"That'd be wonderful . . . "

"Right, then. That's settled. Saturday night, we give ourselves over to the missionaries. Tonight, though, I'm still a cannibal."

And his teeth clamped hard on her ear.

TWELVE

i

Times like this, times of great potential, when he can feel the groundswell rising and rising and ready to break – these are the times when he yearns for wilderness. When he wants to leave the people and the promises, and walk away.

Or so he says, laughing, accusing himself, making it impossibly hard to believe.

He wouldn't be the first, mind you. Even Jesus took his forty days' worth. Call it quality time, a better way to take the phone off the hook. On that level, it's easy to understand: just a little passing isolation, a temporary peace. Rocks and sand and a blinding, burning sky, the chance to be alone with his God, to restore his soul under a desert sun.

Not to run, not to evade his responsibilities. Surely, never that.

And he can't get it anyway, the option isn't there. No available desert, and no time. The best he can manage are those long, solitary walks at night, where he doesn't come in till dawn sometimes.

Ask him where he's been, and he'll say he was out on the town moor, walking on grass and good earth under the stars.

Ask him if he knows the stars, and he'll say no. Not the constellations, he'll say. What he knows is the hand that set them there, that studded the sky with pattern.

Ask him if he doesn't want company, and he'll laugh and say no, that's the last thing he wants. He's got the best company in the world, he'll say, what would he want with more?

ii

Saturday evening: and Rachel stood outside the giant marquee, chewing on a pasty and watching the sky worriedly. It was early yet, more than an hour to go; and the weather was turning sour already, hot and heavy, with thick clouds blotting out the light.

What are you up to, then, big J? What's with all this? First time we've seen a cloud for weeks . . .

A hand closed suddenly, firmly on her neck; she choked, swallowed, turned to find Richard there like an answer to prayer, even if the prayer had only been a grumble.

"What are you up to, kid?"

"Fretting." With a flick of her eyes upward.

Richard didn't even glance at the sky. "Don't fret."

"What if the rain starts? No one's going to come in the rain."

"They'll come. Believe it."

She sighed, smiled. It was hard not to smile, this close to Richard. "I'll believe *you*."

"Well. That'll do. How's the voice?"

"Tired." She'd spent all day in town, she and dozens of others: singing and giving out leaflets, talking to anyone who'd listen. "I'll be okay, though, once I get a drink."

"There are Cokes in the tent there. Help yourself."

"Yeah, right."

"Then find yourself a corner and relax a little. You're too tense, you can't sing if you're all wired up."

"It's the weather, that's all . . . "

"No, it isn't," he said, his strong hand shaking her lightly, side to side. "It's a big night and you've got stage fright. Confess."

"That's supposed to be a secret."

"I don't allow secrets. And by the way, you've also got half your dinner sticking to your face."

His hand released her neck, to brush lightly at the corner of her mouth. She wanted to kiss his fingers, wanted to bite them hard; and did neither, of course, only flounced away into the marquee, tossing her head indignantly at his pursuing laughter.

*　　　*　　　*

Alan Parkinson stood with Jean Dolance and her children deliberately to one side of the marquee, no part of the action.

There were six hundred chairs in this canvas cathedral, with Richard's young disciples moving along the rows, laying out songsheets and pamphlets; and Jean was almost smiling as she said, "He'll never fill it."

"No."

"He will, though," Lisa said defiantly. "Just wait. You don't want him to, but he will."

"Be quiet, Lisa," from her mother; and when the girl only shrugged in response. "And stand up straight. I won't have you slouching. It's disrespectful to Mr Parkinson, and disrespectful to me."

144

"*I* don't slouch," Luther said primly from her other side, stiff-backed and straight-shouldered, standing four-square and triumphant to a wicked world. "Do I, Mother?"

"I should hope not. But your tie's crooked, and one of your socks has slipped. Tidy yourself up, please."

Lisa smirked, as her younger brother fidgeted with his clothing. Alan turned away, hearing his name called; and saw Ted and Arthur struggling with a long trestle table.

"Give us a hand, Alan lad," Ted said. "We want the bookstall set up before anyone comes. There's half a dozen boxes to be fetched in from the car. Boot's open."

But Alan had hardly excused himself to Jean, hardly started towards the wide entrance before he was already redundant, displaced by the disciples. Two of them took the table from the sweating old men; others vanished at a run, laughing in strange languages, fighting for the privilege of carrying books.

Alan stopped in his tracks, watched for a minute, for long enough to see that neither Ted nor Arthur wanted his help now, so many willing hands they had; and then he returned to Jean.

*　　　*　　　*

Rachel had tried to follow Richard's advice. She'd found herself a corner, over where the instruments were stacked; she'd sat on the cool, dry grass, sipped at her Coke and tried to relax, not to worry.

But in the effort not to worry about the weather and tonight, she'd started worrying about her father instead, his strange silences and bitter moods. That was worse, that was the pits. He wasn't coming this evening, largely thanks to her having begged a lift home from someone else; and her relief at his absence only fed her guilt and her sense of helplessness, making her feel contriving and treacherous.

Unable to bear her own thoughts any longer, she'd sought distraction in her guitar, in retuning the strings against the humid air; and now she was strumming it softly, picking out chords at random while she watched the public filing in.

People were coming, as Richard had said they would. There was a strange, murky light beyond the marquee's entrance, a sky like yellow porridge; but still, the people were coming. The back rows were filling nicely, and the first brave few were making their way down towards empty seats at the front.

Rachel watched, all but invisible behind the shelter of a drum-

145

kit and a couple of speakers. She looked at the people's faces, some curious and some reserved, some tense and some excited, and wondered why each of them had chosen to come. How many were already believers and here only to praise, and how many were truly seekers looking for the light. How many had only come to mock. And, of course, how many would leave with their souls made over anew and their lives utterly changed . . .

Watching, looking at the faces, she saw a few that she knew, and then more, and then many: kids from the youth club, adults from the local congregation, even some from her own church the other side of town.

Then she saw one face she'd really never expected, never hoped to find here tonight. She saw Derry. Hands in pockets and head down, scowling at his shoes, clearly wishing himself somewhere, anywhere else; but here none the less, hauled along in the wake of his heavy mother.

His mother headed straight to the front row, with Derry dragging reluctantly behind. Before she could claim seats for them, though, Mrs Bowen was intercepted by one of the chapel elders and taken to join a small group of standing men, deep in conversation.

Derry seized his chance, while Rachel watched. He took one small step backwards, then another; and seeing his mother involved and temporarily forgetful of him, he turned and hurried off up the aisle again.

Not all the way, not out of the marquee. Rachel could almost hear him thinking, wondering if he dared and deciding not. But he found himself a seat right at the back, in the very last row, where he was totally hidden in the growing crowds.

Oh, you . . . Rachel shook her head at him, laughing silently, all delight and all despair; then as his mother turned and looked and didn't find him, she choked abruptly on a giggle that didn't want to stay silent. She hugged the guitar tight, wrapped herself around it, clenched her jaws and swallowed bubble after bubble of rising laughter. She toppled backwards and buried her face in grass, anything to keep the cackles down; and was still rolling, still shaking with a wild hilarity when she banged her head against someone's foot, and looked up to see one of the other musicians staring down at her, more gathering behind.

*   *   *

"Nat . . . "

Helen appeared in the open bathroom door, stood fidgeting

146

with the light-switch cord.

"Problem?" he asked, closing his eyes again, feeling the scalding water tickle at the corners of his mouth.

"No, but we'll be late, if we don't go soon . . . "

"No, we won't. Hang on."

He slid an inch or two lower in the bath, to let the water lap across his face; then he surged up and out in one quick movement, stood naked and dripping, grinning at her.

"Pass us a towel."

She didn't pass it, she brought it; draped it around him and started rubbing him dry, still with that anxious edge to her.

"Nat, are you, are you sure about this? That you want to come?"

"I said so, didn't I?"

"Yes, but . . . It's not your sort of thing. I mean, is it?"

"Maybe not. But it seems to be your sort of thing; and that entitles me to be interested, I think. Doesn't it?"

"Yes. Yes, of course. I only thought – you were spending so long in the bath, I thought maybe you didn't want either of us to go." That last coming out in a rush, her face turned away, fearful of his anger or his agreement, or both.

He gave her neither. He only laughed, patted her cheek lightly with a wet hand, said, "If I didn't want to go, love, I'd say so. And if I didn't want you to go, I'd say that, too. Wouldn't I?"

She nodded mutely.

"Well, then." He twitched the towel out of her hands, knotted it around his waist and headed for the bedroom. "What do you think I should wear? Sunday best, or are we talking low church here, are we talking casual?"

He let her sort through his wardrobe, dressed compliantly in what she chose, and didn't raise a murmur of protest when she hustled him out of the flat with his hair still damp from the bath.

Nat had trained puppies this way when he was younger, when control over a puppy was enough. Once they were broken he'd give them a degree of licence, let them wander further and further afield – and then whistle them sharply to heel, watch them come hurrying back.

Tonight was an experiment, but he was confident of the result. He'd give Helen a taste of freedom, or at least the illusion of it; but when he whistled, when he called an end to the game, that would be that. She'd drop this religious kick and come to heel again, obedient and eager to please.

He anticipated nothing but boredom from this tent-preacher.

147

He'd get his evening's entertainment from her, from the sweet pleasure of watching her run, watching her come back to him.

The evening was clouding over hard, threatening a storm. They didn't have far to go, though, and it was too warm, too sticky for a jacket. He took her hand, playing the game out to its limits and laughing as he did so; and linked like that they walked down the hill and round the corner, towards the pale peaked roof of the marquee.

*   *   *

Derry was looking to be alone when he sidled away from his mother, looking to suffer this evening in solitude; but casting around for a gap, a hole he could hide in, he'd seen a hand half-raised in recognition, Albie with an empty seat beside him.

He'd still rather have been on his own; but spaces were in short supply, and sitting with Albie had to be better than sitting with his mother. Derry inched his way along the row, dropped into the chair beside his friend.

"Hi, what are you – "

They broke off, giggling high and tight. Looked at each other, almost made a silent pact not to ask; but curiosity pushed Derry past the boundaries of common sense.

"You first. What are you doing here?"

Albie shifted awkwardly, stared down at his hands, cracked his knuckles one by one. "Just, I've been talking to Richard a bit, after the club some nights; and I wanted to see what he's got to say tonight. That's all. What about you, then?"

He could lie, of course, it'd be easy. *Same thing, really,* he could say; *I'm just curious. I'm interested, sort of,* he could say that. Wouldn't be much of a lie, even. Anything Richard did was interesting.

Or there was always, *My mam, she was coming and she dragged us along.* Now that really would be a lie. He was here by his own decision and hadn't even wanted to walk down with his mother, only that she was ready at the same time he was and he hadn't been given the choice.

Albie would accept it, probably. He knew Derry's mother. But Derry had his pride; and after so many fights it was the last thing he wanted, to paint himself as meekly giving in to his mother's commands. Tagging along behind her when she whistled.

Come right down to it, he didn't really want to lie at all. Albie hadn't, after all; and Derry's confession was no harder than his must have been.

148

So Derry sat there, flicked his eyes to Albie and away, scanned the marquee without finding what he sought; and said, "Rachel."

Said, "She's right in with this. I mean, she would be, wouldn't she? She's been pushing it all week; and she's got to sing tonight. With the band, and then a couple of solos. And she's scared. She told me, Thursday. So what I thought, I'd just come down. Sort of moral support, yeah?"

"Does she know you're here?"

"No. I didn't say."

"Not much use, then, is it?"

"Well. I can tell her, after. And I just like to hear her sing. Nothing wrong with that, is there?"

"No, sure," but Albie was smirking as he said it. "Nothing wrong with that, mate."

*   *   *

Arthur stood at the marquee's entrance welcoming those he knew, nodding and smiling at those he didn't. He'd been here a while; and looking up the street, seeing how many more people were making their way down, he thought he'd be here a while longer. They'd be lucky to start on time, with all this interest. *Standing room only,* he thought he'd be saying before the end. He tried not to worry about that, tried to persuade himself that between them, God and Richard knew what they were about. The scale of this meeting was starting to frighten him, it was so much larger than he was used to, so much more ambitious; he felt nervous among such a crowd, out of his depth, at heart simply too old to be taking so great a risk.

But still he smiled, nodded, greeted those who greeted him; and privately castigated himself for a man of little faith. Reminded himself that the responsibility didn't fall on his shoulders only, or even largely – there were others to share the burden, and none were frail vessels. If this was what God required of them, they would be given the strength to bear it. That was how His world worked.

And then a hand clutched suddenly, tightly at his arm; and turning, he saw a woman in drab clothes, tight headscarf and long skirt. Her face and clothes nudged sharply at his unready mind, a memory he couldn't place until she spoke.

"Please, is Richard here?"

"Aye, he's here." Arthur had the woman fixed now, remembering an evening's walk, and her abrupt appearance; and her leading

149

Richard off talking and talking, running on at the mouth like a mad thing. "He'll be speaking shortly, once everyone's settled. Just go on in and find a seat."

"But I'd like to see him, you see. I'd like to speak to him privately. Would that be possible, do you think, could you find him for me?"

And somehow it gave Arthur a great deal of pleasure to turn her down flat; to say, "No, I don't think that's a good idea. Not before the meeting. After, maybe; I'm sure he'll be talking to people, after. But he'll not want to be disturbed now." *There's others than you in need tonight, woman; and he'd take you alone if he was asked, I'm sure of that, but I'll not be the one to ask him. It's not the right thing to do, with so much at stake and all of us depending on him.*

Her hands fluttered briefly in protest, she took a breath to argue, to persuade; but Arthur looked deliberately away, waved to a familiar face behind her. After a second, she went with the slow current of newcomers, into the tent.

He smiled inwardly, pleased at having saved Richard that, at least, at such a crucial time. But his attention was caught quickly by a group of teenagers who'd gathered by the chapel fence opposite, trouble in the making.

He'd had his eye on them for a while; but now they were moving, now they were drifting over towards the marquee. Arthur steeled himself. He'd have to turn them away if they gave any hint of having mischief in mind; and that was likely, that was his experience of youngsters. You couldn't trust them, not in a group. Not even a mixed group, as this one was. It used to keep lads on their best behaviour, having a girl's critical eye on them; but not any more. These days, the girls were just as likely to start the ruckus. And the boys might get rowdy just to show off, just to impress.

Arthur made his mind up and began to work his way through the constant stream of new arrivals, to meet the teenagers and send them off with a flea in their ear. The tent would be crowded enough without them, God didn't need their business . . .

*   *   *

It surprised Nat quite how many people were turning up to be preached at on a Saturday evening, especially with the sky promising foul weather before they made it home.

He shuffled forward with Helen clinging to his arm, not to get separated from him in the jostling crowd; and was surprised again

150

by the variety in the people packed around him. Old biddies and social inadequates, he'd expected those and he saw them, labelled them and dismissed them. But there were others too, middle-aged men and their wives who should have been too self-satisfied or too unimaginative to be bothered with a charade like this; and people of his own generation, students and young professionals who should surely be too intelligent to be taken in by the palliative promises of religion. But then, Helen was no fool, and Helen was here. He was here himself, come to that.

Just ahead of him, there was even a milling pack of teenagers, laughing and shoving each other forward: coming to ridicule, presumably, not to pray.

Nat wasn't the only one to doubt their motives. He saw an old man coming to confront them, holding his arm out to deny them entrance; and he smiled, looking forward to the encounter, to see how they would meet the challenge. Might be amusing, that.

But then someone else was there, before the old guy could do more than halt their progress. A youngish man, thirty-odd, blond and handsome with something extra, something that drew the eye and the attention.

"No, let them come in, Arthur. Everyone's welcome tonight, we don't want to start the mission by turning people away."

Stubborn rebellion shifted in a moment, from the kids' sullen faces to the old man's.

"There's no room."

"We'll find room. They can sit on the grass, up at the front. You won't mind that, will you?"

"No, sure. 'Course not," in a quick chorus.

"Richard . . . "

"It'll be fine, Arthur," dropping his arm for a moment round the old man's shoulders, an assertion of utmost confidence. "Come on, kids, I'll show you where to sit."

The teenagers filed into the tent in a cocky parade, while the old man stared distrustfully after. Nat followed, Helen tugging at his arm and murmuring, "That's him, that's Richard, the bloke I met in town."

"Mmm. I guessed."

"You see what I mean, then, do you? He's got something, it really shows . . . "

Nat laughed, spotted a pair of free seats off to one side and hustled her over to claim them. "I'll wait to hear what he's got to say for himself, I'm not susceptible to smooth talking and a pretty face. Not in a man, at any rate . . . "

Helen snorted and rubbed her cheek against his shoulder,

radiant with content. Nat draped his arm around her neck, wishing briefly that she'd make it harder for him sometimes. No one should have it this easy.

The tent filled up and overfilled, latecomers packing in at the back; and meanwhile things got under way with music, a six-piece band that had Nat curling a scornful lip. The musicians were competent, no more; and their material was a dreary imitation of outdated pop, with awkward and insufferably anodyne lyrics about the joys and trials of being Christian. He could have written better himself.

He was just considering a walk-out, wondering what effect that would have on Helen and how he could turn it to his good, when the band finished. There was scattered and uncertain applause, which he used to cover a disdainful snort just loud enough for Helen's ears; and then her new idol Richard jumped up onto the dais at the front and lifted his hands for quiet.

"Welcome to Paradise," he said, in a voice that carried without effort right to the back of the crowded tent. And then, smiling, "That's cheeky of me, I know; a lot of you are locals, you belong here more than I do. But others have come from further afield, and we're especially glad to see you here tonight.

"Again, some of you are believers, you don't need to be told about the glory of God; but others among you will be unconvinced, or downright cynical. I've got a special message for those, and for any here who are unhappy or hurting or scared. I'll talk more about that later; but I just want to hit you with it now, because it's good news, as it always has been. It's the message of the Gospels; and the message is that God loves you, that Christ died for you and that he can live again in your heart tonight, he's only waiting to be asked. That means you personally, each and every one of you. I don't know your names, or your life stories; but I know this much, that God knows it all. He watches you, He loves you, and He grieves for you; and He longs, He hungers for each of you individually to turn to Him. It's a short step, to a glorious salvation; and it's all true. No lies here, no delusions. I can't prove it to you, academically; like all the best puddings, the proof's in the eating. You have to discover it for yourselves. All I can do is give you my word, as a man who's lived with Jesus all my life: there *is* a God, the Bible is a true record of Him and His Son, and salvation is certain for all those with the courage to believe . . . "

Nat wasn't thinking of leaving any more.

He wasn't persuaded either, though he had his doubts about Helen, the way she was up on the edge of her seat, straining to catch every word from her golden boy. But she wasn't alone in that. He was listening himself, listening intently; and so was everyone in the tent, if the silence was any witness.

As Helen had said, this guy had something real, and it had caught Nat as it had caught the rest of them. What he said was nothing, it didn't matter. It was the man himself who counted, who drew all eyes to himself as his voice wove silken bonds to snare his every listener.

That was power, pure and simple; and Nat was devoted to power and the pursuit of power, always had been.

He wasn't bored, not now. On the contrary, he was hungry for more, as hungry as anyone and hungrier than most. This was a tutorial from a master; and proud he might be, but he wasn't too proud to learn.

*   *   *

Billy was paid on Saturdays.

It followed that Billy was drunk on Saturday nights.

This was a Saturday night.

The market closed at four. At half past, Billy had wheeled his empty barrow into line with the others and left it there. He'd gone up to the office and stood patiently smiling at the back of the queue, waiting his turn. A couple of lads had come in after him and jostled him aside, sneering and impatient; but he didn't mind that, not Billy. Not tonight.

At last there was just him left, this side of the desk. Mr Travis had pushed an envelope across; Billy had picked it up, put it in his pocket, turned to go.

"Count it, Billy."

Billy's smile had stretched ingratiatingly. "Oh Jesus, lord, I trust you, Mr Travis."

"I know you do. Count it anyway. And sign for it. You know you have to do that."

Billy did know. This was the only part of Saturdays he didn't like, but Mr Travis never let him get away with it.

He'd sighed, opened the envelope and run the folded notes between his fingers.

"That's right, Mr Travis."

"Is it? How much, then?"

Billy had smiled, shrugged.

"Come on, Billy. Do it properly."

So Billy had laid all the notes out separately on the desk, read the numbers aloud and added them up on his fingers. Mr Travis had helped, when he got muddled.

Then there was the form to be signed, Billy's name to be written down in big curling letters; and then Mr Travis had let him pick the money up and go.

There was only ever one place Billy was likely to go, with money in his pocket and a whole evening ahead: only one place he was wanted, he was welcome.

At six o'clock, he'd walked into the public bar of the 'Lady Grey'.

A group of students at the far end had cheered when they saw him, had whistled and stamped their feet. Billy had grinned, waved, bought himself a pint and carried it straight over to the piano.

That was the only drink he'd had to buy tonight. The students had kept him going after that, lining pints up along the piano top; but they'd made him work, before he was allowed to drink them.

He'd played for hours, anything they asked for. If he'd ever heard it, he could play it. Sometimes he sang in his cracked, reedy voice, when they didn't know the words; but mostly he left the singing to them. It was the playing he loved, the feel of his fingers dancing on the loose and wobbly keys, finding their own way through the music. And the glorious, blissful knowledge that here was one thing that he could do absolutely right.

Finally, though, the students had gone as they always went, too soon: hurrying off to a film or a club or a party, patting him on the shoulder as they left, buying him a whisky for luck and making him promise to come again next week.

Billy had sipped his whisky and played a little longer for himself, trying to hang on to the happiness. Then he'd left the pub with a six-pack of cans under his arm, his reward from the grateful landlord, and made his unsteady way to Paradise.

He had his room there, home sweet home: a cramped little bedsit in a big house. But he didn't dare go home, not yet. He'd done that before too often, gone home with cans under his arm and his head sweet with beer, to be met by his landlady on the stairs. She waited for him, Saturdays; and if he was happy like he was tonight, she took the cans off him and threw him out to spend the night on the streets.

No, Billy was too wise to go home yet. He bought fish and chips and rolled on up the hill from the river, looking for somewhere to sit: somewhere to be comfortable for a while, until all his cans were empty.

He found a tent, a big tent shining with light. Didn't have the nerve to go inside, but settled himself down against the canvas wall, unwrapped his supper and opened a can.

Sat there eating and drinking, listening to the music from inside. A girl's voice, singing old hymns high and lovely; he could play those, he could, just give him a piano. He'd play for her.

But he didn't have a piano, not here. He had nothing but beer and memories, and dreams. Billy sat engulfed by the music, not happy any more, only sad to be who he was, poor Billy all alone on a dark night, shut out from the light within and too scared to go home.

And he cried, he did; poor Billy wept as he listened, as he drank.

*　　　*　　　*

They were back to the music again; but this time it was different, this time it touched even Nat, a little.

He was cynical at the effect it was having, on him and everyone around him: this was what it was for, of course. Religion had always used music as a tool to snare the emotions of its adherents, a substitute for logic. It was manipulation and nothing more; but knowing that couldn't touch the potency of it, or his response. He still leant forward in his chair, still listened intently, still thrilled as he was meant to.

It was a teenage girl who was doing this to him, just a kid armed with a guitar and a microphone and a few old songs. That was why it worked so well; she had sense enough to stick to the classics, and keep it straight and simple. Plus she had a real voice, and she knew how to use it.

Even so – despite the spell she laid on him, despite the tingle she raised in his spine – he was glad none the less when she stopped singing, when she walked quickly off the dais.

Glad for one simple, straightforward reason: that as she stepped off the platform at one side, Richard Gould stepped on at the other.

*　　　*　　　*

Thunder rolled and grumbled in the sweaty air. Lightning poked

155

at the city's rim.

There was no rain, but still Billy worked himself further back, against the giving wall of the big tent. Still he sought shelter against the threat of rain, at the same time searching in his cans for courage to confront it.

If it rained he'd get wet, tent or no tent. If he got wet, his landlady would throw him out for sure. She'd wait for him, however late he left it. She'd listen out, and when she heard his key: "Oh, no," she'd say, "no, don't you come in here like that. Trailing your filth through my clean house, dripping and staining, oh no. Soaking wet and drunk too, you're out tonight, Billy boy, you're not coming in here ... "

Maybe he should go home now, before the rain. But it was still early, she'd catch him anyway, throw him out for being drunk. And he was only halfway through his cans, didn't want her taking them off him.

Maybe he should have another can, and think about it ...

*   *   *

Richard didn't need the microphones. His voice carried of its own accord; and it carried more than his words, more than his simple gospel.

That's what Nat was listening to: the voice and not the words, all the subliminal messages and not the earnest declarations of belief. It wasn't God that interested Nat; and it wasn't God he saw in Richard's performance that night, nor His voice he heard in Richard's preaching. It was only power.

Richard held that vast and disparate audience in the palm of his hand. A phrase could have them laughing, a gesture bring them to the verge of tears; if he'd chosen, he could have brought them to their feet and set them marching that very night, on course to change the world. That was power; and it was what Nat wanted, what he'd been looking for all his life.

Nat knew his goal, and he knew his moment when he saw it; and in that moment, Nat almost did believe in God.

" ... In a minute I'll ask all of you to bow your heads in silent prayer; and what I want then, if there's anyone here tonight who's heard more than me talking to you, anyone who's heard God's voice speaking in their heart, I want them to raise their hands. That's all. Just lift your hands, to show that you've heard and understood the message, and that you want to commit your life to Christ.

"Okay, if you'd all like to bow your heads now, please. You don't need to pray, if you haven't come to faith yet; but I'd ask you to bow your heads anyway. This is a private commitment people are making, it's between themselves and God, they don't want to be stared at . . .

"Now, if you're ready to give yourself to Christ, just lift your hand. If you've heard His word and believed it tonight, if you believe He is your only hope of salvation, raise your hand to say so. That's all I'm asking, just raise your hand . . . All right, sir. I see you. You can put your hand down now . . . Yes. Yes, the lady at the back there. I see you, God sees you. Bless you, sister. Put your hand down . . . "

Beside him, Nat could feel Helen's nervousness, the tremble in her. She believed, that much was obvious; Richard could have sold her anything tonight. And she wanted to lift her hand to say so, to say *You got me* – and she was scared of how Nat would react.

After all, he had the prior claim.

So Nat reached over and closed his fingers around her wrist, good and tight. Felt the utter stillness of her in response, even the tremble fled; and answered that stillness, answered all her doubts and anxieties in one easy movement.

Lifted her hand and his, and held them high.

And five minutes later, when Richard asked for a greater show of faith from these new believers – when he asked them all to come forward, to stand in a group beside the dais – Nat was the first to move, up on his feet and taking Helen with him, his hand locked tight around her elbow.

*   *   *

Lightning twisted the sky like warping steel; thunder snapped it back.

The rain came, slow and heavy like the air, like the thick air.

Outside the tent, Billy huddled as small as he could and pressed against loose canvas, closing his eyes and trying to fool himself with the idea of shelter, trying to let the beer fool him better.

Inside the tent, the worship went on; and why not? It might be chucking it down out there, but hallelujah anyway. They had their God to keep them dry. And if they got wet after all, if the tent leaked or the rain kept on after the show was over, then that must be His plan for the evening and no problem. By definition, not a problem in the world.

* * *

The service ended with half an hour of loud, exultant choruses, hands clapping and arms raised, fingers pointing, heaven this way only.

Afterwards Derry sat still and quiet in his chair, letting the row empty to either side of him as the aisles filled with a milling, murmuring crowd.

Albie wasn't with him any more. Albie had stuck his arm up when Richard was preaching, one more volunteer for the God squad; he'd gone up front with a dozen others, when Richard called. That little group was still together, singled out in their own private circle of chairs: in quarantine from the corrupting world, that's how it looked, and Albie was welcome to it.

It was partly old habit, what used to be force of necessity that kept Derry in his seat, memories of pain and humiliation, trying to use his crutches in a crush of bodies. Partly he saw no need to hurry; no one was getting anywhere very fast, there were that many people blocking the exit. And the rain was coming down hard, and why race to get wet?

Mostly, though, it was a way of getting himself noticed, as he wouldn't, couldn't possibly be in the packed aisles. It worked, his mother proved that by calling to him, beckoning imperiously; he waved blithely back and stayed where he was. Gazed up at the darkening roof and decided he'd stay until the rain found its way through, he'd give her that long. Scanned all the faces he could see without moving his head, looking for her but trying not to look as though he were looking . . .

And then cool hands closed over his eyes and he heard her laugh behind him, heard her say, "Guess who?"

Tilted his head right back as she moved her hands, so that they could look at each other upside down, see how that felt; then she nudged two empty chairs apart and wriggled through.

Said, "I didn't expect to see you here, Derry."

"Didn't you?" He smiled, pleased. "I expected to see you."

"Well, you would, wouldn't you? Smart-arse."

"Wash your mouth out, you. Posh girls don't swear. Nor good Christian girls, neither."

"Oh, is that right? And who says I'm posh, anyway?"

"I do. You talk posh, your dad drives a posh car, you live in a posh house the posh end of town . . . "

"How do you know where I live?"

"You told me." And then, in the face of her transparent disbe-lief, "Well, you told me the street, one time. And I was over there a few days ago, just walking, you know? So I took a look. Dunno which one was yours," lying through his teeth, but at least she couldn't prove it, "but they're all posh down there."

"Just walking, eh?"

"Yeah. I do that a lot, I like it. There's places I haven't been for years, I like to check up on them, sort of. Now I can. See if they've changed . . . "

"Uh-huh."

They gazed at each other for a moment, both of them caught somewhere between laughter and defiance, between confession and denial. Then Rachel changed the subject, with a quick jerk of her head towards the stage. "What about tonight, then, what did you think?"

Derry shrugged. "I liked you. Except it was all bloody hymns again, wasn't it?"

"That's what we're here for, idiot. It's why people came."

"Not me."

"No, well, you're weird, aren't you?" Grinning at him widely, challenging him to deny it.

"One of us is," he said. "How are you getting home, then, your dad coming to pick you up, is he?"

"Not tonight, I've got a lift with Mrs Jopling. That's her, talking to Mr Brougham."

"Oh. Right, then."

"Why, what did you have in mind?"

"Only, I was going to say I'd walk you home. If you wanted. But it doesn't matter."

"*Walk?*"

"Yeah."

"Derry, it's pissing down!"

Which was the second time she'd sworn tonight, but he decided not to point it out. He thought maybe she'd belt him. So he just said, "Yeah," again, as casual as he could manage.

"Weird. *Really* weird. Actually, I didn't want to go just yet anyway, some people are hanging on for a bit, so . . . " And she hesitated, looked back over her shoulder at Mrs Jopling, chewed her lip – and shook her head slowly, regretfully. At least, it looked regretful. "It's no good, she'd never stand for it. She promised Dad she'd see I got home okay. I don't think letting me go off in a thunderstorm with a boy she's never heard of would count, really. I mean, do you?"

Stuff your dad, he wanted to say, but didn't. And then Mrs

Jopling proved her point by calling her away, a little sharply.

She made a move to go, and hesitated; turned back to him, and hesitated again.

"No kisses," she said, "I promised, didn't I?" – and took his hand instead, cool firm fingers folding around his and slipping free too soon. "See you next week, then."

"Eh?"

"Down the club, stupid."

"Oh. Yeah, right. Hey," as she moved away, "this kissing bit . . . "

"What?"

"Well, you promised no hymns, either. And you broke that one."

She stared, her mouth twitching with suppressed giggles. He got to his feet, said, "'Night, Rachel," and walked the other way along the row, hugging himself in delight as he heard her swear the third time, very loudly and right in front of her father's friend.

THIRTEEN

i

Social guru, media pundit, political commentator: it's a role that even his foresight, even his clarity of vision could surely never have predicted for him. It's not, it truly can't be what he wanted. He wouldn't have chosen this.

But he must speak if the Spirit moves him, if God dictates. He must speak for the poor and the disadvantaged, for the homeless and the hungry. That much is a duty. And if an interviewer wants to take him one stage further, to look for root causes and ask about solutions – well, he's never refused to answer a question yet. And he does have all the answers, after all. That's the best of the job; being a mouthpiece for God, he's not vulnerable to doubt.

The journalists love him for it. They've learnt quickly, that he has an opinion on everything and is more than happy to express it; it also hasn't taken them long to notice his habit of backing up words with deeds.

So now they come to him about every local issue, be it political or religious or whatever; and if it wasn't a story before, chances are it will be after.

ii

Jack Dubrowski stood in the sunshine and the rubble, sleeves rolled up and arms folded, watching them work on Cockburn Grove. His thoughts were on mill-wheels turning in circles, because this was all so much like the building of the chapel forty years ago, he was so very much reminded. There were the young enthusiasts, the amateurs, the muscle, shouting and sweating and climbing all over; and here were the few wise heads, the professionals, feet firmly on the ground.

That forty-year lag had changed Jack himself from the one to the other, had brought him down from up. *You're the flyer, Jack lad,* they'd said to him then, *you must have a head for heights. You get on up and show us how it's done.* And he'd done that, in all his youth and foolishness and pride; he'd done headstands on

161

the roof-tree, with twenty feet to fall if his balance went. This time it was, *You were a carpenter, Mr Dubrowski, will you keep an eye on what we're doing? Just give us a shout if we go wrong, that's all, keep us on the straight and narrow* . . .

He'd tried to defy time and good sense, tried to join them on the roof the first day up. But the ladders had made him dizzy; he'd had to be helped down and taken in to his flustered, anxious sister, and even now he winced away from the memory of that humiliation. So he did what he could instead, what they'd asked of him. He stood on the ground and gave them what benefit there was to be drawn from his long experience. Gave them a rocket, too, when they deserved it for shoddy work or carelessness with tools.

So everything was different from forty years ago; but yet it was still the same, it was still people giving their time and labour to build for God and for each other.

Jack heard the growl of an engine in low gear, and turned to see a builder's lorry edging cautiously down the broken road, scaffolding poles rattling and clanking in the back. Mrs Bowen's boy, young Derry, was perched ostentatiously, surely illegally, on the tailgate; and he jumped down as the lorry passed, casual and easy now on his healed legs.

"Hi, Mr Dubrowski. Nice day, yeah? Johnny says I can help him with the scaffolding down on the end house, it'll just be the two of us, he reckons we can finish today if we go for it . . . "

"Indeed." Jack looked at the boy in his smart tracksuit and asked, "Why are you not working today, the gym is open, yes?"

"Yeah, sure, but Mr Jenner gave us the rest of the day off. I'm not skiving, me."

"He seems to give you a lot of time off."

"Well, yeah, I guess he does; but he works us hard when I'm there. And it's not like a proper job, I don't do hours, really. Just when he wants me. Or when I'm not busy I go along, see what needs doing. But he sends us off sometimes. He's got this other kid there, see, Jason, he does the regular work . . . " A shrug, a shuffle of his feet, and, "Um, is Rachel around, is she?"

"No, I think not today. I haven't seen her."

"Oh. Oh, well . . . "

Then the lorry's horn sounded from the far end of the terrace; Derry sketched a half-wave and was off, sprinting.

Jack was busy for the next hour or so, helping to fit a new frame around an old window. That done, he moved back to his place

162

outside, to stand in the sun and watch. To be seen, also. It might be foolish, it might be utterly contrary to the facts, but still he felt very much like a host and the workers all his guests; it seemed a duty on him to be visible, to be available.

After a while he heard slow, shuffling footsteps coming down the road. He glanced round, and smiled.

"Hullo, Billy."

"Hullo, Mr Jack."

"Not working today?"

Billy turned his head away, rubbed at his neck, said, "Not today."

That was strange on a Saturday; but Jack didn't want to pry into Billy's secrets. The man had few enough, in all conscience.

After a minute, "What are they all doing here, Mr Jack?"

"They're fixing up these other houses, Billy."

"What, for people to live in, like?"

"That's right."

"Oh." A pause, and then, "That must be nice, that. To have a house to live in."

Jack didn't know where Billy lived, but it was likely some boarding-house, bad bed and a worse breakfast. Unless he had family to look after him; but if so he surely wouldn't look so wistfully at these unfinished houses, surely wouldn't say, "Who's going to live in them, then, these people, is it?" with quite such a hungry longing in his voice.

"Some of them, yes. Not all, and only for a while, some. But they are to be chapel houses, you see, Billy, we are to buy them with chapel money; so all the chapel helps, who can."

Another, longer pause, while Billy digested that with a series of slow and thoughtful nods. Then, "I'd like to help too, Mr Jack," he said. "I could do that," pointing. "I'm good at pushing barrows, that's my, that's my *job*."

"I know that, Billy. Well, go and ask, if you really want to help. Ask Nat."

"Nat? Who's Nat? I don't know Nat."

"He's in charge. I don't know where he is just now, but ask anyone, they'll find him for you."

And a little after that, still at his post, still watching the houses and the road, the work and the new arrivals, Jack saw a bicycle coming down fast and careless over the broken tarmac, begging for punctures.

It was a girl, long hair flying: Rachel, beyond a doubt. But she was usually not so reckless of her tyres. Jack was ready to tease

163

her, to impute a cause to her hurrying and direct her to the scaffolding, to Derry; but a glance at her face changed his mind, as she jerked to a savage halt beside him. She looked a long, long way from being fit to tease.

"Rachel, good afternoon."

"Hi, Mr Dubrowski." She stepped off the bike, tried to balance it against a skip, and watched it slip and fall with no reaction beyond a tight little shrug. "Where's Nat, d'you know?"

"Here, I think; which house, I am not sure. Shout for him." And then, offered plain with no trimmings, no teasing, "Derry is here also, helping with the scaffolding. Down there, at the end."

"Is he? Oh, right. Thanks . . . "

But it was the middle of the terrace she went to; and it was the young man Nat he heard her shouting for.

iii

"Nat?"

Nathan didn't so much as turn round. He held a hand up in a brief gesture, *wait*, while he watched his newest recruit at work through the window. It wasn't easy, fighting those heavy old wheelbarrows up a narrow ramp of planks; but Billy managed it with aplomb, tipped his load of rubble into the skip and grinned triumphantly as the dust rose in a cloud around him.

Nathan grinned also, gave him a wave of approval, *carry on, Sergeant Billy*. Then he looked round to find Rachel fidgeting, her face strikingly pale and her fingers restless in the dark mess of her hair.

"What's the matter, sweetheart?"

Her head jerked, refusal rather than denial, *not going to say*. "Nat, give me something to knock down. Something I can smash."

He laughed, "You serious?" and then saw that she was, saw that she meant it very deeply. "Okay, then, let's see. That wall out the back there, divides this garden from next door? We don't need that." He'd meant to be thrifty, take it apart gently to save the bricks; but she clearly needed something to pulverise.

"Good. Thanks, Nat."

"Got any gloves?" And seeing her shake her head, "You'll get blisters, mind."

"Don't care."

"Okay, then. We've got plasters, in any case. And, Rachel?"

164

"Yeah, what?"

"Don't be too macho, you haven't got the body mass. Use a sledgehammer, sure, but find yourself a light one."

She just grunted. He smiled and watched her go, wondering what could have got her so worked up. The girl was raging, too mad to speak, almost; and yesterday he'd have put money on her being immune to anything so unChristian and uncontrolled. But maybe even God couldn't keep teenagers level forever.

iv

No job, no home for Billy now, poor Billy.

Billy wasn't telling people, he didn't want them to know; but he'd lost his job. Lost it in the pub, he had. He was always losing things, always leaving things in pubs and them not there when he went back to look. His money, his fags, his hat – all sorts of things. You name it, Billy had lost it in a pub somewhere, sometime.

Now his job, he'd done the same thing with his job.

And that was a joke, that was, but it wasn't funny. Billy wasn't laughing.

He'd been smiling and sunny on Wednesday when he rolled into the market at half three when he should have been there at two. That was a happy thing, all that extra lunchtime. Extra pub-time.

But he wasn't happy long, because his barrow wasn't where he'd left it, where it ought to be. And when he looked, when he asked who'd seen it, who'd shifted it:

"You'd better go and see Mr Travis," one of the stallholders said, shifting her gaze, not looking at him straight.

"But where is it, where's my barrow, then?"

"Just go and see Mr Travis, Billy. He'll explain."

On his way to the office, Billy had seen his barrow. With someone else pushing it, some boy, skinhead with muscles and big boots on. Billy was angry; but he wasn't going to start trouble with a boy like that. He just hurried faster up the stairs.

Mr Travis said, "Billy, where've you been?"

"Lunchtime, Mr Travis. Mr Travis, someone's – "

"It's half-past three, Billy."

"Is it?" All innocence, as only Billy could. "Sorry, Mr Travis. But listen, someone's got my barrow . . . "

"I know someone's got your barrow. Someone's going to keep

165

your barrow, too, if he turns up on time. I'm sorry, Billy, but I've told you before, half a dozen times I've told you."

"What, told me what, Mr Travis? What's the matter, what have I done?"

"You're drunk, Billy. Like you were drunk after lunch yesterday, and the day before. Where are you getting the money from, anyway?"

Billy stared round the office, looked down at his feet, saw them shuffling.

"I'm not drunk," he said.

"Billy, you stink. I could smell the beer on you when you walked in. I could *hear* it, the way you came up those stairs. Where's the money coming from, Billy?"

"Found it," in a mutter. "Found a wallet. Thirty quid, there was."

"Uh-huh. Well, I'm sorry, Billy, but that thirty quid has cost you your job. Three days on the trot is too much. I need people who are reliable, who don't come late and leave early; and especially I need barrow-boys who aren't going to be drunk. Those barrows are heavy, you could really hurt someone one day."

"I'll be careful, Mr Travis, I'm always careful. I never hurt nobody, not all the time I been working here . . . "

"Billy, it's no good arguing. I want you out of here. Your job's gone already, that lad came asking and I wasn't prepared to wait for you any longer."

Billy had argued, of course. He'd pleaded, he'd cried, even; but he'd still lost his job that day. Lost it in the pub, he did.

He'd got really drunk then with the money Mr Travis gave him, money for two weeks' wages. He'd got rolling, steaming, roaring drunk; and he'd forgotten to hide it when the pubs closed, when he had to go home.

So his landlady had caught him, drunk when he shouldn't have been, when he shouldn't have had the money. And because he was drunk, he'd told her what happened; and she told him to leave. Pack and go, she said. Out by Saturday, she said.

And this was Saturday and here he was. Out. Out and about, down and out, out for a duck, on an outing. Carrying everything he owned in two bags and one old cardboard suitcase tied with rope, and nowhere to carry it to, nowhere to go.

Trudging down the hill, because that was a lesson he'd learned time and time again in his tired life, that down was always easier than up.

"Out and down," he muttered. "Out and down, down and out, poor Billy. Poor silly Billy."

He went past the chapel and the school; and then he stopped and went back a little way, because Billy had had an idea. Not a great idea, not one of the world's finest, but not so bad for someone so far down and so far out as Billy was just then.

He'd spent all the day doing what he did best, pushing barrows for them down at the houses. And not getting paid for it. So what Billy thought, Billy's idea was that least they could do, they could give him a roof over his head. Didn't have to be a good roof, any old roof would do.

He wouldn't go down to the houses, because he couldn't sleep in all that muck, he couldn't breathe in the dust; but they had another roof that Billy could use for a bit.

Billy just fancied a bit of camping, this nice hot weather.

v

Anwar Patel was a smooth young man, cool in his shades and his white BMW convertible, loose and easy and unconfined. Had the world at his feet, had Anwar.

Only now he lay at the feet of the world, and the world was kicking him.

He'd spent the evening criss-crossing the city, collecting rents for his mother. He'd taken cheques from students and cash from the unemployed or the deeply dodgy, tearful promises from single mothers backed by the odd threat from their boyfriends. He'd listed complaints about kettles and curtains, leaking roofs and broken beds; he'd smiled and been solemn, joked and shrugged and acted tough. And got a kick from it all, why not?

And there'd been nothing more on his agenda after the last calls in Paradise, nothing he had to do. He could have gone home to his mother's house, to his wife newly imported from Pakistan; or he could have searched out some friends instead. Watched a few videos, driven down to the coast, found a club and drugged himself with dancing, gone home at last in the early hours to a house of sleeping women. It really wouldn't have mattered. The choices were his to be made, which was how he liked it.

What he hadn't accounted for was the possibility of his being on someone else's agenda, being subject to another man's choice.

The last visit he'd made tonight, almost the last on his list, he'd hammered on the door, above the sound of Bhangra music pumping from his car in the street behind him; and the door had opened, hard hands had pulled him inside and the door had closed again.

Anwar had looked into the depths of a terrible smile and seen how real it was, how very much it was meant.

And now his shades were broken, and all his illusion with them. Now his blood was clotting the carpet where he lay, was glue in his nose and a gag in his mouth; now terror held his heart in tight fingers.

A steel-toed boot ground itself slowly into his spine, and at least it wasn't kicking any more; and then there was a hand in his long hair, pulling his head all the way back, showing him that face again, reversed. Showing him that smile.

"Message for your mother," the smile said. "Tell her she doesn't sell Cockburn Grove to the Christians. She sells it to Mr Belderstone, for whatever he wants to pay. You tell her that. That's all."

But that wasn't all, because the message had to be underlined, it had to be emphasised. And the boot did all that, calmly and quietly; and Anwar was quiet too beneath the boot, too far gone for screaming.

And yes, his mother would get the message.

FOURTEEN

All things come to him who waits. It's not quite biblical, maybe, but it's true none the less. And just look: here he is reaping the rewards of his patience, abundant gifts.

Particularly, he's found what he'd been needing above all else, his lieutenant. His right-hand man. A young man, to be sure, barely more than a boy, but that's all right. It's not a problem. Talent and flair, that's what he's been looking for, enthusiasm and fire to complement his own; and that's what he's found in Nathan.

That, and a propensity to war. Which is all right also, war's what we're talking here, after all. Lieutenants, and glory, and war. Like a mighty army, and onward Christian soldiers, all of that. And it's common knowledge that young men make the best soldiers. They'd have to, they've been sacrificed enough.

Not that this lad's heading for sacrifice, oh no. He's been led to Richard in the hour of need; and Richard's strength will support him, even as his supports Richard. Mutual dependency, that's what we're looking at here. Isn't it beautiful?

ii

Sunday: and Rachel had got up early, to go with her mother to communion. Her father was still in bed when they left, which suited her fine.

He was in the kitchen when they got back from church, though; she could hear the sounds of burnt toast being scraped. If she'd been alone, she'd have turned in the hallway and gone upstairs almost without a thought. But she wasn't alone, and she'd just that minute been agreeing with her mother that she was dying for a cup of coffee. Nothing to do, then, but go on in and face the guy, hope and pray that at least they could manage this much, they could have a cup of coffee together as a family and without a fight.

But for once in her life she was praying without faith and

hoping without any foundation. She didn't think she believed in families any more. Not this one, anyway. Not cosy cups of coffee after church, friendly Sunday chats round the kitchen table.

And sure enough, her father looked up frowning, his shadowed eyes red-rimmed from lack of sleep; and on his seeing Rachel the frown deepened, darkened to a scowl.

"Where were you, then?" he demanded. Not even a cursory good-morning, straight into the interrogation. "All yesterday you were out, where were you?"

She stood and faced him, tossed her long hair back and stared him straight in the eye. "Down Paradise. Helping out at the houses till it got dark, then prayer-meeting in the chapel."

"Rachel." Her mother, trying to intercede. "I thought we agreed you weren't to go over that side of town without telling us? Especially not after dark?"

"That's what we *agreed*, yes," she said, getting in quick before he did, laying it all out nice and clear. "That was fine. But what *he* said yesterday, he said I wasn't to go over there at all. Just like that. Drop all the friends I've made, dump all the work I've taken on, just abandon everything. No reason given."

"It's what I want," her father said. "That's reason enough for you."

"No," she said flatly. "No, it isn't. It just *isn't*."

"It'll have to be. I want your promise, that you won't do this again. You can go to services over there if someone takes you and brings you back, but that's all. Especially, you're not to go down to those houses again, under any circumstances whatsoever. Promise me, please."

And she took a deep breath, glanced just quickly at her pale, anxious mother, and said, very politely, "No."

"Rachel . . . "

"No. If I made the promise, I'd only break it; and I won't do that. Not for you, not for anyone." *Especially not for you, I've got my standards.* "I'm sixteen, Dad, I'm entitled to make some decisions for myself. I'm involved with what's happening over there, and I'm going on with it. That's all there is to it. I don't know why you want me out, but I won't quit now."

"I see." He was silent briefly, gazing at her in her stubbornness, her mutiny; then, before her mother could interfere again, "Your bicycle's out the back there, is it? Is it locked?"

Rachel blinked at this abrupt shift, then suddenly understood. Took a second or two to control the sudden beat of anger in her, and answered neutrally, truthfully. "Yes."

"I'll have the key, please."

She nodded, unzipping the bum-bag she wore on her hip to defeat the pocketlessness of leggings. "The key. Of course, you'll have the key. Here it is, Daddy, here's the key." Laying it neatly on the table, *click!* "And here's my purse, too, you'll want that, all my money. Otherwise I might catch a bus, instead of cycling. You'll want to stop that. And here," kicking them off one by one, bending to pick them up, to lay them on the table beside the key and the purse, "here are my trainers. You never know, I just might take it into my head to walk, on a sunny day. You know where my other shoes are, they're in my wardrobe. Just help yourself. And you'd better take the rest too while you're there, all my clothes. Just in case. It's summer, I could go barefoot if I fancied it . . . "

She stood there facing him while her mouth ran on, bitter and accusing; and she watched his hand rise and start to swing. And didn't move, didn't duck or flinch, even, wouldn't give him that much satisfaction.

She was vaguely, dimly aware of her mother's sharp protest, and her father's sharper response; but that wasn't important, wasn't even interesting. What was interesting was how she was suddenly hard up against the kitchen wall here, when she had been standing a couple of metres away. How her cheek was throbbing, burning, growing hotter by the second, must be glowing with the heat by now, dazzling bright, branded with a broad palm. How her father had never hit her in her life before, never ever. How she hadn't thought him capable, and how wrong could she be?

Slowly, carefully, Rachel pushed herself away from the wall, found her balance, and took three paces forward. Stood there, an arm's reach from her father. Faced him – and turned her head a little, tilted it a little.

"Go on, then," she hissed, around the pain in her aching jaw. "Have another go, why don't you? Match them up, I don't want to go around lop-sided."

For a second he hesitated, for a second she thought perhaps he might; and was surprised to find that she didn't actually care, that she might even welcome it if he did. The pain didn't bother her, and it would be nice to have him utterly condemned by his own hand, and in front of a witness, yet.

So she turned the other cheek and taunted him with it, tempted him to a deeper degradation. But he didn't strike her in the end, though he didn't do the other thing either, didn't apologise, didn't slump into tears and beg her forgiveness. He simply walked out of the kitchen and out of the house, got into the car and drove away.

The silence still held, in the kitchen. Rachel listened to the car's

171

departing, and wondered if he was leaving for an hour or the day or forever; and in the ice of the anger still gripping her, found again that she didn't care. Let him go, they could live without him.

Her mother was another problem, gripping the back of a chair, her head jerking between Rachel where she stood and the empty doorway where her husband was gone. But that was for later, it had to be. One thing her father had been right about, now was a time for getting the hell out of here.

She gathered her things from the table with fingers that betrayed her, daring to tremble, to make a mess of picking up the fiddly little key; jammed her feet back into the trainers and went to the door.

"Where, where are you going, Rachel?"

And she just had enough breath, enough control for one more cold and deliberate sentence before she had to clamp her mouth to silence and get moving fast.

She glanced briefly at her mother, looked away again before she could see the tears and the shock, the great need that was in her; and said, "I'm going to Paradise, where the *fuck*," laying into it good and hard like a teenage rebel should, like a beaten and tearful, a much-abused child naturally would, "do you think I'm going?"

And went.

iii

The marquee had become a semi-permanent fixture, here for the summer at least. For the duration. Their regular services attracted a crowd in three figures these days, these glorious days. Far too many for the old wooden chapel. Richard had mooted the possibility of a move, but there'd been no need even for Jean or Alan to find an argument against that. All the old men had frowned and fretted, scratched their heads and looked uncomfortable, waited for someone else to speak; and Richard had smiled, had let the subject drop and not brought it up again.

And meanwhile, until the congregation slumped or the hard weather came, they used the marquee. It was better in any case, far cooler with the sides raised, open to both the breeze and the passers-by. People would walk more happily into a tent than a chapel; or they'd stand around outside, listen to the music, perhaps strain a little to hear what was said between the hymns. And when the service was over, the congregation could linger on the grass outside, mingle with the listeners, absorb them into friendly groups or family picnics or rowdy games of soccer. A tent was better witness, all in all.

Today, Nathan drifted out with the crowd, past the bookstall and into the steady sunshine. He smiled or waved or nodded to familiar faces, all these new friends; paused when a question forced him to, explained that Helen couldn't come, she was at her parents' this weekend, and moved unhurriedly on.

Eavesdropped too, a little. Sampled the conversation here and there:

"What are you up to, then, lurking around?"

"Guarding your bike, aren't I? You didn't lock it. You got to lock it, round here. Lucky I came along . . . "

"Lucky, right. Just chance, was it, you just happened to come this way?"

"Yeah, right. Fluke. Walking past, saw your bike, no lock on it, thought I'd better wait, that's all. What's happened to your face?"

"Mind your own business. Don't *touch!*"

"That's nasty, that. Who's been knocking you about?"

"No one, don't be silly."

"Oh, sure. Just walked into a door, I suppose. C'mon, Rache, what gives? Tell us."

"No, shove off, it's private. Nothing to do with you. And don't call me Rache, okay?"

And though Nathan wasn't watching, he listened and knew what happened almost to the smallest gesture, the lightest eye-contact and the feelings behind it. He heard the soft hiss of a bicycle being wheeled over tarmac, and that was Rachel walking away while Derry stood and watched, stood and ached; and then the silence, and that was Rachel stopping, looking back.

"Well, are you coming, or what?"

"Yeah. Yeah, all right. I'm coming. What's the hurry?"

And those were his footsteps, light and deliberately slow to catch up with her, determined not to hurry.

So Nathan circulated, mingled, gleaned a little here, a little there; and eventually was hailed as the crowd thinned, was called across by Richard.

"Nat. How's it going?"

"It's going well, of course. How else would it be going?"

"Good. And Helen?"

"Oh, she's going well, too," with a grin. "Said to tell you, she's sorry not to be here."

173

"I'm sorry not to see her. You're happy, then, the pair of you? Not with each other, I mean, that's easy to see. With what you're doing, what you've done. The commitments you've made."

"Oh, yes," Nathan assured him, on Helen's behalf and his own. Nothing but certain about that. "No regrets."

"No. I'd have been surprised if you said otherwise. It's hard to regret joy and salvation, even if it comes with a great deal of work attached. Talking of which, I'd like a word . . . "

"As many as you need. I was going down to the houses, that seems to be my job at the moment, but they'll get on well enough without me for a while."

"Good. Come on, let's walk. We can wander down that way, so long as we don't have to rush."

And this was what it was all about, really, what everything was for. To walk with Richard – and at his right hand, yet, and no chance of its being an accident. Accidents didn't happen around Richard. Everything was meant.

To walk with Richard, and see the faces of the people they met: friends and strangers both, believers or not, it didn't matter. Awe and curiosity, they all had it, a sense of coming into contact with something rare and wonderful. Their heads would follow Richard down the street, as a flower follows the sun; and by definition, if they followed Richard then they followed Nathan too.

Not with intention, of course, he was a daytime moon to Richard's sun, sharing the same sky but shining only with a reflected light. Shine he did, though, there he was; and that was the goal. To be there, to be seen to be there. To be known. *Nathan . . . ? Oh, yes. I saw him with Richard. So that's Nathan, is it? He's close to Richard, you could see that. Nathan. Good. I won't forget Nathan . . .*

And they wouldn't, he'd make sure of that. No one in Paradise this summer was going to forget Nathan.

"The point is, Nat, I've been thinking. What we're seeing here in Paradise is a revival, a spiritual rebirth; but it could be more even than that, it could be a revolution.

"What we need to do, we need to broaden the front. We need to be involved in local issues, to show people we're not just concerned about the state of their souls. Christ said, 'Render unto Caesar that which is Caesar's' – but he was living in an occupied country under military law. This is a democracy, and we-the-people *are* Caesar. The power lies with us, to improve our lives and our neighbours' lives; and that's what we should be doing.

174

This has to be a holistic mission, concerned with the whole body of Paradise. And that means the people's health and welfare, it means everything from how good are the schools to how clean are the streets.

"And it's not just a matter of getting on a soap-box and pontificating. I've been doing some of that, and I will do more; but it's not enough. We have to be seen taking action.

"This is where you come in. You've earned yourself some considerable authority in the short time you've been with us, particularly with the young people. That's why you've ended up unofficial overseer down at the houses: because it's the kids who are doing all the rough work down there, and you're the man they look to. Never mind that you've no experience. If they bring you a problem, you give them a sensible solution.

"And that's just what I'm looking for – someone who can do that, who can bond all these youngsters into a problem-solving unit and set them loose on Paradise. Who can direct all that energy and goodwill into projects that are going to benefit the whole community, and keep us right bang upfront in the public's eye.

"I think you can do that, Nat. I think you're my man. You're very new to faith, but that doesn't matter – I'm not asking you to take on any spiritual leadership here, beyond what the Holy Spirit and your own good sense suggest. Just to use the talents you have and the respect you've earned, to work for the good of this mission and Paradise at large.

"Don't say anything now, there's plenty of time. Mull it over, give it some thought. Talk to Helen, talk to anyone whose opinion you value. Talk to God, that goes without saying. Then come back and talk to me, okay?"

"Okay," Nathan said, soft and sure, keeping pace with Richard down the hill. "I'll do that, I'll think it through; but I could tell you now, what my answer's going to be."

"Don't bother," Richard said, smiling. "I already know what your answer's going to be."

iv

Services might be held in the marquee these days, but Sunday School was still where and when it always had been, Sunday afternoons in the chapel. Mrs Bowen still taught the younger class and Mrs Dolance the elder, in two murmuring circles coming

175

together for prayers and choruses at the end.

Even here, though, there were changes. Even the smallest children couldn't miss the thrill in the air this summer. Mrs Bowen was different, for a start: fat and happy now, always smiling, where she used to be fat and solemn and earnest, first on her knees and last to rise. And Mrs Dolance was different too, but that wasn't so good; she was snappier than ever, and snappiest of all with her own daughter Lisa.

But the changes went deeper than the teachers' moods. There were other teachers came in some weeks: younger people, teens and twenties from all over the world, who talked to both groups together about how wonderful it was to have Jesus for a friend. There were trips and outings, and you could bring friends along on those, they didn't have to be chapel-goers. And there were bonfires and barbecues, singsongs and sausages and smoke; and, of course, there was Richard. As he did for the grown-ups, Richard shone like a new star for the children that summer.

But not for everyone. Little Luther Dolance, trained and obedient, acting on orders, addressing his classmates as they waited inside the wire fence to be collected and taken home:

"I don't think he's so great. I think he's vain, and, and arrogant. He's just a stranger, he's not one of us; and he comes shoving in here, grabbing all the glory, putting himself forward. Being on the telly. That's not what Chapel's for. He's just using us, to make himself famous. That's what I think, anyway. And so does my mum."

And Luther might not be loved or reckoned wise in his generation, might not even be liked very much; but still he was something of a power in the land. He was his mother's eyes and ears in Mrs Bowen's class, and his mother had a hard hand against wrongdoers. He was also her voice, and it was as well to listen to what Mrs Dolance thought. They learned that young, in the Sunday School.

Down at the Corner Café, where Arthur was so often treated to a chocolate biscuit after his supper, Arthur was being treated this afternoon to a long tirade with his cup of tea.

" . . . and it's not just the way he behaves," Alan was saying, "the arrogance in him. No one questions his calling, it's just his manner that offends; but more than that, I do question his judgement. Some of these people he's surrounding himself with, total strangers to us, they're no part of Chapel; and yet they're doing things in our name, and with his blessing. You'll excuse me speaking so plain, Arthur, but it's there to be done. They were as much strangers to him, a few weeks since . . . "

"They've come to us from their own churches, Alan," Arthur said slowly, weary already. "They're all known somewhere. And God knows them all, let's not forget that. You couldn't get a better reference."

"Not all of them," Alan said in flat contradiction. "That Evelyn woman, take her. She may talk about God, but she's no true believer. I don't know what she's after with Richard, but there's something. She dangles after him like dags from a sheep's tail."

Arthur blenched at the image, but couldn't deny the strength of it. There was something disturbing about Evelyn Somers, the way she came to services only to linger, only to snare Richard into private conversation afterwards. But, "You can hardly say she speaks for the Chapel, Alan. And it's not up to us to decide where Richard makes his friends."

"No, but he should be more careful, that's all I'm saying. He's made himself very visible, everyone in this city associates him with us now; and he's a responsibility to be careful in the company he keeps. Someone should bring that home to him, or maybe next week we'll find they *are* speaking for the Chapel. We'll find they're the new Council, and we've been voted out, the Lord and us, and it's turned to a chapel for the greater glory of Richard Gould." Alan was making no effort to hide his bitterness now. "We're being swamped, Arthur, that's the danger of it. There's precious few of us, we six, against dozens of these incomers; and they're taking our chapel away from us. That's what I'm afraid of, that we'll wake up one morning and find it's not our chapel any more, our voices count for nothing . . . "

Following the children out, with Lisa at her heel like a sulky dog, Jean Dolance paused in the chapel's doorway; turned her head slowly from one side to the other, eyes narrowed against the sunlight, taking it all in. Laying it up like ammunition.

Some of the small children were still congregated by the chapel wall. Mrs Bowen was with them, and would stay until they'd all been claimed by their parents. Jean summoned Luther with a jerk of her head, and turned her attention out beyond the wire.

There were the usual Sunday stragglers out on the street: families and single mothers, children playing unsupervised, a tight knot of teenagers at the corner.

Over the road, snaring the eye, was the height and breadth and presence of the vast marquee; and even now, even in its quiet time between services it was thronging with people. It was an echo, a symbol, a constant reminder of the power Richard had drawn to himself and the favours he so generously dispensed.

This side, close to the wire, one more figure caught her notice. A man turning between the chapel and the marquee, watching both. A short, balding man with a notebook in his hand and a camera around his neck, tapping a pen against his teeth . . .

"Come along." With a silent prayer of thanks, seeing her path laid out for her so clear, Jean gathered her children and led them through the gate and down the road towards the journalist, his questions, her replies.

v

Derry was down at the houses, up on the roof when he saw the big Volvo nosing its way cautiously off the main road, pulling up as soon as the tarmac started to break apart.

Even from this height he knew the car, and the driver. Rachel's father, that was – and that must be her mam, getting out the other side. He still didn't know what had happened, Rachel wasn't talking; but he knew this much, that it was her parents that had got her so mad. He'd picked that up from what she didn't say, the questions she wouldn't answer.

He looked down the other side of the terrace and saw Rachel at work on the wall again, sledgehammer flying, kicking up a cloud of dust. He thought of yelling down to her, but decided against. She had a livid bruise on her cheek this morning, and a misery inside that she was trying to hide under a brutal temper. Best to keep her and her parents apart, so long as she had that hammer in her hand. She wouldn't bash her dad, maybe – though Derry had guessed, was almost certain that her dad had bashed her – but he wouldn't take any bets on the car . . .

So he walked quick and easy along the ridge of the roof, to the scaffolding he'd helped to erect; and he went down that scaffold like a monkey, taking time to delight in his new body, a hand here and a foot there, swing and stretch and a final jump to ground.

He found the Grants hesitating on the broken road, gazing uncertainly at the row of houses and the dozen workers visible. They were trying to pick Rachel out, obviously; but there was clear relief on Mr Grant's face when he recognised Derry.

That was one advantage of losing his hair, Derry thought wryly, almost the first he'd found – that he was easy to identify, even stripped down to shorts and deck-shoes, even covered with dust

178

and sweat.

"You're Derry, aren't you? Rachel's friend?"

"That's right, Mr Grant."

"Good. Ah, this is my wife . . . "

"Hullo, Derry." A smile that seemed genuine, despite the strain. "Rachel talks about you a lot."

"Yeah? That's nice," smiling back, also genuine. "I talk about her, too. Lots."

"Is she here?"

"Yeah. Yeah, she's here." He didn't offer to take them to her, though, he wasn't going to do that even if they asked. "She's busy, mind."

"Well, we won't disturb her, then. In that case." That was Mr Grant snatching at the opportunity, relieved again, and grateful. "If you could just give her a message for us . . . ?"

"Yeah, sure. No sweat."

"Good. If you could just tell her . . . " He paused, looked to his wife for help, and didn't get any; so he had to go on by himself. Derry almost felt sorry for him. Almost. If it hadn't been for that bruise on Rachel's cheek. Derry's mam beat him up all the time, often raised bruises; but that was different. He wasn't Rachel. "Tell her, I'm sorry for what I said, for what happened this morning. Tell her I want a good long talk with her, we both do, to get everything sorted out; but it can't be today. We're going up to see Richard now, and then we'll be out all evening." Having a good long talk themselves, Derry thought, getting things sorted out between the two of them first. "So tell her, tell her to be careful, going home; and she can get a takeaway for dinner. Here, give her this . . . "

Derry took the ten-pound note, mildly surprised to find himself so trusted, even in a crisis; but, "She can come and have tea with us," he said. "Mam'd be dead pleased."

"Well. That's even better. Give her the money anyway, though. Just in case. And tell her we will have that talk, tomorrow."

"Yeah, sure."

"Thanks." A nod, a twitch of the mouth that was probably the best he could do towards a smile, and he turned back towards the car. His wife lingered, though, for one last word.

"Derry? Keep an eye on her for us. She's maybe forgotten it just now, but she's the only one we've got."

"Yeah, I know." He hesitated, fractionally; then gave her a broad, a beaming smile, and said, "Me, too. She's the only one I've got, too."

*

179

Or the only one he wanted, at any rate. You couldn't say he'd got her, not yet.

And especially you wouldn't have said it, he wouldn't have claimed it when he gave her the message and the tenner, out in the gardens there. When she listened and nodded, took the note and hardly parted her caked lips enough to say thanks, while her eyes said, *What the hell's he doing, sending messages through you? This is private family business and you've got no part in it, Derry Bowen, who asked you to put yourself forward like that?*

Just as well she didn't say it aloud, because he had no answer except to shrug and walk away, and that was no answer at all. His eyes dropped defensively in the face of her anger, her humiliation; and he took in the state of her, dishevelled and filthy, dust in her hair and coating her T-shirt and her shorts and every exposed inch of her skin except where the sweat had streaked it clean.

And he let his tongue run loose and free, said, "God, just look at the state of you. I said you could come to ours for tea, but not like that, you can't. Mam'd go spare. Mr Dubrowski's got a bath, but I don't reckon he'd have you in the house. I wouldn't, anyway. Run a hosepipe out the window, maybe, let you shower on the lawn – "

"Shut up, Derry."

So he did that, he shut up, instantly obedient. Their eyes met, her marked face twisted; she wrapped her arms fiercely around him, butted her head into his shoulder and didn't pull away even when Johnny wolf-whistled raucously from above.

Heat and hard bones, firm muscles and soft sticky clinging filthy skin: he held her and hugged her and wished that he were bigger, wished that he could engulf her entirely within himself.

Instead he unpeeled himself too soon and took her hand, took the lead for once, tugged her away from the houses and the work and hopefully all thoughts of her father. Led her off on a scramble into the wasteland of rubble and destruction.

They clambered up and slid down slopes of artificial scree, took the skin off their hands and scabbed their knees like little children, sweated some more and got dirtier than ever. They heaved stones into the murky pools that lurked behind rusting and broken wire, and retreated choking and screaming with laughter from the vile miasma that rose up at them from the disturbed water. Once a dead dog came up with the stink, and Rachel didn't laugh that time, and neither did he; they'd both seen how its head was almost hanging off, from the great pale gash where someone had cut its throat. They laughed a lot, though, and squabbled amiably about anything and everything, so long as it didn't matter.

At last they came back to the houses, but only to wash roughly in buckets of hot water relayed from Mr Dubrowski's and to collect Rachel's bicycle. They didn't go to Derry's mother for their tea, though. Instead they bought curried rice and chips from the Chinese at the top of his street and ate it with fingers and plastic forks, sitting on a tombstone in the cemetery and passing a bottle of cider between them.

Nor did she have to be careful on the way home; Derry was careful on her behalf, watching her every step of the way. Sometimes she rode her bike, slow and wobbly, while he jogged along beside; sometimes she pushed it, or he did.

They didn't hurry, and they still got there too soon. All the time Derry had been wondering, would she ask him in for a coffee, should he angle for it, or should he just say goodnight and go? He couldn't decide, and it didn't matter anyway because she found something different, a better choice than either. She made coffee and brought it out, and they sat on the doorstep watching the stars appear; then she went inside again, and phoned for a taxi to take him home.

FIFTEEN

i

No surprise, that he becomes counsellor and father-confessor to Michael Grant. Even when he was a child, he says, his playmates used to come to him with their little problems, the sins on their small consciences. The only difference is a question of degree; and come right down to it, that's no difference at all. The problems may have got bigger by the world's definition, but then so's he. His shoulders are broader these days and his legs are strong, he can carry a greater weight for his needing neighbour.

And he'll be glad of that strength now, because it's a heavy burden Michael's brought to him; but he'll be glad also to take it on. It isn't only the law that Richard lives by, that he should bear his brother's burden. It's his pleasure too, he says, it's a part of his great joy.

And he doesn't suffer from Michael's uncertainties. No one could ever accuse him of dithering or doubt. He won't rush into anything, of course, no doubt he'll take it first of all to God; and God will show him a path, lay it out clear and unequivocal. That's how it works, in Richard's life. He says.

And he'll follow that path, step by step in his glowing golden confidence; and all will be for the best, he says, in this best of all possible worlds. As it always is, he says.

ii

Terry was in his office when the phone rang: his private line, the one that didn't go through the company switchboard, the one his secretaries didn't answer.

"Belderstone."

"Terry, it's Carlton Kerr. Are you alone?"

Carlton Kerr – senior partner in Terry's team of architects, and you could say Terry's partner too, certainly privy to many of his secrets. A co-conspirator in the eyes of the law, if the law ever looked in their direction: an accessory before and after and in many cases during the fact. And sounding panicked this morning, sounding very unhappy indeed.

"Yes, I'm alone, Carl." Alone, unwatched and unrecorded, or all Terry's expensive security gadgets had been so much waste of money. "What's the problem?"

"I, um, I'd rather not discuss it on the phone. Can we meet for lunch?"

"Briefly, if you think it's necessary." Terry didn't have the time or the patience for traditional business lunches, unless he was wooing very important clients indeed. He certainly didn't want to lose two or three hours to calm a jittery colleague. "Here, at one-thirty. Give me the gist, though. I don't like surprises."

"Michael Grant's resigned. He was in here just now, gave me his resignation in writing . . . "

"That's unfortunate, but I don't see the problem. He's good, but there are other architects."

"It's not that, I'm not worried about that. It's what's behind this, what made him do it . . . "

"Well, what, then?"

"I don't know, he wouldn't say. He wouldn't say anything, except that he was leaving immediately, no notice. But it was his mood, his attitude . . . I've known him for years, I counted him a friend. But he was, it's hard to explain, utterly formal this morning, not a spare word, just the facts. He was leaving us, here was his resignation, here was the address of his solicitors and would we please arrange all the financial details through them, buying him out of the practice and such, as he was going to be out of the country for a while."

"It'll cost him," Terry mused. "Leaving like that, you can screw him financially."

"I pointed that out. He just nodded, he seemed not to care at all about the money, he only wanted out. That's the thing, Terry. He's been odd for weeks now, very quiet and not working too well; and distant when I tried to discuss it with him. I'd put it down to family problems, but I think I was wrong, now. There was such distance in him this morning, he could hardly bear to speak with me, there has to be a reason for that . . . "

"Yes." Easy enough to guess the reason, and only two questions remaining, really: how much did he know, and what was he going to do about it? "Michael Grant – he's the Christian, isn't he? Tied in with that bloody group down on the site?"

"What? Oh – yes, I believe he is. Why, where's the relevance in that? No point appealing to his better nature, I told you, he was *viciously* cold with me just now. Said what he had to say and walked out before I could so much as offer a handshake and a

183

word of regret. Just as well, actually. I don't think he would have shaken my hand, I think he would have refused . . . "

"Steady, Carl. I'm just thinking aloud, that's all." *And you're talking too loosely, on a telephone line. My end's secure, but I wouldn't bet on yours.* "Come here for one-thirty, we'll talk about it then, over a sandwich and a glass of wine. And try not to worry. I'll tell you this much, if Michael's upset about anything he's come across in the line of business," that should be oblique enough, "he'll likely take it to his church. He won't make trouble himself, he's not the type. And if that church tries to make any more trouble for us, they'll find they picked the wrong team to fight with. I'll stir up so much trouble for them, they won't know which direction to look for the next lot coming . . . "

iii

A week into the holidays, Rachel was already losing the habit of early rising. Her internal clock still woke her at eight, but only barely; and the happy thought, *I don't have to get up yet,* was generally enough to send her drifting back into the slow and easy dreams of summer.

Not today, though. Today her first thought was of her father, underlined by the aching discomfort in her cheek. That was enough to keep her conscious and wondering. She rolled over to face the wall, hitched the duvet up as far as her nose, and remembered that he'd promised her a long talk today, some kind of explanation. Remembered too that it was Monday, a work day, he wouldn't be home till the evening.

No point in thinking about that, then. With all the day ahead of her, she'd either work herself up into another rage, or else turn all sweet and forgiving. And she didn't want to do either. So she said her first casual prayers of the day, just a quiet good-morning to God and the family; then she wriggled even further down under the covers, because maybe they couldn't read her thoughts quite so easily through that thickness of feathers, and a girl was entitled to a little privacy, even from God.

Then she thought about Derry.

That was confusing, blush-worthy, fascinating and horrendous both at once. Some of the things she'd said last night, Lord, you'd think she was drunk. On half a bottle of cider, yet. But then, some of the things *he'd* said . . .

About then she heard her father's car driving off into town.

Good riddance, she thought, in a brief return to savagery; and thought about getting up then, now that the coast was clear. But no, that would be too obvious, to God and her mother both; and besides she was dead warm, massively comfortable, didn't want to move so much as a finger . . .

And didn't, until she heard her father's car coming back again. Which was weird, the church clock hadn't hit ten yet, so what was he doing home? She lifted her head to listen more easily, to be sure of his footsteps coming in; and heard the murmur of his voice in the kitchen and her mother's reply.

And felt a sudden stab of pain in her cheek, started off by the movement; and thought no, she wasn't going to let him think she was hiding.

Kicked herself out of bed, went loudly through to the bathroom – let him hear her moving about, give him a chance to be chicken if he wanted to, jump in his car and run away again – and then back to her room to get dressed, to skimp her Bible reading and her proper prayers, to check out the way she looked in the mirror, bruised cheek vivid under hot eyes.

Just to make the point even louder, to be sure they couldn't miss it, she went back to the bathroom for the final extra little touch; and walked downstairs, walked into the kitchen tall and straight and defiant and smelling noisily of witch-hazel.

Her father was sitting at the table, his jacket off already and his tie loose. Her mother had the ironing-board out, and several chairs heaped with clothes around her. It was all very odd for a Monday morning. And what made it odder, some of those clothes – like the yellow sun-dress on the board right now – Rachel only ever saw on family holidays. They weren't going away till August, last she'd heard . . .

"Rachel. Good, I'm glad you're up." He didn't sound glad, she thought; or look it, either. No artificial smile painting itself across his solemnity. But that was just as well, maybe. Pretence would have been disgusting. "Come and sit down, please. We've got a lot to talk about."

Too right we have. But she tossed her head, so that her hair flew away from her face – another way of drawing attention to her bruises, and so what if she was overdoing it, she had a right to – and said, "I want a coffee, first."

"I'll make it," from her mother. "You just sit down, sweetheart," hands on her shoulders pressing her into a chair, pressing another message into her skin. *Give him a chance, Rachel, don't*

185

be so condemning. At least hear what he's got to say. He is your father . . .

Rachel shrugged the hands away and the message with them, not inclined to generosity this morning. She did stay seated, though; and that was enough, she thought, they couldn't ask more than that.

"Well. Look, Rachel, first thing, obviously. I'm terribly, desperately sorry about what happened yesterday," his eyes straying briefly to her cheek and falling again, to where his hands lay linked and tight on the table. Strange, that, her father too embarrassed to look at her straight. She was used to the other way around. "You were . . . provoking; but that's no excuse, and I'm not offering it as such. I'd like to plead mitigating circumstances, though, if I may."

Plead what you like, mate. She wasn't giving an inch. All she wanted was the facts.

So she said nothing, forcing him to say more; and what he said was, "The point is, love, I've been having a dreadful time at work recently. Not the normal stresses of the job, it's more than that. Something I found out about the company, and some of the jobs we've been doing. It's been preying on my mind, and I'm afraid I've been taking it out on you and your mother. It all came to a head yesterday; and obviously we couldn't go on like that any longer, so I've done what I should have done weeks ago. I resigned this morning."

Rachel stared at him briefly, willing him to go on; but when he didn't, when he obviously wasn't going to: "And that's it, is it?" she snapped. "That's enough?"

"Well, clearly I can't forget what I've learned; but I talked it over with Richard last night, and he doesn't see any need for further action. I've disengaged myself, and yes, I think that's enough. For the moment, at least. We'll just have to see what happens in the future, how the situation changes . . . "

Rachel made a disdainful gesture with her hand. "That wasn't what I meant. I don't give a, a flying fuck about that," almost stumbling over the phrase, the first time she'd ever felt its weight in her mouth; but it rolled out nice and easy once she'd got it started, she could see it becoming a habit. If she went on being this angry, she could. "What I mean is, that's supposed to be enough for me, right? You think I should be satisfied now, all bright and forgiving, is that it?"

"I hope you will," her mother said softly, unhappily. "We've always brought you up to be forgiving."

"Oh, sure. You brought me up to be peace-loving, too. Not to

186

go around belting people. I'm sorry, I'm not in a forgiving mood just now. Maybe if you'd treat me with a bit of respect, it'd be easier. But you can't fob me off like this. I want to *know*. And I reckon I'm entitled. That's my price, Dad," added quietly against the resistance she could see in his face.

"I think she's right, Michael," and her mother's hand gently brushed the hair back from her cheek, another way to underline that Rachel was the injured party here. *Thanks, Mum.* "I think you owe her that much."

Her father thought for a minute, spoke heavily; said, "In justice, perhaps I do. But there are other considerations. I've decided not to report any of this to the police or the Institute; I don't see how I can justify gossiping to my daughter."

"You told Richard," Rachel reminded him.

"Yes, but that's different."

"How?"

"He's an adult."

"Oh, right. That's what it comes down to, is it? You talk to Richard, you're discussing things with an equal, that's fine; but you talk to me, you're gossiping to a child, and that's wrong. I'll be seventeen in a few weeks, Dad. I could leave school, leave home, get married if I wanted; I could get pregnant, any time I choose." *Derry'd cooperate.* "But you still don't think I'm old enough to know what's been tearing this family apart?"

Her father made a helpless gesture. "All right, I'll tell you this much. No more, though, so you can stop leaning on me. If this doesn't satisfy you, that's just tough. My senior partner's been getting business for the firm in ways that are certainly unethical, and on occasion downright illegal."

"What, Uncle Carl?" He was her perfect image of an architect and an adoptive uncle both, tall and thin and precise, fine silvery hair and a neat beard. "Like what? He couldn't do anything really bad, he's too nice . . . "

And she blushed then, feeling her father's eyes on her, realising suddenly just how young she'd sounded. But he smiled, just slightly, and said, "Niceness doesn't preclude criminality, love. And he's been pretty bad. Bad enough that I had to get out. I don't feel good about that, I should have been more positive, confronted him or reported him, one or the other; but I like him too, so I've taken the easy way out."

"Sure, why not?" Rachel agreed absently. "No problem so big it can't be run away from. But what now, then? What are you going to do, look for another job?"

"I'm not certain yet. In the short term, we're going to France.

As to what happens after that, it depends what the situation is when we come back."

"Right. But, hang on a minute." France explained the sundress, and all the ironing. They had a cottage in the Dordogne, a tumbledown farmworker's billet they were renovating. For three years now they'd spent a month there every summer, odd weeks at other times. Rachel loved it, ordinarily. "How long were you thinking of? In France?"

"Four weeks at least, maybe more. Maybe all summer. I want to get my hands dirty. In a clean way, I mean, not with all the muck I've been scrabbling around in here."

"Oh." Rachel could understand that, it was the same impulse that had sent her to smash walls down at the houses. But, "I, um, I really . . . I don't want to go. Not now. There's, there's too much going on here . . . " What with Richard and the mission and Derry, her whole life growing into new and unexpected shapes, it was the last thing she wanted. There'd be nothing left by the time they came back, she'd be a stranger again, with it all to do . . .

"Ah." Her parents looked at each other, across her head; and there was a sudden air of relief in the room, of another problem solved.

"That's all right, Rachel," her mother said, hands busy again, playing affectionately with her hair. "That's fine. You're old enough to stay here, if you want to."

iv

Lisa was upstairs in the bathroom, scrubbing the outside of the toilet bowl when she heard her mother leave the house.

She'd already done the washing-up after breakfast, cleaned the cooker and the kitchen sink and hoovered every room downstairs. After the bathroom, there would be the bedrooms; and by the time she'd finished those no doubt her mother would be back and finding more work to be done. Mrs Dolance would have no idle hands in her house, for the Devil to misdirect.

But with her mother gone this was Lisa's chance, as like as not her only chance today; and she wasn't sure if her nerve would hold out until tomorrow.

So she left her work unfinished, traces of Luther's toothpaste still in the sink and his soapy fingerprints on the tiled splash-back. She took off her nylon overall and washed her hands, went down to the hall and changed slippers for outside shoes.

And was intercepted by Luther, disturbed from his Bible study, his thin voice sharp with questions.

"Where are you going, Lisa? Have you finished? Does Mother know you're going out, did she say you could?"

Lisa stiffened, with her fingers on the handle of the door; then she turned, looked down at her young brother, and answered his questions. Without any of the bad language, the school words that sprang quickly to her mind and almost as far as her lips. No point making trouble worse.

"I'm going out," she said, no point lying either. "No, I haven't finished, and no, Mother doesn't know. All right?"

"She'll be angry."

"I know," Lisa said wearily. That was a fact of life, like breathing, or having to go to the toilet. You did something, anything you wanted to do; and Mother found out, either on her own or because Luther told her. And she was angry, and you were punished for it.

"Well, don't do it, then," Luther said from the safe harbour of his own virtue. "You shouldn't do things that make her angry. Where are you going, anyway?"

"None of your business."

"I'll tell."

Of course you will, you little shit. You always tell. She shrugged, too wise to plead, too experienced to bother. "So tell. She'll find out anyway."

"Tell me where you're going, and she won't. We'll keep it secret. If you tell me."

"I'm going to chapel," she said. "I'm going to say a prayer. Satisfied now?"

Silly question, from the black scowl on his face. "I don't believe you," he said. "You're lying, you're lying about *sacred* things and that's a sin, it's a bad sin. I will tell now, I'll tell Mother you lied to me, and – "

And that was enough for Lisa, enough even for her slow temper. She lifted a hand, pointed a finger and spoke in a hissing whisper; said, "Judge not, Luther. Judge not, that ye be not judged."

And Luther went suddenly pale, took a step backwards, away from her or her finger, or else his own memories of judgement. And Lisa smiled at his fear, and turned, and left the house; pulled the door sharply shut behind her, felt the click of the lock and walked off almost jauntily down the hill.

Lisa was going to the chapel, not a word of a lie; and once there,

189

she would say a prayer. That much was certain. But she wasn't going in order to say that prayer, prayer wasn't the purpose of the visit. Worship, perhaps; you could say that, like so many others, she was going to the chapel to worship. But she was also going to warn.

That was another reason to feel good, the importance of the information she carried, her worth as a messenger; but even so her jauntiness couldn't last, it had to fail as she walked in through the porch. As she came face to face with Nathan Lewis.

Lisa didn't like Nathan, largely because Nathan didn't like her and made no attempt to hide it. All he had to do was look at her – the way he was looking at her now, with that thin mocking smile and the impatient snapping of his fingers – to make her feel exactly her age and condition, to know herself precisely for what she was: a fat and dumpy pubescent girl with greasy hair and skin, badly dressed and trying to hide her water-wrinkled fingers in non-existent pockets. She wasn't allowed pockets, because she couldn't keep her hands out of them. Lisa thought Nathan could probably see that too, could see the entirety of her life reflected in one simple motion, her palms sliding over coarse fabric.

She clasped her hands firmly behind her back, tried to meet him eye to eye, tried to tell him firmly and clearly what she wanted; and didn't make it, could only eye the toggles hanging from his sweatshirt hood and mumble. "Is, is Richard here, please?"

"He's here, yes." With its subtext, *He's a busy man, whyever should he be bothered with the likes of you?*

"Can I, can I see him?" *If it's all right with you . . . ?* She could hear her own subtext too, the pleading in her voice; and she despised herself for being so weak. No wonder he despised her too and did it better, so much more whole-heartedly.

"I'll see. Wait here." Greatly condescending, Nathan walked down the aisle, tapped on the little door under the arm of the cross and opened it. Put his head inside, had a quick murmured conversation; turned and came back with one eyebrow dramatically raised, *well well, wonders will never cease.*

"Go on in, Lisa. He says he'll be delighted to see you." *And what a liar, what a terrible liar he is, and him a Christian too . . .*

There was a desk in the back room that Lisa had never seen before. Richard was sitting there with a pile of letters and a portable computer, she'd obviously interrupted him at work; but then, whatever Richard did was work, one way or another. And he was always doing something. You couldn't see him at all, unless you were prepared to interrupt.

190

And at least he wasn't sitting hunched over the computer, fingers flying, making her wait. No, he'd turned the machine off before she even reached the door; he'd turned his chair away from the desk and was patiently waiting, all golden and glowing and all of it for her. Here was another man who saw truly what she was; but where Nat saw and sneered, Richard saw and loved her just as truly. He did, he really did; and was it any wonder then that she came to worship, as well as to warn?

"Lisa. Come in and sit down. It's lovely to see you here. Are you by yourself this morning?" Meaning, *Have you got away, have you come without your mother the tartar, without even your little brother the spy?*

And she nodded yes to both questions; and gazed at him and smiled, for no good reason except that he was there to be looked at, and that was something good to smile about.

But she wasn't here only to worship. "Richard," she said haltingly, almost flinching from her mother's imagined hand, her snapping voice, *Mr Gould to you, my girl,* "I've, I've got something to tell you, it's important . . . "

"All right, Lisa. Just take your time, and don't worry. Whatever it is, you can trust God to show us an answer to it."

Lisa wasn't sure she'd trust God to tie her shoelaces, these days; but you didn't say that sort of thing to Richard. He might know it anyway, he might read it from your eyes or your heart or your mind, but you still didn't say it.

So she fixed her eyes hard on the wonder of him, and said her first prayer of the day, secretly in her head. *Like mother like daughter,* she thought despairingly; and who could like her mother's daughter after this? A family of spies, they were: her mother spied for the papers, Luther spied for Mother, and now here she was spying for Richard. Never mind motives, they were still all of them doing the same thing, still spying.

"After Sunday School, yesterday," she began, and already she was wincing at the hard shapes of the words in her mouth, their sharp and unforgiving edges. "There was this reporter, just out on the street there; and Mother talked to him, she took him home and answered all his questions . . . "

"I know," Richard said.

Maybe she shouldn't have been surprised at that, maybe she should have remembered that Richard knew everything: that with God and all His angels to spy for him, he surely didn't need Lisa. But, "Oh!" she said, sounding stupid even to herself. "Oh, do you?"

"Well, it's not exactly a secret, sweetheart," he said, laughing at her. "If you want to keep secrets, you shouldn't talk to journalists. Here," handing her a paper, "a girl should read what her own mother is saying. Page five, I think."

And page five it was, of course. Richard didn't make mistakes. He probably didn't know how.

But maybe he didn't know everything, either; because Lisa read the article through, and said, "This isn't all. This isn't everything she told him."

"Isn't it?"

"No. This, this is just the good stuff . . . "

"What," he said, still sounding amused, "you mean she's been passing on all the scandal, too? How Uncle Ted finished off the ginger-nuts after the last Council meeting, and refuses to admit it? How Jack Dubrowski's got an unpaid library fine that dates back a year and a half?"

Lisa shook her head, miserable but determined in the face of this tender teasing. "It isn't them," she whispered. "It's you."

And for a moment then he was utterly still; and if the glow didn't fade, it at least turned inwards and away from Lisa so that it seemed to her that it did fade, just for that moment.

And then it was back, Richard was back in all his blazing brightness. "So what's your mother been saying about me, Lisa?"

Lisa did her spy bit then, as her mother had done it yesterday, as Luther did it all the time. She tangled her chubby hands together in her lap, stared beyond them to where her feet were ploughing ridges in the old carpet, and told him what her mother had said.

"Lots of things. Wicked stuff, all about how you were making a takeover bid for the chapel. How you were bringing in all your own people to run it, and pushing the old Council out. It wasn't true, but I couldn't say so, could I? He wouldn't have listened to me. And, and Mother would have been angry . . .

"But that wasn't the worst of it," hurrying on quickly before he could stop her, or before she lost her nerve and stopped herself. "She said something else. About you and, and that Evelyn Somers. She said that was the story he should be going after. She said you two were, you know, like, having an affair, like that . . . She said you went to her flat at night, or she came to you. She said you walked around hand in hand, when no one could see you. She said you were preaching the Gospel and practising sin. Fornication, she said you were doing . . . "

"I see. Thank you, Lisa."

And again his light seemed briefly dim, seemed to be swallowed up inside himself. It came back only with his smile, and even that might have been a little less rich than usual, a little less comfortable on his face.

"Your mother's made a mistake," he said. "It's nothing to worry about, she simply misunderstood. And the journalist realised that, obviously, and didn't print the story. He only printed the truth. But I'm still glad you came to see me, Lisa. This is what I'm here for, to listen to your concerns. Now let's say a quick prayer, shall we, let's put it all in God's hands, where it belongs . . . "

So Lisa found herself praying in the chapel, as she'd said she would; but prayers didn't work for Lisa these days. Richard had the magic now, he had the monopoly of it in his own two human hands – and when she sneaked a peek while he was praying, when she saw those hands so tightly pressed together, she thought a little private blasphemy. She thought there wasn't really room for that much magic, between those two linked hands.

v

It came as a relief to Helen, to be back among the certainties of Paradise. Things were different at her parents' house, and difficult without Nat; there were too many questions asked, not enough answers to go around. She'd found herself beset by doubts, by caustic fingers digging at the cracks in her new-made faith, the deeper cracks in her confidence.

But coming into the city, simply crossing the border made things better. Helen saw two worlds now, and this was the one she favoured: this island of faith, this beacon she called home.

No Nat at the coach station to meet her, but no surprise, she hadn't expected him. Had barely hoped, even. She took a bus, mapping a route out in her head – to the flat first, then the chapel, the marquee, down the hill to the houses. One of those, she'd find him.

But she didn't need the map at all, she didn't have to walk the least part of that route; God had things organised better. She stepped off the bus, it drove away, Nathan called her name. She startled, stared – and saw him on a bank of grass just across the road, sitting with Richard in the sunshine. *Or sitting with the sunlight in the Richardshine,* she thought, giggling wildly as she waved, as she ran without looking, scaring a passing cyclist half to death.

It was Richard who rose smoothly to his feet, who caught her in his warm strong arms, who absorbed her headlong dash into a welcoming hug. Nat just stayed quietly smiling up at her, his eyes unreadable behind his Ray-Bans; but after a minute he laughed, he said, "Are you going to put my girl down, or what?"

Richard grinned, and gently unhitched himself. Nat reached to curl long fingers around her wrist, to pull her into his lap; and that was it for Helen, that was Paradise pure and simple, Nat's kiss with Richard watching.

It took a minute to get sorted, to get rid of rucksack and jacket and get settled; but soon enough they had it just right, they had it perfect. She was nestled against his chest, cradled in his arms, her head on his shoulder and his breath in her hair. She was blissfully happy, she felt like the smallest and most ultimately trusting of children; any minute now she'd start sucking her thumb. And they'd laugh at her if she did, both of them would, and frankly she didn't give a damn.

"Tell you what," Richard said, somewhere above her. "Why don't you take the afternoon off?"

"No need," Nat said, playing with her hair while she pouted invisibly at him for being a traitor, for doing the right thing. "I don't think we should stop now, Richard. This is important."

"So's Helen," Richard said, earning a richer glow to his halo. "Don't be such a martyr, Nat. Trot off home, the pair of you, and get caught up. But don't forget the Watch meeting tonight, you said you'd do that for me."

"Sure." Nat's fingers stroked the nape of Helen's neck, making her breath catch and her whole scalp prickle with sweat under her heavy hair. "I won't forget. Plenty of time before then, to get caught up."

So they went off hand in hand, Helen in the lead and tugging. There was no talking; he didn't ask about her weekend, she didn't ask about his. She'd hear later, what he wanted her to know.

When they reached his flat she dropped her rucksack just inside the hall, he kicked the door shut behind them; and the bedroom was right there, first exit, but even so they barely made it, they still left a path of scattered clothes behind them.

"Nat . . . ?"

"Helen."

"You don't, you don't think this is sinful, do you? I mean, us not being married and stuff, if we're Christians maybe we shouldn't . . . "

"You want to stop?"

194

"No. *No!* It's just, maybe we have to stop anyway, want to or not. If it's the right thing to do . . . "

"Richard doesn't think it's sinful. He said so."

"Did he? Well, that's okay, then."

"Is it?"

"Yes, of course. Why not?"

"What, Richard's your sole authority, is he? There could be other people with other opinions . . . "

"Oh, sure, you could find someone to say we shouldn't. Mrs Dolance, she'll be saying it already. Mr Parkinson. All those old guys, I expect. They're sweet, but I bet they disapprove. But – yes, I'd rather listen to Richard. He doesn't have opinions, he just *knows* . . . "

"Well. Good, then. Move over, I want an unfair share of this duvet."

Later, dressed now but still nesting on the bed, picking at a Chinese takeaway straight from the cartons:

"What's so important about this meeting tonight, how come you've got to go rushing off?" *How come we couldn't stay the way we were,* she meant, *naked behind closed doors, and only our bodies open?*

"Neighbourhood Watch," Nat explained. "It's the sort of thing Richard wants me for. He hasn't got time for all the meetings people want to see him at, so I'm his representative. And he's right, I should be there. It's a natural extension of this task-force idea. If we're going to be a power in the community, we've got to be *au fait* with the security situation, and we've got to be visibly involved."

Helen nodded dubiously. She could see the wisdom of it, of course, it made perfect sense; but, "Why does it have to be you?" she grumbled. "Why does it have to be you *tonight?*"

"It doesn't have to be me." He put his chopsticks down, reached for her still-bare foot and scratched at the sole with his thumbnail, making her squirm. "Not me alone. It can just as easily be us. You're a resident too, right?"

"I'm not, though," she whispered, breathlessly hopeful. "This is your flat, I don't live here . . . "

"As good as," he said; which wasn't exactly an invitation, *it's high time you did, when are you going to quit wasting rent-money on that other place and move in here with me?* But it was the next best thing, from Helen's point of view. As good as.

Nat had dropped all his political commitments, after that

195

momentous evening in the marquee. Helen had been surprised, almost shocked by the speed with which he abandoned old beliefs and old colleagues, in favour of the new.

But there were definite advantages to this sea-change; and one of them was this, that – in addition to getting her soul saved, finding a purpose to life and the promise of an everlasting joy to come after – she got to share another side of him. She got to walk with his arm around her shoulders, hugging herself tight against him all the way down to the school where the meeting was held; and once there, she got to see Nat doing what he did best, taking charge.

The Chairman had worked slowly and carefully through the agenda, from Apologies for Absence to Any Other Business. The Community Policeman had reported on burglaries and twocking in the area – and then had apologised and talked of auto-crime, of Taking Without Consent. People had worried about the number of empty premises, the encouragement they provided to vandals and tramps. Nat had yawned once or twice, shifted in his seat; and – bored stiff by the meeting, but as ever thrilled by him – Helen had smiled, reached for his hand, nudged him into stillness.

Some representative you are, she'd mouthed at him, too fast to read but the gist surely obvious, *some diplomat, you* . . .

But then they reached Any Other Business; and – clearly contrary to all expectation, the Chairman already stacking his papers and his mouth half open to declare the meeting closed – a man at the back had got to his feet and said, "Yes."

Said, "Yes, please. We need your help."

He was a short man, a tubby little Sikh smiling with shyness, sharp white turban and thick grey beard; and he said, "Please, my wife and I, we wish to attend our daughter's wedding in Manchester this month; but we do not dare to leave our house, do you see?"

"Why's that, then?" the Chairman asked, frowning with irritation.

"It is because of the vandals. The racialists. They have attacked my house, oh, many times, when my wife is in the house, do you see, sometimes even when I myself am in the house; and we do not dare now to leave the house to be empty for one night."

"Well, if you talk to PC Andrews here, give him the address, I'm sure he'll arrange to keep an eye on the place, Mr . . . ?"

"Singh, my name is Singh. But this is not enough. The police, yes, they drive past once or twice in the evening, but the racialists see them coming and keep out of sight, and return when the car is past. We need more help than this."

"Well. I'm sorry, uh, Mr Singh, but I don't see what else we can suggest. Perhaps you should get in touch with some other organisation, though I don't know who. We're not vigilantes, it's not our job to patrol the streets . . . "

And Nat was on his feet in an instant, no boredom, no detachment in him now, all scorn as he said, "Of course it is, that's precisely the job. It's a job that needs doing, and who else is there to do it, who should do it, if not the residents? The police simply can't cope, we all know that; that's why Neighbourhood Watch exists, for crying out loud, so we can help. So that neighbour can watch out for neighbour. And yes, that does mean patrolling the streets. We should work up a rota, get it organised. And it certainly means keeping an eye on each other's houses, to be sure they're safe, left empty. I'll arrange that for you, Mr Singh," charged with confidence now, electric, with every eye on him, "you don't need to worry. Never mind this lot, we'll keep a watch on your house."

"Who's 'we', then?" a voice came back at him, from the floor. "Who are you, lad, come to that? Never seen you at one of these meetings."

"No, but you'll be seeing me again," Nat snapped. "My friends, too. My name's Nathan Lewis, and I'm here on behalf of the Paradise Pentecostal Gospel Hall." Adding, in case there might be too many syllables in that particular mouthful, in case they needed a more straightforward pointer to the truth, "I represent Richard Gould."

SIXTEEN

i

It's true, she does take his hand in the street; but it can't be a romantic gesture, how could it? Surely, anything but. She's not waving, she's drowning. Not cuddling, but clutching.

And one straw of comfort for her, for him, for all of us perhaps: that she's not clutching at straws here. He's no man of straw, to come apart beneath her desperate fingers. That much we can be sure of, surely we can.

That's how to read it, yes, that she grips his hand in a fever of need. And that he meets that need – what else would you expect? – with words of comfort and hope, with a smile that lights up the darkness.

It's more than his smile, though, that sparks so bright tonight. Someone's busy with a camera, the glare of a vicious flash: he gazes across the road, open and ultimately trusting, to see a short man with a long lens and a motor drive, snapping madly to the end of the roll.

– Who, who's that? she asks. What does he want, why the pictures, why me?

– Not you, he says calmly, smiling still. He doesn't want you, Evelyn. It's only a journalist, it's only me he's after. I'm news in this city, I can't escape the newsmen.

– I don't want to be photographed, she says. I don't want to be news.

– Don't worry, he says, you're not.

And if there's a twitch to his perfect face as he says it, a blemish of doubt on his serenity, it's only there a moment; and nothing to worry about because it's dark, it's far too dark for her to see.

ii

Derry was woken by his mother, banging loud and heavy on his door.

"Yeah, what?" he croaked, his voice thick with sleep.

"Phone! It's that Rachel. And she's in a call-box, she says, so move yourself . . . "

And Derry did that, jamming legs into jeans with frantic haste, barging out of his room and across the landing. Snatching the receiver off young Sammy, who was gabbing nonsense into it in high delight. "Rachel? That you?"

"Hi, Derry." There was a breathy giggle in her voice. "Who was that I was just listening to?"

"Oh. My kid brother, Sammy. Sorry, he's a pest."

"He sounds sweet. Maybe you should ask him for lessons, how to chat up girls. He's got a great technique."

"Rachel — are you all right?"

"Yes, sure, why wouldn't I be?"

"I don't know, you sound funny." *You sound drunk.* "And you never phoned me before, and it's half seven in the morning . . . "

"I know that. Um — look, are you going into work this morning?"

"I was, yeah."

"Oh. Okay, then. Doesn't matter."

"What?" And then, registering the background babble behind her voice, "Rachel, where *are* you?"

"At the airport."

"You what, what are you doing there, where are you going?"

"I'm not. I'm just here, that's all. And I thought you might like to come out, I want to talk to someone. But it's okay, if you've got to work I'll just go home again, it's not important really . . . "

"Wait." The airport, that was five miles out of town. There were buses, there had to be buses from somewhere. "I'll come. Just give us half an hour, I'll come."

"What about the gym?"

"I'll phone in sick. It won't matter, they're never busy, mornings. I'll tell George I'm all sweaty and dry-mouthed and my legs have gone wobbly. I just won't tell him why."

She giggled again. *Definitely drunk,* he thought. "You have been taking lessons, haven't you? Come on, then. I'll be up on the roof. And, Derry?"

"Yeah, what?"

"Hurry."

He washed and brushed his teeth in nothing flat, chucked clothes all across his room and finally settled for his gym kit and tracksuit, what he would have been wearing anyway. Going downstairs, he had an idea, a second thought; and delayed just long enough to take his mother by surprise with a sudden hug,

199

and a whispered plea. "Do us a favour, Mam, phone us in sick? George'll believe you, he wouldn't me."

"I'll do no such thing. I'm not lying for you, my son, you bear your own sins . . . "

And she sent him on his way with a sharp cuff on the ear.

No time to fuss around with buses. *Hurry,* she'd said. So he sprinted up to the taxi office and spent his last fiver on a cab to the airport.

I'll be up on the roof, she'd said. So he climbed all the stairs he could find, and automatic doors at last let him out onto a flat roof, and yes, there was Rachel. Not waving, not running to meet him; not even watching the doors for his arrival. She was bent perilously over the perimeter rail, her eyes on the planes below.

He jogged across the concrete, and she did look round briefly as he got closer, did give him a quick smile before turning her attention back to the planes.

"Hi," he said, joining her, leaning his elbows right next to hers on the railing.

Another distracted glance, and you wouldn't think this was the girl who'd been so urgent on the phone. "Thanks for coming," she said, but that was all.

"No sweat," he said; and, "Any time."

And didn't know what to say after that, so just kept quiet, the way she was. Watched the planes, the way she did; though there was little enough to see. Just some passengers boarding a big jet, and their luggage going on at the back.

After a minute, "I got you out of bed, didn't I?" she said, her voice sort of unfocused as if she wasn't really paying much attention to what it was saying.

"Yeah, but no matter. I said, any time."

"I was just thinking, I bet you didn't have any breakfast. You can get food downstairs, or coffee, if you want it . . . "

"Can't," he said equably. "Got no money, I had to blow it on a taxi to get here."

"Oh – *damn* you, Derry Bowen . . . " And she turned to face him, turned to hug him at last, good and tight and just the hint of a kiss below his ear. Then she shoved him away, caught at his hand, pressed a purse into it.

"Here. Go on, get anything you want. Caviar and champagne, I don't care."

And turned back to the planes again, unless it was back to the people.

*

He was back on the roof, back with her in five minutes, hot dog in one hand and coke in the other.

"For *breakfast?*" she said, amused or disgusted, both.

He nodded cheerfully, licking at oozing yellow mustard. "'Snice. Your purse is in my pocket here, but you'll have to fish for it, I haven't got a hand free . . . "

"It can wait. Don't get cocky, boy," with a hard little jab in the ribs; but when he skipped away she pulled him back, held him with an arm around his waist.

"See that plane?" she said conversationally, as the jet began to taxi towards the runway. "My parents are on that plane."

"Yeah?" He stared, from the plane to her. "Where are they off to, then?"

"France. We've got a cottage. But the point is, they're going on their own. Leaving me. I'm old enough to look after myself, apparently. Parents are *weird,*" explosively. "Last week, I wasn't old enough to be out on my own after dark. This week I can be left for a month, money in the bank and *do what you like, dear, of course we trust you . . . *"

Derry munched in silence, while they watched the plane's slow progress; then, "That's good, isn't it? Them going away? No more fights."

"Of course it's good. Sort of. It's just weird, that's all. They've never done things without me, we're a family. Or we were, till it all went sour. That's why they're off now, to get it fixed again, just the two of them. Mum called it a twenty-thousand-mile service. Then I'm supposed to go out in a few weeks' time, and we'll all be cosy together." The plane reached the runway, and turned into the wind; Rachel sighed fretfully. "I just hope it works, that's all. I need it to. I need my family working properly, everything's squiffy without it."

"Yeah. You going to be all right, then? On your own, like?"

"Of course I'll be all right, why wouldn't I be?" But she glanced at him sideways, smiled slyly, said, "So long as I get visited. I'm going to need lots of visits."

"Am I allowed?" he asked, sure of the answer but wanting to hear it anyway. "I mean, your dad, he didn't like me much. I thought maybe he'd said, no Derry . . . "

"My dad," she said, "can go stick his head up an ostrich's bottom, before I let him choose my friends for me. But no, you've got special permission anyway. He said so."

"Yeah? What did he say, then?"

She giggled, as the plane began its take-off run. "What he *said,* he said if I really wanted that bald little squit hanging round me all the time, then he supposed that was okay by him. What he *meant* was that he was sorry for being so nasty before, and he'll make it up to you when we all come back."

"He said that, did he? Bald little squit, he said that?"

"Mmm."

"So what did you say?"

"*I* said he'd better watch out who he went around insulting, 'cos you weren't so little any more, and you had a rotten temper and you'd tear him limb from limb."

"Oh, great. So what did he say then?"

"That was when he stopped calling you a bald little squit, and started calling you King Kong . . . "

And that was when the plane passed almost directly above their heads, with a roar that would have defeated any conversation. But Rachel had turned her back in any case, was watching it out of sight, waving madly, both hands; so just in case her father could see, Derry put both arms round her slender ribs and held her close, held her still while she waved.

iii

Vinny was in Paradise this morning. He'd been in the gym earlier; Jason would have known that anyway, just from the way his skin had prickled first thing when he arrived, from the way he felt so nervous and shivery, jumping at shadows. But if you were lucky, if you didn't know Vinny well enough to smell him on the air, then there was always the roomful of cats downstairs to say that Vinny had been around.

Collecting.

He wasn't here now, but his cats were like a promise, *I'll be back.*

Jason didn't think George had expected the cats, they were just one of Vinny's little surprises. The music was on extra-loud up in reception, to cover the noise; but Jason worked down in the store-rooms, mostly, where he couldn't escape it. The dog was at it too, barking its head off and hurling itself against the door, going crazy almost in its dark room with the smell of all those cats, all the fighting and screaming.

Jason shivered, remembering his own long hours in the stink and terror of that room. He'd promise anything, he'd *do* anything, not to go through that again.

202

But he'd also do anything to get back at the dog for scaring him so much, so long as it was safe to do; and the sound of its great muzzle snuffling at the crack under the door gave him an idea. He left off mopping the concrete floor, went to the cubby-hole under the stairs; came back with a can of fly-spray.

Crouched down, stuck the nozzle noisily into that little crack, waited for the dog to investigate – then gave it a good heavy squirt of the stuff, right up the nose.

Listened to it sneezing and choking behind the door, giggled, hugged himself in delight.

Stood up, turned round.

Saw Vinny watching him.

The bastard must've come in the other way, from the back alley, down the steps and through the open fire-door; and Jason hadn't heard him with all the racket going on down here, hadn't smelt him or sensed him or anything.

And now he stood there with his guilt in his hands and his terror like cold fire tracking across his skin and digging deep, digging right into his bones; and Vinny smiled his crooked smile, licked his broken yellow teeth, took his time, while the old canvas shopping-bag in his hand wriggled and kicked.

Finally, he spoke.

Said, "George not around, then, Jase?"

"Uh, yeah. Yeah, sure, he's upstairs, Vinny . . . "

"Well, better put that away, then, hadn't you? Sharpish, before he hears his dog all snotty and comes down to see why."

Jason did that, relieved but not grateful, not stupid enough to be grateful. This only dug him deeper into the pit.

Then Vinny said, "Right. Job for you, Jase. In the back of the van, couple of tea-chests, wire-netting over the top. Go fetch 'em, and fill 'em up."

"What with?"

"Christ, what do you think? I've got another one here, start you off." And Vinny swung the bag and threw it, the squirming, struggling bag he'd held.

But Jason caught it badly, distracted by another figure moving behind Vinny, someone else coming in through the fire-door. He caught the bag by a corner, just barely getting a grip; and the contents fell out, dived between Vinny's legs and made a dash for freedom.

And was grabbed by Derry, scooped up in firm, gentle hands and cradled close to his chest as he said, "What's going on, where'd the kitten come from? Not yours, is it, Jason?"

203

Jason just shook his head dumbly. Vinny did the talking. "It's a stray," he said. "I've got this place south of the river, I like to pick strays up off the street sometimes. George lets me use his gym," gesturing to the store-room where all the noise was coming from, the wailing of fighting, frightened cats, "there are always a lot of strays around here."

Derry was frowning, looking like he didn't believe a word of it. Jason couldn't blame him for that. Any sensible cat would run a mile sooner than take anything from Vinny.

But just in time here came George down from reception; and Vinny said, "George. I was just telling the lad about my cat sanctuary, see. He saved a runaway for us."

"Is that right?" George took it all in at a glance, and smiled widely; said, "Derry, son, I thought you weren't coming in this morning. Your mother phoned, said you were sick."

"Did she?" Derry went bright red. "Oh, hell. I'm sorry, George, she told me she wouldn't. Um, I'm not sick. I just, I had to see someone, it was urgent . . . "

"Uh-huh. Girl, was it?" And when Derry nodded, "Well, we've all been sixteen, son. Just don't make a habit of it. So you've got one of Vinny's strays there, have you? Well, tell you what," dropping a huge hand on Derry's shoulder and steering him towards the stairs, "it's a cute little thing, that one. Maybe you'd do Vinny a favour, take it off his hands. He's got too many anyway. Maybe that girl of yours'd like a kitten, mmm? Look, here's twenty quid, take it to a vet and get its jabs done, better safe than sorry . . . "

So Derry came to work late, and got bribed for keeping quiet, and hardly did a thing all day for fussing over his bloody kitten; while Jason had to jam half a dozen vicious and terrified cats into two small crates, and got his arms scratched to ribbons doing it, while Vinny just leaned against the door and watched.

Then he had to carry the crates out to the van; and then the room needed cleaning, because there was cat-crap everywhere. He was just dumping a shovelful outside when Vinny came up the steps behind him, said, "Saturday night, Jase. Don't make any plans."

"What, why not?"

"Because I like the way you shovel shit, son."

"Christ, Vinny, give us a break! I got to work for George all bloody day . . . "

"I know. I'll pick you up when the gym closes. Be ready."

And he would be ready, of course he would, no question; just one last sulky mutter, "I'm on curfew, I got to be back at the hostel by ten . . . "

"Just have to shovel quick, then, won't you?" Vinny said, smiling his terrible smile. "You'll be brought back when the job's done. But do it good, and maybe there's a bonus."

And with that he slammed the doors on his shrieking cargo and went to the front of the van, drove off without another word; leaving Jason staring after him, wondering just what Vinny's idea of a bonus was, and whether he really wanted to find out.

iv

Luther slept, and walked strange worlds in his dreams: worlds where he couldn't be safe because no God walked with him, he went naked and unprotected and unsaved.

His sister's hand dragged him suddenly, pinchingly back into the real world; he opened his eyes to the darkness of his own small bedroom, the darker shadow of her body bent over him. And that wasn't much better, because saved he might be, one of the elect and bound for Heaven, but their mother was out all night at a vigil, and without her he sure as anything didn't feel protected.

He tried to pull free of the grip she had on his shoulder; but her other arm swung without warning, caught him stingingly back-handed across the cheek.

"Wake up, Luther," she said, hissing. But he was awake already, he was ahead of her, he knew what she'd say before she said it. "This is judgement." *And you don't fight judgement, you don't resist.* That much she didn't need to say, it was implicit. He knew the rules.

"What do you, what do you want, Lisa?" Sulky and afraid and starting to snivel already, knowing that Lisa would give him reason enough before the night was out.

"I want you to sit up. *Up,*" and she hauled him easily out from under his blankets, up onto his knees on the bed. That was another good reason not to fight Lisa, she was bigger and stronger, savage when Satan used her that way. And Satan was strong in her tonight, Luther could see that even in the dark; he could hear it in her voice, feel the Devil's strength in her fingers, another good reason to be afraid.

"You've been getting me in trouble again, Luther," she said. But it was Satan talking through her really, *You've been getting Me in trouble,* he was saying. "I want you to see what happens to

205

little boys who work their mouths off. I want you to see it first, before you feel it. Look . . . "

And she pulled the curtain back from the window and thrust his face hard up against the glass, to be sure that he saw.

Down in the street, in the gutter right outside their house, something was burning. Something big, with strange blue flames dancing over its darkness.

"What," he whispered, "what is it?"

"It's a little boy whose sister doesn't like him," Satan whispered gleefully, in Lisa's voice. "She poured paraffin all over him, and set him alight. He's frying now, open the window and you'll smell him as he burns, like a doomed soul in hellfire. Like you'll smell yourself in a minute. That's for you too, Luther. That's the judgement."

"You burn." Luther's voice was cracked with terror but driven by truth, even in the face of ultimate evil. "You burn, *you* do. *You.* Not me . . . "

But his sister's hand with the Devil's mind behind it had let go of him already, had picked up a bottle from the floor; and suddenly his head was wet and his pyjamas were soaking. Luther backed away across the bed into the corner, and heard the bottle bounce emptily plastic on the carpet.

And then there was fire suddenly blazing between her fingers, and he saw the devil-light in her eyes.

And he screamed, kicked his feet uselessly at her, pulled the wet blankets over his head; and lay curled in a shivering and terrified ball, waiting to explode in flame and die burning.

And he waited, and waited longer, and didn't burn.

And finally, when he'd sobbed and shivered long enough, he prayed; and was enlightened, a little. Because it wasn't paraffin that had soaked him and his bed, he couldn't smell paraffin at all. It was something else, smelling stronger all the time as it warmed in that little cave of darkness beneath the blankets.

It was pee, that's what it was. Satan was tricksy, Mother said that all the time. He'd moved Lisa to pour her pee all over him and pretend it was paraffin, to punish him for telling truth to Mother.

And the punishment wasn't over yet, it didn't end there. Because Mother would find his bed wet in the morning, and he couldn't tell her true this time, he didn't dare; so then she'd punish him for bedwetting, she'd stand him on the landing with his wet sheets over his head and leave him there until they dried.

And he didn't want to think about that, not at all. So he thought

206

about Satan, and Lisa, and sin: how often she was tempted, how often she fell. She was weak and evil; and her punishment would come, but not from him. Not this time. He would suffer in silence, and God would surely reward him for that, as he was sure to punish Lisa.

And then Luther thought about the burning thing down on the pavement, and wondered what it was. Just old rubbish, that Lisa really had poured paraffin over. Not a boy.

But Lisa was set for Hell if she let the Devil use her. She'd burn, all right. And Luther shivered in his cold, wet bed, and thought about burning. He thought about Lisa burning and burning with all the other sinners, all God's enemies all in the same fire, all burning.

And he made a list of them in his head, and put Lisa at the top because she was too evil to be saved, she was lost, even his mother was starting to believe it. Oh, yes, she'd burn. Lisa and the others, all the ones his mother named sinners and blasphemers, sinners and thieves . . .

v

Billy had done well tonight. His students had been in at the 'Lady Grey', and they'd kept his glass filled for him. They were his favourite people; and he was their favourite piano player, they always told him that.

And then, chucking-out time, he'd been wandering his slow way up from the river – heading for home, you could call it, maybe; but it wasn't really, no home for Billy now, only somewhere to sleep – when he passed a big house, loud music, more students spilling out into the street. Drinking and laughing, talking and shouting, bringing their party out for some air.

Billy tried to squeeze past; but a voice called his name and an arm dropped over his shoulders, curled itself around his neck. Billy whimpered, ducked, tried to wriggle out from under. But he wasn't allowed, the arm just tightened and the voice only laughed. So he looked up to see who it was, who had him now. Whether he ought to be frightened.

He didn't know the face, it was just a boy, another boy who knew Billy. Of course he did, everyone knew Billy. Nothing to be frightened of, a drunken boy shining with sweat, his hair dripping and his T-shirt as sticky as his skin.

"Billy. Hullo, Billy, how are you?" And a roar of laughter, and a swig at the almost-full bottle of wine in his other hand.

"I'm fine, mister, thank you. Thank you for asking. How are you?" Billy knew his manners.

"I'm pissed." And the boy drank from the bottle, and looked at the bottle; and he looked at Billy, and laughed. "Here," he said, "you take this. Birthday present."

"It's not my birthday, mister." Grinning widely because he couldn't manage a laugh and he thought he ought to, it seemed like a good idea.

"No, I know," and the boy almost choked over this one, it was so funny. "It's mine, it's my birthday. I'm twenty-one. This is my party." And he looked at it from the outside, just for a moment, almost from where Billy was standing; and shook his head, and shrugged. Said, "So you, you take this, Billy, all right? Have a drink on me. Everyone else has."

The boy let him go then, and wove his way back into the party, moving unsteadily from friend to friend. Billy weighed the bottle in his hand, and smiled; lifted it to his mouth and drank, and wandered on.

The bottle was half empty by the time he reached the marquee. Even so, he didn't neglect his usual cautious approach, walking all the way around it before sidling in, high-stepping over the ropes and checking that no one was there, no one was watching.

It was just as well that Billy didn't believe in ghosts. It was a frightening place to be alone in, that tent, for a frightened man: with the chairs all laid out in rows for a ghostly audience, and the canvas twitching and flapping in any breeze, and all the shadows moving every time a car drove past with its lights on.

But Billy was getting better, mostly, not so frightened now, except tonight. Tonight was a little bit special, with all the drink that was in him. He couldn't walk the aisle without crashing into chairs, without stumbling over his own feet and jumping at every sliding shadow.

"Steady," he muttered, "whoops!" he giggled, "careful there, Billy son, step careful, they'll hear . . . "

But no one heard, or at any rate no one came; and Billy made it at last to the stage at the far end. Went round behind it and peered underneath, into the three-foot gap between boards above and dying grass below.

He couldn't actually see anything in the utter darkness under there, but he pretended he could. Pretended he could see the shape of his suitcase well hidden, the shape of his bags. Then he sat on the stage and went on drinking, drank until he'd finished the bottle.

He wasn't feeling too wonderful by then, not too fit, our Billy; but he smiled anyway, laughed to spite himself. Waggled the empty bottle in the air in a final toast to the birthday boy and stood up, badly needing a piss.

And was sick, suddenly and violently sick all the way down his front.

He bent over, retching; and retched worse at the stink of it rising to hit him, the foul taste of it in his mouth, coating his teeth and his tongue.

And was still retching, forgetful of all but this most immediate misery, when he felt a warmth and a wetness flowing uncontrollably down his leg.

Billy cried a little then, with all the nastiness of it. He liked to be clean, he liked to keep himself nice. One of the miseries of living in a hole was that he was always dirty and his clothes were worse. And now this, now they were disgusting and he had no way to wash them, no water and no money and no home . . .

He didn't cry for long, though. Not Billy. He pulled his clothes off with fastidious fingers, all his clothes, and stood naked in the darkness; and thought about dragging out his luggage to find new clothes, and giggled, and decided not. Decided to sleep like this, naked on the cool grass in the warm night.

Nodded solemnly to himself, and was still nodding yes, yes indeed when a circle of light appeared right in front of him, and the wall of the marquee started to shake.

It shook a little, stopped, and shook again; and the wall was looking a little baggy suddenly. Drooping inwards. And then there was another circle of light, and they were torches; and there were men's voices, now that he was listening. Now that he was staring, trembling, naked and afraid.

"Just cut 'em," one voice said, good and loud. "Cut the ropes, that's all. That'll bring it down. Weren't you never a boy scout, didn't you go camping?"

And the walls shook, and there was a tremble even in the poles now, an unsteadiness all around him; and Billy only wanted to creep deep into the darkness, into his hole under the stage and hide there.

But he was still standing, still working up the courage to move when suddenly there was more to watch, the shadow of a great arm on the wall right by him, long finger pointing.

And the shadow punched at the wall, and broke through; and it

209

wasn't a finger, no, it was a knife, long and sharp and glinting as it ripped down through the canvas. Long and sharp and laughing.

But it wasn't the knife that was laughing. It was the devil's face that came shoving through the slit, wild eyes staring into Billy's and that crazy laugh dying into silence.

The silence didn't last long, Billy saw to that.

Billy screamed, high and shrill.

Then he turned and ran, naked as he was, nothing in his arms or on his back. He ran from every poor thing that he owned, ran screaming down the hill until he couldn't scream any more, he needed all his breath for running.

He ran till the tarmac turned to stones beneath his feet, and cut him badly; and then, at last, when the pain was worse than the fear, he stopped and turned and looked behind him.

And saw nothing, nobody, no faces. Heard no laughter, nothing.

Drew a slow, sobbing breath and looked about him, wanting only a new place to hide . . .

SEVENTEEN

i

He stands in Paradise and looks at sin; he stands and shivers, with the sun's cloaking warmth across his shoulders.

– It's only mischief, he says. It's kids, he says, that's all.

He says.

He's wrong, though, and he knows he's wrong, he must do; which means he's more than wrong, he's lying.

He'd have to be, really. He can see better than that, he can see that there's more than mischief in this, more than kids playing trash-the-tent.

He knows anger and hatred when he sees them, he knows the smell of evil.

And he knows a warning when he sees one, he's no fool.

So he stands there in the sunshine and looks on the wreckage of the marquee, the great cathedral reduced to a heap of dirty canvas, cut ropes and broken poles; and no doubt he tries not to see it as a symbol. Not to think of mountains laid low and beacons broken, faith damaged and hope destroyed.

Smiles for the cameras, and says no.

– No, he says, this changes nothing, how could it? A few vandals can't disrupt the smooth unfolding of God's plans, he says. This is only foolishness, and it's foolish to attach any importance to it.

– A new marquee has been ordered already, he says, it'll arrive this afternoon.

– Never mind at what cost, he says, money doesn't matter. It's immaterial, he says, the fight is what counts. God's soldiers, he says. That's what we are, we're God's soldiers; and this is camp, he says, this is HQ.

– No, he says, laughing, Jesus is the general. Not me, I just follow orders.

– But the Romans pitched their tents here, he says, and so will we. They weren't frightened off by the local tribesmen, and neither will we be.

– Nor Goths nor Visigoths nor Vandals, he says, will drive us out of Paradise.

And he says it light-heartedly, he says it laughing; but there's a serious message there, for anyone who wants to hear it. A response. *Message received*, he's saying. *We stay*, he's saying; and, *Your move*, he's saying that too.

ii

Jack Dubrowski was taking advantage of the cool morning, working in his garden before the noon sun burned away all his good intentions. This was a miracle summer in more ways than one; but fierce heat sapped his strength and fed his idleness, and it was well to forestall it. A shame to waste the time.

Especially with no work going on along the terrace, no one around. They'd all be up by the school, he thought, where the marquee was. Had been.

It was a bad thing, what had happened to the marquee: bad, but not surprising. Jack had heard about it on the local radio news, first thing this morning; anything that happened in Paradise was news these days. He'd been saddened and worried, but not at all surprised. The only surprise was that it hadn't happened sooner. The kind of kids they had round here, always stealing cars and breaking windows – why had they ever imagined a tent would be safe? Even God's tent?

Still, every cloud was lined with silver, everything happened with God's consent and there was always good to be found somewhere, you only had to look. And Jack didn't have to look far, to see one small goodness growing out of the night's vandalism.

Anita loved to sit in the garden ordinarily, but she'd hardly been out of the house since the building work started. It frightened her, so many people and so much busyness where she was used to solitude, to having no one and nothing move between the houses and the river. Never mind that they were nice kids, always polite and seldom rowdy; they were just too many, and their constant comings and goings left Anita confused and unhappy.

Today, though, Jack had seized the opportunity of their absence. He'd brought Anita out, taking all her frail weight easily on one arm; he'd shown her the row of empty gardens, and her chair set out ready for her, turned toward the sun; and he'd seen her smile and nod and look blissfully content.

And that was how he felt now, blissfully content as he

212

straightened slowly against the ache in his back, dusted dry earth from his hands and turned to look, to check, to be sure. It was more than habit now, to keep such a constant watch on Anita; but today it was all reward and no worry. She was settled and comfortable, a glass of home-made lemonade on the grass beside her, a magazine in her lap. Her face was lifted to the light and her eyes were closing. She'd be asleep any minute now.

Jack nodded to himself, living for the moment as he had learned to do; then he turned and bent again to his weeding, with only a brief yearning for the spine and shoulders of a younger man, the calves and thighs and especially the knees of a boy.

Then Anita screamed.

It was a thin, pale sound with no strength to it, it would have been hardly more than a gasp from anyone else; but it had Jack jerking upright and twisting round, sharp as a young man, anxious as a boy.

Nothing to see – only Anita, pale and trembling, her mouth working soundlessly as though that one feeble scream had taken all her voice away from her.

Jack rubbed at his neck, where a stabbing pain spoke to him in secret, talked of the need to move more slowly. But he defied that and his aching back both, defied his body and the age of it as he hurried over to where Anita rocked in her chair, twisting her hands together.

"Anita, my dear, my sweet one, what is it? What is it has frightened you? Here, have a drink," and he lifted the lemonade to her lips, "take a sip and tell me."

"Jacek . . . " Her thin hands ignored the glass and clutched at him, digging for comfort. "Jacek, I saw a face . . . "

"Where, my love?" *In the cloudless sky, my love, in the air, was it, or was it in the earth?*

"There, there at the window . . . " Not one of their own windows she pointed to with a shaking hand, but further down the terrace. "In the empty house there. Oh, can it have been Papa, is he playing a game with us, is that it? Is it Papa playing games?"

"No, not Papa. Only a workman, I'm sure, Anita, nothing to be frightened of." Nat or one of the other lads, presumably, come down to do a little work after all. But still, "I'll go and see, shall I? Find out who it is?"

"Yes. Thank you, Jacek." And she smiled her vague and grateful smile, said, "Ask him back for a glass of lemonade, won't you, if it's one of the boys we know?"

The boys you know are dead and gone, my love, or else a thousand miles from here and fifty or sixty years from being boys; and do they ever think of you, do you suppose? Do they ever remember the bright laughter and the sparkling eyes, do they remember the name, perhaps, and ask among themselves whatever happened to Anita Dubrowski?

Aloud, he said, "I'll do that, of course. If it's someone you know. If he's not too busy to come."

"Thank you, Jacek. I'll fetch the lemon biscuits." She rose carefully to her feet, and frowned; and said, "Are there any, did I bake biscuits yesterday, Jacek? Do you know, I can't remember?"

You haven't baked for years, my love, my sweet. "I'm not sure," he said. "You go and see."

Jack couldn't tell quite which house, which window Anita had been pointing at. He couldn't see any movement himself. And when he shouted, "Hullo! Who's there, anyone there?", there was no answer. No voice calling in reply, no face returning to its window, no sound of footsteps or unheeding work.

Perhaps Anita had simply imagined it, or misunderstood what she saw. A cloud's reflection, perhaps, moving across the glass? But there were no clouds. A bird, then, a seagull reflected, or a crow. Plenty of those, foul birds feeding on the foul land.

But Anita's eyes had always been sharp and clear, it was the mind behind the eyes that couldn't make sense of the world they saw. She might convert her old brother somehow into a beardless youth, she might look at England and think herself in Poland, but she'd never yet seen what wasn't there.

So Jack climbed over the low wall separating his garden from the next, stepped from order into wilderness and began to search the houses.

Shouting into an open, empty doorway, he thought he heard a response. Not a voice, and you certainly couldn't call it an answer, nothing so direct: only a scuffling sound on the floor above, that might have been someone moving around and might equally well have been rats.

Whatever, it was enough to draw Jack further in. He hadn't bothered with the first two, only stuck his head inside and called, listened to the silence and moved on. But there's a different quality, Jack thought, to the silence of an empty house; and he didn't think this one was empty.

"Hullo, who's there, please?"

Nothing, no reply, only the listening silence. But he went to the

214

stairs nevertheless, set foot on them, started to climb: murmuring soft prayers against his fear and his age, the threat inherent in the gloom and shadows above.

On the seventh step – when he looked down to watch his feet, and that was only because he was old and a little unsteady, of course it was, nothing to do with being afraid to look up – he saw, in the dust and dirt, a footprint.

A naked footprint.

Big and broad, a man's it was, five wide toes and the ball of the foot; and now that he was looking, there was another on the step above, a clear trail of them. Leading up.

For a little while, perhaps for half a minute Jack only stood there, thinking and wondering and uncertain. Then he remembered to pray; and then, finally, he remembered his courage.

He called again, "Hullo, is there anyone here, please? It's me, Jack Dubrowski," and getting no answer he went slowly on up the stairs, following the footprints.

The trail was harder to see on the landing, where the muck was thicker and there were no windows, and all the doors were shut; but he thought it led down to the far end, the furthest door. And when he stood outside that door, when he rapped on it and listened, he thought he heard someone breathing inside. Breathing and shifting and maybe moaning, just a little; or maybe it was only the wind in the chimney, stirring up the dust.

And maybe he was only a short old man, maybe all his strength was gone and all his courage with it, all spent in his foolhardy youth; but still he wasn't going to draw back from this door. Wasn't going to turn and creep away down the stairs, hurry back to his own house and phone for help. Wasn't going to disgrace himself or his faith or his people.

No.

He set his hand on the doorknob, muttering something that wasn't a prayer any more, more like a call to arms. He turned his wrist and felt the latch withdraw, and held it so a moment longer; and then he pushed the door open.

Dusty sunlight made a curtain in the room beyond, drawn from window to floor, with a lurking figure behind. Jack squinted between his fingers, spoke sharply, said, "Who's that, who is that there?"

And was answered with a shifting, huddling movement and a sullen, scared little mutter, "It's nobody, Mr Jack, it's only me . . . "

215

"*Billy?*"

Jack walked forward through the hard light, stood with his back to the window, and saw Billy. Saw more of Billy than he wanted to, indeed, saw his pinched ribs and skinny flanks, all his pale skin streaked with filth and his face with tears.

"What happened to you, Billy? What are you doing here? And like this, why this?"

But Billy only sniffed, and tried to wipe his nose on the back of his hand and smeared snot across his cheek, and shook his head; and Jack said, "All right, Billy. Never mind. We'll talk about it later. For now you need a bath and some clothes, yes? And a meal, too, I'm sure you will be hungry. Come, stand up now. Don't worry, we're not going far, only to my house; and there's no one to see. Not even Anita, if we go the front way. Here, take my hand. And don't cry, there's no need to cry now . . ."

iii

Rachel had been in Paradise all day. She'd got grass-stains on her T-shirt and a nasty cut on her knee, and she'd broken all her nails with hauling at heavy canvas and trying to unpick knotted ropes; but it had been worth it, in the end. They'd cleared the collapsed marquee out of the way, along with the chairs and the staging and everything, to make room for a new one to go up that same afternoon. That was dead right, Rachel thought, the perfect response. It'd show the vandals and the press and the whole damn city that you couldn't stop God's people from witnessing, any more than Canute could stop the tide from coming in.

Then they'd laid the old marquee out on the grass to inspect the damage. It wasn't too bad, really: new guy ropes and poles, a bit of patching and darning, it'd be as good as new. Nat said the chances were they'd be buying it and doing the work themselves. Richard's idea, of course. If they owned their own marquee they'd be free to decorate it, to paint it with God's messages: to turn it into a massive and mobile billboard, long-distance words of love . . .

So they'd started the work already, on the assumption that what Richard wanted would inevitably happen. They'd taken off all the slashed ropes and stays, coiling them up neatly for salvage; which was why Rachel's nails were so sore and bruised and broken. Years of weather and tension had welded some of the knots into a solid mass of fibre, too much for mortal

216

girl to disentangle.

Now she sat ruefully examining those mistreated finger-ends, sat clean and comfortable in Derry's home with Derry's family around her, everyone there except Derry. She'd been mothered by his mother, befriended by his father and wrestled into laughing submission by the two little boys; and she was loving every minute of it. This was what she'd missed the last month or two, the warmth of a family happy with itself. The chapel provided some substitute, to be sure, all one family under God and plenty of love floating around, plenty of encouragement; but it wasn't the same. Blood was thicker even than Communion wine.

The strident chimes of an ice-cream van sounded in the street below. Sammy Bowen looked up hopefully, from where he was driving a model jeep around Rachel's bare feet and ticklishly over her toes. His bigger brother Trevor came charging up from the street, yelling the news; and their mother sighed hugely from her end of the sofa, waving a fat arm towards the table.

"All right, Trevor, son. Fetch my purse over here, there's a good lad."

"No, look," Rachel said, "let me."

Reached into her back pocket, and was stopped twice over: once by Mrs Bowen, "Don't you, girl, you leave your money where it is, you're in my house now," and once again by the sound of footsteps on the stairs.

Only her smile moved then, only the dancing light in her eyes as Derry came in, his hands full of ice-cream.

"What are you . . . ?"

The question made it halfway out, while his face puckered uncertainly; then Sammy was tugging at his tracksuit and Trevor was hauling on his arm, both loudly demanding.

"What makes you think they're for you, then, eh?"

But the game wasn't played with any conviction, he was still darting glances at Rachel; and it was only a moment before he gave the boys a cone each. "There you go. Now get out of here . . . "

His brothers stampeded off down the stairs and into the street. Derry handed another cone to his mother, looked at the two he had left, looked again at Rachel; and said, "Uh, Dad in from work, is he? I got him one, too . . . "

"Aye, he's in our room." Mrs Bowen heaved herself to her feet, holding out an imperious hand. "Give me, I'll take it."

That left Derry with one, left him stranded. Rachel was giggling

217

aloud now, knowing that wasn't helping him any but doing it anyway, loving the sight of him so flustered, so confused.

"Uh," he said, "I, er, I licked this one . . . "

So she bounced to her feet, bent over, and licked it too.

"Now we'll have to share it. Come on, let's go and sit in the sun."

And she tucked her arm through his and drew him through the kitchen to the open back door, to sit on his own back doorstep above his own back yard.

For a while they licked and crunched without talking, passing the cone back and forth between them. Then Rachel popped the last small bite into his mouth, sucked her fingers cheerfully and wiped them on the T-shirt she was wearing.

Which was his cue, deliberately given; and he didn't miss it.

"That's mine," he said, "that T-shirt."

"I know. Your mum said it didn't fit you any more. Too tight all round, she said it was."

"Aye, it is. But what, you're wanting my cast-offs now, are you? What's going on, Rache, what are you doing here?"

Having fun, making friends — finding another perspective on you, sunshine. The family that eats ices together is nicest together. "I got rescued," she said aloud, another answer and just as true, not cheating at all. "I've been down at the marquee all day and I was horrible, all sticky and sweaty and grunge. Bleeding, too," tapping the big plaster on her knee for evidence. "Your mum came down while I was trying to wash the muck out of it, in that little sink in the chapel; and she frog-marched me back here. Drowned me in TCP, she did. Then we had a cup of tea and talked about you; and then I got cheeky and asked if I could have a bath. Only my T-shirt was just too yuck to put on again after, so I scrounged this. Why," half untucking it from her cut-offs with a consciously wicked smile, "do you want it back?"

He shook his head urgently, blushing and grinning both. "Nah, that's okay. That's fine. What d'you do to yourself, then, your knee?"

"Oh, I just knelt on a bit of broken bottle, that's all. Didn't see it, in the grass."

"You want to be careful," he said, his hand reaching shyly to touch, to settle briefly just above the plaster. "You want to look after yourself," he said, just where a more confident boy would surely have said it the other way, *You want looking after.*

"I will," she said, "I do. I am," remembering the house standing empty, all her own, and her whole life her own responsibility.

And didn't know quite where to go from there, and Derry was no help, hypnotised by his own boldness, his hand on her knee; but they were rescued unexpectedly, by a small and fierce shadow that shot across the roof of next door's garage, cleared the wall in a single bound, landed in Rachel's lap and viciously attacked the swinging end of her pony-tail.

Rachel convulsed in laughter, cupped the little kitten in both hands, lifted it to her face and nuzzled it gently while it batted at her nose with tender paws.

"Hullo, gorgeous, where did you come from?" A glance at Derry, turning suspicious at the contented breadth of his smile. "Not yours, is he? You never said you had a kitten."

"He's not ours, no."

"Whose, then, d'you know?"

"Yours. For your birthday. You can't take him away, though," added quickly before she could start to enjoy the idea of company at home. "The kids have adopted him, they'd be ever so upset if he went now. You want to see him, you'll just have to come and visit."

"Uh-huh. What's his name, then? So I know who to ask for, when I come?"

"Dunno. Up to you, ain't it? I said, he's yours. The kids call him 'Cat', if that's any help, but I don't think he's really took to it."

Rachel chuckled, stroked the soft fur, rolled the kitten over in her lap and never mind the sudden pin-pricks of his claws gripping tight in protest at the indignity; and said, "Okay, call him Mortimer."

"Fine." There was a clattering of pans in the kitchen behind them, and Derry swivelled to shout over his shoulder, "Mam, can Rachel stay for tea tonight?"

"Oy!" she protested sharply, "I never . . . "

But his mother's voice came booming back at them, "Of course she's staying, what did you think? The girl's got no flesh, she needs feeding."

"Okay, mate," she said, capitulating in the face of his triumph. "I wasn't going to scrounge; but as it happens, it's dead handy. Nat's called a meeting at the chapel for half past seven, so I haven't got time to go home." And then, sweet revenge, she kissed him full on the mouth and just when he wasn't expecting it. "Thanks for my present," she said, "he's beautiful. Bit early, but never mind that. You'll just have to bring another present to my party, won't you?"

"What party?"

"I'll let you know. And you'll be there, boy. There or dead,

219

those are the choices."

When they went out after tea – not to go anywhere, there was still half an hour before her meeting; just to walk in the sunlight, because tired or not they couldn't sit still any longer – it seemed normal and natural for Rachel to take his hand, and swing it back and forth a little as they walked. Nothing to make a fuss over, just what she felt like.

When a door opened twenty metres ahead and a woman stepped out, Rachel knew her instantly from her clothes. Even from the back they were unmistakable. Rachel stopped dead, and would have tugged at Derry's hand to stop him too, except that she didn't need to. He was already urging her gently back into a shop doorway.

"Two minds with but a single thought," she murmured; and choked on a sudden giggle, bit down hard on the sleeve of his T-shirt to control it.

"Ouch," he said mildly.

"Sorry, was that you?"

"Yeah. Do it again."

She snorted, and looked up the road again to see where Evelyn had got to. "Don't you like her either?"

"She's a screwball. Talks to herself all the time, and she has real stupid rows with people. Flies right off the handle over nothing, half the shops round here have banned her. She had our Trev in tears a couple of times, when he was littler. Sammy just keeps out of her way."

"So do you."

"Yeah, dead right. She scares me," and he didn't sound like he was joking. "How do you know her, then?"

"She comes to services." And Rachel wasn't going to say any more than that, certainly wasn't going to gossip about how Evelyn spent her time at services: sitting as close to Richard as she could, trying to catch his eye, trying to monopolise him beforehand and afterwards. Rachel's conscience was busy enough already at this unkind and unChristian lurking in doorways, she wasn't going to throw any more fuel on that fire.

"Oh, right. Religious nut, is she? That figures."

That earned him an elbow in the ribs. He just laughed, wrapped his arms tight around her, leant his chin on her shoulder and watched with her as Evelyn stalked slowly up the hill.

As she passed an innocuous-looking, empty-seeming car.

As a man appeared suddenly, sitting up after she'd passed; as he slipped out, closed the door with a visible effort at quietness, followed her out of sight.

"Who was that, then?" Derry asked, his breath warm and moist in her ear.

"I don't know . . . " A funny little man he'd been, short and thin and balding; only there wasn't anything funny in what he was doing, following Evelyn around.

"D'you think we ought to go after them? Just to check, like? It's a bit dodgy, blokes following women around, I don't like it. Not on my patch."

Two minds with but a single thought.

She nodded. "Come on, quick. Before we lose them."

Evelyn turned off before she reached the main road at the top of the hill. She took a side-street, the little bald man followed her, and Rachel and Derry followed them both.

"I bet I know where she's going," Rachel said after a few minutes. "Mr Grimes lives just along here." *And that's where Richard's staying . . .*

Sure enough, Evelyn turned into the cul-de-sac where Ted Grimes had his house, one of the few in Paradise with a front garden. And Richard was there, in the garden, seemingly waiting for Evelyn; at any rate, he greeted her with no surprise, only a kiss of welcome.

And the little bald man produced a camera from his pocket, took a photograph of that kiss, melted professionally into a doorway.

Rachel tugged Derry back, quickly out of sight.

"Well, I don't know what he's up to, but I guess it's not our business any more. Richard can look after her, better than we can." *Better than anyone.* "I'll tell him, next time I see him to talk to; someone ought to know. But it looks like she's safe, anyway. That guy's not going to attack her or anything."

"No," Derry agreed. "Can't think why, mind, all that sexy gear she's got on . . . "

Rachel giggled, and punched him. "Shut up, you're horrible. That's not funny a bit."

"Oy, you stop beating me up, you," laughing, pushing her off. "You'll be sorry, else."

"Oh, yeah? What are you going to do about it, then?"

What he did, of course, was make a grab for her. He was meant to.

And while they wrestled, while she was spitting with laughter and fighting hopelessly, helplessly against his new strength, she felt his warm hands on her back, skin on skin under the baggy T-shirt; and stopped fighting, stopped moving at all, was suddenly very sorry indeed.

Licked her lips, spoke slowly, reluctantly; said, "Derry . . . "

That was all, just his name; but it was enough, seemingly. He stepped back, let her go, lifted his hands in a gesture close to apology. She gave him a wan smile, her own version of the same thing, another way to say sorry. *Sorry, but I can't, I daren't. This is getting dangerous* . . .

Then she looked at her watch, said huskily, "Time we were getting back for that meeting, anyway."

"We?"

"Yeah. You're coming too, didn't I tell you?"

And she took his hand to be certain of it, to drag him along if necessary. She'd have to keep him at a little distance, that was becoming obvious, she couldn't trust herself too close these days; but she wasn't going to let him take too much.

When they reached the chapel, they found it comfortably full: most of the seats taken, plenty of conversation, plenty of curiosity.

Nat was at the door, welcoming people as they arrived, knowing them all by name. Looking beyond him, she realised that she could have done the same thing, more or less; and even Derry was finding friends to wave to, people he'd met at the youth club or working down at the houses.

That seemed to be the common link among them, in fact: that they were all young and enthusiastic, all more than simple chapel-goers. Some were local like Rachel herself, some like Nat were students; others had come from America or Australia or France, sent by their churches for the summer. But whoever they were, they were the core of what was stirring in the city, the great revival promised. Richard provided the leadership, the spark, he was the catalyst and the inspiration; but it was this crowd that did most of the work. Rachel thought about that, and wondered just why Nat had called this meeting tonight, what he might have in mind.

Then Derry nudged her over to a seat next to his friend Albie, breaking the thread of speculation; and shortly after, Nat closed the chapel doors and walked slowly down to the front. He perched on a table set to one side and said nothing, made not a gesture; but still the buzz of conversation died a quick death as everyone watched him, waited for him to speak.

"A few days ago," Nat said, "Richard asked me to give some thought to an idea he'd had. He wanted to see us out and about on the streets, more in evidence even than we have been. Not preaching, though, not testifying. Doing practical work, getting involved. Religion's too much an ivory tower sometimes, he was saying, we need to be a visible force for good in the community. Picking up litter and helping old ladies across the street.

"A couple of nights back I went to a meeting of the local Neighbourhood Watch. Which I have to tell you isn't so much watching as dozing – though those of you who've lived here for any length of time won't need telling. There was a man there, an Asian man who wanted to go to his daughter's wedding; only she's a student in Manchester, and they were scared to leave their house over the weekend, for fear of what they might come back to. They're a kind and decent couple and they're living in terror, right here in Paradise.

"And last night, as you all know, our marquee was wrecked by vandals."

A pause, a sip of water from a glass ready on the table.

"Now I've been thinking about this all day, these separate events, and I think they're all part of a single clear pattern. Richard was right, as usual; but we need something more than street-stewardesses, picking up litter and helping old ladies.

"What I see, what I've been shown is a disciplined group of people taking responsibility for their own area. Doing what the Neighbourhood Watch ought to be doing, and isn't; doing far more than the police can hope to do. They haven't got the personnel or the resources, or the local knowledge. We have.

"I think we should be patrolling the streets at night, protecting our property and other people's. Even wearing uniforms, maybe, so we can be identified at a glance, so everyone knows we're around.

"I think we should be leafleting every house in Paradise, telling them we're here. We should give them a phone number where they can call direct and be sure of a response if they're worried or frightened or suspicious. We should know where the pensioners live, and the disabled, and the single mothers with young children.

"I think we should be a help and a comfort to every honest soul in this community; and I think we should be a worry and a bother to every crook, every burglar, every car-thief, every mugger and swindler and vandal that we've got.

"It's ambitious, I know; but I think we can do it. I think we have to do it. The job's there to be done, and we're right here, on the spot; I think this is what we're for, just now.

"Not alone, of course, we won't have to do it alone. Richard and the Council will back us, when they see we're in earnest; and

Richard's got all the contacts we'll need with the police, the local council, the social services, all the civil authorities. The Asian communities, too. I'd like to involve them as soon as possible, to avoid accusations of a Christian Mafia.

"But we have to start it, we have to get the ball rolling.

"Paradise is in our hands, that's what I'm saying, really; and we've got the chance, the opportunity to make it a better place to live."

Another pause, another sip of water; and he lifted his head, ran his eyes slowly across his silent, intense audience.

"Who's with me?" he asked, quite quietly. "I'm looking for lads to help guard the new marquee, as of now; I'm camping in there from tonight, and anyone who wants to join me is very welcome. But that's the lesser issue. What I'm really calling for is volunteers for a private army. God's army, the Christ Commando. No weapons, apart from righteousness and prayer, but I think they'll be enough.

"We're all soldiers already, by definition – but are you ready to wear the uniform?"

EIGHTEEN

i

A voice hails him as he leaves the house, a hand goes up to stay him, a camera clicks and whines. Nothing unusual in that, there's a journalist waiting most mornings nowadays; and it's most often this one, this little bald goblin of a man.

– Richard, Richard! Have a word, can I?

– If you can talk on the trot, he says, checking his watch and smiling, of course smiling. I've a meeting at half past, he says, and barely time to get there.

– Oh, right, got a meeting, have you? Not meeting the girlfriend, then, not this morning?

He barely checks in his smooth progress, barely frowns, barely allows the least distaste to show around his smile.

– I don't have a girlfriend, he says gently. I have a meeting, he says.

– I've got these pictures say you've got a girlfriend. Hugs and kisses and hand-in-hand, that says girlfriend to me. It will to my readers, Richard. Here, see? Keep them, I got copies.

This shouldn't be a surprise, really. He's been warned. He takes the photographs, flicks through them, hands them back.

– Thanks, but no. I don't need these.

– I need a statement, though, Richard. I do. You in love with Evelyn Somers, are you?

He laughs, loud and long and natural.

– Oh dear, you must be desperate for a story, he says, if that's the best you can come up with.

– You didn't answer the question, Richard.

– I love everyone in Paradise, he says. And he couldn't be lying, not possibly, not a chance in the world.

– You still didn't answer the question, Richard.

– That's because it's a stupid question, it's meaningless. What's it supposed to mean? God doesn't discriminate, he loves all of us, equally and without measure; and that's his commandment to us. Love thy neighbour as thyself. I'm not God, I'm not infallible, but I do try. I do my best.

– You don't go back to other women's flats in the middle of the night. You don't walk hand in hand with other women . . .

– Not when your camera's looking my way, apparently.

– So what are you saying, that there's nothing between you and Evelyn? Outright denial, is that it, can I print that?

– No, he says, that's not what I'm saying. Print what you like, he says, it's a free press; but don't come to me for help. I won't lend your stories the credence of a statement, he says.

There's a glimmer of steel at last, a hint of inflexible will; but it's not enough to stop the questions coming.

– No comment, then, is that it? Can I quote you on that?

– You can't quote me at all, he says. And laughs, and says, Quote the Bible instead, it's a better source than I am. Here you are, chapter and verse, he says: 'Therefore thou art inexcusable, O man, whosoever thou art that judgest: for wherein thou judgest another, thou condemnest thyself; for thou that judgest doest the same things.' Romans, chapter two, verse one. God's comment on all tabloids. You want to quote anything, quote that, he says.

ii

Billy had fallen among angels, and was saved.

It was two days since Jack had found him, but Billy didn't count it like that. He wasn't prone to looking back; he liked to be happy, and his history seldom made for happy remembering. So mostly he simply looked forward and hoped. Just now, though, he was happy, he was delighted to remember; but not two separate days, no. Just one long miracle, that's what had overtaken Billy.

It had started with Jack bringing Billy home, giving him a bath and clothes and breakfast. Clothes for his back and food for his belly, and so what if the clothes didn't fit and the food all tasted funny? Billy was glad, he was grateful, he was, yes. He'd been cold and naked and starving of the hunger, and he knew enough to be grateful.

Jack had asked him questions then; and that was the bad bit, because Billy didn't want to talk about voices and faces and the devil in the night. So he didn't, and after a while Jack stopped asking.

Billy didn't want to meet Jack's sister either, not just then, with his face wet from crying at all the questions. Jack took him into the front room, where Billy could be alone, he said; and that's when the miracle grew wings. That's where it turned all golden and gleaming like the sunshine, warm and comfy like a good bed, vivid as a cold bottle on a hot night.

226

There was a piano in the front room, and Jack said Billy could play it, if he wanted. He said go ahead, play it all you like, Billy. That's what he said, and that's what Billy did.

Billy was still playing when he felt a hand grip his shoulder, heard a voice say, "That's enough now, Billy. It's time for elevenses."

It wasn't Jack's voice, though, and it wasn't Jack's hand. Billy looked round, and it was an angel had him by the shoulder, bright gold and glorious. Billy could see fine, he had two good eyes in his head, and he knew an angel when he saw one.

Knew an angel's voice, too, and felt its power.

"I brought you some coffee," Richard said; and Billy's bones melted in his body. "Come and sit over by the window, and tell me where you learned to play like that."

So Billy sat by the window in the sunlight, though it wasn't the sun that dazzled him; and stutteringly said that he never did learn, he never had lessons, no. He'd never seen a piano, not to touch, till he was fifteen and left school and some people took him into a pub to celebrate. They got him drunk, it didn't take much then, his first taste of it, that was; and they sat him down at the piano, they thought it would be funny. And his fingers touched the keys, him laughing and clowning, happy to make his friends laugh; and right then he knew, soon as he touched the keys, soon as he heard the music.

He didn't know much music then, but everything he did know he could play. Everything he'd sung or heard sung in his fifteen years on earth, from nursery rhymes to hymns; he played them all, and wanted never to stop.

And he still didn't want to stop, and didn't have to. He drained his cup of coffee, finished his biscuits and looked at the piano longingly, looked to Richard for approval.

And Richard laughed, and said, "Go on, then. Let's hear some hymns, if you know any."

"Oh, I do. I do, I know lots of hymns, I do. Used to go to church regular, I did . . . "

Eager to prove that, he would have played all the hymns he knew if Richard hadn't gripped his wrists and lifted his hands off the keys, and said, "Enough! But you play wonderfully well, Billy. It's a great gift. You only have to hear a tune once, is that right? And then you can play it?"

Billy nodded eagerly, bouncing on the piano stool. "That's right, Richard, it's easy. You could do it too, anyone can . . . "

"No, they can't, Billy. I know I can't. It's a gift, it comes from

227

God, to make you special. You should be grateful."

"Oh, I am, Richard, I am." Billy was good at being grateful. He'd had it knocked into him all his life, how grateful he ought to be.

"So why don't you go to church any more, Billy?"

Billy looked down at his long, bent fingers, and didn't answer. But Richard only waited, patient as any angel, leaving the question right there in the air between them; and at last Billy had to say something, so he said, "No one to take me."

"No one to bully you, do you mean? No one to drag you along, the way you were dragged as a kid?"

He shook his head, urgent and honest. "No, not that. I mean, we did get dragged, all of us had to go to church; but I liked it. I never told anyone, but I did. I liked the singing."

"But not the sermons, eh?"

Billy giggled and shook his head, still not looking up.

"Well, I can't blame you for that, Billy. No one likes sermons when they're young. But listen, never mind what they told you then, those preachers weren't speaking with God's voice. God did speak to you when you were in church, He spoke to you personally, to Billy Finn. It was the music, don't you understand?

"That's what happens when you sit down at a piano, Billy. God taps you on the shoulder and says move over, let's make this one a duet. Every time you play, you play with God; and He's telling you He loves you, and you're telling Him the exact same thing back again. I can hear it, even if you can't. Doesn't matter if it's a hymn or ragtime or a rugby song, it's right there in the music, every time . . . "

Billy listened, and he believed; he didn't have the option. You can't disbelieve an angel. So Billy learned about Richard's God, and learned to love Him in words as he had in music; learned to pray to Him in words, as he had in music.

And that was Billy's miracle, started two days ago and not finished yet. Billy was saved, Billy was born again and bubbling over with it. He was sleeping on the sofa in the front room, as near the piano as he could get. He played it first thing in the morning and last thing at night and all the hours he was allowed in between; and every phrase, every chord, every note was a conversation, Billy to God and back again.

Sometimes Jack's sister Anita came to listen; and sometimes she came to sit in the garden while Billy was out there digging and weeding, earning his keep. She was funny, Anita was. She called him by the wrong names, and spoke to him in words he didn't understand; but Billy smiled and nodded anyway, and she was happy. She laughed and patted him on the hand, or brought him a lemonade, or a chocolate plum if it was after dinner.

Billy was very grateful then. He loved chocolate plums. It was hard not to steal one or two out of the box on the piano when he was playing, he loved them so much; but he'd never done that. Yet. It would have been ungrateful. And God wouldn't be happy with him. Billy was saved, he was a Christian now, he had to think about that sort of thing.

One thing Billy hadn't done, though, even talking to Richard: he hadn't said what happened that night to leave him naked and fearful, hiding in the houses. Richard had asked, but Billy still didn't want to talk about it. There are some things even angels shouldn't hear.

This morning Billy sat playing quietly, tunelessly for once, his fingers barely stroking the keys as he listened to the sounds of people working further down the terrace. Making all the houses into homes, they were. That was a good Christian thing to do. Maybe this afternoon he'd leave the piano and wheel barrows around for them, to show how grateful he was . . .

He idled through a slow blues they had on the jukebox down at the 'Lady Grey', then remembered he was happy now and played some jaunty Irish jigs he'd heard at a session one time.

Was interrupted by applause; looked round to see Nat in the doorway clapping, with carrier bags at his feet.

"That's good, Billy," Nat said, picking all the bags up and coming in, pushing the door shut behind him. "That's very good."

Billy smiled shyly, ran a hand over his close-cropped hair, fidgeted a little on the piano stool. Nat was foreman, Nat was overseer; Nat was boss, around here. You always had to be careful, with bosses.

"Did you want to see me, Nat?"

"That's right, Billy, yes. I did want to see you. If you can spare the time . . . ?"

"Oh, yes, Nat. Sure thing, of course I can . . . " Already closing the piano lid, turning away from the music, *anything for you, Nat. You're the boss.*

"Good, thanks. Now then, Billy . . . " Nat perched on the arm of a chair, where he could sit and smile at Billy; then he reached into one of his bags, and pulled out a pair of Billy's trousers.

"I think these are yours," Nat said. Billy could only stare wide-mouthed, dry-mouthed, and nod, and feel the trembles starting in his hands.

"Good. You'll be glad to have them back, I expect; Jack's clothes don't fit you very well, do they?" Neither did Billy's own, bought at jumble sales and charity shops, seldom even tried on; but Billy wasn't going to say so. "We've had them all cleaned for you, I took them to the laundrette myself."

"Uh, thanks, Nat . . . " Billy blushed, at the thought of all the holes and stains in his underwear. Giggled and looked down, splayed his fingers on his knees; then made a real effort, a happy Christian effort. *Nothing to be shy about, Nat's my brother now. I'm saved and he's saved and we're all saved together.*

Looked up and smiled at Nat, reached out a hand for his trousers.

And Nat smiled brightly in return, and held the trousers back. Out of Billy's reach.

"You know where we found these, Billy?"

Of course Billy knew; and of course Billy didn't want to say. Talking was too close to remembering, and that was the last, the very last thing he wanted to do. What he wanted to do instead, he wanted to lie. *No, I don't know where you found my trousers. I don't care where you found my trousers, I just want my trousers back, and thank you Nat and goodbye.*

But he couldn't do that. Saved men don't lie, brothers don't lie to each other; and it wouldn't do any good anyway, he could see that. Nat was the boss, and Nat meant business.

So Billy nodded, slow and reluctant.

"It was in the marquee, all this stuff. Under the stage. I guess you'd been sleeping there a while, hadn't you, Billy?"

"Yes. Yes, I didn't, I didn't have anywhere else to go. I'm sorry, Nat . . . "

"Oh, don't be sorry. There's no need. You're welcome to a bit of our grass. If we'd known, we would've found you somewhere more comfortable. You should've said, Billy boy. I'm glad you didn't, though," he added, laying Billy's trousers across his lap and folding them neatly, getting the creases straight. "I think you were there, you see. Weren't you, Billy? I think you were right there when they chopped the tent down, I think you saw them do it and that's why you ran away. I think maybe you even know who they were, eh, Billy? And I think you're going to tell me," his voice soft and quiet and making Billy shiver, making him afraid all over again. "I think you're going to tell me everything that happened, everything you saw and heard and did that night. Aren't you, Billy? Aren't you?"

230

And Billy could say no to ordinary men like Jack, and get away with it; and he could say no to angels like Richard, and get away with that too. Men and angels, they were kind, they understood about being too scared to speak.

Nat was different. Nat was the boss, and you wouldn't have thought he was a brother now, not with his eyes so demanding and his voice only playing games with softness. Nothing for Billy to do but wrap his arms around his sparrow chest, rub them hard against the bitter cold of memory, stare at the floor and mumble.

And tell Nat everything.

iii

Eight o'clock, the gym closed. Usually Jason had to stay for a good half-hour after, to clean up; but *when the gym closes,* that's what Vinny had said. And Jason didn't want to keep Vinny waiting. So at quarter to, hanging around in the foyer with George and Derry, the last customer gone already and all of them only waiting on the clock:

"George, can I, can you let me go at eight tonight? Please? Vinny wants me for something, he said he'd pick me up . . . "

"You'd better be ready, then," George grunted. "Derry, son? You mind doing Jason's work for him, this once?"

Better bloody not mind, Jason thought sullenly. *Cunt never does any fucking work anyway.*

"No, sure," from Derry. "Must be my turn, we ought to share it . . . "

"I'll decide who does what in this gym, son. You can stand in for him this once, but don't make a habit of asking, right, Jase? Derry's too soft to say no, maybe, but I'm not."

George broke off at the sound of light footsteps on the steps outside. A girl put her head round the door, dark hair swinging. "Um, hi. Sorry, I don't want anything, really, just can I wait for Derry, if he's around . . . ?"

George chuckled amiably, like the big fat friendly uncle he looked like and wasn't. "He's right here, pet. Help yourself."

"Is he?" She looked further in, giving Jason a careless, friendly smile, finding Derry in the corner. "Oh, good . . . "

Derry was glancing uncertainly between the three of them, but the girl didn't have any doubts, any hesitations. She went straight over and kissed him, quite unconcerned. "Hullo, you."

"What are you doing here?"

231

She sighed loudly – for her audience, that, as much as for him – and knocked her forehead lightly against his. "Talk about brick walls . . . ! I'm looking for you, dummy. I've been doing righteous and dutiful things all day, and I want a break. I want someone to take me to the cinema and feed me popcorn bit by bit and buy me a hot-dog after. Are you game, or do I go after somebody else?"

"Well, yeah. I mean, no. I mean, of course I will. Only . . . " And Derry caught Jason's eye, looked shifty, looked like he might back out at the last minute. Jason's fists clenched impotently, fear and anger surged and mixed to cloud his vision and leave him on the brink of doing something very stupid. But the girl said,

"Only what, got another date, is that it? Filth. Dung. Insect . . . "

"No. No, stop it, shut *up*." Derry was laughing now, grabbing at her, trying to gag her with his fingers. "I've got to work late, that's all. Got to clean up. D'you want to wait? Be half an hour, maybe."

"Wait? I'll watch, boy. And criticise. I wouldn't trust your housekeeping, I've seen your bedroom . . . "

He jabbed her in the ribs, she kicked him, they fought and giggled their way through into the gym; and Jason watched, and scowled, and wondered what the hell she saw in him.

Vinny was late. Jason sat in the foyer on his own now, sat with his hands pressed tight between his knees, palms together, sweating; and he watched the clock and waited, watched and hoped. Maybe Vinny had forgotten, maybe he'd changed his mind . . .

But at last there were footsteps again, on the concrete steps outside. Light and scurrying footsteps, like the last time: but no miracle, no laughing girl for Jason.

Vinny kicked the door open wide, nodded at Jason, said, "Where's George?"

"In the office."

"Right. You go out to the van. I'll be a minute."

More waiting, but no hope in it this time, no dream of rescue or relief. Jason stood by the bonnet of Vinny's ancient van, picking at rust-spots with his fingers. The doors weren't locked – if ever anything anywhere was safe, then Vinny's van was safe in Paradise – but Jason had sense enough not to get in without permission. He wouldn't even slump against the bonnet, in case Vinny looked on that as a liberty and decided to give him a lesson in respect.

*

232

It was another quarter of an hour before Vinny came out of the gym. No explanation, naturally no apology; just a gesture, *get in*, and they were off.

It had never occurred to Jason before now, to wonder where Vinny lived. He wasn't the sort of man you asked questions about; curiosity was dangerous. If anyone had asked Jason, though, if he'd had to guess, he'd have gone for one of the big estates. A high-rise block, most likely, where the lifts didn't work and half the flats were boarded up and the other half had steel doors and dogs; but in the city, in any case. In the city for sure.

He'd have been wrong, though. He learned that now, and not by asking questions: only by sitting silent and afraid, hunched against the van door as far from Vinny as he could get. He was bleakly surprised when they left the city, surprised again when they crossed the river. Didn't say anything, though; wouldn't say a word unless Vinny wanted him to. Keeping Vinny happy, that's what it was all about tonight. Earning that terrible smile.

South of the river the good roads broke up into a mess of narrow lanes, the city into a scatter of villages that started small and only got smaller as they drove further and further out.

Turned out that Vinny didn't even live in one of these snot-sized villages, though. Where Vinny lived wasn't anywhere at all.

They were halfway down a one-track lane, going way too fast – but quite safe, of course, no worries there; who in the whole fucking world would be brave enough, stupid enough to crash into Vinny's van? – when they passed a sign stuck into a hedge. It was hand-painted, rough uneven white lettering on buckled hardboard; and the sign said, *Staffies. Pups and stud.*

Vinny turned sharp left at the hedge's end and braked hard, skid-stopping on a rutted piece of ground where nothing grew. There were a couple of old caravans up on breeze blocks, sad and weather-stained; and they might as well have had another sign outside, *Vinny Lives Here.*

And Jason thought maybe this was right after all. Maybe the guy was just too different, too frightening to share a building or a street with anyone else. Maybe sharing even a city with Vinny would be too much to handle. If there was only the two of you in a whole bloody city, maybe you'd go mad simply from knowing that Vinny was there, he was around, you might walk round any corner and find him suddenly, right there smiling at you . . .

Behind the caravans were lines of home-made sheds, planks and whole doors and sheets of corrugated iron all nailed and lashed

233

and jointed together half a dozen different ways, with tarpaulins and chicken-wire to cover the gaps.

The sheds were full of dogs. Jason could hear them as soon as the van's engine died, a riot of barking that just went on and on. He could see some of them too, when he got out: could see pale and dark and brindled noses snuffling at the chicken-wire, catch glimpses of squat, heavy bodies and bandy legs.

"Staffies," Vinny said. "I breed 'em. Come on."

And Staffies they were, Staffordshire bull terriers: Jason recognised them when Vinny unlocked the first shed to let half a dozen youngsters run yelping and squabbling out into a big pen. They were common dogs around Paradise. It had been Alsatians when Jason was a kid, then Dobermanns or Rottweilers; now it was Staffordshire bulls. This must be where they all came from, this and places like this. Not directly, though, not from here. Jason couldn't imagine anyone buying a puppy direct from Vinny.

"Right," Vinny said. "Wheelbarrow and shovel, up the end there. Off you go, Jase. Clean them out, scrub the floor down after. Brushes and buckets. I'll be watching."

Jason took a quick look inside the shed, smelt the shit and the rank straw, felt the ache of exhaustion in his bones – and went trudging off to fetch barrow and shovel like a good boy, like a sensible boy always would. Never mind that he'd worked all day for George, and no money in that either; never mind that he'd breach his curfew at the hostel tonight. None of that mattered, here and now. Just keep Vinny smiling . . .

So he did that, he kept Vinny smiling. He mucked out all those kennels, one by one; and then he scrubbed them, down on his hands and knees in the smeared shit on the rough concrete floors. He put down fresh straw and filled empty water-bowls, working his way slowly and wearily down the line.

The last was bigger and much more solid, built of breeze blocks with a proper roof on it. Jason sagged against the wall, waiting for Vinny to finish herding a litter of puppies and their waddling mother out of the exercise pen and back into the half-darkness of their kennel.

"Now this lot's a bit different, Jase," Vinny said, undoing padlocks. "A bit special, this lot is."

Jason only shrugged, too tired to care. Vinny pulled the door open, reached inside and flicked a light on, which made it different, all right. The others didn't have lights.

And what Jason saw in that light, in that shed, when he followed Vinny inside – yes, that was different too. The dogs looked the same, or almost the same; but looks can be very deceptive. Were deceptive, here.

First thing Jason saw was the tea-chests they'd packed the cats into Tuesday morning, shoved up against a wall. No noise coming from them, not now; but he peered in and saw a single cat crouched in the bottom of one, two in the other. They hissed weakly, their fur matted, their faces scabby from fighting.

Next to them was a treadmill, a length of carpet stretched over rollers in a frame. Jason had never seen one before, but he knew what it was. A strong dog could run for hours on one of those, and just get stronger.

Then there were the pens, made of breeze blocks again, with strong metal mesh for the gates. The first had a nursing bitch in it, with half a dozen pups; the other three each held a solitary dog on a chain. Looked like Staffies, they did, more or less: macho Staffies, maybe, Staffies with a nasty streak.

Only they didn't have any ears. Dead giveaway that was, when you saw how their ears had been lopped off right down low, nothing to get your teeth into.

"Pit bulls," Vinny said, but he didn't need to. Jason had figured that out for himself. And what they were for, he'd figured that too.

Jason had to do these pens one by one, because the dogs couldn't be put together, they'd slaughter each other. When he'd finished the last, Vinny fetched a length of cord, stood on a pen wall to push one end through an eye in the ceiling and said, "Here you go, Jase, Promised you a bonus, didn't I? Teach you something."

He went over to the tea-chests, peeled back wire netting and pulled out a cat. He held it round the throat and it didn't even struggle, it just dangled; but then, Jason thought, if Vinny picked him up that way he'd probably just dangle too.

Vinny tied one end of cord around the cat's neck, tight enough to hold it but not to strangle. Then he pulled the other end, drew the cat right up to the ceiling.

"You hang on to that now, Jase. Don't let go."

Jason held the cord, listened to the cat's thin yowling and watched its tail slash the air, its legs scrabble for an impossible purchase on nothing; and saw how it was hanging directly above the puppies' pen.

Vinny opened the gate and whistled the bitch out; caught a couple of tumbling pups who tried to follow, tossed them back inside and slammed the gate.

"Lower away, young Jason. Nice and slow."

Jason paid the cord out hand over hand, inch by inch. The cat swung and twisted and kicked, audibly choking now.

One by one, the puppies heard it and broke off their squabbles, looked up and were momentarily still and silent.

"Far enough. Hold it there."

The cat's tail was still thrashing two feet above the puppies' heads; but the largest of them bunched his hindquarters beneath him with a wriggle, sighted, jumped.

Fell short, fell back, but it didn't matter. Suddenly they were all at it, four squat furies leaping and yapping, colliding in mid-air and trying again. Soon one of them timed it right, got a mouthful of tail and clenched its jaws tight, hung on and dangled.

The extra weight on the string caught Jason unawares; he let six more inches slip through his fingers. Before he could recover it there was another strike, a strangled scream from the cat as a puppy clamped itself to a hind leg.

Jason shot an anxious sideways glance at Vinny, but he was smiling. "That's okay, Jase. Keep it there, let those other lazy buggers get aboard. Then pull it up again, right up to the roof. Trains 'em not to let go, if there's a bit of a fall under 'em."

These vicious little sods showed no signs of letting go, fall or no fall; but Jason waited till the last hysterical puppy had got itself a good mouthful of belly, then he hauled on the cord till the mass of cat and pups was swinging and twisting just below the roof.

After a couple of minutes, Vinny flicked Jason's cheek with his fingertips, stinging like fire. "Let 'em down now."

Jason lowered the animals into the pen; and as soon as its feet touched to ground, the largest pup transferred its grip from leg to throat. Vinny grunted in satisfaction.

Jason couldn't tell exactly when the cat died, buried as it was under an enthusiastic heap of puppies; but soon it was only rags of flesh and fur and bone to be fought over, stains of red.

Then it was straight back to the city, no more thanks than that for all the work he'd put in; and he had to ride in the back of the van, because Vinny wouldn't have him in the front.

"You stink, Jason," he said cheerfully. "You've been crawling around in dogshit, and you stink. I don't want you stinking up my seats."

It's your own bloody dogshit, Jason thought sullenly, *I was doing it for you. And for nothing, too . . .*

And got silently into the back, sat hunched up and sulking in the dark.

*

He didn't even get a lift all the way back to the hostel. He was late for his curfew, of course, and he told Vinny that, said there'd be real trouble if he didn't get in soon; but even so Vinny only drove him over the bridge and into Paradise. He stopped at a garage, jerked the back door open, said,

"Out you get, then."

"What? Vinny . . . "

"Out."

"Come on, man," being stupid for the first time tonight, taking a chance, arguing with Vinny. "You can take me all the way, it's only a couple of minutes and I'm late already, I'll get bollocked . . . "

"Not my problem. Out, I said. Things to do tonight."

So Jason got out, helped by Vinny's fingers twisting savagely at his ear, a sharp thumbnail digging deep into the lobe.

Sent on his way with a cuff and a silent jerk of the head, he walked off scowling, rubbing his throbbing ear and looking for a can to kick. Or a dog, that'd be better, something living. Living but safe, a stand-in for Vinny but nothing like him, something that couldn't bite back . . .

He didn't find a dog, or not one that came close enough to kick. He found a better idea, though. Slouched up an alley, found a house with broken glass topping its walls and graffiti on its gate; and he was that late for curfew, another half an hour wouldn't make any real difference. Either they'd breach him to the police or they wouldn't, he couldn't change their minds for them if he ran all the way back now.

Might as well go back feeling good, feeling satisfied . . .

He went twenty metres back down the hill, took a jump at the wall and scrambled up. Balanced along it to the broken glass and jumped down, onto the car roof and into the yard.

The window he'd spray-painted for them was still solid black except for one corner, where someone had been at it with a knife or something. Stupid gits.

He didn't have any paint on him tonight, didn't know what he was going to do now he was here. Maybe he'd kick the back door in, he still fancied kicking something. The man'd be out as usual; and if the woman was in, well, so much the better. Maybe he'd kick her too. Maybe he'd do more than kick the bitch . . .

There were three steps up to the back door. He took them at a run, rammed his shoulder against the wood to test the locks –

237

– and found himself staggering into the kitchen as the door slammed open with no resistance, not locked or bolted, just on the latch, for God's sake . . .

He caught his balance against the cooker and stood perfectly still, holding his breath, holding himself ready for anything.

No noise in the house, no reaction at all. She mustn't be in, then, even the woman must have gone out for once. That meant Jason had the run of the place, he could do what he liked.

He'd clear out anything saleable, for a start. Hot-wire the car, load it up and run the lot down to George. If it wouldn't start he'd just take what he could carry, jewellery and cash.

Then he'd trash the house, do the whole place over, top to bottom. If they thought they'd had problems before, they had a sweet, sweet surprise on the way . . .

Grinning to himself, giggling aloud, Jason made his way through to the living-room, to check out what was worth taking.

Walked in, and turned the light on.

Stood very still, and wet himself.

iv

It had been a busy day for Nathan, a good day. First thing this morning he'd collected their keys from Mr and Mrs Singh, and seen them off to Manchester for their daughter's wedding. They were staying overnight, and they were still worrying; but Nathan assured them that their house would be protected, every minute they were away. During the real danger time, the hours of darkness, he'd be there himself, he said.

He stayed long enough to see the first shift of house-sitters settled and certain. Then he took the mission's new minibus to a clothing warehouse to take delivery of a job lot that had been rushed through in twenty-four hours, thanks to Richard's name and the mission's money: combat jackets with bespoke shoulder-flashes, *CC* in gold on red tabs.

While he was there, he picked up a couple of pairs of camouflage trousers for himself, desert boots and a choice of headgear – jungle hat, balaclava and beret. He persuaded the trader to throw those in gratis, negotiated a discount for anyone else who wanted to do the dressing-up bit so thoroughly, and drove his booty back to Paradise with a happy grin on his face.

He put in a couple of hours' work down at the houses *pour encourager les autres,* concerned not to let enthusiasm slip in the face of more glamorous possibilities. "Everyone wants to play policeman," he grunted to Helen, sweeping up dust and dead plaster. "I mean, who wouldn't, when you're talking the romance of a uniform and a little brief authority, versus hard work and sweat and filth," pausing to cough and spit disgustedly, "that gets into your lungs and all? I'm turning black from the inside out . . . "

"I wouldn't," Helen said quietly. "I'm not going to."

Nat leant on his broom, cocking his head enquiringly.

"Not the uniform bit," she went on. "I don't like it, it's too militaristic. The name, too, the Christ Commando, I don't think it's right. I'll help where I can, of course I will; but we're a church, not an army."

"Someone's got to take responsibility," he said. "And the police can't, or won't. Would you rather see the vandals running riot and the pensioners terrorised?"

"No, no, of course not. I'm not saying I'm right, Nat. I don't suppose I am, really. It's just the way I feel, is all."

"Well, I'll just have to make you feel differently, then, won't I?" He rested his broom against the wall, twitched hers out of her hand and set it alongside, reached for her and drew her close. "Can't have doubts, so close to the heart of government," he murmured. "I shall use every argument at my disposal," biting gently at her lower lip, "to bring you round to my way of thinking . . . "

And then he bit harder. She caught her breath; he nipped a little flesh between his teeth and crushed it, till she moaned aloud. Then he laughed, kissed the tip of her nose in a mocking salute and said, "Now, anything else bothering you? You've been quiet all week."

"Just, just I never get to see you any more. Not properly, the two of us together. You're always doing things with other people. And I know, I do know it's important, it's God's work and I wasn't going to say anything if you hadn't asked; but, well, it'd be nice if you could make time for me sometimes, that's all. It'd be wonderful. I *miss* you, Nat, I miss you like crazy. Even when you're this close I still feel like I'm missing you, because your mind's off somewhere else . . . "

He smiled, and glanced at his watch.

"Let's do that, then, let's make time for each other. I can make an hour for you right now, if we chuck this. I need a bath anyway; no need to rush it. No need to rush anything. How's that, meet the bill?"

"Yes. Yes, *please*."

*

239

So he took her back to his flat, she shared his bath, he didn't rush anything.

After that it was down to the marquee, all dressed up like a soldier. He took his seat on the platform, and gave his first press conference: announced the formation of the Christ Commando. Television and radio were there, all the local papers and stringers for some of the nationals. Nat smiled into the cameras and fielded the questions, turned them where necessary to say what he wanted to say; and he knew just how he was coming over. This was what the training had been for, all the political seminars and public meetings. He'd sound young and confident, articulate and dedicated, an idealist with a sense of humour and a touch of charm.

He couldn't lose.

Then to the Singhs' house again, taking food for the volunteers. Rachel had found a razor-blade in a plastic frame and was going at a black-painted window, scraping it clean one flake at a time.

"Okay," she said, "I know it doesn't help much, I'm not getting very far; but I was bored. And at least it's something, at least I've *tried*, they'll be able to see I've tried . . . "

"Hey," he said, "you don't have to justify yourself to me. Or the Singhs either. They'll be grateful. You carry on. Oh, and you can pick up a Commando jacket any time, down at the marquee. They don't cost, just help yourself."

She shook her head briefly. "It's too hot for a jacket. I don't know how you can."

"Couldn't get camouflaged T-shirts. But seriously, Rachel, I think you should. I think they're useful."

She glanced at him sideways, turned her attention back to the scraping.

"What's wrong?" he asked, suppressing a smile.

"People'll laugh."

"Not often, not for long. And you've been laughed at before, out witnessing. It's never stopped you yet."

"Well. Derry'll laugh, anyway." And that was it, of course, that was the problem.

"I thought Derry was with us?"

"Not really. Not properly. He never has been, really. He'll hang around, so long as I'm there," with an unexpected blush, half-hidden behind her falling hair, "but he won't wear any uniform. And he'll take the mickey out of me something rotten."

"So beat him up," Nathan said, laughing now. "That's what you usually do, isn't it?"

"Can't any more, he's getting strong. And he fights back these

240

days." But she was smiling at least, thinking about it; and after a little more thought she said, "Do I get sergeant's stripes?"

"Don't be greedy, little 'un. Lance-corporal, maybe."

"That'll do. Anything, so long as he has to salute me," she said meditatively. "And call me sir."

After that there was a meeting with police and community leaders, to calm their fears about vigilantes and sectarianism. That was the crucial hour, when the scheme could have been killed in its infancy or else reduced to impotence, just one more pressure-group striking poses for the media. But for that hour Nat had Richard there to back him, though he still did most of the talking; and afterwards it was smiles and handshakes all round, best wishes and promises of support.

"Congratulations, Nat." That was Richard, throwing an arm over his shoulder as they left. "I knew you were a politician, but I've never heard a case better argued."

Nathan shook his head. "Not my doing, don't congratulate me."

"Well, no, then. Not directly your doing, you were inspired, that's clear. Though even the Spirit can't do the job with unsuitable tools. Are you ready for the bad news now?"

"What's that, then?"

"You've just become a bureaucrat."

"Eh?"

"You've got an organisation to build. You can't just let the Commando happen, it's going to need a lot of strength at the top, a lot of control. You'll have to keep it disciplined; and when I say you, I mean *you*. This one's your baby."

"Oh, I know that. I like it," smiling at him, a secret shared. "It's responsibility," *it's power*, "it's what I've always been looking for. Don't worry, I'll make this work. And *without* turning into a bureaucrat, thanks very much. There'll be volunteers for the paperwork. Now, are you coming down to the marquee for your jacket?"

And Richard laughed, and said, "Not me. I said, this is your show. You're top dog; but they won't believe that, if they see me in your uniform. No, I'm staying strictly in civvies."

Nathan had spent the rest of the day closeted with half a dozen picked lieutenants, drawing up initial routes, rotas and regulations: who would patrol where and when, what they were to look out for, what they might and might not do. Obviously these would be revised by experience, perhaps also by further

241

consultation with the police and others; but at least they provided a groundwork, a basis to operate from.

The later editions of the evening paper featured a colour photo on the front page, Nathan in his military regalia under the headline, *LOCAL CHRISTIANS DECLARE WAR ON CRIME.* In the text, he was referred to as 'generalissimo Nathan Lewis, Richard Gould's right-hand man'. He liked that.

He liked the TV report that evening, too; but what he liked best was the recognition he got in the streets, as he walked round to the Singhs'. A couple of local shopkeepers were just locking up, rolling steel shutters down over their windows; they stopped him, "just wanted to say good luck with it, son; and if you need any help, let us know, eh? Contributions, I mean. We've been done over three times this year, anything that keeps the villains off this patch has got to be worth it."

"We haven't done anything yet," Nathan said, grinning. "But I'm hopeful. Would you come to a meeting, if I asked all the small businesses round here? Our patrols can keep an eye on your premises, obviously, but there may be other ways we can help."

"'Course we'll come. Just let us know, we'll be there. So'll everyone on this street."

And then, cutting down a back alley, he saw some boys smashing bottles against a wall; but one glimpse of his uniform and they scarpered, as they would have done for a policeman.

That rounded off Nathan's day for him like a forerunner, a prophecy of success; and he went whistling down to the Singhs' house, looking forward greatly to the night.

House-sitting for Mr Singh was the Commando's first venture, and Nathan had appointed himself chief sitter for tonight. Other young men from the mission would keep him company in three-hour shifts, but he meant to stay awake all night long.

There had been so many volunteers for this inaugural duty, they'd had to draw straws. Nathan might have picked his own companions, but he didn't want to be seen playing favourites so early. He'd agreed to leave it to chance, or to God; and for this first stretch, nine till midnight, he had one of the Swedish boys with him.

Bengt was wearing a ring on his finger, where none had been before.

"Since three days," he said shyly, when Nathan asked.

"That's quick, isn't it? You only got to know her on the boat coming over . . . "

"It would have been quicker, for me. I have asked Ingrid a

242

month ago, I have been sure already that this was what God wanted for us. But she said," and he smiled now, through his solemnity, "she said only would she say yes when I could ask her in English and properly, not just half a sentence. I have to take her out and talk English all the night, and then ask. I have to try three times, before I don't talk Swedish at all. But it was only a game, she has meant always to marry me. It is what God intends."

"That's wonderful," Nathan said, using one of Richard's tricks, kissing Bengt on the cheek. "When's the wedding, are you going to have it over here? With Richard to marry you?"

A shake of the head. "No. We would like it, but not our families. We should get married in our own church at home. And not yet, I think. Perhaps at Christmas, perhaps next year."

"Well, maybe we'll come over, some of us. If we can. There ought to be someone there, you'll be our first marriage."

"Yes. You think there will be more?"

"I'm sure of it. If the mission lasts. Which means if Richard stays, I suppose – and he's making long-term plans, there's no sign of him leaving."

"Richard will stay as long as God calls him to stay," Bengt said certainly. "And the mission will last as long as God sees a need for it."

"Yes. That's what I meant. You won't be staying beyond the summer, though? You and Ingrid?"

"We cannot. We have college courses and exams, and friends and families. We must find other work than this. But there is much to do."

"Of course . . . "

It felt odd, making slightly stilted, slightly difficult conversation in a stranger's house – and a house made stranger still by the decor, a curious combination of English and Punjabi. Nathan found everything a little gaudy for his taste, a little overdone. There were too many ornaments on the shelves, too many unreadable texts on the walls; the carpets and the chairs were too soft, the curtains too heavy, the television too big and everything too brightly coloured.

Also, the room was stifling. He went to open a window and found that he couldn't, they'd all been nailed, puttied and painted shut. That made sense, in Paradise; but he had to get some air in, if he was going to spend all night here.

He opened the front door wide, went through to the kitchen and did the same at the back, to get a through-draught. That felt better immediately, stirring his hair and cooling his skin; but as soon as he was back in the living-room he heard a crash, the

243

draught grown strong enough to slam the back door and kill itself dead.

Nathan sighed, thought about wedging the door open and decided it could wait.

"Let's sit outside for a while, Ben. It'll be cooler, and we might as well let people know the place is inhabited."

So they perched on the window-sill with their feet on the low front wall, and watched the street as the street watched them.

Later, when the sky had finally consented to get dark this long summer evening, they heard another crash from inside the house: as it might be the back door blowing open again.

Nathan was up in a moment. "You wait, Ben. I'll go see."

He slipped into the hall and pulled the door quietly to behind him, heard someone moving in the kitchen and stood quite still, waiting.

Saw a slim figure, just a dark shade in the dark house, making its way from kitchen to living-room, going in, turning on the light.

Stepped forward then, silent on the thick carpets; closed his hand nice and friendly, nice and tight on the boy's thin neck and said, "Hullo, Jason."

Bengt came in a minute later, to stare at Jason where the boy stood rigid, with Nathan's hand on his neck and a dark stain showing vivid on his pale, filthy jeans.

"Nothing to worry about, Ben," Nathan said. "We've got a visitor, but he won't be any trouble. I think it's best if you go off now, and leave the two of us to talk this through on our own. You might tell the other guys, too. Tell them not to bother with their alarm-clocks, I won't be needing them now. It'll be easier with just the two of us, won't it, Jason?"

And just a little pressure, a little warning squeeze on his neck had Jason nodding, jerking his head up and down until another squeeze told him to stop.

"Well. If you are sure, Nat . . . ?"

"Oh yes, I'm sure. You get yourself off, get to bed."

"There is nothing else you want me to do?"

Nathan thought about it, and smiled brilliantly. "Just the one thing," he said. "You can pray. Pray for young Jason here, he's got a lot on his conscience and I don't think it's going to be an easy night for him."

"Yes, of course. I will pray for you both."

"Thanks, Ben – but concentrate on Jason, eh? He needs it more than I do."

*

244

"What have you been up to, then, Jason?" Laughing lightly, giving him a teasing little shake. "Rolling around in a dung-heap, is that your idea of a good Saturday night? You're very smelly. Even disregarding your little accident. Come on through to the kitchen, let's get you cleaned up a bit."

Nathan's grip didn't slacken until he'd propelled the awkward, unwilling Jason down the passage. Then he closed the back door, leant against it, folded his arms and said, "Take your clothes off, Jason."

"Y'what?"

"Take your clothes off. Put them in that bucket there, we'll leave them to soak."

"What are you, some kind of fucking queer?" muttered defiantly, with yearning looks at the door Nathan was leaning against, the passageway that Nathan could reach in two quick strides. "I'm not stripping off for some – "

"Jason." Nathan kept his voice quiet, matter-of-fact, a little bored. "Do you want to do this the hard way? We did it the hard way last time, if you remember."

Jason flinched, remembering; and slowly, slowly worked one trainer off, and then the other.

"That's better. Put them in the bucket. And everything else. Those trousers are the worst, but I think everything's a bit smelly. Take it all off, you'll be much better company."

"What'm I going to wear, then?"

"Oh, you don't need to wear anything, Jason. It's a warm night, and this is a very warm house."

"What are, what are you going to do?" Stripped down to his underwear now, skinny and ridiculous in Y-fronts and amateur tattoos, "What d'you *want*, fuck it?"

"Oh, I just want to talk, Jason. I want you to bare your soul, that's all. You'll feel so much easier when you've confessed all your sins and done a little penance. Let's have those knickers in the bucket, now. Then you'd better slosh some of that disinfectant over them, and top up with water. Hurry up, kid, we've only got tonight . . . "

"Fucking *shit!*"

This was later, much later, out in the back yard. Jason swore, dropped the razor-blade he was working with and whimpered a little, gazing at his hand. Nathan saw blood welling darkly on the boy's fingers, running in dribbles to his palm.

"Never mind, son. You cut yourself, you know what's the best thing, don't you?"

245

He twisted the nozzle on the hose he held, and a jet of cold water spurted out. Jason yelped, and jumped back; but Nathan played the water over the naked, shivering boy for a second or two longer before cutting off the flow.

"Get on with it, Jason."

"I *cut* myself, you fucker . . . !"

That earned him another short, sharp shower. "Language, Jason. I know you cut yourself. You wouldn't have cut yourself if you hadn't broken the proper tool for the job, would you? Now pick up the razor-blade, and get on with it."

It had been Rachel's example, and the little progress she'd made, that had led Nathan to setting Jason's penance.

"You painted this window out," he'd said, handing over Rachel's little gadget, the blade fixed in a frame. "You can scrape it clean. That seems fair."

"Yeah, okay. Okay, anything . . . "

And Jason had started in willingly enough; but it didn't take him long to learn how hard the work was, and how slow. Soon he'd been whining in protest, and Nathan had had to connect up the hose, to encourage him. That worked for a while; it worked until Jason got seriously rebellious, snapping the paint-scraper in two and throwing the bits over the wall into next-door's yard.

"There," he'd panted, staring stupid defiance at Nathan. "What are you going to do about that, then, eh?"

But Nathan already knew what he was going to do about that. He'd been expecting it for a while, only surprised that it had taken Jason so long; and he'd already discovered that Mr Singh used an old safety razor to keep the edges of his beard neat.

He'd pulled a packet of loose razor-blades from his pocket, and tossed them onto the window-sill.

"You can use those," he'd said. "And don't get clever again, young Jason. Don't push your luck."

And with that advice backed up by a long cold shower that left its victim crouched in a corner huddled and gasping, Jason had taken it very much on board, hadn't got clever at all. Had only got sensible, clamping a razor-blade tight between finger and thumb and scraping away with laudable concentration.

Even now, with the blood still running, his rebellion didn't last. He scrabbled for the blade, picked it up awkwardly and made at least a show of getting back to work.

"Good boy," Nathan said softly, deciding to be satisfied. "Now talk to me, Jason. Don't stop, you can talk and scrape at the same time. Tell me everything: everything you do, and everything you know. But start with tonight, tell me where you've been, to get so much shit on you ... "

Later still, with the short night gone and full light in the sky again, Nathan looked at his watch and laughed. Coiled the hose neatly and tossed it into the kitchen sink, collected the bucket of Jason's clothes and carried it out into the yard.

"Time to go home, Jason."

The boy stood still for a moment, then slumped. Dropped the razor-blade with fingers bleeding from many cuts, dropped his arms onto the window-sill and his head onto his arms, started to cry again.

Nathan ignored him for the time it took to tip the sodden clothes out of the bucket, watch the water drain away, and empty a bottle of bleach over them. Then he chucked that aside and said, "Come on, kid, it's over. Get dressed and scarper. You're not going to bother the Singhs again, are you?"

A shake of the head, a muffled negative.

"And you're not going to tell anyone about what happened tonight, anything stupid like that, right?"

"No," loud and clear this time, "no, I swear ... "

"Good. Off you go, then. Vanish. I'll let you out the back here, don't want you dripping through the house. Oh, and Jason?"

"Y-yeah, what?"

"Don't forget to give that message to George, will you?"

"No, I got it, I'll remember ... "

"Good lad."

He unbolted the garage door and swung it up while Jason forced his legs into saturated jeans and his feet into trainers, pulled his sweatshirt over his head and ran out into the alley, abandoning his underwear altogether.

Grinning to himself, Nathan leant against the wall and watched; and laughed aloud when the run slowed to an awkward, hopping dance as Jason plucked at his wet clothes, as he pushed his hands down inside his jeans for whatever protection, whatever relief they could offer ...

There were other thieves, other vandals than Jason in Paradise; but by his own confession, Jason had been the Singhs' particular tormentor. At any rate, the house should be safe enough left empty for ten minutes, at six in the morning. Nathan locked it up and left it. He was feeling tired and exhilarated both, as always after a night with no sleep, and also deeply contented. *Never laid a finger on him, guv*, he thought, and laughed again. *I was his father confessor, that's all. Supervised his penance. He was very penitent.*

He headed up to the main road, cutting through back alleys for added interest — and shying sharply away from a wooden gate when a heavy weight hit the other side of it, with a volley of barking. That set other dogs off in other yards, up and down the hill; Nathan hurried out of the alley.

He found a newsagent who was working if not officially open, sorting papers for the delivery rounds. Who was quite happy to sell Nathan the local Sunday paper, a tabloid with its editorial policy focused firmly below the belt.

There was a photograph of Richard on the front page. Nothing too surprising in that, he was always news in this city, these days; but the photograph showed him kissing a woman, whom Nathan needed only a moment to identify as Evelyn Somers. And the headline was *MORAL CRUSADER'S ILLICIT LOVE*, and the story was either libel or disaster, unless it was both.

NINETEEN

His reaction is easy to guess, easy to see. No dissembler, he. He tastes corruption on his tongue; his nostrils flare at the stink of it; he wants to go and wash his hands.

After the disgust the anger, burning, cleansing. He must feel as Christ felt at the temple gate, seeing the moneychangers arrayed in all their pride and greed before him; and no doubt like Christ he wants to damage and destroy, to use the weapons of his body and his voice and all the influence he has.

It's no sin, such an anger. He follows his master, in this as in everything. And one thing we can be sure of, his fury's not directed at the obvious target, the journalist who scraped this story from the dregs and residues of a diseased imagination.

No, he sees further than that. He must do. He doesn't watch the game, he watches the player, the hand that moves the pieces.

Last week it was muscle, vandals at the marquee. This week it's more subtle, a story designed to degrade and discredit him and through him the whole mission, the movement that has gripped this city and drawn it so much closer to God; but he'll be seeing the same hand at work.

No chance of its being coincidence. He knows the flavours of conspiracy.

ii

Evelyn Somers sat in her nerves and twitches, in her flat; she looked out of the window, and saw the world.

Saw the world waiting, and was afraid.

First thing this morning, before her first cup of coffee, even, before her first cigarette she'd been up the road to the newsagent, she'd bought a copy of the *Sunday Messenger* and read its messages.

She'd seen herself on the front page, kissing Richard; and since then, ever since then she'd been afraid. She'd been watching the world from the window, and not answering the door.

There were people in the street. The world was watching her. Scooped and resentful journalists sat on car bonnets endlessly smoking and endlessly, endlessly patient. Cameras cocked. They'd all got their photos of Evelyn at the window, staring out; now they wanted more, Evelyn at the door, questioned and consumed.

Other people, too. The local children were out there, laughing and quarrelling and chasing each other but all staying close, all watchful. Neighbours were standing around pretending to clean windows or scrub dog-do off the pavement but in reality just as curious as the children, just as prying.

That strange, sick man from downstairs: he was gone now, off to the club, no doubt, but he'd been out there earlier, talking to the journalists. Telling lies about Evelyn, no doubt. She'd find out tomorrow.

A police car had come by a couple of times, the driver only stopping to say something briefly through his window before he moved on. That was no help, what help was that?

Finally, though, she saw someone else in the street outside, someone who could perhaps help her.

She'd never been fond of Nathan. He was too young, too confident, all drive and ambition; and there was always a sneer in his smile when he talked to her, she could see it clearly. Always scorn to be heard in his voice.

But she couldn't have been more glad to see him now. If anyone could get those monstrous lurking, spying journalists to go away, he was the man. And he was wearing his Commando clothes, his uniform of authority; that'd give him a little extra weight. Or at least it would remind them that he had Richard's weight behind his own. They wouldn't argue with Richard's representative, not in Paradise . . .

So Evelyn watched hopefully, thinking that maybe Nathan would take it all upon himself, maybe he'd go straight up to the journalists and clear them off without even coming to her door.

He didn't do that, though, he only nodded at them, acknowledging their presence, *I'll get to you later*. Then he rang Evelyn's doorbell.

She hid behind the door as she opened it, to escape the photographers' shining lenses; and slammed it again as soon as Nathan was inside, against the shouted questions of the men pressing hard on his heels.

"Come, come in, Nathan, come upstairs. I, oh, I'm so glad to see you, you've no idea. I feel so trapped, those terrible people haunting me like this, you can't imagine . . . I daren't set foot outside, I'm a prisoner, a *prisoner* . . . They'll listen to you, though, I'm sure of that. You tell them. You tell them, this is no way to treat a human being, caging her in her own home . . . "

"It's not the journalists I want to talk to," Nathan said.

"Not . . . ?" She turned to stare at him, startled and anxious, hearing that sneer in his voice again and something more: like flames glimpsed through a furnace door, she thought it might have been, anger deeply and strongly contained. "Oh," she said, "but surely, now you've seen, surely you'll have a word, you'll tell them to go away? Surely you will . . . "

"I'll talk to them," he said. "As they are. As I can do some kind of damage limitation, I suppose. But I'm not going to chase them off, Evelyn. They wouldn't go in any case, and I'm not going to try. Just deserts, I'd call them. The perils of fame. That's what you were fishing for, wasn't it? Your fifteen minutes in the spotlight? Well, you've got it now. Lie back and enjoy it, I would. That's what it's for."

"I don't," she said, "I don't know what you mean. What do you mean, what are you talking about?"

And Nathan pushed past her, picked up the *Messenger* and said, "This is what I mean. What you *did,* Evelyn, what you've *done.* If you don't like the repercussions, that's just tough. You brought it on yourself, sister."

It wasn't brotherly, the way he called her sister. It wasn't brotherly at all. She brushed hair back from her face with a trembling hand, and reached for her cigarettes. "I didn't, I didn't do anything, what am I supposed to have done?"

"You know what you did." But he reminded her anyway, reading extracts from the paper in a savage imitation of her own high voice: "'Yes, of course I love Richard. How could I not love him? We're soul-twins . . . It's the most incredible relationship. It's more, it's so much more than physical . . . I think he's divine. I think he's Christ come again, and I feel so incredibly lucky, so *privileged* to have been chosen. I'm no one special, I'm nothing, but still I'm special to him, that's my miracle . . . '"

He dropped the newspaper then, just let it go so that its sheets scattered across her carpet; and he didn't say a word, he only stood there unmoving, unblinking even, and his eyes lashed her into an awkward, stumbling justification.

"Well, it's true. It's all true, everything I said. They distorted it, I know, they made it sound sordid, but I never said it that way, that's not what I meant. You can't blame me for the way they

251

twisted what I said . . . "

"Can't I?" he asked, quiet and menacing. "I think I can, Evelyn. It's trash, of course," and his foot stirred the strewn pages dismissively, "it's all trash, he's trash that wrote it; but you're trash too. You knew what you were doing. You were making yourself important, weren't you, Evelyn? Feeding your own fantasy, sounding good in your own ears. Building yourself up. Well, let's face it, no one else was going to do that, were they? There's no one else to build you up, because everyone else sees you for what you are, for the trash you are.

"Except Richard, of course. He wouldn't see that. He's very focused, is Richard, he looks for the good in people all the time, and generally he finds it. And if not, if all he finds is vacancy, then he's found himself another job, hasn't he? He just wants to see that vacancy filled, make it a life worth living.

"That's all it was, that's why he gave you so much time, and so much of himself. You're a black hole, Evelyn, and he was trying to stop you sucking everything down into your emptiness. Waste of time, of course, but Richard doesn't admit the impossible.

"So he tried, and failed; and you tried too, didn't you? Suck suck, you went, with a real prize in your sights. A nice juicy mouthful he'd have made, for a lady spider.

"Only he was immune, or just too big to handle. Whatever. You weren't getting anywhere, so you did the other thing. You did this." Kicking at the newsprint again. "You went for damage. Anything to make your mark, to be sure he'd remember you. That's it, isn't it, Evelyn? That's what this is all about. You're just trying to raise a few scars."

She shook her head tremulously, no. He didn't understand. He was saying terrible things and they weren't true, none of them were true. She loved Richard, she truly did; and he loved her. He'd said so, those very words, and such a glow about them . . . She'd never do anything to hurt him, it would be like blotting out the sun. It would be madness. And she wasn't mad, no, no.

"Well, you listen, Evelyn. I've left you alone so far, because I thought you were harmless; but I'm laying down some ground rules now. And if you know what's good for you, you'll follow them. You'll follow them *exactly*.

"I haven't seen Richard yet, to discuss this with him; but I know how he'll react. He'll laugh, because it's nonsense; and he'll be all sweetness and light and forgiveness. He'll have the press eating out of his hand in nothing flat, and then he'll come and talk to you, try to get you straightened out.

"Frankly I think that's a waste of time, I don't think anything could straighten you out. Your mind's so twisted you make Spaghetti Junction look like a country crossroads. But I can't stop him trying.

"What I can do, though, I can stop you making things worse. Are you listening, Evelyn? These are the rules you live by, here on in. Number one, you don't talk to the papers. Not ever again, not about anything, you understand me? If you see a journalist coming, you cross the street. If he comes after you, you run. If he catches you, you say *nothing*. Not a word, not a syllable.

"And number two, you keep away from Richard. I can't keep him away from you, but you don't encourage him to visit, and you certainly don't visit him. You don't visit him, you don't phone him, you don't hang around to catch him after service. If you see him coming, you walk the other way. Run and hide. Duck and cover.

"If you won't do it for his sake, then do it for your own. Because if you break that rule and I catch you doing it, you're going to be feeling very sorry for yourself, very quickly. You're living on my patch here, Evelyn, and I could make you terribly unhappy. I could make you wish you'd never been *born* . . . "

He left her then, left without another word, no repetition and no detail.

Evelyn sat for a long time shivering in her chair by the window, not looking out. The journalists were still there, the world was still there, no doubt, still waiting for her to show; but she didn't care about that now. She closed her eyes and listened to his voice rebounding like an echo that only got louder, never won free.

Eventually she stirred, she rose and gathered together all the scattered sheets of the *Sunday Messenger*. She sat back in her chair again, opened the window and began to tear the paper into neat rectangular strips, page by page. Each strip she gripped between thumb and forefinger, held out of the window and released into the wind's grasp; and even as her eyes watched it snatched away, her fingers were carefully tearing the next.

When she'd finished with the newspaper, when it was all gone, she started on her children's drawings, all she'd been allowed of her children: taking them one by one from the wall, tearing them, letting them go.

Most mornings Kyzer would greet George by the gym door, urgent to be let out after a long night loose in the empty building.

Today, though, there was no visible sign of the dog, only the sound of it, a rumbling growl down in the basement.

George whistled, and got no more response than a staccato barking, like a summons.

Going downstairs he found Kyzer at the far end of the corridor, snuffling around the fire-door, sneezing and growling.

"What, something out there, is there? Well, there better be, this much fuss . . . "

George slid the bolts back, slipped a hand through Kyzer's thick collar and pulled the door open.

Something there, right enough. Young Jason, huddled in the corner of the shadowy well, where the steps led up to the alley. Wrapped in a woman's old brown coat he was, pale and filthy, barefoot and trembling, crusted blood all over his hands.

"Please, George, I'm sorry, but I didn't, I didn't have nowhere else to go. And I got to see you anyway, I got a, a message for you . . . "

"Is that right? Well, you better come in, then." George pulled the stiff-legged, straining Kyzer back out of the way, to let the boy scurry past. Jason smelled strange, harsh and astringent. "Go and have a shower, warm yourself up and wash that stink off, you're making my dog sneeze. Then come and see me in the office. And for God's sake dump that coat, you look stupid."

"Can't, I ain't got nothing else to wear . . . "

"What, nothing?" And when Jason shook his head, George laughed. "They really did you good, didn't they, kid? All right, get some gear out of the shop, then. You know where the keys are. Make a list, you can owe me for it."

Jason nodded wearily, like a boy who was getting well used to owing George. George laughed again and sent Kyzer out for a piss in the alley, jogging up the steps to keep an eye on it. It wasn't safe just to let it run free, kids played around here.

Twenty minutes later, Jason came into the office with wet hair, wearing a tracksuit and a pair of cheap plimsolls from the shop.

"I wrote it down, what I took," he muttered, passing the keys across the desk. "It's not much, honest . . . "

"Smart kid." But the lad was being super-sensible this morning, subdued by whatever it was he went through last night. He hadn't even sat down, though his eyes were red-rimmed with exhaustion; he stayed on his feet, trying to look respectful at a guess, only spoiling it by the way his hands constantly scratched at his chest and legs.

"Stand still, for God's sake, what's the matter with you? Itching powder in the kit, is there?"

Jason shook his head. "I got burns, sort of. They're dead sore . . . "

"Let's see."

Jason rolled a sleeve back, to show patches of vivid red on his scrawny arm.

"Jesus. What did that to you, son?"

"I dunno. Something he put on my clothes. I took 'em off, I couldn't stand it. Found that coat down on the wasteland. And I couldn't think of anywhere to go, except here. I must've been breached at the hostel, I can't go back there . . . "

"You'll have to go back sometime. Stupid to go on the run, you'll just end up in more trouble. But you should see a doctor anyway, if you're like that all over."

Jason nodded, sniffing. "Even my, my hair's gone. You know, down there. I just seen in the shower, it's all gone. And it hurts something awful, down there."

George choked down a laugh with unaccustomed kindness. "I'll get you seen by someone in a bit, kid. They can't breach you if you're in hospital, and they'll take you back if you give them a decent story. But I want the truth, first. What happened?"

"I, I can't tell you, Mr Jenner. Really," and his eyes were shifting desperately around the room while his badly-cut fingers knotted themselves together in the exigencies of fear, "really I can't. He said, I mustn't tell anyone . . . "

"Who said?"

"That Nathan guy. The one who, who . . . "

Who got my name out of you, when he caught you burgling his flat for me . . . "All right," George said calmly. "I know who you mean. So what's this in aid of, then, what did he do you for?"

"I can't, I can't say. Just, there's a message from him. For you, he said I had to give it to you, personal, like . . . "

"Well, I'm here. In person."

"Yeah. Yeah. He said, I had to tell you that whatever you're running on the side from the gym here, you've got to stop. He said he's with the chapel now, he's cleaning up Paradise, and he doesn't want no crooks on his patch, he said. He said run the gym as a straight business or he'll run you out of Paradise, he said. I'm sorry, George," in a whisper, "but that's what he said. And he said I had to tell you, just like that . . . "

George nodded slowly, remembering something else Nathan had said, the first time they'd met. Talking about Jason, about that betrayal. *It's just a question of who he's more scared of, really, isn't it?* And the answer, the evidence was right in front of George now.

He didn't like it at all, that there might be someone else operating in Paradise who scared people more than he did. Except for Vinny, of course, and he didn't count Vinny.

"All right, Jason," he said. "You get on outside, wait by the car. I'll run you up to the hospital, see what they say; and don't worry about the hostel, I'll sort them out. And the police, if you've been breached already. I'll get that straight for you."

You can owe me, we'll add it to your many debts, my son. He didn't say that aloud, though. Jason had been with him long enough, he should understand how it worked by now; and if not, if he saw it only as unfettered kindness, well, that could be useful too. Gratitude might keep the boy obedient, where fear looked like failing or being overridden.

iv

"Hullo. I'm sorry to disturb you on a Sunday, but I'm with the Paradise chapel, and I was wondering if you'd heard or read anything this weekend about the Christ Commando . . . ?"

Rachel didn't feel entirely comfortable taking the good news door to door this way, face to face with strangers. But she had Bengt with her, another team over the road, Nathan and Richard and ultimately God at her back; and with that much support she'd stick with it, all the way to the bottom of the street. She wouldn't go sliding off round the corner to find Derry, though she was sorely tempted. That was the Devil's voice whispering to her; and he wouldn't be working at it so hard if he wasn't getting worried, which only proved how useful this work was . . .

In fact just a quick check of her clipboard told her how useful this was. Okay, a lot of the doors she'd knocked at today had produced hung over and sarcastic students, or sweaty men with beer-guts and sneers, or else nervous Asian women who didn't have the English to understand her. But even that was useful knowledge, it all added to their picture of Paradise; and then there were the others, the people who stood in clear need of the Commando and had been genuinely glad to talk.

She had half a dozen names on her list for follow-up, from pensioners who needed help with shopping and housework to a teenage mother who was heavily in debt and hopelessly confused about benefits. There must be someone who could give her the right advice; Rachel had promised the girl a visit as soon as she'd tracked an expert down. She'd also offered free baby-sitting, confident that Nathan would approve.

This door produced a middle-aged mother of five with a husband away at sea. She wasn't noticeably impressed by Rachel's spiel – "bunch of kids, what use do you think you're going to be? It's kids like you cause most of the trouble round here, anyway. Kids like mine, come to that; and I can't see you lot reforming them" – but she was quite willing to list all her complaints, from greedy landlords and leaking roofs to the stray dogs that terrorised her Yorkshire terrier. Rachel noted them dutifully, gave her a leaflet with the Commando helpline number on it – actually a portable phone that Nat carried around with him – and turned to go.

And heard a whistle, heard her name called in a clear, summoning voice like a bell, a voice she couldn't deny. Looked round and saw Richard on the corner, beckoning. She sprinted, instant and automatic obedience; and,

"Rachel, can I have you for half an hour?"

"Yes, of course." *The rest of my life, if you want it.* "Ben can find someone else to partner him. What's up?"

"You'll have heard about that story in this morning's *Messenger*?"

"Yes, I heard. It's stupid." And it was stupid; but that hadn't stopped everyone gossiping about it, getting on Rachel's nerves with their endless speculation. That felt just as dirty, just as intrusive as the report itself. Which was one reason why Rachel had chosen to partner Bengt on the house-to-house this morning. His English might be very much better these days, but he was still quiet when he was allowed to be. She'd felt a little guilty, using him that way; but needs must when the Devil drives, and the Devil was driving God's people hard that morning, scoring points all down the line.

Richard smiled at Rachel's ferocity, but only briefly. "Yes. But I must go and talk to Evelyn. She spoke to the reporter, there's no questioning that, he didn't make it all up; and she must be deeply confused. She needs help to see things clearly, and I think it can only come from me.

"The point is, though, I'm told there are more journalists hanging around outside her flat. If they see me going in alone, there'll be more photos in the papers tomorrow, more nonsense written. It doesn't hurt me, but it could damage the mission.

"So will you come with me? It'll limit their imaginations, at least, if I have a girl with me. And it might help Evelyn."

And though he wasn't going to mention it, it would obviously help Richard to have a witness who could testify to the innocence of his words and actions. Rachel wasn't blind, she knew there were people in the chapel hierarchy who'd snatch at any opportunity to get at Richard. This story would be seized on with glee; no point giving them more ammunition than they had already.

"Of course I will," she said. "But why me?" She could see why he'd want a woman, but there were dozens of others he could have chosen, surely should have chosen over a teenager.

Richard chuckled. "Because it's only just occurred to me," he confessed. "Or put it another way, say God's chosen you. I saw you, and he put the idea whole into my head; so it must be you he wants me to take."

Nice to feel so sure about things. Rachel could barely remember the days when she was utterly certain herself, when everything that happened was planned. But whether it was God or Richard who wanted her, the answer was still yes. She'd do anything for either one of them.

They hurried through the interconnecting streets towards Evelyn's flat, and the closer they got the faster Richard hustled her along. Rachel didn't understand that urgency, or where it had come from, so suddenly; but she felt it herself or caught it from him, and they were both running as they turned the final corner.

She was expecting journalists and found them, notebooks and cameras and tape-recorders and all. What she hadn't expected, what she couldn't understand was the paper under her feet, little torn strips littering the pavement and strewn across the road. Hundreds of them there must have been, thousands maybe. Newspaper mostly, but there were pictures there too, kids' drawings by the look of the fragments she could see. If Richard hadn't been so urgent she'd have stopped to gather some up for a closer look.

But his hand gripped her arm, dragging her on, no time for curiosity; and even so they didn't make it, they didn't get to Evelyn's door before the journalists got to them.

"Richard, this story — any truth in it?"

"When did you first meet Evelyn Somers?"

"Why did she have her kids taken away from her?"

Rachel flinched back under the onslaught of lenses and

questions, pulled away from Richard and pressed herself against the wall, wanting no part of this. And instantly felt guilty for abandoning him, *some support you turned out to be, girl*; but she didn't need to worry, you never needed to worry about Richard. *You're never alone with Jesus,* she reminded herself forcefully, scornfully. *If you're with God, you're in the majority. By definition.*

And if that was theory, this was the practice she was seeing in front of her now: Richard calm and confident, greeting the journalists by name, quieting them with just the raising of a hand.

"No," he was saying, "the story's nonsense. Gossip and exaggeration. No, I won't be making a detailed statement. Say what you like. Hot air cools fast, you can't sustain a farrago of speculation and innuendo, so why should I worry? I'm more concerned about Evelyn. It can't be much fun for her, having you lot camped on her doorstep. Have you seen her this morning?"

"Oh, we've seen her," one of the journalists replied. "Where do you think all this crap came from?" His foot kicked at the scraps of paper, stirred up a minor storm.

"What do you mean, Peter?" Richard was tense and still suddenly, wholly focused.

"This is what she's been doing, ever since your soldier-boy went in and came out again. I've got pictures. Very odd, she looks. Highly peculiar. Only she stopped an hour back, and we haven't seen her since. We knocked, but she doesn't answer."

"That's hardly surprising. Why don't you all push off, and leave the poor woman alone?"

"Can't do that, Richard. Not till we get a statement. More than our jobs are worth, that would be," added virtuously, with a deliberate smugness.

"Mmm. That's something else you might consider sometime, Peter – just how much your jobs are worth, if this is what they bring you to." But Richard was speaking inattentively, almost automatically, it seemed, his head turned upwards and his eyes scanning Evelyn's blank windows.

"Someone's been in, you said. Was that Nathan Lewis?"

"That's him. In and out."

"Well, if she let him in . . . "

Richard knocked, stepped back a few paces – the journalists falling back too, to make a respectful space for him – and called up. "Evelyn? It's Richard. May I come in?"

With his witness, Rachel thought, though he hadn't mentioned that. Seeing this crowd slavering for a story, she was quite determined; there was no way she was letting him in there alone.

His calling produced no more response than his knock. He waited, briefly, but didn't try again.

"I think we ought to get in there," he said quietly, talking to Rachel now. "Invited or not."

"How can we? Unless you've got a key . . . " *And I hope you haven't, they'd love that, the papers would.*

"Well," he said, "maybe the door isn't actually locked. Nat might not have closed it properly behind him."

And he laid a hand against the wood, and pushed; and sure enough, the door swung open. Richard stepped inside, with Rachel scuttling fast on his heels, and he shut the door again firmly in the face of the astonished press.

"How, how did you know . . . ? That it would just open like that . . . ?"

"I didn't know," he said. "I prayed. Now come on, let's find Evelyn."

And he led the way upstairs at a sprint.

It was Rachel who actually found Evelyn. Richard went one way at the head of the stairs, she went the other. She opened a door, found herself looking into a bedroom and backed out quickly, taking only time enough to register that the bed and the room were empty.

Tried the next door. Bathroom. Put her head in –

– and there was Evelyn, reflected in the mirror. In the bath she was, her glazed eyes staring fixedly into that same mirror so that she seemed to be staring straight at Rachel as she lay pale and still in the still, pink water . . .

v

Helen had left Nat sleeping, snatching a few grudged hours' rest after his all-night vigil and his anger. She'd written him a note and gone for a long hard solo Sunday cycle ride, just a way to pass the time; but she'd passed more than time, she'd passed Evelyn's flat too, and the lurking reporters.

Had thought, *Serves her right, hope she's penned up in there for days*; and had repented the thought almost immediately, no proper wish for a newly Christian girl to be wishing. For penance she'd almost stopped and knocked, almost gone in to talk to the woman, see how she was, if there was anything she needed in her imprisonment.

But then she'd seen Evelyn at the window, making it snow in summer: pale face behind dirty glass, pale hands reaching out to drop little scraps of paper onto the journalistic circus below.

Had thought, *No, thanks. She's cracking up, that lady is. And I'm sorry, I know it's all the more reason to get involved, to try to help – but I can't, that's all. Can't face it. Maybe later, but not, not now . . .*

Had bent lower over the handlebars and hastened past, fast as she could down the hill, speed the best drug she could think of for discomfort in the conscience.

When she came home hours later Nathan was dressed, in uniform again and on the phone, his voice tight and commanding.

" . . . And someone's got Richard, have they? . . . Good, I want him kept an eye on. And the press kept away, that's crucial. He's in no state to say anything. Tell them I'll make a statement later – or no, better, any chance of you finding a room there for a press conference? You and me, you take the medical questions and I'll handle the rest. Can do? . . . Terrific. That's great, Martin. Six o'clock, then, tell them. I'll be up before that, though. Soon as I can."

He hung up, looked at Helen, said, "You picked a fine time to go wandering off, didn't you?"

"Why? What's going on, who was that?"

"Martin Leclerc. *Doctor* Leclerc, and thank Heaven we've got some of our own people up at the hospital."

"Nat, what's *happened*?"

"Evelyn Somers has *happened*," he said savagely. "Slit her wrists with a kitchen knife – and not the first time, according to Martin, she's got scars. Only this time she did it with the papers right there on the doorstep."

"Oh, Jesus . . . " As the oath it was meant for it felt strange in her mouth, like trying to swear with the name of her closest friend; so she turned it into a prayer instead, an appeal. "Is she – is she all right?"

"Depends on your definitions, but she's alive. She shouldn't be, but she is. That's the other half of the story. It was Richard who found her. Well, Rachel, at least he had the sense to take someone with him. Rachel found her in the bath. Richard told her to phone for an ambulance, then wait for it downstairs. And the way he said it, apparently, she didn't think of arguing. She's a smart girl, she didn't open the door, just sat on the stairs till she heard the siren. She let them in, kept the press out. Evelyn went away on a stretcher, and Richard went with her; and Rachel said he looked dreadful. Grey and drained, she said, but Evelyn was looking better. She said.

"Trouble is, she said it to the press. I think they bullied her, and she's only a kid. Anyway, she told them; and they're already calling it Richard's second miracle. It'll be in the papers tomorrow, how he brought Evelyn back from the dead. That's what Rachel said, apparently, she said Evelyn looked dead when she found her."

Helen nodded slowly, trying to take it all in; found one question that needed to be asked. "Where's, where's Rachel now, is someone looking after her?"

Nathan laughed shortly. "Don't worry about her, she's all right. I told you, she's smart. She came here first, to tell me; then she phoned Derry. Had a good cry on his shoulder, then he took her away. She'll be fine."

"Good, that's good. What about poor Evelyn, how is she? Alive, you said, but . . . "

"Don't worry about her, either," he said, his voice flat and harsh. "She's got what she wanted. We managed to get Richard away from her, he's collapsed in another room at the hospital; but she'll be watched round the clock now. All the attention she could ever want, she's going to get."

Helen shivered. "Do you think that was it? Just attention-seeking?"

"Of course that was it. Like the story in the papers. First she made herself sound important; now she wants us all to feel sorry for her. Like you said, poor Evelyn. It works, see?"

"Nat, you're not, you're not being very charitable . . . "

"There's a difference between charity and blindness. It isn't charity to disregard the truth. If we pander to Evelyn now, it'll only compound her problems." He drew a breath, as if he meant to say more; then stopped abruptly, touched her cheek, said, "But look, never mind her. It's a mess, and clearing it up is my problem; but it's not yours. You go run yourself a bath, you're all sweaty. I've got some more phone-calls to make, but I'll come and do your back in a few minutes. We've got to talk anyway, and it looks like I'm going to be busy all evening."

Helen nodded obediently and went to start the bath, barely wondering what it was he wanted to talk about, she was so busy secretly fretting over how she'd passed Evelyn by that morning. God had guided her wheels, perhaps, but she had to apply the brakes herself; and if she'd done that, if she'd stopped and talked to the woman, maybe this wouldn't have happened . . .

*

She soaked in scalding water, feeling her exhausted muscles relax; but Nathan's news had taken all the pleasure out of it. Her mind was taut and sharp and suffering under the lash of guilt, turning in circles: picturing Evelyn in her own red bath and sinking till Richard came, too bright a light, to draw her unkindly back. But no, he couldn't do anything unkind, it wasn't in him. And they couldn't have let her go that way. She was ill, that was all. She could be made better, with prayer or counselling or drugs, whatever it took. And Richard would see that she got it. But oh, how must she be feeling, to have made the choice and gone so far and find the gate barred against her . . . ?

Nathan came through at last, and perched on the side of the bath. She smiled weakly up at him, rubbed her cheek against the back of his hand, wanted to tell him how weak and selfish she'd been, deliberately turning her back on another's blatant need.

But he didn't even let her get started on that difficult confession. He soaped her back, working strong fingers deep; and while he worked, he talked.

He said, "Listen, lovely. All this, it's set me thinking; and what it comes down to is, you and me shouldn't be living together. Not without being married.

"If the press can stir up this much grief," he said, "just from a couple of pictures and a crazy woman's nonsense, what are they going to do when they find me living with my girlfriend? The generalissimo, they call me; and I've got to be high-profile if we're going to make the Commando work. Which means we can't afford to have them catch me out. It's vicars-and-choirboys stuff, they love God's people getting caught *in flagrante*; and we *can't* afford headlines about me living in sin.

"I know," he said, "Richard says it isn't sin. You believe him, I believe him. But that's not the point. We mustn't put him in the situation where he has to defend us, he's got problems enough. And the press could find plenty of people in the chapel who'd disagree. Some of the Council would say a zebra was spotty, if Richard called it striped. And for this they've got the Bible to point at. They'd love to tell the newspapers that Richard's teaching went against the Bible.

"And before you ask," he said, "no, we can't cheat. We can't have two separate addresses and go on sleeping together. We've got to be upfront about things, I'm not lying to anyone.

"If we don't get married," he said, "we're going to have to split up."

And she leant back into the insistent pressure of his hands, and waited for him to ask. Waited to say *yes*, to say *yes please*.

"So what I'll do," he said, "I'll move down into the houses. Now, tonight. They're just about ready now, I'll be quite comfortable in a sleeping-bag until they're properly furnished. We should probably have someone on the premises anyway.

"I think it'll work out well," he said. "I can run the Commando from there too, there'll be plenty of space.

"You can have this place, of course," he said. "I'll sort it out with the landlord tomorrow, get the tenancy transferred to your name.

"Don't look so miserable," he said, smiling, stroking damp hair back from her face. "No one ever said it was easy, being a Christian. This is just one of the hard bits. But it is right, you've got to see that."

Actually all she could see was his face, blurred by tears and retreating.

"I'll have to go now," he said. "They need me up at the hospital. Pack a few things for me, will you, pet? Toothbrush and clean knickers, stuff like that, you know what I like. We'll sort the rest out another day. You just stick it all in boxes or something, and I'll pick it up when it's convenient. There's no hurry. Oh, and anything you need you can keep, of course. That goes without saying. Anything you want . . . "

And then he was gone, and he was the only thing she wanted.

TWENTY

Days later and he's still angry, that's clear to be seen. He used to radiate love and warmth and peace; now he radiates energy. Where he used to shine, he glows.

Once, he was comfortable to be with, he was the calm in the eye of the storm. Not so now. He's all fire and urgency, he is the heat of battle.

But every good general pays heed to his humblest soldiers, even in the very heart of war. With the anger burning in his blood, his pulse beating like a call to arms, he still finds time to sit and listen while Billy plays hymns in the new marquee.

He still finds time to say,

— That's marvellous, Billy. That's truly wonderful.

And to say,

— God doesn't give men talents for nothing, to be let run to waste. Why don't you play for us on Sunday?

And,

— Don't look so scared, I don't mean in here for the multitudes. Not the first time. But we still have an early service in the chapel, eight o'clock. You'd play there, wouldn't you? Just a couple of hymns and something quiet through communion. I think you can do that, Billy. I *know* you can, and I think you should.

And,

— Mrs Dolance plays for us usually, but I'm sure she won't mind standing down. Once she hears how well you play. God speaks through your fingers, Billy, you're a walking miracle . . .

As soon as Lisa came into the house, her mother called her through into the kitchen.

"Where have you been, then?"

She was kneading bread-dough at the table, flour up to her elbows, Luther at her side. That made sense.

Lisa shrugged. "Nowhere."

"I sent you to the shops with Luther. I told you to come straight back."

"Luther came, didn't he?" *Luther's a good boy.* "He had the shopping. It didn't need two of us to carry."

"I said I wanted you straight back. You could have been doing this, saving me the work. Luther says you gave him the slip, he just turned round and you weren't there any more . . . "

Luther's asking for trouble. She gazed at her brother coldly — not angry, only judgemental, and see if he can work it out for himself — and said, "I left him by the chapel. He's a big boy, he can walk home from there by himself."

She hadn't meant to say any more, certainly nothing about how she'd ducked suddenly into the marquee so that he wouldn't see her, looking back; but then, she hadn't planned on turning this into a confrontation. She was ready to sulk and squirm, ready to take the tongue-lashing she expected. What took her by surprise was a sudden flare of anger and an urge to strike back for once, not to take and take like that dough her mother was hammering. An urge to hurt.

And of course she had the weapon for it, right there in her mind, fresh in her memory.

"When I left Luther," she said, *before I went and bought a cigarette from the shop on the corner, before I smoked it,* "I heard Richard talking to that Billy in the marquee."

"Eavesdropping now, is it?" her mother grunted; but if it was meant as a reprimand there was no force behind it. She was interested, as Lisa had known she would be.

"They were talking about you."

And she was more than interested now, she was charged and electric: her floury fingers hooking sharp into Lisa's shoulder and her voice cracking like a whip, saying, "Talking about me, what do you mean, what did they say?"

"Well, it was Richard doing the talking, mostly. Billy just played hymns on that electric piano thing."

"Never mind Billy," and Lisa was being shaken now, she was being hurt; but she didn't care, it was worth it. "Billy doesn't matter, he's too stupid to count. What did Richard say?"

"Billy does count," Lisa panted, triumphant. "That's the point. Richard wants him to play at chapel on Sunday morning. Instead of you," added flat and fierce and final.

There was a pause then, both children staring awed and wary into their mother's sudden stillness. They felt the weight of her silence, and Lisa at least was afraid, almost sorry that she'd seen

266

and snatched the chance to do this, almost wishing she'd left it to someone else to bring the news.

But then her mother spoke, in a soft and hissing voice, water dripping onto hot ashes.

"The thief cometh not," her mother said, "but for to steal, and to kill, and to destroy. Luther?"

"John," Luther said. "Chapter ten, the tenth verse."

"Good boy. It is written, My house shall be called the house of prayer; but ye have made it a den of thieves. Lisa?"

Lisa shrugged. "I don't know. Matthew?"

"And Mark, and Luke. But which verses?"

"I said, I don't *know*."

"Find out, and learn them. Each one has it different; say them to me tonight." But disciplining her daughter was a minor concern at the moment. She closed her eyes, the better to see what was being done; and said, "That's what he is, that Richard. He's a thief. He stole our congregation, he stole the final flowering of all the work we've done all these years, he gathered it to himself, for his own greater glory; and now he steals the chapel too, he leaves us with no role under our own roof. It's not ours any longer, it's not our chapel.

"Well, he's welcome to it," she said. "It's only a building, it's only wood on brick foundations. Our faith rests on something stronger, we don't need that old hut. It's only that I hate to see it stolen and misused, I hate to see the people misled." And her eyes snapped open, and she said, "We have to do something. Lisa – no, Luther. Run and find Mr Parkinson. He'll be at home, this time of a Wednesday. Fetch him here, son, we need to talk. And you, girl – you finish this bread for me, then get to your room and read your Bible. You've those verses to find."

iii

Domenico Santori, passionate Italian, stood on the streets of Paradise and saw how his campaign had been taken away from him, and marvelled.

It was only a couple of days since Richard Gould had phoned him, to say that there would be a protest meeting and a march on the Saturday following. "You're quite right," Richard had said, "we can't sit back and let all this redevelopment go ahead without protest. We're the community that will be affected, we have a right to be heard. You, particularly. You will speak to us at the meeting, won't you?"

Yes, Domenico had said, yes, of course he would speak; but Saturday was too soon, how could he arrange anything in one short week, nobody would come, or nobody who counted . . .

Richard had laughed, had said, "Don't worry about that. Don't worry about anything, in fact. You've been a lone voice crying in the wilderness too long; it's time we took that burden from you. Just come along on Saturday. You'll have an audience, I promise. And it'll be large enough to make the council listen."

At the time, on the phone, Domenico had doubted; but doubt was harder, after Richard came to see him. After he'd seen the depth of the man's commitment, seen how it drove him like a whip. He'd changed since the public meeting, or something had changed for him; or else Domenico had simply misread him, had been dazzled by the smile and missed the fire beneath.

Forty-eight hours later, with Richard's private army in action, doubt was no longer an option for Domenico. He believed. He'd have his audience, and the media and the council and maybe even the country among them.

They were devastatingly efficient, these kids who called themselves the Commando. Monday evening, they'd discussed the text for leaflets and posters. Domenico had been there, co-opted onto the committee, and he'd put forward the name of the printers he always used; but no, that wasn't necessary, they had others in mind, church members who wouldn't charge for the Lord's work.

Tuesday night the posters were there already, big and bright and insistent, and the leaflets were promised for the morning. Interviews had been arranged on local TV and radio, but the interviewers wanted Richard, of course. Domenico had said nothing. Richard would draw the crowds they needed; he wouldn't. Instead, he'd offered to help distribute the leaflets door-to-door. At least that was something he could usefully do.

But Nathan had smiled and said no, there was really no need. The troops would do that, he said.

And now Domenico stood on a corner and watched the troops at work: boys and girls blitzing the street, wearing their combat jackets even in the heat, proud of their uniform and their faith. They knocked on every door and stopped every passer-by; they annexed heavy shopping-bags or calmed screaming babies while they talked, and still didn't stop talking. And it worked, or seemed to. Only Saturday would show for sure, but certainly people took the leaflets and read them, and promised their support.

And certainly Domenico couldn't have achieved anything like this; and yes, of course he was jealous and resentful. How else should he feel, seeing what he had worked for so hard and never achieved, seeing it happen at someone else's command, another man's sudden decision? How else could he feel, having his dreams appropriated and being himself supplanted from the heart of them?

But the cause was what counted, or ought to be. It wasn't power he was passionate for; or not for himself. For the people, yes, for the community. And perhaps this was a path to that goal, perhaps Richard would cede his power to the people somehow, once the battle was won. Till then, best if he kept it; even Domenico could see that. You needed a strong leader, and to have Richard was a gift from God.

There was a girl with string and scissors and a bagful of posters mounted on thick card, making her way from lamppost to lamppost down the street. When she reached the corner, she smiled broadly and said, "Hi. You're Mr Santori, aren't you?"

"That's right. How did you know?"

"Aha! We know everyone on our patch, we do." She was still young enough to enjoy being mysterious; but at the same time honest enough to give her own game away, going on, "I saw you from up the street there, and asked Nathan."

"Oh, aye. Right. I know him." Domenico wondered if this was perhaps a sign of how things were changing in Paradise, that a stray man alone should be so quickly spotted and checked up on. "So who are you, then?"

"Rachel Grant. With the Christ Commando." She grinned suddenly. "Hey, listen to me. Name, rank and serial number. Except we don't have either of those, really. Not yet. Nat says it's all thanks to you, this rally on Saturday?"

Domenico shook his head, a shade regretful. "No. It should have been, maybe, it's the sort of stuff I should've been doing; but it was Richard's idea. He just phoned and told me about it. You lot have done all the legwork."

"That's what we're for," she said, walking on to the next lamppost as she talked, so that he had to follow her. "But Nat said Richard didn't even know about this redevelopment stuff till he learnt it from you. So you did it really. It'll be thanks to you, when we win." And no doubts in her, no ifs or buts; they would win, and it would be thanks to Domenico.

Feeling better, he held two of the stiffened posters back-to-back around the lamppost, while she tied them into place. And when she moved on to the next he went with her, having found a role at last, something he was allowed to do.

Walking past a wall covered with graffiti, she took out a notebook and scribbled. "The council's got a magic machine, we'll get them round to clean that off."

"What's the point?" he asked dispiritedly. "It all comes back again. You can't stop the kids round here."

"I think we can, maybe. Now we're starting to patrol. I think we'll scare them off, or find them better things to do. They're only bored, mostly."

But then she stopped, her eyes fixed on another stretch of wall. *DERRY* it said, or shouted rather in huge letters and vivid colours, except that the final letter was barely sketched in, sign of an artist interrupted. And she said, "I don't know, though, maybe we should talk to people first, maybe they like it. I mean, it gives a wall some character, at least . . . "

Domenico laughed, gifted an unexpected flash of insight. "Know the boy, do you?"

She smiled, shrugged her submission, *okay, you caught me.* "Yeah, I know Derry."

"Boyfriend?"

And she shook her head positively, decisively; and thought about it, and said yes. Said, "Yes. Absolutely, utterly boyfriend. And that better not be fresh, or he's dead. It's my birthday, Saturday," with a sweet *non sequitur* that surely had to mean something, but not to Domenico.

"You are coming on the march, though?"

"Oh, yes. Of course I'm coming. Him too, I'll bring him. He's supposed to work, but he can take a day off. For my birthday he can. He lives here, he ought to be concerned. He ought to be marching, not painting his stupid name on walls . . . "

iv

Helen had come as far as the low wall that surrounded St Giles' Hospital. Conscience and guilt had driven her here; but now sheer chicken-heartedness had stopped her fifty metres short of the gates, which was also fifty metres short of the journalists.

She wasn't sure what they were doing here, days after all the excitement. It could hardly be a fresh story still, hardly deserving of so many newshounds pressed so close to the gates, needing the hospital's security staff to keep them out of the grounds.

270

But whatever the reason, they were there and she was here, and she wasn't going any closer. She wasn't fighting her way through that mob.

And truth, reluctant truth to tell, Helen was nothing but glad of this block, this stop to her good intentions. Conscience and guilt make efficient whipsters, but they have nothing to offer except a sense of duty done: they're all stick, no carrot. This was the very last place on earth Helen wanted to be right now, her intended visit was the very last thing she wanted to do; and it was a burning relief, it was almost a joy to be handed this easy excuse not to do it.

Which of course only made her feel more guilty, only stirred her conscience up to greater feats of savagery against her cringing soul.

So she sat here on the wall, without the will to go forward or the strength to retreat; she sat and prayed silently for one or the other, or some miracle to render both unnecessary. Also she prayed for the woman inside, the patient she'd come to visit. Tried to salve her conscience that way, because surely prayer was worth more than uncomfortable small-talk, wasn't it? Surely it was, it had to be, that was axiomatic . . .

But something was happening now, there was a stir among the journalists. They were packing tighter, calling questions, holding cameras high above their heads to get their pictures unobstructed.

And the object of all their interest came walking quiet and steady along the path from the wards, seemingly quite undisturbed by his waiting reception. At a nod from his golden head, the guards swung one of the gates a little way open; and he squeezed calmly through the gap, and was mobbed.

Helen couldn't hold herself apart from that thrusting, eager rabble. She got to her feet and hurried to the fringes of the press, where she could just make out his voice amid the shouted questions and the constant rattle-and-whine of the cameras.

" . . . How's Evelyn, Richard?"

"Her doctors can answer that question better than I can. You should talk to them."

"How did she seem, then? To you?"

"She seemed well enough. I wasn't with her very long, but we talked a little and said a prayer together. She seemed fine."

"What's she doing at St Giles, then? This is a mental hospital. Why was she transferred from the General? Is she here voluntarily, or has she been sectioned?"

"I'm sorry, I can't possibly answer that question. That must be confidential."

"Would you say she's mad, Richard, or possessed by demons, or what?"

"No, I wouldn't say anything so stupid. I'd say she needs rest and prayer and counselling, and between us we can see that she gets all three."

"Is she on any medication? Tranquillisers, sedatives?"

"Again, that's confidential. Are you?"

"Richard, Richard, what I want to know, Richard, if you could heal her body and bring her back to life again, Richard, how come you couldn't heal her mind? How come she has to be locked away?"

"Listen," he said, "why don't you *listen* to me for a change?" But Helen thought that was a mistake, she hoped they wouldn't do that; because it seemed to her that his voice had lost much of its richness and certainty, much of its magic. It used to be that every word held the promise of a better life, that those who listened to Richard now could become like Richard later. But that was all turned around suddenly, what had seemed gold was only gold plate after all, and that grown thin and ragged, glimpses of base metal showing through. If you listened, you could hear confusion and doubt and simple temper threatening.

Or Helen could, at least.

"Listen," he said again, an error compounded. "I can't heal anyone," he said, as he had said before; the difference being that this time he was believed, at least by one of his audience. "God heals, not me; I'm only a channel. If God chose to heal Evelyn's body with a miracle, perhaps that's because it was necessary, it was the only way to save her. Perhaps He feels she's safe now, she can be left to conventional medicine and the excellent staff here at St Giles. I don't know." And then – as though he'd heard himself suddenly, followed his own advice and listened to the defeat in his voice, like a light extinguished and a beacon overthrown – he tried for a smile and his old disarming shrug. "I don't know," he said, trying to sound as if he did know really, "I'm not privy to God's private counsels."

"But it was a miracle, was it, you are claiming that? She would have died without it?"

"I'm not claiming anything," Richard said. "You're the people who make the claims. All I'm doing is reporting the facts. I lifted Evelyn out of the bath, held her in my arms and prayed for her until the ambulance came. That's all I know, and certainly all you need to know. Only God could tell you more. Ask Him if you want, but don't ask me."

And then a car sounded its horn in the street; Helen looked round and saw Nat leaning across to open the passenger door. Richard pushed through the crush and got in, and the car pulled away.

And Helen only stayed where she was, quietly on the margins where neither man had seen her. She sat on the wall again as the journalists dispersed around her; and that seemed right, that Richard and Nathan should both leave her like this, without a backward glance. Without even being aware of what they did. Betrayal and abandonment, she thought, they were brothers, they should certainly go hand in hand. Having been betrayed by each of them now, she should certainly be abandoned.

It was terribly appropriate, she thought, that she should end up like this, alone in an empty street, sitting on the wall of a mental hospital. On the border.

There was nowhere else she'd rather be. What were her choices? She could sit in the flat and look at all Nathan's abandoned things, look in the mirror at herself; or she could go down to the houses and help to put the final touches to Nathan's new home, help to move him that much further from herself.

And now of course she had the added bonus of this second betrayal, of seeing her guiding light flicker and dim. Richard had been her only source of strength these last days. Her faith was all she had to lean on in her misery, and her faith depended on his; if he was going to fail her, she'd have nothing left to hold the darkness back. And that momentary falter, that glimpse of fallible man – that was failure enough, simply the hint, the implication that he might fail.

Faith can move mountains, but doubt brings disaster; and Helen was doubting now. There was no solidity in anything, if Richard could stumble. She couldn't trust the very wall she sat on, nor the air she breathed . . .

A hand touched her shoulder then, and she screamed; jumped to her feet and ran off along the pavement, looked back to see a security man staring after her, stepping over the wall to follow.

Shook her head frantically, at him and at the whole treacherous world.

Scurried across the street and went on running.

TWENTY-ONE

i

He marches at the head of his people, and no doubt his heart is filled with humility and pride. Humble he must be on his own account, for his own unworthiness; but proud, he should be infinitely proud of those who march behind.

They march from Paradise with banners and music, with faith and prayer and determination. All the long route to the city centre there are people waiting: some to watch, some to cheer, some to join the march. They shout their slogans, they cry for people power and an end to thoughtless greed. A few politicos mingle, try to hawk their papers and their particular views among the marchers; but the Christ Commando is policing this march. The radicals will find themselves arguing their views with young men and women who are very ready to argue back.

There's a small park just over the road from the Civic Centre: trees and squirrels, flowerbeds and wide green lawns. That's where the rally will be held, right under the windows of the city planners. As the march arrives, it loses definition; the long crocodile turns into a milling throng, leaders and followers and hangers-on all mixed chaotically together.

And he feels a touch at his elbow, finds Terry Belderstone at his side.

– A word with you, Mr Gould.

– Yes, of course, he says, smiling, ever willing to listen.

They stand in the obscuring shelter of a tree, and perhaps it's more than leaves and shadow that hides them from the searching disciples, that isolates them for this brief time.

– Well, he says, what is it brings you into our camp, Mr Belderstone?

– I'm not spying, Terry replies, a little huffily. I'm plain to see, he says. I'm curious is all, I'm trying to understand. I'm offering long-term jobs and revitalisation, he says, I'm offering new life and all you do is spit in my face. Are you jealous, he asks, because I've got money and all you've got is words, is that it?

– No, Richard tells him, that's not it.

– Well, what, then? What is it, what's wrong with a business park in Paradise?

– Nothing, in itself. It's what else you want to bring with it. It's a new bridge, new roads, it's tower-blocks instead of terraces; you want to turn Paradise *into* a business park, Mr Belderstone, and its people just fodder for your factories. That's what's wrong. And another thing, he says, quiet and calm and controlled. It's the way you're going about it, he says. It's bribes to the council and thugs vandalising our marquee in the dead of night, he says. It's lies fed to the press that lead a woman to attempted suicide, he says.

– I don't know what you're talking about, Terry replies, just as calm and just as quiet. There are laws of libel, you know, it's as well for you there aren't any witnesses.

– God's my witness, Richard says, you can't escape His eye. And as it happens, I've got proof, he says. I haven't done anything about it yet, but I will if I have to. If you force me to it.

That's what he says, standing bold and straight and armoured with righteousness, throwing down a gauntlet, no foe too great.

ii

It was late, late in the evening and the fair was closing down; and Derry went home with Rachel, his arms full of prizes.

This was her birthday, and her birthday party. They'd been together in a crowd all day, at the march and rally; then they'd been together *en famille*, birthday tea at the Bowens'. Derry's mother had made a cake in secret, with sixteen little candles round the edge and one tall one in the middle; Rachel had blown them all out in one, and Derry had seen her eyes close and her lips move in a silent wish, she wouldn't tell him what. But she hadn't cheated, she said, it was definitely a wish, not a prayer. Wouldn't *pray* for that, she'd said. Wouldn't dare.

Then it was more crowds, and all the fun of the fair. *Win me a coconut*, she'd said, nuzzling at his neck. So between getting sick and dizzy on the rides he'd spent a fortune at the stalls, he'd wasted pounds; but he'd come away with three cuddly toys, two dolls and the coconut she was so set on.

And now, at last, they were together and alone: making their way to Rachel's house, laughing and hot and clinging to each other, only laughing harder every time they had to stop to retrieve the prizes he kept on dropping.

"Don't drop the coconut," she said, stacking fluffy toys into a pyramid under his chin. "It's important."

Wouldn't tell him why, but he found out soon enough. She arranged the toys and dolls on chairs in her living-room, "See, told you it was a party. Pretty crowded, eh?" Then she took his hand, tugged him through to the kitchen and made him hold the coconut steady while she punched its eyes in with a hammer and nail that were ready waiting on the worktop.

"Got this all thought out, haven't you?"

"'Course. Us older women, we think ahead."

She drained a thin, pale liquid into a jug; Derry looked at it, wrinkling his nose in disgust. "Yuck, what's that?"

"Coconut milk, stupid. Haven't you ever . . . ?"

"Nah. You get coconut in boxes, where I come from. And you get milk from bottles, and it don't look like that."

She giggled, and kissed him. "Go on, be brave. Try."

So he dipped a finger in and sucked it suspiciously.

"Well, it's okay. Tastes sort of coconut, really."

"Never!"

"Yeah, it does. But for drinking – I dunno, I'd rather have a can of lager."

"You don't have to drink it straight. This is a party, remember?"

And she showed him half a bottle of Bacardi.

"That's better."

"It'll be better still, in a minute." She took the top off, they had a swig each – "Just one – oy! One, I said . . . !" – and then she tipped the rest in with the coconut milk.

"I learned this off a friend. Poor girl's Malibu, it's gorgeous . . . "

Five minutes later they were snuggled up nice and comfy on the sofa, sharing a glass because one was easier to handle and much more fun to fight over; there were chunks of sweet coconut on a plate on the floor, the telly was on with the sound turned down, they couldn't stop talking and Derry couldn't imagine ever wanting to move again, ever.

"Your boss didn't fuss, then, you taking the day off?"

"Not really. He's dead soft, underneath. I just said it was your birthday, my girl's birthday, I said. He was a bit sarky, it's the busiest day, Saturday, but he didn't mind much. Something funny, though," frowning, trying to remember through the swimminess in his head. "Yeah, that's it, he said to tell you not to get too tied up with them Commandos. Not safe, he said."

"What's he mean, not safe? 'Course it's safe, we make it safe."
She nestled in a little closer under his arm, where it was undeniably safe; looked at the glass in her hand, tilted it up to catch the last drips on her tongue, licked the rim and passed it to him for a refill. That wasn't easy one-handed, aiming straight. Getting harder all the time. "And us girls," she said, "we don't go around alone. Never ever. Never ever ever," giggling, liking the sound of it. "We're perfectly safe."

"Well. It's just what he said, that's all. But he's funny about the whole business. I think he had a row with Nat, he told Trace to cancel his membership and send his money back. And he's cleared all the stockrooms out downstairs, too. Dead fed up about that, he was. Jason's painting 'em now, but George isn't happy."

"What did he used to keep down there?"

"God knows, he never let me see. Kept the doors locked all the time. Pinched stuff, I reckon, he's a bit of a villain, is George . . . You got anything we could stretch this with?" Looking at the glass, what was left in the jug. "Won't last long, else."

"There's some ginger ale, we could stick that in."

And they did that, after five minutes' arguing who was going to fetch it. In the end they went together, hand in hand, tripping over each other's feet and falling altogether in the hall, so that they had to sit on the stairs for a while till the giggling stopped.

They added half a bottle of ginger ale to the jug, and, "Gingibu," Rachel named the fizzing cocktail, grinning. "Yummy."

It tasted strange to Derry, but this evening was all strange tastes and new discoveries; and the bubbles were nice. Back in the living-room he drank a glassful straight down, stretched himself out on the long sofa and settled his head on Rachel's lap, smiled dizzily up at her and watched the world spin away.

He woke to a terrible dryness in his mouth, churning acid in his stomach and an urgent need to piss.

He was lying on his side, his head propped on something firm but giving, something blue. Blue denim, with Rachel's leg inside it. She hadn't left him, then. That weight slumped across his shoulder must be the rest of her, slid sideways in her sleep; and she'd have a dreadful cricked neck in the morning if he left her.

And he had to move anyway, he'd wet himself if he didn't get to a toilet. If he didn't die of thirst first, he was desperate for a glass of water. A *pint* of water . . .

He sat up cautiously, peeling himself away from Rachel so that she slipped all the way down into the dent his own body had made. That looked better. He'd straighten her out properly when he came back down again. Maybe he should wake her up, send her off to bed; but *should* didn't count for much, against what he wanted. And what he wanted was to be cramped and sweaty and uncomfortable, sharing a sofa with Rachel . . .

Standing up made his head reel, and his legs; but worse, it made his stomach twist and churn, an added urgency. He stumbled out into the hall and up the stairs, bruising his shoulder against the wall and using his hands to help when his balance went.

He barely made it to the bathroom, his jaw clenched panic-tight against the sour burning liquids rising in his throat. He lunged towards the toilet, dropped to his knees, wrapped weak arms around the bowl and was comprehensively sick.

Afterwards, he remembered how much he needed a piss, and did that too; then he rinsed his mouth out and drank deeply, straight from the tap, leaning all his weight on the basin.

Sweating and shaken, he thought the carpeted floor looked dead comfortable, just the thing for a quick sit down before he tackled the stairs again.

And sitting, he thought maybe a lie down would be even better, just five minutes to get over it, before he went down to Rachel . . .

Next time he woke it was dim morning, and there was a soft pillow under his head and a duvet over his shoulders. It felt wonderful, even still in his clothes. Just lovely.

This was still the bathroom, though. He could see the toilet bowl by his feet there, the door just a metre from his head. Rachel must've found him, made him comfy and gone to bed . . .

He rolled slowly onto his back, and his shoulder bumped against something. He turned his head to look, found himself eye to eye and sharing a pillow with Rachel.

After the first shock came a surge of panic, a hasty, stupid fumbling below the duvet. Yes, he really did still have all his clothes on. He was too shy to reach, to see if she did.

But then the solemnity of her dark stare melted into a smile. "Hullo," she said in a cracked whisper. "How are you feeling?"

Every cell in his body ached, his head was pounding, pain stabbed like needles at his eyes. "Terrific," he said, and meant it.

"Me too." She closed her eyes and moaned softly, then touched her nose to his. "Did you throw up, too?"

"Yeah."

"Good." She shifted over, within the orbit of his arm; and yes,

278

she was still as dressed as he was, T-shirt and jeans. He kissed her wild hair, and chuckled. And felt her smile against his neck, heard her ask, "What's funny?"

"Us," he said. Then, "You," more honestly. "Not me, I just passed out. But you, you did all this, and it's great. It's perfect." Better than the sofa, but still no threat for either of them.

"Mmm. Clever, aren't I?"

"You're magic."

He wondered vaguely what her parents would think, if they could see him and their magic daughter now; and that thought led on naturally to another, and, "Oh, fuck."

"What?"

"I should've phoned Mam, that's what. When we got in, to say I was staying."

"You didn't know, then. You hadn't been invited. And she knows where you are, she can figure that out. She's no fool."

"She'll still be worrying. And she'll fuss like mad when I go back, she always does."

"It's only because you were so sick before, you can't blame her for being a bit over-protective ... "

"I know. It's just a pain, that's all. I should've phoned."

"Too late now," Rachel said practically.

"Yeah. I'd better go early, though, stop her fretting."

"How early?"

"Well, not yet ... "

She wriggled a little closer, he held her a little tighter; and they both looked at each other, both read the same thought in each other's eyes. *That's close enough, tight enough. Far enough for now. Any more than this, and we're in trouble.*

But her bare toes were playing teasingly with his; and he blinked, thought about that, tried to remember. Finally, had to ask.

"Did you take my trainers off?"

She giggled, made a face. "Yes. And your socks. Dis*gust*ing."

"Well," he said, "that's that, then, isn't it?"

"What's what?"

"You'll just have to marry me now."

And he kissed her quick, to catch the returning giggle on her lips; then tucked her head down against his shoulder, and tangled his fingers securely in her hair to stop anyone snatching her away while he was sleeping.

Later they were both awake again, curled together in their bathroom nest, watching daylight strengthen through the dimpled

279

window; and he said, "What time is it?"

"Dunno."

"I should go," not moving a muscle.

"Mmm." She pushed herself up on one elbow and ran a hand thoughtfully across his scalp. "All right, but you're not going like that."

"Like what?"

"Like this," twisting a length of straggly hair between her fingers. "It looks awful. And no boy sleeps with me," giggling again and making him blush, which only made her giggle more, "nobody sleeps with me without me leaving my mark on them. You sit up, over against the bath there, and take your T-shirt off."

It took a little while longer, before either one of them would move; but eventually he was where she had told him to be, and she had nail-scissors and an electric razor in her hands.

Derry looked at them suspiciously. "What are you going to do, then?"

She draped a towel around his bare shoulders, knelt astride his legs and kissed him quickly. "Trust me."

And he did, of course he did, most things; but, "Your hands are shaking."

"I know. All of me's shaking. And my head hurts, and I just might throw up again. That's why I'm using this," flicking the razor on and off. "Dad says a wet shave is better. Next time, maybe, but I don't want to cut you. Hold still, now . . . "

She took his head between her hands and tilted it firmly. He felt cold metal against his skin, just above the ear, and heard the scissors snip. And held still, and trusted her.

iii

Grace Bowen always liked to clean the chapel early of a Saturday evening, to have it nice for the Sabbath; but she couldn't do that last night, on account of having Derry's girl Rachel round for tea. Those two had gone off to the fair afterwards, but it was too late then, there were the little ones to be got ready for bed and watched over while they slept.

So Grace had set the alarm for six o'clock, politely begging the Lord's pardon for having to work on His day; but then it was His house she'd be cleaning, so He shouldn't mind too much.

As usual, though, she couldn't be comfortable in her bed until she'd heard Derry coming in, her eldest and best-loved safe home again; and tonight he didn't come. Twelve o'clock, one o'clock, the hours ticked past and Sam snored beside her and still the boy stayed out. The fair would have shut down long since, and of course he'd taken Rachel home; and of course that's where he was still, Grace knew that. She wasn't stupid.

But what was he doing there? That was the question that nagged and fretted at her, that kept her eyes wide in the dark against the weariness of her body. Rachel was a good girl, responsible; her own parents were trusting her alone, and she wouldn't betray that trust, nor Richard's, nor the Lord's. Not willingly, at least. But that Derry, he was no believer. And he was sixteen, and burning with his body's hunger; and the slippery tongue he had on him, talk anyone into anything Derry could, if he wanted to . . .

So Grace had lain awake half the night, fretful over the sins of her beloved son; and had risen exhausted in the early morning, had hauled her heavy body down the hill to the chapel and given it a perfunctory sweep through, a wave of the duster, little more than a lick and a promise.

Then, through in the back room rinsing out her cloths, her eyes had caught and snagged on Arthur Brougham's old easy-chair. Soft and comfortable it looked, just right to take a tired woman's weight for five minutes, too early on a Sunday morning . . .

Dozing, she half-woke at noises coming from the chapel proper, quick footsteps and the scrape of chairs. Jean Dolance must have sent her boy Luther down to help set it straight for service. She did that sometimes. He was an obedient lad, Luther, and an early riser. Not like Grace's sweet slugabed. Alone or not he'd be sleeping still, he'd sleep for hours yet; and never a thought for his worried mother, the wicked rascal . . .

And she smiled and closed her eyes and dozed again.

She woke a second time to other noises, a hissing and a crackling that she didn't understand, didn't like. She shook her head, trying to drive back the sleepiness that was still with her, and pushed herself up and out of the chair.

Five paces took her to the door, but the handle was too hot to turn. She stared at it, muzzy and confused; tried again, and burnt her fingers badly.

And smelt something burning other than her own flesh, and saw wisps of smoke coming in under the door.

Heard a sharp explosion, as it might have been a beam snapping in great heat; and started to sweat suddenly, in her crumpled cotton frock.

She hurried to the sink, and the window above; but gave the window no more than a passing glance. It was too small for her generous frame and too well-protected in any case, its bars and chicken-wire defences serving to hold her trapped inside.

She snatched a cloth from the sink and ran to the door again, wrapped the handle around and twisted.

Pushed the door open six inches, a foot – and pulled it hard closed again, seeing the inferno beyond.

Now she broke the window, and screamed for help.

No one heard this early on a Sunday, no one came. Grace dropped to her knees, praying incoherently, burying her face in the filthy cloth; then she hauled herself up again, and went back to the door.

Pushed it open, all the way this time.

Saw how the flames roared and guttered in the sudden draught, saw how much of the floor was gone; and already the heat was stretching the skin across her forehead, drying her sweat and scorching her hair and hands.

She squinted into the smoke and the glow and glamour of the fire; prayed again, *Lord protect me, for Sam's sake and my boys*; and started to murmur aloud as she started to walk. And only got louder, brought her chanting near to a shout as the first flying embers bit cruelly at her clothes and skin.

"Yea," she murmured, "yea," she said. "Though I walk through the valley," she coughed, "the valley of the shadow of death," she yelled as the smoke enwreathed her, "I will fear no evil; for thou," she sobbed, "for thou, for thou art with me . . . "

iv

Derry had insisted on breakfast, before he went. He'd demanded bacon butties; she'd given him muesli, and watched him wolf two big bowls and half a loaf of toast to follow. She'd nibbled on slices of apple to keep him company, wondering aloud how he could possibly do that to himself after last night, but inside she'd had other questions to wonder and worry about. So had he, judging by the way his eyes would meet hers and linger, or else skitter away; by the way his face changed so suddenly and so often between grinning content and fiery blushes.

They hadn't talked much. Once he'd fuelled up he'd kissed her fleetingly, pinched a couple of apples to keep him going on the walk home, and gone. And she'd let him go, had been grateful even to stand at the door and watch him walk away. He'd looked back a couple of times, waving awkwardly; but what had touched her more, what had made her smile was the way his hand kept straying to his head, running down over his newly-shaven scalp.

She was feeling proud, excited, madly pleased with herself and him; but even so, she'd been glad to see him go. She desperately needed some time to herself now. It wouldn't hurt him either, to do a bit of serious thinking; only she couldn't tell him that, he'd only get scared. One day at a time, that was how Derry liked to live. Which was all very well for a summer, but you couldn't run a life that way. Or she couldn't, at least.

So she'd waved him off and shut the door, and for all that she loved him she'd still felt a great wave of relief at having the house to herself again. She'd run upstairs, stripped off yesterday's clothes and had a long, luxurious shower; then she'd spent a couple of hours pottering around, tidying up and getting her head together before going to morning service at her local church. Checking in with God, that was, giving Him an update and trying to find out how He felt about it all.

The bad bit was, if He came out strongly anti-Derry, she thought maybe she wouldn't listen. But He wouldn't do that, He surely wouldn't. It was Him threw them together, after all; and God didn't play games with people, not like that. Not nasty.

So she went to church and got caught up with God, came home and got caught up with her diary, chewing her way through two biros in the process. Then she thought she could just about handle a bite or two of lunch, to go with the next round of paracetamol; and only then, only after that did she put her Commando jacket on and cycle over to Paradise.

She met the smell first, freewheeling down the hill, still a corner and a hundred metres or so from the marquee. Wet, charred wood – she remembered it distinctly, precisely, from when a tramp had set their garden shed on fire, back when she was a kid.

She looked round, trying to spot which house had had a fire; but couldn't see, and had to stop looking at the corner.

No traffic in sight, no sound of cars approaching, so she took a chance for once, swept gracefully around the corner without slowing –

– and now, now she could see.

First she saw the vast red bulk of a fire-engine pulled up off the road, just by the marquee. Three police cars on the grass around it like worker-bees around a queen, blue lights strobing, bright even in the sunshine.

Then she saw the people, gathered in knots and tangles all along the road, the odd policeman keeping a watchful eye; and she saw combat jackets too, her brothers and sisters in the Commando doing a shepherding act of their own to make the policemen's job a little easier.

Finally, she saw what she couldn't see.

She couldn't see the chapel any more.

She coasted to a slow halt by the kerb, got off the bike, began to push; and was intercepted before she'd got very much further.

And was truly, seriously grateful for the interception, for the chance to force a smile and say, "Ingrid, hi. What's, what on earth has happened here, what's happened to the chapel?"

"There was a fire," Ingrid said, taking Rachel's bike from her and leaning it against a lamppost, putting an arm around her shoulders as if it were a friend lost and not a building. "Early this morning, it must have been very quick; they saw it from the marquee, the boys who were sleeping overnight, but it was a blaze already then, and when the fire-engines came there was nothing to save."

"Well, an old wooden hut like that, it was bound to burn fast." Rachel didn't feel any too distressed, though she understood how some people would, the ones who'd been coming here forever. The old guys on the Council, they'd *built* the place, even, they were going to be heartbroken. But, "A blessing it was early," she said. "Nobody around, I mean, to get hurt . . . "

Ingrid was silent, suddenly stiff against her. Rachel looked at her, alarmed. "It didn't, did it? There wasn't anyone inside?"

Ingrid nodded slowly, reluctantly. "The, the firemen found a body. Rachel, it is not certain, we cannot be sure – but Grace came here to clean, very early, and she is missing now."

"Grace?" For the briefest time Rachel could fool herself, could fail to recognise the name; but not for long, already there was a falling, swimming sensation as it fitted, as it locked secure into place, and, "You, you mean Mrs Bowen? Derry's mum? You mean Derry's *mum* was in there, and . . . ?"

"We think so." And Ingrid's arm tightening its grip was surety, was guarantee: no official identification yet, maybe, but the fact was certain.

"But . . . " Rachel shook her head numbly; then turned it more slowly, looking. "Where is he, where's Derry?"

"He was with the police, I think. Now, I don't know."

"The police? What for?" And then, thinking suddenly how odd

284

it was, "Why so many, what are they doing here?"

Peering over the heads of the crowd, she could see men walking in the cinders and ruin of the chapel, bent double, sifting wet ashes with their fingers. Slipping things into plastic bags sometimes, putting samples into little bottles.

"They think it was, I don't know the word, when they think someone started the fire on purpose?"

"Arson," Rachel supplied dully. "But, but they can't think *Derry* . . . ?"

"No, I am sure not. Only routine, for sure. But he is her son, and he lives here, he might have seen someone, he might know something that would help."

"He wasn't even in Paradise this morning, he was, he was over at my place all night . . . " And she looked around, desperate for a policeman to tell that to, for someone in authority to tell her Derry wasn't in trouble; and saw Richard making his way down the road towards her.

Wriggled free from Ingrid's grasp all in a moment and without thinking about it; walked, jogged, ran to meet him, hurled herself into the sure comfort of his arms.

Just a minute, that was all he could spare her before he was called away; but a minute bathed in Richard's love was worth hours or days of anyone else's time. And when he had to go Nathan was there instead with his own quick, tight hug, with a kiss on the cheek and a tug to pull her jacket straight, a murmured order, "Smarten up, soldier."

And while of course she didn't take him seriously, because of course he didn't mean her to, nevertheless she stood a little taller, and wiped the tears from her cheeks with a determined hand and said, "What, what should I do, Nat?" for all the world like a soldier looking for orders.

"What do you want to do?"

"Anything, to help," she said; and then, more honestly, "I want to find Derry."

"Good. That's best, I think. He'll need you. Do you know where he is?"

She shook her head. "With the police, Ingrid said . . . "

"I don't think so, not any more. Not much he could tell them, really. Go ask his father, he'll know if anyone does."

"Yeah, sure." And then, momentarily unsure again, ready to face Derry's grief but more scared of an adult's, "How is Mr Bowen, have you seen him?"

Nathan shook his head, smiled his understanding, patted her

285

lightly on the cheek. "Go find out, soldier. That's the job. Do what you can to help, if Derry isn't there — and yell for someone else if you need them, okay? Don't take on too much. This is a community, burdens are for sharing. Got that?"

"Yes, sure." But it almost came out, 'Yes, sir,' and she was almost giggling as she hurried off, because she'd almost, she'd very nearly saluted.

She'd left her bike behind, but that didn't matter. Ingrid would look after it. She came to Derry's door and knocked, and waited, and knocked again; and at last, at long last there were slow footsteps on the stairs, Mr Bowen coming to answer.

He looked dreadful, pale and dull-eyed with his face filthy and his shirt untucked and little Sammy slung on one hip, sucking his fingers.

"Rachel," he said, and even that seemed to call for a greater effort than it was fair to ask. "Derry's not, Derry's not here . . ."

That wasn't good news, that was cause for worry. But she could only deal with one thing at a time, she could only lift what she could carry. And she lifted Sammy from his father's hip, transferred him to her own; said, "That doesn't matter, Mr Bowen, I'll find him later. Right now I'm here to help you. How's about if I look after the kids for a while, how would that be? Give us a key and I'll get them out from under, give you a chance to get sorted, a bit . . ."

She was being deliberately brisk and efficient, almost impersonal, the only defence she could find against his pain. But it seemed to work for him too, it seemed to be just what he needed. He nodded and went slowly back upstairs, calling for Trevor.

Rachel sat on the bottom step, with Sammy on her knee; and he said, "Our mam's dead, isn't she?"

"That's right, pet. I'm ever so sorry."

"Dad's been crying. But I haven't, I haven't cried. Trev said not to, so we didn't. Derry did, though," terribly solemn. "Derry came home with his head all bald, he looked funny. But then he cried. And he sweared, too. And then he ran away. Where's he gone, Rachel, where's Derry gone?"

"I don't know, love." *He didn't come to me.*

She took Trevor and Sammy to the grass behind the marquee, where they played a desultory game of football in the sunshine. Rachel was in goal, but she didn't have much to save. Mostly she listened to the little boys talking as they kicked the ball between them. Neither was old enough to know at all what death might

286

be; Sammy at least could barely understand that his mother wasn't coming back. It was their honesty that touched her most, more even than their confusion. At one point Trevor asked Sammy if he felt like crying now, assuring him that it would be all right if he did; and she could have hugged the boy for his puzzled shake of the head, for saying, "No. Don't want to. Sorry. Your kick now."

At length, when they grew hungrier than Coke and crisps could satisfy, she took them home. She'd promised them fish-finger sandwiches for tea, but found herself instead handing them over to an aunt, their father's sister. "Thanks, duck, but I'll take them now. They'll be best squashed in with my lot, stop them brooding. I'd take him too, only he'll not come. I can't get any sense out of him. Terrible thing, of course, but that's no reason to behave like a gormless jack-rabbit, and so I told him."

She bore the children off, leaving Rachel with Mr Bowen, a man sadly shrunken: a man she found sitting with his eyes glued to the blank television, mindlessly stroking the kitten Mortimer who lay flattened and loudly purring in his lap.

And no, Rachel couldn't get much sense out of him either, except to understand that he didn't want to be mothered by his sister or fussed over by his wife's chapel friends or even worried about by his son's girlfriend; he really only wanted to be left alone with his sadness and his memories of Grace.

And no, he still didn't know where Derry was, the lad hadn't shown up all afternoon.

With nothing to distract her now, no other responsibilities, finding Derry was suddenly Rachel's only priority; and her continuing failure frightened her badly. No telling what he might do, with his world so splintered. He must be half crazy with grief and anger, he might be needing her desperately – and she couldn't *find* him . . .

There was no one down at the houses, but the marquee was full: everyone was there, except the one she wanted. She found his mate Albie, and made him take her round all their old haunts in Paradise, in case Derry had retreated to the comforts of an earlier life; but they didn't find him.

Then someone, she didn't know his name, just a man from the congregation, he drove her briefly home, in case Derry had gone looking for her there. But there was no sign of him, no note, no message on the answering machine.

She went back to Paradise and talked to Nathan, and half an hour later the Commando was out on the streets, asking everyone they met – "especially the kids," Nathan had said, "concentrate on the kids. If he's been around, they'll know" – but learning nothing, checking in with nothing to report.

The service that night had to be relayed outside the marquee with speakers; it seemed as though every Christian in the city had come to see the charred beams and ashes of the old chapel and to pledge support for its rebuilding. And of course to mourn Derry's mother, to display their united outrage at her death.

But Rachel wasn't among the standing, shifting crowds outside; she was safely at the heart of it, wedged in among friends and comrades, invisible in her uniform and only singing in a whisper tonight so that not even her voice could make her stand out, only her private panic to remind God that at least one girl down here really meant it, when they prayed for Grace's family.

After service she hung around for a while, hoping for another touch of Richard to melt the chill of her anxiety; but she was denied even that much succour, as she saw him going off with Nathan and the chapel elders. Some sort of council of war, presumably. She couldn't butt in on that.

Instead she reclaimed her bicycle from Ingrid and went for one last slow ride around Paradise. Up and down the steep streets, with no thought for her aching legs; she squinted through the thickening light, trying to spot the one figure who could move with that peculiar mix of grace and awkwardness that was Derry, a boy still unaccustomed to his new body and uncertain how to carry the weight of it, how to use the strength.

It was a desperate throw, and like most such an utter waste; and so at last she found herself cycling wearily home. Numbed and exhausted by the day, battered almost into insensibility, she wasn't even praying now, far less hoping. Wanting only to stop, she coasted round the final corner into the cul-de-sac –

– and braked to a sharp halt, because there was a police car there, right in the middle of the road, lights on and doors open and a policeman standing beside it.

He beckoned her, and she wheeled her bike up beside him.

"What's wrong?"

"Do you live here?"

"That's right. Why?"

"Which house?"

Rachel pointed, reluctantly.

"Your parents in? Or anyone? We haven't had an answer from there."

"No, they're away. It's just me. What's going on?"

"Maybe nothing, but we've had reports of a prowler hanging around. I'd better send someone in with you, if you're on your own. Just wait, I'll get a WPC."

Rachel scowled, chewed a thumbnail, asked diffidently, "What's he look like, this prowler?"

"Skinhead. Young lad, apparently – d'you know him?"

Rachel nodded her head and shook it both at the same time, or tried to. Choked down giggles of relief, *got you, sunshine. And bless you for coming here, you blithering moron . . .* and said, "Yeah, I know him. I think. He's not a prowler, he's just upset. He'll be looking for me. You haven't been into the garden, then?"

The policeman shook his head. "Not at the back. The gate's locked. We didn't want to climb over, not without stronger reason."

"No." Derry would've climbed over, though, no question. He'd probably be glad of the peace of it, an empty garden now and Rachel later.

"Best if I come with you, though. Just to check."

"Unh." She understood his concern, but *no, not at all. Best if you don't.* "Okay – but look, stay by the gate, will you? And then if it is him, just go away? That's the last thing he needs just now, is a policeman asking him questions. And no," forestalling the obvious, "he's not on the run. I said, he's just upset."

She sorted out the key to the garden gate, and unlocked it; gestured to the policeman, *you stay here,* and walked through.

"Derry, love? You here?"

Shadows stirred and shifted at the foot of a gnarled old cherry. "Yeah," his voice came back in a hoarse whisper, damaged by too much emotion. "Yeah, I'm here. How did you know?"

"There's only half a million coppers in the street looking for prowlers," she said lightly, turning to wave at the constable by the gate, to wave him away. "Not to mention the whole Commando mobilised in Paradise. We've been *worried,* fool."

He stood up slowly, shrugged against the tree, said nothing.

And she didn't say anything either; she only stepped close, hugged him tight as she could, *lean on me instead, I'm better than any old tree,* and just hoped he could hear.

Eventually she took him into the house, and he leant on her all the way. Rachel put the kettle on, and said, "Where were you, then, where've you been all day?"

Derry shook his head. Didn't know, or couldn't say.

It didn't matter. She ran a hand over his smooth skull and said so, said, "Never mind. You're here now, that's what counts. You make some coffee, okay? I've got to use the phone."

She went through to the hall and rang Derry's number. When his father finally answered, "Mr Bowen? Hullo, it's Rachel. Just to tell you, Derry's turned up. I've got him here. Um, what do you want me to do, should I stick him in a taxi or what? He's not, he's not looking too good, he won't talk . . . "

She waited, giving the guy the time he'd need; then she heard what she'd been hoping to hear, what she'd been angling for.

"No," she heard. "Not, not tonight. Can you keep him there, lass? It's a lot to ask, I know, but . . . "

"No, it isn't. Don't be silly, Mr Bowen. I'll keep him as long as you want me to. Talk to you tomorrow, okay? And, and I hope you have a good night. Try to get some sleep, I'll be praying for you. We all will . . . "

She hung up, blushing; and went back to find the kettle boiling like fury while Derry only sat at the table and watched.

"Oh, you . . . !" she said. "You're hopeless, you are." Bustled about with mugs and coffee, then stopped, looked at him, asked, "Are you hungry?"

He shook his head.

"Okay, let me put it another way. Have you eaten?" Thinking back over the day, "Since you left here, even? Since breakfast?"

Again, a shake of the head.

"Well, you're going to eat now, boy. Hungry or not. You can help us cook it, too. Fetch that box of eggs over . . . "

She force-fed him scrambled eggs and bacon, making a second plate for herself when she remembered that she hadn't eaten either.

Then she ran upstairs to fix the guest-room for him: make up the double bed, put towels and a toothbrush by the washbasin, a pair of Dad's pyjamas under the pillow if he wanted them. No little nests on the bathroom floor tonight. That was for yesterday, and everything had changed since then.

When she came back to Derry, he'd moved at last: he was standing by the door punching the wall, tears streaking his cheeks while soft moans escaped from his slack mouth. As soon as he saw Rachel he turned away, dragged a hand across his face, bit down hard on his crying.

She all but ran across the room, shoved him back against the door and punched him once as he'd been punching the plaster-work, hard and vicious, meaning to hurt.

"Don't you," she hissed. "Don't you *dare* try to cover up on me, Derry Bowen. Cry if you want to, that's okay, that's fine. I'll cry too," and she was already, she could feel the blurring of it, eyes and voice and mind all going together. "But you dare go all macho on me, you just try it, and I'll, I'll . . . "

She didn't have the words to finish, but didn't need them. Because he was crying again now, crying as well, the two of them together; and she couldn't support her own weight properly, let alone the weight of him leaning on her too. So they slid down the door and ended up all tangled on the cool tiled floor, and not so different from last night after all.

No question of camping the night there, though. Not this time. After a bit she pulled herself slowly away from him, said, "Derry." Said, "*Derry!*" as he tried to draw her back again, as she had to use all her strength against him. Said, "Come on, get up. We can't stay here. There's a bed for you upstairs, it'll be good and comfy, let's go, okay . . . ?"

Persuasion and bullying and sheer muscle against his weakness and distress: she got him on his feet and moving, steered him up the stairs and into the guest-room. Pushed him down onto the bed, and for the second time in twenty-four hours found herself fumbling with the laces of his trainers while he lay slack and unresponsive beneath her touch.

"I know, I know," she muttered, more to herself than him as she struggled with tight and clumsy knots. "Now I've got to marry you, right? Might as well, anyway. Might as well be married already, the way we're going. I'll have to wash these socks for you, in the morning . . . "

She looked up then and found his eyes on her, wide and watchful. Remembered then that this wasn't last night nor anything like it really, that he wasn't unconscious this time and they were neither of them drunk.

Straightened quickly, said, "You, you can manage the rest, can't you? Just get undressed and into bed, there's a loo through that door there. Pyjamas under the pillow . . . "

"Don't go," he said.

"I'll be back, I promise. Ten minutes, that's all. Tuck you up, kiss you goodnight . . . " She was desperately trying to be funny now, but it wasn't working.

"Don't *go!*"

So of course she didn't go. She sat on the window-sill and waited while he used the loo, sat and watched while he got undressed and slithered under the duvet and didn't bother with the pyjamas.

Then she turned the light off, sat on the bed and held his hand, tried to make him talk about his mother.

That didn't work, though. It seemed like all he could do was shake, now he wasn't crying any more. She squeezed his hand as tight as she could between both of hers, and still she could feel him trembling inside, under the skin; and that was only one hand, there was all the length and breadth of him shaking too and with nothing to hold on to, nothing to be held by . . .

And so she did just what she'd been so scared of, what seemed so little different from what she'd done yesterday, and yet so vastly more.

She disentangled her hands from his and stripped off quickly in the darkness, trying to be calm about it, trying to trust him or herself or God. God had brought him to this, after all, and then brought him here. He'd brought them together; He'd have nothing to complain of, then, would He? Besides, she was only going to *hold* the guy, for crying out loud. Like what's-her-name in the Bible, Abishag the Shunammite, that was her. She just warmed David up a bit, they didn't bonk . . .

So Rachel slid under the duvet with Derry, wrapped her arms and legs tight around him, kissed him gently, told him that she loved him. Told him to go to sleep.

But he lifted his head and kissed her back, not so gentle; and then again, and this time not gentle at all, but with a mute hunger in it, almost a panic, *show me, then. Show me that you love me . . .*

TWENTY-TWO

i

He kneels in the ashes, in the very heart of destruction; and it's not hard to know what's going on in his head, anyone could see it if they were there to look. He's wide, wide open now.

It's not charred wood he's smelling, though he kneels in a very bed of it; nor is that the taste of ashes in his mouth, though ashes cloud around him, clogging even the air he breathes. No, what he smells, what he tastes is the taint that underlies the fire's residue, the evil that brought it into being.

Sin has its own flavour, specific as salt, and as human. Sin's as natural as sweat, and as easy to wash away. Evil, though, evil is something entirely other; and evil has poisoned the air here and soaked the ground, as petrol must have soaked the old wood to set it so quickly and so fiercely ablaze.

He prays, for sure; but for once it's hard to have any faith in his prayers, it's hard to believe he's getting through. From the look of it, he doesn't believe himself.

He rises with a shudder, and wades through the floating ash to where Nathan waits by the bent and buckled fence; steps over, and glances down with distaste at his ruined trousers.

— They'll wash, Nathan says.

— No, he says. No, I don't think so. Nor this, he says, with a gesture behind him, not wanting even to look again. We can't rebuild here, he says, the stain runs too deep.

— That's very mystical, Nathan says. Too much for me, he says, with a distancing chuckle. But no, he says, we couldn't rebuild here, there'd be no point. The site's too small, he says. Too many of us, we need a proper church now.

They walk away down the hill; and before they come to the houses, they come to the gym.

Stand and look at it, side by side: a golden head and a dark one, two quiet faces with a lingering passion in their eyes.

And they don't say a word, but they gaze at the bones of the building, the lines of it, the big Methodist chapel that it used to be; and each perhaps knows what the other's thinking.

Each is seeing with the other's eyes, perhaps; and probably neither one of them is seeing a gym.

ii

Billy was very happy in his new home.

He was happy simply to have a home, and a room of his own again. Happier still that he'd been useful, that his own work had helped to make this home; and happiest of all to live surrounded by his new family, all his brothers and sisters in Christ.

All that made for a very happy Billy, though he knew this was a sad time for everybody else. Sometimes he felt guilty about that, he thought he should be sad too; and sometimes he was, it was easy to be sad when he thought about poor Sister Grace being all burned up in the fire.

But even there was something to make Billy happy, to make him smile in his sadness: because Richard wanted him to play in the big tent today, for Grace's funeral.

He'd been practising all morning up here in his room, listening to tapes of the hymns and songs that Richard had asked for, playing them through after. He had a cassette recorder that some-one had given him, and he practised on a little electric piano from someone else; and he had a chair to sit on when he practised and a bed to sleep on at night, and a comfy chair and a bookcase with no books in it and a carpet and curtains and a bedside light, and they were all presents from people he didn't know, brothers and sisters he hadn't learnt the names of.

It wasn't just him, he was no one special. Ever since Nathan said the houses were ready to be lived in, people had kept turning up with presents. They had all the furniture they needed now, and all the cookers and washing-machines and pots and pans and everything; but still people came with little things, little extras, "just to make a house a home," they said.

This was very much Billy's home now, although he paid no rent and nothing in it belonged to him. He understood that very well. He'd never thought of owning his own furniture, and he had no thought of it now. But still this room was his room, everyone called it Billy's room; and that meant everything in it was his too, for as long as he stayed. And he loved his bed, his chairs, even his bookcase with no books in it.

That's what he was doing, in fact, now that his practising was over: he was sitting in his room, looking round at all his things,

294

touching them with his eyes and heart and loving them all indiscriminately, as only Billy could.

Voices penetrated his happiness, his sheer joy in life. His window was something else that Billy loved, his to open or his to close; and it was open now and he could hear voices, down in the garden below.

Billy knew those voices. One was Richard and Nathan was the other, and they were both good friends of Billy's. Nathan was scary sometimes, but he was a friend and a brother none the less, and Billy didn't hold the scariness against him. All bosses were scary sometimes, it was part of their job; and Richard might be leader, but Nathan was very definitely boss.

Eavesdropping was a sin, Billy knew that. He used to get belted for it, as a kid. But eavesdropping was spying, was listening at keyholes; it wasn't sitting on your own bed in your own white room, with your window wide open and two friends outside, talking. There was no sin in that.

" . . . Tell me honestly, Nathan. What do you think? If it wasn't kids doing it for kicks, then who was it?"

"Not kids, I'm sure of that. Oh, they're capable, of course they are, I know kids who'd have done it without a second thought; but not like this. Not with the door open, and someone inside."

"That's what's so strange, that Grace couldn't get out in time. Or scare them off, whoever they were. She was nobody's victim, Grace, I can't understand how she got trapped that way."

"I'm not sure we'll ever know that, Richard. Not for certain. Not until we find who did it, anyway."

"Until the police find them, you mean."

"Yes, but I think we need to look too. Okay, they're professionals; but we can saturate this area, and we're already more deeply embedded than they are. We can talk to people who'd have nothing to say to the police."

"Well, of course, if your Commandos hear anything, that'll be very helpful; but take it to the police, Nat. You're not vigilantes."

"No, of course not. Don't worry. Tell you one thing, though: it's got to be the same people who did the marquee. That was to warn us off, but we took no notice, so this is by way of stronger action. Unless it was copycat. I can think of at least two parties who'd be very happy to see us pulling out of Paradise."

"Terry Belderstone's one, I suppose; he knows I can blow his plans apart. I think perhaps I will, now. He's had his chance to withdraw gracefully. But the other?"

"George Jenner, at the gym. He's so bent you'd need a jig to pull him straight again. And I sent him what you might call a quiet warning to behave. This might have been his response. I'll find out, though, Richard. I promise, I'll find out."

Billy shivered in the sunlight, in his nice warm room.

"That's another thing," Richard said. "That gym. We do need premises, and a former church, after all, God's house rededicated to His service: I'd like to see that. Would he sell? We could make him a good offer; and he might be glad to get out, if he's crooked. If he sees the area being cleaned up."

"I think he could be persuaded," Nathan said, laughing, making Billy's skin tingle so hard he had to rub the goose-pimples down. "You ask him nicely; and if he isn't nice back, well, just leave it to me. I'll do the persuading."

iii

Sam Bowen the quiet man, the private soul, had thought about it often, as some people do, as they must; but he'd never imagined it like this. He couldn't have, no one could. He could never have foreseen himself bringing his wife to a tent to bury, under the eyes of television cameras and a vast congregation.

He bore it as well as he could, to keep himself private under all those eyes. He took his place at the front, his sister and younger children to his left and his eldest son to his right; and his eyes turned constantly through the service, one side to the other. He was checking on his family, his own blood, all that was left him; and at the same time he was avoiding the other option, the looking straight ahead. One thing he didn't want to do today, he didn't want to spend too much time looking at that coffin on its trestles, a box too small, far too small to contain his abundant Grace.

His two little boys were preternaturally tidy, their thick hair combed and their fidgety bodies held still in formal and unfamiliar clothes. Derry too was dressed for grief, in a borrowed suit and proper shoes with a shine to them; and of them all, Sam thought, himself included, Derry was the one most obviously grieving. His eyes were bruised and bloodshot, his hands trembled between his knees, he sat stiff and upright and afraid, alone for all his family's being there; and his shaven skull left him twice exposed in his distress, all eyes drawn to it and the nakedness of it giving him nothing to hide behind.

296

But what troubled Sam's mind was a nagging doubt, one heretical question: he simply wasn't certain what it was, that Derry was so grieving for.

Oh, his mother's death had hurt him badly, no question of that. He had run, and had found his shelter where Sam had hoped and prayed even for him to find it; and that was the rub, that was the sticking point right there, because Derry and Rachel weren't speaking to each other any more.

The boy had come home alone, drag-tail and haunted, when they should have been inseparable; and he hadn't been in touch with Rachel since. Sam didn't understand it, and Derry wouldn't talk. Wouldn't sleep, either, wouldn't eat or work or do anything but suffer. And for all that Derry had loved his mam, Sam truly didn't think it was her death he was suffering for.

Even here, even at Grace's funeral the kids were keeping their distance. Derry had stayed hard by his father's side since the cortège had fetched them, wrapping his family around him like a blanket; while Rachel lurked with the choir in their corner, not even joining the long parade of well-wishers coming over to shake hands and murmur consolations.

It seemed inevitable that Rachel should have a solo spot during the service, just to make everything harder. Derry had to screw himself right around then in his seat, not to be looking at her; and her voice was inescapable, short of his ramming his fingers into his ears like a child.

The voice made the song inescapable too, and that was Sam's big problem. It had to be her own choice, her own courage that drove her to it; even Richard wouldn't have made so bold with others' feelings. Sam wanted to curse her, then he wanted to applaud; and could do neither one, could only do what his son was so obviously trying not to do, could only sit and listen.

And Rachel might have been playing and singing just for the three of them, for Sam and for Derry and herself as her fingers fumbled and her voice was lost, as the tears streaked her cheeks, as she drove herself on through a sad and sorrowing version of 'Amazing Grace'.

When the service was over, they followed the coffin out into the sunlight with all the congregation behind them. Most would be staying, congealing in clumps around the marquee to murmur their polite memories of Grace, to smile their wry smiles and finally to help stack chairs and set up tables for the funeral tea.

There were still many people coming further, though, coming

all the way to the cemetery to see Grace put in the ground. That was Sam's one act of rebellion in this long ceremonial; he'd gone against Grace's own expressed wish to be cremated. "She's had flames enough already," he'd said, flat and final; and no one had contradicted him on that.

So Sam and his sister and his three quiet sons filled the first car in the cortège, and the little boys both turned their heads to see how many cars they had behind them. And Sam's head turned too, in equally direct defiance of his sister's hissed command to sit straight; but he wasn't turning to see, he was doing the other thing, turning not to see.

Not to see the ashes and filth behind the buckled wire, where surely there must be little fragments of Grace remaining, because she sure as hell wasn't all together in that too-small box; and how the hell could she possibly have thought she would all be put back together come Judgement Day, if they'd burnt her altogether?

To the cemetery, and another solitary walk ahead of the crowd, Derry equally solitary beside him and the little boys with Joyce behind. A few more words from a book by the graveside, and then the coffin lowered jerkily into the hole, the first scatter of earth falling like a hard, dry rain, no life in it.

People milling and muttering, giving Sam and Derry a little more elbow-room than they allowed themselves; and Derry looking utterly lost, rubbing at his bald head, saying "What," saying "What happens now?"

"Now we go back to the tent," Sam said. "No hurry, they won't be ready yet."

"What for?"

"Tea and sandwiches. Chin up, son, there's a long way to go. But first," he added, "before any of the rest of it, first you talk to Rachel, all right?"

And he turned away quickly as the girl came up, patted her shoulder briefly in welcome and left them together, though he didn't go far. Far enough not to be seen listening, but close enough to listen, just about. This was important. Grace wouldn't have scrupled, where Derry's happiness was concerned.

"Derry," she said, "I've got to tell you, you've got to know. I'm going away, Saturday."

"Away," he repeated; and for that moment, for that one word there was a world of pain in his voice, before he caught it. "Where, then?"

"France. My parents phoned, last night. They've been patient, they did wait longer than they said; but they want me now. It's all arranged, tickets and stuff, so . . . "

"Right. Well. Why not, who's to stop you? You go on, have a nice holiday. Send us a postcard," savage now, not to be heard to be hurting.

And she came right back at him, just as nasty: "It's not a holiday. And there's no point staying here, is there? Not for you. I mean, look at you, you won't even let me *near* you . . . " And she lifted a hand to prove it, and yes, he shied away.

But, "Other way round," he said, and this was it, this was the heart. "Way I remember it, it was you wouldn't let me near, right?"

"Derry, I'm not, just because we slept together one night doesn't mean I'm just available whenever you want me, okay?"

"I needed you," he said, sullen and heavy.

"No, you didn't. Not in the morning. You just wanted to. And what I need, I need to think about it first. And pray about it, and get my head straight somehow because I really don't know what's happening with us at the moment."

"Sure you do, you just told me. What's happening is, you're going away. This is my mam's bloody *funeral,* and you're going away. Thanks a lot, Rache."

"I haven't got any choice, I told you that! But if I did, I think I'd still choose to go. Maybe we need this. You can do some thinking too, it won't hurt. You figure out what you really want from me, see if it comes to anything more than bed. If it does, maybe we can do a deal. If not, not."

And she pushed past Sam and walked away, shaking her head at a word from Richard as she passed; and she must be saying no to all of them if she was saying no to him. She went quickly up the hill to the cemetery gates, passing all the long line of cars and all the drifting people; and she went through the gates and out and kept on walking.

One more sandwich for the rest of us, Sam thought sadly, and turned to find his son at his elbow.

"Dad . . . "

You blew it, kid. Stupid. But Sam only smiled as best he could on the day he buried his Grace, put an arm round Derry's broadening shoulders and said, "Come on, let's go look at the flowers. Everyone's watching, see, they want to see us notice what they brought . . . "

TWENTY-THREE

i

If he burned before, if his anger blazed, he's incandescent with it now. It hurts, to meet his eyes.

Two things he says he wants, and means to have. Means to take, if they're not given freely. Not for himself, of course, he takes only in the name of the Lord; but take he will, no question.

Two things: and the first of those is a new church for his people, and we know already where he's looking to find that, where his choice has fallen.

The other is as simple to say, at least. He wants the truth; he wants to know who it was burned the chapel down, who sent Grace rising to heaven in a pillar of greasy smoke.

And for this too he can at least begin his search in the same place. He can ask the same man.

So that's what he does, he goes to the gym and asks George. One thing at a time, direct and straight from the shoulder.

– You what, George says, you want to *buy* the *gym*?

– That's right, he says, we want to buy the gym. Fair market price, he says.

And when George laughs, and shakes his head, and tells him that's a good one, that is, that's very amusing:

– Put it this way, he says, you've got a choice. You can take the money and run; or you can do the other thing, you can stick it out. But you'll lose, George. That's a promise. It's not the gym that keeps you profitable, he says, it's what you get up to on the side, your nice little earners; and they're history. This is my patch now, he says, it's God's little acre; and if you don't keep your nose clean, I'll run you off. I'll close you down, George, and I might even put you away.

George sits behind his desk and looks at him, plays a pen between his broad fingers and says nothing at all.

– Oh, and by the way, George, what do you know about the chapel burning down?

And as he asks, he unshutters his eyes just a little, gives George a glimpse of the furnace where nothing could walk unscorched; and there's a sharp, happy snap as the pen breaks between

George's fingers, and shards of plastic scatter on the desk.

ii

Waking daily to an empty bed in an empty flat in this her emptied life, Helen felt daily more tempted simply to stay where she was: to curl up tight around the heart of all that emptiness, Nathan's absence; to hug it to her, to lie engulfed and never move again.

Every day so far, though, something had pushed her into dull movement. Habit was strong, habit sneered at her for feeble self-pity; and where that wasn't enough there was always physical need, hunger or her bladder or the phone's persistence. Noticeably missing from the roster, though, was what ought to have come top of the list. She'd listened and listened for God's good voice telling her to rise up and defy the demons of depression, calling her into a bright and hopeful day under the shadow of His arm; and she'd never heard it yet.

Today was the closest she'd got to that, and it was a pretty weak imitation: the voice of her own conscience driving her finally to set bare feet on the carpet – or on the razor-wire barbs of real life, which was how she saw it these days, how she felt every step of her way – and scuttle through to the bathroom.

She set a bath running, just habit again, not to go dirty into a dirty world; and stood long minutes staring at herself in the mirror, at her thinning face and sinking eyes, changes too gross to hide or overlook.

Would you buy second-hand sympathy from this girl? she thought; and shrugged the thought away, no use to her. That was all she had to offer, after all: all the pity that was in her, once-used already to pity herself.

At the Bowens' front door, she didn't even pause in a sudden hunt for courage, as she would have done six months or a month ago. Dead already, dead at heart, she had no access to shyness or nerves any more. She just lifted her hand and knocked.

Waited, and knocked again; and still heard nothing, no voices calling or footsteps hurrying or stumbling or coming any which way down the stairs to answer her.

Another time, then. There was no hurry in any case, she had nothing to give them that they couldn't get in better measure from others. Assuming that they wanted it at all. A wall of words made a pathetic defence against catastrophe, Helen had gleaned that

301

much in recent days. She'd tried so hard, to shore up some fragments among the ruins; and every day there was less to work with, every night her dreams were filled with the sounds of fire and flood, the screams of falling . . .

But walking away, walking up the hill because better that than going down, she saw the airport shuttle at a bus-stop on the main road; and saw Derry getting off, unmistakable even with his head down and shoulders slumped, a slouching cartoon mockery of himself.

He came blindly down the street, not seeing her, seeing nothing at all beyond the ground he walked on, if he was seeing that. Helen stood still and he came to her, and would have walked straight by if she hadn't reached an arm into his path.

"Derry? Have you got a minute?"

His head lifted, and she saw how his eyes were red and wet; and she envied him that, his being able to cry. She couldn't manage it herself, depression was a dust-bowl with no water. And almost she envied him his cause of grief, his mother's brutal ending. Better that than what she carried.

But she said, "I've just been to your flat, but I suppose your father's at work, is he? There wasn't any reply."

"Nah, he's gone over my auntie's house, see the kids. Stay there all weekend, I expect. Want him, did you?"

"Only to say how sorry I am, about your mother," feeling amazed at herself and at him, the two of them so bereft but still trying, still keeping up the cover. "And if there's anything I can do, any time . . . "

"You any good at miracles, then, are you?" And he spoiled it then, met her eye to eye for the first time, an abrupt and savage contact. "'Cos the thing is, see, your friend Richard, he's really let us down this time. Me, he did me fine, no problem. And that, that crazy woman, tried to top herself, know the one? He managed her, didn't he? She was happy dead, says so in this morning's paper, but he dragged her back any old how. Only then it was my mam's turn, and she didn't want to die, no way; but he just stood there and let her, didn't he? Stood there and watched, like the rest of 'em. And when, when they found her, Christ, he did it for the crazy woman, he could've done it for Mam, he could've brought her back too. But he didn't even *try* . . . "

"Derry," she said, from the heart of her own failing faith, "Derry, it's not that easy, it can't be. It's not a tap you turn on, miracles on demand . . . "

"He didn't even try," Derry repeated. "Maybe God had it all

302

lined up ready for him, he only had to ask, like with me, maybe. But he never, he never *tried*, even. So yeah, there's something you can do for me. For both of us, me and my dad. You can tell him, right? Tell him we don't want him, and we don't want any of his bloody soldiers either, coming round at us all the time. Just makes it worse, that's all. We don't want any of you, okay?"

"What," Helen said, trying for a tease, something light-hearted, just to show him how unfair that was, "not even Rachel?"

And she didn't know why but it all went very wrong then, worse than it was already. Derry stiffened and stared at her, paled and turned his face away; and, "Fucking bitch," he said. "Fucking shitty little *bitch*," he said, his voice thickening; and Helen barely had time to wonder whether it was herself or Rachel he meant before he was gone, sprinting all the way down the hill and out of sight, not to show her his tears.

iii

Coming down the track towards the houses, Jack Dubrowski met a rare car coming up, bumping slowly over the broken tarmac. The driver was no one he recognised, a burly man with a beard and a wary scowl.

Jack stepped aside to let the car past, and spotted a briefcase on the passenger seat before the driver's heavyweight stare forced his gaze away. Someone official, then; and not a friend, by the look of him. Not a bearer of good tidings.

Obscurely warned, Jack shifted the shopping-bag he carried from one hand to the other, repossessed the centre of the crumbling road and walked unhurriedly on: setting himself solid and foursquare in the departing driver's mirror, to seem unworried and already defiant.

The door of his house stood open; but that was nothing new these days, with so many kids in and out of the other houses and so many of them in and out of his. Always someone coming to see him, or else to sit with Anita. She adored it, so long as they didn't come in uniform. The girls were all her bosom friends, though she couldn't remember their names from one day to the next and thought them all Polish, all Catholic; and the boys were all her suitors, all paying court to her beauty.

So he walked in smiling to see who was here today, who had throned Anita in the glamour of her own confusions; and found it entirely otherwise, Billy sitting on the stairs and sobbing loudly.

303

"Billy, now, Billy, what's the matter, heh? Hush, you'll frighten Anita, all this noise . . . "

Billy sniffed, and wiped his sleeve across his face, and looked up blinkingly. "Oh, Mr Jack, we've all got to move," he said, "we've got to move house. And I came to say could I come back here again, I don't want to leave my room but I thought I could come here; only it's you too, I've seen the paper and it's just the same . . . "

"Billy, take this shopping and put it in the kitchen. Put it all away for me, you know where everything goes. And put the kettle on for a cup of tea, will you please? And don't worry so. I don't believe any of us are moving house this time."

"But it says, the paper says. Nathan read it to me next door, and what it means, it means we have to move, he said so . . . "

"I don't think so. It means they want us to move, perhaps; but that isn't the same thing. I'm not moving, nor Anita. Nor I think your friends next door. Make the tea, Billy."

He patted Billy abstractedly on the shoulder and went through to where Anita sat with her head turned for once away from the television and towards the window, towards the real world.

"Jacek, what does it mean, this paper, this *eviction order*? What does it mean? We cannot leave our home, we live here . . . "

"And will not leave," Jack promised her, taking the paper from her fretful hands and scanning it quickly, giving her his own strong hand to hold instead. "Come, this is just bureaucracy. Nothing to worry us. Billy is making us a cup of tea; and when we have drunk that, I will go round to see Nathan and Richard, if he is there. We will discuss it, and pray about it; and it will be nothing to worry about, Anita, you will see. It will all be forgotten by Christmas. God will not take us from our home."

He did it once, he thought, *when we were younger; surely, oh, surely He will not do it again, now we are old?*

With Billy and Anita finally settled, a game-show on the television and each of them sinking into their own private and very separate worlds, Jack felt himself free to leave them. He walked next door and into real life again, where eviction orders were important documents and very much to be worried about, and prayer might not be enough of a response.

This second house in the terrace was already becoming known as the offices. Richard had taken over the ground floor, with a couple of willing assistants to keep him organised; while upstairs was Nathan's territory, HQ for the Christ Commando.

Nathan had come downstairs for this, though. He was sitting

with Richard in the front room, the conference room; the door was open, and he hailed Jack as soon as he saw him.

"Come and join us, you should be in on this. You got a notice to quit?"

"Yes. It frightened Anita. Billy, too, it frightened Billy . . . "

"It would. Everything frightens Billy. I hope you told them, this is nothing to be frightened of?"

"Isn't it?"

"No. It's just a chess-game still, just another move. Legally they're in the right, since Mrs Patel sold out to Belderstone; but they're not going to set the bailiffs on us. They can't afford that kind of publicity, we know too much about their operation."

"So what do we do now?"

"Ignore it, more or less. We'll get one of the legal eagles to draft a response, and let the solicitors argue over it. That'll take months. You might have to sign something, I don't know; but don't worry, you won't have to move. Tell Anita."

"I'll tell her," Richard said. "She'll believe it more easily, from me. I'll come and see her in a little while, Jack. When we're through here. Perhaps you and I should have a talk, as well?"

And that was what Jack wanted, what he needed: reassurance stronger than Nathan's casual dismissal. He wanted the same message with Richard's authority stamped on it. So he nodded, and sat down to wait.

And listened, of course. Gleaned a little more advice.

"We'll have to be careful," Nathan said, "never leave the place empty. That goes for you too, Jack."

"Anita never goes out now," he said, and was saddened to hear himself say it. "Only into the garden."

"Well, don't let her. Not even the garden, unless you're around, or one of us. Be sure, be careful. If bailiffs do come and find it empty, they'll just walk in; and once they're in, we're out. Don't trust Billy on his own, either. He'd let 'em in."

"You speak as though we were under siege."

"We are, effectively. We have to act as if we are, we need a siege mentality. And talking about sieges, Richard, what are we going to do about the gym?"

"The chapel," Richard corrected him quietly, solemnly. "God doesn't abandon His houses. You can't deconsecrate a church, whatever the business managers say. And what we're going to do is reclaim it. Turn it back from worship of the body."

"Sure. But how?"

"Peacefully. Peaceful pressure. That's the strategy. Tactics are your department. Just watch your PR, though. We don't want to

305

look like a bully throwing his weight around, putting a local man out of work."

Nathan laughed. "We've got enough on George Jenner. It'd never stick. If we went to the police with what I know, he'd be shut down tomorrow and banged up by Tuesday."

"Not that, either," Richard said. "I don't want the police brought into it. Jesus threw out the moneychangers by himself. That's how we've got to do it, in a clean fight, him and us."

"Peaceful, though, right?"

"Right. You don't go in there with whips. Take your time, Nat, and do it right. Think before you do anything; and if in doubt, talk to me."

"Okay. You're the boss."

"Right."

Jack listened, and learned. And wondered how all this could possibly have grown from the old chapel's little mission; and wondered when and how the old Council had finally been displaced, because that had definitely happened. They hadn't met for a few weeks, even before the chapel burned. There hadn't seemed much point.

He sighed privately, frowned, shook his head in irritation with himself. The old days had been quieter for sure, and very much easier; and yes, he'd enjoyed his position in the congregation, the cachet of being a founder and a Council member. But that was all vanity, and profitless; and it was very much the way of the world, that the old should step aside for the young and vigorous. Richard was achieving so much more than they ever had, it was wickedness even to dream of turning the clock back . . .

A tap on the door-frame and a girl peered in, young Helen; and Jack really did want to turn the clock back then, but not very far and only for her sake, only to have her happy again. She looked like a refugee, with her smile long lost and her eyes so deeply sunken; and that was all wrong, in one newly claimed for God.

She made no effort to hide her misery, nor the cause of it. Her whole body flinched when she saw Nathan, and she had to steady herself physically against the door-jamb.

But she looked past him to Richard, and said, "There's, there's that policeman come back to see you again. About Grace. He's got some more questions, he says . . . "

"All right, Helen. Thanks. Show him in here, would you?"

Even the full force of Richard's smile couldn't get through to Helen now. She only nodded and left, slump-shouldered and despairing. Jack wanted to see Nathan move, go after her, make at

306

least a gesture towards restoration; lacking that, he got to his feet himself.

"I'll go, too. I have nothing more to tell the police."

"There's always something more," Nathan said calmly. "Eternally interested, the police."

And he still made no move to leave himself, nor to hold Jack back.

Jack passed the incoming detective in the hall, with a nod of recognition; stepped outside, but didn't go back to his own house. Not quite yet.

Helen was sitting on a slope of earth and thin grass, on the ill-defined border between the houses and the wasteland. She sat alone, all folded in on herself, hair hanging like a curtain between herself and the world; and Jack felt moved, felt called to draw that curtain back, if only briefly.

This was where looseness led, he thought: looseness in the young people themselves, and then looseness in Richard, to condone and not condemn. Change the world as it might, God didn't change and neither did His laws. Sin was sin and coupling outside the bonds of marriage was fornication, nothing more. The way Jack had heard it, Nathan had finally moved to put things right; only he'd done it badly, broken off the relationship where he should have married the girl. And this was the result, Helen wrapped in shadows, no good advertisement for the chapel or the mission or the Lord Himself.

She held a newspaper screwed and twisted between her hands, the local *Evening Argus*; and when he sat down beside her, cautious of his old bones and totally unheeded by her, he took that as a key, an easy way into conversation.

"Is that today's paper, Helen? I haven't seen it yet."

"Yes," she said, behind her veiling hair. "I, I just bought it, up the top; and I thought, I thought Richard ought to see it. Only he was talking to Nat, to Nathan, so I didn't. I just waited. And then the policeman came."

"Yes. What is there in the paper, that you thought Richard ought to see?"

"Oh, it doesn't matter. He'll know anyway. He knows everything, doesn't he? Just that some reporter got himself in to see Evelyn, in the hospital, and they've printed this whole long article about what she said. I guess even Richard's failures are news, aren't they? And Evelyn went to Heaven, when she died. She says so. Here, see for yourself," thrusting the paper into his hands and scrambling to her feet, kicking up a cloud of harsh dust, making

307

him cough. "She walked down this long tunnel and found the light at the end of it, found Jesus waiting to take her up to Heaven. Only then Richard came and fetched her. You read it, you tell him if you want. But he'll know already, won't he? He was there, he's the bastard brought her back."

And she slid down to level ground and walked away.

iv

"No," said Lisa.

"Yes," her mother said, and slapped her.

Lisa shook her head, only to clear the swimminess out of her brain; and her mother read that as defiance and slapped her again, bony palm as hard against her cheek as tarmac would be hard beneath her knees.

Because that was what her mother wanted, Lisa on her knees on the pavement, out in public; and that's what she got in the end. That's what she always was going to get, and she'd known it and Lisa had known it and no doubt Luther and Mr Parkinson had known it too. Lisa didn't have the stomach for this kind of fight, the head-to-head confrontation.

So she stopped saying no eventually, as she was bound to do. Said yes instead, said, "All right, all right, if you're that fussed," in a thick and sullen mutter; and followed the other three out of the house and round the corner, all the way along to where the old chapel used to be.

Dropped to her knees on the pavement, just like them. And folded her hands together, closed her eyes and thought, *Beam me up, Scotty*. Didn't pray, except to be someone else and somewhere else, anyone and anywhere rather than Lisa Dolance and here, on her knees on the pavement on a busy Saturday afternoon in Paradise.

They were here by appointment: inevitably the first, but not long alone.

In ones and twos others came to join them, perhaps a dozen altogether and all from the original congregation, the old faithful. This party was invitation only, and no new blood, thank you, no young turks. No Richard, nor anyone tainted by Richard's touch. None of the four old men, even, the supplanted Council.

Lisa tasted sour ash on her tongue, breeze-blown from beyond the twisted fence; and she thought that was about right, that fitted. That was the chapel she had in her mouth, all that was left of it: and it was dry and bitter and unpleasant, and who could argue with that?

She hawked and spat, to clear her palate of the taste; and even through her closed eyelids she could see her mother's glare, feel the threat of her hand again.

And then her mother's voice: but not talking to her, thank God. Talking to God, indeed, loud and clear and triumphant.

" . . . Fire cleanses, Lord, fire burns out the dead wood to make room for new growth. That's what we pray for now, Lord, we pray for new growth in this troubled community. We pray for the will and strength to rebuild our chapel here, on this spot; and we pray for guidance in the choice of those who will lead us, that we not be led astray by a smiling face and a glib tongue.

"Because fire cleanses, Lord, fire is Your weapon against wickedness and deceit. Did not Sodom and Gomorrah perish by fire, at Your hand? And did not You say, through Your prophet Ezekiel, in chapter twenty-eight and the eighteenth verse of his book, 'Thou hast defiled thy sanctuaries by the multitude of thine iniquities, by the iniquity of thy traffick; therefore will I bring forth a fire from the midst of thee, it shall devour thee, and I will bring thee to ashes upon the earth in the sight of all them that behold thee'?

"And so has it been with us, Lord, to our tremendous sorrow. Because we were led astray and followed a false prophet into vanity and falsehood, You found it good to send Your fire to destroy the house that we had built to You, and to take from us the soul of our sister Grace.

"But Lord, guide us, and we will build again to Your glory. And until that building is done, we will pray daily here on the pavement, Lord, because You have found us not deserving of a roof or the privacy of walls; and this shall be our penance and atonement, that we pray here, on our knees and in public . . . "

Not me, Lisa thought. *Not again. Not every day. No way.* But she was here now, when she'd said no; and she thought probably she'd be here tomorrow, too. And the day after, and the day after that . . .

Half an hour they'd been here now, while her mother and Mr Parkinson spelled each other at the praying. Half an hour was nothing, they could keep this up all day and half the night if they chose to. They'd done it before.

But already Lisa could hear what she most dreaded, voices from across the street: the giggles and sharp high shouts of children, the husky snigger of a teenager.

Lisa stole a glance without lifting her head, barely lifting her lashes, not to let them know she was looking. Half a dozen young boys in a group, an older lad at a little distance, lounging against a wall.

Lisa winced and closed her eyes again, and really tried to pray now.

A minute later there was a quick patter around her, like a sudden spit of rain; something sharp bit at her parting, lodged in her hair.

She looked up, startled, not hiding anything this time; and saw one of the kids stooping for another handful of gravel, his friends hesitating, torn between the temptation and the risk. Looking to the teenager for approval or encouragement, glancing anxiously across the road for any signs of retribution.

They wouldn't be seeing any of that, though. They'd see Lisa watching, maybe, see her nervousness and laugh; but the rest, Luther and the adults wouldn't pay any attention except perhaps to pray a little harder.

The kid cocked his arm and threw, *look at me, then,* swollen with his own bravery. A shower of stones and dust fell around Mr Parkinson; and his eyes opened, and in a loud voice he said,

"'Blessed are they which are persecuted for righteousness' sake: for theirs is the kingdom of heaven. Blessed are we, brethren, when men revile us, and persecute us, and say all manner of evil against us for His sake.'"

Lisa couldn't see any men, only children crying out for a box round the ear. Nor did she feel blessed by their attention.

But her mother added her voice now. "'Rejoice,'" she said, dark and harsh, "'and be exceeding glad: for great is your reward in heaven: for so persecuted they the prophets which were before you.'"

"'Yea,'" another voice, Lisa couldn't tell whose, "'and all that will live godly in Christ Jesus shall suffer persecution.'"

This wasn't helping. This was asking for it. Lisa saw the teenager bend and straighten, twist and hurl. A crushed Pepsi can caught Mr Parkinson hard in the chest, and all the kids cheered.

"'Love your enemies,'" Mr Parkinson shouted, sounding anything but loving. "'Bless them that curse you, do good to them that hate you, and pray for them which despitefully use you, and persecute you.' And we do pray for these children now, Lord, that You will reach down and touch their hearts, show them their foolish sinfulness . . . "

But seemingly all God had shown the children so far was a source of more ammunition. Everyone had their eyes open now, ducking and dodging. The stones were getting bigger, too. Lisa's mother had a bruise on her cheek; but that wasn't going to stop her praying, any more than her prayers were going to stop those kids from throwing stones.

Lisa wanted to run, she wanted all of them to run before someone got seriously hurt. The others wouldn't, though; and she didn't dare run alone. That would be like an open invitation, *chase me, hurt me, let's go!* And then there would be her mother to face later, and that would be worse. Worse than a stone in the face, maybe.

So Lisa stayed; and because she stayed, she saw the cavalry come to the rescue.

The Commando, rather.

She saw four men in combat jackets come running from the big marquee, dodging the traffic and shouting as they came.

She saw the boys all turn to stare; saw the little kids back off nervously, group together, ready to run.

Saw the teenager toss a stone in his hand, make his mind up and chuck it, hard at the nearest man.

That was Nathan, Lisa saw; and she saw him catch the stone like a cricketer. Saw his arm draw back and snap forward, just like a cricketer.

Heard the boy scream, saw him clutch at his head, saw the sudden leak of blood between his fingers.

Saw him run, off and away with all the kids behind him.

Whatever happened to turning the other cheek? Lisa wondered; but no, Nathan would have no problems with eye-for-eye theology.

Behind her, a triumphant voice:

"'But the Lord is with me as a mighty terrible one: therefore my persecutors shall stumble, and they shall not prevail: they shall be greatly ashamed; for they shall not prosper: their everlasting confusion shall never be forgotten.' Jeremiah 20, verse 11."

And another:

"'Let them be confounded that persecute me, but let not me be confounded: let them be dismayed, but let not me be dismayed: bring upon them the day of evil, and destroy them with double destruction.' Jeremiah 17, verse 18." And a pause, a laugh, "Good old Jeremiah."

Lisa's mother didn't find that at all funny, by the glare on her face. But even she seemed to realise that the time for prayer was gone now. She rose to her feet to face Nathan; and Lisa scrambled up quickly, not wanting to miss a moment of this.

"Fun's over," Nathan said, while two of his companions trotted on up the street a little way, and the other made notes in a book. "Everyone all right?"

Lisa's mother just looked at him.

"Good," he said, taking that to mean yes. "But seriously, Mrs Dolance, there are better places to pray. You're blocking the pavement, to start with. You get some snotty bobby along, and that's obstruction. And it's asking for trouble anyway, with these local kids. Come to the marquee, if you want to pray."

"I go where the Lord leads me," Lisa's mother said loftily, "and pray where His Spirit calls to me to pray. And I do not take instruction from the likes of you. Christ teaches us to suffer persecution and to turn the other cheek, not to break heads and return violence for violence."

And she turned away, the audience over: turned her back on him and his rescue to gaze through the broken fence at the ashes of her queendom.

Nathan shrugged, smiled coldly, went away.

Then it was like Sundays after chapel, the people queueing up to shake hands, to nod and murmur a word or two and ask what time tomorrow.

And finally there were just the four of them left, as there had been at the start: Luther and Lisa and their mother, and Mr Parkinson. And three of them were ready to go, and Lisa at least was just desperate for it, mad keen to get away from here; but Luther stood with his fingers twisted in the twisted wire and his eyes on the ashes, as his mother had stood a few minutes before.

"Was it hellfire," he asked, "that God sent to burn the chapel down?"

"Hellfire's hotter than that, lad," Mr Parkinson said. "And it doesn't go out."

"But it was God's work, He burnt the chapel down?"

"Oh, aye, it was His will, no question. It was a lesson, you see, to be learned the hard way."

"Was Mrs Bowen a sinner, then? She must have been, mustn't she, for God to burn her up like that?"

"Not for us to say, lad. She's gone to judgement, that's all we know. It's for God to judge her, not for us; and not for us to question what He does, neither. Come on, now."

TWENTY-FOUR

i

Put on hold, he hears soft muzak pumping at him; and no doubt he transmutes it in his head, lead into gold, celestial choirs singing. He lives in a world of total significance, where all things come from God and everything matters, even a minute of music.

But then the music is gone, and it's a man's voice that he hears; and even he couldn't change the coldness in that, surely, there must be limits even for him.

– Belderstone here.

– Ah, good. Thank you for finding the time to talk to me.

– To listen. I haven't said I'm talking. I don't know that I've anything to say.

– Oh yes, I think so. On the subject of these eviction orders, I thought perhaps you might like to say that you'd be withdrawing them forthwith.

– And why should I do that, Mr Gould? You'll find them quite legitimate. And I want you off my property.

– I'm sure. I'm sure you do. But you're wasting your time, you see. God is in the midst of us, and we shall not be moved. God shall help us, and that right early. Psalm 46, verse five. More or less. Give or take.

– Is that right? Well, I'll look forward to seeing what God does, then, in the face of a legal warrant. Render unto Caesar that which is Caesar's, Mr Gould. I know my Bible too, even if I can't compete with you.

– No, you can't, really, can you?

– There's more to life than the Bible.

– Certainly there is. Folk wisdom, say: God helps those that help themselves. It's not Scripture, but there's a lot of truth in it none the less. Positive action, that's the key.

– What are you talking about?

– Here's another Bible verse for you. 'And ye shall know the truth, and the truth shall make you free.' John 8, verse 32. It's quite apt; because I do know the truth, you see. Don't I? And the point is, the police have been asking a lot of questions about people who might have been stirred up to violence against us. I've not been very cooperative so far, to be honest with you. But I

313

might have to rethink that, the Lord might lead me to another perspective. And if that happened, if I found myself telling them just *why* we'd got your back up, Mr Belderstone – if I showed them the evidence I've got – well, I don't think the consequences would be too pleasant, would they?

A pause: then,

– Not for any of us. You included, you sanctimonious little shit. I could make life very uncomfortable for you down there. Very uncomfortable indeed.

– Oh, I'm sure you could. Dangerous, even. Burn us out of here, say, and you've got no problems, have you, Mr Belderstone? No opposition any more, no squatters standing in your way.

The line is silent, even the sound of breathing stilled.

– Oh, and by the way, Mr Belderstone? *Did* you have anything to do with the chapel burning down?

Another kind of silence, richer, more heavily textured; and the sudden, loud sound of disconnection.

ii

When Derry came to work on Monday morning, he found a picket outside the gym.

He saw them from a long way off, half a dozen people with placards, grouped around the steps. From that distance he couldn't read either their faces or their messages; but they were Commandos, that much was clear already. All labelled, all in uniform.

Funny, Derry thought. Camouflage was supposed to hide you, make you hard to see; only they used it right the other way around, to make themselves stand out.

Halfway down the hill, he knew some of them from their stances, the way they moved and gestured. That was Nathan, no question; and that little blonde girl he'd seen around, he didn't know her name but no mistaking that head of hair; and the kid at the end there, wasn't that Albie? He thought it was.

Closer still: and now he could make out the bold capitals on their placards, if he squinted. GOD'S HOUSE FOR GOD'S PEOPLE, one said. Another, DRIVE THE BODYCHANGERS OUT OF THE TEMPLE.

They were singing, too. A couple of them clapped in time, the blonde girl raised her arms above her head and swayed from side to side, her eyes shut and her face radiant.

If Rachel was around she'd be there, Derry thought, playing guitar for them. And he scowled, kicked the kerb, *didn't* want to think about Rachel. Never mind that he wasn't being given the choice, that everything reminded him of her and every memory hurt like acid in his guts. He could try, couldn't he?

So he did that, he tried; and seeing the Christians gave him something else to think about, that took him past the picket with barely more than a nod, barely more than a touch of curiosity. Time enough later, to figure out what that was all about. Right now he was thinking about his mother; and his heart was in the fire, and he could hardly see for flames.

But George was waiting for him just inside the door; and big George had more than a touch of curiosity. He had a hefty dose of suspicion, and a lot of questions that he wanted answered right now.

"Friends of yours, are they, Derry? That lot out there?"

"Some of them, yeah. Sort of. I know 'em, anyway."

"Knew they were coming, did you? Know what this is about?"

"No." *Don't know, don't care. They want to make prats of themselves, let them.*

"I wish I could believe you, son. I really wish I could."

"What does that mean?" Derry demanded. "I haven't seen any of them since, since the funeral. I don't give a flying fuck what they're up to, it's nothing to do with me." *Not any more.*

"You would," George said. "Your girl wanted you to, you would. I don't see her out there now, but she around, is she? Coming down later, say?"

"Rachel's in France," Derry said woodenly, and so much for good intentions, for trying not to think about her. *I know she is, I saw her go. Stood on the airport roof and watched her onto the plane. Dunno if she saw me, she didn't wave. And she's not my girl, don't call her that. Not any more.*

"That right? Well, doesn't stop you being a spy, does it?"

"I'm not a spy, Christ, what am I supposed to be spying on?"

"Don't be sweet, son." George's big hand spread itself across Derry's chest, and pushed; and Derry was slammed back against the wall, the breath half knocked out of him. "You've got a foot in both camps, see, Derry; and that's not comfortable, it isn't safe. My point of view, it means you can't be trusted."

"So what, you don't want me to work here any more, is that what you're saying?"

"I'm thinking about it. You're on probation, that's what I'm saying. And watch your step, I'm saying that too. Loud and clear.

315

Like, I might be very unhappy if I found you nosing around in the office, say. Are you getting this?"

Derry nodded slowly.

"Right, then. Jason's not coming in today, Vinny's borrowed him; so jump to it, sonny. We open on time, Christians or not."

"You could call the police," Derry muttered. "If they bother you that much."

He knew it was stupid, as soon as he'd said it; didn't really need George's heavy hand clipping him on the side of the head, jambling all his brains together.

"I might take Kyzer out for some air, mind," George said meditatively. "Maybe I'll chain him to the railings till we open, let him join in the community singing. He'd enjoy that."

Around midday, George sent Derry out to buy some sandwiches for lunch; but he didn't get far. Nowhere near the sandwich shop. He jogged down the steps, turned his head away from the protestors, tried to skitter past them on the trot; friends or not, they could only embarrass him now. Or do worse than embarrass, if they wanted to talk about Rachel.

Somebody wanted to talk about something. A hand caught his elbow as he passed; and he stopped himself only a moment short of actually fighting free. Turned wearily, *why can't you leave me alone? Rachel has,* and let Nathan lead him a little way down the hill, out of the others' hearing.

"Derry, how attached are you to your job?"

Hardly at all now, George is cutting me loose. But he wasn't going to tell Nathan that. "I like it," he said. "Why?"

"This isn't a good place to be working, is why. Word to the wise, Derry. I think you'd be better somewhere else."

"I don't owe you any favours." *Not any more. I haven't got Rachel any more, I don't have to keep you happy.*

"You'd be doing yourself a favour, that's what I'm saying."

"Yeah? How's that, then?"

"Don't go all hostile on me, Derry. It's your welfare I'm thinking of. We want rid of George, you see," Nathan went on. "We want him out of the gym, and preferably right out of Paradise. And the point is . . . "

But Derry was interrupting, shaking his head, genuinely outraged. "You can't do that. You can't *do* that. You don't own this city, you got no right to drive people out . . . "

"Don't be naïve, Derry. Where people like George are concerned, we've got every right. Look, you're not blind, you're not stupid. You know what goes on here, better than I do, probably."

316

Derry shrugged. "Okay, so he's bent. That still doesn't give you the right . . . "

"Yes, it does." Derry's turn to be interrupted now. "It's not just a right, it's every citizen's *duty* to fight crime – and that includes you. That's what I'm saying, I'm worried about you. We're trying to keep them out of it, but if the police did get involved, it's going to mean trouble for you too, if you're still around. You don't want to go down as an accessory."

"I'm not involved in George's scams," Derry said indignantly.

"I know that, but the police don't. And – well, would you trust Jason to tell the truth, say? To stand up for you?"

No, Derry wouldn't. He wouldn't trust anything to Jason, certainly nothing as precious and fragile as the truth. In the back of his mind, a soft voice was listing this month's losses. Mother, girlfriend, contentment, all those were gone already; and now his job looked set to follow. Pushed by George and pulled by Nathan, how could he hope to keep it?

But he said, "I need a job. I do, I need it. Dad's not been to work since, since Mam, and one of us has got to." Not for the money, Derry's wage-packet was a joke. Just to get out, to be busy. Not to spend all day with his father.

"You don't need this job, Derry. Truly, you don't. We'll find you a job, if you want; but seriously, mate. Just get out."

Derry slowly, slowly shook his head. "I did this," he said. "I got this job, all by myself, no help from anyone. I'm not going to chuck it up just 'cos George is in trouble. He's probably going to sack me anyway, but I'll wait for that. I'm not quitting."

Derry thought Nathan might lose his temper then, but he didn't. He just looked away for a moment, turned back again decisively.

"Derry, I didn't want to tell you this, but you're forcing me. So I'm sorry, all right? I wish you didn't have to know."

"Know what?"

"We've been making enquiries, and there's a very good chance that George was behind that fire at the chapel. He didn't set it, but he might well have had it set. He might have been the man that killed your mother."

Derry's turn to look away; and it took him longer, it took everything he had to turn his head back again, to say, "You, you told the police, then?"

"No. Not till we're certain."

"What, you're guessing, is that it?"

"It's more deduction than proof, at this stage. But burning the chapel, that's the same thing as slashing up the old marquee,

317

right? Same mind behind it?"

"Well. Maybe. Could be, yeah."

"Exactly. It could be. And Billy was in the marquee, when it got done; he saw the face of the man who did it. And he's seen the same man again since then."

"So?"

"He saw him here, Derry. Going out' the back way, with George. And the Lord knows, I've given George reason enough to turn against us. I gave him a special reason, between the marquee and the fire. So you could blame me too, you could say I was responsible. I'll take that on my shoulders, if I have to. But I think George may have to answer too. Yes?"

Just then George came out of the gym behind them, came down the steps with Kyzer on a short chain.

George yelled at Derry, to know what the hell he thought he was doing; and Nathan paled suddenly, and pulled away; and Derry hardly noticed either one of them.

Certainly he didn't respond to either one of them. He only walked away, walked a little and then started to run; and didn't go anywhere near the sandwich shop, or back to work that day.

iii

Vinny had got himself a new van for the day, a big transit job. Borrowed it off a mate, he said, smiling. Jason didn't believe that. He couldn't see Vinny having mates. On the other hand, say you had something, a van, say, and Vinny came up to you, said he wanted the use of it – well, you weren't going to say no, were you? Help yourself, Vinny, you'd say. Here's the keys, you'd say. Want me to clean it out for you first?

That was the best thing about it, really, that this van was clean inside. It didn't smell, the way Vinny's did. Vinny still smelt, of course: dogs and drink, fags and old sweat and something else, something peculiarly and frighteningly Vinny. But the seat was wide, Jason could get a good distance between them, out of arm's reach; he could wind the window down, and think positive. Breathe easy.

Nothing to be scared of, after all. Not a thing. He closed his eyes, pressed his face into the wind and saw himself oh so casual, talking to wide-eyed kids: *Vinny? Sure, I know Vinny. Me and him have done jobs together, for George. No trouble. Vinny's all right, he's easy. We're a team.*

And opened his eyes and saw the truth, saw himself in the wing-mirror, oh so scared.

Vinny drove them to a farm, half an hour out of the city. He drove across the farmyard and pulled up in front of a metal-sided barn. He sounded the horn and got out, a quick jerk of his head sending Jason jumping out the other side.

A woman's figure appeared briefly from behind the house, waved and vanished. Vinny grunted, set both hands to the barn's high door and began to push.

Slowly, with much creaking and a tooth-aching squeal, the door started to slide. Jason stepped forward, thinking he should help, that was surely what he was here for and Vinny would surely take it out of his skin if he only stood around watching.

But no, another jerk of Vinny's eloquent head held him still. The heavy door rolled back with no help from Jason, and hot air from inside poured over him like water, smelling bad.

It looked like an aircraft hangar in there, it looked that big; and it looked empty, except for a raised stage in the middle of the floor. That was serious relief to Jason, who'd been imagining all sorts of stuff.

Following Vinny in, blinking his eyes hard against all the dust dancing in the dim light, Jason saw what that stage actually was, and blinked again.

It was a boxing ring, that's what. Squat and solid, ropes and all. Timekeeper's table sat beside it.

"Harvest's coming in next week," Vinny said. "Farmer needs the barn. We take this apart, run it down to the gym. Got it?"

"Yeah. Yeah, sure. But, Vinny," made brave by so much conversation, "what's it for?"

"What's it for, it's for boxing, what d'you think it's for?"

There were dark stains on the canvas, that made Jason wonder a little. Best not to mention them, though.

"Yeah, but – why here?"

"Unlicensed. Bare-knuckle, sometimes. Bad news, if you get caught," and he grinned like someone who had got caught and had thoroughly enjoyed the experience, hadn't found it bad news at all. "So we move it around. Summer, it comes out here; now it goes to the gym for winter. Fold that table up, carry it out."

It was hard work, unmaking that ring and loading every board, every bolt of it into the van. They sweated in the baking barn all

319

afternoon, before they were done. Vinny drank his way through a six-pack of lager, and didn't offer Jason a taste; when he was desperate, when his head was swimming with the heat and he truly couldn't go on, Jason found a tap out in the yard and sucked water from the cup of his hands. And Vinny called him back before he'd had nearly enough, and he went.

At last they were finished, though, and driving back towards the city. Giddy with relief that the day was so nearly over, Jason wet his lips with the last moisture he had in him and asked Vinny a question, pure curiosity.

"Do you, do you do that, then, Vinny, do you box?"

Vinny smiled. "I'm the best, round here," he said. "Had a licence once, when I was a kid; but unlicensed is better. No Queensberry shit. No one beats me, without all that shit."

"Yeah? So why," and this was dodgy ground, this was danger- ous indeed; but he was light-headed, foolish, blundering on, "why only round here, then, why stop here?"

Vinny paused, blinked, looked at him; and returning fear made him suddenly sober again. But all Vinny said was, "This is my territory, see? I don't leave my territory. They want to come here, I'll fight them. I'll fight anyone. And they do come. I've got a reputation."

And then he glanced at the lowering sun and said, "We've got time, before we take this gear to the gym. George won't want us turning up when he's busy. We'll go to my place, you can help us with the dogs. Like last time."

"Yeah, sure, Vinny," Jason said, thinly desperate, thinking, *God, no. Please no. Please not like last time, anything but.* "Any- thing you say . . . "

"That's right, son. That's dead right, that. Isn't it? But you be a good boy, do your work and keep your trap shut," reaching across to knuckle Jason's skull sharply, rattle his brains around, bang the message home; and no, this seat wasn't wide enough after all, to take him out of the reach of Vinny's arm, "don't go gabbing it around and maybe I'll give you a treat. Maybe I'll get you in at the next fight. Afterwards, too. You can stay after, maybe."

Jason didn't ask what came after. He didn't need to. He'd seen the underside of the dismantled boxing ring, and he thought he knew already.

TWENTY-FIVE

i

He lives now in a world of threat and counter-threat, not at all the Paradise he hoped for; but he won't be surprised about that. Nothing ever came easily, to God's chosen people. And he still has his vision, surely, he must still see his golden city like an inverted image of the streets he moves among. He's going to have to fight for it, that's all. He has to play David, and there's more than one Goliath out there.

But he's ready. He has his slingshot, and his ammunition; and better, he has good men and women at his back. He's not alone, like David was. This isn't single combat, for all that it may look like it sometimes.

Best of all, of course, he's got Nathan. His general, his strong right arm.

But though he can delegate the battles, he can't delegate the war, and probably wouldn't want to. He seems all warrior now, no healer, no recruiting-sergeant he. His faith will be a shield for his arm and a helm for his head; and his anger, his clean and pure anger will be a powerful weapon in his hand.

Walking up from the houses he sees Helen getting off a bus.

— Helen, he says, wait, are you going my way?

— I don't know, she says, not smiling as she used to smile at the touch of his voice, the gentle caress of his company. I don't know where you're going, she says, where are you going?

— To the gym, he says, taking the question at face value, or seeming to. Come and join us, he says. On the picket.

— Oh, she says. No, she says, I don't think so. Not today.

Nor any day is what she means. He must know that, but he lets it go. There'll be time for Helen later. She needs him to be a healer, not a warrior; and he's got a war to win.

— Walk with me, then, he says.

— For a bit, she says. I'm going home.

And again he seems to hear nothing more than the simplest message she might be giving him. He nods, smiles, asks her where she's been.

— The hospital, St Giles. I've been visiting Evelyn. Someone's got to do it. Haven't they?

— Yes, he says. Yes, of course. That's well thought of, Helen, very well. I'm glad.

And she should be smiling, she should be basking in the warmth of his praise and approval; but she isn't. She's sad and brooding and defensive, only repeating herself, saying, Someone's got to do it.

Then she says goodbye and leaves him, scuttles off down a side-street just twenty metres short of the gym, short of the picket-line and Nathan.

ii

For Terry Belderstone, the telephone was as good as a petrol bomb, or better. You could start anything with a telephone, if you knew who to call. Start a rumour, start a riot.

Start a war.

Special numbers, Terry carried in his head. Always had done since the early days, when he was just starting out. Jobbing builders walked a thin line on occasion. You needed friendly hands on both sides, just to keep you balanced; and that didn't change. Rich men needed friends too, and old friends were best.

He picked up his preferred phone, the secured line, and dialled. Face to face would be more secure still; but there were limits to Terry's time, and to his patience. He wouldn't be harried out of his normal routine, by Richard Gould or anyone. Besides, Gould probably didn't need bugs. He probably had his tame God standing by, ready to snatch Terry's conversation out of the air and toss it a mile or two over to Paradise; in which case face to face would be no better protection . . .

Terry scowled, and shook his head as his call was answered. No time for fantasies, this was serious business.

"John, it's Terry. Can we talk?" John's phone could be bugged, maybe, or his office could; but who'd bug a bailiff? Burn the place down, sure, that had happened a time or two. But bugs were subtle, they needed finesse and a little care to handle properly. No one was that subtle with bailiffs.

"Aye, go ahead."

"That place you took the eviction orders down for us, you remember?"

"Sure."

"Well, they're refusing to move. And I don't want to go any

322

further with the law, see, John. I've good reasons. But I still want them out. I want them pushed. As hard as you need to, don't hold back. Scare 'em out, smoke 'em out, whatever. But not from your office. Keep it non-attributable."

"I hear you. Money?"

"Usual account. Take what you need." Terry kept a lot of cash in a building society; John could always withdraw what he wanted, to pay for the quiet little jobs that any business finds itself faced with. Of course he creamed off a little for himself, but that was business too, and he wasn't greedy. If he ever did get greedy, he'd regret it. Terry had other friends.

"Right, then."

"Soon as you can, mate. They're costing me money." And prestige, and other things. Terry didn't mind competition, he liked a fight; but he didn't like uncertainty, and Richard Gould made him very uncertain.

"No limits, then?"

"None. Just don't leave any fingerprints."

"Come on, Terry. I won't even be there."

"Sure." John delegated, too. Terry didn't know who'd do the job, didn't care. They'd be efficient, that was all that mattered. That was why John got his business. "But check that they understand that, whoever you send. I don't want anyone picked up for this."

"Terry, man. Was anyone picked up for that last little number? We'll be careful."

"Do that. Oh, and listen, John," casually, just an afterthought, "I don't care how you shift 'em in the end, that's up to you; but one thing you could do for me," *only a little thing,* "and this might work it, should get them out if it's done right . . . "

iii

No job now, he couldn't work for George again.

No job, no girl, no future that he could see; and his mother dead, his father gone dull and silent, his young brothers living with Aunt Joyce so no family either, no life at home. Derry was surviving day to day, but that's all you could say about it. He wasn't living.

This morning he was out for a walk, slouching through the streets of Paradise. Not going anywhere in particular, but not quite wandering at random, either. There were places he didn't

323

want to go, places he didn't even want to think about; and his feet understood that and were keeping him well away, turning him in safe directions at the corners, holding him at neutral.

Or doing their best, at least. It was asking a lot, though, in these streets where all his life lay embedded, where all his dreams had been so suddenly and cruelly twisted into ruin. Probably it was asking too much, or else they weren't quite up to the job. In any case, he found himself eventually walking along by the cemetery railings. Not going in, of course, he wasn't that stupid, not suicidal; but he was there, and he had his eyesight still, misery hadn't made him blind. His memory too, he had that, despair couldn't make him forget.

So he looked through the railings and saw the mess of dead flowers and drying earth that marked his mother's grave, and the spot where he had last talked to Rachel.

He didn't linger, his feet had that much sense in them still, or else they were driven by shame at having brought him here. He had to make a conscious effort, though, to jerk his eyes away; and even then they found more to see in the cemetery, somewhere else to focus.

There were two figures standing in the shadow of a tree. One was jittery and nervous, constantly afidget; while the other stood calmly and dangerously still, his camouflage not even trying to hide the confidence in him, or the power he held. Derry didn't need to see their faces to know that one was Jason, and Nathan was the other.

Derry couldn't imagine what those two would be talking about, and didn't want to try. Something unpleasant, for sure, something sinister – it would have to be, to make Nathan lurk in the shadows that way. To make him talk to Jason at all.

Whatever, it was well out of Derry's shrinking world. Leave it, he wasn't even going to wonder.

Nor wander, any further. Enough was enough; and Dad would be sitting at home waiting for his lunch, getting hungry and doing nothing about it. That much at least Derry could do, he could see his father fed.

He let himself into the flat and found a parcel, unexpectedly on the living-room table.

"That came," his dad said from the sofa, waving an unfocused hand. "It's for you."

It wasn't a parcel, really, it was a padded envelope, fat and soft

324

and yielding to his hands; and it had come from France, airmail and special delivery, must have cost pounds and pounds to send.

He held it tremblingly, and was too scared to open it until his father said, "Anything to eat, then, lad?"

"Yeah. Yeah, sure. Bangers. Just, just wait a minute, till I open this . . . "

He slid his finger under the sellotape and peeled it away carefully, not to tear even the envelope; worked the end open, and slipped his hand inside.

And didn't believe what he was feeling until he pulled it out and saw it in the light; and still didn't believe it, till he read the note that came with it:

Hair today, gone tomorrow (giggle, giggle). It's too hot to wear all this, so I thought we might as well match. Hang it on your wall, like a trophy.

Love,

Scalped Squaw.

PS. Airport, Saturday week, half eleven. Be there, or be in big, BIG trouble. R.

And his father had to wait a while longer for his lunch, while Derry stood with his shaven head bowed, like a young monk praying; while his hands clutched and his fingers embedded themselves in the long dark pigtail that had once been Rachel's hair.

But he didn't hang it on his wall, no, not even above his bed. He coiled it up and hid it beneath his pillow instead, like a purely private trophy, not for sharing.

TWENTY-SIX

i

Others judge him, yes, and blame him too. He can't have expected to make so many enemies, this side of the lines.

Never mind the malcontents, the rumourmongers, the Alan Parkinsons and Jean Dolances. Their cold and loveless creed has no place in his church. Let them split off and splinter away, and good riddance.

No, what must grieve him more is to see the old men eyeing him askance, his uncle among them. They miss their chapel, they're distressed by Grace's death and distrustful of change. They're too old for this, war is a young man's country; and that knowledge only makes them the more resentful. So they murmur among themselves and say that things have gone too far, that Richard's overreached himself and hence this retribution. It's the work of evil men, they say; but Richard brought it down, and God allowed it. It's a judgement, is what they're saying.

Which must hurt him deeply, to see their faith in him fading and twisting into doubt. But he still has his Commando, tight and true. There he can trust absolutely, and does.

And he still has the attention of this city, large congregations and the media's eye; and above all, of course, he still has his own faith, his guiding light. That's one certainty in a shifting world. He still has his God; and there's a judgement he can trust, there's Someone who won't doubt or listen to rumour or hesitate when the going gets rough. God will still be seeing him clear, God knows him through and through – and with that sight and in that knowledge, God set him here with a job to do.

And surely that's enough, who could challenge that?

ii

Jason had never seen the gym look like this before.

Nothing magical about the transformation, mind. He'd done it himself, mostly, with a lot of sweat, a bit of help from George, the occasional kick from Vinny – and that helped more, that really got him going. Jason could do anything with Vinny's smile to encourage him, Vinny's boot to urge him along.

All the machines, all the weights were stacked tight against one wall now; and in the centre of the cleared space was the boxing ring, roped up and ready.

And all around the ring was a crowd of men, packed elbow to elbow and more coming in every minute. They were smoking and swigging from cans, talking loudly, laughing and coughing and spitting on the floor; and they were what made the real difference, more than all of Jason's sweat. It wasn't a gym any longer, with this lot here. It was an arena.

"Good evening, gentlemen." George's voice boomed across the gym, crushing conversation rather than cutting through it. "Welcome to the Paradise Gym, and some top boxing entertainment. There'll be half a dozen bouts for you tonight, climaxing of course with our own local champion, Vinny Armstrong, versus a challenger from Lossiemouth, Kevin Campbell."

Cheers and catcalls, and some wit shouting, "Send 'im back to Flossiemouth, Vinny! On a stretcher!"

Jason giggled.

"Thank you, gentlemen, thank you. You'll be seeing Vinny later. In the meantime, we've some younger talent to entertain you with, including a couple of lads making their professional débuts. All fights to be fifteen rounds, of two minutes each; referee to judge, if they go the distance. And now, let me introduce you to your referee tonight, Mr Calvin Chase . . . "

George had dug up a thin, tired-looking man to act as timekeeper. His name was Norman, his clothes must have come from Oxfam and he had a quarter-bottle of gin in his pocket, that he took nips from when he thought no one was looking.

Jason was dogsbody, keeping the corners supplied with water-bottles and towels, running errands for the trainers. He had a chair next to Norman, though, and he did get to sit down sometimes; so he noticed the gin, and Norman's habit of watching the fight rather than the clock. Many of the rounds were lasting more than two minutes. Once Jason nudged his shoulder, and muttered, "Time, mate," to remind him; but Norman just scowled at him, "Piss off, kid," and let the boxers exchange another flurry of punches before he rang the bell.

They were crude bouts, those opening fights, with no science about them and not a lot of talent, clumsy blows clumsily

327

countered. For the audience it seemed to be only the outcome that mattered, to settle the many private bets being laid around the gym.

Things were different, when Vinny stepped into the ring. The constant babble of comment and wagers died to a whisper, and even that was shushed into silence. People came in from the toilets and from private conversations, private deals being finalised outside; the only movement was a slow press of bodies inward, as those at the back strained for a better view.

Vinny was wearing an old faded singlet and long shorts, and didn't look at all like a boxer. Concrete-hard he looked, all scars and tattoos and muscles like cables under his skin, thin and tough. Dangerous, too, he looked deadly dangerous; just not at all like a boxer.

His opponent Campbell was maybe ten years younger and maybe two stone heavier, and none of that was fat. Now he did look like a boxer. He even had the moves right, ducking and weaving and sparring at shadows while Vinny just stood in his corner, rubbing his gloves together and smiling, smiling.

George was in the ring talking to the referee, Campbell's manager was in there too with a couple of hangers-on, someone else had sneaked in with a camcorder to get the preliminaries on tape; it was starting to look quite crowded, when the ref called the two fighters to the middle.

Vinny walked over, stared and smiled, made a vague gesture towards touching his glove to Campbell's. Campbell jigged and bounced, muttered something inaudible – and head-butted Vinny in the teeth.

Howls of protest from the crowd, a milling confusion of bodies in the ring: Jason saw Campbell being restrained, being hauled back to his corner while Vinny leant against the ropes, reached a glove up to his mouth and brought it away smeared with blood, spat a tooth onto the floor. George was talking to him urgently, but he didn't seem to be listening. Then the referee was leaning over the ropes snapping his fingers, and Jason had work to do, handing up towels and a bucket of water.

That was when the police chose to walk in.

There were only a couple of them, one sergeant and a constable against a couple of hundred fight fans; but they came dressed in their authority and they brought silence with them, spreading it across the restless and resentful crowd as they squeezed their way through to the ring.

Nothing cowed or submissive about that silence, though. It was wary but hostile, that calm-before-the-storm that's so very badly misnamed, that isn't calm at all, is tight and stretched and ready to snap. The police obviously sensed that; they looked uncomfortable in their uniforms, made little gestures to keep this all low-key, *let's not get excited, just a few questions, nothing to get worked up about . . .*

When they reached the ringside George was ready, was waiting for them: looming massively above their heads, his arms stretched out along the ropes to make a closed door of his wide body, to keep them down there on the floor.

But his voice was polite, incongruous, almost ingratiating: "Yes, gentlemen, how can I help?"

"A word in your ear, Mr Jenner. If you wouldn't mind."

George bent obligingly six inches lower across the ropes.

The sergeant sighed, exchanged a glance like a shrug with his companion and said, "We weren't notified, you see, Mr Jenner. Didn't know this meeting was happening."

"Is that right? I'm sorry, sergeant. I'll have words with my secretary. You certainly should have been informed. Caused any problems, has it? Traffic, parking, like that?"

"Nothing to worry about, no. I'd like to see your licence, though. If you don't mind."

"Licence?"

"From the Boxing Board of Control, George." It was a sudden shift, from Mr Jenner to George; and George reacted as suddenly, stepping through the ropes and jumping lightly down.

"Yes, there's a problem there, sergeant; it hasn't come, you see. I've been on the phone to them this afternoon, they say it's definitely been sent out, everything's in order, it's just the post office messing things up again . . . "

He was lying through his teeth, of course. Jason knew it, the listening crowd knew it, the police undoubtedly knew it. But his voice was calm and persuasive, his big hand was friendly on the sergeant's shoulder, and there was nothing at all friendly about the watching, waiting men around them. The police did what was only sensible, backed off and walked away; asked George to bring the licence in when it arrived, said they'd be double-checking with the Board in the morning, left all the decisions to their superiors. And there'd be no prosecution even when George failed to show, when the Board denied all knowledge. George would get a visit, perhaps, he'd pay a hefty bribe in preference to a fine, and that would be that, everyone happy. No further action. Jason turned his eyes back to the ring.

And saw what no one else was seeing, because they were all still watching the police being escorted out in George's shadow: saw Vinny smile, blood on his teeth, and saw him slam a rabbit-punch hard into the back of Campbell's neck.

Campbell didn't make a sound, he just slumped forward to hang across the ropes like washing on a line. Then people noticed, then people swarmed around the fallen man; his manager screamed at the referee and his mates yelled threats at Vinny, making gestures but not going near, not braving the threat of that bloody smile.

And Jason was busy handing up towels again, handing up water while the crowd grew restive, starting a slow hand-clap and chanting for the fight.

Jason thought they'd had it already, and he knew who'd won.

Soon, though – too soon for Campbell by the look of him, swaying on his feet, water dripping from his hair and his eyes unfocused – they were clearing the ring and the referee was beckoning the two fighters to try again with the handshake. Honours even, perhaps he was thinking, wipe the slate clean and start from scratch.

This time it was Vinny got in first with the head-butt, brow to brow, sending Campbell reeling back to the ropes. The referee tried to intervene as Vinny followed, tried to haul him off; but Norman the timekeeper muttered, "Fed up with this, let him do it," and struck the bell to start the round.

The referee stepped back with a shrug, *get on with it, then*; and Vinny got on with it. One punch, viciously low in the gut; and as Campbell doubled over, Vinny grabbed his head and drove a knee hard into his face. Jason heard the crunch of crushed cartilage even above the crowd's noise, as Campbell's nose was pulped.

A couple of hard punches on the back of the head, and Campbell was down; and he might be finished already, but Vinny wasn't.

"Bad move, that," Norman wheezed, laughing, as Vinny's boot smashed into the fallen man's kidneys. "Head-butting Vinny, knew that was a bad move ... "

Worst move Campbell ever made, by the look of it: by the look of him just lying there, his body juddering and jerking at Vinny's feet. The ref went through the formalities, counted Campbell out and raised Vinny's arm in triumph; and all through it Vinny just went on kicking, until there were so many people swarming into the ring he didn't have room to swing. Even that didn't stop him stamping one last time on Campbell's head before he turned away.

It took them a while, it took frighteningly long to get Campbell on his feet and out of the ring; but they managed it at last, just when Jason was starting to think they needed a stretcher in here and an ambulance outside. Or maybe even a hearse.

Could've looked worse than it was, though. Jason had been on the toe-end of Vinny's kicking a time or two himself, one time for real; and he was still walking around. This had been harder and heavier, but then Campbell was a bigger man. He'd survive.

Half an hour later Jason was busy again, feeling important, feeling flattered that they let him stay even though he had to work for the privilege.

Take the ropes off the ring, George said, coil them up neatly, put them out of the way. Unscrew the corner-posts, and don't lose the screws. Take the canvas off the floor, and fold it up.

Jason did all of that, while the crowd thinned around him, the uninvited going home, poor suckers, never to know what they were missing. Then, with the ring reduced to a sturdy wooden stage, George and Vinny and half a dozen others took hold of one side, and lifted it; stood the whole thing on end and turned it over so that it wasn't a stage any more, it was a pit with a rim chest-high. Jason looked down into it, looked at all the stains and gouges that disfigured the wood, and grinned contentedly.

Already he could hear dogs snarling and barking, right here in the gym; and he was here too, he was admitted, was trusted, was a part of it.

Felt great.

*   *   *

On the rough ground opposite the gym, two figures were sitting on a mound of earth: sitting quiet and still and wearing black, not in uniform tonight.

One was murmuring into a handset, saying, "There's another dog going in now. The men come out to get them, then they knock to get back in. Two or three people on the door, inside."

The handset hissed and crackled, and spoke. "Stand by. Report any change. Keep out of trouble. God bless."

*   *   *

331

His troops, his spies might not be in uniform, but Nathan was; and so was his audience, a chief inspector and a superintendent, the senior policemen in Paradise.

"Put it this way," Nathan was saying. "We've got unlicensed boxing, for a start, and unlicensed gambling to go with it; and your men have been inside, they've seen what's going on and they've come straight out again. It's not very impressive, is it, Superintendent? Particularly in view of what's happening there now. It's not going to look good in the papers. We've got photographs too, papers love photos. Especially these, night-sights on the camera, dead sinister stuff. We've got your men going in and coming out again, nice and chummy with George; and what we're getting now, we're getting the dogs. Those dogs are going to be front page of the *Chronicle* tomorrow. It's just a question of what's the story they print with the pictures: whether we're talking 'Police Swoop' or 'Police Do Nothing'."

"Are you *threatening* me, Mr Lewis?" Superintendent Malone enquired, quite mildly.

"No, not at all. Simply stating facts. We will be giving the story to the press; and you are a part of the story, we've involved you from the start. The outcome is very much in your hands, that's more or less all I'm saying."

"More or less?"

"Yes. One other thing I'm saying, that we don't like this sort of thing happening on our patch. You're supposed to police this community; and God knows, we don't want the job. As long as you're doing it, we'll work with you, that's what the Commando's for. But you quit, you stand back, you close your eyes and you won't know what's hit you. We'll take over on the streets for a start, we'll take care of Mr Jenner and all his kind; but that will only be a start. Because then we'll be moving on to you, Superintendent. We've got the media in our back pockets, don't forget, we can have the whole country looking in on Paradise. If we don't like the way you do your job, you could lose it very, very quickly, Mr Malone. And yes, you want to think of that as a threat, go right ahead. Why not?"

And he turned and marched out of there, back straight and boot-heels clicking, very much the soldier on the very eve of battle.

*   *   *

Vinny's brindled pit bull was in the pit tonight, with a white bull mastiff. That wasn't a good move, either. Whoever owned the mastiff should've learned from the earlier fight, should've known not to go up against Vinny. Jason only saw the dogs at it for a few seconds before he was jostled and shoved to the back by eager punters, but already the mastiff had been brindled itself, with its own blood.

This far back, Jason couldn't see a thing; so he went to the wall where the machines were stacked, and clambered up onto a shoulder-press. From there he could look over the heads of the crowding men, and down into the pit. He could see the dogs rolling and tumbling, slamming against the wooden sides, bruising themselves on the corner braces; and he could see how the mastiff's jaws snapped and slid across the pit bull's skull where its ears should've been, leaving just a runnel of blood.

Vinny's dog was smarter, or else it was tougher, perhaps, or better trained. Or maybe a pit bull would always have the edge over a mastiff, or Vinny's dogs over anyone else's. Whatever. Jason saw it catch the mastiff's shoulder, and he heard the bone crack and the white dog scream; and while it was still screaming the pit bull shifted its grip unexpectedly, shoulder to throat.

And then it just hung on, as pit bulls do: dug its teeth in and locked its jaws, spread its legs for purchase and never mind how much its victim struggled.

And never mind the spray of hot blood in its face suddenly, the taste and the stink of it and the howling mob bent over the walls of the pit above its head. The dog hung on, its jaws clenched ever tighter, biting through thick fur, crushing flesh and windpipe; and then it tossed and jerked its head from side to side, tugged and tore without ever loosening its grip until it had ripped the mastiff's throat wide open.

Jason saw it all, from his vantage point. He clung tight with sweat-slicked hands and screamed as the men below were screaming, as the dog screamed in the pit, as long as breath was there for screaming with.

And when it was over, when the mastiff lay slack and red and wet on the wooden floor, moving only when the pit bull dragged at it, the men all turned away laughing and shaking their heads, settling their bets. Even the mastiff's owner only shrugged and turned his back, no interest now, only a mess for someone else to clear up.

It was Vinny who hoisted himself over the wall of the pit, once he'd collected all his winnings. His dog was still worrying at its fallen opponent, licking the blood at its neck; and when Vinny whistled, he got only a growl in response.

Which was another bad move, even pit bulls make mistakes. Vinny kicked it, hard; watched it back suddenly into a corner, saw its haunches tense to spring and kicked it again, quite unconcerned.

And the dog yelped and shivered, and stood still for Vinny to muzzle, to collar and chain it and lift it out slung across his shoulder, blood-spattered as it was.

Then Vinny looked up, looked straight at Jason and whistled again.

No fool, Jason, no bad moves for him tonight. He came when he was called, when he was whistled for: came slithering down from his high point, came dodging through the milling men to see what Vinny wanted.

"Get that cleaned up," Vinny said, a jerk of his head to indicate the pit. "Sharp now, they'll be ready for the next soon."

"What shall I, what shall I do with, you know . . . "

"Stick it in a sack, bring it out. Just don't get blood on the floor, or George'll have your guts."

George had his guts already, Jason thought, unless he'd sold them on to Vinny. Seemed like that, sometimes. But he fetched a black plastic rubbish-bag and clambered obediently into the pit.

Raw meat, that's all, he thought, giggling at the way the mastiff's head was half-severed from its body, the way it flopped around as he pulled the sack over its hindquarters, the way it leaked a little more blood from the raw wound of its throat.

But its eyes stared at him, dead or not; the smell made him queasy and its legs wouldn't cooperate, they didn't want to be bagged up and chucked away. Jason wasn't giggling by the time he finally got the top of the bag bunched up and tied in a knot; no, he was down on his knees in the blood, his jeans were wet and sticking to him, he was sweating and gagging and halfway to throwing up right there in the pit.

"Come on, Jase, step on it," Vinny said, leering at him over the side, making obscene gestures with a mop.

"Yeah. Yeah, okay, Vinny, I'm coming . . . "

The sack was slippery now and its contents heavy; Jason had to dig his fingers right through the plastic and into still-warm fur to keep a grip on it, to save leaving smudges of blood on George's floors.

Vinny had parked some way down the hill from the gym tonight. He took Jason down to the van and put his dog in the back, clipping its chain to a welded bracket; then he nodded at the dark wasteland stretching away from the road.

"Come on."

This was hard going for Jason, with the sack of dead dog getting heavier by the minute and his grip slipping again. Twice he nearly dropped it, once he actually did; but Vinny didn't wait, he just kept on walking, so that Jason had to run stumbling after to catch up.

Finally Vinny stopped, on the edge of a sudden pool of water. There was some broken wire that used to fence it off, a fallen sign warning of danger; and Vinny gestured, said, "Stick a couple of rocks in the sack and chuck it in, Jase. It'll have company down there."

From the stink that rose up after the splash, Jason believed him.

Then it was back up towards the gym, Jason wondering how many more times he'd have to do this tonight, how late they'd keep him afterwards with all the cleaning up: how he'd explain the state of himself when he finally got back to the hostel, all blood and stinking. Wondered if it was worth it, and shied quickly away from answering that one, because the answer was obvious but so were the alternatives. Jason knew boys who'd got across George; he'd seen tonight what could happen if you got across Vinny.

No bad moves. Not tonight, not ever.

So he made a good move instead, one of the few: he lifted his eyes before they reached the gym, and stopped dead. Stared up the hill at what was white and quiet, coming down; then jumped forward to snatch at Vinny's arm, to stammer, "Vinny, look . . . "

Vinny cuffed him off, then looked where he was pointing.

"Raid," he said, as the police van coasted to the gym door with its lights and engine off, with half a dozen cars following like infantry after a tank. "Come on."

"Where?"

"The van, Jase. Don't be stupid."

"But, but, we've got to tell George, warn him . . . "

"How are you going to do that, then?" Vinny was smiling dreamily, sounded as if he really wanted an answer.

"We could, we could go in the back . . . "

"They know there's a back way, there'll be more of them out there. It's too late for George now. George is going to get busted. And this is George's place, right? He's going down, hard. Forget George. You stick with me, Jase."

And a hand tight on his elbow, just to make sure that Jason did.

335

They stayed where they were long enough to see a policeman smash his way in with a sledgehammer, with a dozen men at his heels. Then, as the noise of the raid rose behind them, dogs barking and many voices yelling, they went back to the van.

Jason was thinking of getaways, even now. *Vinny, I got to go, I got to get back to the hostel, I'm late already, they'll breach me . . .* He didn't know if that would count as a bad move or not, the mood Vinny was in; and never got a chance to find out either way, because someone met them at the van, rising from the shadows on the wasteland.

Someone with an iron bar in his hands.

"You." Campbell's voice was slurred by more than his accent and his hatred. "You, you shitfuck. You're dead, you . . . "

Jason still thought the man should be in hospital, the way he sounded, the way he lurched onto the ill-lit pavement. And he'd have to be sick in his head, to come after Vinny in that state. Wasn't once enough?

Jason looked around for help, but couldn't see anyone. Campbell must've slipped his minders somehow, and come back on his own.

Well, he was going to be sorry. Too late to help him now.

Campbell swung the bar roundly at Vinny's head, but Vinny just ducked under it and kicked his knee as he twisted.

He staggered, swore, flailed again. This time Vinny stepped back to let the bar whistle past his face, then came forward, fast. A butt to the head had Campbell reeling; a knee in the groin finished him, had him down and retching.

But Vinny still wasn't finished. Vinny didn't stop, that was Campbell's lesson for tonight. Vinny had to be interrupted, or he just kept going and going.

Right now he was going with the iron bar, on Campbell's ribs and spine and kidneys while the man grunted and swayed on all fours like an animal; and then, even as Jason screamed to stop him, on the back of Campbell's head.

Jason heard the cracking, splintering noise that made, saw the dent that it left, the deep depression in Campbell's skull as he dropped like a rock, face down on the pavement.

*   *   *

Nathan was keeping his troops well back out of the way, by

order: they stood in a huddle on the rough ground opposite the gym, listening to the sounds of the raid, frustrated and critical.

A sudden scream from further down the hill had them all turning as one, all staring. Nathan saw two figures standing, a man and a boy, it looked like, and a third flat out on the ground.

At last something to do, something to prove themselves more than informers. Nathan snapped his fingers, took his men with him as he ran.

They were heard coming, a little too soon; he saw their heads jerk up, saw that the boy was Jason. Smiled to himself, even as he shouted. "You two, don't move! Stay right there!"

And the man smiled too, which was odd; Nathan could see that quite clearly, though he couldn't see anything much else about the guy. Just a crewcut head, and a smile.

And then the man went round the back of a parked van and opened the doors. Nathan only ran faster, until he saw what came out of the van, what came hurtling up the hill towards him.

Then Nathan screamed.

*   *   *

Jason was close to total paralysis by now, as it sank in that maybe he'd just seen murder done, he was maybe the only witness.

Vinny dragged him stumbling to the van, shoved him in the back, tossed the iron bar in after, slammed the doors. Jason only wanted to hide, to be any place but here; but closing his eyes and wishing didn't help. A sudden jerk sent him sliding, so that his eyes opened as his hands grabbed for support. He saw the world again, caught in Vinny's headlights through the windscreen of the van; clung to a handhold and watched it like television.

He saw four or five young men in a loose group and all of them moving, dodging and ducking and dragging each other free as the dog snarled and twisted in the centre of their circle, snapped and leapt and dodged their flying boots in its turn.

Another of them was hanging back, pressed against a streetlight, not moving an inch; and Jason recognised Nathan's pale face, just as the van's engine roared.

As it headed straight for that dogfight, accelerating hard.

*   *   *

From where he was standing Nathan could see the van quite clearly, see it coming, see that there wasn't room for it to pass on the narrow road with his lads jumping around the way they were. But he couldn't so much as cry a warning, couldn't have opened his jaw that wide. All he could do was slit his eyes against the headlights' glare, stand with his back jammed hard against the strength of steel – all that was keeping him upright, almost, that streetlight and the stiffness of terror in his legs – and wait. He was safe here, at least.

Safe from the van, at least . . .

Time stretched, as time can; and stretched just far enough for his troops to see their danger. Their shouting shrilled into panic, and there were sudden shadows breaking the light, tumbling through. Then a soft thud, audible even above the racing engine; and then the van was past, was gone and off and away.

No peace even in its absence, though, no silence. Rather a thin voice of pain, breathing hard and sobbing.

"Christ bless us, who's hurt?" A voice, from Nathan's left; and a sudden rush of denials, "Not me", "I'm all right", "Okay over here . . . "

And Nathan could move now, because it was clear to him even before he saw; he pushed away from that good, that useful light, walked unsteadily to the middle of the road and looked down at the pooling blood, the twitching body. "It's the dog," he said, his voice still shaking as his hands and his mind were shaking, "it's just the dog, that's all. He hit his own fucking dog . . . "

And there was a touch of silence there, Nathan could feel it, just a hesitation before habit took them over, before they grouped very much around him, looked to him, said, "What do we do now, Nat?"

"See which way that van went," Nathan said, busking it, making it up as he went along. "Anyone get the number?"

Silence. Of course they hadn't got the number, if he hadn't.

"Okay, never mind. Maybe the police did, he'll have gone straight past them. Someone go tell them what's happened; and tell them we need an ambulance," with a glance back at the prone body on the pavement.

"And a vet," another voice interrupted, "they've got someone with them, I think, for the dogs. He'd better come and see to this one."

Nathan wanted to say no to that; he wanted to say, *No, leave that to me, I'll do that. With a length of wood, a bottle, half a brick, anything that's handy.*

But he didn't, of course. Instead he said, "Anyone see their faces, know who they were?"

338

Silence again, only one voice pointing out, "Not if you didn't, Nat, you were in the lead there, you saw them best."

Which was true, of course; and he almost smiled as he shook his head, as he said, "Barely got a glance. Couldn't even give a description, really."

TWENTY-SEVEN

i

He hasn't slept at all this night just gone, nor will there be much chance even to catnap in the day to come; but that doesn't matter. He won't be feeling tired, not any more. Nor shaken, nor angry. The peace of the dawn, an hour of solitary prayer under God's clear sky: it's more than a recharge, you can tell just by looking. He's been washed through and through by the first light of the day, and that's all he needs to set him up.

So he rises from his knees, brushes soil and grit from his jeans and walks away from the river, back over the waste ground to the houses; where Nathan meets him, his uniform fresh and his hair wet from a hasty shower. Nathan hasn't slept either.

This is a catch-up session, a mutual briefing. Nathan's spent much of the night with the police, making statements, supporting his men, asking questions on his own account; while Richard's been at the hospital.

— They wouldn't let me in to see the man Campbell, Richard says, he's in a coma, he's in intensive care and no one's getting in. But they've given us a room, he says, it's practically a broom cupboard but it's very close to the unit.

— I don't see the use of that, Nathan says, what's the point?

— Prayer's the point, of course. Prayer is always the point. I want a team in there twenty-four hours a day. We can pray anywhere, and we must; but this room can be a focal point, a powerhouse of prayer.

— You mean you're going to shout at God until he listens, Nathan says, grinning; and Richard grins back.

— That's about the size of it, he says.

— Better if they'd let you in, Nathan says, you could lay hands on him and give us all another miracle.

But Richard's shaking his head already, even before Nathan gets to that last word.

— Answered prayer is always a miracle, he says, but sometimes it's better not to ask God to shout back. We'll just pray, he says, and let God work through the doctors' hands.

— Okay, I'll organise some shifts. We'll have that room buzzing.

— Good lad. Now, what's your news?

340

And Nathan smiles just a little, as he gives it.

– George is in real trouble, he says, what with Campbell, and the press coming when we whistled. Without that, they'd have fined a few people and forgotten about it, even with us on their backs; but now they're really throwing the book at him.

– There's no suggestion that he was involved in the attack on Campbell, surely?

– None at all, but that's not going to save him. If you ask me George'll be very, very lucky if he keeps himself out of prison. Either way, the gym's finished.

Richard nods. Then,

– The police haven't identified those people you saw?

– Well, if they have, they haven't said; but I don't think so. One lad, one older man: it's not much to go on, is it? And the men from the dogfight won't say a word . . .

ii

Back at the airport again, the third time this summer; back on the roof, watching the planes and praying to a God he didn't believe in, that this time wouldn't be like the last.

He was an hour early, and her flight was dead on time; Derry watched it all the way to earth, restless with nerves. He'd heard somewhere that most accidents happened at take-off or landing.

But when it was down safe, when it had taxied up to the terminal and finally come to a halt, he was still jittering, still tight as a wire; and that had nothing to do with statistics. He waited till the doors were open, the stairs were in place – and then he couldn't do it, couldn't wait any longer. Didn't want to see her at this distance, from this angle. Too much like last time, when he'd almost wanted to jump . . .

So he turned and ran inside, ran down all the stairs to the arrivals gate; and he waited there instead, with a crowd of others.

It took longer than he'd thought, there was time enough to fret himself sick, near enough. But at last people started coming through, strangers with trolleys or burdened with bags; and at last, at long long last one of the trolleys wasn't being wheeled by a stranger. Rachel's dad, no problem spotting him; and her mum beside him, easy, he'd know her anywhere.

The girl with them wasn't Rachel, though. He thought they'd fetched the wrong girl home, except that she was waving wildly, trying to pretend she wasn't a stranger at all.

341

And now she was through the last barrier, past the last uniform and hurrying, running up to him, this dark skinny beauty with the shaven head. She grabbed his hands and stared at him, her eyes narrowed and intense, no way for a stranger to behave. So okay, she was Rachel really, of course she was; and still very much the same underneath, under the suntan and the soft velvet stubble. Still supercharged, unexpected, scary.

"How've you been?" she demanded, solemn and direct, *don't lie to me, don't try to fob me off.*

Derry shrugged. "Not too hot," he said; but then, not lying at all, "Better now," he said that too.

That earned him an extra squeeze of the hands, hard enough to hurt, almost; and she smiled for the first time, briefly, before giving him a black scowl.

"You've grown," she said accusingly. "That's cheating, when I'm not here."

"Not in two weeks, I haven't."

"You have. Look, you're taller than me," and she proved it, having to go up on her toes to press her nose against his. "I'm not having this, Derry Bowen, I'm not cricking my neck for you. You get something done about it, have your spine shortened. Do some more running, wear those legs away a bit . . . "

She was kicking his shins as she said it, and that really was hard enough to hurt. He shoved her away; then grabbed her, all nervousness forgotten, and held her too close to kick, muttering threats into her ear. She snorted, relaxed against him, turned her face up for a kiss and never mind any crick in her neck.

After a minute she wriggled free again, too soon.

"How long have you got off work, just the morning, is it?"

He shook his head. "I quit. Tell you later," as she started to frown, "I don't want to talk about it now."

"What do you want to talk about, then?"

"Anything. What was France like?"

"Hot. French. Little bit lonely," and she wrinkled her nose at him as he grinned, came right back at him, dead nasty. "You were here when we went, weren't you? Up on the roof. I saw you."

"Yeah. I was here." He'd seen her too, long-haired and distant and lost to him forever.

"Why didn't you wave?"

Because I thought you wouldn't wave back. But he chickened out, cheated, said, "Why didn't you?" Looked over her shoulder before she could reply and said, "Your parents are waiting."

"Well, go talk to them, then. Say hullo."

"What, me?"

"Yes," she said, laughing at him, "you. Big brave Derry Bowen. Go on, make me proud. And ask them to look after my stuff, tell them I'm not coming back yet."

And she turned him round, put her hands on his shoulders and gave him a firm push, didn't give him any choice at all. So he walked the ten or twelve difficult metres to where her parents waited, met the adult amusement of their smiles and said, "Um . . . "

"Come to take her away, have you, Derry?" Mr Grant said, amazingly making it easy for him.

"Uh, yeah. If that's okay, I mean . . . "

"That's fine, we're sick to death of her. Just have her home in reasonable time, please. Ten o'clock, say. All right?"

"Yeah, sure. Ten, right."

"Good. Here, you'd better take this," fishing his wallet out and handing Derry a wad of folded notes, "she'll need feeding sometime today. Eats like a horse."

A friendly nod and he was off, wheeling the luggage-trolley away with his wife just a wink and a smile behind him: leaving Derry standing rock-still in the bustling crowd till Rachel came, slipped her arm through his, tugged him back to earth.

"He was nice," Derry said, wondering.

"Well, he is. Can be," a late correction, with a giggle attached.

"Yeah, but look, he even gave me money to take you out . . . "

"Terrific. How much, and where are we going?"

"Dunno, I haven't . . . " He looked at the notes in his hand, and scowled. "Shit, this stuff's no use, it's all French. What am I supposed to do with that?"

Next thing he knew she was sighing, banging her head against his shoulder; then she tugged him round, pointed him towards a *bureau de change* and propelled him forward with both hands on the small of his back.

iii

It was Arthur's birthday, though there was nobody to remember that, no one who knew; and if he wasn't actually a year older than yesterday, that wasn't going to stop him feeling it.

He oughtn't to grumble, he knew that. Stumping around Paradise and seeing so many of those combat jackets, so many young faces with their bright smiles and their burning faith: he ought to be praising God, not scowling resentfully and feeling displaced. He'd had his time and his task, done it to the best of his ability. Now seemingly it was time to step aside.

It was hard, though. Too hard, maybe; at least, he hadn't done it yet. He was still here. Hanging around the marquee today, alternately patronised and ignored as he tried to understand what was happening.

The talk was all of the old Methodist chapel, the Paradise Gym it was now. There'd been a police raid there last night, Arthur had heard about it on the radio this morning; and the kids were saying now was the time to strike, now they could force the owner to sell up and hand the place over.

Arthur didn't like that. He hadn't liked any part of this campaign of Nathan's. Buying the building back for God was a noble notion, if it had been on the market and God's will; but the one it wasn't, and the other was surely doubtful.

All Arthur wanted to do was rebuild the old chapel, on the old site: now, quickly, before winter and while they had the manpower. They could do that easily. The youngsters had picked up the skills they'd need, working down on the houses; and the elders had done it all before, they had the experience.

But no one was listening to Arthur any more. It was all Richard now; and Richard said no, Richard said wait, the Lord will provide, Richard said.

And maybe he was right, maybe they would get the gym; but Arthur didn't want it, wouldn't take it as a gift. When Richard and his glow were gone, the dull realities of bricks and mortar would remain. Rising damp and falling slates, and worse – and they might have money now, but for how long? And at what cost?

No, Arthur wasn't happy; but no longer a power in the land, he was learning to keep his tongue still, not to speak his mind. He resented the tolerance of these young people, as much as their arrogance; they would always make time to listen, and they would never ever agree.

But Richard came in just then, and Arthur was still susceptible to magic. He still smiled merely at the sight of that young man, even if the smile had a little wryness to it these days; he still sat a little straighter in his chair, and tried to look less like a man totally overtaken by events.

"Arthur." Richard paused, of course, always happy to acknowledge the former régime; even to ask advice, though he seldom took it. "How are you?"

"Concerned."

344

"I know. We're riding the whirlwind here, Arthur, and I think we're all concerned. But we've the Lord at our back, and it's He who's using the spurs. All we can do is trust, and pray."

Easy enough for Richard, trust came as natural as breathing to a man like him. To Arthur, not. He had to work at it. Oh, he trusted God, right enough, but precious few men.

He was going to say so, no holding back; but there was a sudden yell shrill enough to hurt even in the dead air of the marquee, and Richard staggered a pace as a figure with cropped hair leapt on him from behind, twined legs around his waist and both arms round his neck.

"Guess who? No peeking . . . "

"Rachel," he said instantly. And then, twisting his head round to meet her eye to eye, "No, I'm wrong. It's a monkey. Hullo, monkey."

"Watch it, you, or I'll ride you all day long." But she jumped down and hugged him normally, said, "How's business, then?"

"Booming. You should be in uniform, we could use your help."

"Not me, I've gone AWOL till Monday." And her eyes moved to the marquee's entrance, where another shaven-headed figure lurked, hands in pockets, shifting his weight from foot to foot; and even Arthur smiled, and Richard laughed out loud.

"I see. How are the hormones?"

"Buzzing, thanks."

"That's good. You get back to him, then. And Rachel," as she turned, a final thought to take with her, "you just enjoy yourself, I don't want to lay anything heavy on you; but I don't think you're AWOL at all, I think that counts as detached duty."

She paused, thought about it, shook her head. "Can't be. It's too much fun, when it isn't just muddle. I'll be at service tomorrow, and I'm bringing the parents, so dig up a good sermon. Nice to see you, Mr Brougham. 'Bye now."

She ran then, out and away, snatching Derry's hand and tugging him off into the bright day, where Arthur's eyes couldn't follow. The light was grey here in the marquee, except where Richard walked; in here he could see all too clearly, and mostly what he saw was uniforms, mostly what he heard was calls to war.

iv

Released at last – or free to go, at least: not the same thing, not the same thing at all – George found himself waited for, hailed even before he got out of the police station.

"Mr Jenner!" A voice from behind him, a voice with a smile in it, amused by its own good manners, perhaps. Young man's voice, and George had had it up to here with polite young men. He didn't stop, didn't even turn to look.

But, "George, wait up," the voice said in high delight, "you don't want to go out there, all those cameras, all those questions. Haven't you had enough questions?"

And yes he had, of course he had, too many. So he stopped, and turned; and saw the uniform first, his eyes bleary and slow after a night of no sleep and a day's hard schooling. Saw the combat jacket and trousers, army boots and forage cap.

And then the face beneath the cap: Nathan Lewis, leading player in George's bad summer season . . .

"George," he was saying, all smiles, "George, don't go rushing out there, you won't like it. Pressmen, George. Television. You're in the news."

Yes, and who put me there? George wasn't fooled. These people were good.

"What the hell do you want?" he asked, knowing all too well what Nathan wanted.

"We want to help, George. That's why I came down, really, to see if we could help. I brought the chequebook," and he patted his jacket pocket. "We'd have put up bail for you, if you'd needed it. I want you to know that."

"You think I'd touch your fucking money?"

"Money's money, George, wherever it comes from. And if you really want to know what I think, I think you'll end up taking all the money we offer you, and be glad to have it. That's what I think."

"Oh, is that right?"

"I think it is. Your business can't survive this; and the last thing you need is an expensive property round your neck. On the other hand, large amounts of ready cash, that must be about your top priority; and that's what we're offering. Come and talk to us, that's all I'm saying. Let's be civilised, okay?"

George looked at him, saw the cocky stance and the arrogant smile, all the body-language of triumph and contempt, and didn't feel at all civilised.

Didn't pulp him either, though. He'd save that for later. Just now, the little shit was right.

"When?" George asked flatly.

"Soon as you like, George. Come now, if you like. I've got the

346

car out back, we can go and find Richard right this minute."

"No. Not now." He needed to think, to talk things over with a few people; above all, to get his head around what had happened. He had to be sure he was seeing things straight, before he set anything in motion. "Not today."

"Fair enough. You call the shots. But not tomorrow, either. Don't want to talk business on the Sabbath."

"Monday, then. Monday morning."

"Good enough. Monday morning it is. Now, can I give you a lift anywhere?"

"No."

"You don't want to go through those reporters, George. That's a gauntlet."

George's fingers flexed once, and were still. "Listen, you scum," he said, very quiet, very controlled. "I'll take your fucking money if I have to, I'll screw you for every penny I can and be glad to do it; because you're right there, money's money. But I won't ride in your car, I won't eat with you or shake your hand, I won't breathe the same air as you longer than I have to." *And I don't just mean like we are now, face to face. Air's universal, it goes planet-wide. Soon as I can fix it, I won't be sharing any of that air with you.* "Got that clear, have you?"

"Oh, absolutely." Nathan's smile didn't lose a fraction of its brilliance; this was his happy hunting ground, and he was hunting. "Clear as crystal, George. We'll keep it as businesslike as you could wish. In and out, no messing."

"And one thing else."

"What's that, then?"

"Who grassed me up? You tell me that."

"Ah. I'm afraid we did, George. I warned you before, I wasn't having you messing about on my patch."

"Not that. I know that. But someone told you, or you'd have gone for the boxing and missed the dogs." Playing it dead straight now, hungry for information.

"Mmm. I'm not sure I can tell you that, George. In all conscience. I was given the wink, sure; but strictly in confidence."

"Confidence be buggered. I want to know."

"Tell you what, then. We'll make a private deal, shall we, just you and me? I'll tell you, the day we complete on the purchase. The day we get the documents. Not the keys, we want them as soon as possible, as soon as the police are finished in there. But when everything's fixed and firm, when the gym's ours beyond all question: that day, I'll tell you who it was. I promise. How's that?"

347

"I want it now."

Nathan shook his head. "Not before we complete. That's the deal, George, take it or leave it. Just remember, vengeance is a dish best eaten cold."

George took it, of course, he didn't have the option. Took it with a nod, no handshake; and turned and walked away, walked down the corridor and out to where the sun glinted off a dozen camera lenses, all of them pointed at him.

After he'd barged his way through, after he'd shrugged off the last persistent little bitch a hundred yards down the road, he hesitated briefly, where to go now; then turned down the hill, towards the gym. The building would still be sealed off, no doubt, full of police going through his private papers, no question of his getting in. But his car was there, and his dog might still be there, if they hadn't taken him to the pound. George wanted his dog, quite urgently.

On the way, he saw Derry across the street with a girl under his arm. New girl by the look of her, a skinhead, not the longhair he'd been so gone on before. They were twined as tight as Siamese twins, joined all the way down from shoulder to hip, heads leant together for private whispers. But while George watched they broke apart suddenly, to laugh and fight and run like children; and just as Derry caught her, just as he tucked her back against his side he seemed to remember the world again. Looked around, to see if it was watching; and saw that it was.

Saw George.

And flinched, and looked away. Not at his girl, just away, just somewhere else.

And then he hurried her off, round the first corner they came to; and George stood monumentally still, gazing after them and thinking that at least one of his questions had been answered, and that the most important, the most urgent of them.

Thinking that maybe he didn't need private deals with Nathan Lewis after all: which loosened the chains just a little, left him a little more free.

v

They went to meet Derry's father after work, because Derry insisted that they should.

"I always do, now," he said flatly. "Dad likes it."

348

"Can't you miss? Just once?"

"No," unusually digging his heels in, making Rachel wonder. "It'll be nice for him if we're both there. He likes you."

"Well, I like him, too. But won't tomorrow do? I've had enough of other people, even nice ones. I don't want to be polite any more, I don't want to be dutiful," twisting the can out of his hands and taking a good long undutiful slug, "I just want to be with you. Eat, drink and be merry. No parents."

"I talked to your dad," Derry said, and she really didn't understand this stubbornness, it wasn't like him at all, "you can talk to mine. Anyway, I've got to cook his tea."

"You what?"

"I've got to cook his tea. Please, Rache? We can go out after, get a pizza, whatever you fancy. I just want to see him straight first."

And if he was asking now it was only for her company, not her permission; he was going whatever she said, whatever she did. She was more than curious now, she was intrigued.

"Can you cook?" she asked innocently, as if there were nothing else going on in her head, no greater questions.

"I manage."

"This I want to see." Up on her feet, big easy smile, reach for his hand and tug. "Let's go."

They'd spent half the afternoon in the park, lying semi-conscious under the sun, skin gluing itself to sticky skin while they shared two wicked cans of warm lager. Rachel had been too relaxed, too happy even to talk until Derry had grown restless, until he'd asked for the time three times in fifteen minutes. But now they left the still heat and the panting dogs, the restful sounds of white-skirted women playing bowls; they walked away from peace and pure content, back into the busy traffic of Paradise, and Rachel couldn't see why anyone would want to.

Derry set an urgent pace through the streets, so that she had to skip a little to keep up with him. When she protested, only half laughing, he just said, "Don't want to miss him," and hurried on. He kept a hand on her elbow, not to lose her along the way; but all his mind, all his energy was focused on getting there, and none at all on her. And that felt weird, she wasn't used to being anything other than first with him and certainly hadn't expected it today.

Derry's father worked for a private security firm, contracted to provide cover at the local hospital. Judging by what he said himself, his job mostly consisted of checking parking permits and

349

clamping cars that weren't entitled to be there.

"We used to paste warnings on their windscreens," he'd told her, chuckling, "but clamping's better. That makes them really mad. And then we charge 'em fifty quid to take it off. But I'm not a security guard, really. Just a carpark attendant."

"Don't you mind?" she'd asked.

"No, love. A job's a job, you've got to be grateful these days. I do my time, I get paid, there's a pension at the end if I'm lucky, if the firm doesn't go bust. It's just life; and it's not the important part, it's not what counts."

And he'd glanced quickly at Derry then, who was wrestling his brothers across the floor; and back to her, and *that's what counts*, his eyes had been saying, *my rowdy sons, the life that's in them, that I gave to them.*

And yes, she liked Sam Bowen, liked him a lot. How could she not?

They reached the hospital with plenty of time in hand, thanks to Derry's urging; sat on a wall to wait, and she said, "Derry, pet, what's the big deal about meeting your dad?"

He shook his head, not looking at her, his eyes as fidgety as his fingers on her arm. "Nothing. Just, I don't want to miss him, that's all . . ."

"Liar. That isn't all; or it doesn't explain, anyway. Your dad's a grown man, he can find his own way home, he can get his own tea if he has to. So what's so important?"

Derry only shrugged, didn't answer that.

"Derry, *talk* to me, damn you . . ."

That got through to him, at least a little way. "I can't," he said, finally turning to face her. "Not now. Just wait . . ."

And then he drew her close and hugged her, more for his own comfort than for hers; and like that they waited, heads bowed together under the heady, heavy sun.

Ten, fifteen minutes, and at last Derry's father came. He came like a man with no life in him, like a zombie, pale and uncertain; and Rachel finally understood Derry's determination to be here. She wasn't at all sure Mr Bowen could find his own way home, in this state.

She conjured up a smile, though, or a reasonable facsimile of a smile to greet this unreasonable facsimile of Derry's dad; and he tried the same thing, tried a smile back. His mouth cracked open, gave them glimpses of teeth.

"Well," he said, looking from one to the other, "if it isn't the

350

terrible twins. Hullo, Rachel. Like the haircut."

But there was no truth in the smile or the wisecracks, no life at
all, he was running on empty. Rachel hugged him, Derry punched
his arm, pinched his cap and put it on Rachel's head, and they
walked out of the hospital grounds three abreast and very like a
family; and it was all pretence, all shadow.

Mr Bowen hardly said another word on the way to the flat.
Rachel talked with increasing desperation, telling him all about
France and all about coming home again, her day with Derry.
Meanwhile he was walking more and more slowly, so that by the
last stretch she had his arm tucked firmly through hers, hoping to
look like a daughter on good terms with her dad while she felt
more like a nurse with an invalid patient, lending her young
strength just to keep him on his feet.

Home at last, Derry settled his father in front of the television
with a glass of brown ale; then he took Rachel through to the
kitchen, and shut the door.

"Derry, what's wrong with him?"

"Dunno. He's lost it, is all. He's like this all the time now, I
don't know what to do with him. He won't go to the doctor, I
tried that. There's nothing wrong with him, he says. But he cries,
all of a sudden, like, he can't stop himself. And he doesn't talk, he
doesn't do nothing. I bullied him back to work this week, see if
that would help, but . . . " A little shrug, a gesture of helplessness,
see for yourself.

"Why didn't you tell me?" she asked fiercely.

"How could I? But I had to come. He doesn't eat, if I don't
stand over him."

"Of course you had to come," hugging him gently. "I just can't
believe it, that's all. He was all right when I saw him at the, at
your mum's funeral. I mean, he was sad, but he wasn't brain-
dead. Something must've happened, since then . . . "

"I reckon things just stopped happening," Derry said. "There
was just him and me left suddenly, no kids or nothing; and he lost
it. It's like he just doesn't care any more . . . "

"Derry man, he still cares, don't be stupid. He's just sick.
Depressed, or something. Have you talked to anyone?"

Derry shook his head.

"Well, you should. Go to the doctor yourself, if you can't get
your dad there. Tell him."

"Her. But I can't, anyway. I can't explain. I couldn't even tell
you."

"She'll understand. She's trained, she's seen this sort of thing

351

before. It's just grief or whatever, he's got all tangled up with it in his head." And when Derry only stood there, miserable in the circle of her arms, she said, "Look, would you like me to talk to Richard?"

"What good would that do?"

"He can *help*," she said sharply, wanting to shake him. "You should've gone to him yourself, you know you should, that's what he's for. Even if you don't believe in prayer and that, he could still help. You shouldn't be dealing with this by yourself, you'll get ill too. And I need you healthy, Derry Bowen. I do."

He moved at that, running his fingers through the fuzz on her head till she wanted to purr with pleasure. "I thought, I thought you'd gone, I thought that was it, finished, over . . . "

"I did go. I came back. And don't you get all morbid on me, I can't be doing with it. Where shall we go tonight?" If he wanted to change the subject, she'd bloody well do it properly.

"Wherever you want. We can do anything, so long as it's over before ten. I'm going to be dead good about that, get you home on time. Show your dad he can trust me."

"Hey, let's not go overboard about this, okay? If he said ten, ten thirty's soon enough. You're my boyfriend, he's not supposed to trust you." Then she rubbed her cheek against his shoulder, squinted up at him sideways and said, "Do you think we ought to go out? Maybe we should stay, keep your dad company . . . "

Derry shook his head. "There's no point, Rache. Really there isn't. I've done that, all the time you've been away," with a quick smile, *didn't have anything else to do, with you away,* "and he doesn't want to talk or anything. He just watches telly and goes to bed. Hardly knows I'm there half the time."

"You don't know that," she objected. "He might be glad to have someone else around, even if he doesn't show it."

"Maybe," Derry said doubtfully. "But it's you I want to be with, not my dad; and not here, I'm sick to death of the place. I've got to get out, or I'll go crazy."

Rachel looked at him, and remembered something she'd decided in France: that there was such a thing as being too unselfish, too virtuous. Just another form of self-indulgence, that was, it was sinful by definition and made you too smug to live.

So, "Tell you what, then," she said, "let's go to the beach, yeah? You can run around and scream if you want, stuff like that, make you feel better. I'll throw sticks for you to fetch. And we can eat hot dogs and ice-cream and make sandcastles, like the first day I met you. Sound good?"

"Sounds great."

"Right, then. But first, we'll give your dad a treat. *I'm* going to cook his tea for him; you can watch, and learn. Chef's assistant, you can be. Chief potato-peeler, that's about your level . . . "

TWENTY-EIGHT

i

Confrontation comes sooner than he can have expected it this morning, and from a surely unexpected quarter.

– I should be there too, says little Arnold Saltley.

– Arnold, whatever for?

– Because I'm treasurer. I'm still treasurer, even though you want me to go.

– Arnold, that's not true, he says. I don't want you to go. It's only that I think you'd be happier, if you passed the job on. It's got too big for you, you've said that yourself.

– Even so, Arnold says, giving Richard another glimpse of the stubbornness that has kept him in place when all his old friends are gone: overruled, outvoted, often simply ignored but still there, still clinging, still scowling in corners and holding everyone back. Maybe that's right, Arnold says, maybe the job's outgrown me, but I've not given it up yet. Someone has to keep your feet on the ground, he says. And your people may outnumber ours, he says, but we're still here, and we deserve a voice. We deserve some representation, he says.

– Arnold, I've never denied that. Your voice is always welcome. But . . .

– But nothing, Arnold says. I'm treasurer, I'm responsible for money. So I have to be there, he concludes, triumphant; and we shouldn't be talking like this anyway, not on the Sabbath. Not business talk, on the Lord's day. Tomorrow will be soon enough, he says, I'll see you tomorrow, with him.

– Yes, Richard says, resigned to it at last. Tomorrow, then, he says; but, Arnold?

– Well, what?

– Leave the talking to me. You're welcome as a witness, and *ex officio*, but leave all the talking to me.

– Oh aye, says Arnold. Oh, I'll leave the talking to you, he says, why not? That's what we've been doing all summer, no reason to stop now . . .

The marquee was awash with rumours before the service, but they broke over Helen like waves over a rock, broke and ran away and left no mark.

Service itself was all fire, all passion. Richard's preaching was electric, his aura crackled and spat; and Helen watched and listened and felt nothing, too far away even for Richard to reach now. Fireproof, she seemed to be. Like sand, or glass – or like sand in a glass, perhaps, and running out.

Afterwards, when the people mingled and mixed, talked and hugged and laughed together – well, she was no part of that either, not any more. These were her friends and more than friends, her brothers and sisters by adoption; and she felt lost among them. She flinched back from their welcoming hands, turned her head away, made herself deaf to their calling.

She took her dull and listless way between them, and came out into the endless sunshine of this relentless, mocking summer. *Busy old fool, unruly Sun* – and dishonest with it, offering so much: throwing down warmth and light and all the metaphors you could want for love and hope and rebirth, all the promises she'd seen and seized a few short months before.

And all of them as empty and insubstantial as the sunlight, nothing there to hold to, nothing but illusion and loss . . .

It was quieter around the corner, along the side of the marquee. Helen stepped over ropes and pegs till she felt far enough from the crowds, where her solitariness would look deliberate. Like a sign, *do not disturb*. She sat down on dry grass and baked earth, leant back against the canvas wall and closed her eyes.

This way she could still hear, still feel, still smell the world around her, and yet not participate in it; and that was what she wanted, to shut it out but not yet cut it off. Down at the houses she'd be drawn in, she'd be involved and open and exposed, not fireproof at all; and her only other option was to go back to the flat, to sit among all her ghosts of happiness and count them off on her fingers, when they fled. Too many walls that way, too many doors locking hard behind her. That must have been how Evelyn felt, she thought sometimes, often: one last door slammed against her, one door too many . . .

She shook her head against even the thought of that – but she should, she must visit Evelyn again, and soon; tomorrow, she had nothing to do tomorrow, or any day next week, she'd visit Evelyn

– and sat still again. Still in the world, still making that hard choice.

Listening, she heard music above the distant voices. Not the electric piano, not Rachel's guitar or Steven's drums. Mouth organ, that's what it was. Being blown soft and easy, but getting louder, coming closer.

The tent wall moved at her back, something brushed her bare arm, someone grunted and settled beside her, and went on playing.

Helen scowled in her own private darkness, hitched herself an inch or two away. Pulled her knees up to her chest and wrapped her arms around them, dropped her head, maybe she'd look like she was praying. Maybe then they'd leave her alone.

But no, the music just went on; and finally, Helen opened her eyes and turned her head.

Billy smiled at her shyly.

"Billy," she said, while he tapped the harmonica professionally against his knee, shaking out the spittle, "what are you doing here?"

"Playing my mouth organ," he said innocently. Sly little Billy, thought poor Helen looked lonely, didn't want to say so straight. "Richard gave it me, isn't it good?"

But, "No, I mean, with this lot?" She couldn't say 'us lot', not any more. She felt like a sheep worked out of the flock and abandoned, all marks of membership removed. One man's work, and he didn't even need a dog to do it. "You don't belong here . . . "

"Yes, I do." He sounded quite hurt; but that was tough. Helen hurt, let the world hurt with her for a bit. Wouldn't hurt. "I'm a believer. I believe in God the Father, God the Son and God the Holy Ghost. Richard says it's the best thing in the world, to be a believer."

"It's a point of view," Helen said; and stopped talking, weary of it.

She closed her eyes and heard Billy's music again, a sweet, slow version of 'Forever Young'. Too late for him, she thought; he was getting old already, or he wouldn't be giving himself away like that, looking back to when Dylan was asking all the questions and writing all the prayers.

Not too late for her, though. She was young still, she could be young forever. Fool them all, do a Peter Pan act. Second star on the right, straight on till morning.

"There's Richard," Billy said suddenly. So of course Helen

356

looked, and saw Richard; and saw Nathan with him, and didn't even turn her head away. They were what she came for, what she stayed for, what she dreaded most, these glimpses and casual encounters.

"I love Richard," Billy said.

"Sure. We all love Richard." He didn't give them any choice, did he?

"Yes, that's right. We all do," echoing her, except that for her it was only something inevitable and obvious, like *we're all going to die,* and for Billy it was clearly still a delight. "And Richard loves us, too. I think Richard loves everyone."

"I'm sure he does," she said, exhausted by the burden of it, the knowledge of being so much loved.

Billy went quiet then, and she had the feeling that he was building up to something, some revelation she didn't want to hear or respond to.

And sure enough,

"I'm scared of Nathan," Billy said.

"Yeah," she said, no room for anything but honesty these days. "Me too, Billy."

"But I love him too," Billy said stoutly. "He's my brother, I have to love him."

"Yeah," Helen said again. "It's a killer, isn't it? Unless it's a joke. But I don't hear any cosmic laughter, do you?"

Billy only looked at her, not understanding; but she couldn't help that, or him. She was far past helping others, couldn't even help herself any more. Slipping and sliding, that was all, falling towards the pictures in her head.

Falling towards Evelyn.

iii

Billy didn't drink any more, except at service when they passed the great cup from hand to hand, saying *This is His blood which was given for us; drink this, and remember Him.* Only it wasn't blood, it was wine and Billy drank it happily, one big gulp every Sunday; but that was all, that was all he drank now.

Now when he felt thirsty – when he was happy, when he was sad or confused or frightened, when he was with his friends or when he was alone – he remembered the Bible verse that Richard had made him learn by heart. *You only need one,* Richard had said, *that's all anyone needs; there's enough truth in one verse to*

357

*last a lifetime. But everyone needs their own, and this one's yours,
Billy boy, this one's for you.*

"But whosoever drinketh of the water that I shall give him,"
and Billy saw streams and rivers in his mind, waterfalls sparkling
like diamonds in sunshine, "shall never thirst; but the water that I
shall give him shall be in him a well of water springing up into
everlasting life."

Billy could lose himself in that, and forget all about being
thirsty. *Never thirst,* he said to himself often, many times a day,
I'm saved, I don't need to be thirsty ever again.

And that made him happy; but what made him sad was seeing
other people thirsty, not knowing about the Water of Life; or
knowing it, seeing it and turning away, not drinking.

That's what Helen was doing, he thought. She was so sad, she
frightened him a little. He didn't know what to say to her. So in
the end he left her sitting by the big tent, he said goodbye and got
up and walked away. And it was hot, and he was miserable, and
he felt very thirsty indeed.

Never thirst, he said to himself, but still felt thirsty.

"But whosoever drinketh . . . " he started murmuring softly as
he walked; that was his verse, his refuge, and he said it again and
again and still felt thirsty, seeing pictures of pints in his head,
feeling the weight of whisky in his hand. And he had money, a
little, they gave him a little money every week; and it was Sunday
afternoon but there was still time before the pubs closed, he could
still get himself a drink . . .

Only he didn't do that any more. Sad or not, thirsty or not, he
was saved now and he didn't drink. He said his verse louder and
walked more quickly down to the houses, a good long way from
any pub.

Saved or not, Billy was still superstitious; but even sticking rel-
igiously to all his rituals, *this hand in my pocket playing with my
lucky stone and this one swinging free, that's lucky, and please
God let me find someone nice to talk to,* this didn't look like his
lucky day. Through all his loud, determined optimism, he could
feel the unresponsiveness of Heaven, the emptiness of the houses.
Could see it too, walking all the way down the long terrace and
looking in at all the windows as he passed. Sunday after chapel
was always a bad time to find people, and today even Jack and
Anita had gone out. To the Polish Club, Billy remembered now,
too late. They were having a party.

Still, when he came to the end of the terrace he went inside,
changed boots for slippers and started to search. Prayers were

always answered, Richard said that often, you only had to believe hard enough; so Billy believed very hard that there was someone, anyone sitting quiet somewhere in the houses, waiting to be talked to. All he had to do was find them.

Everyone still talked about 'the houses', but that was habit rather than description. Except for Jack's on the end, there were no separate houses left. Separate doors outside, yes, and staircases within; and most of the residents talked about living in number seven or number eleven, it helped people to find you. But in reality it was a single building now, one long college.

Billy went upstairs first, touching base in his own bedroom, touching a talisman or two just to settle his soul; and then he made his way methodically down passages and across landings, checking every bedroom. Just in case.

No one there.

So he did the same downstairs, where the summer's workers had done more than knock doorways through from one house to the next: where they'd demolished whole walls to make new spaces, and added more windows to light them. Billy went through common-rooms and prayer rooms and kitchens, came finally to the offices and still hadn't found a single soul to speak to.

Accepted at last that the houses really were empty, that he was on his own here when he most needed company to ease his raging thirst; but remembered too that a Christian is never alone, Richard had told him that, and that God was the best company ever.

Billy was still a little scared of God, shy of opening a conversation and nervous of the consequences; but he could be braver here in Richard's office, where something of Richard's spirit seemed to cling. Even the battered old auction-room furniture was friendly. Here Billy could be comfortable with himself, and maybe with God too.

So he dropped awkwardly to his knees, folded his hands and started to say his prayers.

After he'd said the 'Our Father' and the 'God Bless' he couldn't think of anything else to say, he didn't know any other prayers. He couldn't remember words the way he could music. It had taken him days to learn his Bible verse.

But Richard said praying was just like talking really, you didn't have to have proper prayers to say; and above all else Billy wanted someone to talk to. So he took a deep breath, clenched his hands a little more tightly, and started talking to God.

Once he'd started, there seemed to be an awful lot to say. He told God all about Helen and how sad she was, and how he worried about her; and about how that worry made him thirsty, and how hard it was not to be drinking.

He talked and talked, and had no idea what the time was or how long he'd been there, talking.

He forgot altogether about the world outside that room, until it broke in on him with fire and glass, with fear and terrible faces.

iv

Jason didn't want to be here, didn't want anything to do with this; but he had no choices left. Even running wasn't an option any more. He could run from the police, from the hostel, he'd done all that, but he wasn't going to run from Vinny. Vinny might come looking.

So instead he was crouched in the back of Vinny's van smelling of petrol and deep shit scared, utterly out of his depth; and the van was jolting and bumping, shaking the bottles Jason held in his shaking hands.

Vinny stopped the van and got out, but Jason didn't move, his hands didn't stop shaking. The bottles clinked together in a swift staccato, until Vinny pulled the back doors open.

"Out," he said; and Jason moved then, Jason got out sharp, holding his bottles carefully upright, well away from his body.

"Up there, then. You first."

Looking around, Jason saw that they'd parked right by the river, on a broken stretch of road. Ahead of him there was fifty metres of rough ground which turned suddenly into gardens, running up to a single row of houses standing proud of the wasteland.

At least he knew where he was now. As to what he was here for, he'd always known that.

"What if, what if they see us?"

"What if they do?"

"Christ, Vinny, you could get ten years for this . . . "

"Not me, Jase. I don't do time. And they won't find you, will they? They're looking already, maybe; but they won't come and look where I've put you. You're safe with me. So move."

And he took a Zippo lighter from his pocket and flicked it idly into life. Sparks flew on the wind and Jason gasped, jumped back, hurried up onto the wasteland crouching low and scurrying while fear twisted his face into something close to a smile. It was almost funny, that, the idea of being safe with Vinny. He could almost laugh at anyone who chose to put those two words together, except that of course nobody laughed at Vinny, it simply wasn't safe . . .

Jason found shelter behind some tangled shrubs; then, hearing Vinny's soft chuckle at his back and the click of the lighter, he started forward again, following an old stone wall up towards the houses. Thank Christ there was no one out in the gardens. It was a hot sunny Sunday, but this was where the Christians lived, maybe they were all at church. Maybe Vinny had actually thought about this, unless he'd just hit lucky.

Whatever, there wasn't anyone around. No faces at the windows either, that Jason could see; no figures moving behind the glass. *Maybe God's on our side*, he thought; and was almost praying on the last quick sprint, to keep it so.

Vinny strolled casually up after him, bright-eyed and smiling.

"Right, then."

They were standing on a gravel path running the full length of the terrace, between the houses and the gardens. Each house had a back door, eight or ten of them; but Vinny didn't seem at all bothered. He just walked down the path, looking quickly in at all the windows; and eventually he stopped, stood still, stood looking for maybe ten seconds before he beckoned Jason.

"This one," he said, halting him with a hand against his chest, just short of the window. "Give us some fireworks, Jase. One, two and then back to the van, quick as you like."

Jason looked at the Zippo held out on Vinny's hard palm, and said, "No." Heard the whine in his own voice as he said, "No, you do it, Vinny. Please?"

Vinny smiled, folded his hand into a fist around the lighter and cracked Jason's skull with his knuckles, just the once. Jason didn't even flinch, he'd learned not to do that, it only made things worse.

"Do it," he heard Vinny say; and Jason did.

He held both his bottles by their necks, took the lighter from Vinny.

"One at a time, boy," Vinny said, the words coming soft and slurred around his bad teeth. "Don't want an accident, do we? Put the other one down."

So Jason set one bottle against the wall, and held the other at arm's length.

He flicked the lighter open, spun the wheel with his thumb, saw

361

it spark and catch in the fitful breeze.

Touched the flame to the rag wick hanging from the bottle's neck and saw it flare, pale in the sunlight; and cocked his arm and threw, straight at the window from a metre's distance.

The window smashed and the bottle went through; and Jason grinned at the guttural cough inside, the sudden light.

"The other one," Vinny whispered in his ear. "Hurry."

Jason hurried, snatching up the other petrol bomb, lighting it, throwing it through the broken window into the smoke and heat of the fire inside; and he was already turning to run, not needing Vinny's grip on his arm to encourage him, when he heard some-one screaming in there.

And he stopped, jerked away from Vinny, turned back to look; and saw the blundering figure of a man, up on his feet and burning.

v

Billy felt the heat, and screamed as the air burned around him.

Howling, he thrust himself to his feet, "Jesus *God*," he wept, "help me now, oh Jesus help me I'm dying . . . "

And he was, or he was dead already and in Hell with the flames rising around him and nothing to breathe but smoke and fire and burning, burning air. He wept and screamed, howled and prayed and staggered through fire to the window, where the face of a demon smiled at him through the broken glass.

And Billy screamed again, turned back to the fire and prayed screaming.

"Lord Jesus GOD help me now, help Billy . . . "

And the flames flickered and died before his outstretched hands, and Billy was left coughing in the smoke and filth and stink of the dead fire, and he didn't have a blister on his skin.

vi

Jason didn't see, when the fires went out.

Vinny was watching at the window, but not Jason.

Jason was standing with his back to the wall and his eyes closed, fists clenched. He heard the man sobbing and screaming the other side of the wall and sobbed himself, wanted to scream.

362

He thought he could feel the fire's heat, coming through the bricks; and tried to tell himself that it was only where the sun had warmed them, but still he thought he could feel them getting hotter, even in his body's shadow.

And then the screams stopped and he thought the man was dead, maybe, all burned up and gone.

He heard Vinny in the silence after, heard him laughing, swearing; and Jason still didn't look, didn't at all want to see. Only there was suddenly another voice too, a happy babble from inside the room, and then he had to look.

He saw Vinny backed off a pace or two, laughing but not smiling, not enjoying this; and he saw a little smoke drifting out of the broken window, but that was all. No leaping flames, no cinders, no residues of burning man.

So he looked in and saw that the fire was out, was gone; and the man was kneeling on broken glass, crying and shouting hallelujah and praying for deliverance from demons.

Jason thought he'd had that already.

But no one was praying for Jason, no one delivered him. Vinny's hand locked like a claw around his arm and dragged him away across the gardens, down to the van. There Vinny's hard fingers jabbed at him, Vinny's open palms cuffed him dizzy, cuffed him till his nose bled; and Vinny said, "What did you do, Jason? What did you put in those bottles?"

"Petrol," Jason gasped, slumped over the bonnet of the van, watching blood drip and run across the rusting paintwork. "I swear, petrol. Like you told me, from the can . . . "

"I don't think so. I don't think it was petrol. I think you fucked up, Jase."

Vinny thrust him into the back of the van like an animal, like one of his dogs; and Jason curled into a ball like a frightened animal, and only curled up tighter when he slid from one side to the other and back again, Vinny's driving adding more bruises to what Vinny's hands had already given him.

vii

There was a thin, dirty smoke rising above Vinny's place, birds wheeling in alarm. George saw it from some distance down the lane and would happily have stopped and turned and gone home again, if he weren't so driven. He really didn't want to know what

363

burned on Vinny's land.

But he parked beside the van, and got out; and coughed in an eddy of stinking smoke and followed the sound of voices, yelps of pain down to where a cat's body twitched and danced inside a burning tyre, Vinny's idea of a Sunday evening bonfire. Even the earth was burning, in a ring around the tyre. Vinny stood close by with Jason's head trapped under his arm, his knuckles working a hard rhythm on the boy's skull.

"That's how petrol burns, Jase," Vinny was saying. "See that?" to a kid who wasn't seeing anything, who had his face forced into Vinny's side and could hardly be breathing down there. "That's how petrol burns. It doesn't go *out*, Jason, it doesn't flare up and go *out*."

"What's going on, Vinny?"

Vinny looked up, nodded through the smoke. "Little chemistry lesson, George. Nothing to worry." One final crack of knuckles on bone, and he pushed Jason away. George registered the state of the boy, tears and filth; but he wasn't interested. Jason wasn't useful any longer.

Vinny was, though, more and more. Vinny was *needed*.

"Got a job for you, Vin."

Vinny said nothing, he only threw another tyre and some green branches on top of the cat's kicking body, making a thicker smoke.

"I can't do it myself, I can't risk it. Got to keep my nose clean. But they won't touch you; and I want this done, Vinny, done soon." God, how he wanted it done! "That kid, Derry – he's the one grassed on me, I'd put my life on it. I want him hurt, Vin." And when Vinny still didn't react, "I can pay," George added hurriedly. "I'm selling the gym. More than it's worth, they're giving me. I can pay a good price . . . "

"Sure you can, George," Vinny said cheerfully. "But not me. I don't work for you any more."

"It can wait a bit, if you're busy. Maybe I don't come first now, I can see that, without the regular work; but it'd only be an hour, Vinny, it's nothing . . . "

But Vinny was shaking his head as he stalked around his bonfire, smiling in the smoke. "You're a loser, George," slow and sweet and final, "you've lost, and I don't work for losers."

"For Christ's sake, Vinny man, I'm offering good money here . . . "

"I don't need your money. I don't work for you any more."

"So who, then? Who do you bloody work for, if not me?"

Vinny lifted his head, cracked his knuckles slowly, finger by

364

finger; said, "Goodbye, George."

George took one, two steps towards him, and stopped. Thought better of it, wouldn't pit even his bulk and strength against Vinny's viciousness, even in anger.

He retreated scowling to his car, and had the door open already when a voice stopped him.

"Mr Jenner?"

Half a whisper, half a sob: George turned to see Jason edging round the corner of the caravan.

"Well?" And when the boy didn't come any closer, when he only stood there shivering, looking over his shoulder to see if Vinny was coming through the smoke behind him: "What the fuck do you want, Jason? I haven't got time to piss about."

"Do you, do you really think it was Derry, then? Grassed you up, I mean?"

"Yeah," George said, remembering the shifty look on him. "Yeah, I do. Stands to reason. Why?"

"Would you, would you pay me? Like you would Vinny, I mean, if I did him over for you?"

George almost laughed at that, would have done any other day of his life. But this wasn't a day for laughing; and never mind that Jason was a skinny kid with snot smeared across his face, smelling of dogshit and terror. Put money in his pocket, say an iron bar or a baseball bat in his hands, he could be vicious too. No question of that; and that was all George needed.

"Not as much," he said. "I wouldn't pay you as much as Vinny, it's class you pay for, see? But yes, I'd pay. What do you want money for, Vin charging you rent, is he?"

Taking it out in kind, more like, George thought, seeing Jason's shiver. But why not? That's what the kid was there for, to be exploited. Always had been. That's what kids were for.

"I want to get away, Mr Jenner," in a heartfelt whisper. "I just, I just want to get right away from here. Go to London, I don't know, anywhere. Away, that's all I want . . . "

"Okay, son." George made his mind up quickly. "You do this little job for me, and I'll see you right. Do it well, mind. A proper job."

"I will, Mr Jenner. I promise."

"Good lad, then." And George took a couple of tenners from his pocket, folded them up and pressed them into Jason's scabby, filthy fingers. "There, that's on account. Come and find me when it's done, you know my number."

Jason nodded, clenching both hands around the cash. Then he stiffened as Vinny's whistle rose above the dogs' barking, down by the sheds; and he turned and ran like an obedient dog to the feet of his master, and George wondered if he'd ever have the nerve to break away, even if he had the money.

Well, it was no problem of his. He drove away from Vinny's in the half-light, wondering if Jason was up to the job or not; and wondering too just who it was Vinny was working for now, who he thought would come out a winner from all this mess.

The only thing he was sure of, it wouldn't be Richard and his fucking church. They'd get theirs, just like Derry was going to get his; George would see to that. Pay for it, if necessary.

TWENTY-NINE

i

Oh, yes.

Yes.

This is right, this is so right.

As soon as he walks through the door, he must feel it. Every place has its aura, every building its true heart; and all the trappings of commercialism can't disguise it, nor the odours of recent evil conceal.

Not from him. Surely, not from him.

The feet of generations have walked where his feet now echo their solitary way; voices still sing in the silence. It's not mortar that bonds these brick walls, it's prayer. He'll hear that.

He looks at all the stacked machinery, and won't be seeing it. No, what he'll see, he'll see the flames of Pentecost leaping from face to face in an endless dance; and that's history or prophecy or both, but his eyes are sharp, he'll see them in the here and now also, see them quiver and tense, ready to set the world alight, waiting only for the people.

He stands by the dog-pit and closes his eyes, breathes in; and yes, he can smell the blood and the pain and the fear, how could he not, with all his senses so alive? But he'll be smelling bread and wine also, the body and blood of his Lord, and he'll know he can make this place clean. It's clean already, at heart.

And – prophecy again – soon it will be the burning, vibrant heart of God's great mission to this city. He must feel that. The new Jerusalem is only just around the corner; and oh, it's going to be so glorious . . .

ii

There were marks of scorching on the walls and smoke-stains on the ceiling; the air was heavy with the stink of fire, for all that they had the door and the window open and joss-sticks burning in all four corners of the room.

Nathan stood in the centre, turning slowly and breathing

deeply. What he smelt, what he tasted was war; and he was in charge of the defences. It was Richard's office that had been attacked, but Richard didn't count in this. This was Commando business.

Nathan smiled, and beckoned one of his lieutenants in from the corridor.

"Joe, go into town and price some stuff for us. We need a safe. Fireproof. And big, it's got to take a lot. We could've lost all Richard's papers in this. It'll cost a bomb – ouch, sorry, no pun intended – but we've got to protect our data."

"Be safer in a bank," Joe suggested.

"We need it on hand; and I'd rather trust our own security anyway. Now we know that we need it. They may come back for a second try, but they won't catch us napping again. So: a good safe, intruder alarms, outside lights, all of that. Price it all. And baseball bats, while you're about it. Good ones."

"You serious?"

Nathan nodded. "I'm serious, Joe. Billy could've died in here on Sunday; Grace did die, back in the old chapel. That's twice, and if they come at us a third time I want to be ready. I'm not asking anyone to go up against petrol bombs with their bare hands. Billy survived, but you can't count on miracles. Here on in, we take no chances. Pray about it, if you're not happy," seeing Joe's patent unease, "but every peace-keeping force goes armed. It's just self-defence, Joe. Defence of the community. Someone's got to fight for Paradise."

Outside he found Billy more or less where he'd expected, sitting on a pile of rubble in the sunshine, staring at the rolled and folded carpet. Even after a day in the open with a fresh breeze blowing, it still stank of petrol.

"What's happening, Billy?"

A shake of the head, an instant smile, both of them tinged with Billy's usual nervousness. "Nothing, Nat."

"Can't have you sitting doing nothing, Billy. You'd better talk to me," added quickly before Billy could jump to his feet and run away, in search of something to do that was a very long way from Nathan. "You figured it out yet, what happened on Sunday? When the fire went out?"

Billy frowned, puzzled that he needed to ask. "It was a miracle, Nat. Richard says so. I prayed, and God saved me."

"Okay, good," with a clap on the shoulder. "So what about what happened after? Tell me again, about the man outside."

"It wasn't a man. I said, it wasn't a man. It was the devil, he'd

368

come to gloat, he'd come to take me away into all the fires of Hell; but God saved me, and put the fires out."

Nathan sighed, and tightened his grip. "I think you can do a little better than that, Billy boy. What did he look like, this devil?"

"Like the devil. I've *told* you, Nat. And the police, I told the police too. They didn't believe me either. Ask Richard, Richard believes me."

Nathan had asked Richard. *It's what Billy believes,* Richard had said. *And up to a point I'm with him on this, I think he saw evil out there. Someone totally without conscience or scruple, and that's not a bad definition. Whatever he saw, it scared him to the very depths of his soul. Don't trouble him any further, Nathan, he's troubled enough.*

But Nathan needed more, he needed a description, and he was going to trouble Billy till he got one. Looking for an angle, he said, "It's not that I don't believe you, Billy. But I think your devils wear human bodies; and I want to find them, to stop them scaring you again. Maybe God won't give you a miracle next time."

"There won't be a next time," Billy said, clutching frantically at Nathan's arm. "Will there, Nat? No next time, please no next time . . . "

"Most things come in threes," Nathan said, "and that's twice now you've seen devils. Once in the marquee, way back before you came here; and once again on Sunday. If you want to stop the third time, you've got to help me now. Tell me what they look like. Did this devil look like that one, the one who chased you out of the marquee?"

Billy shuddered, and nodded vigorously. "Yes, of course he did. He's the same, it's all the same devil. Of course it is. There isn't more than one. And I've seen him three times already, I saw him at the gym, I told you that. So there won't be a next time, will there? Will there . . . ?"

iii

School soon, and she didn't want it, she wasn't ready to go back. Hadn't done any work over the holidays, except her true work, spreading the word. Wearing the uniform, fighting the good fight. She thought there was going to be trouble, maybe, when she made it clear that she wasn't putting it all aside for a year, hanging the uniform up till her exams were over. No way was she going to do that.

369

And there was Derry, too – something to be proud of there, something achieved. Derry definitely counted as work. And she wasn't going to shelve him either, school or no school, A-levels or not.

Rachel grinned at the sudden image of Derry sitting passively shelved above her desk – between her teddy-bear and her photo albums, say, to be looked at and joked about and taken down only when needed. Handy, that would be. She'd like that.

Except that she wouldn't, of course. Not really. He was better the way he was, elusive and unpredictable, all awkward corners and sudden surprises. Troublesome and difficult, but never more trouble than he was worth . . .

"Share 'em or save 'em, sister." That was Kathy, her partner for the morning, nudging her in the ribs, laughing at her; and only laughing louder when Rachel blushed.

"Sorry, I was, I was just . . . " *Just getting caught with my brain halfway to marshmallow, soft and sweet and lurid pink; and thank the Lord you can't read my mind . . .*

"I know what you were just," Kathy said, reading her mind like a headline. "Where is he, then, bottom of the next street, isn't it?"

"Halfway down."

"Well, go on, if you want to. I can manage."

Rachel shook her head, stubborn in the face of temptation. "I said I'd come round with you, and I will. He can wait till we're finished."

"Sure he can. Can you?"

"*Yes,*" fiercely determined. "Derry doesn't, he hasn't got a monopoly over me. This is important too."

Kathy put an arm round her shoulders then, and hugged her. "Come on, then. Who's next?"

Rachel checked her clipboard. "Mr Colbert. It's pension day, so he'll want some shopping done; and he's probably got some laundry for the van to collect, only we'll have to lean on him about that, he gets embarrassed."

This was the role Rachel had found for herself in the Commando, where she felt happiest: as a home help, rather than a vigilante. Let the young men watch for trouble, that wasn't a job for her. She'd walk people's dogs for them and clean their windows, dig their allotments and disinfect their toilets, and feel herself just as useful. Or more so, because she could talk about God while she worked, and they'd listen to her where they wouldn't to the lads.

So they called on Mr Colbert for his pension-book and his

shopping list; they played with his cat, asked about his distant family and bullied him gently into confessing that there was a bagful of damp sheets in the bathroom.

With that off his mind, he was chattier. He came to the door as they left, and a group of passing teenagers nudged his mind, seemingly, and turned his conversation.

"Those kids," he said, "they're not from round here. Know what they come for, do you?"

"No, what's that, Mr Colbert?"

"Drugs," he said. "They do, I've seen 'em. There's a bloke just up the road here, he's got kids at the door all hours. In and out in two minutes. What's that, then, if it's not drugs? Straight from school, some of them, still in their uniforms. Then they go down those empty houses at the bottom of the street, where no one's going to see what they're up to. It's disgusting. You lot talk about cleaning up this area, that's where you should start. Get the drugs out. They're filth, these drug-peddlers. And the kids who buy them, they're no better. Run them all out, that's what you should be doing."

"What d'you think?" Kathy asked, when they finally got away. "Is he for real, or is he losing his marbles?"

"He doesn't like kids," Rachel said cautiously. "And how would he know, anyway? He never gets out, that's why we have to do his shopping."

"Oh, he spends half his time sitting on the wall there outside his door, just watching the street. He'd know, if anyone would."

"Or he'd make it up. Could be there's just someone he's got a grudge against, he wants to make trouble for."

"You're not saying we should ignore it, are you? Someone maybe dealing drugs to schoolkids, on our patch . . . "

"I just don't think we should take his word for it, that's all. He can be pretty nasty sometimes, I've heard him."

"Even so, we've got to tell someone. That's one of the reasons we do this, right, to keep our ears open? We'll tell Nat, then it's out of our hands. If he takes it seriously, he can come and talk to Mr Colbert himself."

"You can tell Nat," Rachel said, ducking the issue hard. "If you must. Not me, I don't want anything to do with it."

"Rachel, what's wrong?"

"It's just, I don't want to be a copper's nark, you know? It's not what I signed up for. And that's what it feels like, even telling Nat. Even if it's true, and we don't know that, remember, we should, we should talk to them, not turn them in . . . "

371

"We're only going to tell Nat, Rachel. He's not the police, he's one of us. He can talk to them as well as we can. Better, they'll listen to him. Round here, blokes carry all the authority."

"Yeah. I suppose . . . " But she still didn't like it, so she chickened out altogether. Looked at her watch, and said, "Listen, can you cope by yourself now? Sorry, but I really should get down to Derry's. His dad's coming home for lunch, I said I'd cook something, I'm giving Derry lessons . . . "

And got the hell, got the devil out of there.

iv

Alan Parkinson was labouring for the Lord; and nothing meta-phorical about it, not today. He was getting his hands dirty, and his boots and his clothes and his hair. He was sweating in the sunshine, hungry for his lunch; and in his heart he was jubilant. His mind ran with the hard verses of his hard God, the promise of a life of grinding toil – and this was it, he'd seized that promise and made it good and would be rewarded.

In the sweat of thy face shalt thou eat bread, till thou return unto the ground, it said in Genesis, *for out of it wast thou taken: for dust thou art, and unto dust shalt thou return.* And it was in the dust that he was working now, dust and ashes caked his sweating skin and his lips and the back of his dry throat. Nor was he going to stop yet, even for a pull at his bottle of tap-water. This wasn't penance, this was praise, and he owed as much as his body could bear to pay.

The long planks that had been walls and roof and floor to the old chapel weren't even wood any longer, only charcoal. They snapped and crumbled under his stamping feet; he stooped and gathered the pieces with his hands, filled the wheelbarrow time and again, emptied it into the skip on the road.

He didn't work alone, though. He had help, other hands work-ing in the soft and clinging ash, gloved with the filth of it: softer hands than his but no less eager, no less driven.

As Alan worked, he prayed and dreamed alternately: dreamed of the chapel he would build here, God's own house remade, and prayed for its soon completion. The land was theirs now, Richard had ceded it and they would have fresh deeds drawn up to fix it in law, unchallengeable. Then they would build, with their hands, as the old men had before them; and this time his place would be at the front as of right, with Jean beside him and no incomers to displace them, no ambitious young men, no Richards.

Jean was visiting friends and colleagues now, the heart's-blood of the old chapel, seeing how many she could bring back to the fold. She would build the congregation, as Alan built the house; and that was right, it wouldn't be fitting for a woman to labour with her hands. Male and female created He them, and each had their role to play, each had their work, not interchangeable.

Besides, she'd sent her representative. It was young Luther who toiled beside Alan, shovelling muck into the barrow and dragging half-burnt timbers to the skip; and no more than Alan was the lad looking to rest. He attacked the work with a frenzy, something far stronger than obedience to his mother's orders. His eyes burned with the vision of a new chapel rising from the ashes of the old, a chapel they could call their own; and like Alan he would work until he broke, to see it happen here.

v

Helen and Evelyn walked the gravel paths of the hospital gardens, between flat lawns and trees in ordered ranks; and it was like walking on the moon, Helen thought, two separate moonwalks, they were so cut off from the world, from other people, from each other.

"Could you," Evelyn said, "it isn't fair to ask, I know that, I shouldn't ask and you mustn't if it's difficult, but could you just let me have some money for cigarettes? We're not locked up here, we're encouraged to get out, I can go down to the shops any time I want; but they don't give you any money, do you see? It's so ironic, it's so typical, they say go, they say go to the shops, but they don't give you what you need . . . "

Helen had been ready for this, at least. It was the same question, every time she came; and of course it had to be the same answer, what else could she do? She gave Evelyn a fiver, but that was for later, this time she'd come prepared. She had twenty Marlboro in her bag, and a box of matches.

"Oh, thank you, bless you, Helen. Oh, that's good of you. Oh, that's so *good*," lighting up and drawing the smoke deep. "We're not allowed to smoke inside, can you believe it? Not at all, there isn't even one room set aside. It's too much, really it is. People are ill when they come here, they have problems, they shouldn't have to put up with that as well. I've told them it's not fair, they're asking too much; but they don't listen. Well, you wouldn't expect them to, would you? Petty bureaucrats . . . "

"Let's sit down," Helen said; and they sat on the grass in the sunshine, inside the wall, and Evelyn blew smoke like a wall between them, and laid down words like another wall behind the smoke.

And Helen listened and nodded or shook her head, smiled or frowned without really hearing, only following the beats and rhythms of Evelyn's high voice. This wasn't what she was here for. Soon, though, they'd come to it soon. They always did.

"It's very good," Evelyn said, "the sunshine. Just to sit here in the sun, in the light. It's so dark in there, they burn the lights all day but it's still dark. It's the soul of the place, I think, it has a dark soul. Out here is better. It's like a metaphor, really, don't you think? To come from there to here, from their cold lights into God's good sunshine."

And this was it, Helen thought, it had to be. Another angle, but the same old news.

"It's the quality of the light," Evelyn said, "that's what makes the difference. They keep asking me about it, but it can't be put into words. You don't know light, you can't know what true light is until you've been where I've been. Oh, if only I could tell you, Helen: to be so close, to have come to the very gates of Heaven before Richard called me back . . . The light's pure there, it *sings* somehow, as if it lived itself. Perhaps what we call angels are creatures of light, or only Heaven's light and nothing more, touching the earth for a moment, the messenger and the message both in one . . . Don't you think?"

"I don't know, Evelyn. I haven't seen."

"No, but you will, Helen. In the end, at the last, we'll all see. We'll all stand in that light, and be burned clean. That's my theology now, that's my belief. There isn't a hell, except what we make for ourselves. God doesn't want us to suffer, why would He? We don't take our sins with us. I felt so *clean*, as clean as the light, I felt entitled, welcomed . . . "

And Helen sat beside her in her own private hell, so totally walled off; sat in the depth of her personal suffering and listened, and heard every word of it.

THIRTY

i

It's not often he has trouble with a journalist. Generally they love him: his open heart and his easy smile, his beauty and his truth. Good pictures and good copy, and what more could they ask?

Today, though, today he's in trouble. And with a woman, too – barely more than a girl, even, young and fluffy and shouldn't be a problem at all. He should be wrapping her round his finger, dangling her on a string and making her dance to his own soft singing. That's what he does to girls, and he trails a chain of still-tender hearts to prove it.

But not this one. She won't wrap, won't dangle, won't dance. She's on a mission as much as he is, and she's very directed. He's showing her round the old gym, the chapel-in-waiting; but he's looking to the future, and she keeps harping on the past.

– I'm surprised, she says, that you'd even be thinking of taking on such a commitment. Isn't what you've achieved already proving too much to handle?

– No, not at all, he says, laughing. It's not my achievement for a start, he says, it's God's; and He's big enough, He can handle anything.

– Seriously, Mr Gould.

– I am serious, he says. God is doing a great, a wonderful thing in this city.

– Is that right? she says, challenging. Isn't it true to say that things really haven't been going that well recently? I'm not talking bums-on-seats here, I know you get a lot of attention, but hasn't the dream all turned rather sour?

– In what way? he asks. I hate to seem disingenuous, he says, but I don't think I know what you're talking about. There's nothing sour in my dreams, he says.

– I'm talking about violence, Mr Gould. I'm talking about arson and fire-bombs and *murder*; and an attempted suicide, and vigilantes on the streets, and . . .

– Grace's death was a tragedy, he says, for her family and for all of us. Privately, I think it was a tragedy also for those who set the fire. I don't think they knew she was there. It must be a very heavy burden on their consciences.

– Not so heavy it stopped them doing it again a few days ago, down at your HQ. I understand someone nearly died in that attack, too.

– We've no evidence that it was the same people, Richard says, a little snappily. Let's leave the guesswork, shall we? Yes, we have been attacked; clearly we've made enemies who want to drive us out of Paradise. But they won't achieve anything, we're here to stay. Every day we're making headway: learning a little more, meeting a few more people, touching a few more hearts. Frankly, our enemies don't stand a chance. They'll be made over, like Paul on the Damascus road; or else they'll be washed away and gone. It's inevitable, that's the lesson of history. You can't stop a tidal wave, and they only waste their time in trying. And incidentally, he adds with a smile like a slap on the wrist, light and teasing and significant, the Commando isn't a vigilante group, he says. So don't write that, will you?

– Don't tell me what to write, Mr Gould.

– Write the truth, he says.

– I will, she says, meeting his gaze, no hint of compromise in her.

– Well, that's all right, then. Isn't it?

– I'll write what I see, she says.

ii

Derry had a job again, one which he didn't want at all and couldn't possibly have turned down. It was designer work, it was made for him and it fitted like a glove; it was so good you could call it a miracle, almost, and he'd never been comfortable with miracles and wasn't comfortable now.

He was working at the gym again, caretaker and handyman. Not so different from before, except that he wasn't working for George any more, he was working for Nathan. And even that wasn't so different really, because you couldn't trust George an inch, and Derry didn't trust Nathan either.

But the money was good, a fair rate for the job, which made it a hell of a lot more than George had paid him. And home was five minutes' walk away, and he liked the work, even if he spent most of his day with a bunch of eager Christians who weren't even getting paid for it; and, of course, there was Rachel.

She was in and out, helping or hindering or holding back, it depended on her mood; but she was around, that was what counted. She was there.

Today she'd been helping, she'd been part of a team taking the wall-mirrors down. But that was done now, the others had gone, Derry was up a step-ladder plugging holes and Rachel was bored.

She sat on a tool-box, eating an orange and making I-want-to-go-home noises; and when Derry ignored her, she started flicking orange-pips at him.

"Don't do that," he said. "I swept up already."

"I know." She climbed up behind him, to feed him the last piece of orange; but then she tickled him to make him choke, the ladders wobbled dangerously, and he yelled at her.

"Jesus, Rache! You got shit for brains, or what?"

She jumped down, stalked away, came back glaring; and for a second they balanced on the very edge of a row. But Derry sighed, put his Polyfilla down and said, "Sorry. You scared me, that's all. I don't want you hurt."

"I'm rubber," she said shortly. "I bounce."

"Yeah, well, I don't want me hurt either."

"No, and God only knows what you're made of these days. Concrete, I reckon. From the skull down. Next time you can just stick with the seven-stone weakling bit, okay? None of this muscleman stuff, you've got too heavy to throw around. Too big to bully. Bald and skinny, that's how I like my men. And short. You've blown it, buster. You can go find someone your own size . . ."

He grinned, perfectly reassured; sat down on the steps and pulled her closer, stroked the soft suede of her head till she stopped talking. Then, "Look, I'll be done in five minutes. Why don't you go and have a shower?"

"Are you saying I *smell*, Derry Bowen?"

"Yeah. Get some clothes out of the shop, too, that's disgusting," picking at the T-shirt she wore, damp and dirty after a hot day's work.

"Can we?" she queried, suddenly sounding desperate.

"Why not? You lot bought the place. Lock, stock and barrel, Richard said. And you can't sell the club gear to anyone, it's got the logo all over. Might as well wear it, I reckon."

"Oh, *magic* . . ."

Twenty minutes later, they came out of the gym damp and scuffling still, at the end of a happy fight: Rachel had found the stopcock and turned the water off in the middle of Derry's shower.

He called pax, locked up, claimed her hand; and,

"I do feel virtuous," Rachel said. "Tired and clean, there's nothing like it. And all the evening still to come . . . "

"What d'you want to do, then? After we feed Dad?"

"Dance," she said. "Can we?"

"Thought you were tired."

"Never too tired to dance. It's Wednesday, there must be a disco somewhere."

And she wrapped both hands around his wrist and towed him up to the junction, as if to prove herself still fizzing, ever ready to bop.

They bought a cauliflower and a pint of milk and headed for Derry's, where his father would be waiting for them, on sick leave now after Richard had persuaded him to a doctor; but they didn't get that far.

Their route took them past a run of derelict properties, burned out and boarded up. Parked in the street outside was the Commando's own APC, the battle bus they called it: a Ford transit with seats for twelve, brightly painted and armoured with faith. And there on the pavement were half a dozen shock troops in uniform, the hardest of the hard young men. The Church Militant. Nathan was with them, standing out by sheer force of will; and with them too, sitting slumped on a wall and seemingly under arrest, were three frightened kids. Two boys and a girl in school clothes and ties, barely in their teens. And here came a fourth out of the house behind them, where the boards had been levered off the doorway: with a Commando locked tight on each arm, this lad was stumbling and swaying between them, filth running like vomit out of his mouth. He had to be on something, glue or stronger.

Rachel moaned slightly under her breath.

"What?" Derry asked, fixing his grip on her hand in case she tried to slither away. He lost her too often to the Commando, didn't want to lose her now.

"Just, I know what this is. Kathy must've told Nat. I wish she hadn't."

"What are they doing, anyway?"

"Playing policemen." Rachel stood still, against Derry's tugging; and then, "I'm sorry," she said, "I'm going to have to help them."

"Don't look like they need any help to me."

"Not them, you idiot," jerking free now, pushing him away, "those kids. They look scared out of their wits . . . "

378

I would be, Derry thought, *with Nat on my back. Nat and his private army.*

He trailed reluctantly in Rachel's wake, heard her ask, "Where are you taking them?"

"Down the houses," Nathan said. "Just for a while, Rachel, don't look so worried. I'll get Dr Jonah over to have a look at them, that lad wants something to bring him down; the others just need a good scare and a bit of a talking-to. So we'll do that and run them home, have a word with their parents, maybe. It's better than the police, isn't it? Well, isn't it?"

"Yeah. I suppose . . . "

"All right, then. You and I can have a talk later. This is what we're for, Rachel. Among other things."

She nodded vaguely, promising nothing and still not looking reassured; then she made a move through the young men, towards the wall where the kids were sitting.

Derry held her up with an urgent hand on her arm.

"Come up to ours when you're finished," he said. "Please?"

"I don't know, Derry. I don't know how late I'll be . . . "

"Doesn't matter. I need you."

"No, you don't. Not as much as they do, not tonight. You can cook cauliflower cheese," she said, wilfully misunderstanding.

Derry ignored that. "You come to us, right? You mustn't go home on your own, it isn't safe."

"I can get a taxi."

"You can get me," he said. "I'm cheaper."

She gave in at last, with no words, only a tight sighing hug that he took for a promise. Then she went over to the wall where the kids were sitting, sending the watchful young men back with a contemptuous jerk of her head, *they don't need standing over, leave them to me. They're not your prisoners.* Except that they were, of course, and the young men stayed very watchful.

Derry saw her sit down beside the girl and put an arm around her shoulders. He saw how the girl tried to shrug her away, and failed, and hunched tighter into herself; and he thought that would work no better than the shrugging. You had to go at it harder than that, to put Rachel off. He knew . . .

Then, walking away, exchanging nods with Nat and the others, he saw a police car pass. The driver slowed to watch what was happening, but didn't stop; and that was typical, Derry thought, losing his grin entirely. That was the police all over. They wouldn't interfere, if they saw their job being done for them.

Or sometimes they didn't do it anyway, regardless. Like with Derry's mam, they hadn't done their job there, they hadn't found who killed her. Didn't seem interested any more, even, didn't seem to be looking.

He shoved his hands deep into tracksuit pockets, drew his head down into his shoulders, walked on home as if he were walking into a wind, his mental gears slipping between murder and cheese sauce.

iii

Nathan was feeling happy, very happy with his day's work; and he still had the night to come, it wasn't over yet. Not by a long chalk.

Things could go wrong yet, he still had that tension to keep him high and tight; but so far, he couldn't have scripted it better. Even the police had cooperated, by refusing to cooperate. He'd passed on what Kathy had told him, like a dutiful citizen should, and the desk sergeant had been deeply, devoutly uninterested. *I'll make a note of it, sir*, she'd said, *have one of our cars keep an eye out*; but her body-language had been saying something entirely different. *Who d'you think you are*, it was saying, *trying to run our patch for us, telling us our jobs? Nobody pulls our strings*, it was saying, *we don't dance to anybody's tune. Push off and play soldiers somewhere else* . . .

Which left Nathan free to play it his way: public protector and helpmeet, virtually writing his own headlines. *Local Christians Take Action After Police Do Nothing*, perhaps. Or, *Chapel Moves to Stamp Out Drugs in Paradise.*

But the job needed doing first, before he called the papers in; and the best bit of this job was still there for the doing.

Dr Jonah had already taken one of the kids off to hospital, the one who'd been out of his head on solvents. Nathan had sent a car to the boy's house to collect his mother. *All part of the service, ma'am.* Now the other three were being loaded into the battle bus, for their own journeys home. They'd been lucky. Nathan had confiscated the fractional amounts of cannabis they'd been carrying, along with their cigarettes and papers, and he'd taken their names and addresses for his files; but apart from that he'd promised them no action. He wouldn't even tell their parents, let alone the police.

And the price of this generosity? Information, of course. He'd made no bones about that, he'd named his price and they'd met it; and if there was honour among thieves it was certainly

380

news to him.

He saw them off with a wave and a smile, *see you around, kids; but don't let me see you doing this again, I don't want you brought back here*. He could see Rachel's shaven head through the window of the bus; she was sitting with the weeping girl, a friend in need, the gentler face of the Commando. Nathan made a note, he must be sure to have that talk with Rachel. An army runs on discipline, and its officers depend on loyalty from the troops; and she'd been ill-disciplined and disloyal both. He'd have to get her straightened out about that.

But meantime, there was work to do. He turned and walked back into the houses, as the bus drove away.

Half a dozen of his closest lieutenants were waiting for him in the office, the same young men who'd been with him on the bust this afternoon. Eager, dedicated soldiers for Christ, these: in an earlier age they'd have been crusaders, or Jesuit missionaries – or maybe, just maybe they'd have been inquisitors in the court of Philip II.

Certainly they were willing to fight; and that's what he asked of them tonight.

"It's a lesson, that's all," he said softly, earnestly. "An object-lesson, a deterrent. Nobody gets hurt, but everybody gets the message. This is our back yard, and we're going to keep it clean any way we have to. We've got to protect the kids."

He broke off as the door opened behind him, looked round to see Billy with a long, heavy box in his arms.

"I found them, Nat. Just where you said they were."

"Good lad, Billy. Just stick them on the table, thanks."

Billy put the box down and opened it, lifted out a baseball bat and swung it experimentally. Nat flinched, feeling the room suddenly smaller than before, the ceiling lower and himself more fragile.

"Careful, Billy. You'll hurt someone."

Billy shook his head. "Not me, Nat. I'm always careful." He put the bat back in the box, smiled at it, said, "Are you going to play a game?"

"Not tonight, Billy. It'll be getting dark soon."

"That's right. It'll be getting dark. What do you want them for, then?"

Nat might easily have lied for the sake of peace, to keep things easy; but his men were listening and he wanted no hint of doubt, no question about the rightness of this night's work.

"We're going to put the fear of God into some bad people, Billy," he said. "They've been selling drugs to schoolkids, right

381

here in Paradise; and we're going to stop them, that's all. We're going to run them out of town."

Billy thought about that, and said, "Can I come too?"

"I don't think you'd better, Billy-boy."

"Oh, yes," and Billy nodded definitely, determinedly. "Yes, I better had. It's God's work, isn't it? It's for God. I want to work for God too, I want to bat for God." He giggled, and hefted the bat again. Everyone ducked. "He's calling me. That's why I didn't know what to do with myself tonight. This is what He wants me to do. That's why you're all going, isn't it? Because God's calling you?" And when they reluctantly nodded, "Well, He's calling me too. And you can't argue with that."

And of course they couldn't, so Billy came too.

iv

Not all brothers were equal, no question about that; and these were very important brothers indeed. They had a cup of tea and biscuits, and prayed for a while; and then they took their baseball bats and climbed into the battle bus. And Billy went proudly with his brothers, and sat in the front next to Nathan.

"Where's Richard?" Billy asked. "He should be here, to bless us on our way."

"He doesn't know what we're doing, Billy. We'll tell him about it afterwards."

"Oh." Billy thought about that, tried to understand the idea of doing something without Richard's approval, failed utterly. "Don't you think we ought to tell him now?"

"No. This is my job. Are you sure you want to come?"

"Oh, yes," Billy said quickly, before Nat could stop the bus and put him out on the street. "I want to come. God wants me to come. But . . . "

"But what?"

"Richard won't, Richard won't *mind,* he won't be angry with us?"

"Look, Billy, I told you. I'm in charge of the Commando, I decide." And Nat did slam the brakes on now, did bring the bus to a hard stop. "Are you with us, or not? Would you rather just get out here? I'm not taking anyone along for the ride, you've got to be committed."

"I want to come," Billy said desperately, said again. "I do, yes. I'm with you, Nat. I was just, just asking . . . "

382

"All right, then." Nat started the bus again, and glanced over with a smile that helped a little to settle Billy's pounding heart. "Don't worry so much. Richard won't mind, why should he? This is the Lord's work too. It's the sharp end, that's all."

Billy nodded, mute and grateful.

It wasn't a long drive, just five minutes from the river to the top of the hill, where the main road marked the border of Paradise. Nathan parked in a back alley, then faced his troops.

"That's the flat," he said, "number 17, on the right there. We're not going in this way, though, we'll go round the front. We've got nothing to hide. And one last reminder, we're not here to hurt anyone. Defend yourselves if you're attacked, and look out for each other; but don't start anything. Got it?"

There was a general chorus of agreement, and only Billy's voice raised in query, now they were here and he couldn't be left behind any more: "Shouldn't we turn the other cheek, if they attack us? That's what it says in the Bible . . . "

Nat chuckled, but it wasn't a happy sound. "You can do that if you want to, Billy, but I don't think it's a good idea. This is eye-for-an-eye country. And it says that in the Bible, too."

Billy subsided then. One of his other brothers said a final prayer, for strength and courage and protection from evil; then they all got out of the bus and walked round onto the street.

"He lives alone," Nathan murmured as they clustered in front of number 17. "At least, that's what the kids said; but there are people in and out all the time, no telling what we'll find inside. Be ready for anything. Billy, you stick with Len, all right? Do what he tells you, and don't do anything else."

"Sure, Nat."

Billy grinned at brother Len, who nodded to Nathan and took Billy's arm, tugging him gently to the back.

"We'll be the rearguard, Billy," he said. "Just till we know what's what."

"Ready, then?"

A murmur of agreement, a single voice saying, "Christ be with us," loud and clear and triumphant; and Nathan lifted his baseball bat and knocked hard on the panelled door.

Three times he knocked, and had no answer; and he was just stepping back, just lining the bat up to swing, to smash the lock, when brother Micky stopped him. "Wait. Someone's coming."

A moment later the door opened a few inches, and a woman's voice said, "What do you want?"

383

"Dave," Nathan said. "I want Dave."

"He's not in."

"Well, never mind," Nathan said, and even from the back Billy shivered, at the sound of the smile in his voice. "You can give him a message, can't you?"

And then Nathan put the end of his bat against the door, and pushed abruptly; there was a gasp from the shadows inside, a stumbling noise, and the door swung open wide.

She was barely a woman that stood there, hanging on to the wall and staring: barely more than a girl, and vastly pregnant. Vastly frightened, too, her eyes wide in her thin face, seeing only the threat of them, their uniforms and weapons.

"Micky," Nat said, "can you take care of her?"

"Sure. Someone's got to. You come out of there, honey," and Micky took the girl by the hand and drew her out. "Come and sit here, on the wall. And listen, got somewhere else to go tonight, have you? Got a home to go to? Be a good idea, you don't want to stay here."

"I want to stay with Dave," she said, whisperingly defiant.

"No, you don't, honey. Believe me, you don't. Besides, Dave's not staying. He's finished here."

"That's the message," Nathan said from behind her, making her jump. "That's what I want you to tell him. Tell him his time's up. Party's over, tell him that. Tell him he's not welcome in Paradise, or anywhere in this city. By the way, where does he keep his stash?"

"Dunno what you mean," sullenly.

"Don't be silly, pet lamb," Micky said, with an arm round her shoulders and a gentle shake. "He's been dealing from here, and we don't like that; but it's his trouble, it's not yours. Don't involve yourself, you've got other things on your mind. Tell us where the stuff is, or we'll just have to tear the place apart, looking for it. We're not going to hurt Dave," he added quickly. "We're making a point, is all. He's been screwing up our kids."

The girl only tightened her lips, turned her head away.

"Okay," Nathan said. "Let's find it. Stay with her, Micky."

"You got it."

Nathan led his troops through the door and up the stairs. Behind him, Billy heard the girl's voice rising in a shriek: "You can't go in there! Get out of there, that's private, you can't just fucking barge in . . . "

Somewhere ahead of him, someone laughed; and Billy grinned too, because that's just what they had done, they had fucking barged in – *sorry about the bad word, God* – and of course they

384

could. They were the Commando and this was Paradise, and there wasn't anyone to stop them.

All the rooms in the flat had glass doors. Nathan stood on the landing, and sent his men through them.

"Iain, Joel, Stefan – you take the bedrooms. Len, Billy, go on through to the back, kitchen and bathroom. Be quick; but don't get carried away, don't forget to search. I want those drugs found."

"Sure, Nat, we'll find them. That apart, how far do we go?"

"All the way, Len." And Nat grinned suddenly, said, "You don't leave one stone standing on another."

Then he walked into the living-room with Len and Billy at his heels, on their way through to the kitchen; and he swung his baseball bat, casual and one-armed, and smashed the television.

It took a couple of minutes for Billy to get into this, to get his head around it. At first he had to keep asking Len, "Is it all right if I break this, then?"

But Len was ripping up the lino in the bathroom and checking the floorboards underneath, too busy to come and see. He just shouted through, yes every time; and soon Billy stopped asking. He waggled his bat around in a cupboard full of glasses, giggling as they shattered. He picked up piles of plates, and dropped them; he opened a window, chucked out a bowl full of washing-up and heard it smash in the yard beneath. That set a dog barking down the street, but Billy didn't care.

He'd just found a shelf full of jars of jam and pickled onions, and was making up his mind which wall to throw them at when he heard Micky's voice calling, his feet running up the stairs.

"It's okay, Nat, Linda's coming up. She'll show us."

"Good. Everyone on hold, please."

Reluctantly, Billy put the jars down and joined the others in the living-room. The girl Linda made her slow and heavy way up the stairs; then she stood in the doorway and stared, and started crying.

"He'll kill me," she said. "He'll fucking kill me . . . "

"No, he won't," Nat said confidently. "He won't lay a finger on you. You won't be here, anyway. I've decided, we're not leaving you in this mess. We'll take you back with us tonight, and sort something out tomorrow. Don't worry, Linda, you'll be seen to. Now, quick, where does he keep his drugs?"

"Have you finished, then?" she demanded, shuffling through an ankle-deep tangle of tape on the carpet, where Nathan had been busy with the videos. "Will you just go?"

"The sooner you show us," Nathan said, "the sooner we'll be gone. You, too. You don't want to be here when he gets back."

"Don't fucking tell me what I want." But there was no edge even to her defiance now. She fetched a sheet of newspaper, took it to the far corner of the room and spread it foolishly over the carpet, by where a giant yucca was growing in a big-bellied chamberpot.

"I can't lift it," she said, stepping back. "It just lifts out, but I can't manage."

Nathan gripped the stem of the plant with both hands, and jerked upwards; and it did just lift out, earth and roots and all contained within an inner pot. Nathan set it politely on the newspaper, and looked into the chamberpot. Reached in and lifted up handfuls of foil-wrapped cubes and little plastic envelopes.

"Good," he said blandly. "Joel, let's have some pictures."

Joel photographed the yucca, and the pot, and the drugs in the pot, while Linda moaned and hid her face in case he wanted to photograph her too. Then they laid all the drugs out on a sheet, and Joel photographed that; and then Nat took them all to the toilet and flushed them away.

Then he came back to the living-room, picked up the yucca one-handed and threw it like a javelin through the window, without bothering to open the window first.

Billy giggled; Linda screamed.

"You bastard!" she yelled, crying again as the video followed the yucca. "You fucking shit, you promised . . . "

"No, I didn't," Nathan said. "It's a hard lesson, I know, but Dave's got to learn. You go on out, we won't be long now."

Linda spat at him, and walked awkwardly out of the room. Billy heard her fumbling her way down the stairs, still sobbing; Nathan looked around and said, "Where's Micky?"

No answer, except a sudden cracking noise from the bathroom, the sound of a heavy weight falling. Len twitched an eyebrow, went to see; came back grinning.

"He's doing some very serious work on the lavatory, Nat. Good as a sledgehammer, these things," twiddling his bat in his hand.

"Right. Leave him to it, then. Billy, you go down after Linda, will you? Take her round to the van, get her settled. Here's the keys. We'll be out in a minute."

Ever obedient to his captain, Billy trotted down the stairs with the keys jingling in his hand and only a passing regret for those pots of jam, those clean white walls. That would have been fun;

but this was important. Which made him important too, among all these important brothers.

Coming out into the street, he found a small crowd gathered on the pavement opposite. A safe distance to be curious from; Billy recognised that, he'd measured it often enough himself.

Linda wasn't there, though, not sitting on the wall like she was before. He looked up the street, and saw her just turning the corner that would take her to the back alley, and the van.

Billy ran after. "Linda! Linda, wait for me. I've got the keys, you can't get in without me. I'm Billy, Linda . . . "

And then he reached the corner, and looked for her –

– and saw her, yes, saw her pressed against the wall, knuckles crammed into her mouth for sheer terror; and no wonder, because standing right there beside her was Billy's devil, wreathed in smoke and smiling.

And Billy didn't have his knuckles anywhere near his mouth, no, and no time to get them there either.

Billy just screamed, and screamed.

v

For once, Jason had a job to do that he was keen on: so keen, so eager that he'd actually asked to go with Vinny into Paradise this evening.

"You can come. You can do the shopping." Vinny wasn't like George, he didn't ask questions; and neither did Jason. He didn't ask what Vinny was doing in town, or why he was taking one of his dogs with him. Jason was only glad he got to sit up front this time, he didn't want to know.

They went to a supermarket first. Vinny sat in his van in the carpark while Jason filled a trolley for him, under orders. White bread, margarine, dried milk, instant coffee and tins, dozens of tins. Jason did the cooking now: open a tin, heat it up, put it in front of Vinny with half a dozen slices of bread. The dogs ate better, the fighting dogs got real meat. Not from a supermarket, that came from a butcher in one of Vinny's deals, and some weeks it didn't smell too good. The dogs wolfed it, though; and so would Jason have, given half a chance. Jason mostly lived off bread and marge.

The shopping was boxed up and stowed in the back with the

muzzled dog; then Vinny drove off, after making his own kind of arrangement to pick Jason up again.

"Be back here," he said. "After the pubs."

That could mean eleven, could mean one o'clock. Jason would be here at eleven.

But he was free now, if only for an evening; and the first thing Jason did was spend some of George's money.

He all but ran to the nearest chippie, ordered pie and chips and a jumbo sausage and guzzled them in the street outside, swigging at a Coke to wash the food down quick as he could. Taste didn't matter, he only wanted to feel full again.

He wadded polystyrene tray and paper wrappings into a ball and kicked them into the gutter, twisted and crushed the can and kicked that too, grinning at the clatter of it.

A voice called his name, footsteps came running over the road: "Jase, man, where've you *been,* what've you been *doing,* Christ, I haven't seen you for *months* . . . "

Jason snarled, shoved the boy up against the wall, hard; gave him just a quick glimpse of the blade he was carrying, that he'd sneaked out of Vinny's caravan. Said, "Shut your fuckin' mouth, Lee. You don't go shouting me up like that, right?"

"Jesus, Jase . . . "

"And you haven't fuckin' seen me, neither. Got it? Like you said, you haven't seen me for months, and you still haven't."

"All *right,* Jase, I got it, let me go, will you? Jesus . . . "

Jason stood away from him, jerked his head.

"Now get the hell away from me, all right?"

Lee backed off and hurried away, almost running, looking back over his shoulder as he went. Jason grinned again, savage and sure of himself, walking on air; but there was a lesson to be learned. Too many people round here knew his face, he was going to have to be careful.

Going up the hill, he saw one of Nathan's crowd playing soldiers in his stupid uniform, pasting notices on boarded-up doors and windows.

Jason ducked up the back alley, not to be seen, and found that the guy had been here already; there were posters on the back gates of all the empty houses.

WARNING! the posters said. *This property is under the protection of the Christ Commando, and may be inspected at any time. Do Not Trespass!*

Jason shivered, hearing Nathan's voice behind the warning,

remembering Nathan's sense of punishment.

There was a pair of empty flats for sale opposite where Derry lived, that had been left alone both by the vandals and the vigilantes. No notices on the back gate here, thank God; so Jason took a run and a jump at it, caught the top of the wall and hauled himself over.

He climbed the steps to the upper flat, glancing up and down the alley and watching the windows opposite. He felt dangerously exposed up here, above the sheltering wall; but upstairs was where he wanted to be, for the view he'd get.

Three good kicks sent the door crashing open. The first thing Jason did inside was push it to again, and wedge it shut with a good thick splinter from where the frame had split around the lock. He'd made a fair bit of noise out there, but God, this area, they'd be used to that. And he'd been quick. If anyone did look out now, there'd be nothing to see.

It was murky in there, with no lights and grey nets over all the windows. The air was warm and stale, thick with a summer's dust. Jason coughed, and made his way quickly through to the flat's front bedroom.

He had a perfect sight of Derry's door from here. He knelt by the window, twitched the net curtain a few inches aside and settled down to watch.

He was watching for Derry, wanting to catch him alone and vulnerable; but the first bald head he saw wasn't Derry's. He thought it was, when he saw a skinny teenager with no hair jumping out of a minibus on the corner. Took him a second to remember that Derry wasn't skinny any more; then another second, a closer look to realise this wasn't a boy anyway. Derry's girl, that's who it was, that Rachel he talked about all the time. Looked stupid like that, with all her hair shaved off. Sexy too, though. Christ, he'd like to give her one. Be like raping a nun, that would, he'd enjoy that . . .

She ran up to Derry's door and drummed on it hard with both fists. Then she shuffle-danced impatiently on the step until Derry answered; and already Jason knew he had no chance of getting Derry on his own tonight. Not before eleven, anyway, when he had to be back in the carpark.

He slipped out the back again, pulled the door closed behind him and slithered over the wall into the alley. A bunch of little kids watched him curiously, but he just stared them down and hurried to the corner.

Derry and Rachel were going off up the hill, hands in each other's pockets and no hurry. They were so wrapped up in themselves, Jason figured they weren't likely to look round; so he followed them for a couple of minutes, as far as the main road. They went straight over there, not heading down into town or waiting at any of the bus-stops; and Jason remembered something Derry had said at the gym once, that Rachel lived over in the posh north of the city. They were heading that way now.

Jason scowled and shook his head, decided to let them go. It wasn't safe, following them any further: not with the wide town moor to cross, no doorways there he could duck into if they did look back. Too bad. He'd like to know where Rachel lived. That'd be useful, it was giving him all sorts of good ideas . . .

At a loose end now until eleven, Jason wandered the streets and alleys, tasting his home turf again and wishing himself back here, wishing himself safe. No use pretending, though. He shouldn't be here, this was stupid, he was just laying himself open . . .

He'd get a few cans of lager and drink himself happy for an hour or two, in a corner of the supermarket carpark. That's what he'd do. But one more corner turned brought him into the fringes of a gathering crowd; and beyond their muttering heads he could see a flat with its door kicked in, people in combat jackets at the upstairs windows. *Time to get out of here, Jase.* The last thing he wanted was to run into Nathan. Even curiosity couldn't hold him against the threat of that.

So he peeled himself around the edges of the crowd, found a way into an alley, and took it.

And ran into Vinny instead, just standing there with a joint in his hand, inhaling deeply.

"Jase. What are you doing here, Jase?" The question whispered softly, soft and murderous.

"Nothing, Vinny. Just, just walking, like, and there were all these people. What's going on?"

Vinny didn't answer, he only looked at Jason and took another drag on the joint, letting smoke trickle out of his nose and mouth. Then a pregnant girl came out of the street in a hurry, saw Vinny and suddenly wasn't in a hurry any more, wasn't going anywhere, only huddled herself against the wall and chewed her knuckles in a panic; and she was followed by a man in a combat jacket, who saw Vinny and stopped too, and started screaming.

"Jase."

Vinny turned and walked away from the screaming man and the sobbing girl both; and at his word Jason trotted obediently at

390

his heels. Down past that same minibus that Rachel had got out of earlier, with religious slogans painted big and bright all over it, to where Vinny's van was parked behind it.

There was another man, a stranger standing beside the van with Vinny's dog muzzled and chained at his side.

"What is it, then?"

"It's the Christians," Vinny said. "Put the dog back in. Wait till they go, and see what they left you." And then the slightest, the least significant of pauses; and, "Those people are pissing me off," Vinny said.

THIRTY-ONE

i

He isn't angry, no, that's evident: he keeps his anger in reserve, to use as a weapon against the godless only. But he is disturbed, he must be, seeing things happen in his name that were never a part of his vision.

So he walks with Nathan, up from the houses to the old gym, which still no one except Richard has learnt to call the chapel; and on the way he says,

— I think you need to throttle back, Nat. Direct action is all very well, I applaud it; but when it comes to trashing people's homes, and scaring a pregnant girl out of her wits . . .

— She wasn't as scared as Billy, Nat murmurs as though he's only half listening, as though his mind is following its own track through this story. Billy met his devil in the alley, he says, did you know?

— Yes, I've talked to Billy. That's not the point at issue.

— No, Nat agrees. The point is, this guy was selling drugs to schoolkids, and the police weren't interested. What did you want us to do, turn a blind eye?

— No. I'm not disputing the need, it's your methods that concern me. That girl, and the sheer violence of what you did. Even the papers have reacted badly, they're talking about vigilantes again, and the American experience . . .

— We'd have looked after that girl if she'd let us. If she hadn't gone running off. Someone took care of her, anyway; she was back at her mum's the next day. I found out who she was and sent people round to check. And if you want to talk about the papers, have you looked at the letters columns? It's the punters' reaction I'm interested in, and they love it, they're grateful. They're not worried by horror-stories about gunfights in Los Angeles, why should they be? We don't carry guns.

— You carried baseball bats.

— And used them, on toilets and televisions. Look, it *worked*, Richard, that's the point. That's what matters. Nobody got hurt, there's one drug-dealer less on the streets of Paradise, and an object-lesson for the others.

— No doubt. But you're the Christ Commando, after all. Christ was a man of peace, he preached gentleness; you work under His name, you should follow His teachings.

— I'd rather follow his example, Nathan says, smiling.

And his smile speaks of moneychangers, and of whips; and for once Richard has no answer.

ii

Terry Belderstone wasn't happy, he felt let down; and that did call for a face-to-face meeting, it was the sort of message that wouldn't come over so well down a telephone. People might misunderstand. Even an old friend might just underestimate Terry's deep and legitimate grievance, and mistake the call for a simple slap on the wrist.

So he'd summoned John to a meeting, a long way from home turf for both of them. *Meet me at the coast,* he'd said. *The lighthouse carpark, three o'clock. Don't be late.*

Driving over the rough causeway at half past three, his tyres churning through puddles left by the retreating tide, he reflected that John must have had a difficult time of it, crossing even half an hour earlier; and was still smiling when he reached the small carpark, to find John moodily waiting by the wall.

Terry stopped his car, and sat still until John walked over; and then he waited a few seconds longer before pressing the button that wound his window down.

"Bloody hell, Terry," John said explosively, "where the hell have you been? Three, you said; and I nearly wrecked my bloody car to get here, I thought you must be over already, thought you must've come over this morning. God knows why you'd want to spend a day here, but that's what I thought. And the notice-board said the crossing wasn't safe till a quarter past, and bloody right, too . . . "

Terry said nothing till the tirade was over; and then he ignored it completely. "That job I asked you to see to," he said, "I understand your man messed it up, is that right?"

"No," John said. "Vinny doesn't mess things up. It went wrong, but that's not Vinny's fault. You put a couple of Molotovs through a window, you expect the place to burn, don't you? I mean, don't you?"

"So why didn't it?"

"Christ knows. Miracle, the papers said. Did you see that? They called it another bloody miracle."

393

"I saw." Terry looked up at John, and said, "I've got no time for miracles. You understand? I want that job done, properly and soon. Both parts. I want them off my property, even if you have to destroy the property to achieve it; and I want all the papers in that office destroyed, in any case."

John sucked air through his teeth, shook his head doubtfully. "Won't be so easy now, Terry mate. They'll have those soldiers of theirs on guard now, it won't be easy to get past them. And likely they'll have shifted anything valuable out of there already, put it in the bank."

"I don't think so. They're cocky, they've got God on their side; they'll think they're as safe as any bank. So prove them wrong."

"What's so important, then? What are you so fussed about, some religious nut's paperwork? What have they got on you, Tel?"

"Never you mind what," Terry said; and now the message was getting through, this was why he did this face to face. Because big as he was, John's face paled suddenly and his legs took him an involuntary pace backwards from the strength of Terry's stare. "Don't ask questions," Terry said, "knowledge is dangerous. And I want that lot feeling the danger. No more miracles, John. No excuses. Those houses'll burn, the same as their old chapel burned. That gym they've taken over, too. Burn the lot, if you need to. Just do the job."

John ran a hand over his face and looked at it curiously, as if surprised to see how he was sweating; but he nodded, and said, "Yeah, sure. Don't suppose Vinny'll need encouraging anyway, he took it very personal, like, when it didn't work the last time. He'll like another crack."

"See that he gets it right, this time. Tell him."

"You've not met Vinny, have you?" John murmured; and turned and walked away before Terry could respond.

Terry sat in his car and watched him drive away, drumming his fingers lightly on the wheel and thinking how much trouble those few people in Paradise had caused him. Impossible to believe, that they should be so hard to shift. Unless you believed in miracles, of course; which Terry didn't. Emphatically not. Even money couldn't buy miracles.

Conflagrations, though, it could certainly buy conflagrations; and Christians certainly burned, that was well established throughout history. One fire might have gone out, but the next one wouldn't; and if there were any Christians in the middle of it, well, Terry wouldn't mind that.

Wouldn't mind a bit.

Anita looked out of her window and saw soldiers, and was sore afraid.

These were the hard young men of her terror; and they shouldn't be here, she hadn't got that far yet, she was deliberately too young for this.

But there they were, parading in uniform on the broken ground below her window, marching or driving off to only the good Lord knew where and for what dreadful purpose. Or they sat in gangs on the stony ground with their jackets off and their faces turned to the sun, their voices loud and their laughter louder. Girls, too, they had girls who aped their uniforms and their manners, who sat and laughed with them and spoke the language of the invader, and didn't speak Polish at all.

After dark they patrolled the street, and no sign of any girls with them then: only the young men and always in groups. They spoke in softer voices and swung long truncheons through the air and looked eager to use them, to break and smash and destroy; and Anita watched from her window instead of sleeping, and was afraid.

She wouldn't go out the front at all now. She wouldn't walk under those young men's eyes, to be humiliated by their lusts and her own terror. No wonder her friends never came to visit any longer, with that gauntlet to run; no wonder she had to pass her long days alone.

Jacek was a brave boy, he still went to work each day; she'd even seen him chatting with the soldiers. Not collaborating, of course, he was no collaborator; but it made good sense not to antagonise them, these young men far from home. Better to keep them easy, even at the cost of a little pride.

It was a dangerous game to play, though, standing smiling under their cold eyes, too close to those long clubs. Anita's heart walked a wire every time she saw. It was chiefly for her own sake that he did it, to keep her a little safer while he was gone; but still she wished that he wouldn't, still she wished he'd stay home with her and never go out again.

Nor did the soldiers keep to the street in front. Sometimes she went into the garden to hang out the washing or pick flowers for the dining-room, or simply to sit a little while in the sun; and more than once she'd seen them out there too, between the gardens and the river. Each time they'd smiled and been polite, greeted her by name and lifted their clubs only in salute, but each time she'd scuttled back inside as quickly as she might, and not gone out again that day.

Today, there was no one out at the back; Anita had checked that, from behind her curtains. The soldiers were all on the waste ground in front of the houses, laughing and shouting. She could hear them even with the windows closed on this hot day, the curtains pulled. She sat over her sewing and tried not to listen to their noise: tried to pretend that there had been no war and no invasion, that there were no soldiers and that any imminent knock on the door would be only a girlfriend come to call, or a boy with flowers and a shy invitation, would she care to walk in the park this bright sunny day?

But her needle slipped in her sweating fingers; and yet when she raised those fingers to her aching temples they were cold, cold as a lavender compress but far less comforting.

She rose, to go to the bathroom and wash; but she'd taken only two paces towards the door when the window shattered behind her. She gasped and turned, clutching the chair-back for support. The curtain still moved from the force of whatever had struck it, whatever had broken the window. The soldiers weren't shouting or laughing now, the sounds of breaking glass had silenced them; but Anita could hear their feet running towards the house, and that was worse. That was nightmare. After the weeks of tension, of pressure, of threat unspoken and danger barely kept in check, now came what she had dreaded so long. Just one of them grown tired of waiting, frustrated, wanting blood: he picks up a rock, weighs it in his hand and throws. And with the shatter of the window everything else is broken too, all the restraints. All Jacek's good work forgotten. Now they were coming, as she had always known they would come: coming to do harm, to rape, to smash and destroy. She was her country, and what they had done to her country they would willingly do to her . . .

But Anita could run, at least. They wouldn't take her as easily as they had taken her home town, so quickly they'd done that, just there one morning on the street and everything under control, everything in their hands.

She shook off the paralysis of terror and dragged herself through the house from front to back, grabbing at door-frames and furniture, her arms pulling her on when her legs were weak. Wrenched the back door open, and staggered outside; and thank the good God the soldiers were young and impetuous and hadn't planned this, hadn't sent anyone to watch the gardens.

She ran over the lawn and between Jacek's vegetable beds, and heard distant knocking as she ran: those deadly young men hammering on her door, just a moment short of breaking it down.

There was a wall at the bottom of the long garden, but it was old and badly needed mending, there was a place where the bricks had tumbled and Anita could scramble through the gap. No path on the other side, only rough and broken ground, falling away steeply to the river; but she was out of sight from the house down here. They would take a few minutes to search, before they thought to look for her through the windows; and when they looked, they would see nothing.

There was comfort in that, if none in the sound of their voices that she could hear now, thinly calling her name. Wolves they sounded like, wolves howling on the trail.

No time to rest. She scrabbled and slipped down to where there was a path, an old road that ran beside the river. There she hesitated a second: left or right? Which was better? It didn't matter; in an occupied city both ways were dangerous. She turned right, the way that would bring her more quickly out into the country, where she might find people to help her and somewhere to hide, somewhere she could get a message to Jacek.

But she didn't get as far as the country. She didn't get very far at all before there was a man standing blocking her way; and she couldn't see him clearly, squinting into the sun the way she was, but he shouldn't be there really, there shouldn't be anyone, not down here, no one ever came down here . . .

He spoke to her, but she couldn't understand him. He didn't look like a soldier, wasn't in uniform but wasn't speaking Polish either. And then he seized her arms and lifted her almost off the ground, lifted her to his face like he was going to eat her; and that's what his smile said too, that she was food and had come there for the eating.

She could see him better now, his dark face and his filthy smile; she could smell his breath, even, and that was worse even than the smell of her fear, rank on her body. Her weak, gnarled hands pressed at him, tried to push him away; but he only laughed, and shook her, and dropped her down.

Broken tarmac stung her hands, terror cut at her mind like shards of glass; and when she tried to crawl away, he seized her by the hair and lifted her cruelly to his face again, and bit her chewingly to swallow her screaming.

Helen saw it all, from where she sat in the shadow of a bridge that was never built, just the first rough ramparts raised before the money dematerialised.

She often came down here these days for the privacy of it, to encompass herself with solitude. She could sit for hours in this hopeless silence, where the voice of the city had been broken by neglect: sit and watch the river run, and sink so far into desolation that she was no longer afraid even of her own despair.

Today she saw a man walking on the road below her; and she shivered, and pressed closer against the bank of earth and rubble where he shouldn't see her, because even in the bright sunlight he carried his darkness like a cloak about him. But though he frightened her, still it was only like watching something frightening on television, as all her life now was like watching television. Nothing was real, nothing could truly touch her.

She watched him pass, and the aura of his malevolence passed with him; and then it was more than ever like television, because at a distance she saw an old woman appear suddenly on the road ahead of him. They were stick-figures from here, and she couldn't see clearly with that aura of his clouding everything about him, but she could see enough.

She saw how he raised the woman and let her fall, and lifted her again; how he held her as if for a kiss, and then how his hands misused her, then his feet.

How long he took to do it.

Helen watched it all from where she sat, as though she were watching television; and when he was finished, when he walked away and left the old woman broken and still on the roadway, still she sat and watched for a while longer.

He was long out of sight before she moved. She stood and walked over the rough ground towards the houses, and even then she didn't go down to the road.

She found the Commando frenetic, hiving like bees, in and out of the long terrace.

"She's not here," she heard someone report, loud enough for his voice to carry even over the distance she kept between herself and Nathan. "That's definite. Even if she was hiding, we'd have found her."

"Crazy old cow." Helen heard that too, and the total lack of affection that underlay it. Amazing, that no one else heard the truth of Nathan in his voice; he gave himself away to her with every word he spoke. Not that it mattered.

Helen caught someone's arm as he hurried past. "Who's not here," she asked, "who've you lost?" *Apart from me.*

The boy looked at her as though she were more than lost, as though she were totally forgotten already. Only good manners gave her an answer. "Miss Dubrowski," he said. "Anita. We were playing baseball, and we broke her window; and when we went to apologise and mend it for her, she was not there. But Jack says she should be, and so we are worried. We are making a big search."

Helen nodded wisely. "I thought it might be her," she said. "Don't worry about a search, I know where she is."

Helen led half a dozen of them straight there, along the bottom road. She had Nathan at her elbow, too close: and that closeness was enough to turn this real, no television now, no changing channels or watching the white noise.

The old woman wasn't dead, or anywhere close to it. Helen heard the obligatory murmur of prayer behind her, as her companions thanked God for it. Some of her companions, at any rate: Nathan's mouth was tight and angry, saying nothing.

Anita had moved just a few metres in the twenty minutes since the man had left her, and she'd clearly paid all too dearly for even that little distance. She'd pulled herself off the road, and now lay huddled against a slab of broken concrete, slack-jawed and dribbling, her face streaked with filth and her fingers twitching at her torn clothes.

Nathan made a noise of deep disgust, and gestured to the others. "Help her," he said. "Get her back to the houses. Dr Jonah's on his way over, I called him straight away. He'll settle her down."

Helen didn't make a move, didn't need Nathan's hand tight on her arm to restrain her. Real or not, Anita's troubles were no troubles of hers: counted for nothing, against Nathan's hand tight on her arm.

Anita screamed when they tried to move her, a thin wail without air or body, fragile as her hold on sanity. They couldn't see what had been done to her, much – there were bruises and bite-marks on her face but no bones broken, they thought, certainly no blood – but she meant that scream, she was surely hurting.

Nathan sent a couple of boys running for the battle bus and the doctor. It wouldn't be easy driving, but they could bring the vehicle part of the way at least, and there was a stretcher in the back.

He said nothing, while they waited. The rest of the team was clustered around Anita, one of the girls talking to her while the others prayed; but Nathan stood apart, kept his grip on Helen's arm and said not a word.

The bus came at last, bumping slowly over the broken road. The doctor jumped out and ran to his patient, while the boys brought the stretcher behind him. Helen didn't watch, but she heard another scream from Anita, then a soft moan, then nothing more; and a minute later the stretcher was carried back and slid into the bus bearing a blanketed form.

Nathan didn't even ask Dr Jonah how she was, how she'd be. He only stood and watched, and perforce Helen stood with him. As the team climbed aboard, one of the boys asked if they weren't coming; and then Nathan spoke, then he said, "No. We'll be along later. I want a word with Helen, in private."

The boy nodded, and pulled the door shut.

No room to turn here, so they watched the bus reverse slowly around the corner and out of sight. Then, when they were alone in this nightmare country, Nathan said, "So tell me about it, Helen. Tell me how you could sit there — where were you, up there somewhere, was it? — tell me how you could sit up there and watch while an old lady was being tortured. Tell me how you could do that, because I don't understand."

Helen just shrugged. She didn't believe him, she thought he could understand that. She thought he could do it himself without batting an eyelid; he could probably do the torturing, come to that. But she wasn't going to challenge him. Why bother? It didn't matter now, what he thought of her or she of him.

Then he struck her.

It was a brutal, dizzying blow that set her rocking, would have sent her stumbling over the road and into the river if he hadn't caught her head with his other hand and held her still, held her upright.

"Talk to me, Helen," he hissed, twisting her hair in his hand, dragging her onto tiptoe against the pain of it. "Tell me how it was. Or are you saving it for the papers, is that it? Do you want to sit up on the dais at a news conference and tell the world instead, tell them all how it felt to do nothing, to betray Richard and me and this whole movement, never mind Anita? Is that what you're after?"

She gave him something then: not a lot, just a soft whimper and a momentary shake of the head, but it was enough. He released his grip, allowed her to scuttle back a metre or two before his voice caught her, held her again just as tightly.

"Well," he said cruelly, contentedly, "if you won't talk to the papers and you won't talk to me here, just the two of us, we'll have to do this formally, I'm afraid. I think you're sick, Helen. I think you're dangerously ill, if you can watch an old woman's agony and do nothing to stop it. I don't think we can afford to carry you with us any longer. But it's not my decision, of course. I'll convene a meeting for tomorrow night, I'll get Richard there and Dr Jonah, a few other people. Sort of a star chamber, I suppose you'd call it. You can try to explain yourself to them, and then we'll decide what's best to do. Seven-thirty, at the houses. Don't be late. And you'd better not be around much before then, all things considered. Best if you keep away, I think."

And he smiled, nodded dismissal, and walked off down the road and away; but the bruises that he'd left on her arm and on her face were enough to keep this real for Helen, still not television, still no chance to change channel.

So that it did matter after all, it mattered a terrible great deal, and her pain was far greater than Anita's, although she wasn't screaming.

Not aloud.

THIRTY-TWO

i

They've given Anita a room to herself, at his request; but that seems to be about all he can do for her. No miracles this time round. He's prayed over her, and laid hands on her; but she shrieked at his touch, and paddled her hands in the air to waft him away.

The doctors say to give her time, to give her peace. And whether it's what they meant or not, what she's getting is a constant prayer vigil at her bedside, a twenty-four hour hotline to God, hot and humming.

Richard hasn't left her yet, except for one hour when he walked around the other wards shedding peace and hope and dreams of health as a tree sheds blossom. The journalists followed him on walkabout, gleefully gathering copy: and he knows what the stories will say. *If he can heal strangers and unbelievers,* they're going to ask, *why can't he heal his own?* He's told them, of course, he's answered that question more than once; but they're journalists, they don't listen. That's understood.

Meanwhile, he sits by Anita's bed with her brother Jack beside him, members of the Commando, other friends. He leads them all in prayer, spoken or silent, they follow his lead as ever; and anyone who wants to see him has to come and see him here.

As Nathan, now:

– You will be there, won't you, Richard? Seven-thirty, down at the houses. It's important that you're there.

– I suppose I can come, yes, he says, with a regretful glance at Anita's slack face, her dark bruises. *I'd rather be here,* he's saying; and aloud he says it another way, says, I'm not sure about this, though, Nat. Not this way, not a trial . . .

– It's not a trial, Nat says briskly, no one wants to judge her. An explanation, he says, that's all.

– Well, leave it to me, then, just let me talk to her in private. She'll talk to me. She couldn't to you, perhaps, things are complicated between you; but she'll talk to me . . .

But Nat's shaking his head already, saying, I think we all need to hear it, Richard. What she did reflects on all of us; and I think she owes us that much, a public explanation. It won't be easy for her, I do know that; but it's necessary. Not a trial, but I think she has to work a little, I think that's fair. That's justice.

And Nathan's sense of fairness or justice may not accord with Richard's, or with his sense of Helen's needs; but every general has to back his commanders in the field. It's a matter of discipline. So he nods, and says,

– I'll be there.

Nathan glances at Anita and says, Has she talked yet? Has she said anything, about the guy who attacked her?

– Only a little, Richard says, and only in Polish. A werewolf, Jack tells me; that's what she was talking about.

– Terrific, says Nathan. Babbling old bag, he says, why can't she get her head straight?

And Richard only smiles, not listening to the words: listening only to the buried affection he clearly hears in Nathan's voice, the true gold beneath his affected harshness.

ii

It had been a terrible day for Rachel, and it wasn't getting any better. Not worse, mind, it could hardly do that, she couldn't imagine it getting worse; but nothing that happened helped, and nothing that might help showed any signs of happening.

The latest thing was Nathan tying her up in this kangaroo court of his, asking her to stand in as Helen's friend.

"You won't have to say anything," he said. "She just needs someone to sit with her, and give her a shoulder to cry on if she gets upset."

Rachel thought she'd get upset all right, confronted by Nathan at his nastiest and a jury of Commandos. Let him say what he liked, this was definitely a trial. And *not today,* she thought, *for God's sake not today, just leave me alone.* But she couldn't say that, so, "Why me?" she demanded. "It's not like I'm any special friend of Helen's . . . "

"I don't think Helen has any special friends," Nathan said solemnly.

"Even so. Find someone, I don't know, tougher than me, someone who can stand up for her better. Someone *older,* for crying out loud. I'm only seventeen, I'm younger than she is . . . "

"Not in outlook, love," and Nathan was grinning at her now, irresistibly sexy in spite of everything, her deep mistrust and her

403

spindizzy mind. "Not in wisdom; and that's what Helen needs, just a bit of good Christian wisdom and a hand to hold. I can't think of anyone better, or I'd be asking them, wouldn't I?"

One thing for sure, he certainly wouldn't be asking Rachel if he knew what was going on in her head, what she was trying to adjust to this dreadful day. But she nodded numbly, *sorry, Helen, I'll do a rotten job for you; but that's life, sister,* and said yes.

Said, "All right. Of course. If that's what you think . . . "

"Good girl. And don't worry, pet, it'll be fine." He stooped and kissed her cheek, and moved on before she'd made up her mind to flinch away.

One blessing, there was some time yet before the court convened: time to walk and think, and be alone.

She walked out of the houses wishing she hadn't come at all today, feeling betrayed, feeling conspired against, even God ganging up on her. She should have followed her first impulse and kept right away, and never mind that old myth about things being easier to bear if you kept busy . . .

Fifty metres down the hill and there was suddenly a voice behind her calling her name, footsteps running and skidding to catch up.

She didn't look round, didn't need to. Derry appeared, whooping; grabbed her arm as a brake to stop himself plunging on into the river and then held on to it possessively, elbow in one hand and wrist in the other.

"Where are you going, then?" he demanded. "You don't go walking around on your own, not down here. Christ, that old girl was attacked down here, that was only yesterday. You got no sense, or what?"

Rachel hadn't thought of that, it simply hadn't occurred to her that she might be walking into danger; but this wasn't the best way to hear it. Not today, and especially not from Derry.

She jerked free with a scowl, took a couple of slow, deep breaths not to say anything worse than she wanted to, and said, "Leave it, Derry. I'll be fine."

"Of course you will. Now. I'm here." And he was blithely reaching for her hand, loud and brash and confident, not picking up any messages; so that she had to put both hands behind her and dance a couple of paces backwards, out of reach.

"Derry. Listen to me. Just leave me alone, okay? I don't want you right now." *I don't want anyone, but particularly not you.*

She was still working hard, not to be gratuitously vicious; but apparently that was vicious enough, that stung. She saw him flinch, and twist a little away; but even then, even with his eyes bleeding hurt at her, he didn't go. "I'm not leaving you down here. What's wrong, anyway, what have I done?"

What had he *done?* Sweet Jesus . . .

She didn't even try to answer him, she only turned and walked off, and heard his unwelcome footsteps dogging her; and turned again to say, "For God's sake, Derry, can't you take a hint? I don't bloody want you!"

He grinned weakly, squinting his eyes against the sun or against the glow of her anger; and said, "You know, your language, it's getting really bad. I must be a bad influence or something, you never used to swear. Used to be a good girl, before you met me . . . "

And that was enough, that was altogether too much. Rachel stooped and snatched up a handful of gravel and stones, chucked them at him hard, meaning to hit.

Said, "Fuck off, Derry Bowen. Just, just fuck right off, all right?"

And ran this time, off and away down the road; and heard behind her the blessed silence of his feet not following, though she could feel his eyes following her all the way.

Running felt good, it felt like she could run right out of her body and leave all its problems behind her; and when she couldn't run any longer, when she had to drop onto a bench or die, that felt good too. Her brain was buzzing, her heart was working so hard she could feel it right in her bones, her poor legs trembled and ached and even her sweat was comfortably and familiarly her own, all salt and Rachel. She closed her eyes, stretched out under the lowering sun and thought maybe she wouldn't go back, she'd just stay here and drift . . .

Except that she wouldn't be left alone, they'd come looking. Not fair to put them through that, to have them thinking she was another Anita, attacked by a wolf-man and left for dead.

No, better to go back. Better that than being fetched . . .

She didn't rush into it, she certainly didn't run; but when she was ready — ready as she'd ever be, at least, with everything changed and new and terrible — she walked slowly back into her life again.

Halfway there she saw Derry, standing on a ridge of rubble a couple of hundred metres up from the river, where he must have been watching for her all this while. Neither one of them waved, or made any move towards each other. Derry was a problem again, but he was very much a problem for later. She had herself

405

to sort out first.

She was well late back at the houses, almost twenty minutes and almost deliberately so. Certainly she was hoping they'd have got fed up waiting, and found someone else to hold Helen's hand.

But she went to the room anyway, to show willing; and found Richard and Nathan waiting there, half a dozen others, no Helen.

"You're late," Nathan said, knuckling her skull lightly, no heat in it and not at all perturbed at how quickly she ducked away. "Where've you been, with Derry? Well, no matter, Helen hasn't turned up either. Come on, we'll go fetch her. Just you and me, I think."

He didn't give her a chance to say no, he took her elbow and led her straight out to his car.

They passed Derry on the brief drive up to Helen's flat. He was standing on the rough ground opposite the gym, where he could watch what went on down at the houses. He stared fixedly at the car as they drove past; Nathan sounded the horn and waved, Rachel just looked stonily ahead. Whatever happened now between the two of them, she wasn't going to start it through a car window.

The curtains were pulled and the lights were out at Helen's flat, no signs of life. Nathan hammered on the door, and got no reply; but when Rachel expected him to turn away and leave it, when her soul was secretly singing with this unexpected relief, he fished in his pocket instead and pulled out a bunch of keys.

It took her a couple of seconds to remember that he used to live here himself, this was his flat before it was Helen's. By that time he'd found the right key and was letting them in.

"Do you think we should?" Rachel murmured, hesitating on the doorstep.

"Sure, why not?"

"Well, it's her home . . . "

"Not mine any more, you mean?" Nathan grinned at her. "But she might be sick. We ought to check, at least."

Besides, you've got the keys and you're going to look anyway, right or wrong. Right? Right.

Standing uncomfortably in the living-room, watching Nathan rummage through a pile of notes by the phone, Rachel slowly realised what felt so strange about this invasion: which was that it didn't look like an invasion at all. You'd never have known that Nathan didn't live here any more. In himself he seemed totally at

406

home, totally relaxed; but more than that, Helen couldn't have changed anything since he left. His posters on the walls, his clutter on the mantelpiece – Rachel could even see his old dental appointments still pinned up above the phone, along with half a dozen postcards that she was willing to bet had all been sent to him.

Poor thing, she thought. *He walked out on her, but she's still trying to live within his life. Maybe she pretends he's still around, if all his stuff's still here. His fault, he should've cleared out properly if he was going. He probably gets a kick out of it, though, he's the type . . .*

Nathan looked up at her suddenly, as though he was hearing her thoughts loud and clear.

"Have a look in the bathroom, will you? Just to be sure."

Rachel shuddered, remembering finding Evelyn adrift in her own blood. "Please, no. Not the bathroom."

Nathan remembered then, if he hadn't before, though Rachel rather thought he had. "All right. I'll do the bathroom. You take the bedroom, okay?"

"Okay. What am I looking for, exactly?"

He shrugged. "Anything that might tell us where she's gone. She used to read her post in bed, maybe she had a letter or an invite. Maybe she left me a note, she must've known I'd come looking. Just see what you can find."

Helen had left Nathan a note. There was a sealed envelope with his name on, propped up against the clock on the bedside table.

Somehow that was what Rachel saw first, turning the light on in the curtained room. She saw the envelope, perhaps because that was what she was looking for; she walked over and picked it up, and was already turning to call him when she saw also how the bedclothes were humped over a still form, how a fan of red hair was spread across the pillow.

"Helen . . . ?"

Wondering if she were really asleep or only faking, only hiding down there, Rachel drew the duvet slowly down from Helen's face.

She lay comfortably on her side, no tension in her. Her skin didn't so much as twitch, so she probably was sleeping. And looked as though she needed to, so pale above the satin green of her pyjamas, she must be ill. They couldn't drag her down to the houses in this state. But she should know that they'd been; and maybe they could help, maybe Dr Jonah should see her . . .

Rachel grasped her shoulder, shook her lightly – and snatched her hand back too late, already burned by the coldness of that touch, even while a colder sweat prickled on her scalp.

Disturbed, Helen slid slowly onto her back and her head toppled off the pillow, so that Rachel could see how she was wax-pale on one side of her face only. The other was mottled purple, and even now her eyes didn't open; and Rachel's fingers were still rubbing themselves together, trying to rub away the chill of her in those shimmering pyjamas . . .

Rachel stepped back from the bed thinking *Evelyn,* thinking baths full of blood. She opened her mouth to yell for Nathan, then changed her mind ridiculously, didn't want to shout in this room, didn't want to wake Helen now. And then blessedly didn't need to shout because she heard him coming anyway, coming in.

"Jesus fucking *Christ!*" she heard; and then she was pushed aside as Nathan strode over to the bed, lifted Helen's slack arm and fumbled for a pulse.

No point in that, she thought but didn't say.

After a second Nathan glanced up at her, said, "Get Richard. Now. *Hurry.*"

And that made sense, at least, that felt right; though Nathan clearly was hoping for another miracle, and Rachel was dead sure there wouldn't be one. Not this time, Helen was too long gone from here, even Richard couldn't call her back.

Nathan was prepared to try, though, all by himself until Richard came; Rachel's last sight of him, he was swinging his hand viciously across Helen's cheek, "Come on, you bitch, you fucking little shit, snap out of it, come *on* . . . "

Out of the door and down the hill, running again; and again she was running to escape. Not to fetch Richard — no point hurrying for that, despite Nathan — but only to leave Helen behind. Not to have the touch-memory of cold meat on her fingers, that was what counted.

Halfway there, she met the battle bus coming up with Dr Jonah at the wheel. He braked just long enough for Richard to jump out, then revved the engine and roared away again, blaring his horn at the intersection as he drove through a red light.

"You know," Rachel said, gasping, stumbling into Richard's arms. "Don't you?"

Even now, Richard found the time for a quick smile as he hugged her.

"Nothing magic," he said. "Nathan phoned."

"Oh." She hadn't thought of the telephone. Perhaps she hadn't wanted to; better to have come running, perhaps, than to wait in that cold flat and watch Nathan bullying a corpse. "Well," she said, "shouldn't you be going, then? It was you he wanted." And then, feeling suddenly bitter, "Dr Jonah can't help. You neither, but Nathan wants a miracle."

"Miracles wait on the Lord," Richard said, quite sternly. "Five minutes either way, what's that to God? And you're in my charge too."

"I'm all right."

"Are you?"

"Well. I will be."

"Yes," he said, "that at least I'm sure of; but a little help wouldn't go amiss. You could use a hand to hold. Go and find Derry, he'll look after you. That's what he's for."

A wink, a grin, a quick kiss on the cheek and Richard was off, jog-trotting up the hill, covering a lot of ground fast. Rachel watched him out of sight, thinking that he couldn't know everything after all, or he would have changed his prescription. Derry was no safe harbour tonight.

No sign of him still hanging around, though, so at least she wouldn't have to fight him off again. He'd panic, of course, as soon as he heard about Helen; and then he'd pass that panic to everyone else, trying to find her.

Well, let him. Rachel lived at the centre of a web, family and friends and boyfriend and church all interwoven: every which way she turned she saw love in abundance, so much love it was choking her. She had to tear free of it tonight, whatever damage she did.

No, Derry could whistle for her. And the rest of them, they could make an orchestra of whistlers, whistle up the wind, it still wouldn't work. She wasn't running to anyone.

So she didn't run, she walked; and she walked alone and slow, heading ultimately for home but not in any hurry. She walked up through Paradise – past Derry's door to prove she wasn't hiding from him, ready to send him away if he appeared – and over the road to where the streets turned a little smarter, semis rather than terraces, houses rather than flats.

It was the same route she'd walked so often with Derry at the end of an evening, her feet were doing that automatically, turning at all the right corners. And how he loved doing that, the responsibility of it, seeing her home and keeping her safe.

Didn't make a very good job of it, though. Did you, boy? You may not be asked again.

Maybe he wouldn't wait to be asked, though. A couple of times, looking round, she saw a figure some way behind her; and that could well be Derry. Probably was. She couldn't tell for sure in the fading light, but it made sense. He wouldn't come close after the last time. He'd been lurking all evening, watching her from a distance, and he was lurking still.

This was a sop to his conscience, Rachel supposed, a way he could pretend he was still taking care of her. Still seeing her safe home.

Bit late for that, boy. Might as well see Helen safe, for all the good you can do either one of us now.

She thought about Helen, of course she did, not trying to outrun her now. She thought about Helen and hugged herself for her own warmth, against that memory of cold; and tried again to rub the touch of it off her hand, where it was clinging.

But the shock of finding her had passed already, and even the horror was fading. And the grief, the regret, the guilt, all the emotional baggage-train that came after could be elbowed aside. Real enough, all of it — and no more than Helen was owed, because they'd let her down badly, they must have done — but it couldn't hope to stand up to Rachel's other anxieties tonight. Helen had died, and Rachel had found her dead; but all of that could be tucked away somewhere private, left alone to ripen or rot in its own time.

She thought about Helen for a while and then stopped, more or less, finding worse things to occupy her mind. And she thought about Derry a little; and confirmed her suspicions on the long, straight path across the moor. Nowhere for him to hide there, he was just a distant figure who walked when she walked and stopped when she stopped, like a shadow long detached. And then she forgot him too, more or less. Give or take. He wanted to lurk, okay, let him lurk; but no closer than that, nothing bolder than lurking. If he got bold, she'd tear him apart.

Off the moor and almost home: and she wasn't thinking at all on this last lap, only turning her head in the soft breeze to catch the movement of it through her short short hair, hoping her parents would be out or in bed already. Bad enough to have to tell them about Helen; worse, to have to say who found her. Impossible, to tell them about anything else.

A couple of times she thought she heard light footsteps running, though there was no one to be seen. Once she fancied she caught a glimpse of a shadow moving, drawing back into an alley's mouth as she passed. Derry being chivalrous to the last, seeing her all the way and trying so hard not to let her see him. Thinking he was clever, no doubt, keeping to the alleys, keeping parallel. *Stupid pillock,* she thought, *irresponsible bloody nerd* – she'd be frightened if she didn't know it was him. Didn't he realise how scary he was acting, spying on a solitary girl, following her in the dark? Serve him right if he got picked up for it, plenty of police round here this time of night . . .

Not enough, though. Not when you needed them. And she did need them, because it wasn't Derry.

She learned that at last at the head of her own little cul-de-sac, only metres from the garden gate. She was trying to spot lights through the neighbours' trees, see if her parents were home, when she heard the running footsteps directly behind her and coming closer, coming hard. Not even giving her time to turn before there was a clubbing pain on the back of her neck, and the pavement spinning up to catch her.

And then there was dizziness and feeling sick, and struggling not to throw up; and being dragged away from the streetlights by someone who surely wasn't Derry.

He crouched over her, breathing hard in his black balaclava, nothing to see of him but eyes; and something was glimmering in his hand and pricking hard at her neck.

"This is for Derry, right?" coming at her in a thin hiss while one hand jerked at her clothes, while the other kept the knife at her throat. "You tell him that, you tell him. His turn later, I'm going to carve him good; but this first, this is for him. This'll carve him, all right. And you, you don't move, right, you don't make a sound or I carve you too . . . "

And that hand was at her jeans now, knuckles pressing into her stomach while the fingers fumbled with the buttons; and she whimpered, and prayed secretly, silently, *Jesus help me now, come on, I need it, you've got to, help me now, JESUS! help me . . .*

And nothing, no miracle: no sudden policeman, no angel, no Derry or Dad or stray dog or anything. No one to help her and her jeans were open now and his hand was inside her knickers and there was nothing she could do but save herself and she had to do that, she didn't have the choice.

So she lashed out, gasping, never mind the knife. Caught him by surprise, caught him on the jaw and heard his mouth snap shut, heard him yelp as he bit his tongue; and kicked out with both legs at once, sent him sprawling.

Heard the knife clatter out of his hand but still didn't back off, didn't call for help. There was no help, she knew that now, not from Derry or the police or her family or God or anyone. Even though he'd dragged her to the alley behind her own house, even though there was a light she could see in her parents' bedroom, still she couldn't trust them to come, she couldn't trust anyone. She had to do it herself.

So she threw herself at the scrambling, skinny figure, fingers clawing at the eyes behind his woollen mask and her voice screaming, yes, but not for help: screaming in accusation, screaming to make him afraid as he had frightened her.

"I'm pregnant, you little shit," she screamed, sobbing, kicking, nails at his throat. "You fucker, you filthy fucking shit, I'm *pregnant . . . !*"

And she went on screaming, even after he'd torn himself away from her, scratched and bleeding behind his balaclava; even after he'd run off she didn't stop, she went on screaming that enormity into the night until her parents came to take her inside.

THIRTY-THREE

i

Again, he does not get to bed this night.

He's pulled some strings, talked to some people; and as a result Helen was brought here, to this small room in the hospital, rather than the mortuary.

The one night is all he's been allowed. At breakfast time she has to leave, to join the cold queue for a post-mortem. But during these hours of darkness, she is his.

And that's appropriate, surely that's fitting, for this is a dark hour indeed, or was meant to be. He must see Satan's hand in this, clear as day. This ultimate expression of Helen's sadness can only be His cruel work; the hopelessness and the bottle of pills to hand, the one temptation she no longer had the strength to resist. And the extra little twist, that the emptied bottle of paracetamol in the bathroom had been Nathan's own, left behind like so much else – like Helen – when he moved out: yes, that has the great Enemy's personal touch. That's wicked.

But the Devil is a forgetful devil, or else His long dull anger blinds Him to the truth. He may seek to wrap Richard in Helen's darkness and the darkness of her death, but it won't work. Richard makes his own light, it isn't all the reflected glory of his God. Richard sees his way clear, in the darkest night.

And so now he closes the door on the world and spends the night alone with Helen's clay; and not for us to wonder what he does behind that door. That he grieves, we can be certain. Any death is a great distress, one of his own is greater; and a death sought out, self-made, cannot be less than a terrible sorrow to him. He will surely, he must blame himself, even where no blame can possibly attach.

But his grief is private, and what it drives him to. Perhaps he only watches over her this night and prays that she may find rest and peace in Heaven, where she couldn't find either in Paradise. Or perhaps he does more, perhaps he lays his hands upon her; perhaps he prays to see her rise like Lazarus and live again. It's not unlikely. Christ taught His apostles to raise the dead, He ordered them to do it. And if anyone deserves a second chance, it must

413

be Helen.

But if he asks, he's answered, flat and final. When they come for Helen in the morning, when they bring their metal box on wheels and knock politely at the still-closed door, he opens it alone and silent. He admits them to the presence of the still-dead, the unrisen Helen; and they lift her and lay her in and cover her over with perhaps a little more care, a little more respect than she might receive if they weren't being watched.

He sees them wheel her off to her appointment with a knife; and he turns and walks the other way, to where some of the Commando have waited all night down the corridor.

ii

It was still early, not nine o'clock when Derry arrived; but Rachel was up already when she should have been in bed, out in the garden but not in the sunshine, standing hunched in a tree's shadow hugging herself when she should have been watching for him. Except she didn't know he was coming, seemingly, because the first thing she said when she saw him, she said,

"What the hell are you doing here?"

"Your mum . . . " It was hard to talk when he was snatching for breath, sweating and shaking from that cruel run, three miles in no time at all; harder still in the face of a cold antagonism. But he pushed the words out somehow, said, "Your mum phoned. She said, she said you'd been *attacked* . . . "

He could see the signs of it on her now, bruises on her bare arms and shadows under her eyes. But she turned away from him quickly, saying, "Christ, why doesn't she just call the papers? Quicker than telling everybody, one by one . . . "

"I'm not everybody," he said, baffled. "Am I? Come on, Rache. She said I should come . . . "

"What for?"

What *for*? Jesus . . . "Maybe she thought you'd want me here," he said, all need now, all pleading.

"Well, she was wrong, wasn't she?" thrown at him brutally, over her shoulder; and then, "Don't *touch* me!" as he reached for her, for some sign of tenderness. She twisted away, walked up towards the house, said, "Just, just go away, Derry, all right? Just sod off and leave me alone . . . "

It was the same message as yesterday, and he couldn't bear it twice. Not even long enough to ask why. He turned and

414

blundered out of the garden, wishing only that he had the strength to run again, to get away the faster; and looking back only once as he fumbled with the gate, to see her disappear inside and slam the door against him.

Heading back, he had to break into a jog a couple of times because the only alternative was breaking into tears, right there in the street, in public; but each time he was walking again inside a hundred metres. Once he had to stop altogether and sit on a wall for a while, his legs too weak to hold him.

So he was still some distance short of the moor, still sniffing and shivering in his sweat when he heard the soft hiss of a bicycle's tyres right beside him, and looked round to see Rachel.

He didn't stop, and neither did she. He just went on walking, watching his feet because he couldn't bear to look at her; and he saw how her wheels wobbled dangerously in and out of the gutter, going too slow to keep a proper balance.

After a minute, as if they'd had a whole conversation during this awkward silent progress, she said, "Okay, then. Airport. Soon as you can."

And then she was gone, racing away, taking the corner into traffic stupidly fast so that he screamed after her to be careful, far too late for her to hear.

And then he stood still, then he hugged a streetlight, laughing and not minding a bit now what anybody thought, what he looked like; and then he panicked beautifully, deliciously, because he was miles from home in his running gear, he had no money and he didn't know how the hell he was going to get to the airport.

Twenty minutes later he was there, money in his pocket and a fierce tension building in his throat. He wanted to sing, but only as a wire sings in the wind. On his way into the terminal building he passed Rachel's bike, padlocked to a fence; he patted the saddle for luck, and felt it still warm under his fingers. She could only have been here a minute, it was a hard ride from the city.

He ran up all the stairs to the roof and she was there, waiting where they'd stood before, eyes on the tarmac below.

He went to stand beside her, gripped the rail as she was gripping it, their hands a foot apart. She looked as sweat-sticky as he was, and as frightened.

"You were quick," she said. "I thought you'd be longer."

He grinned, a little embarrassed. "I knocked on your door, asked your mam for the bus fare. Told her why, and she gave us ten quid and called a taxi. She wasn't very friendly, though," remembering the coolness of her, how she wouldn't chat while they waited. "She said we had to talk, but . . . What happened with this bastard, then? Tell us."

Her whole body twitched. "Later," she said. "Not now."

That'll keep, she was saying; but that just meant there was something else, something more important. "So what," he said, "what's going on? You were wrong all yesterday . . . "

He was angling for an apology, maybe, as well as an explanation; at least a sign of warmth, of things put back in place again. Something to break that choking tension.

He didn't get it, though, not so much as the least measure of a smile. Only two dark and searching eyes, and two flat words.

"I'm pregnant," she said, and waited.

Derry's world rocked. He clenched both hands tight on the rail to steady himself, breathed slow and deep to fight the dizziness; at last turned his head to find her still watching him, still waiting.

"You can't be," he said. *Please, please God . . .* "It's a mistake."

"I did the tests twice," she said bitterly, betrayed. "Two different kits, same result. I'm going to the doctor this afternoon, but she won't say any different. It's real, Derry. Believe it." And then, when he shook his head, "You only have to do it once, you know. That's all it takes."

He shook his head again, against the contempt in her voice; and heard himself saying, "So who did you do it with, then? Who else?"

He saw her hand only as a blur, but then he was seeing everything blurred just now. The sting of it across his cheek, though, that was sharp enough, that was focused; and her voice came over loud and clear, swearing like he'd never heard her, like he didn't think she could.

He drew a hand down over his eyes to clear them, looked at her straight and infinitely disillusioned, and said, "It can't be mine. It *can't.* I can't have kids, Rachel. They told me that. All the radiotherapy I had to have, they couldn't keep me safe; and there wasn't much point worrying about it. I was going to die, right? So I got kind of fried down there. If you're pregnant, it was somebody else."

That stopped her swearing, at least, stopped her dead for a moment; but then she said, "No. Nobody else. I swear," saying it wearily now, all the anger snatched out of her. "You must've got more miracled than we knew, even. What would you call it? Reconstituted, I suppose. Reconstituted balls, that's what you've got. Some miracle, eh?"

And again he was spindizzy in the world, and had to grip the railing simply to keep his feet; and when he could lift his head again he said, "No," he said, "come here," and held one careful arm out to her. "Please? Now?"

"What?" she demanded, cat-cautious and distrustful.

"You," he said, pulling her close, wrapping both arms around her suddenly in a burning frenzy, rubbing his head against hers stubble to stubble, burying his face in her neck. "You," he said, "you're my miracle."

"Derry, man, get off . . . "

"No, I mean it," and he wouldn't let her fight or wriggle free, he used all his new strength to hold her still. "Everything I ever wanted, you give me," he said; and then suddenly, with a spasm of chill, "You do, you do want it, don't you?"

"I don't *want* it," she said. "I never *wanted* anything less in my life. But it's here, so there's nothing to discuss, is there? I'm not having an abortion. And I won't give it away, either. I did this, and it's mine to keep."

"Ours," he whispered. "*Ours.*"

"Well. All right, then. Ours. One way or another."

"That's what I mean," he said. "You give me everything. You're my miracle," he said again, still barely able to believe it.

"Soft git," she murmured; but he thought maybe she was beginning to believe it too, he could feel her starting to relax against him, shifting her body into comfort.

He clung tight for a minute longer, feeling the reality of her and the leaping relief in himself, the overleaping joy; and then, suddenly anxious, "You shouldn't be shooting round on the bike like that, not if you're pregnant, you got to be careful . . . "

"Oh, God. Don't you start," and her head battered painfully at his shoulder. "I'm not made of tissue-paper, and neither's the baby, all right?"

"Well. You be careful, that's all. We can go back in a taxi," he decided, "I've got the money. Get one with a roof-rack, that'll take your bike. And," tucking her up comfortably against him again, while he looked further ahead, "we can get married soon as you like, get Richard to do it, is he allowed to? He must be, he buried, he buried my mam, he must do weddings too. And, and you don't have to give everything up just 'cos you're going to have a kid. You could quit school for a year, say, come and live with me and my dad, we can all look after each other; and then you can go back and do your exams, and college after if you want to, and I'll stay home and look after the kid, I'd like that . . . "

417

But then she put her hand over his mouth, and, "Derry, stop. Just, just stop, all right? Don't go making plans, it's too soon. I've got to talk to my parents, other people, I can't decide anything yet. They do know, they found out last night, but we couldn't talk then, they had the doctor round to give me a jab, I was right out of it after that, that creep . . . "

And he could feel her shudder just at the memory of it, and he wanted to hear about that, too, there was someone in this town he had to murder; but one thing at least they did have to get settled, here and now. "Okay," he said, "no plans; but you will marry me? You *will*?"

She looked up at him uncertainly. "That's planning."

"Yeah, but it's got nothing to do with your parents or anybody. Will you?"

"Do you really want to? I mean, never mind the baby, if it was just you and me, would you want to?"

"I always did," he said. "Marrying helps, Dad says. Used to say." *Before Mam died, and he stopped talking.*

Rachel's lips twitched. "You're weird, Derry Bowen. Boys aren't supposed to want to get married. They're not supposed to want kids, either."

He shrugged. "I used to want everything in a hurry, 'cos I had to; and I still do, even if I don't have to any more." And then he grinned, rocked her from side to side, said, "You'll look lovely all skinhead, in a big white dress. Get your dad to buy you something dead expensive . . . "

She stiffened against him, all but pushed him away. "Derry, I can't do that."

"Why not? He can afford it."

"No, not that. I can't wear white." And when he stared at her, she gestured impatiently. "Derry, I'm *pregnant*. And I'm not going to lie about it, I'm not going to pretend. So I can't go up the aisle in white, making out I'm a virgin. How can I?"

He took her by the shoulders, almost angry. "You *are* a virgin, stupid. Where it counts, you are," over her spluttering protests. "In your head. That night my mam died, that wasn't sex, what we did then. That was, I dunno, medicine or something."

"Therapy," she suggested faintly.

"Yeah, right. That. Not sex. And you want white, you wear white. Your dad says any different, tell him to come see me."

"Derry, man." She sounded breathless, shaking her head, and he couldn't read her for once, didn't understand what she was feeling. "If I, if I listen to you, then that makes me the second-ever virgin birth, you realise that? Me and Mary. As in the Virgin

418

Mary, Mother of God, you know? *That* Mary."

"Yeah," he said, pleased with the idea. "So?"

"So that's blasphemy of the most horrendous kind, and you're probably going to go straight to hell for even *thinking* about it, but oh God, I do love you," she said, which was all that had been missing from his day.

So he kissed her, and then he kissed her eyes where she was crying; and then he said, "You coming too, then?"

"Where?"

"Down to hell. When I go."

"Expect so. Expect I'll have to, for listening to you. Virgin birth, for God's sake . . . We'll all go. All three of us, hand in hand and stuff the lot of them. Deal?"

"Deal."

iii

Nothing had gone right for Jason in the last two days, since he'd got himself stranded. Nothing had gone right for him all summer, really; but this was the pits, this was as bad as anything and worse than most.

He'd thought it was different last night, he was riding high for a while there, but even that had turned bad in the end.

So now he was back, hiding out in the flat opposite Derry's because he couldn't think of anywhere better to go. Except away, of course, right away, the hell out of here. That'd be best, that's what he should be doing. He should be twocking a car right now and just going, never mind where so long as it wasn't Paradise or anywhere in this filthy city.

He'd almost done that the first night, after he'd missed his rendezvous with Vinny. After *Vinny* had missed it, rather. Bastard just didn't turn up, and Jason had been stuck, marooned in the only place that was worse for him than being at Vinny's.

He'd almost done it, then. He'd found the car, a Golf GTi with a dozy owner who'd forgotten the alarm; smashed a quarter light and got in, scaffed the ignition and driven away inside twenty seconds. Not bad, seeing how out of practice he was.

But there wasn't any bloody petrol in the car, it was running on empty; and while Jason still had some of George's cash, he wasn't fool enough to try filling up at a garage. They'd have the cops on him straight after they'd taken his money. No way he looked old enough to be driving a GTi around. Same thing if he drove off

419

without paying, they'd be after him in no time. And he could outdrive any bloody cop, sure he could, but this wasn't the right time to be hotting around . . .

So he'd only taken the car down to the waste ground and burnt it out, a flaring beacon to his frustration and his fear; then he'd scuttled through Paradise, dodging police and Commando patrols until he came to this flat, the safest place he could think of to hole up.

That was the first night, curled in his clothes in a nest of curtains, hungry and nervous and jumping at noises.

Yesterday he'd gone out once, just to the corner shop; he'd bought a loaf of bread and a jar of peanut butter and come sneaking back again. It was dead hard to spread peanut butter with his fingers, so he'd mostly just eaten it in lumps straight from the jar, with the bread dry and water from the tap after, drinking from his hands like an animal.

Then last night – no, he didn't want to think about last night. One more thing he'd fucked up, that was all.

And today he hadn't been out at all, he didn't dare. He'd watched the street a little from the window, he'd seen Derry go racing off in the morning, not come back; he'd daydreamed about doing that job for George, catching Derry alone and private and really going to town on him. George would see him safe, if he just got the job done; and then he'd be safe from George too, maybe. If the job was done.

Only daydreams – he didn't have the knife any more, wasn't fool enough to take Derry on without it – but daydreams were all he had left. He felt trapped here, banged up inside invisible borders, even Vinny's place inaccessible to him now, the wrong side of the river.

All luck had left him too, he had no more luck than hope; because in the middle of the afternoon, broad daylight and plenty of life, plenty of people on the streets, he heard voices just below the window and a key scratching at the lock.

One panicked glance out showed him a young couple waiting while a man sorted through a tagged bunch of keys: the estate agent, surely, come to show some people round. Today of all days, when the sodding place had been for sale six months or more . . .

Jason thought maybe the woman had seen him looking; but whatever, he wasn't going to wait to find out. He was up and moving already, sprinting through the flat and never mind the noise he made, doors banging behind him as he leapt out at the back, ran halfway down the steps to the yard and vaulted the wall into the back alley.

And landed just twenty metres from a Commando patrol, three young men dressed in their assumed authority.

"Hey, you! Wait there . . . "

Jason wasn't waiting for anyone. He twisted round and ran again, skidding down the hill with the Commandos in hot pursuit.

But going downhill was only taking him closer to their headquarters, and the chance of running into more of them. So the next corner he came to, he turned sharp left; and again at the next, to take him up to the main road again. Maybe if he could just get over that they'd let him go, that was the border, maybe they didn't operate outside Paradise . . .

Daydreams, for sure; because he was starting to wheeze already, and running uphill was harder work and they were gaining all the time, he could hear them almost on his heels now, strong and purposeful. But he lowered his head and ran blindly on, not giving up for once in his life, not going to let the luck beat him this time – and then suddenly there was a frenzied yapping from behind him and some ginger mongrel fucking *dog* was there, dancing round his legs and snapping at his heels.

It was just too much for Jason. His toe caught in soft fur even as he tried to dodge, and he went staggering off the pavement and slammed into a parked van, and a hand grabbed his arm tight and said, "That's far enough for you, lad."

"Get off, get off of me," Jason gasped, trying to wriggle free, not having a prayer. "You're not a cop, you got no right to hold me. That's assault, that is . . . "

"Citizen's arrest," the young man said equably. "I arrest you on suspicion of breaking and entering. You're not obliged to say anything, but anything you do say may be used in evidence. There you are, nice and formal. Now, do you want to tell me what you were doing back there, or shall we go and see?"

"Get stuffed," Jason said, and kicked out at the dog that was sniffing around his feet again.

"Oy!" with a rough shake. "No need for that. What about that flat, Björn?"

"It is for sale," another Commando said, trotting up to join them. "The agent is there now, he says someone has been camping in it, and the back door is all smashed. He will come and see us later, when he has had it mended."

"Breaking and entering," Jason's captor said happily. "Like I said. Okay, let's take him down the houses. Give Nat a call, tell

421

him we need the battle bus. You may be lucky yet," to Jason, "maybe they won't press charges, if we ask. Just depends how cooperative you are. The estate agents like us, you see. What's your name?"

Jason just spat.

"That's not cooperative, stupid. Look, do you *want* to end up in a police cell tonight?"

No, he didn't; it was the last thing he wanted, with memories of that little knife lost and doubtless found by now, his fingerprints all over. So he told the guy his name was Jason Dewey; and that was relayed over the walkie-talkie, and even from where he stood five metres away and still breathing noisily, still half-deafened by his own labouring heartbeat, Jason could hear Nathan's laughter coming through.

"Well, well. Jason Dewey, home again. How've you been, then, Jason? Keeping fit? You don't look too good. Bit pale, bit thin. Not been getting out much, I expect, is that it? Not eating properly?"

They were in an office down in that terrace where all the Christians hung out, where the petrol bombs hadn't worked. Just the two of them, just him and Nathan: Nathan perched on the corner of a desk broadly smiling, Jason sitting where he'd been told to sit, cowering in an armchair, sullen and afraid.

"Look," Jason said desperately when Nathan paused, seemed to wait for a reply. "Just, just say what you want, okay? I'll do it, I'll do anything . . . "

"Of course you will. But all in good time, Jase. All in good time. You do look hungry. Man shall not live by bread alone, you know. Nor even bread and peanut butter." He grinned amiably, went to the door, put his head out and said something; Jason couldn't see who he was talking to, didn't hear what was said. He only sat miserably silent and dreamed of heroic acts: of a leap out through the open window, a mad plunging run over the wasteland to the river, a good clean dive and a swim to the further bank and safety.

And of course didn't move a finger, wouldn't move a muscle without Nathan's permission.

Nathan sat down and started reading letters, making notes, ignoring Jason altogether. After a few minutes a girl brought in a tray: steaming curry and rice, and a can of Coke. Jason's mouth flooded with saliva, just at the smell of it. Even through his fear he felt his stomach stir with hunger. Nathan thanked the girl abstractedly; she put it down on the desk and left without speaking, sharing a smile equally between the two of them.

Nathan skimmed through a couple more letters, then glanced up and said, "Well, go on, then. Eat. Don't let it get cold."

Jason stared at him, at the tray, at Nathan again. "You mean, it's for me?"

"Of course, for you. You need it more than I do."

Jason snatched the tray, carried it back into the recesses of his chair. He spooned the food frantically from plate to mouth, tasting nothing, not caring even that Nathan was watching and laughing at him.

"Those are nasty scratches you've got on your neck there, Jase," Nathan said suddenly; and Jason did care then. That was enough to stop him eating, to have him stiff and still, watching Nathan warily with his mouth half open, half full.

"You've been fighting, I expect," Nathan went on cheerfully. "You shouldn't do it, you know – but it's no use preaching, is it? Boys fight. Like dogs, dogs fight. Don't they?"

Jason still didn't move. It was Nathan who did, walking from desk to window, waving to someone down by the river.

"We have to be careful these days," he said, "we have to keep a guard on watch down there. Did you hear we got fire-bombed? Did you hear that, did the news get that far?"

Then he tapped Jason lightly on the head and said, "Eat. You've stopped eating. You have to eat. Clear your plate, Jason."

So Jason did, he ate every last grain of rice without having tasted one; and felt them all churning in his stomach afterwards, liable to come up again if Nathan said one more word, made him just a tremor more afraid. He wrapped both hands round the can and sipped at it like medicine, but it didn't make him feel better. Nothing could.

"You asked me what I wanted," Nathan said softly, somewhere behind him. He didn't look round. "And you're right, there is something I want from you, Jason. Same thing as before, what I always want from you: just information, that's all. You're my fifth column, sunshine, you're my spy. You know what's what.

"Thing is, you see, Jase, there's a devil in Paradise. Or a wolf. He's been seen, several times; and he's been trouble for us every time we see him. I want to know who he is, and where to find him; and I think maybe you can help me there. Can't you, Jason?"

"I don't," Jason muttered with the taste of acid sharp in his throat, on his tongue, "I don't know what you mean. I don't know no devils."

"Sure you do. You know this one. He drives a van and he keeps dogs. And boys, I think he keeps boys too, sometimes. Or one boy, anyway. Isn't that right, Jason?"

Jason swallowed, felt his mind reel and his skin slick with a chilly sweat. He clenched his jaw, shoved himself awkwardly to his feet, looked round desperately while his mouth filled – and felt Nathan's hand clamp hard on the back of his neck, was thrust across the room to the window so that he could vomit onto the flowerbed below.

And as he stood there bent over and spewing, Nathan's hand stayed firmly on his neck and Nathan's voice went quietly on above him, cataloguing his terror.

"See, what it is, Jason, Billy's devil had a boy with him, when he bombed this place a couple of Sundays back. We're sure about that, Billy saw them.

"And then, that night the police raided the gym, someone set his dog on us. On *me*, Jason," and the hand spasmed briefly, just as there was another spurt of sour bile rising in Jason's throat. He almost choked, trying to spew and scream at once.

"Billy's not much good at descriptions, and I couldn't see clearly, it was pretty dark out there; but I'm sure it was the same man, Jase. I've got a feeling.

"He had a boy with him that time, too. I think the police want to talk to that boy."

Jason moaned, and retched.

"And then there was poor Rachel, of course, she got attacked last night, did you hear? She's not sure who it was, not certain sure, not to swear to it in court; so she hasn't told the police who she thinks it might have been. Yet. But she did tell them she left him marked, scratches on his throat, she said. And of course they've got the knife he left behind, I expect they're checking the fingerprints on that right now . . . "

There was nothing left in Jason to come out, except the acid taste of fear; and all the hawking, all the spitting in the world wouldn't shift that.

His clothes felt damp against his skin, his eyes and nose were running, he had dribbled something on his chin. Nathan hauled him upright, put a wad of tissues in his hand and pushed him back into the chair again.

"That's how it is, Jason," he said calmly. "Indecent assault, attempted rape, arson and attempted murder, that's how it looks to the police. That's the trouble this boy is in. It's big stuff. But we can help, we're pretty big stuff ourselves these days. We can offer shelter and protection, and a good lawyer if it ever got that far.

"So how's about it, Jase? Tell me who this devil is, and where I

424

find him. That's all you have to do."

Jason shook his head despairingly. "He'll kill me," he said, plain and factual.

"No. I told you, we can offer protection for as long as you need it. We'll keep you here until he's put away," as if that was a benefit, something to be grateful for. "You'll have a room, regular meals and people on the watch for you twenty-four hours a day. You'll be safe as houses, I promise. And these houses are pretty safe. They don't even burn, remember?"

And Jason looked into the width and depth of Nathan's smile and broke, as he always did.

Told Nathan what he wanted to know, and felt something warm and wet and terrible happening to him even as he shaped Vinny's name in his mouth, even before he'd said it.

THIRTY-FOUR

i

It must make him sad to see these children here now, but he doesn't show it. He surprises them by smiling at their news, not even grave, let alone reproachful. He tells them a new life, a new soul is always a cause for celebration. Then he makes Derry fidget and Rachel blush by talking about sin: by saying that loving the sinner is easy, but sometimes it's possible even to love the sin.

– I'm glad it happened, he says, I think it was the right thing, I think maybe it was Derry's salvation that night; and I want you both to look on this baby as a reward, not a punishment. Will you do that for me?

Derry looks as though he's wishing for hair to hide behind, a great long mop of it like Rachel used to have; but Rachel, no, not her. She looks at him straight and fierce, eye to eye, and says,

– That's silly, it's not like that. It's not either of those. It's a *baby,* that's all, it's just a baby. And it's ours. That's all, she says, it's just ours.

All their feelings are sharp-edged and a little vicious this morning, driven by fear. They're afraid of the future, of course they are; and they're afraid of each other, too. They sit side by side but a foot apart on the sofa, just two fingers tightly linked as though they can't bear any greater contact, as though it might cut too deeply and expose too much.

They're here to talk about weddings. What else?

He'll want to be the one who marries them. These two kids of all his wide parish, he'll want to be the one. He must think he's entitled.

But he's being cautious, he's saying if instead of when. It's not their love he doubts, he's quite clear on that. It's himself he won't make promises for.

God has a way of breaking His servants' promises at need; and it's He who defines that need, He makes the choices.

Nathan smiled a little, smiled wickedly as he drove, thinking of Jason. There was some confusion among the Commando, whether he was under arrest or in protective custody; but either way it really didn't matter. Jason was so shit scared since he'd turned God's evidence, he hadn't set foot beyond the room they'd given him. No need to lock that door or put a guard outside. The whole room simply stank of fear, it oozed out of Jason like sweat.

Even that, though, even the stink of fear was an improvement. Nathan had had to send a couple of lads up, to induce Jason to take a bath. *Check that he washes behind his ears,* Nathan had said; and from the noises that came down he rather thought they'd taken him literally, or even done the dirty deed themselves to be certain sure. While the boys were in the bathroom, he'd found Jason some fresh gear and had his old clothes burned. There was a double purpose to that, because choosing what Jason wore was close kin to sewing big arrows all over his kit. If he chose to run out on them, a boy in a bright orange tracksuit shouldn't be too difficult to spot.

Nathan didn't know the country south of the river, he'd never had any call to discover it; student life mostly kept within the city bounds, or else looked to the coast and northward. Nor could he see a way to tap into the Commando's pool of local knowledge, because this was very much a solo effort he was on, very much a secret mission.

Jason would keep his mouth shut, no worries there. And no one else need ever know, except his visitee. But that necessary secrecy did leave Nathan dependent on Jason's crude maps for guidance, smeared and almost indecipherable sheets he'd wrung out of the boy under threat of taking him along in the flesh; and that dependence did result in his getting lost very soon after crossing the river.

Jason's going to regret this, he thought, reversing grimly into a filthy farmyard and backtracking for the third time in ten minutes, while a thin mud-coated collie loped snarling beside the car, snapping at the tyres. Nathan twitched the wheel spitefully, but the dog danced clear just as the rear of the car slammed across the lane, aimed at crushing it into the hedge. *He's going to regret it deeply. First thing he can do, he can clean the car for me; but that's only the first thing. Nobody sends me driving in circles, least of all that whingeing little shit . . .*

There was no one around to ask for directions; but logically that was all to the good. No one to ask meant no one to see, and he didn't want people remembering a strange car nosing around the lanes. As they would have cause to remember . . .

It was a relief finally to find the right track in this tangled country, and to see the sign that confirmed it. "Something about Staffs," Jason had said, "I dunno, don't hit me, I can't *remember* . . . " When he'd explained what he meant, Nathan had forborne to hit him; and in fact the boy had remembered well enough. *Staffies. Pups and stud*, crudely painted and leaning perilously out of the hedge; that was it, had to be. There couldn't possibly be two.

Relief also, driving slowly past the turning, to see dead ground and a pair of ancient caravans but no van, no signs of occupation. No Vinny. "He should be out," Jason had said, whimpering a little, "that time of day, he *should* be. Usually is. But I can't, I can't promise, like. It ain't my fault if he's there, is it? I mean, is it?"

Nathan might have thought it was, if he had been; but Vinny wasn't there, and Jason was suddenly scoring points all down the line. Except for his maps, of course, he'd still have to pay for his maps.

Nathan reversed into the turning, to put the car out of sight from the lane but be ready for a quick getaway if it was needed; then he sat still for a moment, crossed himself with an ironical chuckle and an upward wink, and got out of the car.

The noise of the dogs hit him like something physical, a solidity of air. Nathan was instantly tense – though sheer volume had little enough to do with that, one dog would have been plenty, and it needn't even bark – and wondered how the master of the property put up with such a racket. No question about Jason, he'd stuck it only through fear and force of circumstance; but Vinny presumably had the choice.

But then, maybe they didn't bark around Vinny. The way Jason talked about him – and Billy too, Billy was just the same on much shorter acquaintance – Vinny should stand ten foot tall in his clawed feet, and that not counting the horns. He should breathe smoke and fire, like any self-respecting devil, and would no doubt have little trouble quelling a pack of rowdy dogs. Just a glance would do it, surely, would bring them to an awed and obedient silence. Rather as it did with Jason. That boy was Vinny's dog, and would be again if they met up again. Something to watch out for, that was. Couldn't afford a double agent lurking in the houses, right at the heart of their organisation.

Just depends who he's most scared of, Nathan reminded himself; and resolved with a smile to pay some more attention to that, to be certain of the boy.

Jason's cartography hadn't been limited to the lanes, and the route from Paradise; he'd charted the extent of Vinny's holding too, to give some idea of what was where.

So Nathan could stand now and look, and know that the caravan on the left was where Vinny ate and slept, while the one straight ahead was his office, if you chose to call it that. At any rate it was where he took his visitors when he had them, where he made his deals. The first rough shed was where he stored petrol and oil for his van, paraffin for his heaters, food for his dogs; where he kept his tools; where he had kept Jason too, when he had him. But that was all the same thing, because Jason had never been more than a tool of Vinny's. Probably his finest hour, Nathan thought. Till now. Till he became a tool of Nathan's instead.

Nathan moved quickly, after that first minute of looking. He didn't want some casual passer-by to see him here; only Vinny should know or guess who it was who'd called in his absence. Nor did he want still to be around when Vinny himself returned. He was curious to see the man more clearly, smugly eager to see him in retreat; but not here, not on Vinny's own turf and the two of them alone.

So he ran quickly over to the first of the two caravans, and tried the door. Open: Jason had said that, that Vinny never locked anything. "Doesn't need to," Jason had said. "Who's going to mess with Vinny?"

Well, me, for one, Nathan thought, looking inside. This was living quarters, clearly: a couple of worn blankets muddled on a mattress, filthy clothes heaped in corners, a calor gas cooker and a table stacked with tins. Nothing to interest him in there. Besides, the place stank.

The other caravan might have proved more profitable. Nathan had been hoping so, at least. Jason hadn't been allowed in there, so there might be secrets. But if there were, Nathan couldn't find them in the few minutes he allowed himself to look. A couple of greasy armchairs and a desk; and the desk contained nothing but stud records for the dogs, made out in a clumsy, unaccustomed hand and claiming prize-winning lineages that Nathan didn't believe for a moment. If Vinny kept honest records about any of his transactions, he clearly didn't keep them here.

And so out of the caravans, and down to the dogs. They were still rapt in a frenzy of barking, setting each other to fresh riots; Nathan stood on the path that led down between their jerry-built kennels, watching edgily to see if the frantic, scrabbling bodies showed any signs of getting through the wire.

They didn't; so, a little reassured, he started down the slope towards the more solid-looking building at the bottom, where Jason said the pit bulls were kept behind padlocks and on chains.

He walked a little carefully, because in each hand he carried a five-gallon drum of petrol from Vinny's capacious store.

When he drove away fifteen minutes later, he left a thickening column of dark smoke rising behind him, and the air filled with screaming.

And just as well he left when he did, just as well he'd hurried; because he came bonnet-to-bonnet with a rusty blue van in the lanes and barely avoided a collision, the van was being driven so fast and braked so late. And then the van's driver only sat in the middle of the narrow lane and waited, leaning on his horn, until Nathan reversed into a gateway to let him pass.

Nathan couldn't see his face, for the sun reflecting off the windscreen; but he remembered the van. This was Vinny on his way home, no question of it.

"Have a nice day," Nathan murmured, grinning tightly at the van's shrinking reflection in his mirror as he drove away.

THIRTY-FIVE

i

He stands upon a high place, and looks out over his kingdom; and he surely must be pleased with what he sees.

He came up to the roof of the gym with Rachel's father to talk about some building work, his vision and Michael's reality, the artist and the architect; but Michael's gone down now while he stays aloft. From here he can see all Paradise around him, from the long terraces on the slope above to the waste ground that borders the river.

But it isn't only geography. He can see through to the heart, we know that, he can see the soul; and he can see how much has changed in the few short months of summer. He sees how the streets are clear of graffiti and broken glass, how there are no stray dogs running in the alleys nor stray teenagers lurking with menace on the corners. He sees pensioners treated with respect, the disabled and disadvantaged encouraged, helped where encouragement is not enough. And he sees the houses below him, standing alone and proud like a ship in a sea of rubble, a busy focus for the young army that's done all this.

All this, of course, is only a beginning, first steps in a long march; but God has promised this city to His people, that's why they're marching. It's what he's been saying all summer, that there's a promise to be redeemed. He should know, he's a witness to it.

If he's sad, if any sadness touches him as he surveys his triumph, it must be the sadness of Moses: permitted to see, but not to share. Always the vanguard, always the visionary going into darkness; he can look, but he'd better not touch.

That's life, though. Or it's his life, at any rate. That's his burden, that's his cross, that's the cup he drinks from.

His fingers lift to touch his jacket pocket, stiff with a hidden letter, his Master's voice.

And it saddens him, perhaps; but that's the way the communion bread is crumbled.

Vinny had only kept one memory of the day just gone, only one moment that he meant to carry with him through the days ahead. He had his own insight into what was important, what mattered and what did not.

His home had been destroyed and everything he owned was gone, except for the van; but that wasn't it.

His only clothes were scorched and stank of smoke, he tasted ashes in his dry mouth and his skin was angry, burnt and blistered; some of his tattoos would be permanently scarred and twisted out of true; but that wasn't it.

His dogs were dead or run away, but mostly dead; and that wasn't it either. Some he'd killed himself, the ones that crawled out of their collapsing, blazing kennels with their fur on fire and their raw flesh seared and bubbling. He'd taken an iron bar and walked through the eddying smoke while his caravans burned behind him; he'd walked untroubled through the flames and the pitiful screaming, and he'd crushed skulls as he went, any living, burning thing he saw.

At the foot of the slope was his special kennel, his particular pleasure, made of breeze blocks and wouldn't burn. But the padlocked door had been kicked in, and there was a light inside that wasn't electric. Vinny walked into the heat and the stink and the choking smoke of it, and saw that while concrete and breeze block wouldn't burn, straw of course would; and so would living flesh, if well doused with petrol first. All his pit bulls had been roasted in their pens.

But that, even that wasn't what remained with him now the day and the long night were over.

What he chose to keep, what he carried forward for future reckoning wasn't what had been done, rather who had done it: who had left their allegiance signed like a glory in the earth.

Flames had flickered and burned even on the dead ground in front of the caravans, far enough away for there not to be any confusion about it. Nothing accidental here, this was a message. The earth burned in the shape of a neat cross, light danced over that symbol of light and branded it deep into the lifeless soil; and that was what Vinny had chosen to remember.

And now he was back in Paradise, watching the Christians: or more exactly watching a grass, watching a blabbermouth who'd gone over to the Christians, who was going to be very sorry later.

Vinny stood on the hill in the shadow of a parked truck and watched all the coming and going down at the terrace of houses, the Christians' HQ; and what he watched most particularly was Jason, crept out to clean a car, maybe thinking he was safe from being seen in this early light.

He was very wrong, if that's what he was thinking. Vinny had watched for hours already, since before the darkness shaded into dawn. He remembered the car, as well as the cross; and he hadn't been at all surprised to see Jason.

Nor at all sorry, either.

iii

It had been a long, strange summer for Albie, and he was almost glad that the intensity of it was almost over. His GCSE results had been good, and he'd be back at school next week to start sixth form. That would eat into his time, sharply reducing the work he could do for the Commando, for Richard and for God; but it would be welcome as well as resented, both at once. He could use a breathing-space, time out to take stock a little.

He'd come a long, long way these last few months – farther than the Americans, he thought, farther than the Australians, even though he hadn't shifted a metre off his home ground. Farther than anyone, except Derry. He hadn't been to the gates of death and back.

But then, Derry and Albie were on different roads. They talked together sometimes, and in common with most of his colleagues Albie found the guy utterly bewildering. How he could be born and raised by a believer, how he could work for and with believers all day, how he could be head over heels in love with a believer and above all how he could be healed by faith, how he could see a miracle from the inside and still not believe himself – it made no sense to Albie, who had been brought to faith so easily, when all his background and culture was against it. When his family, indeed, was so angry against it they'd had the rabbi round more than once to argue with him.

But Derry was Rachel's job, everyone in the Commando recognised that. Albie talked to him, sure, but he didn't preach. He was just glad to have one friend surviving from the old days, like a finger's-hold on his past, even if that friendship had to be rebuilt on new and uncertain ground for both of them. They'd both been born again, this summer.

Today Albie had been helping with the conversion work in the old gym, swinging a pickaxe with Derry and a couple of older lads, breaking up the concrete flooring down in the basement. It was hard work when you weren't used to it – or when you weren't a body-builder type, like Derry was turning into – and Albie was knackered by midday.

So they'd delegated him to run up to the shops for lunch, sandwiches and soft drinks and chocolate; and so he came down the steps into the street, dust in his hair and his clothes and his throat, his arms and shoulders burning with exhaustion, happy as a sandboy and whistling between hacking coughs.

·The weather had been stuck on sunshine all summer long – *since Richard came,* he thought, and pretty much believed it, that there was a connection – and it was far too warm for the combat jacket he'd pulled on as he left. But the pockets were handy, Albie carried any number of things in his pockets; and Nathan liked them to wear the uniform when they were out and about in Paradise. *You're always on duty,* he said, *you're always on call; and I want us inescapable, a constant visible presence on the streets. It'll be a comfort for the vulnerable, and a warning to the wicked.*

So Albie wore his jacket in the heat, like the good soldier he was. He wore it open, though, not to seem too regimented; and shoved hands in already-bulging pockets and never mind if that looked scruffy for a soldier, he might be on duty but he wasn't on parade.

He took the back alleys in preference to the streets, second nature to a teenager in Paradise, an old habit he didn't want to kill. Alleys were interesting, you found the most amazing stuff dumped out sometimes.

No treasure today, but he found a can right under his feet as if it had been put there specially, red and round and ripe for kicking; and that transported him from Paradise to sheer heaven. The sun on his back and a can to kick, his soul saved and no hurry in the world, friends waiting and lunch to come: he couldn't have dreamed a better day.

He kicked his can, and woke every sun-dozy dog up the alley. Half the back gates rattled with the pressure of their bodies, and the air filled with barking. None of the dogs were loose, though – no strays in Paradise these days, and people were learning to keep their pets in the yard, not the street – so he only grinned, and kicked the can again.

And whistled until the cough came back to remind him how dry his throat was; and dreamed a little of being loved as Derry was, of another girl as fire-bright as Rachel; and barely saw, paid no attention to the old and rust-ridden van ahead of him, until the door opened as he passed and someone got out.

Someone, or something.

Albie was aware of twisted teeth and shining, twisted skin, baldness and blisters and a smell that made him gag; but black-stained fingers closed on him, and he was aware of nothing then but flooding pain, too much even to scream for.

It filled him as a bath might be filled from its plug-hole, filth and waste bubbling up from beneath; and that was almost the worst of it, that those hands might be waking it and drawing it up but it was all there already, it all came from inside.

And it rose in his blood and in his bones, it swirled and spun his mind to a dizzy sickness and dragged him down, dragged him deep, deep and down . . .

iv

Derry ran a wheelbarrow up the ramp, tipped rubble into the filling skip; then he retreated backwards to the pavement, and turned to go inside again.

And then, finally, he saw her.

She had to bite down on an unexpected giggle, he looked so gormless for a second, so totally taken aback. Then he grinned a little uncertainly, visibly forgot what he'd meant to do next and walked over, leaving the wheelbarrow stranded.

"Hullo."

"Hi."

He grinned again, fidgeted, rubbed his face on his arm and his filthy hands on his shorts. It wasn't just the state of him holding him back; but today she was impatient with that caution, today the last thing she needed was a boyfriend scared to touch.

So she resolved that the easy way, reaching out to grab his arm and pull him down onto the wall beside her.

"Careful," he said, squirming away, still trying to keep an inch or two of distance, of safety between them. "I'm all mucky."

"Jesus, Derry. Do you really think I care?"

That stilled him in an instant, as it was meant to. He always listened when she swore. He looked down at his hands, and

435

nodded; said, "Okay. All right," as if she'd asked a totally differ-ent question, and came the other way. Shifted right up against her, put both his arms round her, kissed her dry-lipped and dusty.

"How are you, then?" he asked anxiously, as if everything might have changed since yesterday. "You're all right, you're not being sick or anything?"

"No," she said, laughing at him a little and glad of the chance, "I'm not being sick or anything. I feel fine."

"Good. Only I didn't expect to see you, I thought you'd be off looking for Albie, everyone else is; and then I thought maybe you weren't feeling well, and they'd sent you away . . . "

"Derry, I'm fine, all right?"

"All right, okay, good. If you're sure. I worry," he said, mean-ing *I love you.*

"I love you," she said, meaning *Don't worry, everything's going to be all right, the baby and us and everything.*

He smiled a little smugly, a little pleased with himself, as if that was the only news he was already sure of; and then he said, "So why aren't you, then?"

"Why aren't I what?"

"Off looking for Albie."

"Oh, that. Don't see the point. He's not a lost dog, he won't come running if we shout for him. He just met some friends, I reckon, and went off."

"What, with our lunch-money?"

"Reckon so. Listen, are you going to pack up here, or what?"

"Yeah, sure," he said, as if the idea had been in his head all the time. "If you want me to."

She nodded. "I want to go to the beach." She wanted an idyll, she wanted to walk hand in hand and barefoot through the surf and talk sensibly, easy and undisturbed.

"Okay. Wait while I shower?"

"If you're quick."

"Promise."

He went scrambling up the steps, leaving Rachel to collect the forgotten barrow and wheel it away inside for him, where it stood a chance of still being there tomorrow.

Where she would have stuck to the busy streets, straight up to the main road and the bus-stop, Derry asserted himself for once, tugging her into the quieter alleys. *Where he can play shield and defender,* she thought with a malicious grin, hiding it against his T-shirt as she tucked herself obediently under his arm. She'd already had one lecture from him, not to wander around here alone. Never mind that it was her own territory she'd been attacked on, or that she'd been taken in the street and not the alley. It did his ego good to lay down rules, and her no harm to follow them. Statistically he was right anyway, these alleys were definitely dodgy . . .

And then he wheeled her round a corner, and they found a group of little kids gathered together in a whispering huddle, staring at something on a garage door.

"What is that?"

"Look," he said, no help at all. She didn't want to look, she had a bad feeling about this. The way those kids were – excited but tight, on edge, falling back now to let them see better – and the way Derry felt against her side, suddenly so watchful, so afraid: it all said *No* to her, said *No, don't listen to him, don't look, you don't want to know.*

But she did look at last, reluctantly, she didn't have the option; and what she saw made her gasp, almost made her scream until she saw it clearly. And even then she didn't want to go any nearer, certainly didn't want to touch.

What she saw was a combat jacket, one of their own: a Commando jacket, no mistaking that.

And it hung suspended like a cross on a garage door, the fabric nailed to the wood like a crucifixion missing only its proper body. And what made it very much worse – what added to the idea that the body had just stepped out for a fag and a tea-break and would be back in a minute or two, back in position and in agony – what made her question her eyes and her sanity both was the blood.

Blood dripping fresh and glistening from the empty jacket; blood oozing from a dozen wounds, dribbling from sleeves and hem to run down the garage door and dry in streaks and runnels on the concrete below.

THIRTY-SIX

i

Consternation at the airport: the check-in girl almost in tears, as she labels his bags for Sydney via Amsterdam.

– Are you, she says – trying to be jocular, and failing – are you running out on us, Mr Gould?

He laughs, delightedly; then sobers to a smile, shakes his head.

– No, he says, I'm not running out on you. I've had a call, he says, that's all.

From God or just from Sydney, he doesn't say.

– But you are, she says, you are coming *back?* We do need you, she says, we need you so much . . .

– No, you don't. It was only ever God you needed, never me. And you've got momentum, nothing's going to stop you now. It's a great leap into light this city's taking; you'll be a beacon, he says. Even from Australia.

– That means you're not coming back. Doesn't it? *Doesn't* it?

– No, he says, it doesn't mean that at all. Only that I can't say for sure, he says, God is not predictable; I go where he sends me. *If* I don't come back, you'll manage fine, he says; but put it this way, it's a return ticket. And you've just labelled my bags, you know what I'm taking. Does it look to you as if I'm emigrating?

She smiles at last, at least partially reassured. One small suitcase and a duffel bag – might last her two weeks, in Ibiza. Might not.

– Send us a postcard, then, she says; because she knows postcards have magic, you always come back before your postcards, that's the rule.

– Of course I will, Yvette.

And now she really smiles. And never mind that she's wearing her name-badge as the rules require, she didn't see him read it.

ii

Going back to Vinny's in the very early light, practically a dawn raid, Nathan wasn't fool enough to go alone.

This time he took the battle bus, filled with troops. "I've got an idea who might have Albie," he said, knowing with an utmost certainty who had Albie. "Someone I've run across recently. He's a dangerous man, he might do something like this. I think we should go and see."

"What does Richard say?" someone asked.

"Richard's gone to Australia," Nathan said. "Remember?"

Of course they hadn't remembered, it was too sudden, too much of a shock, too startling to hold in the mind. Except for Nathan, who relished the opportunity. *We're on our own now,* and that was precisely how he wanted it. No miracles today. Strategy and tactics, guts and maybe a little sheer bloody-mindedness would win this one. Richard wasn't a feature any more.

"Joel," he said, "bring your camera. And someone bring the baseball bats. Just in case," he said.

Usually they sang in the bus, hymns and choruses and Jesus rock and reggae; but not today. Today they prayed, mostly in murmurs, in groups of two and three as the seating had them.

Nathan's memory did better than Jason's maps, taking them straight there; and then even the praying died into silence as they looked at where they'd come to, what they'd reached.

Even Nathan who'd been here before, who'd done the damage and knew what to expect, or thought he did: even he was rocked a little, even he had to be still and stare for a second or two before rolling the bus off the road and parking on the scarred earth, where he'd branded it with a cross for the Commando, *X marks the spot.*

No movement, no van or other vehicle, no sign of any life at all. Probably it had been a mistake to come. Whether he had Albie or not, Vinny clearly wasn't here. And it could be dangerous for Nathan to expose himself to too many questions.

But still, he was glad to see it: to jump out of the van and land with his boots in ash, to draw a lungful of air and almost choke on the grittiness of it, and the smell of recent burning.

He heard sounds of disembarkation behind him, sounds of coughing, voices muttering; then the first question.

"Nat, what in the world *happened* here? Looks like a thunderbolt hit it."

"Maybe it did," he said neutrally. "What I hear, the guy had done more than enough to deserve it. But never mind the questions, let's just have a look around. And be careful."

He was more than careful himself, he was ultra-cautious as he made his way past the scorched skeletons and blackened, fallen panels of Vinny's caravans. He didn't really think anyone was lurking in this turmoil of destruction; but on the other hand, he did think that Albie had been snatched for bait as much as retribution. And he did think that the crucified jacket was a challenge; and Vinny would surely know they'd come here. What Nathan expected to find was another message, like the blood on the jacket.

What he found first, what he caught his toe against and all but stumbled over in the long shadows was a soft body. He looked down into a rising mass of flies; looked through them, and saw graphic evidence that Vinny had been down this way at least once since the fire. It was a dead dog, only a dog, but it hadn't died in the flames.

Checking his path more carefully he saw more corpses, many more, leading him like an easy trail to the roofless ruin of the furthest kennel, where Vinny had kept his pit bulls.

Nathan made his way cautiously towards it, finding no more life *en route* than those swarming flies. The door was a charred joke, which fell from its hinges when he kicked it; but someone had been active here since the fire went out. The corrugated iron sheets that had made the roof were stacked on one side, instead of lying all over as they must have fallen when the wooden rafters burned through.

The breeze block pens still stood, only blackened by the fire and their metal mesh gates twisted out of true. Nathan looked into one and saw a heap of bodies burned through to the bone, too dry and dead even to interest the flies.

He smiled, and glanced into the next.

He was still standing, hands spread on the high pen wall and staring into its darkness, when his men came to find him.

"Nat? There's nothing here . . . "

"There's something here," he said softly. "Come and see."

He'd been expecting a message of some sort, and this was it.

It wasn't Albie that he'd found, but it might as well have been. It might have been better if it was; at least that would have left no room for extrapolation, for thinking, *He went through this, and isn't here any longer; so what, what the hell, what kind of living hell is he going through now?*

Nathan climbed over the wall into the pen, and instantly felt the

440

difference under his feet, even through thick rubber soles. Everything was sticky in here, and the ash on the concrete floor had caked into lumps which were still damp; which meant both that Albie was not long gone, and that he had at least been alive when he left. When he was taken. This blood was fresh.

Nathan bent to retrieve the articles that lay scattered on the concrete, gluing themselves slowly to it; and someone checked him, someone said, "Nat, don't you, don't you think we should leave things as they are? For the police, I mean?"

And he looked up just briefly, just long enough to say, "What police?"

Then he gathered, and straightened with items in his arms and stains on his uniform; and someone said, "Well, we've got to, haven't we? We've got to tell them? I mean, this is kidnap, and it looks, it looks like *torture* . . . "

"Listen," Nathan said, high-stepping over the wall again and handing his burdens around, *share and enjoy.* "Albie was one of our men, right? He was one of *us.* If you think we've just been playing at soldiers all this time, then you'd better think again. I'm not giving this job over to the bloody police. He was taken from us, and we'll get him back again. And while we're doing it, we'll teach these people not to mess with the Commando. Clear?"

There was an evasive mutter around him, which didn't match with any army he knew of.

"Is that *clear?*" he demanded, with a snap in his voice.

And they stiffened, straightened, all but saluted; and they said, "Yes, *sir,*" without the faintest trace of irony in them.

"Right, then. Back to the bus. And bring that stuff," as if they'd thought to do anything else with the chains and weights and rusty iron blades that clung so to their fingers.

Nathan led the way out, heard them obediently at his back; and knew that he could say, he could do, he could get away with anything today.

Get away with murder, if he had to.

*　　　*　　　*

Terry Belderstone could be patient, when he needed that. He'd outwaited business associates many a time, simply sat silent on a deal until it hatched to his advantage.

Other times, he could be savage in his urgency. As now.

He felt he'd been patient long enough, or too long. All his plans were on hold, he was losing money while Richard Gould and the legions of God occupied his property and held a blackmailing sword above his head. He wanted them out, he wanted them running so scared they wouldn't ever stop to look behind them.

So he picked up the phone and dialled; and when it was answered he kept things simple and direct.

"John," he said, "why is nothing happening?"

"Oh. Terry." And oddly he didn't even sound surprised, let alone jumpy as he should have been. "Yeah, good, I'm glad you called."

"Why?" People weren't supposed to be glad, when Terry phoned in this mood. When they'd given him cause to.

"Saves me ringing you, don't it? Listen, you just keep an eye on the local news tonight."

"What am I watching for?" Terry didn't like conversations where his only contribution was to ask questions, but this one seemed to be outrunning him by some distance.

"No good asking me, mate, Vinny doesn't talk much. But I had this from him straight, he's organising something. God knows what. It'll get you off the hook, though. Vinny's a bit eccentric in his methods, maybe, but he takes a job on, it gets done."

"I am not," Terry said softly, "on anybody's hook. Is that clear?"

"Sure, Terry, sure."

"It's just a job I want done, is all. A messiness that I want cleared up."

"Okay, if you say so. Whatever. It'll all be cleared up tonight, I guarantee."

"Very well, then. But your head's on this one, John, I'll not take another failure. See your man doesn't let you down."

John chuckled, the thing Terry had least expected him to do; and said again, as he'd said at their last meeting, "You've not met Vinny, have you?"

And then he hung up before Terry could, cut him off and left him bewildered and frustrated, angry but hopeful.

Terry didn't know what was going on here, and he didn't like it; but one thing was certain, he wasn't going to sit quietly at home tonight and watch television.

He'd be there in Paradise to see it all live, to check it out in person, to be sure.

*   *   *

Billy didn't like funerals, they scared him. He always wanted to open the box up before they buried it or burned it, to make sure the person inside really wasn't screaming. He'd felt that way at

442

Grace's, even with the piano to keep him busy.

He was glad that Helen's parents were taking her away, so there wouldn't be a funeral here. There was a service instead, a memorial service they called it; but they hadn't asked Billy to play, so he wasn't going. He wasn't sure that Helen wouldn't be there in her box, for people to say goodbye to.

Everyone else went, almost. Billy sat on a heap of rubble in front of the houses and counted them all away. They went off in little groups, some of them packing into cars and some of them walking. It wasn't very far to go; and they couldn't go in the battle bus, because Nat had that. Nat and his soldiers.

Billy thought it was funny, that Nat wasn't going to Helen's service. Helen was scared of Nat, he remembered that; but he also remembered before, when Nat had been her boyfriend. She'd loved him then, and Billy thought he ought to be there.

But she'd loved Billy too, she told him so; and Billy wasn't going. Maybe Nat was like Billy, maybe he didn't like funerals. Maybe he didn't want to think of a big box with Helen in it.

Little boxes were different, though, little boxes were all right. Billy had a little box, and he knew just what he wanted in that.

When he'd counted everyone out and the houses were empty, Billy went back inside. He went upstairs to Nat's room, where he stood by the door for a moment, sweating and breathing hard. Even the idea of this had frightened him a little, and doing it frightened him a lot. He was more scared of Nat than Helen had ever been, Billy was sure of that.

There weren't any locks on the bedroom doors. Everyone was trusted. Billy felt very bad, breaking that trust; but he'd prayed about it, he'd prayed *Lord Jesus, make it right, what I do. It's for Helen.* And there wasn't anyone here to catch him anyway, all the houses were empty. Billy knew that, he'd counted with little stones in his hands, to make sure he didn't go wrong.

So he opened Nat's door, and walked in.

He knew what he wanted, and where it was. He'd carried it up here himself, when Nat asked him to. It was a cardboard box, and Nat kept it under his bed.

So Billy got down on his knees and tugged it out with trembling hands, thinking how many fingerprints he was leaving, how awful it would be if Nat found out. He wasn't taking much, and what he wanted wasn't even Nat's; but still Billy thought he might die. Might die of fear, before Nat even started.

So hurry, hurry. Leave the door open to hear if the bus comes back, and hurry . . .

The box was full of things that Nat had brought back from Helen's, the day she died. If she was dead, if she wasn't kicking and screaming in her box, the way Billy dreamed about the dead.

Billy knew some of the box's secrets, because he'd carried it up to help Nat.

"I thought you fetched all your things from Helen's before," he'd said; and Nat had smiled.

"Not all of them, Billy," he'd said. "Only what I needed here. And actually not all of this is mine. Some of it counts as Helen's. But I'd like to have something to remember her by; and there's some stuff I wouldn't want her parents to find, it would only upset them. You know what I mean, photographs, personal things."

Billy hadn't really known what he meant, no; but he'd remembered. And now he was back, rooting through the box for a photograph and maybe something else if he could find it, something of Helen's to remember her by. Nothing that might possibly be Nat's.

He found the photos first, a thick wadge of envelopes held together with a rubber band.

Opening one at random, he soon learned what Nat had meant, why he wouldn't want Helen's parents to see them. Some were pictures of Nat with no clothes on; but most of them were Helen. Billy hoped that they were old pictures, because he didn't think a Christian girl should have posed like that, or a Christian boy been there with a camera. He pushed them hastily back into the envelope, and felt unhappy even opening the next.

This was better, though, this was just Helen and Nat on holiday. Billy wasn't sure why Nat would have hidden these at all, unless he wanted everyone to forget that him and Helen had ever been together.

Billy found just what he wanted in this envelope, the perfect picture: a close-up of Helen on her own, laughing into the camera, alive and happy and free. That was just right, that had to go into his box.

And he was just wondering what else might be in Nathan's box that could go instead into his, when he heard footsteps in the empty house; and looked up to see a figure standing in the doorway, a shadow against the light.

And nearly screamed for sheer terror, until he recognised who it was and realised he'd only counted wrong, he'd forgotten one of them.

444

And then was just as scared all over again, when the shadow said, "What are you doing, sicko, going through his stuff? Want me to tell him, do you, is that what you want? Is it?"

And Billy stammered no, and swore his heart away to keep this secret.

*   *   *

George wrapped the chain twice around his knuckles, and looked at it with a vague, unfocused longing. What he wanted, what he wanted most in the world was to slam that improved fist into someone's face, and feel the bones break. He didn't much care whose face, whose bones, he'd take any of them – Richard Gould, Nathan Lewis, Derry. Any policeman in the city. Young Jason, for not putting Derry in hospital the way George had paid him to.

But he grimaced, and shook his head, and tamely clipped the chain to Kyzer's collar. And that was what angered, what outraged him most about this summer's end: that he'd been tamed, driven to being sensible and quiet and not making waves. It was his best chance of not going to prison, his solicitor said. If he kept his head down like a model citizen, kept right away from Paradise.

So that's what he did. He lived in his little council semi in the suburbs, he was polite to the neighbours and didn't so much as swear at the local kids when they were kicking up a racket. And he always kept the dog leashed and muzzled, to demonstrate how responsible he was. Tamed like an animal, to avoid being caged like an animal.

And like a raging animal he wanted to pulp and rend anyone who crossed him, just about anyone who crossed his path; and he never once let it show.

Until today, when he walked down to his garden gate, turned up the street – and stopped, dead in his tracks.

Saw the filthy blue van so badly parked ten yards away, and just stood there realising that it wasn't over after all. Waiting for it all to begin again.

And his fist clenched inside the doubled chain, and that wasn't only to hold Kyzer back against his pulling.

The van's door opened, and a figure stepped out; and oh no, this wasn't what he'd been told at all, this wasn't keeping his head down or not making waves, oh no.

This was Vinny, of course it was, no one else would ever drive his van; but it was Vinny as even George had never seen him,

445

never dreamed of seeing him.

Vinny swayed the short distance from the van, and it was hard not to step back or turn away. Too hard for Kyzer. Its growl turned to a whimper, it backed up against its chain and tried to pull George home. And that was a Rottweiler trained to fight, guaranteed not to be scared of anything in the wide world.

The skin on Vinny's face and hands was raw and blistered, black with filth. His crew-cut had been scorched away, and the scalp showed livid red. His clothes were burned right through in patches; and they stank, they looked as if they were rotting on his body.

Even his smile was worse than George remembered, and his breath smelt putrid.

"George," Vinny said, smiling, breathing all over him. "Got a little job for you, George."

No nonsense now about Vinny working for George. And no small talk either, no polite enquiries about what the hell had happened, to make this mess of him. "Uh, okay, Vinny." *Whatever.* "What do you want?"

"All those kids you ran, in Paradise. Regular little network, wasn't it? Twockers and thieves. I want them, George, I want them all tonight. Except for Jason, you won't get Jason now."

"Christ." That was just what he wasn't supposed to be doing, running his old contacts in Paradise. But he wasn't going to argue. He drew a hand over his bullet head, and it came away damp. "What do you, what do you want them for, Vin?"

"I want a riot. I want you to buy me a riot tonight. You fix it, I'll tell you where."

"Tonight? That's not, that's not much time, these lads aren't easy to find . . . "

"You find them, George. You do it." Vinny leaned closer, hissing in his ear, and George couldn't suppress a shudder of revulsion just at the touch of Vinny's clothes against his. "I'll show you something, George. I'll show you what I've got in my van."

And George went with him, hauling a stiff-legged and whining Kyzer after him; and George saw what was in the back of Vinny's van, and then he threw up in the gutter.

*   *   *

Jack was in his bedroom, desultorily putting things into boxes, when he saw Billy through the window.

Billy was down the bottom of next door's garden, on his knees,

446

scrabbling the earth up with his hands; and that was strange enough to lift Jack out of his own preoccupations, worrying enough to take him downstairs and out.

"Billy?" he called, hurrying down the path. "Billy, what are you doing there?"

Billy startled, and looked over his shoulder with a furtive guilt. "Mr Jack! I thought, I thought you were at the service, everybody's gone to the service . . . "

"No, Billy. I didn't want to go." Jack hunkered down cautiously and said, "I was up at the hospital, with Anita; and then she fell asleep, and I thought it would be a good time to come and do some packing. Did you know we are moving?"

"Yes," Billy said mournfully. "I think it's sad, I don't like it. Everybody's going. Helen's," *Helen's in a box*, "Helen's gone, and Bengt and Ingrid have gone back to, to *Sweden*," triumphant in his remembering, even through his melancholy, "and some of the others have to go back to college soon, and now you're going too. Everybody's going. Even *Richard's* gone," remembering suddenly, saying it with a breathy horror, the worst news in the world.

"I'm sorry," Jack said, more touched than he'd expected or wanted to be. "I don't want to go, Billy. But it's Anita, she's too frightened to come back here now. Richard found us a very nice flat, with a warden to help when we're ill; and it's not far away, so you can come to visit," and no, he really didn't want to go. He wasn't so old that he needed sheltered housing, like a blanket between himself and the world. That was all for Anita. But he wasn't too sorry to be separated from Nathan and his Commando, especially lacking Richard to temper that young man's enthusiasms. No more than Anita was Jack fond of the uniforms.

"What are you doing here, Billy?" he asked again, seeing a flat cardboard box at Billy's side, and the marks where his fingers had scraped at the baked earth.

Billy blushed. "It's, it's like my own little service, Mr Jack. I wanted Helen to know I was thinking of her. So I thought I'd bury some things of Helen's here. I wouldn't mind coming here, to put flowers and think of her. But all I've got is a picture," and he glanced nervously about him as he said it, as if he shouldn't have even that, "and I can't make a proper hole, it's too hard."

"You need a spade," Jack said patiently. "Come on, we'll go and fetch one. And maybe I can find something to put in your box, yes? We have some flowers that Helen gave Anita, that she dried; we will put one of those in. Anita would be happy to do that, I am sure . . . "

So they did that, they dug a hole and buried a box in lieu of a coffin, a dead flower and a photograph in lieu of a dead girl; and they marked the place with a cross of wood and string. And Jack said a prayer, and then stood to attention with his spade while Billy played *Abide With Me* in a slow lament on his harmonica, while tears flowed down his face.

*   *   *

Derry did go to the service, but only for Rachel's sake, to be a hand to hold against her memories, and company after.

Only when he got there he found that he wasn't needed after all, Rachel was letting others do his job for him. The service was held in the big marquee, like when they buried his mother; and Rachel was right up the front, in a tight huddle with her friends from the Commando. Derry couldn't push his way into a pack like that, and wasn't going to hang around on the fringes, feeling awkward and waiting to be noticed.

So he took a seat at the back, and sat through the service trying not to listen to the words, not to hear echoes. He thought he'd catch Rachel on the way out, but he wasn't the only one who'd thought of that, either. She came past him with a couple of girls, arm in arm in arm; and when he called her name she didn't seem to hear, or didn't want to.

They were having a wake, he'd heard, down at the houses; and he could follow them there, he supposed, he could amuse himself for hours watching Rachel turn to others for the support she obviously didn't need from him . . .

Thanks, but no thanks. He had better things to do. When she wanted him — *if* she wanted him, if she remembered she did actually have a boyfriend for times like this — she could come and find him, she knew where he lived.

Except that he didn't go home, he was too restless and fretful. He just walked around for a while, not finding any of those better things to do: feeling sulky and jealous, not pleased with himself but managing to blame Rachel for that too.

Eventually he fetched up outside the hospital, where a woman was selling flowers from a stall. Like everything else, flowers made him think of Rachel, and he certainly wasn't buying any for her. But there'd been flowers in the marquee too, flowers for the absent Helen; and that gave him an idea, something that definitely counted as a better thing to do.

*

He bought a couple of bunches, he didn't care what, big and bright and colourful was all that counted; and he carried them down to the cemetery where his mother was buried.

She had a headstone now, thanks to Richard. He'd arranged it, got the chapel to pay for it; he'd even written the words, more or less. Officially he'd discussed it with them, but that was back when Derry's dad was totally brain-dead, and Derry himself didn't have any ideas. It made no sense to him, his warm, gaudy, enveloping mother written down on cold stone. So he'd just shrugged and said yes, sure, whatever; and he couldn't remember his dad saying anything more.

Now he sat back on his heels and looked at her name chiselled in marble, and it still didn't make much sense. Flowers were better, loud flowers in garish colours, that she would have liked and laughed at. He put those in the little vase that stood half-buried in the earth, and fetched some water for them in a plastic cup that was rolling around in the wind.

After that he sat for a while picking grass and weeds off the settling mound, clagging his nails up with earth and imagining just what she would've said if she'd seen them like that.

He didn't talk to her, he didn't believe in ghosts or angels, he just thought she was dead; but it felt good simply being here and thinking about her. That's what graves were for, he reckoned. Helen's parents were having her cremated; but then they wouldn't have anywhere to go, to remember their daughter.

He was still there, crumbling lumps of earth between his fingers to make it all look good and smooth and tidy like she would have liked it, when he heard slow footsteps coming down the path and stopping right behind him.

For a moment he thought it was Rachel, he thought she'd read his mind and come to find him. So he turned round with her name already halfway to his lips, and a smile behind; and had to check back quick, because it wasn't Rachel at all, it was his father.

That was almost as good, though. Better, even.

Derry stood up and brushed the dirt off his knees, said, "Hi, Dad," calm and quiet, as if it was dead regular for the two of them to meet each other here.

"Son." His father nodded, not taking his eyes from the grave. "She's being looked after, then. That's good."

"Yeah. Yeah, she's being looked after. Listen, did you want to be alone for a bit? I'll wait for you by the gate . . . "

"No. No, don't worry, lad. I only came to see. That stone's

449

good, I like that." Mr Bowen nodded a couple of times, then said, "So why aren't you at work, then, it's a work day, isn't it?"

"Yeah, it is. But there was that service I wanted to be at, and – well, I'm on the skive, I suppose. That's all. Doesn't matter, there's no one there to check, and I can make it up later. I just wanted some time away from it today."

"Tell you what, then, son." And here came a miracle: a suggestion, a firm idea from his father. "Why don't you and me get the boys, and we'll take them to the beach? School starts next week, they'll be glad of the treat."

"Great. Terrific, yeah, let's do that. Let's go."

"You could bring your girl, if you want to. If she's around."

Derry thought about that, about running down to the houses and rooting Rachel out. It felt briefly ideal; but she might not want to come. She might even be vicious about it, how could he think of playing on a day so solemn, the day they said farewell to Helen? Or the day Richard buggered off, come to that, she wouldn't be finding that easy to handle.

Chickenshit, he accused himself scornfully; but better that than the other thing, better to dodge bad news than have it to carry.

"No," he said, "best leave her for the moment. She's busy with that crew of hers. I'll catch up with her tonight. We'll make it just family, okay? It'll be great . . . "

So they borrowed Derry's young brothers from his aunt, took them to the coast and played at families. It was easy out there where nothing was real, nothing was even attached to anything real. Derry bought ice-creams and built sandcastles with the kids, and managed not to think about Rachel for maybe an hour at a stretch, about as good as he ever got; and then the ice-cream melted and the tide came in, and they all came home again.

Aunt Joyce made them both stay for tea, "I've cooked it for you special, so you can sit and eat it, you're not strangers here for all that you seem like it sometimes, not calling round from one week to the next." Then Derry saw the little boys to bed, an old ritual all but forgotten in his much-rewritten life; and it was after eight o'clock before they got away, and he'd be lucky if he got to see Rachel at all tonight, she'd likely gone home by now.

Five minutes passed at the bus-stop, then ten, fifteen; and two fire engines went by and a police-car with its siren wailing, but there was no sign of any bus.

"Ah, come on, Derry son," his dad said at last. "We'll walk, it's not that far. Twenty minutes."

"Bet the buses come when we're bang between stops. Three of them together . . . "

But no buses came at all, and Derry was starting to feel more than a twinge of interest before they were halfway home. They'd seen two more police cars and a van with darkened windows and a grille lowered like a visor across its windscreen, and they were all heading for Paradise.

"You know what, dad? I reckon something's doing. This is getting like the night they raided the dogfight."

"Like this every night, on this road. They could be heading anywhere."

And he was right, of course, this was the main highway through the west of the city, from suburbs to centre; but even so, Derry was getting interested. There still hadn't been any buses.

*　　　*　　　*

It had started in a pub on the main road, with a couple of kids being thrown out because they were under age and the landlord wouldn't serve them.

Two minutes later they were in the carpark with a bunch of mates, swearing and jeering at his customers as they went in and writing filth with their fingers on any car that needed washing, smearing muck on any car that didn't.

He went out in a rage to chase them off, and he was a big man, kids trod carefully with him in their light; but there were ten or twelve of them by this time, and they didn't scatter and run. They spat at him, and made threats. One smashed the quarter light of a Mini, and grinned; and then they were all doing it, running through the carpark breaking windscreens and stabbing tyres, yelling and screaming above the rising wail of alarms going off all around them.

His wife called to him from the doorway to come inside, to ring the police; not to be a hero, she said, it wasn't worth it. They had knives, she said. Ring the police.

That's what he did, reluctantly. He asked his customers to leave by the other door, or else to stay where they were if they felt it was safer; then, as the first brick came through a window into the lounge bar, he rang the police.

Even then, with the phone in his hand, he hesitated briefly. He had another number on the wall there, for the Christ Commando. He'd heard good reports of them from a couple of fellow publicans further down towards the river: how they'd been on the spot when help was needed, nipped trouble in the bud, identified

451

troublemakers and under-age drinkers and stopped a fight or two.

But he was only on the fringes of Paradise up here, hadn't seen much of them since they left their card. And this was looking serious, it was going to need more than vigilantes. Vigilantes couldn't bang people up in police cells overnight and take them to court in the morning. He didn't want those little shits pacified, he wanted them punished; he wanted them bruised and beaten and crying for their mothers . . .

So he rang the police.

The first squad car was met with a hail of missiles, and left more quickly than it had arrived. Seeing that, the publican and his wife and their few remaining customers decided not to wait. They abandoned the pub and made a sprint for safety, while those of their cars that weren't already burning at the back were hotting up and down the street in front, lads in ski-masks practising hand-brake turns with others spread-eagled and screaming on the roofs.

And ten or twelve became twenty or thirty, and it might have been fifty before the fire-engines came and were stoned away again. And the police were waiting for riot-gear and reinforcements, too few to do anything but divert traffic and watch as fifty became a hundred and a dozen of those swarmed on the pub's roof like prisoners in a jail, ripping off slates and hurling them down for their mates to dodge.

Then there were enough police at least to control the margins, to contain the numbers and keep it where it was, keep it local. So the hundred stayed at about a hundred, though some few of them were coming and going all the time in speeding cars, the police too few to block off every road and alley.

It wasn't long before the kids up on the roof came tumbling down the fire-escape just in time, as the lower windows of the pub flickered and glowed and glass began to shatter of its own accord, no help from brick or stone.

Vinny sat in his van some distance down the road, the far side of the police cordon, behind the journalists and the ambulances and the fire-engines with their windscreens starred by rocks.

He saw how the Commandos who came to help were turned away by the police, sworn at as rudely and treated as roughly as the teenagers who came to watch and cheer and join in.

And Vinny smiled and drove away, heading down the hill into the very heart of Paradise.

Not enough, to say that Albie trawled pain in the darkness. Not enough to say that he caught and held it, nor even to turn that around and say that it held him, that he lay tangled in his own nerve-net helpless and hopeless, friendless and floating, rapt in agony.

He'd been taken to the very edges of experience, out where nothing is ever less than its own pure self, where everything transmutes but is never, ever diluted. And words invariably, inevitably dilute, offering only a reduction. There are never enough words for the real thing.

So Albie lay, that much is certain, is indisputable; but he lay in something more than simple darkness. Call it the ever-dark, the never-to-be-light. And he knew what it was, that's how things work out there on the margins, they may transmute but they don't have any secrets. Albie didn't expect ever to see light again.

And he lay without moving, even when the world rocked and rolled him. And he suffered something greater than pain and sharper than terror, worse than a cocktail of the two. Constant companions both, pain and terror, and neither one slacking, both sharpening their hooks against his bones. But now they were transmuted, conjoined with slow and cruel time to make something that stretched wider and dug deeper, that pulled Albie beyond the limits of his body and brought him to a new reality.

Brought him here, to the ever-dark: where no light would ever come, where terror never eased its grip, where pain searched and searched and never found an end.

And Albie knew where he was, Albie had a word for it. Albie was in Hell, and God was a liar; there was no salvation from this.

*   *   *

Rachel had phoned Derry's at least half a dozen times today. After the last she'd run up and hammered indignantly on the door, in case their phone was on the blink. Getting no answer then either, she'd shoved a rude note through the letter-box – *Oy, pigling. Where are you, then? I'm hungry, and I want my dinner. If you don't come soon, I'll get my dad over to collect me, and up yours, mate* – and gone back to help unhappy Jack with his packing.

Still no Derry, but in fact she stayed for dinner after all, because Billy was cooking and he always needed help. And afterwards – waiting just a little longer, just in case – she hung around in one of the common-rooms drinking coffee and discussing the only topic of the day, Richard's hurried departure. Having nothing new to say about it, only putting off the time when she really would have to phone her father for a lift.

That's where she was when they first heard of trouble at the Queen's Arms. Nathan took a squad of men and hurried off in the battle bus; and Rachel found it hard to suppress an interior chuckle half an hour later when the bus came back again, sent home by uncooperative policemen. Nathan was on the phone immediately he came in, bullying his way through to a Chief Superintendent, but he still got no joy. They'd have liked Richard on hand, because they were talking to all the community leaders, and too bad he wasn't available; but the Commando, no. This was a job for the professionals.

Nathan relayed that with vitriol to his troops, then dropped into a chair and sulked.

"Look," one of the women said after a minute, going to a map on the wall, "you said the police have got the trouble pretty much penned in around here, is that right, Nat?"

He barely glanced up. "Yeah, that's right. So what?"

"So all this," with a sweep of her hand across the map, "should be safe; and that's our territory. That's where we've got a lot of people who're going to be scared stiff right now. I think we should be out there. Shouldn't we?"

Murmurs of agreement, of approval; and they were moving already, talking it through, who would go to see whom and who would just patrol the streets, to be on hand wherever there was a need for reassurance.

Nathan stayed where he was, shifted just one hand in gesture to his hard boys, to keep them where they were; said, "No. You go if you want to, it's safe enough; but we're staying. That's not our job, fetching clean knickers for old women who've wet themselves. I'm not having that."

Someone murmured then, something about pride; and Nat flashed back hard and fast, "It's nothing to do with pride, it's just fitting the tools to the job. The police may not be able to contain this all night. The kids round here, they see a riot on the news, they'll want one of their own. It's no use if we're spread about all over Paradise, we need to be here and ready. If you see anything out there, *anything*, you call in, right? And watch your backs. That's all."

It was plenty enough for Rachel. She wasn't going out tonight. She was barely seventeen and pregnant, and you had to draw a line somewhere. In her case, Derry and her parents had both drawn lines independently, and she wouldn't push against either one of those; so she went to call her father. If there was a riot brewing, better to get home now before anyone panicked.

But the phone had gone dead, turned up its toes and got wired in to the Celestial Exchange, there was no dialling tone or anything; and she didn't know what to do then. Nathan would have his portable, she could ask to use that; but she couldn't stand Nathan in this mood, hard and vicious. She didn't even want to go back to tell him that the line was dead. *Leave it for someone else,* she thought. *Chicken,* she thought.

Ordinarily she'd ask someone to run her over, no problem; but this wasn't an ordinary night. The battle bus was out of bounds, Nathan wouldn't let that go in case he needed it for his game of big tough macho heroes; and she could hear what other cars they had leaving now, as people scattered to the four corners of Paradise.

Nothing to worry about. As soon as her dad heard, he'd be over like a shot to see her safe; and meantime, she was in no danger here. She rubbed her stomach gently, *okay, little one? Not getting scared, not getting fretful in there?* and went upstairs to find a window with a better view.

She could see the bottom of Derry's street from up there, but no distant figure that might be Derry coming to find her. She thought maybe there was a flicker of light against the sky that might be a pub burning; certainly there was the nearer, brighter flashing of a blue police light, and another moving along the skyline, chasing a pillar of white that had to be the police helicopter with its searchlight on.

Suddenly another source of light, a lot nearer: yellow and fierce, and that was a fire for sure. Except that it was moving, there was a fire rolling down the hill, down the dead road, heading right for the houses . . .

*　　　*　　　*

George thought he might have recognised the boy in the back of Vinny's van, though he certainly wouldn't swear to it. The lad's parents couldn't have been sure of him like that, masked in blood and filth, dark scabbing sockets where his eyes should have been weeping. But still there was something about him, George rather thought he'd seen him around. In a Commando jacket.

So now he was taking Kyzer for a stroll along old, familiar routes, heading for the gym and the houses beyond. Down here the riot was nothing but a distant sound of battle, punctured by the rising and falling-away of sirens; he wondered if that was what Vinny had wanted, to draw the hard men of the Commando out of the way and leave the houses vulnerable.

Could be, but George guessed not. Vinny was harder than anyone, and relished any chance to prove it. And he could find plenty of like-minded men to back him up, if the odds were weighted against him. He hadn't asked George, but that meant nothing now. George was a loser.

Down past the gym, caged in scaffolding; Kyzer wanted to go in, but George dragged it on with a kick and a curse. Nothing doing there.

Further on, though, by the unmade road that led down to the houses: there was something doing there, all right. A tight knot of men, only shadows that far from the streetlights, clustered a cautious distance away from a van that looked a lot like Vinny's. And yes, there was Vinny, he was unmistakable. Pitch dark, you could still recognise Vinny. Looked like he was sluicing the van down, inside and out; but Vinny never washed his van. Hadn't even got Jason to do it, when he had the boy as a slave.

So it wasn't water he was sluicing around. *Guess what?* George thought, grinning in the darkness, seeing how the road ran all but straight down to the terrace of houses. *A calling-card, that's what. Vinny being polite, announcing his arrival.*

A couple of the men joined Vinny at the van now, started to push while Vinny walked along beside and steered one-handed through the open window.

Finally, when it had picked up a bit of speed, Vinny gestured the men away and let the van roll past him. At the last second he struck a match and tossed it casually into the back, through the open doors.

In the sudden flare of light, before he had to turn his eyes away, George saw or thought he saw more than he'd expected, and far more than he wanted to see. He saw – or thought he saw – a movement that was more than the movement of flame, a movement of black within the rolling orange; and thought no, Vinny wasn't dumping evidence, he was blazoning it across the night. *Vinny is here,* he was saying – and he was sending the boy to take the message, still living and still in the van.

*　　　*　　　*

The only good thing that Nathan could see about this whole long

456

day was that he'd learned just how loyal his central corps, his shock troops were prepared to be. That loyalty might have been inspired by Richard, might be given nominally to God; but it came to him, personal and direct.

But loyalty or no loyalty, he was running out of time. *No police,* he'd said, *we'll handle this ourselves*; and he'd conspicuously failed to do so. All day he'd been searching for Albie, and what he'd learned amounted to a fat nothing. George had been sighted in Paradise, but Nathan couldn't find him; and no one would admit even to knowing Vinny. They were lying, of course, but no matter how hard he leant on them, it seemed that Vinny could lean a little harder. *Just a matter of who they're most scared of,* and Jason was the only one he'd had opportunity to tutor in the more esoteric degrees of fear. Vinny clearly took classes.

And now this riot was going on, it was a situation tailor-made for the Commando to operate side by side with the police, and they'd been sent away like schoolboys. And no, it wasn't a good day for Nathan.

So he sat in the common-room with his men around him, muscular Christianity running to waste; and his mind was a total blank, he couldn't think where to go from here.

And then suddenly he didn't need to, because Rachel came bursting in from upstairs with her eyes bugging out. He glared at her, and she said, "Nat, quick, there's a, a burning car, it's coming down the hill straight for us . . . "

And here was blessed action at last, something to do. He ran to the nearest door with his men behind him, saw the flaming vehicle careering down the road and started shouting orders.

"Rachel, back into the house and get everyone out, in case it hits the building. Micky, Joe – fire extinguishers, you know where they are. Run."

Any more warning, any more time and he might have done better, might have figured out a way to stop the fireball dead or divert it onto the wasteland where it could be no danger to anyone. But time was the one thing he was short of; nothing more he could do but stand and watch as it ran out altogether, as the blazing van – he could see it more clearly now, lit by its own fierce light – came bumping faster down the last few metres of road, took a sudden swerve from a pothole and smashed head on into the battle bus.

Then the boys were back from the house with two extinguishers each. Nathan grabbed one and led them cautiously towards the inferno.

"Should I call the fire brigade?" someone asked behind him.

He shook his head. "We can deal with this. Just let it burn out if we have to, it's far enough from the houses not to hurt ... "

He aimed his extinguisher and squeezed the trigger experimentally, felt it cough and saw how the flames bowed back before the chemical cloud. He nodded contentedly. "We can deal with this," he said again. "Two of you this side, someone come round with me. Don't get any closer than you have to, though. No heroics. The bus's tank is nearly empty, but it might still go up with a bang."

And he ran in a wide circle around the back of the van – and stopped, staring, seeing something other than the fire moving in that inferno.

Seeing a figure suddenly come plunging out all flames, its distorted mouth stretched in a terrible silence, as though it were already screaming in another world.

Jumping back with a scream of his own, as Albie came to embrace him like a brother.

*   *   *

With no responsibilities left tonight – his dad safe home and happy with the telly and Rachel surely off with hers by now, she got dead impatient when she was hungry – Derry was free to go siren-chasing, and find out what had stopped the buses.

He loped up to the main road, thinking that it was quiet like a Sunday: it wasn't only buses, there were no taxis either, hardly any cars at all. Except police cars, plenty of those; and one of them stopped right by him, the driver wound down his window, and,

"You! Where the hell d'you think you're going?"

Derry gestured. "Down there. Why?"

"You are not, son. You turn round and go home. Right now."

"I'm not doing anything."

"Wrong. You're doing one thing. You're going home. Hear me?"

"What's going on, then?"

"Look, are you deaf?" The policeman swung his door open, set one foot on the ground, and Derry back-pedalled quickly.

"Okay, okay, I'm going! See?"

"Right, then."

The police car stayed where it was, watching, until he'd turned off the main road; then he heard it speed away.

*

And then he went to see the action anyway. He wasn't going home on some copper's say-so. This time he stuck to the back alleys, the routes that were second nature to him, and the only people he met were going the same way on the same errand.

He could see the fire's light against the sky before he saw what was burning, hear the sounds of riot before he saw a single rioter or a single cop.

The cops weren't hard to find, though, you just turned a corner and there they were; and this lot were no friendlier. Especially to teenage boys. Probably thought he was reinforcements, all set to join in from the blind side. He tried to sneak past the cordon with a news camera crew, but they hauled him out of that and almost beat him up, threatened to arrest him if he didn't go home; and Derry decided that hanging around just wasn't worth it. He'd see more on the telly, back at home.

And then it occurred to him that Rachel would be seeing all this on the telly too, and might be worrying; 'specially if she phoned up and his dad told her he'd gone out to see the fun.

So he jog-trotted back and first thing he did when he got in, he picked up the phone and called her.

Got her mother, and said, "Hi, Mrs Grant. It's Derry. Can I speak to Rachel, please?"

"She's not here," the answer came back, sharp and anxious. "We were hoping she was with you."

"No, I haven't seen her. I was out. She put a note through my door, though, said she was going to call her dad for a lift. That was before tea, that was hours ago . . . "

"Well, she didn't call. We've tried phoning the houses, and we can't get through. We tried you, too, some time ago, but there wasn't any answer. What's it like over there, Derry?"

"Not too bad," he said, trying to be reassuring while inside he started to panic. "The trouble's further down, halfway into town from here. I've just been to see, but you can't get close. Look, I'll go down the houses, shall I, see if she's there?"

"I wish you would," Mrs Grant said. "And, Derry? Call us. As soon as you can, whether she's there or not, whatever the news is. We thought we might come over, but . . . "

"Better if I find her first," he said. "No point you chasing round where you don't know the streets. Don't worry, okay? I'll find her." *She's my girl.*

He hung up, explained to his father in six words – "Got to look for Rachel, Dad," – and took the stairs in as many steps. No jogging now, he ran hard down the hill, taking every short cut that he knew.

Came past the big marquee and across the grass, recklessly plunging down the slope, risking a ricked ankle or worse; onto the road again, over at the traffic-lights without even looking, barely hearing the blare of a horn behind him; and on down to the dark gym, and past it.

But stopped short of the houses, a long way short.

Stopped in a hurry, because he saw a familiar silhouette on the road ahead of him, just at the turning that led down where he wanted to go. A broad and heavy man, thick neck and shaven head, with a broad and heavy dog on a short chain: George Jenner and Kyzer, out walking in Paradise.

Derry wondered why those two should be walking down that particular road, and didn't like any of the answers he came up with.

So he sidled off the road, out of the light quick, in case George turned round. He scrambled over rough ground till he could see the houses; and what he saw made him moan aloud for pure fear.

Because what he saw was fire, two vehicles well ablaze. In the fire's light he could see a bunch of people clustered round something on the ground. It looked like a burning person, but he didn't want to believe that, didn't even want to think about it; and didn't really have the time, because he could see something else, too.

He could see another bunch of men, making their way down the road towards the fire; and it looked like they were all carrying weapons. And George was just a little way behind them, with that bastard dog of his and his own big grudge against everyone at the houses . . .

*   *   *

Terry wasn't fool enough to drive a Jaguar around the streets of Paradise any night of the week, let alone with a riot brewing. Nor was he frightened of being on foot and alone; he could look after himself.

So he parked his car safely in the centre of town, and walked. No buses running, of course, and the taxis wouldn't go west tonight.

Coming from the centre, he came to the riot first; or at least to the fringes of the riot, the noise and smoke of it. It was the noise that hit him most forcefully, even harder than lurid glimpses of the pub on fire: the sounds of racing engines and young voices yelling, police megaphones and sirens, all topped off by the helicopter

460

clattering overhead, seeming to ride on the solid finger of its searchlight.

A police cordon warned him away, and he didn't stop to argue. He had no interest in this, beyond a little human curiosity. For Terry, and he hoped for many others, the main event lay elsewhere: unannounced and maybe even unbegun as yet, but surely looming.

Ten minutes' steady walking brought him to the long terraces at the heart of Paradise, where he found the little children out playing riots, as they'd seen their big brothers doing on the telly. He was glad he hadn't brought his Jag, seeing kids who couldn't be more than eight or nine throwing stones and cans and broken bottles at every car that passed.

There was a television van parked in one street, with its windscreen smashed. The crew was down at the corner, filming possibly the self-same kids who'd done it, while the driver stood by the vehicle, wearily surveying the damage.

"They need a bloody good thrashing, mate," he said, as Terry caught his eye. "They don't get it, though. I've got three myself, and Christ knows, I've never laid a hand on one of 'em. Can't do it, it's not in me. But this lot, now – just let me catch the one who did this, I'll slay him. Put half a brick through the window, missed me by that much," his fingers showing the width. "Parents, that's what they need. Proper parents, who know the job . . . "

And that's what they got just then, or one of them did. There was a mass of young boys in the street, throwing stones for the camera. One ran a few yards further, to get closer to a retreating car, and just at that moment a woman came around the corner and bellowed at him. He checked, looked for support, saw his mates backing off fast; and then he was dragged away by the collar while his mother's free hand beat him around the head and shoulders, while he yelped and kicked, while the camera followed every move.

The driver chuckled delightedly, and even Terry grinned; and then he looked round to find the camera trained on him, using him as visual commentary.

He scowled and turned and strode away, but even as he reached the corner he felt the camera still on his back, still following.

*   *   *

Billy was in his room when he heard Rachel raise the alarm. He'd seen fires and street fights, and they scared him badly. So he'd

461

retreated, he'd shut the door on the fiery world. He didn't have to pull the curtains because his window looked the other way, across the river; but he did, he pulled the curtains anyway, to make himself feel safer.

Then he listened to some music, and played along softly on his mouth-organ. That didn't stop him hearing footsteps on the stairs, or Rachel's clear voice shouting in the passage; but he hoped maybe he could pull the music like a curtain over that as well, just let it pass, let it go away.

Only then she thumped on the door and pushed it open without even waiting for him to say "Come in," and nobody ever did that in the houses, not *ever*.

"Billy, didn't you hear me? There's a fire outside, we've got to evacuate the houses."

That was all the news she needed. Billy really was very scared of fire. He came out of his room fast, not even stopping to pick up his precious tape recorder, carrying only the mouth-organ he already had in his hand.

Then Rachel said, "Billy, are you feeling very brave?"

And no, he wasn't; but of course he had to say yes, even while his feet fidgeted to run.

"Thing is, this place is such a maze," Rachel said, looking up the passage and down, a little frantic. "I don't know who's in, I don't know if anybody's in at all; but it takes so long to check. So could you help me, Billy? Could you go that way, and look in every room, and tell people to come downstairs if you find any? Quick as you can? I'll go the other way, and meet you down in the big common-room. And don't be scared," she added with a thin smile, "we're not all going to get burned up while we do it. I promise."

Billy nodded nervously. One glance out of the passage window had shown him the fire burning up the battle bus.

"And do check every door, even if you think they're out. Someone might be sleeping."

Billy watched Rachel first, saw how she hammered on the first door she came to and then stuck her head in, came out and ran on to the next; and then he did the same, going the other way. Hammer and look, out and run, all through the complicated chain of houses. Room after room, hammer and look, out and run – and when he came to a room that wasn't empty, he was halfway out already before he realised. And then he realised who it was, and almost ran anyway.

But Jason looked over his shoulder, from where he was kneeling

462

on the bed watching the fire; and he said, "What do you want, sicko?"

"F-f-fire," Billy stammered, "there's a fire . . . "

"I know. I can see it. So?"

"We've got to get out, we've all got to meet down in the common-room."

"Who says?"

"Rachel."

Jason just shrugged, and looked out of the window again. Billy hesitated, not knowing what to do now, and after a second Jason turned back to him. "I'm not coming, sicko. But listen," getting to his feet suddenly and coming over, "you don't tell anyone, right? You don't say you saw me here. 'Cos if you do, I'd have to tell Nathan I found you going through his room, and I don't think he'd like that, do you?"

Billy shook his head vigorously. "I won't say," he said desperately. "I won't say a word . . . "

"Right, then. Shut the door after you." Jason slapped his cheek contemptuously, and went back to the window.

Billy ducked out of the room and did as he was told, closed the door behind him; and stood for a second rubbing his cheek and hating Jason and being scared of him and knowing he shouldn't do either, before he remembered the fire and started to run again, hammer and look, out and run.

And when he found Rachel again, down in the common-room, she looked at him alone and said, "You didn't find anyone either?"

And Billy shook his head, and said no.

Said, "No, there isn't, there isn't anybody here, Rachel. Just us."

*　　　　*　　　　*

They killed the fires on the twitching body after Nathan had fought it off, after it had fallen; they left the vehicles to burn and zapped this nightmare figure instead, but couldn't zap the nightmare.

Someone said "Albie," and someone else said "Yes," and never mind how they knew. They didn't recognise him, nothing so easy, no one could have recognised this cindered monstrosity; but there wasn't any doubt about it.

Nathan stood looking for a moment, then said, "Somebody take him inside. Please."

A second's stillness, that stretched and stretched; then one man moved, and another joined him. Together they bent, to lift Albie's body; and as they lifted him, his head fell back and he screamed, thin and high like a kettle's whistle.

They dropped him, and he screamed again, and bucked like a fish at Nathan's feet.

"Jesus Christ, he's not *dead* yet?" Nathan ran a hand over his sweat-slicked face, looked around his men, didn't know what to say. "Look, just, just get him inside, right? Get a stretcher, anything, just get him away from me. And call the doc."

And then he turned his back on their appalled and questioning eyes, staring around the darkening horizon for some kind of help, greatly out of his depth and going under; and maybe there was a God after all, maybe He really was in the business of doling out miracles, because Nathan saw just what he needed.

He saw men coming slow and dangerous down the hill, swinging clubs and iron bars in their hands.

"No, leave him," Nathan snapped. "As you were. We've got trouble."

"But Nat, we can't – "

"Use your eyes, will you?" His arm stabbed out to show them, and they fell silent as they saw.

"The bats. Where are they?"

A brief pause, then someone ventured, "In the bus. I think. In the back there . . . "

And the bus, of course, was burning. Might explode at any moment.

But this at least was something Nathan could do and be applauded for, something he could get right. He wasn't afraid, not in that way. Being a hero had always come easy.

So he ran to the back of the bus despite their protests, seized the hot handle and wrenched it open. Flames leapt towards this new access of air; he ducked, sheltered his face with his arm and peered beneath it.

Yes, there were the baseball bats, in their cardboard box on the floor; and there was fire on the seat in front of them, and the box was starting to smoulder.

Nathan snatched at it and dragged it out, and never mind the sting of it on his palms, or the lick of flame across his cheek.

He dumped the box on the ground and tipped the bats out with a kick.

"Grab one, quick." And when they hesitated, remembering one last time who they were and what they'd been preaching all summer, "Go on, then, *arm* yourselves! Those bastards up there

464

aren't coming to talk . . . !"

And whether it was discipline that did it or loyalty, mindless following where Nathan led; whether it was God's call to His soldiers, because God's never been a pacifist in His own cause; whether it was self-defence or self-interest or whatever the reason, Nathan's army armed itself and marched up the hill to meet the war.

*   *   *

Jason saw the fight starting, from his window. It was hard to make anything out clearly in the dark and the firelight, but he saw the two groups come together and break apart, he saw people in clinches, people swinging clubs. People staggering and falling. And he saw Vinny quite clearly, his face lit red and laughing.

He moved quickly then. Vinny would win, of course, no question of that; and afterwards he'd have a bone or two to pick with Jason. And knowing Vinny he'd pick them with his nails, out of Jason's living body.

Jason just wanted to get the hell out, he was sick tired of being scared all the time. If it wasn't Vinny or George it was Nathan, and he couldn't take it any more.

Before he left, though, he was going to settle up with Nathan, all his scores at once.

He checked out of a back window and saw Rachel and Billy making their way over the broken ground, scrambling awkwardly towards the river with only the light from the houses to guide them.

Good. They were out of the way, and there wouldn't be anyone else left in the houses.

Jason had already stuffed a sports bag with clothes, all he needed. He'd get by. He slung the bag over his shoulder and trotted quickly downstairs. They were making a hell of a noise out front, shouting and screaming and a dog come from somewhere, barking like crazy. But what with the riot up at the Queen, it was going to be a while before the police even noticed the fuss down here.

Good again. Give 'em plenty of time, let 'em all kill each other, that'd suit Jason.

There were half a dozen working kitchens along the length of the terrace, and they all had calor gas cookers. No mains gas, down here. Jason dumped his bag by a back door and made his way

465

from one to the next, working as fast as he could: spilling meths and white spirit and five-gallon drums of cooking oil, anything that would burn. The gas cylinders were stored outside for safety, but it didn't take long to bring them all in and dump them where they'd help the fire best.

He opened their nozzles one by one, and retreated down the terrace with his lighter working.

Then he grabbed his bag and slipped outside. Slammed the door and that was that, he was free of them at last. He looked the way Rachel and Billy had gone, thinking of going after them – the sicko would be no problem, and he had unfinished business with Rachel – but decided not, decided just to let that ride.

Getting away was all that counted tonight. Find himself a car, and go.

As he ran off into the night, a brighter light began to show through the windows of the houses behind him.

*   *   *

This was how battles ought to be, how Nathan had always imagined them: smoke and noise and strangeness, rushing and screaming and standing still, tension and adrenalin and not a hint, not a whisper of fear.

He felt immune, invulnerable, like a god discovering the clumsiness of mortals. A man came at him, brandishing a hatchet; Nathan slipped sideways, and swung his baseball bat to catch him hard across the chest. The man grunted, swayed; and before he could do more than count his broken ribs, Nathan swung again, savagely into his face. The man sprawled backwards, his nose dissolving in a rush of blood.

Nathan laughed. This was *easy*.

Another man coming past, running; running to or running from, starting something or fleeing something else. It didn't matter. Nathan tripped him, and cracked the back of his skull as he struggled to rise. After that, he stopped struggling.

The fight had spread itself all down the length of the terrace now. Nathan ran to a high point, a heap of rubble, to give himself an overview; and saw chaos and confusion, saw some figures wrestling each other, rolling on the ground, while others sparred at a distance, jabbed and parried with their clubs and jumped back out of reach. Saw wounded on both sides, dragging themselves into the dark.

Heard a frenzied barking behind him, and wheeled round fast.

Saw one more figure, a big, broad man with a dog on a short chain at his side.

Heard his own name, "Nathan Lewis," murmured softly, heard it through all that noise, in tones of supreme satisfaction; and heard also the rustle of chain, as the dog was let slip.

And just had time then to feel the fear that had been so wonderfully absent, had time to feel stark terror catch like cold steel at his bones before the rushing weight of the dog was on him, and he was falling, and its hot jaws were hacking at his face.

*   *   *

Derry saw the dog go down on Nathan, and he didn't feel a thing. He saw people fighting, people hurt – people dying, maybe, and some of them he knew. And all it meant was that Rachel was in more danger than he'd dreamt, if she was here; and he couldn't get to her this way. Impossible, to cross that ground without getting caught in the war.

So he circled around it, stumbling over broken stones, falling and bruising himself and feeling nothing.

He came to the back of the houses, never thinking to look behind him, never thinking that anyone might follow.

Cold shock killed the heat of his anxiety then, as he saw the light of fire inside the houses, at half a dozen different windows. He stood still, staring; and then thought, *No*, thought, *She can't be in there, she's too smart, she'll be out of there and gone, she'll be fine* . . .

Didn't know what to do now, except stand and look. Couldn't think where to go to find his escaped Rachel; so didn't go anywhere, and so found her. So saw her coming back.

And moaned with a chill terror, but would have gone to her anyway, terrified or not; would have gone flying to the rescue if a massive hand hadn't closed on his neck just then, if a hoarse voice hadn't whispered, "Hullo, Derry son. I want a word with you . . . "

*   *   *

Rachel had led Billy by the hand, out of the houses and down to the road by the river. Out of all harm's way, she thought. They could stop here, until they'd decided what to do. She thought.

467

She couldn't have been more wrong. All the decisions, all their safety lay in other, hotter hands now; though the first she knew of it was when Billy screamed and ran off sobbing into the darkness.

"Billy, what the *fuck . . . ?*"

She stared after him for a moment, made a move to follow; but the devil was standing right behind her, his hot hands reaching already.

"No one here," he said as he took his grip, "no one here gets out alive."

Just the touch of those hard fingers was enough, more than enough to subdue Rachel. This was more than bad, this was the worst thing in the world; but she had nothing to set against him, no will to protect herself or her baby. She stumbled obediently at his side as he led her back to the houses, heading for God alone knew what degradation and what terror, but not even trying to escape.

Distantly she was aware of a known voice shouting her name; even more distantly she looked, and saw Derry. But he would be no help, he was trapped and taken too, struggling in George's hands. George would tear him apart, she thought.

The houses were on fire, and she didn't understand how that had happened, but it didn't matter now. All that did matter was this grinning, terrible devil with his fingers like irons burning into her skin, digging deep.

She flinched away from his clamorous face and the sight of the houses burning, watched only her feet slipping and tripping on rocks, until he jerked her to a standstill.

Then she had to look at him.

The fire glowed red on his tattoos and his pustulous skin, and his eyes were exultant, reflecting the blaze. His mouth was open, a bad tongue licking at foul teeth; and Rachel wasn't thinking any too clearly any more, terror had made her stupid, but one thought was bright and clear and obvious, *he's going to eat me.*

Only then there was a scream, another scream from the darkness, somewhere close; close enough to make the devil turn his head.

And a rock hit him in those broken teeth, and rocked him hard. His fingers fell away from Rachel's shoulder, he took a step back, and she saw blood dribble and run from his mouth.

Then another rock hit him, on the side of the head.

Rachel looked where he did, and saw Billy; and remembered, this had always been Billy's other talent. *Never play throwing-games with Billy,* that was a lesson quickly learned. He had a powerful arm and a wickedly good eye, and he thought it was funny if you missed your catch and the ball or the frisbee clipped you on the head.

But he wasn't throwing any more rocks, two had quite outdone his courage. He didn't even have the sense to run away again; like Rachel, he was caught and held just by the devil's eye.

But seemingly even the devil could only hold one at once, because Rachel was free of it now. She screamed at Billy to run, and when he didn't she snatched up a stone and tried throwing it herself, tried to save him as he had saved her.

Magic doesn't strike twice, though, and she lacked his arm and eye. Her stone was lost in darkness, and she wasn't brave enough to do the only other thing, to hurl herself physically on the devil and scratch his evil eyes out.

She was crying now, choking on her tears; and so too was Billy crying, as the devil reached him.

And the devil seized him and lifted him, and carried him into the burning houses; and a couple of seconds later there was a great explosion, and all the windows burst out and a door flew off its hinges and the police helicopter came swooping overhead with its searchlight stabbing, like a guide to light Billy's soul its way to heaven.

*   *   *

The explosion sent shards of glass cutting the air like shrapnel, slashing at George's head and back, one sharp chance for Derry; and he didn't waste that chance, using head and elbows and feet to break free during George's moment of cursing distraction.

Rachel was still there, full in view, standing like a dummy in the light; but Derry couldn't go to her, wouldn't lead danger in that direction. One thing he was sure of, George would be coming after him.

So he ran the other way, off over the waste ground in the dark. And sure enough heard George behind him; but that was okay, that meant Rachel should be safe. Knowing that, Derry wasn't so scared now. He'd back himself against George any day, in a game of hide-and-seek around the rocks and rubble.

He kept low, not to be silhouetted against the distant street-lights; dodged from side to side as he ran, doubled back on himself a couple of times, finally ducked under a slab of broken concrete that jutted out like a shelf above the ground. Lay still and quiet, blessing the fitness that George had encouraged in him, and

469

saw his former boss go heavily past. Saw him pause and quest, forward and back, like a dog sniffing the air for scent of a lost quarry; and finally heard him curse and saw him guess, saw him heading off at random and wrong.

Slipped out of shelter and went quietly the other way, barely even troubling to run, just jogging nice and easy on this dodgy ground.

And would have made it, easy; could have got back to find Rachel and see her safe with no more fuss at all if a light hadn't speared suddenly out of the sky and pinned him where he was, standing tall and exposed on a ridge of rubble.

He heard a bellow and here came George plunging straight towards him, twenty metres away and charging like a bull, no dodging this.

Derry stood frozen and fearful again, lit like a beacon to draw his own death close. Because this was death, no question. Let George get his hands on him, and Derry was dead.

And George's hands were stretched out already, fingers set to clutch and tear and destroy; and still Derry only stood there. No point running now, the helicopter would only follow him, noisily picking him out for his murderer to chase. And it was too late anyway, no time to run, George was too close. Nothing to do but stand, and hope . . .

And for once hope was doing its stuff, miracles weren't over yet in Paradise. Because George wasn't looking where his feet were going, only at Derry; and Derry could see what George hadn't, a pool of dead water between them.

He stood on the pool's edge and just stared at George, stared and stared; and George stared back, and kept on coming. Six paces to go now, five and four and surely he was going too fast to stop, he was like a ship, he couldn't slow that great weight in a moment. And three paces and two and that's when he saw the water, when his body jerked and twisted but still kept on coming, and he fell tumbling and bellowing into the pool.

Now was the time for Derry to run again, to get the hell out of there; but he didn't, he stood a minute longer while the helicopter still hung overhead, its light shifting now between him and the pool.

Because Derry remembered two things, even in all this chaos, even with Rachel out there somewhere needing finding, needing him. Two things he remembered, and the first of them was that George – big George, strong as an ox, preached fitness, ran a gym – had told him once, he'd never learnt to swim.

470

And the other was what Nathan had said to him the day Derry quit working for George.

He might have been the man that killed your mother.

And Derry believed it suddenly, after tonight. Believed it with a passion, an utter conviction.

And stood for a minute looking down at George as he flailed in the deep water, as he scrabbled at the loose rubble of the bank and drifted away, drifted out and went under and rose again; and then Derry turned and walked away, to leave the police the only witnesses, their light the last thing George would see.

*   *   *

Jason had found just the car, a flash sports model left where no one should be stupid enough to leave a car like that, its owner slumming in Paradise or come to watch the riots.

He'd bypassed the alarm, no hassle; had started the engine and driven away, all in under a minute.

His sights were on the far horizons. With a full tank of petrol he'd get some way in this, and then he could leapfrog, dump this and find another. He could be in London by morning.

But he couldn't resist one last look at what he'd done, the houses ablaze from end to end. No fucking miracle this time, this time they'd burn all right. And he'd do a fly-past, flat out at a hundred plus, like a V-sign and a victory roll.

And that's what he did, he burnt the air with his speed as he raced down the hill. The police were too busy to pick him up, too slow to catch him if they did; he was cocksure tonight, loud and laughing and alone.

Until suddenly Vinny was there in his wrecked and ravaged body, limping out from under a streetlight with his clothes in smoking rags, spreading his arms wide. Meaning *Stop right there, Jase,* meaning *I want you.*

And Jason sweated and swore, whimpered and just had time to choose; and made his choice, and leant hard on the accelerator and twitched the wheel to make the car run straight at Vinny.

But Vinny wasn't there any more, only his grin remaining seared behind Jason's eyes, and there was nothing but the car's low bonnet between Jason and the streetlight, and then there was nothing at all.

THIRTY-SEVEN

i

He steps off the bus pure gold, bright in this land of light, outshining any sun. Come from summer's end to early spring, he never sees the winter of the world. Never looks back, never reads the papers.

He's met by the woman who runs the mission here in this town like Alice, the woman who wrote him the letter.

— Thank God you've got here, she says. I didn't believe it, when I heard you were really coming. Don't know why I wrote, really, it was such a long shot . . .

— It was the Lord leading you, he says. Isn't that clear, isn't that obvious? As the Lord has led me since. As soon as I read your letter, I knew I had to come.

— Well, we need you. So many children sick, and the doctors can't touch it . . .

— It's not me you need, he says with a smile, with a shake of the head. It's not me, nothing I can do. It's only God. I can't make anything happen, he says, I can't promise miracles.

— Ah, but God wouldn't have sent you, would He? If He didn't mean something to happen?

— It's a point of view, he says, laughing aloud now. Making it abundantly clear that yes, it's his own point of view. It's certainly a long way to come, he says, and I can't think of any other reason He'd drag me all this way. I mean, can you? he asks.

— Not a one, she says.

Which is maybe another minor miracle, that she doesn't read the papers either.

Round to the back of the bus they go, for his luggage; and,

— Blow me, she says, is this all you brought?

— I like to travel light, he says. And laughs again.

ii

They'd cleared the site of the old chapel now, and were ready to start building. They held a rededication service on site before the first concrete was mixed; and plenty of the old guard, the original congregation was there for that. All four of the former Council came, turning back in their confusion to what should be safe, what was known and familiar.

They'd find even this was different, though, Lisa thought, as she watched them almost lurking at the back of the small crowd. They'd lost their place. A new building called for a new voice; and no question whose voice it would be. Alan Parkinson and her mother between them had this deal well sewn up.

Just to rub that in, just to snub the old men further, there was a private prayer-cum-business meeting after the service, back at chez Dolance. No more than a dozen people were invited, the core of the new chapel's strength; and the former Council was very pointedly not counted among that number.

Nor was Lisa, of course, but she was allowed to fetch and carry, to serve coffee and biscuits to the adults. Luther was there as of right, sitting on a cushion at his mother's side.

It was Mr Parkinson who made everything happen today, brought it all out like poison from a wound: and that simply by talking about his new chapel.

"We've to be pure," he said, he kept harping on that. "We've to keep ourselves pure, as best we can. We mustn't introduce corruption, or we'll taint everything we do. That's what happened, that's what went wrong with the old chapel. They let Richard in, they gave everything over to Richard," and no hatred in his voice now, not like before. Richard had handed him everything he'd ever wanted, on a plate. "And Richard was a proud man, he had the sin of arrogance; and that destroyed him and all his works, and it destroyed the chapel too. It was Richard's pride burnt the old chapel down, for all that a human hand set light to it. It was sin killed Sister Grace. And we've to learn from that, sin breeds like a virus. Everyone sins," he said, "we can't escape it, it would be sin itself to think that we could; but we mustn't let sin influence our work for the Lord. We must watch ourselves," he said, "and watch each other; and whatever we see that's wrong, we mustn't hold back from saying. In public, if need be. We must accuse each other, so long as it's done from love; and we must accuse ourselves."

And Luther was fidgeting so much that Lisa could hardly take her eyes off him, she was so interested. Their mother nudged him hard, but he went on fretting, shifting on his cushion, rubbing his arms, tying his fingers into knots.

Mr Parkinson prayed then, for purity and the strength to confess faults, and to point out faults in others. That last wouldn't take much strength, Lisa thought; or if it did most of them gathered in that room had it already, in abundance.

And then Luther let it all hang out, right in the middle of the prayers. Luther screamed, and sprawled sobbing on the floor, and confessed.

"It was me, it was me, I did it, I'm not pure, I did it, I killed her, I killed Sister Grace . . . "

They quieted him at last, by letting him kneel in the centre of the circle and confess properly. Lisa sat in a corner where she wouldn't be noticed, and memorised every word.

"God told me to do it," Luther said. "It was a judgement. I knew it was right. I *did*. Mother said the chapel had been stolen, Richard had stolen it, he was, he was misusing it, she said. And that's wrong, that shouldn't be allowed, he was leading people astray. And a chapel's only wood, Mother said, it's only a building. So I prayed about it, and God made a judgement, He said to burn the chapel down.

"So I went down early in the morning, like sometimes to set the chairs out; and I took the paraffin and a box of matches, and I poured it in all the corners and I set fire to it, and then I came home. And I didn't know Sister Grace was in the Council room, I didn't *know*. And it must've been a judgement on her, mustn't it, she must've been very wicked for God to burn her like in Hell already, and she died . . . "

They sent Luther off to pray alone in his room, while the adults talked; and Lisa stayed quietly in her corner, and somehow even her mother didn't notice her there.

They talked for an hour or more, and all it came down to was, *Do nothing*. There's no value, they said, in telling the police at this stage. What would be the point? they asked. Luther's under age, he's not responsible, there can be no question of punishment. He needs prayer and support and proper training, they said, and we can give him that. His mother can give him that, they said.

So no, they said, we'll tell no one about this. And Luther mustn't tell anyone either, you must see to that, Jean. No more hysterical outbursts, they said. He was moved to speak this time, perhaps, it was obviously important that we know; but he mustn't be moved this way again.

"He'll say nothing," Lisa's mother said grimly. "I can promise you that."

474

And nor would any of them, they all made the same promise; but no one thought to ask Lisa. They left her to her mother, perhaps, or assumed that she and her brother were one flesh.

Wrong.

Lisa thought she might tell everyone, if she felt called to it. If she didn't get better treatment, here on in, Lisa thought she might tell the world.

And she smiled to herself, thinking about that; and thought she might well tell the world. Better treatment or not, blackmail or no.

iii

Michael Grant was in his study, doing some groundwork towards the goal of setting up his own architectural practice, when Rachel knocked.

Just that simple sound cost him a pang, a sense of irretrievable loss. A timid little one-knuckle tapping was all she could manage in these dreadful days, so different from the happy banging of his cocky, confident daughter's fist just a few short months ago. And in those days she came straight in after, carried on the passage of her own noise, she didn't wait for his acknowledgement.

But in those days Rachel had been a hair-bound hustler for God, very much her own person but recognisably his daughter and Jessie's. Now she was a shaven stranger, eternally pale under her tan, perhaps her own person still but at least a little someone else's and barely recognisable at all. That made it logical, he supposed, that she should knock differently on his study door. It wasn't a symptom of the change, it was only a reminder, *don't treat me like the same girl, because I'm not.*

No, indeed.

But still it was no effort to smile when he saw her, she was a stranger easy to love; and maybe she'd come to talk, the way she didn't any more.

"Something I can do for you, pet?"

She shook her head, and he wasn't at all surprised. Disappointed, but not surprised. Maybe she talked to Derry, but he wouldn't even bet on that. They were having a hard time of it, those kids, tense and prickling whenever they were together, though it seemed they couldn't bear to be apart. And Michael was sure she didn't pray much any more, so she wasn't even talking to God, and surely to God she needed someone to talk to; but

475

apparently not him, or not today.

"Uncle Carl's here," she said.

It was difficult to push himself to his feet when Rachel showed his former partner – *and all the time Terry Belderstone's partner,* a cold internal reminder, *taking bribes and back-handers and the Lord knows what else besides* – into the room; more difficult still to shake hands. The sense of personal betrayal ran very deep.

But he did it, for his own self-respect and for Carlton's sake too, under Rachel's wide and watchful eyes. She looked at Carlton as if he were a Mafia boss – or a Terry Belderstone, perhaps – rather than her familiar and beloved adoptive uncle.

Michael sent her away as soon as Carlton was settled, shaking his head to her offer of something fetched from the kitchen. "You get back to that lad of yours, love," *back to one of your high-tension, sharp-edged silences under the trees in the garden, where you'll play with each other's fingers for hours and never dare touch each other's feelings.* "We'll look after ourselves if we want anything."

"Yeah. Okay. Shout if you want, though." Half a smile, shared awkwardly between them, and she was gone. Michael closed the door behind her, went back to his desk.

Sat behind it for the distancing it offered, and said, "Well, then, Carlton."

"Michael." Just his name, but it came with a gesture clumsier than Carlton's former grace and more eloquent: an awkward spreading of the hands, half a shrug, a twist of the mouth. *I know this is embarrassing for you,* his hands said, *it's embarrassing for both of us.* But *there's nothing I can do about that,* was the shrug's contribution; and, *I'm sorry, but it's going to get worse,* was written all over his face.

"Did you want a drink? Tea or coffee? Something stronger?" He could play the good host, at least, even if there was no chance of playing the good friend.

"No. No, thank you. I won't stay long. I want, I only want . . . "

And his face worked, but still he couldn't say it. *Ah,* Michael thought. *Good Samaritan, then. Well, maybe. Maybe I can manage that.*

"Some kind of help, is it?" he suggested neutrally, committing himself to nothing.

"Not really, no," and Carlton's mouth smiled a little, independent of his faded blue eyes. "Though if you could manage to remember that I was never a bad man, I think that might help a

476

little. Most people are going to find it difficult."

"Are you in trouble, Carlton?" Surprising, how upset he was at the thought. Old feelings didn't die so easily after all; and maybe there was hope still for Rachel and Derry.

"Not yet," Carlton said, with another of those fragile little smiles, "but I'm going to be. I'm going to the authorities, Michael. I have to, now. I thought you were entitled to know first, before the papers get it. You might want to go away again, for the next week or two."

"No." There would be journalists, no doubt; there might even be headlines, if they dug deeply enough. Or if Carlton said too much. *The Man Who Didn't Blow The Whistle. Christian Stays Silent In Face Of Fraud.* That probably made him some kind of accessory. But he'd run from truth once this summer; neither truth nor lies could shift him now. "But, I don't understand. Why now? I mean, the, the danger's over, isn't it? Richard was surely the threat, and he's gone, he won't be coming back now. The stuff I gave him," *and should I be telling you this? Probably not, but there you go, here you are. It's a gift, for old times' sake,* "the documentation, he kept all that down at the houses. It'll be nothing but ashes. And I saw Belderstone in the paper just yesterday, being bullish about his business park, now that he has access to the land again . . . "

"That's just the point," Carlton said softly, the hurt beginning to show. "He wants to go ahead as if nothing had happened. That's why things did happen, just so that Terry could carry on as normal. And that's, that's not right. I'm not a bad man, Michael; and this is wicked. People *died* for this. I see them at night, you know, I count them off in my head: one man burned to death in the fire, one man drowned, one lad crashed in a stolen car. Guilty or innocent, it doesn't matter, they're still dead. And some people are still in hospital, there was that boy who had his face ripped off by the dog, monstrous damage, *monstrous* – and Terry made it happen, you know. All of it."

"Do you know that?"

Carlton nodded. "I'm totally satisfied. I *saw* him. Oh, not in the flesh," as Michael stared, "on television. But he was in Paradise that night, and smiling. He was a happy man. And whatever for, if he wasn't overseeing that carnage? He had people killed, to protect himself and his balance-sheet. I can't live with that. And the evidence is burnt now, what you had, or else he's got it; so there's only me to expose him. And I must, that's all. I *must*."

Michael nodded. He was right, of course; it was only a surprise that he should see it so clearly. Not a bad man at all, in the end.

"It may mean prison, Carl."

"Oh, I know. I'm sure it will, unless my health goes first. It would have to, really, wouldn't it? But I'm prepared," he said, looking manifestly unprepared. "It's unavoidable, I have to do this."

They talked a few minutes longer, then Michael walked him back to his car, offered to go to the police station with him and was almost disappointed to find that he wasn't needed, that Carlton had at least had the foresight to arrange for a solicitor to be there.

So they said goodbye on the pavement, under the eyes of Michael's daughter and her boyfriend if they were watching, if they were seeing anything outside themselves; and this time shaking hands wasn't hard at all, he was glad to do it.

ENVOI

It was Christmas Eve, and Derry wasn't sleeping.

He lay edged right over on his side of the bed, flat on his back, his eyes so well adjusted to the darkness that he could see every crack in the ceiling. The streets were quiet now, after the last of the singing pissheads had gone home; nothing to listen to but the occasional car, distant sirens, Rachel's breathing.

That was slow and deep, and he spent some time trying to work out if it was sleep-sounds like it ought to be, or if she was awake like him and just pretending. The way things had been between them the last week or so it could be either, and he wouldn't be able to tell. The magic had been turned off, it wasn't working any more.

So he adjusted his own breathing to match hers, the closest he could get to her right now. And that was what answered the question for him, in the end: when he had to start catching and tripping over the air in his throat just to keep in time, and he realised that she was crying, as quietly as she possibly could.

He twisted over in a moment to where she lay with her back to him, hunched tight and trembling. He wrapped his arms around her, drew her in against him, tried to engulf her with his body, not to give her any choice at all.

"Don't, Rache," he whispered, husky with his own threat of tears. "Don't cry, we can, we can do this," lying through his teeth now, "we can sort it out ... "

And like that, murmuring anything whether it made sense or not, whether it was true or not. Holding her and stroking her swelling belly and pushing his fingers through her growing hair until at last she lay passive and quiescent in his arms, unrecognisably Rachel, not his sparky love at all.

So he turned her, rolled her over to face him because she wouldn't do even that much herself, kissed her wet eyes and said, "What, then?"

"You," she said, as if he didn't know already. But he couldn't lie any more, he couldn't say *What about me?* or anything like it; so he said nothing, which left it open for her to say what she said next, the impossible thing.

She touched his face with her fingers, like a blind stranger trying to learn him; and said, "You don't love me any more."

"Rache, no . . . "

"You don't," she said wearily, exhausted by misery, as if she were merely reporting, with no strength left to fight for what she wanted. "I gave up everything I ever valued, for you. It's all gone now. I'm pregnant, I'm out of school, I've left home; and it's all too soon, it shouldn't be happening to me yet, I'm too *young* for this. I don't, I don't think I even believe in God any more, and that's you too, that's living with you. I want it to work, Derry, I do; but," and here it came, and she was starting to cry again, "but this is *Christmas,* it ought to, it ought to be the best day of the year, it always used to be at home. And, and you're not even *talking* to me, and I don't know what I've done, and I'm so scared . . . "

And Derry held her, and rocked her, and wouldn't let her go even when she struggled; and he kissed her and said no, told her she was all wrong, she was a crazy woman. He loved her more than ever, he said, her and her baby coming. He loved them both, they meant the world to him. And he'd been a pig, he said, and he was sorry; and it was just something on his mind, he'd tell her later, tomorrow sometime, that was a promise . . .

And all of that was true, except the last bit; and Rachel believed it, or believed it enough. The tension ebbed out of her slowly, he chased it away with gentle, frightened hands, and she nestled more comfortably against his side. He kissed her hair and said happy Christmas, and she twitched a bit, sniffed a bit, said after all this she'd better get a stocking in the morning, or he was dead.

And at last she fell asleep, and this time he was certain of it, because she snored lightly into his armpit. And he fidgeted with the loose cotton of her pyjamas, and told her again that he loved her, trying to get himself into her dreams.

And still he didn't sleep, there was no question of his sleeping. He thought he'd likely be awake all night, trying to make plans for tomorrow – how to give Rachel the best day of her life, how to keep his dad happy too, what the hell he could say to both of them about this last week, what they might possibly believe.

Thinking a little about the future, a lot about this summer past and not, not at all about the pain reborn and ripening in his leg.